Raves for *Spellcast* and *Spellcrossed*:

"There's a vast but little known overlap between fans of fantasy and fans o_____ d Barbara Ashford hits the sweet spot _____ umorous, emotional, he _____, Barbara, for making r_____ anted Evening' stuck in _____

—Ca_____ selling
_____ series

"[A] novel about the transformative power of the theater . . . a woman with an unsettled past . . . and the intersecting coincidences that move her toward the future. Maggie is relatable and her journey compelling. Four stars."
—*RT Book Reviews*

"[A] charming fantasy novel. Maggie Graham is enchanted and bemused by the Crossroads Theatre . . . but it takes Maggie a while to really grasp just how magical it is. . . . A slightly bittersweet but appropriate conclusion left me wanting more, in fine theatrical tradition."   —*Locus*

"If you're worried because, like me, you're not a theater buff, please don't let that stop you from picking up this touching and heartfelt tale . . . The story that unfolds is so stirring, that it'll stay with you long after the last page . . . This book, this author, these characters they're keepers."
—The Spinecracker

"*Spellcast* had me spellbound, and *Spellcrossed* was no different. [It] moved me to tears more than a few times, and was equally heartwarming and heartbreaking. . . . Magic and the magic of musical theatre intertwine seamlessly to create a read worth savoring. I can't recommend this series highly enough!"   —My Bookish Ways

"A fantastic sequel in a magical, emotional, heartwarming series. [It's] an emotional roller coaster full of surprises, both good and bad. If you're a fan of romance, vivid writing, well-crafted and relatable characters, then I suggest you give Ashford's series a try."   —Addicted 2 Heroines

SPELLS AT THE CROSSROADS

Spellcast

❖

Spellcrossed

Barbara Ashford

DAW BOOKS, INC.

DONALD A. WOLLHEIM, FOUNDER

375 Hudson Street, New York, NY 10014

ELIZABETH R. WOLLHEIM
SHEILA E. GILBERT
PUBLISHERS

www.dawbooks.com

First Printing, September 2014
1 2 3 4 5 6 7 8 9

AUTHOR'S NOTE

Before I began writing fiction, I wrote musicals. And before I wrote musicals, I acted in them—in summer stock and dinner theatres all over the country. In swanky hotels and quaint country inns, in a converted church in upstate New York and in a dilapidated barn in Southbury, Connecticut.

I acted in brilliant shows and schlocky ones, in air-conditioned comfort and in stifling summer heat. I soldiered through wardrobe malfunctions and choreographic collisions, props that went missing and revolving sets that refused to revolve, blood packs that leaked before the fatal gunshot went off and gunshots that failed to go off altogether. I performed for audiences who were enthralled, audiences who were indifferent, and audiences who were much more interested in the dinner buffet than the show. I worked with gifted performers as well as dreadful ones, with directors who were inspirational and others who were downright sadistic. I met people who slipped out of my life after the curtain came down, others who became lifelong friends, and—at the Southbury Playhouse—my future husband.

I poured those experiences and many more into *Spellcast* and *Spellcrossed*, the two novels that make up this omnibus. And I poured myself into protagonist Maggie Graham, giving her my string of jobs, my hometown, my sense of humor, and—most of all—my love for the theatre.

The Southbury Playhouse is gone now, demolished to build a shopping center. But I'll always remember the seasons I spent there. I hope the time you spend at the Crossroads Theatre will prove memorable as well, and that its magical spell will linger long after you close this book.

Barbara Ashford

To learn more about the world
of the Crossroads Theatre,
visit www.barbara-ashford.com.

SPELLCAST

ACKNOWLEDGMENTS

Bear with me. A lot of people helped me create this book and I'm going to thank all of them!

My writing friends who provided feedback and critiques: Dr. Karl Korri, Michele Korri, Kate Marshall, Michael Samerdyke, Shara Saunsaucie White, Susan Sielinski, Dave Stier.

My friends and colleagues in the theatre who filled in the blanks, refreshed my memory, and corrected my technical errors: Sargent Aborn (Tams-Witmark), Jay Dias, Richard Ginsburg, Andrew Gmoser, Michael Kamtman, Richard Norton, Buck Ross, Steven Silverstein.

The helpful residents of the Green Mountain State who assisted with research, in particular: Patricia Buck (Dover Historical Society), Julie Moore (Wilmington Historical Society), Ned Phoenix (Estey Organ Museum), Stephanie Ryan (*The Bennington Banner*).

My sister and niece—Cathy Klenk and Carter Klenk-Morse—for details of Wilmington and Brooklyn. And menu suggestions! And my brother-in-law Ellis Underkoffler whose photo inspired the appearance of the Crossroads Theatre.

My editor, Sheila Gilbert, who said, "You know, you should write a fantasy that draws on your theatre background." God forbid I think of it!

And the actors, staff, and crew members I've been privileged to work with, especially my husband, David Lofink. Our long run began after we starred opposite each other in *Bedroom Farce* at another barn theatre—the Southbury Playhouse. He is the inspiration for everything I write, and this book is dedicated to him.

OVERTURE

*I*T HAS BEGUN. *The annual migration to this small corner of the world.*

Tomorrow, they will arrive, just as they have for so many years. Bewitched, bothered, and bewildered, to quote the old song title.

Most will find a logical way to explain why they have come here: an impromptu desire to travel, a chance turning at a crossroads, a series of unremarkable coincidences that brought them to this place on this day. Only a few will simply accept what is happening and embrace it. The world looks upon them as dreamers or mystics or fools. But they are the ones who come closest to grasping the truth.

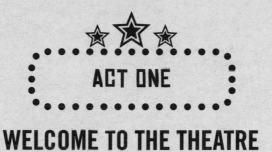

ACT ONE

WELCOME TO THE THEATRE

CHAPTER 1

SOME ENCHANTED EVENING

ON A SCALE OF ONE TO TEN, the day had registered 9.5 on the Suck Scale even before I climbed into the bathtub with my bottle of Talisker. First, the "I'm sorry, but the recent merger means that we'll have to let some people go" speech at work. Then, the horrifically exuberant letter from some college classmate that exclaimed, "Hurry, Maggie! Only a few days left to register for our tenth reunion!"

Now, it appeared to be snowing. Inside my bathroom.

I gazed heavenward and frowned. A few moments ago, the crack in the ceiling had merely struck me as a depressing metaphor for my life. Now, it had blossomed into a giant spiderweb.

Mesmerized by whisky and the sheer improbability of yet another disaster, I watched the web expand. Like a character in a movie who stands on the frozen lake while you're shouting at the screen, "The ice is breaking up, you moron!"

When the first chunk of plaster struck my knee, I grabbed the Talisker and scrambled to safety. Seconds later, a chunk the size of my microwave plummeted into the tub, sending a small tidal wave lapping across my feet.

I stared at the icebergs of plaster floating in the tub, at the gaping hole in my ceiling, at the water racing down the hallway. Then I did what any strong, self-reliant New Yorker would do after surviving the loss of her job and the reminder of ten years of lackluster achievement on both personal and professional fronts. I cried.

After which I blew my nose, drained the tub, mopped up the mess, dried myself off, and called Jorge, the super. By the time he rang the doorbell, I was already packing.

❧❧

I reviewed my options to the accompaniment of Jorge's sorrowful ruminations in Spanish.

No way was I staying in my apartment. It was just too damn depressing.

I could scurry down to Delaware, but I knew I'd run afoul of my mother's bullshit detector. Realizing that some major life crisis had prompted my spur-of-the-moment visit, she'd interrogate me ruthlessly until I came clean. And then I'd have her desperation to deal with on top of mine.

A colleague's apartment? Half my coworkers had lost their jobs in today's bloodbath. The rest felt guilty about hanging on to them. Either way, they didn't need me showing up on their doorsteps, and I didn't need to relive the whole saga with them.

Friends from college? The few I kept in touch with were scattered around the country.

Friends in the city? None.

Still clutching the pair of socks I'd been rolling up, I sank onto my futon. Two years in the city, zero friends. There were the other residents of my brownstone, most of whom I knew by sight rather than name, my colleagues at HelpLink, a few blind dates that my colleagues had arranged, but no real friends. The nice West Indian greengrocer who occasionally tossed an extra mango in my bag didn't really count.

I hauled out the stash of travel books I'd been collecting since I got the job at HelpLink. I'd never gone anywhere, but I had two weeks' severance and two years of meager savings, and if ever I needed to escape Brooklyn, it was now.

I weighed the relative merits of Southern hospitality, Rocky Mountain vistas, and Pacific coastlines before deciding I couldn't afford to splurge on airfare. Then I picked up a guide to New England's bed and breakfasts.

And bing! I had the answer.

What could be more New Englandy than Vermont? The

perfect place to retreat, relax, regroup. Patchwork quilts on
the bed. Rocking chairs on the porch. Groves of maples.
Babbling brooks. Cows.

Normally, I would have spent hours researching ameni-
ties and prices. But if I was going to spend the next God
knows how many months winging it, I figured I might as
well start now.

The next morning, I threw an overnight bag into my ancient Honda Civic and headed north. My spirit of adventure
faded somewhere on I-91. Everyone in Connecticut and
Massachusetts seemed to be fleeing their respective states.
It was like gold had been discovered in the Green Mountains or I'd inadvertently entered an alternate universe
where lemmings could drive. After six endless hours, I
bailed onto a two-lane road and set off in search of a quaint
country hideaway.

The road wound through dense stands of trees that still
wore that new-leaf green that had adorned New York a
month earlier. Eventually, the forest gave way to rolling
countryside that looked like it had posed for a *Vermont Life*
calendar. Stone walls surrounded fields where black-and-
white Holsteins grazed. Purple wildflowers ran riot in a
meadow, while daffodils hugged the foundations of a dilapidated shed.

I passed farmhouses and barns, a Buddhist meditation
center and a blacksmith's forge, but the closest thing to a
town was a collection of rundown mobile homes that had
definitely not posed for a *Vermont Life* calendar. I was beginning to regret the whole winging-it thing when the road
came to an abrupt end.

A sign informed me that I had reached the township of
Hillandale, evidently Vermont's version of the Twin Cities
since Hill lay a mile to the north and Dale three miles to the
south. Logic and my sore butt called for a right turn toward
Hill, but the same instinct that had made me bail told me to
turn left.

As I rumbled over a wooden trestle bridge, I glimpsed a
man crouched on a slab of rock on the stream bank below.
A little girl clung to his hand, staring intently at the opposite bank.

"Who knows what might be under those tree roots, Mag-

gie! Pirate treasure. Or a family of gnomes. Or a gateway to another world."

I pulled over, astonished and angry to find tears burning my eyes. A couple of deep breaths banished the unwanted memory, but my first glimpse of Dale was a little blurry.

Once it came into focus, it proved to be the quintessential New England town, minus the fall foliage. White church steeples. Open fields. Virgin forest. A stream gleaming like polished brass in the last rays of sunlight still peeking over the mountains.

A green-and-white sign welcomed me to Dale, founded in seventeen-something-or-other. I felt like I'd reached the promised land.

I passed a deserted lunch stand and a well-manicured cemetery. Then I spied a large white barn in a meadow. My foot came off the gas pedal as if it had a mind of its own.

It wasn't your typical Vermont barn. Narrow windows along one side formed five Gothic arches. A tall cupola with the same slatted windows sprouted from the roof. Atop it, a spire pointed heavenward, furthering the barn's odd resemblance to a cathedral. Or a Wiccan house of worship. For under the steep central gable, there was an enormous five-pointed star.

I hit the brake. Architectural anomalies aside, I had the weird feeling that I'd seen the barn before. But that was impossible. I'd never been in Dale in my life.

"Need help, miss?"

The words jolted me out of my reverie. A pickup truck had pulled up next to me. An old guy in a John Deere cap regarded me from the passenger side, patiently awaiting my response. It was such a far cry from the typical New York reaction that I just stared at him. Then I stammered, "No. Thanks. I was just . . ."

Gawking at a barn like a stupid tourist.

"If you're looking for the crossroads—"

"Coffee. I could really use some coffee."

"Chatterbox Café. Next to the hotel."

A hotel sounded promising. Maybe I'd skip the bed and breakfast and crash there.

As I continued down the road, the rearview mirror reflected the shrinking image of the barn. It seemed forlorn somehow. But that was as much a product of my overactive imagination as that earlier moment of déjà vu.

The town looked anything but forlorn. White clapboard houses lined the street, most with porches and many with rocking chairs. No B&B signs on the front lawns, just an elderly couple sitting in a pair of Adirondack chairs and a little boy throwing a Frisbee to an enthusiastic golden retriever.

There were a surprising number of cars on the road, most heading in the opposite direction. Traffic slowed to a crawl at the village green. I circled the roundabout, fighting the absurd desire to take another look at the barn. After my second circuit, I became absorbed in the town.

The tree-lined street, neat shops, and small white Congregational church created a setting so perfectly Norman Rockwell that I began to suspect it was secretly Ira Levin. But the women looked normal enough in jeans and sweaters. Nary a Stepford Wife in sight.

As I escaped the traffic circle, the Norman Rockwell aura imploded. A screaming pink neon sign advertised Hallee's. Judging from the lingerie in the window, Hallee's was a shopping mecca for New England hookers. Two doors down, a gingerbready building with dragons flanking the front door turned out to be the Mandarin Chalet. Bea's Hive of Beauty and a pub named Duck Inn revealed a strange local penchant for puns.

The Golden Bough Hotel turned out to be a colonnaded edifice that looked like it had been transplanted from a Tennessee Williams play. Next to it, as promised by my Good Samaritan, was the Chatterbox Café.

Placards in the front window announced "Free WiFi" and "Bikers Welcome," neither of which I'd expected in a country town like Dale. I slowed as two ladies exited the café and got into their car. Their flowered dresses and elaborate hats suggested they were off to a revival meeting. I waited for them to back out, then whipped into the vacated parking space.

My arrival seemed to be the cue for a general exodus

from the Chatterbox. In addition to bikers, Dale's tourist trade included Goths, Renaissance fair refugees, and a small Asian street gang.

Time warped as I stepped inside. Patrons and décor seemed to have escaped from the set of *Happy Days* or *Bye Bye Birdie*. In one of the booths lining the left wall, an AARP couple hunkered down over their early bird specials. A noisy group of tweens crowded around the table in the front window, gobbling ice cream sundaes. The linoleum counter with its soda fountain stools reminded me of the Eckerd's drugstore Nana used to take me to when I was little. Same red vinyl seats on the stools. Same glass domes covering the cakes and pies. Same pleasantly stout waitresses in powder blue uniforms.

One of them ambled over as I slumped onto a stool.

"Long day, huh?" Frannie or Francie—there was a dark smear in the middle of her name tag—clucked sympathetically.

"Very."

"Coffee?" she asked, already reaching for the pot.

"Please." I must have sounded desperate, because she shot me a quizzical look over her shoulder. "Cream, no sugar."

Wondering if I looked as frazzled as I'd sounded, I stole a glance at the long mirror behind the counter. The black flecks in the ancient glass made my auburn hair look polka-dotted, while my face seemed to be showing early signs of bubonic plague. My gaze drifted over a framed photograph next to the mirror, then snapped back as I recognized the barn.

Frannie/Francie jerked her head toward it. "Yep. That's the Crossroads Theatre."

"If you're looking for the crossroads . . ."

Maybe that was why the barn had looked so familiar. I'd spent my first season in summer stock at the Southford Playhouse, a converted barn that seated about one hundred people uncomfortably. Bats made occasional appearances, drawing gasps from the audience and stealing focus from the performers. We made a hundred bucks a week, which included living quarters in a dilapidated rooming house nicknamed Anatevka after the village in *Fiddler on the Roof*. And performed in front of a mottled black-and-gray backdrop that we dubbed The Shroud.

Hands down, the best ten weeks of my life.

The mirror reflected back my smile. Quickly descending to earth again, I asked, "Is there a bed and breakfast in the area?"

Frannie/Francie sniffed. "There's one over to Hill calls itself that. Charge you an arm and a leg and give you toast in the morning. But the theatre folk all stay at the Bough."

As she plunked a plastic travel mug on the counter, I quickly said, "Cardboard is fine."

"This is better," she assured me as she poured. "Ten cents off each refill. Think of the savings." I was still doing the math when she added, "Be ready in a jiff. I know you don't want to be late."

"Late?"

"To see the cast lists."

"Cast lists?"

Frannie/Francie froze in the act of snapping the lid on my travel mug. "You mean you haven't auditioned yet?"

I shook my head. "I'm just up for a few—"

"Well, you better head right on over. Auditions close in ten minutes."

I may have inherited my father's love for acting, but that was more than offset by my mother's practicality. I'd given theatre a try, but when I turned thirty, I wrapped my acting dreams in mothballs and got a real job.

As I reached for my coffee, Frannie/Francie snatched up the travel mug and placed it under the counter. "I'll just keep this for you."

"You're holding my coffee hostage?"

"It'll taste even better after you audition."

"Oh, come on . . ."

When I ignored her shooing motions, she flung back the counter's bridge and marched toward me. I headed for the door, still complaining that I really wanted my coffee and I really, really didn't want to audition.

"Sure you do. It'll be fun."

No, it would only remind me that I'd failed as an actress.

Just as I'd failed as a college admissions counselor, a tele-marketer, and a HelpLink representative.

"You'll do fine. Don't worry about your hair."

She followed me out of the café and stood at the curb while I got into my car. As I eased into traffic, I heard her shout, "Break a leg, hon!"

"Break yours," I muttered.

A quick check of the rearview mirror at the roundabout proved she was still standing guard, ruining any chance of sneaking back to the Golden Bough. Resigned to searching for the overpriced B&B she had disdained, I headed north.

As soon as the barn came into view, my heart started racing. And—right on cue—my foot came off the gas pedal. Clearly, my body wanted me to stop, even if my mind was firmly against the idea.

What the hell. It couldn't hurt to look at the place.

I eased my car down the narrow lane, trying to avoid deep ruts that looked like they had been carved by the Con-estoga wagons of Dale's original settlers. A white farm-house sprawled atop a hill, overlooking the meadow and barn much the way the house in *Psycho* looms over the Bates Motel. As I drifted closer, I glimpsed a couple of out-buildings and what might be a small pond. Beyond that stretched the forest primeval.

There were close to two dozen cars in the gravel lot, sporting license plates from all over the Northeast; I even spotted a few from the South.

Even more astonishing were the hopefuls milling around the picnic tables. In addition to the motley crew I'd glimpsed leaving the Chatterbox, I saw a Rocky Balboa clone in a muscle shirt, Luca Brasi's twin brother, two Le-gally Blonde sorority chicks, a black Rasta dude, a white Rasta wannabe, and an elderly man in a walker serenading a mousy-looking woman with a quavering rendition of "Some Enchanted Evening." A few clutched sheet music, but most were empty-handed and looked as bewildered as I felt.

Up close, the theatre was as unimpressive as its prospec-tive actors. The timbers of the barn were more of a sun-bleached gray than white. Ivy crept over its stone foundations to snake up the wood slats. Atop the cupola, a black weather vane in the shape of something vaguely mammalian creaked in the gusting breeze. Shivering, I slipped through the open front door.

Warmth enveloped me. Not merely the physical sensation of walking into a heated building, but something more—like the embrace of an old friend. I shook my head impatiently; no use getting sentimental about the good old days of summer stock.

The small lobby was empty save for an elderly woman sitting in the box office. She looked up from her magazine and examined me over her reading glasses. Her patrician New England face – bone structure to die for—only added to the impression that she was looking down her nose at me. Then she smiled and morphed into the elegant but warmhearted fairy godmother the Disney animators should have given Cinderella.

"Reinhard will be out in a moment."

I nodded politely and made a mental note to flee before then. There was still time to look around, though; beyond the two sets of double doors that led to the house, the current victim had just launched into a quavering a cappella version of "Born to Be Wild."

A flyer impaled to the wall with a thumbtack advertised next weekend's Memorial Day parade. Another flyer— bright pink—advertised the "Spring into Summer Sale" at Hallee's. All corsets twenty-five percent off.

A poster between the house doors revealed that Janet Mackenzie was the theatre's producer, while Rowan Mackenzie was its director. Doubtless some chirpy husband-and-wife team with pretensions of artistic brilliance. They clearly loved musicals because that was all they were doing: *Brigadoon*, *Carousel*—hoary chestnuts both—and an original show called *The Sea-Wife*. Book and lyrics by Rowan Mackenzie. He'd probably bombed in real theatre, but had enough money to start his own to soothe his wounded ego.

God only knew what *The Sea-Wife* was about; if there were mermaids involved, I was doomed. I'd be perfect for the comic lead in *Brigadoon*, but I'd always despised *Carousel*. Maybe because the story hit a little too close to home. Abusive ne'er-do-well woos small-town girl, who continues to adore him no matter what kind of crap he pulls. Returns to earth years after his death to square things with his wife and daughter. Misty-eyed finale with everyone singing some plodding anthem of hope and love.

To be fair, Daddy never hit us. And it was only during that last year that he began vanishing for weeks at a time. Then Mom kicked him out and he vanished for good.

A weight descended on my chest. I shrugged it off. I had no intention of wallowing in the past. Or spending the summer singing about bonnie Jean and real nice clambakes. Or auditioning for the Crossroads Theatre.

Belatedly, I realized that "Born to Be Wild" had concluded. Before I could beat a hasty retreat, one of the house doors opened. A middle-aged man clutching a clipboard strode toward me.

"Name?" he demanded, pen poised.

"No. Sorry. I'm not—"

"Name."

"No. See, I'm not here for the auditions."

"Name!"

The Teutonic bullying brought out my Scotch-Irish temper. "Dorothy Gale. From Kansas."

His deepening frown chiseled new lines into his forehead. "And I am Glinda, the Good Witch of the North."

"As if," a voice proclaimed behind me. "That's my role."

I turned to discover a plumpish young man posed dramatically in the entranceway. His pink shirt *was* roughly the color of Glinda's gown, but he wore ordinary blue jeans rather than a chiffon skirt and, in lieu of a wand, trailed a plum-colored sweater across the floor.

"Reinhard bullies everyone," he said as he breezed toward us. "But he's really a pussycat. I'm Hal. Welcome to the Crossroads."

"Maggie."

"Ha!" With a triumphant grin, Reinhard scribbled down my name.

"Hal as in Hallee's?" I ventured.

"Aren't you the little Miss Marple? Actually, I'm only half of Hallee's. My other half—"

"Better half," Reinhard muttered.

Hal stuck out his tongue. "Lee's closing up shop for me. I have to be here when the cast lists go up. So exciting."

His radiant smile dimmed as he studied me. In my black tunic and sweatpants, I resembled a lumpish ninja. Doubtless, Hal wished he'd brought along one of those twenty-five-percent-off corsets.

The smile returned with so little effort that it had to be genuine. "You'll be wonderful. I have a sixth sense about these things. Next week, after you're settled, you come into the shop. I have a green sarong that'll look fabulous with that hair."

Reinhard sighed heavily. "Last name."

"Graham. I bet you own the Mandarin Chalet."

"His wife does," Hal volunteered. "Reinhard is a pediatrician."

With that wonderful bedside manner, he probably terrified the local children into good health.

"Mei-Yin also does our choreography. I, of course, do costumes. And set design. Lee—"

"She will find all of this out later," Reinhard interrupted. "Now, she auditions."

I cast a despairing look at each of my fairy godmothers, but Hal just beamed and the lady in the box office waggled her fingers.

I knew I should turn around and walk out. But something—curiosity? instinct? my father's musical theatre genes?—impelled me to follow Reinhard into the house.

The doors whispered shut behind us, cutting off the light from the lobby. We stood motionless in the aisle, allowing our eyes to adjust to the dimness.

I'm a sucker for darkened theatres. There's an air of hushed anticipation, more patient and mysterious than the hush that descends before the curtain rises. As if the theatre holds secrets that it will reveal only to those who will surrender to its magic and allow it to carry them away to another place, another time, another world.

Beneath the odors of dust and old upholstery, I smelled paint and fresh-cut wood, as if the theatre had been erected that morning instead of decades ago. And something more elusive that made me think of warm summer earth and a thick mulch of pine needles.

A shiver crawled up my back. I rubbed my arms, firmly quelling my imagination and the emerging crop of goose bumps.

Mr. "Born to Be Wild" must have left via another door, for the stage was empty. Thick clouds of dust motes lent a Brigadoony mistiness to the pool of light center stage. The music director's head peeped over the rim of the orchestra pit, hair gleaming like a newly minted penny. In the center section of the house, I spotted the dark silhouette of the director.

My stomach went into freefall.

"Break a leg, sweetie."

I started at Hal's whisper, unaware that he'd slipped in behind us. As Reinhard edged past me, I whispered that I didn't have any material, that I hadn't brought a resume or headshot. He ignored my running monologue and marched down the aisle. And once again, I trotted after him like an obedient puppy.

I mounted the five steps to the stage with the alacrity of Marie Antoinette en route to the guillotine. Then I remembered that I was a New Yorker, for God's sake. And once upon a time, people had paid to see me perform. I straightened my slumping shoulders and strode onto the stage as if I owned it.

A shock of static electricity stopped me in my tracks. And with it, that weird sense of coming home that I had felt when I stepped inside the barn.

Get a grip, Graham.

I took a deep breath, let it out, and walked into the pool of light.

"Good afternoon. And welcome."

Although I knew the invisible director was just adopting the same soothing tone I used on HelpLink calls, my heartbeat slowed from rabbit speed to human.

"I'd like you to read a scene first. Something from *Brigadoon.*"

I couldn't place his faint accent, but it was also strangely soothing.

"If you please, Reinhard."

Reinhard thrust a piece of paper at me. Meg and Jeff. Funny, secondary-lead stuff. No sweat. Hearing Jeff's lines delivered in a German accent reminded me how absurd this whole thing was.

"Very nice," Rowan Mackenzie said when I finished. He probably said that to everyone, but a warm glow blossomed in my stomach.

"What will you be singing for us today?"

Exit warm glow, stage left.

I shot a panicked glance at the music director, who just stared up expectantly from his piano in the pit. I couldn't think of anything. Neither the uptempo number nor the ballad I'd always used for auditions. I tried to remember the plodding anthem from *Carousel*, but all I came up with was "A Real Nice Clambake."

Then a title popped into my head. Before I could stop myself, I blurted it out.

I had to hand it to the music director; the guy didn't miss a beat. Never mind that it was a man's song. And a major cheese-fest. With a rippling arpeggio, he launched into the intro of "Some Enchanted Evening."

In spite of my horror, I noted that Penny Hair had chosen a good key for me. Silently blessing him, I dove in. The first verse was shaky, but by the second, I'd begun to enjoy mocking the sappy lyrics and over-ripe music.

But at the end of the bridge, something strange happened. I found myself remembering how I'd felt when I met Michael freshman year. And how Eric burst out laughing when I bumped into him at the Cineplex and drenched him with Diet Coke. That giddy, unexpected "Oh, my God" magic that warms you like single malt whisky and leaves you cold and shivering at the same time.

And just like that, I was singing my heart out. My voice soared during that final verse, only to drop to a choked whisper at the end. The last note was still hanging in the air when Hal shouted "Brava!" and began clapping. The silhouetted head turned, and the applause stopped.

Just as abruptly, my chick-flick sentimentality evaporated. Moisture prickled my armpits and forehead, that awful cold dampness that actors call flop sweat. I hung my head, desperately searching for a trap in the floor so I could plummet quietly to my death.

"Now as to your availability . . ."

"She came in late." Reinhard's disapproving voice boomed out of the darkness. "She did not fill out the form."

"Thank you, Reinhard. Rehearsals begin after Memorial Day. The season ends in mid-August. We hope our actors will be able to join us for the entire summer, but that's not always possible. I need to accommodate everyone's schedule when I make casting decisions, so if you could tell me your availability . . ."

"Oh, I'm available. Free as the wind. No job. No husband at home. Not even any home to speak of since the bathroom ceiling caved in."

Realizing that I sounded more pathetic than amusing, I shut my mouth. The ensuing silence brought on another wave of flop sweat.

He'd given me the perfect cue and I'd blown it. I should have politely but firmly told him that I wasn't looking for a job. Not here, anyway. I had to get back to Brooklyn. File for unemployment. Check out job sites.

As I opened my mouth to explain, he said, "Thank you. Would you please wait outside? The stage door is to your right."

I slunk into the wings where a work light guided me to the door. As I stepped into the real world, the little old man with the walker advanced carefully over the grass.

"Such a lovely song. Not so often you hear a girl sing it."

The familiar cadences of New York restored my spirits.

"We danced to it at our wedding, Rachel and me." As I glanced around, he added, "No, no. She passed away a few months ago."

"I'm so sorry."

"Fifty-two years we were married."

"Wow. That's terrific. Sometimes it feels like I've gone that long without a date."

"A nice young thing like you? You've got plenty of time to find Mr. Right. Who knows? Maybe here. Look at my granddaughter, Sarah." He jerked his head over his shoulder. "The one with the blue hair who's eating up whatever Jack Kerouac's dishing out."

I smothered a laugh; the kid his granddaughter was with did look like a young Jack Kerouac.

"The two of you drove all the way up from the city?" I asked.

"You're a New Yorker, too?" he exclaimed. Because of course, to New Yorkers, there is only one city.

"Transplanted," I admitted.

"Born and bred." He thumped his chest proudly and listed a little to starboard, but steadied himself before I had to leap to the rescue. "Prospect Park."

"Crown Heights."

"We're practically neighbors! Well. Would have been. I live with my daughter now. Over in Manchester."

"If you don't mind my asking . . ."

"Ask."

"Are you an actor?"

"Dentist. Retired. Bernie Cohen."

"Maggie Graham. But you auditioned?"

"Me and Sarah both."

"How did you even find this place?"

"Well, it's funny . . ." His gaze moved past me, and he whispered, "I'll tell you later. Here comes Hermann Goering with the cast lists."

It seemed impossible that Rowan Mackenzie had made his decisions so quickly; I'd known directors who spent days mulling over their choices. But Hal was tacking sheets of paper to the side of the barn.

The buzz of conversation died, replaced by a silence so profound I could hear the creak of the weather vane and the soft whistle of Dr. Cohen's breathing.

Reinhard surveyed us, frowning. "The cast lists are up. Three copies. So do not crowd."

We darted nervous glances at each other, uncertain if this was our cue to inspect the lists and reluctant to move without Reinhard's permission. He nodded, clearly pleased by our obedience, then said, "Now. You look."

In the general stampede that ensued, I stuck close to Dr. Cohen so he wouldn't be trampled. There were excited exclamations as people found their names. A few retreated in obvious elation. Most just looked confused. But clearly, everyone had gotten a role, because there were no tears or brave "It's an honor to be nominated" smiles.

After the first wave subsided, I edged forward with Dr. Cohen and his granddaughter. Once again, my heart was pounding like a demented bongo, but I tried to appear nonchalant as I scanned the list.

Brigadoon: Chorus. Chorus? I nailed that scene. And he put me in the chorus?

The Sea-Wife: Chorus. Again.

Carousel: Nettie. Who the hell was Nettie? The tough-talking carousel owner?

The ear-shattering squeal of a pig being slaughtered turned out to be Dr. Cohen's granddaughter. "Grandpa, I got Louise!"

"That's wonderful, sweetheart!" He angled away from her to mouth, "Who's Louise?"

"I think that's the daughter in *Carousel*," I whispered. "With the big ballet number."

"Ballet?" He glanced at Sarah who was jumping up and down, plump bosoms, belly, and thighs quivering like Jell-O. "Oy. So who's this Mr. Lundie? If he's got a ballet number, I don't want to know."

"You're safe. He's the village elder who explains the miracle of Brigadoon."

"What miracle?" Luca Brasi demanded, shouldering a geeky accountant type aside.

"Of why the town vanishes into the mists and returns for one day every hundred years."

"Cool." One of the Legally Blondes nodded solemnly.

"What about this Heavenly Friend in *Carousel*?" the shorter church lady asked.

"I think he . . . she's a sort of angel."

As the church lady preened, the straw hat of her taller companion loomed behind her shoulder. "And Mrs. Mullin?"

I suddenly remembered who Nettie was: not the tough-talking carousel owner but the salt-of-the-earth woman who sings the plodding anthem whose name had eluded me earlier: "You'll Never Walk Alone." As well as "June Is Bustin' Out All Over." And the fucking clambake song.

It wasn't the age thing I minded. Much. I was rarely cast as the ingénue, even when I was the right age to play one. I'd played Mrs. Kendal in *The Elephant Man*, the Witch in *Into the Woods*. But those were sexy, witty, glamorous roles. Starring roles. Not well-meaning, anthem-singing, clambake-loving frumps.

"Does anybody know who Mrs. Mullin is?" the second church lady pleaded.

"I think she's the owner of the carousel," I replied.

"And Carrie?"

"Hey! *I'm* Harry."

"Not Harry. *Carrie*."

"What about this guy Charlie?"

In moments, I was surrounded, spitting out plot synopses and character snapshots. It was clear most of them knew nothing about these shows. What the hell were they doing here? More importantly, what the hell was I doing here? Chorus in some dreadful original musical. An anonymous villager in *Brigadoon*. And Our Lady of the Clambake.

Rowan Mackenzie must be blind. Or on crack. Why would he cast me as Nettie when he had his pick of not one, but two church ladies? Or cast the geeky accountant as sinister Jigger when he was clearly made to play the insufferable Mr. Snow? And what bonnie Jean in her right mind would go home with Luca Brasi?

What made it more confusing was that some of the casting was spot on. Dr. Cohen was perfect for wise old Mr. Lundie. And Jack Kerouac would be great as the brooding guy who nearly destroys Brigadoon. So how come some of Rowan Mackenzie's picks were so right and others so woefully wrong?

There was an onslaught of shushing as Reinhard waved his clipboard.

"Rehearsals start after Memorial Day. You will be paid one hundred dollars a week. You will live at the Golden Bough. No charge. You will have breakfast at the Chatterbox. No charge. All this is spelled out in the contract. But you do not sign now. Tonight, we celebrate. Dinner at the Mandarin Chalet. No charge. Rooms at the Golden Bough. No charge. Tomorrow, ten o'clock, company meeting. Here. You meet the director. You meet the staff. You make up your minds. Any questions?"

Only about a thousand. But they could wait. I'd take the free food and the free night's lodging. Hell, I'd even stick around for the company meeting to get a look at the demented Rowan Mackenzie. After that, I would hit the road.

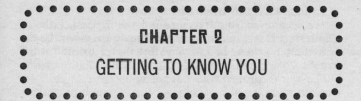

CHAPTER 2
GETTING TO KNOW YOU

THE NEXT MORNING FOUND ME AT THE CHATTERBOX, surprisingly well-rested but no closer to understanding the method behind Mackenzie's casting madness. My plan to pump Hal for information had failed miserably when I ended up at a dinner table with six other bemused cast members and Javier, captain of the stage crew, who was long on charm but short on facts.

Later, I'd voiced my doubts to my roommate, the mousy-looking woman who'd been on the receiving end of Bernie Cohen's serenade. Nancy possessed either a high degree of inner serenity or a low tolerance for late-night chat. All I discovered was that she was a librarian who lived just over the border in Massachusetts with her mother, that she had learned about the auditions while visiting Javier's antique store, and that she had been cast in what should have been my role as Meg in *Brigadoon*. I crawled into bed, pulled the patchwork quilt over my head, and tried to banish the image of Reinhard chortling with unholy glee as he paired us up.

Breakfast proved equally unenlightening. I found allies in Lou—the Luca Brasi look-alike—and Kevin—the Jack Kerouac clone. Everyone else shrugged off my concerns.

Bernie Cohen patted my hand. "So we go to the theatre. We listen to their spiel. What's the harm?"

Frannie (she'd cleaned her name tag) clucked and refilled my coffee cup. "You gotta learn to relax, hon. Things are different in Dale."

"That's what I'm afraid of."

We decamped for the theatre, most of the cast clutching Chatterbox travel mugs, proof that they were in for the duration. Didn't these people have lives to return to? Jobs? Families? Was the Crossroads Theatre some kind of bizarre public works project, the human equivalent of cash for clunkers? Was it a nest of cultists? Was I the only one asking these questions?

"You're not a clunker," Bernie assured me as we settled into our seats in the second row. "And as for cults ... what cult would have Hermann Goering as its front man? For that, you want a face like *his*."

He could only mean Javier, who was strolling onto the stage with his arm around a young woman in overalls. That had to be his wife, Catherine, who was in charge of set construction. If Javier had been tight-lipped about Rowan Mackenzie, he'd had no such reservations about Catherine. In true newlywed fashion, he'd gushed about her artistic nature, her extraordinary handcrafted furniture, her business sense, her natural beauty.

Thanks to Javier, I also knew that the penny-haired music director was Catherine's father. Alex was the kind of man who epitomized nice: pleasant face, friendly smile. If I wanted a recruiting officer for my cult, I'd pick Alex, hands down.

Lee and Hal were clearly a case of opposites attracting. Where Hal talked nonstop, hands flying to punctuate his words, Lee was quiet. Hal wore another vivid shirt—this one buttercup yellow—Lee, a white T-shirt and jeans. And while Hal might be cute in a "pinch those Dutch boy cheeks" kind of way, Lee was drop-dead gorgeous, an impossible amalgam of Kanye West, Derek Jeter, and Beyoncé.

In terms of odd couples, however, Reinhard and Mei-Yin had them beat. She'd been in the kitchen last night, but given "Chinese-American choreographer" to work with, I had imagined an ethereal beauty whose haunted expression testified to Reinhard's bullying and their loveless marriage. The reality was a short, middle-aged barrel of a woman whose piercing voice silenced all conversation and produced a scramble onstage as the staff lined up. Even Reinhard jumped to obey, drill sergeant deferring to commanding officer.

Helen, my box-office fairy godmother, had to be related to the sandy-haired, middle-aged woman standing next to her. Mother and daughter? Aunt and niece? While they shared the same fabulous bone structure, the younger woman's hatchet face held none of Helen's sweetness. "Formidable" was one descriptor that came to mind. "Ball buster" was another.

Reinhard introduced her as Janet Mackenzie. Owner of the "Bates mansion," the Golden Bough, and the Crossroads Theatre. She was also in charge of hospitality. I studied that unsmiling face, tried to imagine her serving up cupcakes and punch, and felt a quick stab of pity for her husband.

As Reinhard launched into a dramatic reading of our contract, I leaned toward Bernie to whisper, "So where's our illustrious director?"

"Waiting to make a big entrance, maybe."

Reinhard paused and glared at us over his ubiquitous clipboard. "There is a question?"

"No. Sorry," I called out and turned my attention to our contract.

Ridiculous to call it that. The one-page document merely spelled out everything Reinhard had told us yesterday and listed our roles. No grounds for dismissal. Not even a line for a signature. Nothing, in fact, that made the "contract" unforceable as a legal document.

Why should I be surprised? Nothing about this place was normal.

Impatiently, I eyed the wings, willing Rowan Mackenzie to show up. I pictured a gaunt man dressed in black, with a melancholy expression, a tragic past, and some horrible deformity. A blend of Dracula, the Phantom of the Opera, and Quasimodo.

I was still debating the hump when Reinhard's stentorian voice faltered. The heads of every staff member jerked right. Murmurs rose from the company. One of the Legally Blondes squeaked. Ashley or Brittany. I still couldn't tell them apart.

A slender man walked onstage. No discernible hump. He wore black jeans, but the shirt was disappointingly beige. His hair was black, too. He wore it loose and very Viggo Mortensen, which was fine for *The Lord of the Rings* but seemed affected for a resident of Vermont rather than Middle Earth. But at least it was clean. Was I the only woman in the world who had watched that movie and wondered why the dwarf always had clean hair while the king looked like he shampooed with lard?

Rowan's vampiric pallor fit nicely with my preconceived image. His stature did not; he was only an inch or so taller than fairy godmother Helen. But he radiated a quiet confidence that gave you the sense that he was in control of himself, the theatre, and everyone in it.

"If there are no questions, I will turn you over to your director, Rowan Mackenzie." With a flourish of his clipboard, Reinhard stepped back, allowing Rowan to assume center stage.

"Thank you, Reinhard. On behalf of the entire staff, I'd like to welcome you to the Crossroads Theatre."

That voice. Yesterday's nerves had kept me from fully appreciating it. Soft and intimate, as if he were speaking only to you, yet each word carried clearly. He augmented its power by allowing his gaze to roam slowly across the front rows, ensuring that each person felt embraced by his welcome.

"I had a chance to meet you briefly yesterday. In the weeks to come, I hope to get to know you better."

Forget about directing. He should have been a therapist. Or a hypnotist. Or a snake charmer.

You are getting sleepy . . . sleepy . . . you want to join our company . . . you want to turn your life savings over to me . . .

"Svengali," I whispered.

Bernie started as if emerging from a dream. "But lovely teeth."

"Your contract outlines the basic information about your stay with us."

Rowan's gaze lingered on me, as if he'd sensed my silent derision. I slumped a little lower in my seat.

"After this meeting, Reinhard will give you a tour of the

theatre and our adjacent outbuildings. He'll also have you fill out a short information form—name, address, cell phone, that sort of thing—and hand out scripts and vocal books to those of you in *Brigadoon*. Be sure to refer to the pages outlining the changes and cuts I've made."

One demerit for dissing the shades of Lerner and Loewe.

"Alex will give you an audio recording of your vocal part. Please let him know which format you'd prefer—tape, CD, or MP3."

Okay. Bonus point for organization.

"Some of you will want to return home until rehearsals begin next Tuesday. However, if you cannot afford to do so or you've come from a great distance, you're welcome to stay at the Golden Bough this week as our guest."

Double bonus points for generosity.

"I've been part of this theatre for many years. The staff and I have mounted dozens of shows with actors who have little or no experience. I'm sure you're wondering how we manage that."

Well, the answer is simple. We take you into a subterranean room where we grow these giant pods . . .

"Well, the answer is simple."

I jerked erect in my seat.

"Hard work."

I wondered sourly if his little smile was directed at me.

"Learning the dances, the songs, the staging. Understanding the characters. Bringing them to life. Working as a team. There will be times when you'll want to quit. When you'll think it's not worth it. But . . ." A pause while that penetrating gaze swept over us again. "If you trust me and allow yourselves to believe that we can make the impossible happen on this stage, we'll have a summer to remember all our lives."

A self-deprecating shrug to undercut the rhetoric. A paternal smile to embrace the huddled masses. You could almost feel the entire cast heaving a collective sigh.

"Thank you for listening so patiently. I look forward to sharing our season at the Crossroads."

Cue curtain. Cue applause. Reinhard herded everyone stage left for the tour. I exited stage right in pursuit of Svengali. Seeing no one in the shadowy wings, I groped my way toward the stage door, flung it open, and bellowed, "Rowan!"

"Can I help you?" a soft voice inquired just behind me.

With an unfeminine screech, I spun around and promptly bashed my head into something. "Jesus, don't do that."

"I'm sorry . . . Maggie, isn't it?"

"Yes, I . . ." For some reason, I couldn't catch my breath. I was hyperventilating like mad and my ears were ringing. Brilliant gold sparks flashed before me like fireflies. A fog of black spots narrowed my field of vision to the pale oval of Rowan's face.

"Maggie?"

This was ridiculous. I hadn't hit my head that hard. I clutched the doorframe and tried to take deep, calming breaths, but my knees buckled.

Strong arms lifted me as if I were Legally Blonde weight instead of a size twelve if the pants were cut just right and had elastic in the waistband. I floated past the picnic tables and into the meadow beyond, silently assuring myself that I had never fainted in my life and was not about to start now.

My first sensation on regaining consciousness was breathing in a sweet, floral scent. My brain finally processed it as honeysuckle. Since it was far too early for honeysuckle to be blooming, it must be Rowan's cologne. What kind of a man wore honeysuckle cologne? He was either boldly confident about his masculinity or totally gay. Or both.

Sunlight warmed my left cheek. Something hard dug into my right. Rowan Mackenzie's heartbeat thudded in my ear. It seemed unusually slow, but maybe he was a Zen master as well as a weightlifter.

I kept my eyes closed while I considered how to repair my shattered dignity. Fingers probed the back of my head gently before brushing against my forehead. So cool, those fingers, and incredibly soothing. As was the voice that murmured my name. My body relaxed. Then tensed as other voices intruded on my pleasant stupor.

"Oh, my God. Is she all right? Should I call 911?"

Hal, of course.

"She fainted," Rowan replied. "I think she bumped her head."

"Oh, poor thing."

Fairy godmother Helen.

"Should I get Reinhard?" A man's voice. Lee, maybe?

"It's just a bump on the head." A woman's voice this time, sharp and authoritative. "Hal, stop hopping around and fetch a damp cloth and a glass of water. The rest of you, back to the theatre."

The thud of retreating footsteps and the murmur of worried voices. A silence broken only by the ecstatic warbling of a robin. And then: "Isn't it a bit early for you to start sweeping women off their feet, Rowan?"

The same female voice as before, but softer now. And venomous.

"I didn't sweep, Janet. Merely caught her before she fell."

I could feel her studying me and tried not to flinch.

"I wouldn't have picked her as the fainting type."

"The air was a little close backstage."

"The air is whatever you—"

"As Maggie can tell you since she regained consciousness several minutes ago."

Busted.

I considered a theatrical fluttering of my eyelashes, but contented myself with simply opening my eyes and staring up at Janet.

Her gaze traveled over me. "Well. At least this one can act."

As she walked toward the theatre, I sat up and gingerly felt the back of my head. No gaping wound. No blood. Just a small but painful lump.

"Is she really in charge of hospitality?" I asked.

"One of life's little ironies," Rowan replied. "But her charm wasn't directed at you."

"I imagine working together can be a strain on any marriage."

Rowan's smile betrayed creases at the corners of his eyes. "Good thing we're not married, then."

"Oh. I just assumed . . . because of the last name . . ."

"It's a common name in Dale."

"Fourth cousins or something."

The smile vanished. "Something."

He gazed up at the Bates mansion, absently stroking the

braided silver chain around his throat. I took advantage of his momentary absorption to study him.

The boyishly smooth cheeks belonged with a softer face. His was all angles—long nose, jutting cheekbones, sharp chin, swooping black-winged eyebrows. Even his eyes were slightly slanted. From the house, they had looked hazel, but up close, they were definitely green. Cat eyes. Or a fox, maybe.

Abruptly, those cat-or-maybe-fox eyes shifted back to me. "You're sure you're all right? No dizziness?"

I shook my head and started to get up, but he forestalled me with a hand on my shoulder. "Wait a bit. Just to be sure."

I rubbed my cheek, fingertips probing a small indentation.

"You wanted to ask me something, I believe."

As I tried to remember what, I realized why I had a dented cheek. His shirt buttons were small but decidedly pointy.

"Are those made out of bone?" I blurted.

Startled, he stared down at his shirtfront, then nodded solemnly. "The bones of former cast members. Who proved . . . troublesome."

For a second—okay, maybe a few seconds—I just stared at him. Then I realized he was screwing with me. He leaned back on his hands, completely unperturbed by my scowl.

"Actually, they're antler tines. And no, I don't race after bucks and wrest their antlers from their heads with my bare hands."

"Of course not. You wait until they shed their antlers, then drag them to the scene shop and saw them up. Along with the bodies of cast members who proved troublesome."

"I'll have to try that next year. Meanwhile, I'll continue to order my shirts online."

"From Last-of-the-Mohicans-Menswear.com?"

The antler tines bounced as he laughed. "I assume you didn't follow me to discuss my taste in clothes."

I shifted uncomfortably, dug a pebble out from under my butt, and said, "It's about the theatre. It seems a bit . . . unconventional."

He nodded, waiting.

"I've done some acting before."

"I gathered that."

I resisted the urge to preen. This was not about my ego. At least, I didn't think it was.

"If you're concerned about your Equity status . . ." he began.

"I wish."

I'd never made it into the actors' union. Just four years in out-of-the-way non-Equity theatres, holding down a series of dead-end jobs to pay the bills. Any lingering urge to preen vanished.

"Look. Can I be blunt?"

"Please."

I scrambled to my feet. He rose with far more grace, one hand extended in case I showed signs of imminent collapse. I was struck again by his height. Or lack of it. Maybe an inch taller than me and I'm hardly statuesque.

Realizing I was staring again, I forced my mind back on track. "Most of the people in there have never been on a stage in their lives. They don't even know why they came here."

"Why did *you* come here?"

"I was looking for a B&B and Frannie held my coffee hostage . . ." I took a deep breath and tried again. "Some of your choices are a little hard to understand. I mean, casting Luca . . . Lou as Charlie, and Sarah as Louise—"

"And Nancy in the role you wanted."

"That's not what this is about," I said, silently vowing to slug him if he quoted that annoying theatre truism: "There are no small roles, only small actors."

"You could play Meg with your eyes shut. Why should I offer you that role?"

"Because that's what directors do!"

"I don't."

"Yeah. I got that. What I don't get is why."

His gaze moved skyward, then returned to me. "I cast people in the roles they need, not necessarily the ones they'd be good at."

I need to be an anonymous Villager? And Our Lady of the Clambake?

Those green eyes held mine. Flecks of gold danced in their depths, like the sparks I'd seen right before I fainted.

"You're right. This is not your typical summer stock theatre. We're here—I'm here—to serve the players as much as
the players are here to serve the show. Ask the staff. Most
of them wandered to the theatre the same way you did. And
they were just as unsure why. But they found something
here that had been . . . lacking in their lives. Something they
didn't even know they were looking for. I know it sounds
crazy, but it's worked for a very long time. Why not give it a
chance? What have you got to lose?"

"Well, in no particular order of importance, my unemployment benefits, my apartment, my sanity . . ."

He laughed and held up his hands in surrender. "Rehearsals don't start for another week. Think about it. If you
decide to join us, we'll be pleased to have you. If not . . ." He
shrugged. "The theatre will always be here." His smile
faded.

Before I could barrage him with more questions, the
stage door banged open and Hal appeared, a cloth in one
hand and a mug in the other. I was surprised to discover
fairy godmother Helen leaning against the side of the barn.
Hal raced past her, spilling most of the water en route.

"It's my coffee mug, but I don't have germs. Are you feeling better? You nearly gave me a heart attack." He held up
the dripping cloth. "Do you want this? Or the water?"

"No. But thanks for bringing them."

He slapped the cloth on his forehead and gulped down
the water. "So. Is she staying? Are you staying? You have to.
You can't walk out after that dramatic beginning."

When I hesitated, Rowan replied, "She's thinking about
it."

"What's to think about?" Hal hooked his arm in mine
and led me toward the theatre. "I'm an artistic genius. Even
when forced to design an entire season of happy villager
drag." He shot a reproachful look over his shoulder at
Rowan. "Alex is a love. Helen's an angel. She's feeling better," he called and received an appropriately angelic smile
in response. "Mei-Yin's a terror, but you'll get used to her.
And Reinhard. They're really both—"

"Pussycats?"

"Absolutely."

"Is Rowan a pussycat, too?" I inquired sweetly.

Hal burst out laughing.

"I'll take that as a no."

"Rowan is brilliant and insightful and deliciously mysterious."

"Yes, Hal. Thank you."

Rowan's tone would have squelched anyone else. "You have to see him in action to understand. But you will. Because you simply have to stay. Doesn't she, Helen?"

"Yes, I think she does." Helen's expression was thoughtful. "She made Rowan laugh."

"You made Rowan laugh?" Hal echoed in an awed whisper. "The very first day?"

I heard a sigh behind me. "The staff suffers from the illusion that I am . . . dour."

"It took me a whole season to get him to laugh," Hal said.

"How'd you do it?" I asked as he ushered me into the theatre.

"Showed up at the final cast party dressed as Titania, Queen of the Fairies."

My laughter faded when I spied Janet—Bitch Queen of Hospitality—watching us from the shadows. Then I laughed again. It seemed safer than thumbing my nose at her.

❦

On my return to Brooklyn, I Googled "Crossroads Theatre" and discovered half a dozen throughout the country, but nothing other than a White Pages listing for the one I had stumbled upon.

I monitored the progress on my bathroom ceiling. Updated my resume. Wondered what Rowan Mackenzie thought was lacking in my life. Added a new folder to my Web favorites list with links to nonprofit job sites. Considered the benefits of a change of scene. Filled out the online application for unemployment. Made a list of pros and cons about spending the summer at the Crossroads. The cons took up an entire column. Under pros, I wrote three words: "I want to."

I threw the list away. Opened an online banking account where my unemployment checks could be directly deposited. Notified the post office about forwarding my mail. Put an ad on Craigslist and found a normal-sounding college intern to sublet until August 15. Thanked God I no longer had a landline that could betray my absence to my mother.

Then I packed my bags and returned to Dale.

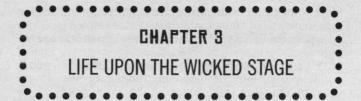

CHAPTER 3
LIFE UPON THE WICKED STAGE

AS I UNFOLDED MYSELF FROM MY CIVIC, a bass voice bellowed, "Yo! Brooklyn!"

Shading my eyes against the late afternoon sun, I discovered Lou and biker chick Bobbie on the third floor porch of the Golden Bough. The beefy guy who had been cast as carousel barker Billy Bigelow completed the trifecta of muscle shirts and tattoos.

"Yo, Joizey!" I bellowed back, feeling an absurd glow at his warm greeting.

"Need help with your stuff?"

"No, I'm—"

"We'll be right down."

As they stampeded toward the French doors, I winced, waiting for the porch to collapse under them. Their voices echoed like distant thunder from the bowels of the hotel, but returned to normal shouting volume as they reached the front doors.

While the guys wrestled over my two suitcases, Bobbie rolled her eyes and said, "You should've got here earlier. You missed the Memorial Day parade. Hal had a float."

"A float?"

"For that crazy shop of his," Lou said. "With guys posed like mannequins, wearing fishnet stockings and corsets and nighties and shit."

"Bunch of faggots," Nick muttered.

Bobbie jabbed her elbow in his ribs. "Hallee's caters to

39

men and women of discerning taste, including the tristate
gay, transgender, and cross-dressing communities."

"You sound like you're quoting from a promotional bro-
chure."

"She is," Lou said, earning an elbow in his ribs as well.

"Gay or straight," Bobbie said, "those drag queens were
hot. Lou thought so, didn't you, Lou?"

Lou punched her shoulder. She punched his harder.
They grinned at each other. I tried to picture them as the
sweet young lovers in *Brigadoon* and failed.

"What room you in?" Lou called over his shoulder as I
followed them into the hotel.

"I was in 304 the night after auditions."

"Right under Nick and me!"

Which explained the ominous thuds I'd heard overhead.
Thrusting aside visions of another ceiling cave-in, I managed a smile and said, "Just let me pick up my key . . ."

But they were already marching up the stairs, Bobbie
leading the men in a chorus of "I'll Go Home with Bonnie
Jean."

With its oak paneling, discreetly clustered sofas and
chairs, and pools of lamplight, the Golden Bough called to
mind a miniature version of New York's Algonquin Hotel.
It even had a resident house cat like the Algonquin, a gray
tabby I'd met on my previous stay with the improbable
name of Iolanthe. If the upholstery was a bit threadbare
and the cat a bit arthritic, it only added to the hotel's
charm.

The air was thick with the contrary odors of dust and
lemon oil. Shadows drowsed in corners and curdled like
thunderclouds below the high ceiling. It was the kind of
place you'd expect to find uniformed bellhops darting up
and down the carved staircase, ladies with bustles and para-
sols exchanging pleasantries with gentlemen in frock coats.

Instead, actors hunched over scripts and mouthed the
lyrics of the songs flowing through their earbuds. In the adjacent lounge, someone pounded out chords on the piano
for a group of singers hesitantly crooning, "Brigadoon,
Brig-a-doo-oon."

Helen smiled as I approached the reception desk.
Janet—predictably—frowned. Iolanthe, lounging atop the

counter, regarded me with sleepy eyes roughly the same green as Rowan's.

"So you're back," Janet said by way of greeting.

"I didn't want to break his heart," I replied with deliberate vagueness.

"I'm sure Hal will be delighted," she said dryly.

"We're all delighted." Helen shot a reproachful glance at her daughter/niece/second cousin.

"Has everyone come back?"

"Some of the younger ones like Sarah and Ronnie can't join us until school's out," Helen replied.

"But everyone accepted their parts?"

"Why, yes. Didn't you think they would?"

"Well, you know. Jobs, families . . ."

Helen waved those away. "Goodness, I can't remember the last time we had a no-show."

"Six years ago," Janet said. "Lee."

"That's right." Helen smiled fondly. "He refused twice, didn't he? But once he joined us, he never left."

"Kind of like a Roach Motel," Janet noted. "The actors come in, but they can't get out."

Helen looked mildly alarmed. "We certainly don't have roaches in Dale. Or bedbugs."

Janet snorted, then lifted a skeleton key from the board behind the reception desk and slapped it on the counter. Clearly, they didn't have much in the way of security in Dale, either.

Helen slid a manila envelope across the desk, her perfectly manicured nails at odds with knuckles that were thick and swollen with arthritis. "Your welcome packet. Plus a copy of your contract and information sheet. In case you forgot to bring yours. You can drop them off here." She patted the wooden inbox at her elbow, currently filled by Iolanthe. "Be sure to check the message board for schedule changes," she added, gesturing to a corkboard that sported the banner "Welcome, Crossroads cast!"

"Phones," Janet prompted.

"Oh, yes. On your last visit, you probably noticed there were no phones in the rooms. And that cell phone reception is a little . . . iffy. The best place for making calls is the third floor porch. Or the road into town."

"Or the hill in the new cemetery," Janet said.

I must have looked appalled because Helen quickly added, "You can always use the house phones. There's one in the lobby and one on the second floor."

"For credit card, calling card, and local calls only." With that gracious remark, Janet walked into the office and closed the door behind her.

I decided I'd better shell out a few bucks for a Skype subscription. I had to be able to talk to prospective employers in private without fear of losing them in mid-conversation. And I had to maintain the fiction that I was still in New York during my Sunday morning check-in call to my mother.

❧❧

The next morning, after breakfast at the Chatterbox, I bundled Bernie and Nancy into my car and drove to the theatre.

"I'll give you the cut-rate tour," Bernie volunteered as he maneuvered cautiously along the uneven brick path. "Since you were too busy knocking yourself out to go on the last one. To our right, the Crossroads Theatre."

"That I remember."

"Over there is the rehearsal studio. Also known as the Smokehouse."

"Because there used to be one on that site back in the nineteenth century," Nancy explained.

"Back there's the Mill." Bernie nodded to a three-story building of dark wood that resembled the House of the Seven Gables without the gables. "Scene shop. Storage. And a loft on the top floor where Catherine and Javier live. Very cozy, Reinhard says. And speak of the devil . . ."

He shouted a greeting to Reinhard, who was hurrying along the covered breezeway that connected the theatre to the Mill.

"Right on time," Reinhard called. "Good. I will see you inside. Mind the step up, Bernie."

"Will do."

As Reinhard ducked into the Smokehouse, I asked, "Since when are you two so chummy?"

"Since I found out he's Swiss."

"Not . . . German."

"A bad habit," Bernie admitted. "Making assumptions. To hear that accent and start wondering what his family might have done to mine during the war." He shook his head impatiently. "Who needs sad thoughts on our first day? We have to . . . what's the saying? Break a hip?"

"Leg, Bernie. Break a leg."

"I thought you only said that before a performance," Nancy said.

"Morning, noon, and night, we should say it. We need all the luck we can get."

The rehearsal studio was utilitarian but cheerful with pale yellow walls and a bank of open windows. Like the stage, its hardwood floor was pegged rather than nailed; the architects who had restored the post-and-beam barn had brought the same eye for historical accuracy to this building, down to the wooden latches on the doors.

A dance barre was mounted on one wall, but there were no mirrors. Probably to spare us the horror of watching ourselves blunder through the choreography. A battered upright piano sat in a corner. The aroma of coffee wafted from the kitchenette along the back wall, but I was already jittery from three cups of Chatterbox coffee.

As I took a seat in the semicircle of folding chairs, Reinhard stalked toward me and brandished my vocal-chorus part. "Welcome back, Dorothy Gale."

Somehow, holding that booklet made everything real. I was in summer stock again. I was doing a show.

"What, no snappy comeback?"

My fingers caressed the black cover. "Tams-Witmark," I finally managed, whispering the name of the licensing company like a prayer.

An unexpected smile softened Reinhard's craggy features. "Welcome back," he repeated. Then he frowned. "No fainting today."

His frown deepened as the Legally Blondes darted into the studio. "The schedule said ten o'clock. Not 10:04."

As they slunk toward the two empty chairs, Rowan laid down his pen and folded his hands on the table. A breathless silence replaced the murmur of conversation.

"Welcome back, everyone. I know some of you have had

a chance to get to know each other this past week, but for the benefit of those who just arrived, let's begin with introductions."

Given the mix of race and ethnicity among the cast, our Brigadoon was going to be a lot more diverse than your typical eighteenth-century Scottish village. The mix of occupations was pretty staggering, too: corporate execs and lawyers, teachers and chefs, computer wonks like the Rastas, auto mechanic Lou, and college dropout/aspiring writer/part-time musician Kevin.

I missed the mark on Nick (a bartender rather than a bouncer) and Bobbie (a home health aide), but I'd pegged many of my cast mates correctly. Church ladies Romaine and Albertha were members of an African Methodist Episcopal congregation in Baltimore. Maya the flower child worked in a New Age bookstore/crystal shop. The Legally Blondes had just finished their junior year of college and were members of Tri Delt sorority.

Top honors for the best introduction went to a twig-like Goth with purple hair who announced, "I have taken the name Kalma, in honor of the Finnish goddess of death whose name means Corpse Stench." Even Rowan blinked at that one.

I found myself wondering what he thought these people needed. Bernie might need to heal from his wife's recent death. Nick definitely needed to get over his homophobia. Caren, the yappy woman who went on and on about her husband the lawyer and their lovely condo on the golf course, just needed to shut up.

Introductions concluded, Rowan called for a read-through. When he explained that this meant reading the dialogue aloud, the principals had a collective panic attack.

"I don't expect a polished performance," he assured them. "But since many of you have never been in a show, it's better to tackle your nerves now rather than opening night."

A few chuckles. A couple of rueful smiles. And voila! Panic gone. If I could bottle what the guy was selling, I'd be a billionaire.

The line readings ranged from leaden to overenthusiastic, but Rowan's benign expression never faltered. As we worked through the script, my respect for him grew. He'd made subtle changes in dialogue, removing references that were hopelessly outdated and altering lines to make Jeff less smarmy, Fiona a bit tougher, and Tommy less of a vacillating dickweed. Librettist Alan Jay Lerner might be spinning in his grave, but the net effect was to make the characters feel more like real people.

After Bernie read the last line, Rowan and Reinhard applauded. The principals grinned. Even I felt triumphant, and I'd just sat there for the last hour.

"Let's take a five-minute break," Rowan suggested. "The bathroom is next to the kitchen. To avoid lines, I suggest you avail yourselves of the ones in the Dungeon as well. When you return, I'll leave you in Reinhard's capable hands for a crash course in stage directions. Please stack your chairs against that wall before you go. And remember—five minutes only!"

"Smoke 'em if you got 'em!" Lou bellowed, prompting a general exodus.

As I rolled Bernie's walker up to his chair, I asked, "What's the Dungeon? Or don't I want to know?"

"You don't have to play nursemaid. Go. Mingle. Get to know the nice single men."

"You're a nice single man. And I'm not playing nursemaid. What's the Dungeon?"

"The basement. Dressing rooms, costume room, the what-do-you-call-it where you sit before the show . . ."

Before I could say, "Green room," the voice behind me did. At least this time I didn't screech. Or bash my head.

"You've got to stop doing that."

"The Dungeon green room is for the musicians," Rowan said, ignoring my comment. "It's next to the pit entrance. The actors' green room is backstage left."

Bernie groaned. "Pit entrance. Backstage left. You give me a headache with all that theatre lingo."

"Wait until Reinhard gets through with you."

"I heard that!" Reinhard called from across the room.

As Bernie pulled his walker closer, Rowan said, "You can sit this one out if you'd like."

Bernie shook his head and pushed himself up. "Long as you don't have me doing Highland flings, I'll be fine."

We spent our remaining three minutes studying the un-framed posters on the wall above the dance barre. Rowan had apparently gotten his start as a librettist by adapting Shakespearean plays. His taste in musicals was almost as old-fashioned; *Into the Woods* was the most contemporary of the bunch.

"Do they ever do shows from this century?" I whispered.

"It's Dale," Bernie whispered back. "They want Rodgers and Hammerstein, Lerner and Loewe . . ."

"Punch and Judy. Funny about the dates."

Bernie peered at the poster for *Once Upon a Mattress*. "What's so funny?"

"No years."

"Who needs years? You hang 'em in the lobby, you know what's playing."

Before I could reply, Reinhard shouted, "Back to work, everyone!" And I joined the returning horde for Theatre 101.

Reinhard lined us up facing the bank of windows. "We will now pretend that we are standing on the stage. The windows are the audience. The part of the stage nearest the audience is called downstage. The part farthest away from them is called upstage. So. When you move toward the audience, you are crossing . . .?" He glanced around and nodded as Legally Blonde Ashley raised a tentative hand.

"Downstage?" she ventured.

Reinhard beamed. "Correct! Now. Stage left is your left—when you are onstage facing the audience." He turned toward the windows and pointed left. "So. I am pointing . . .?"

"Stage left," we chorused.

Like the Scarecrow in *The Wizard of Oz*, his left arm came down and his right snapped up. "And now I am pointing . . .?"

"Stage right!"

"Of course, people do go both ways," I muttered.

"Is there a question? No? Moving on."

He marched us upstage and down, stage left and right. Taught us about the wings located on either side of the stage and the apron that extended in front of the curtain. Pointed out the gaffer tape on the floor that outlined the dimensions of the performing area. Explained sight lines and cheating front instead of facing the actor you were talking to.

I should have been bored out of my skull. Instead, I marveled at how much fun I was having.

Half an hour later, he shooed us to the dressing rooms to change for dance class. On our return, Mei-Yin greeted us wearing a tracksuit and a scowl, shouted "LINE UP!" and stalked past us like a general inspecting her troops, all the while shaking her head and muttering to herself. Finally, she stabbed an accusatory forefinger at Legally Blonde Brittany. "YOU! BLONDE girl! You ever DANCE or you just know how to DRESS the part?"

Clad in black leotard and tights, Brittany had already drawn her fair share of envious stares from the women and admiring ones from the men. Her ponytail bobbed as she nodded.

"I studied ballet, ma'am. At the LouAlma School of Dance in—"

"I don't need your RESUME! What else?"

"Jazz and modern. In college. And one class of—"

"You're DANCE CAPTAIN. Warm them up!"

With that, Mei-Yin stamped out of the Smokehouse. Although she slammed the door behind her, we could still hear her shout, "Shoot me NOW, Rowan. Just put a GUN to my head and pull the TRIGGER!"

I joined a few of the braver cast members at the windows.

"What's she doing?" Brittany asked from the safety of the kitchenette.

"Beating her fist against the side of the barn," Kalma replied.

"Every year they get WORSE!"

"And her head," Kalma added.

"Reinhard's coming out the stage door." A guy named Gary picked up the play-by-play. "He's patting her shoulder, trying to calm her down . . ."

Mei-Yin's howl would have made a banshee quail.

"It doesn't seem to be working," Gary noted.

I caught a flash of movement high under the eaves of the barn. For the first time, I noticed the small balcony project-

ing out from the wall facing the Mill. Slatted wooden blinds
jerked open, revealing a figure framed in the glass door.

"'But, soft! what light through yonder window breaks?'"
Gary quoted.

"I think it's Rowan," Nick replied with a fine disregard
for Shakespeare.

The glass door slid open. Rowan stepped outside, walked
to the end of the balcony, and leaned over the railing.

Mei-Yin shook her fist at him. "What am I? A MIRA-
CLE WORKER?"

"'O! speak again, bright angel.'"

"Now you're just showing off," I said.

Gary grinned. "Twelve years teaching high school English."

Whatever Rowan said made Mei-Yin throw up her
hands and stomp into the meadow.

"'Good night, good night! parting is such sweet...'
whoops, here comes Reinhard."

With commendable cool, Brittany shouted, "Stretch,
everybody, stretch!"

The window brigade barely made it back in line before
Reinhard burst through the door. He'd evidently been dragging his fingers through his short hair because it was standing on end like gray porcupine quills. Unless his wife's voice
alone had produced that effect.

"Everything will be fine," he assured us in a hoarse whisper.
"Always, she is like this the first day. It is her artistic nature. Not
to worry." He shot a quick look over his shoulder. "But best to
hide backpacks. And mugs. Any objects that can be thrown,
yes?" With those comforting words, he scuttled out.

Before we could act on his advice, Mei-Yin stalked into
the Smokehouse and stripped off her jacket. The leotard
underneath revealed the arms and torso of a weightlifter.
Several people surreptitiously nudged their vocal books toward the walls.

"All right, then." Mei-Yin favored us with an unexpectedly benign smile. "Let's begin!"

Compared to Mei-Yin, Reinhard was indeed a pussycat.
While Rowan worked with the principals, he herded the

chorus into the theatre to stage our first number. I had to give him major points for patience as he relayed Rowan's blocking. It's just hard to remain enthusiastic when you're being moved around the stage like a chess piece.

Evening brought our first music rehearsal. When I walked into the Smokehouse, Alex waved me over to the piano and held out a flash drive. "I'm afraid your vocal lines are going to be jumping all over the place. That'll teach you to have a big range," he added with a grin. "You'll be singing alto most of the time. But I need you on the second soprano line at a couple of points. Better find a seat in the DMZ between the two sections."

"No problem." I pocketed the flash drive. "Sorry for the last-minute scramble."

"Oh, I created the files after auditions." He flashed that mischievous grin again. "I'm good, aren't I?"

"You're . . . amazing. How did you know I'd be back?"

"Everybody comes back. I can't remember the last time we had a no-show."

"Six years ago. Lee."

His ruddy eyebrows soared. "You're pretty amazing yourself."

"Janet."

"Ah. Janet."

Astonishing how he could convey respect, ruefulness, and genuine affection in just three syllables.

"Janet's a tough cookie," he admitted. "But her heart's in the right place."

"I'm just relieved to know she has one."

He laughed and turned to the milling crowd. "Okay, let's get started." Several people groaned, and he shook his finger at them. "Some of you probably think you can't sing. Well, that's nonsense. If you can breathe, you can sing. And that's what we're going to concentrate on tonight: breathing and relaxing. Tomorrow, we'll get into the real work."

We breathed lying on our backs. We breathed standing up straight. We hissed like snakes to practice breath control. We blew imaginary bubbles to relax our lips. We worked on diction by repeating tongue twisters like "fluffy, floppy puppy" and "red leather, yellow leather" and "unique New York."

Then he moved on to physical warm-ups: neck rolls and shoulder rolls, leg stretches and propeller arms, reaching for the ceiling and bending from the waist to touch the floor.

"Okay, shake it out. Arms, legs, heads. You can't sing with tension in your body. Now, open your mouths and yawn." His voice swooped up and down, and we imitated him, sounding like inmates of Bedlam on a bad day.

We chanted "Ah," staggering our breathing to create a wall of sound on every conceivable note known to man until I expected the monolith from *2001: A Space Odyssey* to appear. We climbed up the scale by half steps, intoning "Ah, A, E, Oh, Oo" like the caterpillar in *Alice in Wonderland*. In between chords, Alex shouted out instructions: "Drop those jaws! . . .Give me a nice, full sound! . . . Full does not mean loud, people. Listen to your neighbors. Blend. . . . Don't push. Drop out when it gets too high."

Two hours later, self-consciousness had given way to a strangely tribal sense of community. Every cast became a community, of course. But I'd never seen it happen the first day of rehearsal.

Only in the last few minutes did we open our vocal books. Like Rowan, Alex had no fear of editing. He'd cut reprises, chopped verses and choruses from some of the longer songs, trimmed dance numbers and the endless chase scene at the top of Act Two. A troupe of professionals might be able to pull the full show together in three weeks, but those cuts gave me a glimmer of hope that we could, too.

"As you can see from the list of cuts, the chorus will not be singing the 'Prologue.' I'm just using the music to bridge us into that opening scene." Alex raised one palm and gazed skyward before returning his attention to us. "When I do that, I'm asking the shades of Lerner and Loewe for forgiveness.

"Moving on to 'Brigadoon.' It's written for the full chorus, but we're going to add voices a few at a time." Hand and gaze moved heavenward again. "The practical reason is to prevent the chorus from drowning out the actors' lines. But there's another."

Alex's fingers softly sounded the opening chords of "Brigadoon" on the piano.

"We're trying to create a sense of mystery here. Of wonder."

His voice was gentle, like a father telling a bedtime story to his children.

"Listen to the music. A new day is dawning. The people of Brigadoon are starting to stir. Half-awake, half-asleep, caught between the otherworld and this one."

He fell silent, allowing us to appreciate a soaring high note.

"Slowly, the village emerges from the mist. And the villagers awaken from their dream."

His voice gained power with the music, building to Brigadoon's triumphant assertion of faith and hope.

"A hundred years slip by while they sleep. But they only age a single night. And wake as if it's the next morning. Because once again, the miracle has occurred!"

Music and words echoed in the sudden silence. For a moment, we all sat there. Then Alex rubbed his arms. "I get goose bumps just thinking about it."

So did I. Judging from the half-open mouths and dazed expressions around me, so did everyone else in the room.

"Okay, people. That's it for tonight. Practice those breathing exercises. Five minutes on the floor before bed. Five minutes standing in the morning."

"Alex is a lot like Rowan," Nancy observed as we crawled into our beds after our five minutes on the floor. "The way he does things, I mean."

"How *does* Rowan do things?"

Nancy rolled toward me, the lace around the neck of her flannel nightgown peeking over the patchwork quilt. "Well, we didn't do any acting. Just exercises and games. Is that . . . typical?"

"Well, it helps to break the ice and build trust before you get into the scene work."

"But we've only got a couple weeks to put the show together."

"Don't remind me," I muttered.

"It's funny. The exercises seemed silly at first, but I felt good while I was doing them. Rowan makes you feel like you're a real actor. That by opening night, you'll be wonderful."

"That *is* just like Alex."

"But do you feel like that now?"

Reluctantly, I shook my head.

"I noticed it at our meal breaks," Nancy confided. "I left the Smokehouse feeling on top of the world, and by the time I got to town, all my doubts were back."

I frowned. The same thing had happened to me. I'd left the music rehearsal on a real high, flattered that Alex had asked me and Gary to work with the chorus an hour or two each week until he was finished teaching. Now, I found myself dreading the extra work and recalling everything that had gone wrong during rehearsal: how shrill the sopranos sounded, how the basses seemed incapable of blending with the rest of us, how yappy Caren giggled each time she stumbled over her "fluffy, floppy puppy."

"It's only natural to have doubts," I said, as much to reassure myself as Nancy.

"Of course. Don't mind me." She snapped off the lamp on the nightstand between our beds. "I'm just tired."

Footsteps thudded overhead. Springs screeched next door as someone bounded onto a bed. Toilets flushed in the hall. A door banged shut.

Long after silence had descended, I lay awake, puzzling over a director who cast actors in the roles they needed, a dictatorial stage manager who made me enjoy Theatre 101, a music director who cast a spell with his words. Wondering if I was making way too much out of their perfectly ordinary desire to build up our confidence and meld us into a company.

Maybe it was only natural that somewhere between the theatre and the hotel, their spells wore off and our giddy confidence waned. And like the villagers emerging from the mists of Brigadoon, we awoke to reality.

The thought coincided with the sound of muffled footsteps in the hallway. An oddly irregular rhythm. Five steps, then silence. Five more steps, then silence again. It didn't take a vivid imagination to picture someone pausing outside each room.

Like a good New Yorker, I'd locked our door and put the

chain on before crawling into bed, but I still stiffened as the footsteps stopped outside our room.

I heard something brush across the wooden door. My knotted muscles relaxed. Warmth suffused my body. As if gentle arms had enfolded me, I felt embraced by a sense of comfort and safety and peace.

Too tired to question or doubt or do anything other than accept what I had been offered, I closed my eyes and surrendered to the Golden Bough.

CHAPTER 4

TENDER SHEPHERD

MY REHEARSAL DAYS QUICKLY ASSUMED A pattern. Breakfast at the Chatterbox. Dance rehearsal with Mei-Yin. A quick lunch picked up at the Chatterbox or the roadside grill known as the Ptomaine Stand. Blocking with Reinhard in the afternoon. Take-out pizza from Nonna Teresa's or take-out Chinese from the Mandarin Chalet or—less frequently—an honest-to-God sit-down dinner at Duck Inn or the Golden Bough. Then music rehearsal with Alex.

On the nights Alex worked with the principals, Gary led the men into the Dungeon, while I pounded out the women's vocal parts on the piano in the Smokehouse. The hour or two a week Alex had requested quickly became an hour or two a day.

After rehearsals ended, we adjourned to the lounge of the Bough. Helen played bartender, providing a sympathetic ear along with pints of Vermont microbrews. Promptly at midnight, Janet appeared in the doorway to announce that the bar was closed. We learned to talk and drink fast.

Every afternoon, Helen arrived at the theatre with a wicker basket over her arm like Little Red Riding Hood. By day four, we concluded that she brought Rowan his lunch. Nancy, our resident mole among the principals, lent credence to this surmise by reporting that Rowan always brought a strawberry milkshake with him to the Smokehouse when rehearsals resumed. If he ate solid food as well, it was consumed out of sight in his office under the eaves.

Helen's basket always contained a treat for the cast as well: oatmeal raisin cookies, corn muffins, cranberry nut bread. Her energy amazed me. She looked so delicate, almost frail, yet she managed to run the hotel, handle advance ticket sales, and bring us comfort food.

The rest of the staff was equally adept at multitasking. Reinhard still kept office hours several times a week. Hal had his lingerie shop, Javier his antique store. Mei-Yin managed the Chalet with Max, Reinhard's son from a previous marriage. Alex taught at Hillandale High. Lee had a small legal practice.

I gleaned those tidbits from Hal during a costume fitting squeezed into the brutal schedule. But even he had only the haziest information about Janet.

"She must be well-off to keep the theatre going all these years," I ventured.

"Her husbands were."

"Husbands? How many has she had?"

"Two, I think."

"What happened to them?" I asked, immediately casting her in the role of Black Widow.

"They died. Of natural causes," he added pointedly. "She's been a widow for years. Like Helen." Hal sighed. "Helen was only married a year, poor thing. And after her husband died, she never remarried."

When I wondered aloud how the Golden Bough managed to turn a profit with our non-paying cast as its only residents, Hal assured me that the hotel would be full once *Brigadoon* opened, and that it did a brisk business during fall foliage and ski seasons.

My cautious feelers revealed that a number of my cast mates had experienced the same extremes of giddy confidence and stomach-churning doubt that Nancy and I had discussed. Everyone simply assumed our doubts surfaced when the staff cheerleaders were absent. Or as Bobbie put it, "If they told us we sucked this early, who'd stick around for opening night?"

The phenomenon nagged at me, but I was too exhausted to obsess about it. I worked harder that first week than I

ever had in my life. Which made our Act One run-through
doubly painful.

Richard marched through the role of the conflicted
Tommy with the pained determination of a boss eager to
conclude an unpleasant performance review. Ashley did
better with Fiona during the infrequent moments you could
hear her. Nancy and Will lacked any semblance of comic
timing, a serious drawback for the "funny" couple in the
show.

On the plus side, Kevin delivered a strong performance
as brooding Harry Beaton. And if Bernie stumbled over his
speeches and delivered them in the accents of Brooklyn
rather than Scotland, he perfectly captured the gentle humor and wisdom of Mr. Lundie.

I'd been wondering how Alex would coax a lyric tenor
from Lou. Now I discovered that he'd dropped Lou's songs
a fifth. While it was strange to hear "I'll Go Home with
Bonnie Jean" sung in a booming bass, Lou's "hoisting a few
with the boys" approach worked.

Even more amazing was his awkward yet sweetly sincere
rendition of "Come to Me, Bend to Me." Although Bobbie
was supposed to respond in dance, Mei-Yin had wisely cut
much of the ballet and assigned the trickiest parts to Brittany and Maya. Yet with a few simple movements, Bobbie
managed to convey the sensitive nature lurking beneath
her tough exterior.

When the number ended, we broke into spontaneous applause. Lou and Bobbie clowned a bit, but as Rowan
brought us back to order, a look passed between them, as
sweet as those they had exchanged as Charlie and Jean.

Was that why they were here—to find each other? But
how could Rowan Mackenzie have realized that at auditions?

After three interminable hours, Kevin shouted Harry's
line about the end of the miracle. He raced offstage, the
men raced after him, and the staff applauded; everyone had
come that night to lend moral support. Relief turned to
dread as Rowan mounted the steps to the stage.

"Well, I'm sure that felt more like a stagger-through than
a run-through. Believe me, it's always like that the first time
you put everything together."

As he reviewed our accomplishments, the collective tension gave way to renewed confidence. Sure, we were still stumbling over our choreography, flubbing our vocals, groping for lines and characters. But we had made it through Act One.

The only problem was, it shouldn't have been possible.

At Southford, we'd rehearsed an entire show in a week. But we were professionals. That encompassed far more than simply arriving with music and lines memorized. We had a common language. We knew upstage from down, a quarter note from a half. We could execute a plié or a grapevine or a step-ball-change without a lengthy demonstration.

True, Alex and Mei-Yin had simplified the music and choreography, but it should have taken weeks for our cast to reach this level. And although I had just seen the evidence of our success, I still couldn't understand how we had achieved it.

I watched as Rowan drew aside the principals for notes. When they returned to the group, they looked liked worshippers who had come face-to-face with their god of choice. Which might explain their confidence but did little to solve the mystery of how that translated into credible performances.

I was on the verge of broaching my questions to Nancy that night when she suddenly burst into tears. Stunned, I grabbed the box of Kleenex from the nightstand's lower shelf. Nancy plucked out a tissue, blew her nose, and declared, "I was awful."

"No, you weren't!" I protested, assuming my supportive HelpLink expression.

Nancy grimaced.

Wondering if I'd lost the knack of the supportive HelpLink expression, I added, "You had all your lines down cold."

Which is almost as bad as going backstage after a terrible performance and telling an actor that his costumes looked great.

I tried again. "What did Rowan say?"

"He told me I was off to a good start, but I needed to think more about Meg's character. And then he asked how I felt about her."

"How *do* you feel about her?"

Nancy ripped another tissue from the box. "I think she's pathetic! Throwing herself at Jeff. So desperate and grasping and needy. As if having a man—any man—is the most important thing in the world."

I took a moment to digest that, then asked, "Did you tell Rowan that?"

"I didn't have to tell him. He knew."

I was beginning to think Rowan Mackenzie knew way too much about way too many things. But I had a more immediate problem. I plopped down beside Nancy and squeezed her hand; she didn't seem like the hugging type.

"He asked me to find her strengths as well as her weaknesses. To look at the things I disliked about her and try to turn them into something positive."

It wasn't exactly Stanislavsky, but it was better than suggesting that the real reason Nancy disliked Meg so much was that the character possessed qualities that she lacked.

I jumped up and pulled a notebook and pencil from my carryall. "We'll make a list. Meg's strengths in one column and her weaknesses in another."

Ten minutes later, the qualities Nancy perceived as weaknesses filled the entire column. Under strengths, I'd scribbled "Tenacious." But at least she'd stopped crying.

"Now, let's look at the weaknesses and flip them so they're strengths."

Nancy stared at item #1: Pushy. Then looked up at me, wire-rimmed glasses shining in the lamplight. "Self-confident?" she ventured.

"Self-confident. Great! Item #2: Desperate."

"Maybe that should go with 'Tenacious.'"

I drew an arrow between them. We filled in "Flirt" opposite "Tramp," "Earthy" opposite "Obsessed with Sex," "Eternal Optimist" opposite "Completely Clueless about a Future with Jeff."

"This is great," I assured her. "Sure, Meg's been around the block, but she's held onto her hopes. And her sense of humor."

"Put 'Humor' under strengths. No. Make it . . . 'Rueful Self-Awareness.'"

"Maybe she realizes Jeff won't work out. But even if he

isn't Mr. Right, someone else might come along. And until then, she'll manage just fine on her own."

"Ooh! 'Self-sufficient.' Write that under 'Strengths.'" Nancy watched me scribble for a moment, then said, "Rowan should have cast you as Meg. You're so much like her."

"Well, the string of failures with men is familiar."

The notebook shuddered as Nancy's forefinger stabbed the phrase "Rueful Self-Awareness." Shuddered again as I stabbed "Eternal Optimist" and said, "Not so much."

I couldn't even remember the last time I'd gone out with a man, unless you counted the lunch when my boss fired me. My two serious relationships were case studies in Mr. Wrong. Michael—gay. Eric—commitment-phobe and asshole. Okay, only an asshole after he got salmonella poisoning from my deviled eggs and changed from The Guy Who Might Be the One to The Guy Who Stopped Calling.

As far back as elementary school, I'd yearned for the wrong boy, sighing over brooding Allan Parkinson and ignoring Tommy Barnett who nicknamed me Maggie Graham Cracker Crust and made up this stupid song about me. How was I supposed to know that "She's So Crusty" was a ten-year-old's idea of a romantic serenade?

"Don't make the mistake I did," my mother told me in one of our rare heart-to-hearts. "Don't fall for a man who's forever chasing rainbows."

The thing was, I'd seen her photo albums. She looked radiant in some of those pictures. Later, of course, the radiance leached away, leaving the anxious, pinch-faced woman I knew. I'd always wondered if it was my fault. If having a kid strained their marriage. Or if it was because I was so totally Daddy's little girl.

Add that guilt to my string of professional failures, my appallingly small circle of friends, my "I look great as long as I don't stand naked in front of a full-length mirror" physique . . .

God. I was a total loser.

Nancy, however, looked quite cheerful. At least one of us had been buoyed by our exercise.

"I know it's late, but would you mind running Jeff's lines with me in Scene Three?"

I plastered a smile on my face. "Let's do it!"

No good deed goes unpunished. The next morning—our first day off—Nancy rushed into our room with Will in tow.

"I told him about your list," she announced, "and he wants to try it."

"That's great! Let me know how it goes."

As Will's eager expression faded, I realized I'd miss the key point: he wanted to try it with me.

"There's no trick," I assured him. "You just make two columns—"

"But you have to be there," Nancy said. "To ask the right questions." She held out my notebook and pencil like an acolyte offering the high priestess her tools for the mystical rite.

By midafternoon, "Craft Your Character with Maggie" had become the game of choice among the principals. Kevin's list took two hours to develop and involved an extensive backstory undreamed of by Alan Jay Lerner that included Harry Beaton's childhood trauma as a bed wetter, the recurring bouts of eczema that had prompted his aversion to weaving, and his penchant for masturbating in the heather on the hill.

At least Bernie was done in fifteen minutes. And brought his own paper and pencil.

"Now I get it," he said, folding his list into a neat square.

"You already had it. You know Mr. Lundie inside and—"

"Lundie, Schmundie. It's you I'm talking about. Miss Tough New Yorker. Ha! You're a pussycat. Just like Reinhard."

"Pussycat, schmussycat."

"What? It's so bad to help people? That's what you do for a living."

I considered telling him this was hardly the kind of work I performed—had performed—at HelpLink. For one thing, I was seldom on the front lines; I trained and supervised those who were. If answering the phone could be considered the front lines. We weren't social workers or counselors. We were middlemen, providing the information callers needed to *find* a social worker or counselor. Hence, the all-important "Link" in HelpLink. On the rare occasion I covered the phones, I gave callers the information that would lead them on the next stage of their journey down the Yellow Brick Road to wellness and effected a speedy disconnect.

Helping once removed. That's what I specialized in. This hands-on thing was a lot harder. Sure, I'd always enjoyed picking apart characters to discover what made them tick. And I got a warm glow when a fellow cast member had that "Aha!" moment. But spending an entire day doing that was exhausting. Especially since I needed to do my laundry, answer my e-mails, and apply to any job in the five boroughs that looked remotely promising.

And I really needed to avoid pissing Rowan off by playing director behind his back.

"Do you know why you're here?" I asked Bernie.

The wrinkles on his face realigned as his smile morphed into a frown. "I auditioned. Same as you."

"But why?"

"It just felt like the right thing to do. Sarah and I were passing through town. We saw the barn." Bernie shrugged.

It was eerily reminiscent of my experience.

"How does it make you feel? Working here?"

"Again with the psychoanalysis?"

"No. Really."

Bernie cocked his head, considering. It increased his resemblance to a bright-eyed, balding sparrow.

"I feel ... good. Tired, but good. I haven't slept so well since Rachel passed. I wake up in the morning excited. Instead of wondering how I'll fill the hours until bedtime. And the exercise must be good for me. These old hips haven't felt so strong in years." He leaned forward, bright sparrow eyes intent. "And what about you, Maggie Graham? Why are you here?"

"I'm still trying to work that out."

"Well, you keep working." Bernie pushed himself up from the table. "I'm going to grab a nap before movie night."

I groaned, wondering how I could have forgotten. Hal had started the tradition when he joined the staff. Every season began with a Judy Garland double feature: *A Star is Born* and *Summer Stock*. Hal provided the DVDs, Nonna's

provided giant wedges, and Helen served some of her trademark desserts.

It had seemed like a fun idea when Hal mentioned it at
my costume fitting. But I would gladly have traded movie
night for a long walk. Or a long shower. Or even a solitary
vigil in the laundry room. At least there I could ponder the
mystery of Rowan Mackenzie undisturbed. And that of a
seventy-four-year-old widower who had found an astonishing new lease on life.

I was no closer to solving either mystery when I trudged up
to my room that night, canvas bag of laundry slung over my
shoulder. It was well after midnight and although I'd taken
the fire stairs to avoid passing anywhere near the office, I
eased the door open cautiously in case Janet was prowling
around. When I saw the robed figure outside my room, I
caught my breath.

Helen turned toward me, her lips parted in a round "O"
of surprise, the fingers of her right hand splayed across my
door.

That explained one mystery; clearly, Helen was the unseen visitor I'd heard that first night. Before I could ask why
she was lurking outside my room, she started down the hall,
beckoning me to follow. Her destination became apparent
when she walked through the small sitting room and eased
open the French doors to the porch.

"It's not too cold for you?" she asked, eyeing my T-shirt.

I leaned on the railing, breathing in the crisp air. "It feels
wonderful. I've been trapped inside all day."

With its twin lines of streetlamps, Main Street resembled
a landing strip. Hallee's glowed pinkly in the distance, but
the other shops were dark. The curved sickle of the moon
floated among a thousand stars that seemed much closer
and brighter than they did in New York. But as always, it
was the silence that struck me most. The first few nights, I'd
found it unsettling, accustomed to the nighttime mix of si-
rens, car alarms, muted conversations from other apart-
ments, the occasional not-so-muted argument on the street.
Now, the quiet felt restful.

Which reminded me of Helen's visitations.

As if I had spoken, she asked, "You promise you won't laugh?"

I nodded.

"It's ... a sort of ritual. I stop by each room at night and ... bless those inside." She plucked nervously at the sash of her baby blue robe. "I suppose that sounds silly."

Actually, it sounded sweet. Just the sort of thing Helen would do.

"I heard you once. Just footsteps and something brushing against the door. I thought at first it was a burglar."

"In Dale? We don't even lock our doors at night."

"The thing is, after you ... blessed us ... I felt this amazing sense of ... well, peace."

Helen clapped her hands like a delighted child. "Maybe it really works."

It certainly seemed to. I hadn't felt such peace since I was small enough to believe that my parents' presence would protect me from anything that went bump in the night.

Helen's bright smile faded as I stared at her. "This may sound stupid, but you're not some sort of ... witch, are you?"

"Goodness, no. But I've always suspected my great-great grandmother was. A white witch," she added quickly.

"Like Glinda?"

Helen smiled. "Minus the puffy gown. I never knew her, of course, but her book was handed down to me."

"A book of ... spells?"

Her smile grew. "Recipes. And herbals. Some are quite effective. I haven't had a deer in my garden for years. Of course, that might be due to the boys on staff."

My puzzlement must have shown because she laughed and quickly pressed her fingertips to her mouth. "They urinate around the perimeter of the garden. Lee started it, and men being what they are, it escalated into a ..."

"Pissing contest?"

A giggle escaped Helen's fingertips. "Javier's mostly taken it over, since he lives so close. And has a weak bladder," she added in a whisper. "I'd just as soon use my garlic and Tabasco spray, but it's become something of a tradition."

I made a mental note to pump Hal for details, but couldn't resist asking, "Does Rowan ...?"

"Oh, no. That wouldn't work at all."

Before I could question that unusual statement, Helen said, "It's terribly late. And you have a busy week ahead."

Right on cue, I yawned.

"Oh, dear. I've kept you far too long." Helen's anxious frown deepened. "You won't tell anyone? About the blessing? It's really quite harmless, but . . ."

I crossed my heart. "They'll never hear it from me."

Helen's hug filled me with the same peace and contentment as her blessing. Maybe it was just the feel of her arms around me. Daddy had been the hugger in our family. After he left, my mother managed a few awkward ones when I left for college or came home for a visit.

"Do you have any children?" I blurted.

Helen's hands cupped my cheeks, but her gaze drifted past me to embrace the Golden Bough and its sleeping inhabitants.

"Dozens of them."

CHAPTER 5

BEWITCHED, BOTHERED, AND BEWILDERED

MY "DAY OFF" MADE ME REALIZE I could take only so much nonstop togetherness. I tried holing up in my room at lunch, but nibbling fruit, bread, and cheese on my bed was depressing. Plus I got crumbs everywhere. Walking through town meant inevitable encounters with other cast members, the friendly citizens of Dale, or the staff.

Except Rowan. I never saw him in town. I rarely even saw him on the grounds of the theatre. Once rehearsal was over, he hightailed it to his office. Clearly, he had a low tolerance for togetherness, too.

Finally, I took a brisk walk around the meadow during our lunch break. To my dismay, Caren tagged after me, chattering nonstop. When I informed her—politely—that I needed some time alone, her crestfallen look left me feeling guilty and pissed off about feeling guilty. I grimly trudged past the pond, resigned to crumb-filled bedding. Then I spotted a hand-painted sign describing a trail through the neighboring woodland.

The next day, I waited for everyone to head out to lunch, liberally sprayed myself with "Bug Away," and marched off in search of solitude.

I quickly discovered that the sign painter had used the term "trail" rather loosely. I wasn't expecting paved walkways, but I did assume there would be some sort of path. With signs along the way. And maybe a bench or two.

Instead, I found myself doing a Lewis and Clark through

the wilderness, hoping that the red splotches adorning the tree trunks were more than the random results of a local paintball battle. Fortunately, the trees were so enormous that only a few saplings and shrubs had managed to spring up on the forest floor, reducing my need for a machete. The dense canopy blocked most of the sunlight, so I had to tread cautiously. Still, it was wonderfully peaceful. The only things breaking the silence were the twittering of birds, the soft crunch of dead pine needles and leaves, and my occasional curses when I stumbled over an unseen hazard.

I was catching my breath after one such hazard when I heard the singing. A man's voice, faint but discernible. I was too far away to make out the words, but the unfamiliar tune was achingly beautiful.

I wasn't aware of leaving the trail. And by the time I realized there were no paint splotches to guide me, I no longer cared that I might be lost. Like a sailor out of legend, I had to follow that siren call.

My steps kept pace with the long, sustained notes of the melody. As it shifted into a variation, I found myself moving faster, only to slow again as the chorus returned. No longer a sailor, but a strand of seaweed, caught in the relentless ebb and flow of the music.

The language of the song was as unfamiliar as the tune, but the longing in that clear voice made my throat tighten. Its mingled blend of hope and despair, joy and melancholy were so palpable that I discovered my hands outstretched before me as if to grasp those emotions.

His voice soared again to that pure, high note, and my spirit soared with it. It faded to a whisper, and helpless tears welled in my eyes. It caught in his throat, emerging as a ragged cry, halfway between a sob and a growl, and I had to clutch at the trunk of a tree until the dizziness passed.

My chest ached with the effort to breathe. My pulse raced with the urgency to reach him. With every step, the inchoate yearning inside me grew stronger, a longing for something that remained just out of reach, just beyond conscious desire. And with it, the hope that if I found the source of that voice, I would understand my yearning and find what I was seeking.

I broke into a trot, weaving among the tree trunks.

Something caught at my hair, and I clawed free, barely aware of the twigs scratching my hands. Something snagged my foot, and I stumbled, cursing the tangle of vines for slowing me down.

Only when I felt water trickling down my shins did I realize I must have splashed through a small stream. Only when I felt the ache in my legs and the burning rasp of my breath did I discover I was running heedlessly fast.

A wall of stone suddenly loomed before me. As I veered away, my feet skidded on some loose pebbles. I lurched sideways, arms flailing as I tried to regain my balance. I only succeeded in scraping my hands on the rough bark of a pine as I fell.

The singing stopped.

If I hadn't felt the cry tearing at my throat, I would have thought a wounded animal had made it. And like a wounded animal, I collapsed onto the pine needles and curled into a ball.

I don't know how long I lay there. Minutes, probably, although it felt like hours. Slowly, I returned to myself, aware of the painful throbbing in my left knee, the sharp stinging when I flexed my hands, sweat cooling on my back, pine needles tickling my cheek. If there was such a thing at the end of days as the Rapture, this was how it would feel to be left behind. Or worse, to be given a glimpse of heaven and have it snatched away.

Dismissing that thought as overly dramatic, I pushed myself to my feet and took a few cautious steps. Nothing broken, thank God. But dancing would be hell for the next couple of days.

I knew the road through Dale ran north to south. Which meant the woods were west of the theatre. If I could figure out which way east was, I might emerge from this little fiasco intact. Unfortunately, the few shafts of sunlight penetrating the canopy made it difficult to get any sense of direction.

As I searched for additional clues, I belatedly discovered that the stone wall belonged to a small hut. I examined the skid marks I'd left in the thick mulch of leaves and pine needles, wishing I were more like Natty Bumppo. Or any moderately adequate, modern-day Pathfinder.

Desperate to avoid calling Reinhard's emergency number, I made a slow circle, seeking consensus from skid marks and sun on the direction I should take. Then I froze, my brain finally registering what my eyes had just passed over.

A figure stood a few feet away. A man. A man who had crept toward me with Bumppo-esque stealth, blending so perfectly into the patchwork of sunlight and shadow that I'd neither seen nor heard him approach.

Then it all clicked and I snapped, "Do you always sneak up on people?"

"I could ask you the same thing," Rowan replied.

Hard to believe that mild voice was the same one I'd heard earlier. But it had to have been Rowan singing. He had cast a spell just talking about our contract.

In the two weeks I'd known him, I'd seen him in various modes: the polite acquaintance, the rueful hypnotist, the earnest teacher, the avuncular director. It was difficult to find any of them in the blank-faced stranger walking toward me.

Neither his manner nor his expression revealed anger, yet somehow, it filled the forest. The birds fell silent. A cold breeze buffeted my face. The shadows deepened under the trees. He even seemed to grow taller and more threatening with every slow, inexorable step.

Without conscious thought, I backed away. He drew up short, his head snapping back as if I'd slapped him.

The breeze died. The sun came out from behind a cloud. The birds resumed their twittering. And Rowan looked like Rowan again.

"Forgive me. I frightened you."

I shook my head, but the lines between those wild-winged brows deepened.

"Are you hurt?"

"I fell." I sounded like a six-year-old about to burst into tears because of the nasty boo-boos on her hands and knees.

He reached me in a few long strides and gently guided me toward a fallen tree. After easing me onto it, he went down on one knee. Like a courtier before a queen. Or a suitor asking for my hand in marriage.

When he actually asked for my hand, I nearly fell off the log.

"Your hands," he repeated patiently. "Are they badly scraped?"

When I continued to gawk at him, he simply took my right hand in his and turned it palm up. His fingertips glided across the abraded flesh, trailing cool relief in their wake.

He just has cold hands. Nothing weird about that.

He also had beautiful hands, the pale skin unusually smooth for a man. Each long tapering finger had a perfect little crescent moon at the tip of each nail. He and Helen had to go to the same manicurist.

So he's the human equivalent of a Mexican hairless. So what? Or maybe he's the original hairy ape and he waxes. And gets manicures. Nothing weird about that, either. Lots of men do it. I don't know any, but . . .

He turned his attention to my left hand, and I sighed, doubts subsiding along with the stinging in my palm. His hands descended to my sore knee. I closed my eyes, enjoying the gentleness of his massaging fingertips.

Then Nancy's words popped into my head: "I didn't have to tell him. He knew."

I flinched.

Rowan's hands fell still. "What is it?"

Not "Did I hurt you?" which would have been the logical question. Because he knew he wasn't hurting me. Just as he knew exactly where I was hurting before he did the whole laying-on-of-hands thing.

"Maggie?"

So he's a hands-on healer. Nothing . . . okay that is weird. But not impossibly weird.

Abruptly, he rose and stalked away, shoving his fists into the pockets of his jeans.

I'm alone in the forest with my director, that's all. A director who casts people according to need and happens to be a hairless hands-on healer who lives on strawberry milkshakes and only leaves the grounds of the theatre when he hikes into the forest to sing in tongues.

I examined my palms. They still looked red and raw, although they didn't hurt as much.

"I've frightened you again."

I shook my head.

"Come on, Maggie! You're shaking like a leaf and you're staring at me like I'm a . . . . ."

"What?" I whispered. "What are you?"

Just like that, the mask slipped over his features. Not the blank face of anger I'd seen moments ago, but the distant expression I'd noted the morning I'd bashed my head. As if he'd withdrawn into private memories or some secret place where no one could possibly reach him. And then it was gone, replaced so swiftly by an expression of ordinary frustration that I wondered if I was making all this shit up.

"I'm a good reader of faces and body language. A useful skill for a director. When I walked toward you, you held up your hands to stop me."

"I did?"

"That's when I noticed your palms. And when I saw your limp—yes, you were limping—I thought I should ascertain how badly you were hurt in case I had to carry you back to the theatre. Which I'm prepared to do. Although two miles is a long way to walk with a woman slung over your shoulders. Any other questions?"

Dozens flooded my overheated brain. But I was tired and sore and still too dazed to trust myself to frame them, never mind process the answers. When I shook my head, he walked back to me and extended his hands to help me to my feet.

A thick red weal creased each palm. Smaller ones marred his fingertips.

I took his hands without comment, but the tightening of his jaw proved that he'd noticed my slight hesitation and the direction of my gaze.

He drew my left arm around his waist and wrapped his right one around mine. Entwined like kids in a three-legged race, we hobbled through the woods for a bit. Then I eased free.

"I'm just a little stiff," I assured him. "I'll be fine if we go slow."

He stuck close to my side in case I needed help. At the steeper spots, his arm snaked around my waist to support me, the embrace as impersonal as any medic's. When the ground leveled off again, he stepped away. Once or twice, he nodded as if pleased by my progress. But the silence seemed to pulsate with my unspoken questions and his lingering resentment.

Finally, I stopped. As I struggled to find the right words, his expression hardened.

"They're burns."

"What?"

"The marks. On my hands. Burns."

"No . . . that wasn't . . . I just wanted to apologize. For disturbing you. I didn't mean to. Or to spy on you. I just . . ." I shrugged helplessly. "I heard you singing."

The tension had drained out of him during my fumbling explanation. He nodded, unsurprised. He'd probably encountered similar reactions so often that he'd learned to hide in the woods before allowing himself the pleasure—the release—of singing.

We walked on, the silence a little less forbidding now. Which gave me the courage to say, "Could I ask you one question?"

His chest rose and fell as he nodded. I wasn't sure if he was heaving a resigned sigh or bracing himself.

"The song. What's it called?"

From his short exhalation of breath, I decided he'd been bracing himself.

"It's usually translated as 'The Mist-Covered Mountains.'"

"Gaelic!" I exclaimed. "That was the language."

He nodded, grasping my elbow to guide me around a fallen birch.

"What's it about? Other than mist-covered mountains." At his sidelong look, I added, "Okay, that's two questions, but—"

"Home. It's about home. The places you once walked. The people you once knew. The welcome that awaits you when . . . if . . . you return."

"An exile's song."

His head snapped toward me. "Why would you say that?"

"It sounded like a lament. But not without hope."

Slowly, he nodded.

Had he been born in Scotland? That would explain the

trace of an accent I'd detected the first day. And the Gaelic. Had something happened to drive him from his native land? Or prevent him from returning?

"Ask." A small smile—more of a grimace—tugged at the corner of his mouth.

"I was just wondering if you were born in Scotland."

"Yes. And before that vivid imagination of yours runs wild, let me assure you that I am not a Scottish serial killer hiding out in the hinterlands of Vermont."

"Hey, you were the one who said you chopped up cast members for buttons."

"I was joking." The green eyes narrowed. "But the idea is growing on me."

"So I guess I shouldn't ask about the hut."

"You mean the *cottage*?"

From the way he emphasized the word, it was clear that he took exception to the term "hut." But a one-room building barely ten paces wide hardly qualified as a cottage. Unless it was located in Brigadoon.

"What's a cottage doing out in the middle of nowhere?"

"It was built a long time ago. Back in the 1700s, the Mackenzies received a land grant of two hundred acres. There are only twenty acres left, but that's more than enough for someone to get lost. Especially—"

"A city slicker like me?"

"Especially since they adjoin the Green Mountain National Forest."

I thought of reminding him that I would never have gotten lost in the first place if not for his singing, but common sense told me to avoid that sensitive subject.

"So the first Mackenzies lived in—"

"My turn. Why were you walking in the woods? You don't strike me as a nature lover."

"I like nature." I batted away a cloud of gnats and saw him turn his head to hide a smile. "I do! I just . . . this was the only quiet place I could find. Away from everything."

"You needed to get away?"

"Yes! We rehearse together. We eat together. We even sleep together. I needed some private time."

"You didn't find any on your day off?"

"Romaine called an extra chorus rehearsal. And then there was movie night. And—"

"And coaching the principals."

I stopped short. "Who told you?"

"I believe you just did."

My withering look had no effect whatsoever on him. "Okay, Columbo. You want to tell me how you figured that out?"

"Elementary, my dear Watson," he replied, blithely mixing detectives. "If a couple of the principals had improved in the space of a single day, I simply would have assumed they'd had time to process my comments. When all of them improved, I began to wonder if they had outside help. You were the natural suspect."

"It wasn't something I planned. Nancy was upset after the run-through and—"

"Upset?" he asked, his voice sharp.

"She was . . . well . . . crying."

I didn't understand the passionate explosion of Gaelic, but he was obviously swearing.

"She's fine now. Rowan! She's fine."

He stopped swearing, but his frown remained.

"She was just frustrated. So I asked her what you'd suggested. And then all I did—I swear to God—was draw a line down a piece of paper, and write 'Strengths' in one column and 'Weaknesses' in another."

"And ask a few questions."

He was smiling again, thank God.

"A few," I admitted. "But mostly, it came from her. And then she told Will, and Will told Ashley and Richard, and before I knew it . . ."

"The line was forming to the right."

"I wasn't coaching them. Or trying to play director. Or—"

"I'm not angry at you, Maggie. Only at myself. For letting Nancy down. I should have realized . . ." With an impatient wave, he dismissed whatever he'd started to say. "I'm glad you were there for her. For all of them."

"That's me. Maggie Graham. Helping Professional."

He regarded me gravely. "Did you dislike it so much?"

"No," I replied, surprising myself. "It was kind of fun, actually. But by the end of the day, I was feeling a bit overwhelmed."

"It's important to have boundaries."

"Yeah. Well, next time Kevin launches into Harry Beaton's masturbatory fantasies, I'll send him straight to you."

Rowan's laughter startled the birds into momentary silence.

"Oh, to have been a fly on the wall," he mused. "You should be grateful he isn't singing 'Come to Me, Bend to Me.'"

"Or you."

"Me?"

"With your voice? Are you kidding? I'd come in a heartbeat."

I recognized the potential for double entendre at the exact moment that Rowan's eyebrows rose. A wave of heat flushed my body and traveled swiftly faceward.

"Come *to* you," I clarified. "And . . ."

"Bend?" he inquired with a polite smile.

"Oh, look. We're back on the trail. See? The red blotch?"

"Yes."

But he was gazing at my face, not the tree.

"We were talking about boundaries," I said firmly.

"Yes. Boundaries are . . . essential." For a moment, he withdrew into that other place again. Then his expression sharpened. "I'm glad you could help your cast mates, Maggie. But I don't want you to neglect your work."

"Actually, I was wondering if that *was* my work. If that's why you'd cast me."

He shook his head, but refused to say more.

"What? I have to learn it for myself? Like Dorothy in *The Wizard of Oz?*"

"Something like that. Ask me again at the end of the season if you like."

"I will. But if you give me some crap about my heart's desire being in my own backyard and there's no place like home, I'm going to be pissed."

"Duly noted."

"Which, by the way, is a completely dumbass moral. Dorothy had already figured that out before the twister. Glinda could have just told the poor kid to click her heels together while she was in Munchkinland. But no! She sends her traipsing off to Oz to learn what she already learned from Professor Marvel."

Rowan regarded me with mingled amusement and wariness. "I'll have to share your insights with the staff."

"Your staff is obsessed with *The Wizard of Oz*?"

He grimaced. "If I tell you a secret, will you swear not to tell anyone?"

"Is this another bones-of-the-cast-members secret?"

"No. A real one."

I crossed my heart and waited expectantly.

"Every summer, the staff puts on a performance for the cast. The Crossroads Follies, we call it. This year, it's *The Wizard of Oz*."

As he described the Follies, his face lit up like a kid's on Christmas morning, his body trembling with suppressed excitement. It was a side of him I'd never seen and I marveled at the transformation.

"A few days before the performance, we hand out ballots. The cast has to decide who's playing which part and write the name of the staff member next to the role. The person who gets the most right wins a week's salary. Of course, there's always a fair amount of side wagers, too."

Suddenly, the light snapped out. He scuffed at the leaf mold with the toe of his boot. No longer a kid at Christmas but an awkward adolescent whose voice had broken when he asked a girl out on a date.

"It's just silliness," he muttered.

"It sounds great."

Three little words and the light snapped back on.

"Helen would be perfect for Glinda," I continued, wanting to keep it shining. "But I suppose Hal will insist on playing her. You're obviously the Wizard." I paused to gauge his reaction, but he just shrugged. "The big question is who's playing the Wicked Witch." My palms moved through the air as if balancing weights. "Janet. Mei-Yin. Janet. Mei-Yin."

Without warning, the light died again. Following the direction of his gaze, I peered through the trees. What I'd thought was a clearing in the woods was actually the meadow by the theatre. I wondered if he shared my regret at arriving at our destination.

As we approached the edge of the woods, I saw a small knot of people in the picnic area. Two were pacing. The rest huddled together in what appeared to be a very serious conversation.

"Do you think there's been an accident?" I asked.

"Only yours. Come on."

We were still hidden in the trees when they all turned and gazed in our direction. Like bird dogs on point. Then they hurried toward us. It was the staff, I realized as our paths converged. Everybody except Alex. Even Javier and Hal who should be at their shops.

I glanced at my watch. "We're ten minutes late to rehearsal and they send out an all points bulletin?"

"I'm never late. I imagine they were concerned."

"But how did they—?"

"Let's not keep them waiting."

"Which means I've used up my quota of questions for the day."

"Which means you're not the only one who likes privacy."

I added mental telepathy to Rowan's growing list of skills and kept my mouth shut. He squeezed my shoulder, perhaps to apologize for his brusqueness. Then the pressure increased and I realized that, in spite of his words a moment ago, he wanted me to stop.

"Will you do something for me?"

Struck by his serious expression, I nodded.

"Don't mention the scars to the cast. The staff knows. But I wouldn't want the actors to feel . . . uncomfortable."

Again, I nodded.

"Thank you."

As he started walking, I blurted out, "You're all right now, though?"

His eyes widened. I was on the verge of yet another apology when he smiled. A smile so unexpectedly sweet that the breath caught in my throat.

"Maggie Graham. Helping Professional. Yes. I'm all right now."

The smile vanished. In a few purposeful strides, he slipped from confidant to director again.

I doubted I would ever understand the man. Or be able

to anticipate his quicksilver changes of mood. Reason told me not to try. There were too many mysteries, too many secrets. But how could I think of him without hearing that song resonating inside of me, without seeing the scars on his body and imagining the others on his soul?

One thing I did know. It wasn't the burns on his hands that he wanted to keep secret, but the other scars. The ones I'd glimpsed when he had extended his hands to help me off the log. The ones that usually remained hidden beneath the cuffs of his long-sleeved shirt.

Jagged white scars. Created by a knife gouging deep through the flesh and arteries and veins of his wrists.

CHAPTER 6
EVERYBODY SAYS DON'T

FOR THE REST OF THE DAY, the speculative glances of the staff followed me. So I was less than receptive when Alex beckoned me toward the piano during a break in our music rehearsal.

"Don't start," I warned him before he could speak. "Catherine and Javier think I overreacted. Lee and Hal advised me to stay focused on the show. I've endured Reinhard's bullying, Helen's sighs, and Janet's innuendos. And an outpouring of sweetness from Mei-Yin that was far more disturbing than Rowan's singing."

Alex wiped an invisible streak of dust from the top of the piano and said, "Ah."

"I take it you've heard him sing?"

"Yes."

"Are you going to tell me I overreacted?"

"That's hard to say. What was he singing?"

I hesitated, knowing how Rowan valued his privacy. But if the staff knew about his scars, there seemed little harm in telling Alex the name of the song.

When I did, he just said, "Ah." Again.

"Is that bad?"

"No. Probably not important at all. Just the natural curiosity of a music director."

Which seemed way too pat.

Before I could pursue it, Alex said, "Rowan's fine. Right

now, the staff is more concerned about you. We don't want you to get hurt."

"I'm already hurt," I replied, holding up my palms.

Then I finally realized what he was getting at—what they'd all been getting at.

"My God. You're afraid I'm going to fall for him."

"It's happened before. Not for years," he added quickly. "Rowan takes his responsibility to the cast very seriously. That's why he keeps his distance. But you know what it's like during a summer stock season."

Passions blooming right and left, only to die a quick death as soon as you emerged from the hothouse of the theatre.

"Which is why I'm not likely to get caught up in that," I reminded him.

"Of course not." Alex waved his hand impatiently. "Look, forget I said anything. I worry too much. Catherine always says so. Maybe it's because I have a daughter. I have this alarming tendency to take up sword and shield in defense of every young woman who crosses my path, whether or not she needs protection. So when I go into my father act, just remind me that you're a strong woman who's fully capable of—Maggie? Honey, are you okay?"

It was the "honey" that did me in. I managed to control my voice long enough to say, "I'm just ... I'm more tired than I thought. Would you mind if I skipped the rest of rehearsal?"

I bolted for the door before he could answer. Concerned faces turned toward me. Someone called my name. I yelled, "My knee's killing me," which was the best I could come up with on the spur of the moment.

As I hobbled down the brick path, I heard footsteps pounding after me. Then Gary shouting my name. I had almost made it to the parking lot when he grabbed my arm.

"Slow down. You'll only make it worse."

"I'm fine. Let me go."

"You're not fine." But he released my arm and stepped back. "Look, I don't know what happened in there—"

"Nothing happened! I've just had a really long day and I want to go back to the hotel."

"Fine. I'll drive you."

"I don't need you to drive me."

"You don't have to talk. And I won't ask questions. But you're too upset to drive."

"It's half a mile!"

"I don't care if it's half a block. I'm driving. Now give me the keys and get in the goddamn car!"

We both kept our parts of the bargain: I didn't talk and Gary didn't ask questions. By the time he pulled up in front of the hotel, I was calm. Calmer. Yelling at him had provided a viable alternative to tears.

He put the car in park and we sat there, staring through the windshield.

"Thank you," I said.

"Thank *you*. It's not often I get a chance to unleash my inner caveman."

My smile faded when I saw how tightly he was gripping the steering wheel.

"Look, I know I said I wouldn't ask questions. But I saw you coming out of the woods with him. And if he hurt you—"

"No! God. Nothing like that. I fell while I was walking. And Rowan helped me back."

His fingers relaxed. For the first time since leaving the theatre, he looked at me. "Then . . . ? Sorry."

"I just snapped, okay? The staff's been at me all afternoon. Making a huge deal out of nothing. And then Alex . . . he was just being kind and protective and . . ."

Fatherly.

". . . I had a meltdown. God. Poor Alex. He'll be frantic."

And probably sending out an APB to the entire staff that I'd gone 'round the bend.

"Look. Keep my car. Go back to rehearsal and tell him— tell everybody—that I'm fine."

"Are you?" Gary asked quietly.

His genuine concern deserved more than a quick brush-off. I took a deep breath, let it out, and said, "The thing is . . . I lost my father."

Strictly speaking, he had lost us. I saw him twice after Mom kicked him out. Got an occasional postcard after that—places like Sedona and Stonehenge and Machu Picchu. But we hadn't seen or heard from him in twenty years.

"Alex was all fatherly and it . . . brought up a lot of stuff."

It felt weird talking about it. Especially with someone I barely knew. Mom never mentioned him. We'd had the obligatory "Daddy still loves you and this isn't your fault" speech when he left—the kind of thing you say to an eight-year-old. I was in high school before she told me about the times he'd vanish for a week or a month, the repeated absences that cost him his teaching job, the series of part-time jobs he lost the same way, the drug use.

It did little to ease the pain of his absence, but at least I stopped blaming her for the divorce. And understood why she'd thrown out all the shit he'd collected over the years: the programs and photos and newspaper clippings from his "career" as an actor; the books on folklore and mythology and New Age mysticism. She threw out his old cast albums, too, but I found them stacked beside the garbage can and hid them under my bed. I'd carted them from apartment to apartment, even though I didn't own a turntable to play them on. Stupid. As stupid as my occasional Google searches for Jack Sinclair.

Another thing Mom had thrown out: Sinclair. She resumed her maiden name and after the divorce changed mine to Graham as well. A little bit of paperwork, a modest fee, and bam! I was somebody else. And he hadn't even objected.

I kept it simple for Gary. I'd had a lot of experience turning our family psychodrama into an ordinary tale of a marriage gone sour and a single mom raising her kid alone. Still, my calm delivery was pretty impressive when only minutes ago, I'd been on the verge of tears, childishly longing for a father like Alex.

I definitely needed a real day off.

When I finished, Gary sighed. "I lost my dad last year."

He meant that his father had died, of course. For all I knew, mine had, too. There were too many Jack Sinclairs in the world to find one via Google. When I narrowed the search parameters with our Wilmington address or his college or the few other personal tidbits I knew about him, no results came up. Like Mom, he'd been an only child, so there were no aunts or uncles to turn to. And by the time I started looking for him, my grandparents had passed away.

He might be using another name. He might have started another family. He might be chanting mantras in Tibet or chewing coca leaves in Peru or drinking Sterno on skid row. In the end, death and a twenty-year absence amounted to pretty much the same thing.

"If you ever need to talk ... or feel like you're on the verge of another meltdown ..." Gary shrugged, suddenly awkward. "Feel free to call your friendly neighborhood caveman."

He waited until I was inside the hotel vestibule before driving off. I waved one last time and pulled open the door.

Helen stood in the lobby, staring anxiously at me. Clearly, Alex had broken a speed record getting out that APB. But it was Janet who asked, "What happened?"

I went through the whole spiel again. Janet eyed me like a lioness stalking a wounded gazelle. Helen gathered me in her arms. I gave her a quick, hard hug and pulled away.

"If you start being motherly, I'll have another meltdown."

"Why don't I make us some tea? Chamomile, skullcap, St. John's wort. Very calming."

Before I could beg off, she hurried toward the hotel office. Leaving me with the lioness.

Janet waved me toward an easy chair, then sat in the one opposite, leaving Iolanthe, sprawled on the settee, to referee. Ignoring the "No Smoking" sign on the wall behind her chair, she pulled a pack of Parliaments and a lighter from the pocket of her cardigan. With elaborate care, she removed a cigarette, lit it, and took a deep drag, all the while watching me.

"Do you want some advice?"

"No."

Her smile did little to dispel the image of a stalking lioness.

"I like you, Maggie."

I clamped my lips together to keep from gaping. If brittle sarcasm was her response to people she liked, I shuddered to think how she treated her enemies.

"You're not as tough as you'd like people to believe, but you say what you think and I like that. Please don't feel obligated to return the compliment."

"I won't."

Her smile widened as she leaned back and crossed her legs. "Are you the kind of woman who can enjoy sex without requiring romance?"

Didn't see that one coming.

"I'm flattered by your interest, Janet, but you're really not my type."

"Because if you are," she continued, ignoring my comeback, "you might consider sleeping with Rowan."

This time, I did gape. Then I got to my feet. "I am not having this conversation."

"Of course you are. You're fascinated."

I sat down.

"He needs a woman. Well, a man would suffice. It has in the past. But he seems to like you. And you seem to like him."

My head had snapped back against the cushion, like a bantamweight boxer who'd gotten sucker punched by the heavyweight champion of the world. I took a deep breath, gripping the arms of the chair to steady myself. I'd stood up to Reinhard that first day; I wasn't about to let Janet get the better of me.

I crossed my legs, deliberately imitating her. "I didn't realize a producer's responsibilities included pimping for the director. Or does this come under the general heading of hospitality?"

"You'd enjoy him."

"Are you speaking from personal experience?"

Janet laughed and flicked ash into the brass spittoon next to her chair. "God, no. I'd never sleep with Rowan. But he has a powerful effect on people. As you discovered this afternoon."

She was the first person on the staff to admit that. The others had either skirted the issue or tried to make me believe I had imagined the whole thing.

Janet was watching me with a satisfied smile. "What you experienced today was quite intense, wasn't it?"

"But not remotely sexual."

"Mmm. But just imagine experiencing that same intensity—physical and emotional—during sex. I see from your blushes that you are. Oh, for God's sake, stop bobbing up and down like a jack-in-the-box."

I could feel the sheer force of her will urging me back into my chair. But this time, I stayed on my feet.

"Is this something you do every summer? Scope out the cast looking for someone to put into Rowan's bed?"

She shrugged. "Most of the women who come here are too vulnerable."

"And I'm not?"

"Not to romance. That's why I'm proposing this. But before you decide, you need to consider two things."

"Please. Enlighten me."

"Love has no role in this relationship. It's simply a sexual affair that ends when the season does. More importantly, you'll have to forgo your compulsion to play social worker."

"I don't—"

"You can't help Rowan. You cannot heal his wounds or grant him redemption or make him forget the past. Believe me, others have tried. And failed."

My legs were shaking. I would have given anything to sink into my chair—or at least grip the back for support—but I refused to give Janet that satisfaction.

"You'd never make this proposition unless you had a vested interest in the outcome. So what's in it for you?"

Janet's approving nod further infuriated me.

"You've worked in stock. You know how volatile the atmosphere can be. Well, that's more than usually true here."

"Because of Rowan."

She shrugged.

"If Rowan's happy, everybody's happy."

"Something like that."

"And all I have to do is spread my legs."

Janet took a long drag on her cigarette, blew the smoke toward the ceiling, and smiled. "With Rowan, you wouldn't even have to do that."

Before I could ask her what the hell that meant, she added, "Stop acting like some poor sacrificial lamb. If that's all I wanted, I could choose anyone. Sex with Rowan would probably do you a world of good."

"Probably? What happened to experiencing intensity beyond my wildest dreams?"

"Well, that's the risk, of course. That you would enter into this affair with the best intentions and still be unable to resist his . . ."

"Charms?"

"If you like. So a lot depends on how well you know yourself. And how much of a gambler you are." Her smile vanished as she leaned forward. "If you have any doubts, stay away from him. Or you'll be hurt. Deeply, terribly, irreparably hurt."

"By Rowan."

"By your inability to follow the rules I've just laid out. Rowan has little to do with it. He can't help what he is."

"And what exactly is he?"

"Rowan is incapable of love. And he is equally incapable of change."

As I absorbed that damning judgment, I heard a clatter behind me.

"That's not true."

God only knew how long Helen had been standing there or how much she'd heard. Enough to upset her; the cups and saucers were still rattling on the silver tea tray. But she sailed into the lobby like a queen and carefully lowered the tray onto the coffee table between Janet's chair and mine.

"Rowan *is* capable of love. And change."

"Helen, you see, is a romantic. She still cries when the village reappears at the end of *Brigadoon*, proving that true love can work miracles."

"While you don't believe in love at all."

"Oh, I believe in love. I've seen what it can do. The unhappiness it can cause. The lives it can ruin."

Helen was the calm one now. It was Janet whose voice shook with emotion, whose features were twisted with anger. I wasn't sure what lay behind this exchange, but clearly, they had been waging this battle for years. The funny thing was, although I disliked Janet, I pretty much shared her opinion about true love.

"You're wrong about Rowan," Helen said. "And about me. And it's very wrong of you to try and mold Maggie into the kind of woman you've become."

"What kind of woman is that?"

"Bitter. And lonely. If I've been unhappy—"

"If?"

". . . the joy I've known has more than made up for it."

Janet crushed out her cigarette on the rim of the spittoon and rose. "I'll leave you to your joy. Think about what I said, Maggie."

Neither Helen nor I moved until the office door closed behind her. I let out the breath I hadn't realized I was holding. Helen sank onto the settee.

For once, I had the sense to keep my mouth shut. Or maybe I was still too stunned by my conversation with Janet and the turn it had taken at the end.

Iolanthe butted Helen's hand. Absently, she stroked the fur beneath the cat's left ear. "You must forgive Janet. Sometimes, she's . . . overzealous."

"Ya think?"

Helen sighed. "You must find all of this very strange."

"Very."

"The staff really does try to do its best for the cast."

"Even Janet?"

"Whatever she told you was the truth. As she sees it. But don't be guided by her. Or by me, either. Trust your own instincts, Maggie."

"If I did that, I'd be on the road to New York now."

"Have some tea instead."

"I don't suppose you have anything stronger?"

"Why, yes. Lagavulin. Single malt. Would you like a glass?"

"I'd like a bottle. I think I need to get drunk."

Helen nodded solemnly. "That's a marvelous idea."

As she gently dislodged Iolanthe from her lap, I took a deep breath. "What I felt today in the forest was real, Helen. As real as the scars on Rowan's wrists."

Caught in the act of rising, Helen sank back onto the settee. After a long moment, she said, "That was a bad time for Rowan. As you can imagine. But it was many years ago." Then she asked, "Which song was he singing?"

The question was beginning to take on a surreal quality.

When I told her, she sighed. "Yes, of course. He's always nostalgic for home at this time of year." With a determined nod, she rose. "I'm going to fetch the Lagavulin. And you and I are going to forget about the theatre's oddities and Janet's scheming and Rowan's . . ."

"And Rowan."

"Yes. And get gloriously, wonderfully tipsy."

CHAPTER 7
PUTTING IT TOGETHER

THE ONLY PROBLEM WITH GETTING gloriously, wonderfully tipsy was waking up miserably, horribly hung over.

When I crawled into the Chatterbox the next morning, Lou gave a low whistle and said, "Man. You look like shit." Nick suggested a breakfast of raw eggs and Worcestershire sauce, then hastily retreated when I threatened to vomit on him. Romaine clucked. Brittany offered me her under-eye concealer. Nancy—God bless her—silently passed me a bottle of Tylenol.

I had little dancing in Act Two, so it was easy to obey Reinhard's stern instructions to take it easy during rehearsal. Singing proved more painful, thanks to the proverbial twelve drummers drumming in my head.

I had no contact with Rowan until our lunch break. When I lingered to clarify a bit of blocking, he replied, "Check with Reinhard," and strode away.

I stared after him, torn between surprise and resentment. I hardly expected yesterday's encounter to render us Best Friends Forever, but I did expect the same courtesy he extended to everyone else in the cast. Maybe he was self-conscious in the face of the staff's less-than-surreptitious surveillance. Or uncomfortable because I'd seen his scars. I just hoped to God he hadn't ascribed my meltdown to some burgeoning passion.

Our first full run-through on the set did little to restore

my spirits. The malevolent fog machine churned out so much mist that the actors were invisible. The small footbridge I had to cross during "Vendors' Calls" lurched so alarmingly that I feared I would tumble into the orchestra pit. Wheeled carts collided in MacConnachy Square. Dancers stumbling through their steps during the wedding sequence gave new meaning to the term Highland reel.

The highlight was when Kevin's kilt slipped off during the chase. Like the dedicated method actor he had become, he wore what every eighteenth-century Scotsman wore under his kilt—nothing. So the last we saw of Harry Beaton before he plunged to his death was the gleam of his pale but muscular buttocks.

That was Sunday, the first day of Hell Week. Hell Week was really only three days. It just seemed much, much longer.

Farewell to our day off Monday. We worked Act One in the morning, Act Two in the afternoon, and then moved on to tech rehearsal at night. Four hours of Reinhard calling cue lines so we could shuffle to our next position while Javier and the stage crew practiced set changes and Lee punched up the proper lighting or sound effect on his console.

Tuesday afternoon, we worked the problem scenes in the Smokehouse, while the crew made frantic final adjustments to the set.

Dress rehearsal Tuesday night. No calling for lines. No stopping unless disaster struck.

Last chance to put music and lyrics together while wheeling carts or hefting kegs of ale or holding up bolts of woolen cloth. Last chance to master singing and dancing in bulky skirts and petticoats. Last chance to achieve some sort of balance between the musicians in the pit and the singers onstage. Last chance to make the set changes smooth, the costume changes quick, the special effects brilliant.

Last chance to get it right.

Or not.

"Bad dress rehearsal, great opening night," Hal assured me the next afternoon as he slid another pin into the hem of my forest green gown.

"Yeah. I know the saying."

After Helen finished her crash course on applying theatrical makeup, I'd gone to the costume shop for a final fitting. In my case, it was more of a salvage job. During dress rehearsal, I'd managed to rip my hem not once but twice during my mad dash out the stage door, around the barn, and into the lobby for my breathless entrance through the back of the house for "Vendors' Calls."

Hal put down his pincushion and gazed up at me. Yet another man kneeling at my feet. "Relax. In eight hours, it'll all be over. Now walk for me."

I grimly marched between the costume racks and his cluttered sewing table.

"Turn. Slowly!" He scrutinized the bottom of my skirt and grimaced. "Is one of your legs shorter than the other?"

"That must be it. God knows the hem couldn't be uneven."

Hal pursed his lips. "Someone's a little bitchy."

"God. Yes. Sorry. I'm just . . ."

"Exhausted? Nervous? Still recovering from your tryst in the forest?"

I snatched up a pair of scissors and brandished them.

Hal rolled his eyes. "What? Death by pinking shears?"

"Very slow. Very painful."

"Well, put them down and stand still. I can't possibly adjust for your withered leg when you're flouncing around."

I obeyed, impatient to get back to the hotel. I needed to check my e-mail to see if I'd gotten any response to the resumes I'd sent out. I needed to go through a week's worth of forwarded mail and pay bills. I needed to squeeze in a nap, get a shower, and eat dinner before heading back here for opening night.

My stomach executed a nauseating flip-flop; it better be a light dinner.

Still brooding, my gaze was caught by a sketch on Hal's sewing table. I unearthed it from the detritus and studied it in disbelief.

"This is the program?"

Hal glanced up, then nodded and returned to his work. "This. Is the program."

A single 8½ x 11 page folded in half. A drawing of the barn on the cover with *Brigadoon* written below it. Cast list on the left-hand page. Scenes and songs on the right. Names of the production staff on the back.

Where were the ads from local vendors? The listing of the "Angels" whose donations helped to support the theatre? The "Who's Who in the Cast?" The notification about the next production and the time-honored director's notes on this one? My middle school had created better programs.

"You're always bitching about not having enough money for new costumes," I reminded him. "Why don't you solicit ads? Or hit up the wealthy folk of Dale for donations?"

"They're not that wealthy. And they help out."

That was true. I'd seen familiar faces among the stage crew, including Beatrix, Reinhard's daughter from his first marriage and owner of Bea's Hive of Beauty. Frannie and her Chatterbox cronies ushered. And the all-volunteer pit band included some of Alex's students as well as folks from town. But still . . .

"I don't know how you people stay in business."

"Stop fidgeting."

"How tough is it to turn out a program that looks professional?"

"Take it up with Helen. She does the programs."

"God. What am I doing here?"

Hal sat back on his heels. "Right now, you're getting your hem fixed. After that, you're going to relax. Tonight, you'll be utterly brilliant—"

"If I don't tumble off the Bridge of Doom."

"And then you'll have a fabulous time at the cast party."

"That's another thing! Who throws a cast party on opening night? It's supposed to be closing night of the show."

"We have one then, too," Hal replied calmly. "But after all the hard work everyone's put in, we deserve a celebration tonight."

"I'm too tired to celebrate."

"Everyone says that. And everyone ends up dancing the night away."

"Even Rowan?"

Hal returned his attention to my hem. "Rowan's not much for dancing."

"Or mingling. Or leaving the grounds of the theatre. I think he actually lives here."

Expecting Hal to laugh, his silence was revelatory.

"My God. He does live here. That's not just his office under the eaves. It's his . . . lair."

"You make him sound like the Phantom of the Opera. It's a lovely loft apartment with exposed beams, hardwood floors—"

"A giant organ."

"I know nothing about the size of Rowan's organ." Hal managed to wink, leer, and waggle his eyebrows suggestively all at the same time. "Perhaps you could fill me in."

"Perhaps I could slap you silly."

"I'm not into S&M. Although I do look fabulous in black. Makes my fair hair and complexion pop. Still, I'm not sure I should go that route tonight. It might play funereal rather than elegant. Maybe just a spot of color. A violet tie, say . . ."

As Hal nattered on about clothing options, I turned over the latest piece of the Rowan Mackenzie puzzle. So far it resembled an early Picasso, all dislocated features and oddly angled limbs.

But we had the morning off tomorrow. That would give me time to Google phobias. And "The Mist-Covered Mountains." And see if I could fill in a few more pieces of the puzzle.

CHAPTER 8
THERE'S NO BUSINESS LIKE SHOW BUSINESS

AT 7:45, WE FILED INTO THE GREEN ROOM. It looked like all the others I'd been in, except it was actually painted green. This one had the usual dilapidated couches, two easy chairs with stuffing creeping out of the arms like fluffy caterpillars, a coffee table with a book under one broken leg to keep it level, a card table with four folding chairs, and a kitchenette with one working burner.

Someone probably Helen—had hung crepe paper garlands and filled the table with lemonade, a plate of orange slices, a bowl of herb tea bags, and one of those plastic honey bears. The homey touches failed to alleviate the tension in the room. Not just the nervous anticipation that always precedes an opening, but the sweaty, barely suppressed sense of imminent doom.

Only Bernie seemed immune. He'd been depressed since Rowan assigned Hector, one of the tenors in the chorus, to guide him on and off the stage for each entrance and exit. But tonight, his gnomish face was alight with barely suppressed excitement.

"So. Give," I whispered.

"Rowan's going to let me walk on alone for the ending. I practiced all afternoon." He thumped the floor with the heavy cane he was using for the show. "Just had to get my sea legs."

"But with the mist . . . and the dark . . ."

"I'll be fine."

I hoped he was right. Still, his determination cheered me; after Rowan's decision, he'd seemed to dwindle, becoming a tired old man before my eyes.

"Nervous?" he asked.

"A little," I admitted.

"You're a pro. Nothing to worry about. Them, I'm not so sure."

I glanced around the sea of plaid. Nancy was mouthing the words to one of her songs. Bobbie was twisting the lace at the neck of her gown. Kevin checked the clasps on his kilt for the hundredth time. Lou was nowhere in sight; he'd probably ducked out for a cigarette.

I was surprised to see Richard's dark head bent to Ashley's blonde one. Unlike Will and Nancy, their relationship had been awkward onstage and off. Maybe it was the fifteen-year age gap. Or the wider gap in background and personality. Or the never-to-be-spoken-about-but-potentially-uncomfortable issue of race that separated a black executive from Massachusetts and a white sorority girl from Virginia. Probably a combination of all those factors.

But they had apparently surmounted their differences. Just getting to know each other better or yet another example of Rowan Mackenzie's casting magic?

Right on cue, the door to the green room opened and he stepped inside. Immediately, all conversation ceased.

"Hello, everyone. I just wanted ... where's Lou?"

"Right here, boss." Lou edged past Rowan, trailing the aromas of cigarette smoke and Old Spice aftershave.

"I just wanted to thank you all for your hard work. I know it hasn't been easy. And I know you've all had your doubts about whether we could pull this off. Well, tonight, we'll prove that we can."

His intent gaze swept across every face, just as it had the morning of our first company meeting. Then he said, "Take the hands of the people standing next to you. Close your eyes. And just breathe. Slow and deep."

A few weeks ago, there would have been a lot of eye rolling and grimaces. But we had shared a lot since then, including dozens of group exercises that helped us to relax and focus and connect with each other.

His soft voice urged us to feel the hands we were holding, to notice the energy passing through them. And as he spoke, I felt it. A strange tingling sensation that followed the path Rowan described. Up through my arms and down through my torso. Warming my belly like whisky. Flushing my body with heat as it reached my groin. Flowing down through my legs and into my toes, only to circle back again to fill my belly, my lungs, my throat, my head.

Faster now, as if the energy moving through me was feeding on the energy of the others. A stream surging through us and between us, racing around our circle, gaining power with every breath, every heartbeat, pulsing through every body, every mind, leaping from cell to cell, too strong to contain a moment longer.

"Let it go!"

The energy burst free on a wave of sighs and groans. I opened my eyes to find Rowan watching us, his lips parted, his eyes heavy lidded. Almost as if he had just climaxed. Which, I suddenly realized, was exactly how I felt. Drained and exhilarated, relaxed and keyed up all at the same time.

For a long moment, we savored the release and the silence. Then Rowan straightened.

"I want you to step onto that stage with confidence. To trust yourself. To trust each other. And believe that you're ready. Because you are. Tonight, we will create magic in this theatre."

His smile embraced us. Then he slipped out the door.

It opened again a moment later to admit Reinhard, wearing black pants and a black shirt like everyone on the crew. Reinhard had dressed for the occasion, though, adding a black tie to his ensemble.

He examined us critically and nodded. "You will be wonderful." It sounded more like a command than a prediction, but it made us smile, dispelling the lingering effects of the dream-state Rowan had conjured.

"Places, please, for the top of Act One."

Richard kissed Ashley on the cheek. Lou kissed Bobbie on the mouth. Will hugged Nancy. Brittany hugged me. Kevin glowered, already in character.

We silently filed to our positions accompanied by Reinhard's taped announcement forbidding the taking of photographs and reminding the audience to turn off all cell phones. Not that anyone would get reception inside the theatre.

I joined the members of the chorus onstage. Listened to the faint sounds from the unseen audience: the rustling of programs, the creak of the old seats, the murmur of conversation. As the house lights dimmed, the sounds faded, replaced by a hushed anticipation.

The drone of horns issued from the pit. Then woodwinds and violins broke into a wild skirling that made my heart pound.

The work light that had guided us onstage went dark. The overture segued into the slower, softer music of the "Prologue." The fog machine hummed. The red velvet curtain slid open. The lights slowly came up.

A murmured "Ahh" rose from the house as the audience got its first glimpse of the stage. Because of Lee's lighting design, we remained invisible behind the painted scrim. The audience saw only Hal's shadowy maze of tree branches and the deep, swirling blues of the nighttime sky.

Richard and Will clumped onstage, and the music ended. The audience chuckled at Will's zingers and warmed to Richard as he tried to puzzle out what was missing in his current relationship. Their delivery was so natural you could almost believe their conversation was spontaneous rather than scripted.

As our cue approached, an electric current rippled through me, similar to the energy Rowan had conjured backstage, but far stronger. Like we were being charged by some giant battery. Each time the charge passed through us, the current grew stronger, not only feeding us, but feeding on us, gaining power from our collective energy.

A shiver slid down my spine. My fingertips tingled. My nipples grew hard.

Hector's fingers dug into my shoulder. Brittany squeezed my hand so hard it hurt. I wanted to laugh or scream or fling out my arms, but I couldn't. We had to contain the energy, just as we had during Rowan's meditation.

Was he doing this? Were we? I only knew I'd never experienced this on any opening night. It was as if I was truly alive, truly aware for the first time in my life. As if we were all awakening like the villagers of Brigadoon, realizing that something impossible and wonderful was happening.

The furor raging through me slowly began to fade until it was just a comfortable glow. Allowing me to breathe again, to remember where I was, to hear our cue.

Kalma hummed the opening notes of "Brigadoon." Three of us joined in, then four more. Then Kalma began to sing. The first time we heard her clear soprano, we'd all marveled that such a sound could come out of the throat of a girl whose name meant Corpse Stench. But tonight, it was so sweetly ethereal that it seemed to come from another world.

The rest of the chorus added their voices to hers. For once, we didn't have to fight to keep the sound soft so that the men's dialogue could be heard. We simply allowed the hushed expectancy of Brigadoon's dawn to fill our minds and our spirits before emerging from our lips.

At the height of the song, the chorus dropped out, leaving the orchestra to finish the number. For a moment, we stood there, still ensnared by the strange connection between us. Then it just . . . snapped off.

Kalma nudged me toward the stage door. We raced around the side of the barn and bolted through the front door of the theatre, panting. Helen handed us our market baskets. Janet flicked off the lobby lights. Then she and Helen cracked open the doors so we could slip inside.

Seeing the packed house gave me a jolt. Either Janet had papered it with complimentary tickets or everyone in Dale had shown up. After that first glimpse, I was too caught by the spectacle onstage to think about it.

The lights changed and the thatched roofs of Brigadoon became visible through the gauzy scrim. As it rose, ghostly figures emerged from the dissipating mist, shaking off the effects of their hundred-year sleep as they wandered into the square for market day.

I came out of my daze in time to echo Kalma's line, drawing a startled "Oh!" from an elderly woman sitting in one of the aisle seats. Still singing, I sauntered down the aisle.

As the tempo quickened, I walked faster, heart and feet keeping rhythm with the growing urgency of the music. I skipped across the shaky footbridge over the pit, sure-footed as a mule, nimble as a gazelle, and stepped onto the stage just as early morning sunlight flooded Brigadoon, and chorus and orchestra burst into the bustle and excitement of "Down on MacConnachy Square."

❧❧

Most of that night was a dizzying blur, but some moments were etched clearly in my memory. Ashley's shining face as she allowed Richard to coax her into walking through "The Heather on the Hill." The audience laughter punctuating Nancy's comic lament "The Love of My Life"; Lou and Bobbie, touchingly solemn at the wedding. Kevin's terrifying explosion of motion and emotion in the sword dance. And Bernie's triumphant grin as he slowly walked through the town square to welcome Richard back to Brigadoon.

And it wasn't just the performers who rose to the occasion. The mist curdled obediently around our ankles. Lee's lighting captured every shift in emotion. Catherine's promontory was as solid as if it were actually made of rock. The decades-old kilts swung as jauntily as if they had come off the weaver's loom that morning, while the costumes Hal had constructed looked like perfectly preserved clothing from the eighteenth century.

Sure, there were mistakes—harmonies that were off, lines that were flubbed, dance steps that were clumsy—but we recovered and we went on. And by the time our voices blended in the final, majestic chorus and Richard swept Ashley up in his arms, the mistakes had faded to insignificance.

Rowan was right. We did create magic.

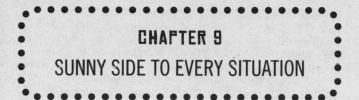

M OST OF THE MEN OPTED TO SHOWER at the theatre. The women piled into cars and raced back to the
hotel to change for the cast party.

When you're twenty and gorgeous like Brittany, you can
blow dry your hair, throw on a tank top and jeans, and look
spectacular. When you're thirty-two and not gorgeous, you
have to blow dry your hair, coax the tangles into submission, apply mousse for a casually tousled look, artfully create cheekbones with two shades of blusher, go for a
sensuous, smoky-eyed look and abandon it after realizing
you look like an exhausted raccoon, try on three outfits,
discard them all, and finally settle on a kicky sundress that
shows off your best features (cleavage) and hides your
worst (hips).

My car was the last to arrive.

"Oh, look!" Nancy exclaimed as we pulled into the theatre parking lot. "Isn't it pretty?"

In addition to the pale amber of solar lights, two rows of
luminarias snaked up the hill. There were dozens of them,
candles glowing softly in their brown paper bags. Lights
blazed from the house, dimming now and then as shadowy
groups of people passed by the windows on the ground
floor. As we approached, the faint strains of recorded music
grew louder, as did the hum of conversation and occasional
bursts of laughter.

All resemblance to the Bates mansion vanished as I

stepped inside. From the crystal chandelier to the decorative moldings to the marble floor, the foyer radiated the same wealth and elegance as its owner. Absently greeting staff and cast, I drifted through the house, gawking.

The parlor, a symphony of soothing golds and browns and greens with silk upholstery on the settees and Persian rugs on the floors. The dining room, where people crowded around a table large enough to conduct surgery on Paul Bunyan to sample the array of hot and cold dishes. The living room, lit by a crackling fire and filled with people sprawled in leather armchairs and sofas.

The sunroom was empty; clearly, everyone who'd come this far had moved right out onto the patio. Through the windows, I could see groups of people chatting, their faces aglow in the illumination of the paper lanterns strung through the trees.

"Are you finished sightseeing?"

I turned at the sound of Hal's voice. "Oh. My. God."

"Yes, it's pretty fabulous. And speaking of . . ." He seized my hands and held me at arms' length. "Hello, gorgeous. I always knew you'd clean up nice. Great tits, by the way. The men will be far too busy staring at them to notice your withered leg. Oh, thank God," he added as Lee approached carrying a small china plate. "I'm starving."

He opened his mouth like a baby bird demanding to be fed, and Lee obediently popped a caviar-topped crostino into his mouth.

"Ain't it great to have rich friends?" Lee observed.

"I wouldn't exactly call Janet a friend, but . . . yeah."

"She pulls out all the stops for these affairs. You noticed the buckets of champagne in the dining room, I hope?"

"I was too blinded by the silver serving trays."

Hal hooked his arm through mine and led me toward the feast. "If you're very good, I'll stand guard while you sneak upstairs and peek in all the bedrooms."

"Doesn't she get lonely? Rattling around this enormous house?"

"Janet's pretty self-sufficient," Lee said dryly.

"And Helen's here most of the year," Hal added.

"Helen? Helen lives with Janet?"

Hal glanced uncertainly at Lee. "Well . . . yeah. She only stays at the Bough during the season."

"They *are* mother and daughter, aren't they?"

Again, Hal glanced at Lee, who said, "You didn't know that?"

"I guessed. God. Poor Helen. I mean, it's not *Mommie Dearest*, but still . . ."

"There you are!" Gary exclaimed, elbowing through the crowd. "I was wondering when you were going to show."

"You think all this beauty just happens? It takes hours of hard work."

"Well, it was worth it. You look terrific."

I am a liberated woman. I believe in inner beauty and have never thought you need a runway model's body to be attractive. That said, being the object of masculine admiration—straight and gay—is a major ego booster.

"No one's said a word about how I look," Hal complained.

"You look fabulous," Lee said. "Now stop fishing for compliments." When Hal began to protest, he popped a scallop into his mouth.

"This is why I'm fat," Hal moaned.

"Tell him he's not fat," Lee said. "I'm getting more champagne."

"That's right! Run away!" As Lee made his way toward the sideboard, Hal dropped his mock outrage and smiled. "He adores me."

"You're a lucky man," Gary said.

"Luck had nothing to do with it. I worked on him a whole season before he finally succumbed." Hal sighed. "We had one glorious night together before I went back to California. We e-mailed all winter, but I despaired of ever seeing him again. Then Helen called and told me that the man who'd been doing costume and set design—this dreadful queen with absolutely no taste—well, anyway, he resigned. And guess who got the job? Everyone kept mum about it until I appeared at the first staff meeting. You should have seen Lee's face!"

"What about my face?" Lee asked, miraculously balancing four brimming champagne flutes in his upraised hands and hugging a bottle under his arm.

"The day I returned to the theatre," Hal said, plucking two flutes from Lee and handing one to me. "When you devoured me with your eyes."

Lee handed the third flute to Gary and raised his own in a toast. "Here's to finding the true loves of our lives."

I laughed at the reference to Nancy's song. Then I noticed Gary's expression. So did Lee, apparently, for he asked, "What? Don't believe in true love?"

"Not so much since my wife dumped me."

After a brief moment of shocked silence, Lee said, "Shit. I'm sorry, man."

"Oh, God, I feel like an idiot!" Hal exclaimed. "Babbling on and on about us when all the time, you were dying inside."

"Look, guys. It's okay. Really. I'm the one who should apologize for spoiling the party."

"Don't be silly," I said. "Friends are supposed to help each other." Before I could do more than squeeze Gary's arm, I heard Lou's familiar bellow.

"Brooklyn! When did you get here?"

"Just a few minutes ago."

"Some spread, huh? But where the hell's Rowan?"

"Got me." I turned to Lee and Hal. "Have you guys seen him?"

Hal glanced at Lee, who just shrugged. "Rowan's not much for parties."

"Yeah, but it's the cast party," Lou said. "He's gotta come for that, right?"

Their silence spoke volumes.

"You're kidding me," I said. "He can't even show up for five minutes? Just to say 'Great job, everybody?'"

"He said that when he stopped into the green room after the show," Lee reminded us.

"But—"

"Let it go, Maggie."

I subsided before the quiet warning in Lee's voice.

Lou shook his head. "That sucks. I mean, that totally sucks."

"What totally sucks?" Bobbie inquired, squeezing between Gary and Lou.

"Rowan. He's not coming."

"At all?" She bit her lip and glanced from Lee to Hal. "He's disappointed, isn't he?"

"Of course not!" Lee exclaimed.

Bobbie looked so forlorn that I wanted to put my arm around her. Lou beat me to it. "See?" he demanded, voice and color rising. "See what you've done? She's upset!"

"Lower your voice," Lee said. "Before the whole room hears you."

Instead, Lou lowered his head, looking like a bull about to charge. "I don't care who hears me! He's got no right to go and upset Bobbie. She worked her ass off tonight. We all did!"

All conversation in the immediate vicinity had stopped. Now, it started up again, a dozen voices clamoring to know what Lou was shouting about, who had upset Bobbie, what was that about Rowan, and on and on until Lee shouted, "Will everybody please shut up?"

Everybody shut up.

"Here's the deal. Rowan doesn't like parties. Not even cast parties. He's never attended one. It's one of his little quirks."

"Phobias," Hal interjected. "A phobia. About crowds."

"He came to the green room," Lou pointed out. "Before and after the show."

"Look, he's just weird," Lee said, wisely avoiding the issue of the on-again, off-again phobia. "But it's got nothing to do with you guys."

Alex chimed in to reaffirm Rowan's pride in us. Reinhard ordered us to enjoy ourselves. Helen added her calming voice, Mei-Yin her hectoring one. Heads nodded in agreement, but I could feel the energy drain out of the party and see disappointment on every face.

As I edged out of the dining room, I bumped into Janet.

"What's the problem?" she asked in her usual cut-to-the-chase manner.

"We just found out Rowan isn't coming."

"Did you expect him to?"

"Well . . . yes."

She gave a snort. "Pigs will fly before Rowan Mackenzie darkens this doorstep."

"You mean you didn't invite him?"

"Of course I invited him. It's a game we play. I politely invite him. He politely declines."

"Maybe if he really felt welcome—"

"It's very rude to lecture the hostess, dear. Trust me. Nothing will convince Rowan Mackenzie to attend this party."

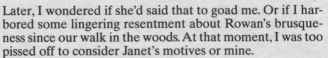

Later, I wondered if she'd said that to goad me. Or if I harbored some lingering resentment about Rowan's brusqueness since our walk in the woods. At that moment, I was too pissed off to consider Janet's motives or mine.

I charged down the hill, brimming with righteous indignation. The front doors of the theatre were locked, but the stage door opened easily.

I was momentarily blinded by the ghost light. Ours had been cobbled together by clamping the light bulb's metal cage to a battered mic stand. Superstition claimed it would ward off specters. Its more practical purpose was to prevent accidents when non-spectral personnel entered a darkened theatre. While I appreciated the tradition, it took nearly a minute before the afterimage of the megawatt bulb faded enough for me to mount the stairs to Rowan's apartment.

The muffled sound of music grew louder as I approached. Fiddle, flute, and squeezebox combined in a spirited reel, accompanied by the softer patter of a bodhran. Rowan was either following his Celtic muse or preserving the spirit of *Brigadoon* offstage.

I knocked softly and received no answer. Knocked again. Still nothing. Finally, I reached for the wooden latch. The door cracked open and I cautiously poked my head inside.

There was just enough light to make out a tall wooden file cabinet, an old-fashioned rolltop desk, and the bookcases lining the walls. Clearly, Rowan's office. The lack of windows struck me as odd until I looked up. Beyond the heavy exposed beams, four skylights had been set into the sloping roof. A cool breeze wafted through the apartment, so they must admit air as well as light. Unless the sliding doors to the balcony were open. It was hard to tell; the lamplight in the bedroom to the left illuminated little more than an armoire and the slatted wooden blinds screening the balcony.

As I opened my mouth to announce my presence, Rowan strode into the bedroom doorway.

He was barefoot and wore a long silk dressing gown that looked like something out of a Victorian melodrama. His hair hung in loose, damp waves around his shoulders. It didn't take a rocket scientist to figure out he'd just emerged from the shower. Or that he'd known someone had invaded his privacy before he saw me. Or that he was furious.

"I knocked. Twice. And when I didn't get an answer—"

"Get out."

I swallowed hard. "I wanted to—"

"I don't care what you wanted. This is my home!"

"I know. And I'm—"

"No one walks into someone's home unannounced. And no one walks into mine uninvited. Do you understand?"

"I just—"

"Do you understand?"

He was absolutely right. If he'd sauntered into my apartment in Brooklyn, I would have raised holy hell. But I never responded well to bullying, however justified.

I gave him glare for glare and calmly said, "Fuck you." And had the enormous satisfaction of seeing those green eyes widen with shock.

"I'm sorry I walked in on you. It was completely inappropriate and it'll never happen again. But before I go, you should know that you've let down the entire cast."

I waited a moment, hoping for a response. When none was forthcoming, I took a step back and reached for the door.

"What do you mean?"

"I mean they expected you to come to the cast party."

"I never—"

"I know. We all know. The staff spent ten minutes explaining how you never attend parties. Look, nobody expects you to come to movie night or hang out after rehearsal. But we did expect you'd show up for a few minutes tonight. To celebrate with us."

"I came backstage—"

"It's not enough," I said flatly. "And you should know that."

"I'm sure they will enjoy themselves without my presence," he said stiffly.

"But they won't! They're not! That's what I'm trying to tell you. If you could have seen their faces ... I thought Bobbie was going to cry."

His mouth tightened. Even from across the room, I could see the muscle twitching in his jaw. A blast of cold air gusted through the apartment. Then he slammed his fist against the doorframe so hard I could feel the reverberation through the floor.

"Am I always to be held hostage to this place?"

The raw anguish in his voice shocked me even more than his words. As I tried to summon a response, his hand rose to grope at his neck. That's when I noticed the thick red weal. The same sort of burn mark I'd seen on his hands. Circling his throat like the silver chain he wore every day to hide it.

The frenetic music had segued into something quiet. I sought the same level of calm for my voice.

"The morning after auditions, you told me you were here to serve the players."

The hand at his throat knotted into a fist.

"You said that everyone who came here was searching for something they needed. Well right now, everyone at that cast party needs you. Maybe it's silly. And childish. Or just the typical insecurity of actors who never tire of hearing how wonderful they are. But they need to hear that. And they need to hear it from you."

He'd turned while I was speaking, bracing himself against the doorframe. As he bowed his head, the long hair drifted across his face, shielding it from my view. Instead of feeling pleased at my victory, I felt miserable. And ashamed.

"Look. I'll tell them I spoke to you. That you told me how proud you were. And how much you wished you could make an exception and come to the party. But you couldn't. Because of your phobia about crowds. Or something. I'll think of something. A feud with Janet, maybe. They'd believe that. I'll make them believe it. It'll be okay."

When he failed to move or acknowledge my words, I whispered, "Forgive me."

The last thing I saw before I pulled the door closed was Rowan lowering his head onto his forearm.

The Janet thing worked like a charm. People were still disappointed, but everyone believed that a long-standing feud prevented Rowan from entering her house.

It took Hal all of three minutes to corner me in the foyer. Instead of demanding the juicy details, he observed me carefully, led me into a sumptuous powder room, and closed the door behind us.

"You really did talk with him."

I nodded.

"Was it awful?"

I nodded again.

"Oh, sweetie." He hugged me hard. "Don't worry. It'll be okay."

"No. It won't."

"Maybe Helen should talk with him. She can always—"

"No! Just let it go, Hal."

I tried to enjoy the party, but I kept hearing Rowan's anguished cry. Finally, I gave up the pretense and headed for the front door.

A buzz of excited conversation made me hesitate. Curious, I followed the crowd hurrying toward the back of the house. I heard startled exclamations, soft cries of pleasure. The words rippled back to me:

"He's here."

"He's outside."

"On the patio."

I couldn't get any closer than the sunroom. Peering through a window, I saw the entire cast huddled close to the house. A good ten feet separated those in front from the shadowy figure standing under the big maple. Obviously, they were still unsure whether there was any truth to the phobia explanation. I almost smiled, but I was having too much trouble breathing.

The staff clustered together at the far end of the patio. Hal's mouth hung open, but the rest did a better job of concealing their shock.

Rowan wore his usual linen shirt and black jeans. The silver necklace was around his throat. He'd tied his damp hair back. A paper lantern hanging from the lower branches of the maple lent a rosy glow to his pallid features. He looked tired, but very calm and completely in control of his emotions.

It was so quiet you could hear the dull chirp of crickets and the faint tinkle of wind chimes as a breeze touched them. Rowan stepped out from under the tree, but stopped just beyond the slates of the patio. Given Janet's comment about Rowan never darkening her doorstep, the feud had seemed a plausible invention, but now I wondered if her words were true. If so, he would find my behavior even more unforgivable.

"I was reminded recently that a director's responsibility to his cast does not end when the curtain comes down."

Janet's head snapped toward my window, and I resisted the urge to shrink back.

"As you know, I am not someone who normally attends parties. But I wanted to come here to thank you again for your hard work. I asked more of you than you probably thought you could give, but sitting in that theatre tonight, I watched each of you dig deep and bring something fresh and wonderful and ... magical ... to that stage. And it seemed only right to celebrate that accomplishment together."

His smile was slow to form, but as sweet as I had seen it that day in the woods.

"I'm proud of you," he said quietly. "So very proud."

I heard a muffled sob. A few sniffles.

"This does not mean I shall begin attending movie night," he added with mock severity. "Even for the Barbra Streisand double feature."

After the laughter subsided, Rowan spread his hands. "That is quite enough speechmaking. Please. Return to the party and enjoy yourselves."

For an awkward moment, everyone just stood there. Then Lou strode forward and engulfed poor Rowan in a bearlike embrace.

I expected that to be the signal for the entire cast to converge on him. Instead, they exercised admirable restraint, approaching singly and in pairs like courtiers paying homage to their king. A possibly phobic but nevertheless gracious king who put the welfare of his subjects before his personal desires. And seeing the warmth with which he greeted each person, I felt renewed shame at the way I'd behaved.

I considered slinking away, but disdained that as cowardly—and unfair to Rowan, who deserved at least a word of thanks for breaking his policy.

The staff was staring toward the sunroom in the familiar bird-dog-on-point attitude. If they'd made a fuss after our walk in the woods, I could only imagine what I was in for now.

I was reconsidering my decision to remain when Reinhard detached himself from the group and started toward the house. Obviously, the others had elected him as their delegate. I'd have chosen Helen or Hal or Alex, but given my tendency toward meltdowns with both Alex and Helen, and Hal's tendency toward drama, perhaps Reinhard was a better choice.

He closed the sunroom door behind him and glanced around to ensure that we were alone.

"I see you lost the coin toss," I said.

He heaved an impatient sigh. "I said to leave you alone. But do they listen? No! Just talk to her, they say. Make sure she is all right. And don't make her cry."

"Poor Alex."

"Poor Alex is outside drinking champagne. Poor Reinhard is here. So. You are all right?"

I hesitated, wondering if I should tell him what had happened or if that would be a further violation of Rowan's privacy. But someone on staff had to know what he was feeling.

"I'm okay," I finally said. "But he's not."

In a few terse sentences, I described our confrontation. Reinhard scrubbed the top of his head, sending his hair into porcupine mode. Then he sank onto the love seat near the windows.

"He actually said that? About being held hostage?"

"Yes."

"That is not good."

"That is not good," I agreed.

"He has not spoken that way in many years."

"That doesn't mean he wasn't feeling that way."

"I am aware of that!" His scowl faded, and he sighed. "Forgive me. I bark. Mei-Yin always tells me this."

Mei-Yin was a more than adequate barker herself, but I decided this was not the time to mention that. Instead, I sat down beside him and said, "I deserved it for stating the obvious."

Reinhard patted my hand. "Poor Maggie. Always, you are the one in the middle. Why is that?"

"Because I'm nosy and pushy and can't let well enough alone."

"Yes. That is true."

I smiled at that, but he had swiveled around on the loveseat to gaze out the window.

"Such a strange man," he mused. "I have known him a long time and sometimes, I think I do not know him at all. Helen, she knows him best. And Alex. Because they write the shows together. And now you come here. Shaking things up."

Reinhard fixed me with an unnerving stare. I hoped to God he wasn't going to suggest I go to bed with Rowan, too.

"Maybe a little shaking up is good. For Rowan. For the theatre. For everyone. No one on staff talks back. Well, Janet. The rest of us wheedle and suggest and encourage. But you! You confront him. You make him talk about things he does not wish to talk about."

"That's definitely not good."

"But . . ." Reinhard held up his forefinger. "You also make him laugh. You make him think. You make him . . . change."

"That's good. Right?"

"That, Dorothy Gale, is astonishing."

So much for Janet's assessment of Rowan. I preferred to think Reinhard's was more accurate.

"So what do we do now?" I asked.

"You want my advice? Say no and I am not offended."

"Yes," I replied, surprising myself.

"Have you ever fished? Not worms on a hook, but real fishing with a fly rod."

I saw my six-year-old self standing on the banks of the Brandywine, holding up a long stick so my father could tie an imaginary lure on the imaginary string. Felt my father's hands guiding my arm as I cast. Heard his patient voice telling me not to hurl the line like a Wiffle ball, but to flick it like you were swatting a fly.

His excited whisper as he predicted that the Giant Brandywine Fish could never resist the lure of the twenty-winged blue dragonfly. His delighted laugh as he described the string snaking through the air and landing in a perfect line atop the tumbling waters. His shout of triumph as he pulled me back into his arms, both of us straining to reel in the mighty fish. And his bellow of disappointment as it sprouted twenty giant dragonfly wings and sailed skyward, cleverly eluding the mere mortals who sought to capture it.

"No, I've never done much fishing."

"Well, maybe it will make sense anyway. Rowan is like a trout. He cannot be hauled into a boat like a crab in a pot. He has to be played. For that you need patience and skill. Give him too much line, he will slip away. Pull too hard, you will hurt him. And yourself."

"I am *not* trying to land Rowan."

"God forbid! That kind of heartache you don't want. But friendship, maybe, is not such a bad thing."

"If he'd allow it."

"Pooh! He is not God Almighty. Although he acts like it most of the time."

"But he's no ordinary man, either."

Reinhard studied me silently. "No. He is not. And that is all I will say about that. Rowan is entitled to his privacy. Just as you are."

"Me?"

"I ask about fishing and the expressions fly across your face. Happy, bitter, angry, determined. All in ten seconds. And I know there is a story there. But do I ask you to share it? No! It is your story. Your past. To share or not."

I stared at the intertwined flowers on the rug at my feet. "You're very observant."

"Yes. But you are also very bad at hiding your feelings." I sighed. "That is not good."

"Maybe not for you. But it is refreshing to find someone so . . ."

"Transparent?"

"Honest."

I looked up at him. "Ditto."

Reinhard nodded briskly and rose. "So. We are done talking. You are all right. I will tell the others. They will not pester you." He paused at the door and jerked his head toward Rowan, who was chatting with Ashley and Richard. "Talk with him. Tonight."

"I was going to! Jeez. Talk about pushy."

"Little girl, you know nothing of pushy until you have lived with Mei-Yin for twenty years." He glanced at the patio, where Mei-Yin was shaking a meaty forefinger in Hal's face. Then he sighed happily. "Such a woman."

As he marched across the patio to give his report, the cast began drifting back into the house. Caren grabbed my arm, babbling excitedly about Rowan's unexpected arrival. I nodded politely and excused myself as soon as she paused for breath.

He was alone now and watching me. My heart went into rabbit beat as I approached. Before I could speak, he said, "I'd like to apologize for my rudeness."

"Please. Don't. When it comes to rudeness, I've got you beat by a mile." His brief smile encouraged me to add, "I just wanted to thank you. For coming tonight. You don't know how much it meant to everybody."

"Of course I do." His smile was just as brief and just as cool. "I've always known that my cast—all my casts— wanted me to share this night with them. I chose not to. I simply . . . drew a line and refused to cross it."

Without thinking, I looked at his feet, still firmly planted in the grass just inches from the edge of the patio.

"Yes," he remarked. "I suppose I'm still drawing a line."

"But you came. That's the important thing. I know how hard that must have been."

"No, Maggie. You don't."

Although his voice was quiet and free of accusation, I winced.

"It's not your fault. You couldn't possibly understand . . . the history."

"Between you and Janet?"

"It goes back far longer than that. To the people who originally owned this land. And my folk."

He made it sound like the Hatfields and the McCoys, the sort of blood feud that went on for generations. Of course, some of the Scottish clans were notorious for their long-standing enmity, but that was centuries ago.

I recalled the audience cheers during the "Entrance of the Clans," each group trying to outshout the others to support its . . . folk. But it was one thing to indulge in some friendly rivalry during a performance of *Brigadoon*. Quite another to refuse to cross the threshold of a long-dead enemy who had committed some crime against your equally moldering ancestor.

"You won't come inside, will you?"

"Never."

His quiet finality was more disturbing than if he had shouted.

"Why don't you leave?" I asked. "If you're so unhappy. Get out of here and start over someplace new."

The silence stretched for so long that I assumed he would refuse to answer. But finally he said, "My home is here. My work. And in spite of that display of self-pity you witnessed tonight, I am not unhappy."

I didn't believe him. And since he was skilled at reading faces, he probably knew that. But instead of disputing his statement or pressing him further, I asked, "So we're okay?"

"Of course."

Again, I didn't believe him. He'd been avoiding me all week and what I'd witnessed tonight had only made him more uncomfortable.

"I am . . . it's hard for me. To break old habits. Including my habit of retreating from people." He cocked his head, observing me as if I were some interesting new strain of bacteria that he'd discovered under his microscope. "What do you want from me, Maggie?"

I wanted to know how he had transformed a bunch of non-actors into the troupe that had just brought off an incredible opening night. I wanted to know how his singing had created such longing inside me. I wanted to know how any man could soothe doubts and ease fears and create that mesmerizing current of power I'd felt backstage.

But he was not about to reveal those secrets to me. So I simply said, "I want us to be able to work together. And be comfortable around each other. I don't expect us to become best friends. Or sip champagne by candlelight and share our deepest, darkest secrets."

"That's good," he said with a thoughtful nod. "I don't really like champagne."

A slow smile blossomed on his face. Mischievous as a little boy who had scored a point. And like a temperamental little girl who knew she'd gotten zinged, I stuck out my tongue. That made him laugh, which sealed the victory for me. Making Rowan laugh seemed the greatest contribution I could make to this weird company.

"It's a deal, then," he said. "No champagne. No candlelit confessions."

He stuck out his hand. I shook it firmly, the ridge of his scar bumpy under my fingertips.

As he walked away, I reflected that the pact was about as ironclad as my contract. Its two prohibitions left the door wide open for me to pursue all those questions I had refrained from asking. Which raised yet another question about this strange theatre and the man who ran it: what did Rowan Mackenzie want from me?

ENTR'ACTE
THE JOURNAL OF ROWAN MACKENZIE

Sleepless. Again.

Reread Act One of *By Iron, Bound*. And finally realize what has been nagging at me.

She reminds me of Jamie.

Her stubbornness. Her sense of humor. Her kindness, too, though she tries hard to keep that hidden. Like Jamie, she heard me singing "The Mist-Covered Mountains." Like Jamie, she was shaken to the core. She even fell outside the cottage he helped me build. The hut, as she called it.

I do not believe in fate. Or ghosts. But when she appeared in my apartment tonight, I could almost hear their voices: the old Mackenzie witch and Jamie.

I taunted the witch and was punished by the iron collar and her curse. I rejected Jamie's offer of friendship with a blatant display of power that shamed and humiliated him. Yet later, he was able to joke about it. Another trait they share. As well as a boundless capacity to beat against the barriers I take such care to erect.

She's pushed for a few weeks. Jamie pushed for nearly sixty years. Dragging me to that first ceilidh in the barn. Encouraging me to use my powers to help those who had lost loved ones in the war. Refusing to let me do it from the shadows, but insisting that I mingle with them. Become part of their community.

Even the theatre was his idea. I merely brought the vision to life by calling to the Mackenzie descendants each spring.

And it all began with his simple gift of milk and strawberries, offered with the innocence and courage and curiosity only a child possesses. A gift for me. The nameless specter in the forest. The accursed one. Little more than an animal after so many years of isolation.

I ate the food he brought. Drank the whisky. Wore the clothes. All gone now. But the cottage still stands. And in it, the furniture we built and the earthenware jug that held the whisky. I am surrounded by Jamie there.

And here. I've only to walk into the next room to see the melodeon he taught me to play, the books he brought me, the battered copy of his schoolboy primer from which I learned to read and write.

So many gifts, the greatest of which I can only preserve in memory: his trust, his friendship, his love. In return, I gave him the necklace. It was just a bitter reminder of the mistakes I had made, the home I had lost. An easy gift to bestow and a selfish one; I was saving my home as well as his. But the greater gift of a true and loving friendship? That, I withheld. I allowed him close, but not too close. I never even told him what his friendship meant to me.

On nights like this, I wonder what would have happened if I had risked more. Would I have broken the curse? Or destroyed him? Both, I think. Too easy to let friendship slip into another sort of closeness. With the others, sex was merely a pleasurable release. Except Helen, of course. And look how that turned out. If I had exercised the same caution with her that I did with Jamie, she, too, might have found a loving partner, raised a family, known real happiness.

Useless to speculate. And foolish to conjure memories that can only fuel my emotions. When will I learn? But if I still struggle to control my power after more than two centuries, why should I be surprised that I cannot master my emotions, either?

In spite of all she has seen, she seems intrigued rather than enthralled. Unwilling to venture too close, to risk too much. In that, she is like me rather than Jamie. But while that wariness will protect her now, it will make it harder for her as the season progresses.

If she is to discover what I hoped for when I cast her, she'll have to let down her guard and look into the dark places of her spirit. And then she will be vulnerable. Which makes it even more imperative that I avoid another misstep, another reckless loss of control. This next week will be difficult, but once Midsummer has passed, I will be calmer. I must be calmer.

Only she can decide how much to risk, how far to travel. My job is to keep her safe on the journey. To let her choose her own path, but remain close enough to support her. Just as I did on that long walk back to the theatre.

It is my responsibility to establish the boundaries and adhere to them. However unsettling the parallels between her and the man who was my best, my truest friend in this world, she is not Jamie. I must remember that.

And accept that even Maggie Graham, Helping Professional, cannot help me.

ACT TWO

THINGS ARE SELDOM
WHAT THEY SEEM

CHAPTER 10
MUSIC OF THE NIGHT

IN THE WAKE OF *BRIGADOON*'S OPENING, the Bough was bursting at the seams with visitors and the company members joining us for *The Sea-Wife*. Bernie's granddaughter Sarah was back. And the Asian street gang, although I knew by now that they were really members of a church youth group.

Their arrival coincided with the first departures, including Nancy's. She had used up all her vacation time and would have to commute to the theater for weekday performances. A week ago, I'd complained to Rowan about the lack of privacy, but now I realized how much I would miss our late-night chats and our endless speculations about all the weirdness here. Having her stay over on the weekends just wasn't the same as sharing the day-to-day craziness.

And rehearsing one show during the day and turning in a dazzling performance on another at night was bound to push us to the brink of insanity. Thank God, *The Sea-Wife* had fewer musical numbers and a lot less choreography.

It took place in the Orkney Islands during the mid-nineteenth century and was based on the legend of the selkies, the mythical creatures who were seals in the sea, but could shed their skins on land to become human. In some ways, the story reminded me of *Brigadoon,* but there was no "true love makes miracles happen" ending. Selkie-woman loves schoolteacher, but longs for her true home. Schoolteacher loves selkie, but refuses to hold her prisoner.

She goes back to the sea. He mourns. Curtain. Okay, maybe the changes he undergoes will help him find love again, but by the end of the read-through, I'd concluded that Rowan's view of true love was even bleaker than mine.

One aspect of the story intrigued me, though: the selkie-woman who is trapped on land, unable to return to her home. For about five seconds, I congratulated myself on discovering Rowan's secret: the guy was a seal. Then logic kicked in and I knew he'd simply been drawn to the legend because it somehow paralleled his mysterious past.

Maya was the perfect choice to play the selkie; she always seemed to have one foot in another world. Sweet-natured Hector would have to go to the dark side to portray James, the fisherman who steals her skin. Caren was playing Hector's jealous wife. If she had exaggerated the challenges of playing a nameless villager in *Brigadoon*, I dreaded to think what she'd be like now that she had a leading role.

But I was far more worried about Gary. He'd shrugged off our concern at the cast party, but playing the school-teacher was bound to dredge up a lot of painful issues about his failed marriage. No matter how much support we offered, the next few weeks would be difficult for him.

And daunting for all of us. If we butchered *Brigadoon*, Lerner and Loewe were unlikely to rise from their graves to berate us. But Rowan and Alex had created this show, and we all felt the added pressure of bringing their vision to life.

Rowan was obviously nervous about our ability to do so. We'd gotten used to his preternatural calm, his "everything will be wonderful" vibe. Now, the Smokehouse crackled with his pent-up energy, leaving everyone unsettled.

His mania peaked the morning he broke us into family groups and asked us to come up with our personal storylines and relationships to the other island families. Then he had us share our stories and improvise scenes based on what was said.

I was playing Bernie's daughter. Kalma and Sarah were my younger sisters. All we knew about our family was our professions: Bernie was a pauper, his daughters were straw plaiters. Apparently, straw plaiting was big business in the Orkney Islands way back when. Another useful skill to add to my resume. Too bad I wasn't applying for a job in Colonial Williamsburg.

Still, we all got into the role-play—especially Rowan, who paced back and forth, unable to keep still as our families revealed long-standing grudges, secret romances, and personal tragedies. In spite of his mania—or maybe because of it—we ended the rehearsal totally stoked. No longer anonymous villagers, but living, breathing people.

As everyone raced off to grab lunch, I watched him stalking restlessly around the Smokehouse. As I hesitated, Reinhard's head came up. He shot me a warning look, then sighed and waved me forward.

After telling Rowan how much I'd enjoyed our improvs, I said, "You know, you and Alex might consider doing your next musical as a staged reading first. That way you could get feedback from the cast. And the audience. Then rewrite over the winter and present the full show the following summer."

Rowan galloped toward me. "That's exactly what we should do. I don't know why I didn't think of it."

For the last week, he'd barely spoken to me. Now, he hugged me so hard the breath whooshed out of me. Tremors coursed through his body, like the purring of a giant cat. The aroma of honeysuckle was so overpowering I had to turn my head away.

Caught by my movement, he pulled back to peer at me. Golden light flashed in his eyes. Sweat beaded his upper lip. His tongue flicked out to taste it. I clung to his arms, dizzy and breathless and a little bit terrified.

"Rowan."

Reinhard's voice, close to my ear. I hadn't even realized he'd left his chair.

Rowan dropped his hands and stepped back. "Heady stuff, the creative process," he said with a rueful smile. "Imagine what poor Alex had to put up with during our collaboration."

I nodded, still caught up in whatever had just happened.

"Lunch," Reinhard prompted.

When I just stood there, his hand descended on my shoulder.

"Right. Lunch."

At the doorway, I glanced back. Rowan was sitting at the table, studying the script. The pages shook in his hands.

❧❧

Although he seemed a little calmer in the afternoon, we were all glad that the theatre was dark that night; his mania was so infectious that *Brigadoon* would have been a train wreck. We were happier still that Mei-Yin had invited us all to the Chalet for a free dinner.

I was hurrying toward the parking lot when I spotted Helen at one of the picnic tables. She waved me over and smiled as I slid onto the bench opposite her.

"How was rehearsal?" she asked.

"Rowan's driving us crazy."

"He's always a little nervous when he begins rehearsals for his new show. He'll settle down in a day or two." She pushed a small pile of papers toward me. "Hal mentioned that you might like to help with the program."

Some were yellowed with age, the paper stiff between my fingers, but each program was a single sheet of paper folded in half.

Choosing my words carefully so I wouldn't offend her, I said, "I know Rowan's adapted plays in the past, but *The Sea-Wife* is his first original script. Let's make this opening really special. Expand the program. Send out press releases. Invite critics to review the show."

"Oh, my . . ."

"That's what theatres do, Helen. A world premiere will bring in lots of new business. That's got to be a good thing."

Or not, judging from Helen's expression.

"I'll mention your ideas at our staff meeting."

As she pushed herself up from the picnic bench, I noticed how tired she looked and cursed myself for shoving more work on her shoulders.

"I didn't mean you had to do it. Just give me a flash drive with the *Brigadoon* program and I'll draft something for *The Sea-Wife* that you can . . . Helen? Are you okay?"

She cocked her head, her expression faintly quizzical, as if she were listening to something I couldn't hear. Then her gaze focused and she smiled.

"Just a little tired."

"Let me drive you up to the house."

"Don't be silly. It's . . ." She glanced at the hill, and her smile faltered. "Well, if it's not too much trouble."

I dashed around the table and took her arm, but she gently freed herself and glanced around to see if anyone had noticed.

"Oh, dear," she murmured.

I followed the direction of her gaze and grimaced when I saw Caren hurrying toward us.

"Helen, you look dreadful!" she announced with a breathtaking lack of tact. "Should I get Reinhard?"

"No!" Helen and I exclaimed. Hoping to speed Caron on her way, I added, "I'm just going to drive Helen up to the house."

Caren latched onto Helen's arm. "I'll help! I'm dying to get another peek inside. Did Janet do the decorating or was that you? I redecorated my condo last year. I thought of hiring someone, but I just couldn't see spending the money. Especially since I knew exactly what I wanted and everyone says I have marvelous taste. Not to brag or anything. It's a sort of gift."

Short of ripping Helen's arm off at the shoulder, I saw no way of prying Caren loose. It took less than a minute to follow the gravel road around the back of the hill to the house, but Caren's running monologue about her fabulous new furnishings made it seem much longer. When I stopped the car under the portico, she scrambled out of the backseat to help Helen into the house, cooing soothing banalities like "There we are" and "Just one more step up" as if Helen suffered from dementia instead of weariness.

We walked through a little mudroom and into an enormous country kitchen that could have graced an interior design magazine: stainless steel appliances, miles of cabinets, marble countertops, terra-cotta floor. As we headed toward the foyer, Helen paused. "I would love a glass of lemonade. Caren, dear, would you mind? I think there's a pitcher in the fridge."

Caren cannonaded back down the hallway, and Helen and I let out simultaneous sighs.

"She's very nice," Helen whispered, "but just a bit . . . taxing."

I followed her up the stairs and into a bedroom that was ... well ... Helen. All soft blues and pinks. Ruffled pillows on the flowered bedspread. Ruffled canopy over the bed. Ruffled curtains at the windows. Even a ruffled skirt around the dressing table. It was the kind of bedroom a furniture catalog would describe as a young girl's dream. Well, some young girls. I went directly from my "all-things-unicorn" phase to plastering my walls with posters of R.E.M., Nirvana, and Broadway musicals.

Helen sank into the rocking chair and leaned her head back. "I do love this room. Such a wonderful view, don't you think?"

The open window next to the bed overlooked the patio. Patios. The one next to the house where we had greeted Rowan and a larger one at the bottom of a flight of stone steps. Beyond it, a series of walled terraces led to Helen's beloved garden. The boys must be pissing up a storm because it was filled with bright splashes of color. A cobblestone path wound through low green hedges to a small pond. The faint sound of splashing water vied with the tinkle of wind chimes and the more strident chorus of birds saluting the sunset.

Beyond the garden, an open field stretched toward the woods like Walt Whitman's sea of grass. The evening sky was a glory of pinks and purples and blues, as if special-ordered to complement Helen's garden.

"My mother would be so jealous."

"Is she a gardener, too?"

"Well, our backyard's about the size of your bedroom. But she grows roses. And has a little herb garden. When I was a kid, I used to cut lavender and make sachets out of old pantyhose."

"I still do that! You'll have to help me this year. It'll be such fun."

"What will be fun?"

Enter Caren with lemonade pitcher and glasses on a silver tray.

"Harvesting herbs. Thank you, dear. Just set that on the dressing table. And—oh, would it be dreadful of me to ask another favor?"

"Of course not!"

"I meant to cut some fresh flowers, but . . ."

"I'll do it! I love flowers. We have a beautiful garden at home . . ."

After she described it in excruciating detail, Helen directed her to the gardening shed. "You'll find everything you need there. The good vases are in the sideboard in the dining room. The everyday ones are in the hutch in the kitchen."

As Caren raced down the stairs, I poured two glasses of lemonade and sank into the easy chair near the window. "If I hear about her rich husband or her fabulous vacations or her marvelous condo one more time . . ."

"Poor thing. She's so insecure."

"*She's* insecure? I've got no job. No man. And an apartment the size of your kitchen."

"Yes, dear," Helen said, completely unfazed by my confession. "But what Caren sees is your sense of humor and your confidence and your strength. That's why she's drawn to you. Why she follows you around like a puppy."

Guilt warred with annoyance at Helen's assessment. Guilt won. I silently vowed to be a little nicer to Caren—or a lot more adept at avoiding her.

Helen turned the conversation to *The Sea-Wife*. Her admiration for Rowan's talent was obvious. But as she described his work, her voice grew soft, her expression tender. As if she were talking about a beloved son. Or simply, her beloved.

Helen and Rowan? She was at least twenty years his senior. It was just too kinky.

I breathed a little easier when she began talking about the other staff members.

"Reinhard got involved with the theatre after his first wife died. He played Captain von Trapp in *The Sound of Music*."

"Talk about perfect casting."

"And guess who his Maria was?"

"No."

Helen giggled. "Mei-Yin was a good forty pounds lighter in those days, but just as bossy. My, she looked stunning in that nun's habit. No wonder Reinhard fell in love with her. By the end of the summer, everyone knew they would spend the rest of their lives together."

"Sort of like Lee and Hal."

"You've heard all about them, I suppose? Yes, Hal loves to tell that story. He's such a romantic. Now, Javier's big role was Sky Masterson in *Guys and Dolls*."

"The Slick Charmer."

"Of course, he's not like that at all. Well, he *is* charming. But underneath, he's quite shy."

It seemed a stretch to call Javier shy. Maybe he was just good at putting up a front. Like me.

"I suppose Catherine played Sarah."

"No, Catherine built the set. She'd assisted on other shows, but that was her first as our construction chief. She and Javier started talking at one of the cast parties and discovered a mutual love of antique furniture . . ."

"And the rest is history." I shook my head, smiling. "You make this place sound like Match.com."

For a moment, Helen looked blank. Then she laughed. "Oh, yes. I've seen that advertised on TV. It sounds so . . . modern. Have you ever tried it?"

"No. But it's got to be better than chatting up some guy in a bar. Or hoping to meet Mr. Right during summer stock."

"Well, you never know. Look at Lou and Bobbie."

"I suppose you knew they'd be perfect together."

"Why, of course. Didn't you?"

"Actually . . . yes. They seemed like best buds from the moment they met."

"That's important, I think. Sexual attraction . . . well, it's all very exciting. But you need to be friends as well as lovers."

Ten years after college graduation, Michael and I were still friends, albeit long-distance ones. We'd never made it to lover status, of course. But there had been that instant spark when we met. For me, anyway. Same with Eric. But when the spark fizzled with him, there was nothing left to hold us together.

Helen idly smoothed her skirt. "Anyone on the horizon now?"

"Not unless it's a very distant horizon."

There were plenty of sparks with Rowan, but everyone felt those. Who could help it? The soft voice that seemed to speak to you alone. The penetrating gaze that made you feel like you were the most important person in the world.

And today, when he hugged me . . .

Sparks. Big-time. Along with the potential for big-time third-degree burns.

Eager to abandon the depressing topic of my nonexistent love life, I asked, "Did you ever tread the proverbial boards?"

Helen smiled. "Just once. I played Mabel in *The Pirates of Penzance*." She closed her eyes, humming softly to herself. *Pirates* was one of the few Gilbert and Sullivan shows I knew, so I recognized "Poor Wandering One."

"I was just sixteen that summer. And I had the most beautiful costume. A white lace gown with four layers of ruffles on the skirt and mother-of-pearl beads on the bodice. A pink satin sash. And sweet little white kid slippers. Rowan said I looked like a princess."

"I bet you . . . wait. I'm confused. If you were sixteen, how could Rowan have seen you?"

Helen's eyes flew open. "In a cast photo, of course. We *did* have photography back then. Daguerreotypes," she added, her mouth curving in a mischievous smile.

"Okay, okay." I hesitated a moment, then plunged in. "How about Rowan? Did he ever do any acting?"

"He prefers to work behind the scenes."

With that singing voice, he'd have to. Otherwise, he'd start a riot in the theatre.

"How long has he been directing here?"

"Oh, quite a while." Helen's nose crinkled in thought. "At least twenty years."

Which made him closer to fifty than the forty I'd suspected he was. Although a wunderkind like Rowan could have leaped right into the director's job after college.

"What was he like back then?"

"Much the same as he is now. A bit more aloof, perhaps."

"Is that possible?"

"He's made great strides," Helen said firmly. "Especially during these last few weeks."

None of the staff had said anything about my bullying him into attending the cast party, but I knew they had to be talking about it. My cheeks grew warm under Helen's penetrating gaze. For the millionth time, I wished I could control my stupid blushes. Maybe if I got out in the sun more, my freckles would multiply and provide some protective coloration.

In lieu of camouflage, I rose and gazed out the window again. The brilliant colors of the sky were fading, the chorus of birdsong reduced to a few halfhearted chirps. Post lanterns near the house and along the drive created creamy pools of light, but I could barely make out Caren's shadowy figure darting around the garden like a demented bumblebee.

The wispy clouds faded from rose to violet, the deep blue of the sky to the softer blue-gray of a Prospect Park pigeon. I tried to remember the last time I had watched a sunset. In the winter, it was always dark by the time I left the office. And the rest of the year, I just jumped on the subway, then hurried down the street with the other worker bees buzzing back to their hives.

I did a lot of racing around here, too. It was nice to slow down, to allow myself to surrender to the calming hush of twilight. Or to the spell of Midsummer.

My stomach growled, reminding me of our dinner. I turned back and discovered that Helen had fallen asleep. Her color looked better, but maybe that was just the light filtering through the pink lampshade. As I debated whether to wake her or simply tiptoe out, I heard Caren's footsteps on the stairs.

"Here we are!" she sang as she waltzed through the doorway.

Helen jolted awake. "Oh! I must have drifted off."

Her gaze slowly focused on the Delft vase Caren cradled. Okay, maybe she did have marvelous taste; the tall spikes of iris and foxgloves were perfect for Helen's room.

As Caren set the vase on a chest of drawers, Helen gasped. "It's nearly dusk!"

"I'm sorry it took me so long," Caren said. "But I don't suppose anyone will mind if we're a little late for dinner."

Helen clearly minded. She jumped to her feet and shooed us into the hall. As we reached the top of the stairs, the front door banged shut.

"Helen? Are you home?"

"Up here, Janet."

"Have you seen—? Good Lord. Why did you cut so many flowers? It looks like a goddamn funeral parlor in here."

Caren's soft exclamation fell somewhere between a squeak and a moan.

"Don't mind her," Helen whispered. "I'm sure they look lovely."

Janet stopped short when she saw us. "What are you doing here? You're supposed to be at the Chalet."

Before I could reply, Caren said, "Helen wasn't feeling well, so Maggie and I—"

"What do you mean? What's the matter?"

"Nothing's the matter," Helen said. "I was feeling a little tired and—"

"Did you call Dr. Hearn?"

"There's no need to call Dr. Hearn," Helen replied, her voice as sharp as Janet's. "I had a lovely visit with the girls. But they have to leave now. It's very late."

"Yes. You're right." Janet strode to the front door and flung it open.

"Umm . . . we drove," I mumbled.

"From the theatre?" Janet's gaze snapped back to Helen. She choked back whatever remark she wanted to make and marched toward the back of the house. I scampered after her, calling farewells to Helen and stealing a glance at my watch. We were going to be *really* late for dinner. It was so hard to judge time around Midsummer; the uncertain gray of twilight seemed to linger for hours.

As we pulled away, I looked in the rearview mirror and saw Janet slump against one of the pillars supporting the portico. For the first time, I wondered if Helen had a serious health problem. No one rushes to call a doctor simply because her mother feels tired.

The house had barely disappeared from view when Caren said, "Could you stop the car?"

I braked next to one of the post lanterns. Caren looked so queasy that I pressed the button on the armrest to lower her window.

"If I ask you something, will you be completely honest with me?"

Praying it was not going to be a "Why can't we be friends?" conversation, I said, "Sure."

"Did you think the house looked like a funeral parlor?"

I might have laughed, but Caren seemed to be on the verge of tears.

"The house looked beautiful."

Which was true. It looked like a beautiful funeral parlor. Or a thriving florist's shop. Where else would you find three giant vases of flowers in the foyer alone?

"I think I overdid it. Danny always says I overdo. That I try too hard. Do you think I try too hard?"

"Janet was just busting your chops. You know how she is."

"But do you think—?"

"I think you need to take a deep breath and let this go."

"I can feel it happening. When I overdo it, I mean."

"Deep breath."

"But I just can't seem to stop myself."

"You can if you take a deep breath!"

Caren took a deep, shuddering breath and let it out. So did I. The lovely calm that had descended upon me while I watched the sunset had vanished.

"Better?" I asked.

"No."

"Well . . . keep breathing."

In terms of interventions, this one was the equivalent of "Shut up and stop bothering me." Further proof that my HelpLink skills were eroding at an alarming rate. By the time I found a new job, I'd probably be advising callers to get a fucking life.

As we started downhill again, Caren shouted, "Stop!"

I slammed on the brakes. "Shit! Was it a deer?"

"No. Down there. In the meadow."

All I could see were the dark silhouettes of trees. And Caren with her head stuck out the window like a dog.

"Go down a little more," she ordered. "Then turn off your lights."

I heaved a gusty sigh and let the car drift around the curve of the hill. As we cleared the trees, the barn came into view, a pale rectangle amid the varying shades of gray in the meadow. I braked yet again, shoved the gearshift to park, and switched off the headlights.

It took a moment for my eyes to adjust to the dimness. Then I caught my breath.

Fireflies drifted through the meadow. Hundreds of them. Or perhaps the flash of their golden reflections in the pond created that illusion. Mesmerized, I watched them blink on and off like the "twinkie" lights my mother hung on the Christmas tree every year.

"Have you ever seen so many?" Caren whispered, gazing raptly through the windshield.

"No," I whispered back.

Not even during those picnics in Brandywine Park. I closed my eyes, summoning the smoke and smell of grilling meat hanging in the air along the river. My mother chiding me for gobbling my hot dog too fast, my father waving away her objections, just as eager as I was for twilight.

Climbing up Monkey Hill, past Brandywine Zoo's small brick primate house to the abandoned pavilion near the summit. My delighted laughter mingling with Daddy's when the first fireflies appeared. Grass tickling our bare feet as we stalked them. His soft voice warning me to be gentle as I captured one between my cupped palms. The light flashing through my fingers, turning them rosy, then pale.

I pretended they were fairies. And I, of course, was their princess, trapped in mortal form. Had I dreamed that up or was it one of my father's stories? He had a million of them.

"Isn't it awful early for fireflies?" Caren whispered.

"What? Oh, I don't know."

They blinked faster now. Pheromones—or whatever insects had—kicking into high gear at the proximity of so many potential mates. One thing was certain: there would be one helluva love fest in the meadow tonight.

Suddenly, Caren leaned forward. "Do you hear that?"

I heard the drone of the idling motor. The harsh ratchet of night insects. The whispers of leaves and pine needles as the breeze shifted. And Caren's sudden intake of breath.

I glanced over and discovered her straining against her seat belt, hands gripping the dashboard. When I returned my gaze to the meadow, I gasped, too.

The fireflies had abandoned their stately dance. A single glowing ball of light raced toward the trees. I glimpsed something dark at its center. Heard a faint burst of laughter, wild and exuberant. And something barely audible in response—high-pitched and silvery, like the rippling glissando of a harp.

In spite of the warmth of the evening, I shivered. My fingers ached and my chest felt constricted. Belatedly, I realized I was clutching the steering wheel in a death grip and straining against my seat belt just like Caren.

The music—the sound, whatever it was—had already faded. I slumped back and took a deep, steadying breath. Then jerked erect as Caren flung open the car door. She raced across the drive, but by the time I switched on the headlights, she was gone.

I scrambled out of the car and shouted her name. Off to the left, I heard a loud crashing in the underbrush. I shouted again, but the crashing just grew fainter.

Shit.

I yanked open the glove compartment. Fumbled for the flashlight. Flicked it on and was rewarded by a gleam of light with the total wattage of one firefly.

Shit!

I leaned on the horn. Three long, nasal blasts. But I knew no amount of calling or cursing or honking would bring her back. Any more than they would have restrained me the afternoon I'd heard Rowan singing.

Frantically, I dug my phone out of my carryall and pressed it on. While I waited for the Verizon Wireless logo to morph into my display, I fished out my packet of Kleenex and stuck a tissue in my right ear. If the harp music came back, I'd be prepared.

I pressed Reinhard's speed dial and waited impatiently for him to pick up. When he didn't, I glanced at the display. No service available.

Shit, shit, shit!

Helplessly, I watched the fireflies move deeper into the woods, no longer a single glowing ball but a dozen clusters of golden light bobbing among the trees. I'd tripped over my feet in broad daylight. Caren could easily break her leg in that dark forest. Or her neck.

"Caren, God damn it, get your ass back here now!"

The roar of an engine answered. Twin white lights blinded me. The SUV jerked to a halt. Four doors flew open. Reinhard leaped out of the driver's side. I was so glad to see his frowning face I could have kissed it.

I raced toward him, babbling about Caren and the fireflies and the harp music. Reinhard grasped my shoulders, murmuring, "Slower, Maggie, slower." My stress level plummeted from incipient hysteria to "This is still bad, but I don't have to cope with it alone."

"Catherine, drive Maggie back to the house. Hal, go with them. Lee, Javier, Alex. Come with me."

I wondered how they'd all managed to squeeze into one vehicle. Then I realized there was another behind Reinhard's. The cavalry galloping to the rescue. But how had they known we needed rescuing? Had they seen my headlights from the theatre?

Reinhard had already plunged into the woods with the others, their flashlights an eerie coda to the earlier brilliance of the fireflies. Shaking, I let Catherine and Hal bundle me into my car. Catherine maneuvered the Civic around and drove us slowly back to the house.

Helen and Janet were waiting at the top of the drive.

"What happened?" Janet demanded.

While Catherine explained, Hal gently plucked the tissue from my right ear and pressed it into my hand.

"This is all my fault," Helen said. "If I hadn't fallen asleep—"

"It's not your fault," Janet snapped. "She left fifteen minutes ago." Her furious gaze returned to me. "What were you doing?"

"Caren was afraid she'd gone overboard on the flowers."

"It took you fifteen minutes to agree?"

"No! It took me five minutes to assure her that you were a ball buster and she wasn't a total loser. Then she spotted the fireflies and things went . . . downhill."

I was almost grateful to Janet for being her usual combative self. It allowed me to unleash my anger rather than dissolve into tears.

"Why don't we all go inside?" Helen suggested. "I'll make tea."

Before anyone could respond, the lights flashing in the woods winked out.

We all froze, Helen still gesturing toward the house, Hal reaching for my arm. Like we were posing for a diorama at the Museum of Natural History. I'd just begun to breathe again when I heard a low rumble like distant thunder that crescendoed to a shocking howl.

It was Janet—naturally—who broke the silence that followed.

"Well. I think we can safely assume that's the end of Rowan's Midsummer celebration. The next few days should be ever so jolly." She sighed and shook her head. "You couldn't have kept driving while you explained she wasn't a total loser?"

"If I'd known Rowan was going to perform the Dance of the Fucking Fireflies, I would have."

Janet snorted. "Well, I've heard our local Wiccans described many ways before, but never as fireflies."

"Wiccans?"

"They hold their Midsummer ritual in the woods."

"Those weren't Wiccans. They were fireflies. Swarming around Rowan."

"I'm sure there *were* fireflies," Janet replied in the soothing tone of a psychiatrist talking to a delusional patient. "The meadow's thick with them this time of year. But they don't swarm."

Catherine's arm snaked around my shoulder. "The light's tricky around dusk. Maybe you saw lanterns."

Helen squeezed my hand. "I suppose you heard music, too?"

"Well . . . sort of. Like . . . harps."

"Usually it's drums," Janet remarked. "Harps make for a pleasant change."

Before I could argue, Reinhard's SUV thundered up the drive. Javier held the door while Lee helped Caren out of the car. She looked dazed but unhurt except for a rip in the right knee of her jeans. Then she saw us all standing there and burst into tears.

"Just what we need," Janet muttered. "More drama."

"Cut her a break!" I whispered as Helen hurried over to Caren.

"Where's Dad?" Catherine asked.

For the first time, I realized Alex wasn't with them.

"He stayed behind," Lee said. "To look for Rowan."

Janet rolled her eyes. "Well, that's a waste of time."

"Maybe it is," Lee replied, an edge to his voice. "But Alex wanted to try."

"Argue about it later," Reinhard said. "Let's get these girls into the house."

Everyone was too busy fussing over Caren to respond to my continued protestations about what I had witnessed. They guided us to the living room and sat us down on one of the sofas. Janet sloshed whisky into two glasses and shoved them at us. I gulped mine gratefully. Caren took a small sip and made a face.

"Sorry," Janet said. "Would you prefer an amusing chardonnay?"

Reinhard shot her a look, and she subsided.

They clustered around us like so many fireflies: Reinhard perched on the coffee table, examining Caren's knee; Helen sitting on Caren's left, holding her hand; Catherine on my right, patting my forearm; Lee and Javier behind the sofa, their hands on our shoulders.

Janet stood next to Reinhard and stared down at Caren. "You've had a little shock, that's all. From wandering around the woods at night."

A soft litany of voices joined hers.

"We always have fireflies at Midsummer."

"But the ball of light? That came from the lanterns."

"The lanterns that the Williams carry."

I didn't believe a word of it. Yet I could feel my head nodding obediently.

"Rowan celebrates with them every year."

"They meet in the meadow."

"And sing. And play instruments."

"And march into the woods for their ritual."

I lifted my glass and discovered someone had refilled it. I drained it and shuddered as the whisky's heat settled in my belly.

"You decided to follow them, Caren."

"And got lost."

"But you're fine now."

"No need to be frightened."

"No need to think about it at all."

The tension had left my body. Maybe that was the whisky. I glanced over at Caren and found her gazing up at Janet, her head bobbing in agreement.

Just like mine.

I shifted uneasily. The watchful eyes and soothing voices made me as uncomfortable as the hands pressing down on my shoulders. Equally disturbing was Hal's odd expression. When he caught me watching him, he turned away.

"Maggie."

My head jerked toward Janet.

"You and Caren should go now. Enjoy your dinner. Get a good night's sleep."

She and Reinhard escorted us out. I glanced back as I left the living room. Lee had his arms around Hal, whose face was crumpled up like a kid about to cry.

All the way to the car, Caren babbled apologies. I kept thinking about Hal's unhappy face and Rowan's terrifying howl, wondering what the hell had happened tonight.

"Will Rowan be okay?" I asked Reinhard.

"Yes, of course. There will be other Midsummers."

I couldn't understand why he had to forgo this one. Wiccans wouldn't have gone ballistic if Caren had interrupted their ritual. It wasn't like they sacrificed babies or anything.

Reinhard's smile was warm and reassuring. So why didn't I feel reassured? Yet when he patted my shoulder and opened the car door, I obediently slid inside.

As we started down the hill, Caren exclaimed, "I don't know what possessed me to go running after those Wiccans. I'm a Presbyterian!"

I let her chatter on until we reached the hotel. As she unbuckled her seat belt, I grabbed her arm. "Caren. What did you really see in the meadow?"

"You mean the Wiccans?"

"No. Before." When she just stared at me, I prompted, "The fireflies?"

"Oh. Right. They were something."

"And the ball of light?"

"The lanterns? Yeah, I saw them, too."

I tried again. "And the music?"

"I heard . . . something. Just for a moment. Then it went away." She glanced down and moaned. "Just look at that hole! My favorite jeans, too. Well, it serves me right. I'm starving. I hope there's some food left."

I got out of the car, but just stood there, frowning.

"Maggie?"

"I think I'll skip dinner."

"Oh, but you have to come. It just won't be—"

"I really don't feel like it."

"Are you sick? Should I call—?"

"No! Just a killer headache. I'll be fine if I lie down for awhile."

I sent her on her way, then climbed the stairs to my room and flung myself on the bed.

Everything Caren had said—everything the staff had told us—sounded reasonable. The light *was* tricky at dusk. Fireflies *didn't* swarm. Could I swear in a court of law that they had surrounded Rowan? Or that I'd seen a glowing ball of light and not the glow of a couple dozen lanterns?

I'd experienced the mesmerizing effect of Alex's voice at that first music rehearsal. And the urgency to obey Janet when she ordered me back to my chair during our memorable chat in the lobby of the Bough. At the cast party, Reinhard had discerned each disquieting emotion evoked by the memories of my father. And with a hug or a blessing, Helen could fill me with peace.

I'd chalked it up to charm or insight or simply strength of will. Now, I wondered if it was something more, if they had actually reshaped our perceptions as they calmed us.

The thought made me shake my head. This wasn't *The Manchurian Candidate*, for God's sake. And if they had brainwashed us, why had it only worked on Caren? Was she simply more susceptible?

I opened my laptop, clicked on the Skype icon, and pulled on my headphones. My breath blew out in a sigh of pure relief when Nancy picked up.

"Hey. It's me. Maggie."

"What's the matter?"

"Nothing."

"You sound funny."

"I just . . . I need to talk to someone normal."

Silence. Then: "Let me get my glass of wine."

"Better get the bottle, Nancy. This might take awhile."

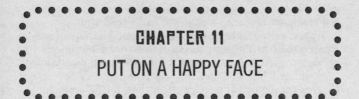

CHAPTER 11
PUT ON A HAPPY FACE

DISCUSSING THE EVENING'S BIZARRE EVENTS with Nancy helped calm me down, but brought me no closer to understanding what had actually happened. Only the staff could provide those answers. And none of them would break ranks. Except—maybe—Hal.

Moments after I hung up with Nancy, someone knocked at the door. As I opened it, Lou and Bobbie thrust out six-packs of beer, Brittany and Kalma, pints of the Chatter-box's hand-packed ice cream. Gary cradled fortune cookies in his palms.

Caren shyly held up a carton of takeout. "Shrimp and snow peas."

My favorite.

I hugged her. I hugged all of them. We crammed into my room and sat up for hours, talking and laughing and groan-ing over the vague fortunes our cookies contained. Maybe it was just another example of the summer stock law of fast-blooming friendships, but I felt closer to them after a month than I had to my colleagues at HelpLink after two years. And their cheerfully normal company kept me from obsessing about the Midsummer madness.

My questions resurfaced during the company meeting the next morning. Reinhard brusquely announced that Rowan was "under the weather" and declared the woods off limits to avoid "unfortunate accidents."

"You think I am treating you like children, yes? Well,

141

until I can rely upon certain members of this cast to exercise common sense, this is how it must be for all."

Caren wilted under his glare. I fumed. Neither of us had wanted to go blundering through the woods, but in order to conceal that little fact, we had to be cast as the village idiots.

Reinhard blocked two of the company scenes in Act One, snapping out stage directions like a drill sergeant. At our lunch break, I decided to brave another wave of Teutonic wrath and attempt a frontal assault. He gave me the opening I needed by asking how I was feeling.

"I don't know which was more unsettling: what I saw in the meadow or what happened at Janet's."

Reinhard didn't bat an eye. "What do you mean?"

"The brainwashing."

"Is that what you call it?"

"What would you call it?"

"Calming two young women on the verge of hysterics."

"Then explain to me why one young woman's memories of last night differ so drastically from the other's."

Reinhard's frosty expression shifted to exasperation. "Because you are as stubborn as a rock." Then he sighed and pinched the bridge of his nose, looking so tired that my anger faded.

"You were honest with me at the cast party," I reminded him. "When you said Rowan wasn't . . . ordinary."

"And I also said that was all I intended to say on the subject. About last night, I can only tell you it was not anything bad."

"Maybe I should just ask Rowan."

Reinhard sighed again. "You can't. He is not in his apartment."

"He hasn't come back?"

Reinhard shook his head.

"Should we call the police?"

"No!"

"But he might be hurt! He could have fallen or—"

"Rowan knows every inch of those woods. He'll be back. We must give him a little time."

A somber Alex awaited us at our afternoon music rehearsal. Everyone else probably attributed his mood to the folk songs we were learning; lost love and grief featured prominently in both "The Great Selkie of Sule Skerry" and "The Water is Wide." Judging from his haggard face, I guessed he'd spent the night combing the woods in vain for Rowan.

After rehearsal, I made my way to Hallee's. The latest window display featured scantily clad mannequins frolicking in a forest glade, their corsets, panties, and bras like so many brightly colored flowers. The single male mannequin sported a scarlet thong and a donkey's head that rested in the lap of a female mannequin in a shimmering negligee of green silk. Hal's tribute to *A Midsummer Night's Dream*.

If only our Midsummer had been so dreamy.

Although it was after 6:00, the door opened when I turned the knob. As I stepped inside, the bell chimed the opening notes of "People" from *Funny Girl*. From somewhere in the back, Hal called, "Sorry, we're closed."

He slipped through the pink velveteen curtains, wrestling with a mound of fabric, and stopped dead when he saw me.

"Oh, sweetie, are you okay?"

I meant to demand explanations. But one look at his worried face and I was fluttering my hands like a fledgling bird and fighting back tears. I hardly ever cried, but lately, one kind word and I sprang a leak.

He hurried toward me, enfolding me in a fierce hug and yards of green tulle. I babbled an apology, but he just shushed me. Finally, he stepped back, wiping first my eyes then his with the tulle.

"Sorry," I managed. "I'm still kind of shaky after last night. And now Rowan's disappeared—"

"That's not your fault."

"We ruined his Midsummer."

"Caren ruined it. Stupid cow."

"That's not fair."

"No. But saying it makes me feel better. Stupid, stupid cow. There."

I hesitated, then said, "What happened . . . at Janet's . . ."

"They meant well. Really."

Hal's eyes pleaded with me to believe him. And part of

me did. Hurting a cast member violated the code of the Crossroads. But the code had to be pretty flexible if it included brainwashing.

"They're like Rowan, aren't they? The same power. Only not as strong."

His gaze slid away, and I realized how foolish I'd been to hope that he would tell me the truth. How could he? Lee was part of it and Lee was the center of his world.

"It's okay, Hal. It's not your fault. It's not anybody's fault, I guess. But that doesn't change the fact that Rowan's vanished."

"He'll be back."

"That's what Reinhard said."

"Because it's true."

"This has happened before?"

"The Midsummer thing? No. But there have been other times . . ." Hal shrugged. "Rowan's moody. Like all artistic geniuses. But he'll be back before the curtain goes up."

Curtain time rolled around. Still no Rowan.

"You don't suppose something awful happened?" Nancy, back for the Wednesday night performance of *Brigadoon*, looked as worried as I felt.

I shrugged helplessly.

Janet surprised us by showing up in the green room. One look at her face told me Rowan was still MIA. Reinhard glanced at the wall clock for the tenth time in ten minutes. By 8:05, he had yet to call places. Standard operating procedure at other theatres, but the Crossroads observed its eight o'clock curtain time with relentless punctuality.

Suddenly, Janet and Reinhard went into bird dog mode. The green room door swung open. Rowan entered, looking so drawn and pale that I could almost believe he *was* sick. His regulation linen shirt and black jeans were stained and wrinkled, but his hair was neatly tied back with a leather thong.

Ignoring his supposed phobia about crowds, the cast clustered around, exclaiming with relief and making sympathetic noises. Caren hung back, watching Rowan like a nervous schoolgirl expecting a reprimand from her favorite teacher. His quick smile brought her rushing forward to join the others.

"I apologize for my tardiness. And for missing rehearsal today."

His voice was hoarse. I imagined that awful howl tearing at his throat and shuddered.

"I appreciate your concern. But now, let's focus on the show."

As we formed our customary circle, Reinhard leaned forward to whisper something. When Rowan shook his head, Reinhard stepped back, but continued to watch him anxiously.

We closed our eyes and clasped hands, breathing together in silence. Instead of soothing me, the ritual brought back disturbing images of the previous night, the gentle pressure of Brittany's hand and Nancy's an unpleasant reminder of the staff touching me.

I told myself that Rowan had not been part of that, that the energy he summoned could never hurt me, that we needed this strange connection in order to turn in the best possible performance. But my body remained tense, my mind churning, my emotions a jumble of resentment and confusion and lingering concern about Rowan.

"We all have concerns."

My eyes flew open at this deviation from the script.

"We might be missing our families. Worrying about our jobs. Questioning why we're here. Questioning what this theatre is all about."

His words were clearly directed at me. Had someone on the staff told him what had happened last night? Or did he just know?

"This is not the time for those concerns. Tonight, we have only one purpose: to present this show."

Nancy squeezed my hand. Could she feel my separateness? Could everyone sense it?

"Some members of our audience probably know *Brigadoon* by heart. Others will be watching it for the first time. They all deserve the best performance we can give."

As the quiet words washed over me, I studied Rowan. The drooping shoulders that belied the confident voice. The deep lines bracketing his mouth. The two grooves etched between his brows.

I wanted to tell him that everything would be all right,

just as he had reassured us so many times. I wanted to promise that he would rediscover the joy that had been snatched away from him last night. Mostly, I wanted to put my arms around him and urge him to let go of his disappointment, of his responsibilities, of the bonds that held him hostage to this place.

His voice trailed off. The smile that curved his mouth was so sweet and tender it made me ache.

"Don't worry," he said, his voice little more than a whisper. "Just acknowledge your concerns as you breathe in."

I closed my eyes and took a shaky breath, filling my lungs with the confusion and doubts of the last twenty-four hours.

"And let them go as you breathe out."

Around the circle, people exhaled in a long, collective sigh. I released my breath and felt the tension drain away.

All of my questions would be there in the morning. For now, I was just relieved to feel the connection between us once more. For a few minutes, I'd felt like Tommy, standing forlornly on the hilltop, scanning the empty valley where the village had once stood. For better or worse, I was back in Brigadoon.

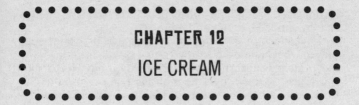

CHAPTER 12
ICE CREAM

THE ENSUING DAYS PROVED that Brigadoon's foundations were still shaky.

"Maybe we're just tired," Brittany said as we trudged into the women's dressing room after another lackluster performance.

"Or maybe," Romaine said, "we all got a little too cocky after opening night. We should thank the good Lord for our success instead of taking the credit ourselves."

I suspected Rowan had more to do with it than God, but I hated to think the credit—or blame—was entirely his. That reduced us to marionettes, dancing on the strings he pulled. Which was uncomfortably reminiscent of how I had felt during the staff's brainwashing.

I slumped into my chair at one of the makeup tables. The mirrors on the wall reflected multiple images of cast mates grimly hanging up costumes and packing up their gear.

Nancy slid into the chair next to mine. Our gazes met in the mirror.

"Do you think we're in this funk because of what happened to Rowan?" she whispered.

"I don't know."

If we had been swept up in his pre-Midsummer mania, we could easily catch his post-Midsummer depression. But his mania had been obvious; the only evidence I could find of his depression was how *we* were feeling. And how the staff tiptoed around him, observing his behavior as intently as they studied Caren's and mine.

Rehearsals of *The Sea-Wife* were just as dispirited. I played what had now become known as "the list thing" with the principals. Caren was wildly excited, but Hector and Maya just went through the motions. Gary refused to participate at all, saying, "Trust me, I know way more about this character than I want to."

I quizzed Maya about Wicca and got a crash course in Reiki healing and chakra alignment as well. The way practitioners moved energy around sounded similar to what Rowan did, but nothing like the staff's brainwashing.

I researched hypnosis on the Web. And energy healing. And firefly behavior. Two hours later, I shut down my laptop. Just what I needed. Another "like father, like daughter" moment. During that last year, he'd spent countless hours doing "research," too. Shut away in the basement when I left for school. Still closeted there when I came home. Sometimes, I'd hear him muttering to himself or strumming the same chord over and over on his guitar.

The Saturday matinee of *Brigadoon* went a little better. And the free dinner afterward—catered by the Mandarin Chalet—helped everyone relax. Rowan showed up long enough to fill his paper plate with chicken and bean sprouts. Then he retreated to his apartment. The previous week, he had surprised everyone by eating with us, putting to rest the rumor that he existed exclusively on strawberry milkshakes.

Spurred by that memory, I made an impulsive trip to town. When I returned, the cast was buzzing excitedly about Reinhard's announcement of the Crossroads Follies. In light of their renewed spirits, I considered stowing my purchases in the green room fridge. My idea—which had initially seemed as fun and foolish as the Follies—just seemed stupid now. But maybe it would make Rowan smile.

As I mounted the stairs to his apartment, my courage evaporated. I left the bags outside his door, knocked firmly, and turned tail.

I'd made it halfway down the stairs when I heard the door open. I froze, hoping the shadows would conceal me.

Rowan's puzzled "Maggie?" proved the futility of that strategy.

I turned to find him silhouetted in the doorway. He bent down and picked up the two small bags. Paper rustled as he examined the contents.

"By way of apology," I said. "For wrecking your Midsummer." When he just stared at me, I babbled, "It was supposed to make you laugh. Because you always drink strawberry milkshakes at lunch."

The silence from the top of the stairs lengthened. Sweat broke out under my arms.

"But obviously, it's not funny. So I'll go now."

"You brought me milk and strawberries?"

His voice sounded odd. Strained.

"Ice cream and strawberries." Had he even looked in the second bag? How do you mistake a pint of vanilla ice cream for a milk carton? "It was a joke. A coals-to-Newcastle thing. Because you drink—"

"Yes. I see."

Slowly, he descended the stairs, the bags dangling from his fingertips like they contained dead rats. He stopped two steps above me. The small light on the stage manager's desk revealed little of his expression, but I thought he was frowning.

"Look, I'm sorry I bothered you."

"Don't apologize. It was very ... neighborly."

"Neighborly?"

"Kind. Thoughtful." He cleared his throat and descended another step. He was definitely frowning. "Unexpected. An unexpected gift."

"It's just ice cream and strawberries."

"Yes. Still. Thank you."

We lapsed into silence. His stare was becoming really unnerving.

"Okay. Well. I'd better get ready for the show."

I glanced back as I reached the stage. He was still standing there, watching me.

❧❧

Rowan's strange reaction made me wonder if I'd made matters worse, but he seemed perfectly at ease when he led warm-ups. Even better, our performance bounced back to pre-Midsummer standards.

After the Sunday matinee, laughter filled the dressing room, a refreshing change from the morose silence of the last few days. Women dashed from costume racks to makeup tables, eager to vacate the theatre and enjoy their evening off.

As the dressing room emptied, Nancy whispered, "So everything's back to normal."

"I guess."

"And all it took was ice cream and strawberries?"

"Or the prospect of the Follies," I replied, still uncertain what had effected the change.

"'Ours is not to reason why,'" she quoted. "Any plans for your day off?"

"The usual. Laundry. E-mail. Job hunting."

And I really needed to start work on *Carousel*. Or at least read it without flinging the script across the room. Maybe that was why Rowan thought I needed to play Nettie—to learn self-control.

I examined my reflection critically. The heavy stage makeup congealing in every line on my face made me resemble a saddlebag that had been left out in the sun for a few centuries. I made a mental note to remember the look; it would be perfect for good ol' Nettie.

As I reached for my jar of cold cream, I heard Nancy's quick intake of breath and looked up to find Rowan reflected in the mirror.

Nancy's head swiveled back and forth like she was watching a tennis match. Finally, she announced, "I've got to be going. See you both Wednesday."

Rowan stepped into the dressing room to allow Nancy to exit. From behind his shoulder, she jabbed her thumb at him, raised an imaginary telephone to her ear, and mouthed, "Call me." I glared at her and heard her chuckle as she retreated down the hallway.

Rowan cleared his throat. "I just wanted to thank you again for your thoughtfulness. And to apologize if I seemed ungrateful."

"No. Just . . . confused."

"Yes. Well." His gaze swept the costume racks, the mirrors, the floor—pretty much everything except me. "Helen tells me you're working on a new program design."

"Nothing too different," I assured him. "Or expensive."

"Perhaps we could discuss it tomorrow."

"Tomorrow?"

"I realize it's your day off, but I thought we might have lunch."

"Lunch?"

"A working lunch. My treat."

"Your . . . ?" I stopped myself before I parroted his words again.

"Treat. Yes."

Lunch with Rowan. His treat. Strawberry milkshakes for two and whatever solid food he usually consumed.

"Okay."

His wandering gaze finally settled on me. "Shall we say noon?"

"Noon, it is."

He turned to go, then hesitated. "Dress for walking."

"Walking?" I asked, reverting to parrot mode.

"There's something I'd like to show you. In the woods."

I couldn't help myself. "Boy, if I had a nickel for every time a guy's used *that* line."

For a moment, his face went blank. Then he smiled. And all the weirdness of the last few days evaporated. Rowan was happy. I was happy. God's in his heaven, all's right with the world.

Still smiling, he shook his head. "What I want to show you is a wonder of nature."

"Yeah. That's what they all say."

His laughter made me giddy.

When I reminded him that the woods were off limits, he just shrugged and said, "Not if you're with me." I was a little skeptical, though, when he revealed that the wonder of nature was a beach. I'd never imagined there was a lake hidden in the depths of the woods. He refused to give me any details, just pointed his finger at me and said, "High noon. At the picnic area."

After he left, I swiveled back to the mirror and told my

reflection that this was a business meeting. I would treat it with the same professionalism that I would treat any business meeting.

The woman in the mirror nodded gravely. Then a goofy smile blossomed on her face. When I shook my finger at her, she laughed.

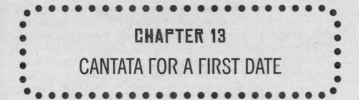

CHAPTER 13
CANTATA FOR A FIRST DATE

COULDN'T VERY WELL GO TO HALLEE'S and have Hal pepper me with questions about my sudden need for a bathing suit. After my frantic search of the Internet revealed zero malls in the vicinity of Dale, I drove to the JC Penney in Bennington.

At 10:30, I raced into a dressing room with an armful of possibilities. I tugged on one suit after another before choosing a one-piece black suit with a little gold clip cinching the draping at the waist. The deep V of the bodice revealed some nice cleavage. I could always wrap a towel around my hips and rip it off right before I plunged into the water.

11:30: Back at the hotel for another shower; wriggling in and out of swimsuits had left me drenched.

11:50: Bathing suit on under canvas pants and T-shirt "Bug Away" sprayed over exposed areas. Water bottle and bath towel in carryall.

11:52: Out the door and into the car.

11:53: Out of the car and back up to my room to grab the mock-up of the program and my notebook and pen in case I needed to jot down Rowan's suggestions. And a bra and panties so I wouldn't have to wear my damp bathing suit all afternoon.

At 11:58, I pulled into the theatre parking lot. I was surprised to find another car parked next to Catherine's Prius and tried to recall which staff member drove a Lexus. Hid-

den behind the open door of my car, I tugged at the crotch
of my swimsuit. The prospect of a long hike on a warm day
while swaddled in polyester grew less appealing as I walked
to the picnic area.

I was still debating whether to change when I spied Janet
and Rowan leaving the theatre accompanied by a man and
a woman in business suits. I used their momentary distraction to race to the Dungeon. Five minutes later, I emerged,
blissfully unencumbered by the swimsuit, and found Rowan
sitting on a picnic table. Janet—thank God—was nowhere
in sight.

He hopped off the table as I approached.

"Who were the suits?" I asked.

He shrugged. "Bankers."

Recalling my mother's early struggles to meet the mortgage payments on our row house, their presence signaled
only one thing. "Is the theatre in trouble?"

"Of course not. I thought we'd picnic in the woods if
that's all right with you."

"Look, I've had a little experience with fundraising. If
there's anything I can do—"

"You can stop worrying about the theatre and enjoy
yourself."

He bent down and slid a bulging knapsack out from under the bench. As he hefted it onto his shoulders, I exclaimed, "My God! What have you got in there?"

"Lunch."

"For all of Dale?"

"I wasn't sure what you liked. So I brought a little of
everything. Shall we go?"

I tried to turn the conversation back to the bankers, but
his monosyllabic responses made it clear he had no desire to
talk about them. The oblique approach of mentioning that
increased publicity might bring in additional revenue proved
as unsuccessful as the frontal assault. Finally, I shut up.

A mile passed in silence. Rowan tramped along the trail
with the enthusiasm of a soldier on the Bataan death march.
Sweat beaded his forehead and upper lip. Every few minutes, he grimaced and shifted the weight of his forty-ton
knapsack. When I caught him rubbing his chest, I finally

realized what was happening. Controlling my panic, I quietly ordered him to lie down.

His head jerked toward me. "What?"

"I think you're having a heart attack. I want you to lie down and try to remain calm."

"Maggie . . ."

"Lie down and remain calm, damn it!"

As I dropped to my knees and rummaged in my carryall for my cell phone, Rowan said, "Maggie. I am not having a heart attack."

I searched his face for any evidence of pain and found only faint amusement.

"It's hot. The knapsack is heavy. And I'm a bit . . ."

"Preoccupied? Unsettled? Upset?"

"Something like that."

"Those damn bankers."

His mouth curved in a rueful smile. "You're as tenacious as a pit bull."

"It's one of my best qualities. You're sure you're not having a heart attack?"

"Quite sure."

"So. The bankers."

As we walked, he explained that Janet's investments had taken a nosedive. And Janet's investments supported the theatre. In good years, it usually managed to break even, but the last few years hadn't been good. And while she was in no danger of losing the property, it had become clear to everyone on the staff that something had to change.

"We've discussed various options. Taking out a second mortgage. Refinancing the current one. Selling off some acreage." He grimaced.

"What about incorporating as a nonprofit?"

"I don't want a board of directors telling me how to run my theatre."

"So choose board members who believe in your theatre! Which includes everyone in Dale. Call up some of the other nonprofit theatres in the state. Pick their executive directors' brains. If Lee doesn't know about this stuff, find a lawyer who does. Someone who'll sit down for an initial question and answer session without soaking you. And do it soon. It might take a year to incorporate. Longer still for grants . . . what?"

Rowan had stopped walking and was watching me. "You're very passionate about this."

"Aren't you?"

"Yes. But the theatre . . . it's my life. It's just one summer in yours."

"I'd still hate to see it go under. It's special. Weird but special."

"I wasn't sure you felt that way. After Midsummer."

And there it was—the proverbial six-hundred-pound gorilla in the room. Or woods, in this case. I waited for him to say more, but he just shifted the weight of his knapsack and started walking again.

Instead of inundating him with questions about Midsummer, I returned to the subject of publicity. He was clearly uneasy, but I expected that; raising the theatre's profile might bring unwelcome scrutiny into his mysterious past—and his equally mysterious powers. But at least he seemed willing to consider my suggestions.

When I brought up salary freezes, though, he shook his head.

"Helen and Janet don't even accept a salary. As for the others . . . you know how much they make? A hundred dollars a week. Same as the cast."

And they didn't even get a free room.

"Alex and Reinhard and Mei-Yin make a good living, but they deserve salaries for all the hours they put in. And the younger members of the staff need the extra money."

"Lee's a lawyer," I ventured.

"Half his practice is pro bono work. Hal's business is just starting to make a profit. Same with Catherine and Javier. And in spite of that, they all volunteered to forgo their salaries this summer. That's how dedicated they are. But I'll be damned if I let them work for nothing! We've survived bad times before and we will now."

He took a deep breath, shook his head, and said, "Forgive me. I'm ruining the afternoon."

"My fault. I shouldn't have beat you over the head about the bankers."

"Let's make an addendum to our pact—no wallowing in guilt."

We shook hands and moved on. Occasionally, Rowan would point out something in the woods—a deep indentation in a bank of ferns where a deer had lain, the tracks of fox and opossum imprinted on a muddy stream bank. I found it wonderfully exotic, but part of my enthusiasm stemmed from his obvious love for these wild places. When the conversation faltered, the silence felt companionable rather than grim, both of us content to listen to the scolding of squirrels, the throaty purrs of wood pigeons, and the intermittent rat-a-tat-tat of a woodpecker.

Typical city girl, I failed to recognize where he was leading me until we entered the little clearing where I had fallen.

"I didn't know the beach was near here."

"Yes."

"Thank God. I'm starving. And hot." I nodded toward the hut and added, "You never did tell me who lived there."

"I did. I still do. From time to time."

I glanced at him to see if he was joking, but his expression was perfectly serious.

"That's where you were at Midsummer."

He nodded.

"And nobody thought to look for you there?"

"I made a point of being elsewhere when they did. Come on. It's just over this rise."

As we crested the top, I temporarily forgot about the beach and simply stared at the enormous tree straddling the next hill. Five men with their arms outstretched might have managed to circle the thick trunk. Dozens of branches sprouted from it, reaching out and up to create a leafy canopy so dense that nothing grew in its shade. Part of the slope had fallen away, carving out a hollow space among the roots. Perfect for pirate treasure or a family of gnomes. Daddy would have loved it.

"It must be ancient," I whispered.

"Nearly two hundred years old," Rowan replied just as softly.

As I started down the slope, he gently took my arm.

Maybe he knew I wouldn't be able to take my eyes off the tree. With every step, my head tilted farther back until my neck ached as I craned to see the top. Crisp leaves whispered underfoot like mothers shushing their children in church, reinforcing the sense that this was a sacred place.

Up close, the twisted roots looked fantastical, spilling down and over and into the soil like tangled tendrils of hair. I ducked under a low-hanging branch and knelt to brush off the leaves, surprised that the roots were narrow enough to cup in my hand. How could something so thin hold up such an incredible weight?

I stroked the tree, savoring the contrast between the smooth bark and the strange gullies coursing through it. It was as easy to imagine a dryad emerging from that trunk as it was to picture a family of gnomes living in the cavern under its roots.

And it was a cavern, not merely the small hollow I had thought. A wonderful playhouse for a child—or a hiding place for a man who didn't want to be found by his staff.

The leaves crackled as I stretched out full-length on the ground. I stared up into the latticework of branches, wishing my climbing skills were half as good as they had been in my youth. But another part of me shrank from such an act; somehow, it seemed sacrilegious.

Rowan crouched beside me, smiling. "You didn't believe me. When I told you it was a wonder of nature."

"I thought that was the beach."

He frowned. "It was. It is."

"So there are two wonders of nature out here?"

"Maggie." Rowan rested his palm against the tree's trunk. "*This* is the beech."

For a long moment, I simply stared at him. "It's . . . a beech . . . tree."

He nodded, his expression wary.

I burst into helpless laughter. Rowan stared at me like I had lost my mind. Finally I managed to wheeze out, "I thought you meant . . . a beach. With sand. And water."

"In the middle of the woods?"

"That's what I said when you told me!"

He shook his head, a smile tugging at his mouth.

"I thought there was a lake. Or a river. Something." I

convulsed helplessly, hands holding my aching stomach. "I even went out . . . and bought . . . a bathing suit!"

I'd read books where people yelped with laughter. Or barked. Or brayed. The sound that emerged from Rowan's mouth was more of a bellow that tailed off into a series of high-pitched yips. He laughed so hard, he lost his balance and sat down hard on the roots. That elicited a genuine yelp, which set me off again. We fell back into the leaves, our laughter slowly easing to a duet of moans and sighs.

"I brought bottled water," Rowan said. "If you change into your bathing suit, I'll pour it over you."

With a supreme effort, I rolled onto my side so I could treat him to the full effect of my glare. He grinned at me, unrepentant, then scrambled to his feet, brushed off the leaves and twigs, and hefted his knapsack.

I groaned. "Can't we eat here?"

"We're not going far. And it'll be worth it."

"Another wonder of nature?"

"Actually, yes."

I allowed him to help me to my feet and clung to his hand as we sidestepped down the beech's hill and marched up the next. As I stumbled over the top, a cool breeze caressed my face. My hand tightened on Rowan's as I gazed out at the limitless expanse of earth and sky before us.

Round-backed hills rolled west in undulating waves of green that faded to a misty blue in the distance. Fat-bellied clouds drifted over them, their shadows chasing each other across the nearest hillside. Farther west, storm clouds curdled in the sky, gray and purple and cream.

I tottered through the sparse grass. The pressure of Rowan's fingers warned me to stop before I reached the edge of our little plateau, but I could see the silver thread of a river at the bottom of the gorge and hear the faint thunder of its water as it tumbled over rocks and boulders.

The sun emerged from behind a cloud as if to bless us, and my eyes closed against its sudden brilliance. When I opened them, I found Rowan watching me.

"You're right," I said. "It was definitely worth it."

I knew this was the place where he sang. He must have stood here countless times, enjoying the play of sunlight and shadow on the hills, watching storm clouds roll in to veil the mountaintops in mist. Sharing this with me was a gift even greater than the magnificent beech.

"Thank you," I whispered.

He just smiled and plucked a leaf from my hair.

I felt strangely shy, as if our relationship had shifted and there could be no going back to the give-and-take we usually shared. As I helped him spread a faded quilt on the grass, I kept stealing glances at him for any hint that he shared those feelings, but he seemed perfectly at ease.

My shyness receded as he began unpacking lunch. Or rather, unveiling it. Linen napkins swaddled bottles of lemonade, white wine, and spring water. Linen placemats and dishtowels protected china plates, crystal goblets, silver utensils. My mouth hung open as he arranged them on the quilt. When he presented the food, I nearly dislocated my jaw.

Poached salmon on a bed of fennel fronds. Cold grilled quail with mustard vinaigrette. Wild rice salad with pecans and dried apricots. Haricots verts and new potatoes with walnuts and Stilton. A French baguette and a tiny cup of sweet butter. A selection of cheeses. A china bowl of strawberries to accompany the lemon curd tart.

When he placed my plate in front of me, I simply stared at it. Then stared at him.

His shoulders moved awkwardly, as if his shirt had suddenly shrunk two sizes. "I just wanted it to be nice."

"Nice? Nice is cold cuts and beer. This is . . ." I waved my hand helplessly. "It's . . . I'm . . ."

"Speechless?"

"Well. I'm rarely speechless."

"I've noticed."

I ripped off a chunk of baguette and threw it at him. Grinning, he snatched it out of the air and took a bite.

"You and Janet must have the same caterer."

He shook his head and mumbled something unintelligible.

"You don't mean to tell me Helen made all this."

"No, I did."

I laughed.

"I *did!*" he protested.

"You. Made all this."

"Catherine was kind enough to help with the shopping. I couldn't get everything delivered on such short notice. And I don't usually keep a side of salmon around the apartment."

"Or a covey of quail?"

"Actually, I made that for supper the other night. I just refrigerated the leftovers and—"

"Okay, now you're scaring me."

He laughed. "With everything you've seen and heard this summer, what scares you is the fact that I can cook?"

"I bet you're kind to animals, too."

"Yes, but I beat my staff regularly." He shook his head, still smiling. "I just like to cook, Maggie. It relaxes me. Now what would you like to drink?"

I eyed the wine longingly and decided I'd better stick with lemonade. As he filled my glass, I ventured, "So if you're a gourmet chef, why does Helen bring you lunch every day?"

He sighed. "She likes bringing me lunch. Just as she likes baking for the cast. She's one of those people who's happiest caring for others."

"Yeah, I've heard of them."

"And it makes my life easier. I'm lucky if I have fifteen minutes to eat. There's always a cast problem or a set problem or some other problem." Suddenly, he stiffened. "Helen doesn't pay for lunch. I've set up accounts with the shops in town. My salary doesn't allow me many luxuries, but it does put clothes on my back and food on my table."

Guilt swamped me as I realized this spread must have cost him a week's salary. "You really shouldn't have, Rowan."

"Shouldn't have what?"

"Done all . . . this."

"It was fun. I can't remember the last time I cooked for someone." He raised his glass. "No wallowing. Remember?"

Our glasses clinked with the musicality of fine crystal.

"So how did you manage to create this feast in that little apartment of yours?"

"It's not so little. Nearly two thousand square feet."

I choked on my lemonade. "You're kidding."

"Ah, that's right. You didn't see much of it that night. It runs pretty much the length of the theatre."

"My God. Do you have any idea what you'd pay for that kind of space in New York?"

"I shudder to think. So what's your apartment like?"

"A hovel. Okay, not a hovel. But not much bigger than your office. Still, the park's pretty close. Prospect Park. The site of my last picnic."

I regaled him with the deviled egg debacle, expecting him to smile like everyone else who'd heard the story. Instead, he frowned and said, "He should have laughed it off."

"Maybe when he quit vomiting, he did. But it was a little late by then."

"That should be the story you told your grandchildren. How Grandma gave Grandpa salmonella poisoning and he fell in love with her anyway."

"You have a strange sense of romance."

"Maybe. But I would have laughed."

The quiet intensity of his voice sent a wave of heat surging into my cheeks. Another settled a good deal lower in my body. I dug into my food, grateful when he turned the conversation to my life in New York.

The more I talked, though, the less interesting that life sounded. My discouragement increased when he asked about some of my previous jobs. I tried to dredge up funny stories, but somehow each ended with me getting fired or quitting or drifting to another job as unfulfilling as the last.

Maybe that was why I switched to wine. After the second glass, I could joke about my lackluster career and pretend I didn't notice how brittle my laughter sounded.

I was relieved when he asked about my previous summer stock experience. On safer ground, I soon had him laughing with my description of our quarters in rundown Anatevka, the mottled black-and-gray shroud that served as our backdrop, and the romantic foibles of my cast mates, including the guy who left his wife for one of the musicians, the woman who came out as a lesbian after sleeping with a townie, and the gay guys who formed a ménage-a-trois with our female stage manager.

"All in one summer?" he asked.

"All in one show."

That prompted him to pour a glass of wine for himself. "Where did you fit into all that?"

"Mother confessor. People were always showing up at my door to share their woes."

"A Helping Professional even then."

"No. Just a telemarketer. But my mother still had a fit when I quit my job and ran away to the theatre."

"Life upon the wicked stage," he mused.

"That and the fact that my father—"

After a short silence, Rowan quietly prompted, "Your father?"

"He was an actor, too. For awhile." I shrugged. "Not much to tell."

"Then why has all the light left your face?"

"Because I don't want to bore you with the story of my parents' divorce, okay?"

"Okay."

"I'm surprised Janet didn't fill you in on all the gory details."

"She did. So did Alex. He was worried about you."

"The whole thing was stupid. I don't know what's the matter with me. It's been ages since I've thought about my father. But these last few weeks . . ." I glared at Rowan. "I suppose that's your doing. Somehow."

"Maybe it's just being back in summer stock."

"Yeah. Right. And those were Wiccans in the woods at Midsummer."

He folded his napkin neatly and laid it beside his plate. "You're very good at that. Using anger or humor to turn aside questions that are too personal."

"And you're not?"

"Yes. We've both developed similar methods of coping with the circumstances of our lives. I'm not sure whether they've helped us or hurt us. But we *have* learned to cope."

"Lunch and psychoanalysis. It's my lucky day."

I wanted to take back the words as soon as I spat them out. Not only did they sound hateful, but they proved his point.

I wasn't stupid. I knew all about using anger to hide fear. Making fun of myself before someone else could. Slipping into whatever role would work best for the moment. Maybe that's why acting came so naturally. I'd spent most of my life doing it. It just got so damn exhausting sometimes.

And it was really annoying that Rowan saw right through my game and called me on it.

Striving for a calm I didn't feel, I asked, "Would you like to look at my mock-up of the program?"

"Maybe later. Would you care for some lemon tart?"

"I'd love some."

The sticky-sweetness of my tone evoked a very small smile. He sliced the tart and sprinkled a few strawberries atop my piece. I waited in polite but turbulent silence for him to serve himself. Then I lifted a forkful to my mouth.

It was delicious. I could hardly get it down without choking.

After two bites, I flung my fork down and demanded, "Why do you have to push so hard?"

"Because I think you're worth it. And because I want you to be happy and I don't think you are."

I bit down hard on my lower lip.

"Why do *you* push so hard?"

I stared at my plate. "Mostly . . . because I'm scared."

The words hung there for a long moment. Then he asked, "Of me?"

"No. Sometimes. But mostly, just . . . scared. That the things I love about this place are an illusion. That after I leave, my life will go back to the way it was."

That the friendships I've made here will peter out like all the others. That I'll always be alone.

"That I'm just going to drift through life . . ."

Like my father.

The aroma of honeysuckle sweetened the air. A crow cawed, a hoarse, mocking jeer. The sun drifted in and out of the clouds, alternately dulling the silver and burnishing it to a high sheen. Rowan's long-fingered hands rested quietly on his knees. Mine were fisted in my lap.

"You don't have to be afraid of me, Maggie. Or fear that everything at the Crossroads is an illusion. I know it's hard not to worry about the future, but maybe by the end of the summer, you'll have a better sense of what you want."

I nodded mechanically; I'd told myself the same things a dozen times since I'd arrived here.

"One thing I do know—you're not a drifter. You're too strong, too stubborn. But what's the harm of allowing yourself to drift for the next two months? Drift and play and dream. Theatre speaks to the child in all of us. The part that still believes in magic. That wants to inhabit other lives, other places. That can burst into laughter or dance or song because we're filled with joy."

My head jerked up. "And believe a painted set is an enchanted village. And fireflies are fairies. And gnomes live under tree roots." I didn't bother disguising the bitterness in my voice. "I believed that kind of crap when I was a kid. And then ..."

"Then your father left. And took the magic with him."

"There was never any magic. Just make believe."

"You're wrong, Maggie. There is magic in the world. Maybe that's why you're here. To rediscover it."

"And you're here to make the magic happen?"

His gaze slid away as he studied the clouds. "I can't offer you a scientific explanation. Any more than I can explain how a psychic works. Or a faith healer. You probably don't believe their powers are genuine."

It seemed more likely that those who claimed to possess them were just preying on gullible people. But I'd felt Rowan's power before every performance and it sure as hell felt real.

"I'm not pulling any strings, Maggie. I'm more like ... the catalyst. The battery that charges the cast. And is charged *by* them. The power flows both ways. And I can only describe that as magical."

Although his description perfectly captured what I felt at the beginning of every performance, I was still astonished that he would admit so much to me.

"You can't always control it, can you?"

He took a deep breath and let it out slowly. "When I'm under the sway of some strong emotion — anger, grief, joy — yes, it's more difficult then. That's what happened at Midsummer. When I left the theatre and saw the fireflies ... I was so happy, you see. And they were so beautiful. The power just ... burst free. And they flocked to me. Surrounding me in light, their wings beating faster than my heart, their spirits singing with mine ..."

His voice trailed off, his face suffused with longing. Then he shrugged. "I suppose that sounds ridiculous."

I shook my head. "It sounds like . . . what I saw. What I thought I saw. Before the staff fed me that crap about Wiccans and their lanterns."

"They were trying to protect me. And calm Caren. She's not as . . . resilient . . . as you."

I felt anything but resilient. The things he was telling me were incredible, impossible. And yet they were the only explanations that made any sense.

"They have the same sort of power you do."

With obvious reluctance, he nodded.

"But . . . how? Where does it come from?"

"Maybe every person possesses it to some degree. But few tap into it. I haven't always used my gift well. Especially when I was young. I was foolish and arrogant. Enthralled by my abilities. Disdainful of those I considered ordinary. I made mistakes. I . . . hurt people. But I'm older now and wiser, I hope. And I hope you'll believe that I would never deliberately hurt a member of my company. Neither would the staff."

I groped for an answer that would be honest. The power that helped us during performances could just as easily hurt us if he became angry. And while the staff might have been protecting him, their manipulation still felt wrong.

When I told him that, he sighed. "Maybe it was. We're only . . . we all make mistakes. But we're committed to the cast. To your welfare. That's why I told you so much. Maybe that was a mistake, too. But I know you've been troubled. And it was starting to drive a wedge between you and the staff. Between you and me. I want you to be able to trust me. To trust the good things that we're doing here."

"And so . . . the picnic."

I should have known it was just an excuse to allay my suspicions. But the bitter twisting of my stomach still surprised me.

"This was just supposed to be fun. I didn't plan on . . ." His thumb absently traced the scars on his fingertips. Then he frowned and folded his hands. "It's been a long time since I've talked with anyone. About myself."

It sounded like the truth. If he was using his power to convince me, I couldn't detect it. And he seemed as genuinely uncomfortable as I did.

"I'm not exactly a whiz at sharing, either," I admitted. "In case you hadn't noticed. It's a whole lot easier to tell other people how to fix their lives than it is to fix your own."

"You don't need fixing, Maggie."

"Just a tune-up."

"We all need that. From time to time."

Our eyes met, held. Goose bumps popped up on my arms. Warmth flooded my loins. My flesh tingled as if his fingertips were running lightly over my body. I closed my eyes, dizzy and unmoored, wondering whether it was the intimacy of his gaze or further evidence of his power. Or just too much wine in the middle of the afternoon.

"Eat your tart," Rowan said. "I slaved over it. Afterward, we'll talk about the program."

The spell dissipated, but his eyes still warmed me, and the golden light dancing in their depths made me shiver with pleasure.

No wonder I forgot to ask about the strange music I'd heard at Midsummer.

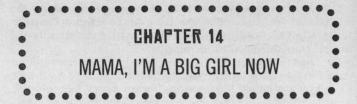

CHAPTER 14
MAMA, I'M A BIG GIRL NOW

FOR THE NEXT FEW DAYS, I was like a child torn between savoring her secret and chanting, "I know something you don't know." The mere sight of Rowan left me
giddy, excited, and a little scared. Thankfully, he behaved
like a grown-up, treating me with an easy combination of
friendliness and professionalism, and the fever abated.

Although Rowan refused to invite any theatre critics,
he did let me send out press releases. And create a nicer
program. He insisted Ashley and Bernie come with me to
solicit underwriting because people would recognize them
from *Brigadoon*. I suspected he wanted her Southern
charm and his Brooklyn folksiness to offset my pit bull
aggressiveness.

We only had to make one stop. The owner of Dale's
General Store—my Good Samaritan in the John Deere
cap—agreed to print it in return for an ad on the back
cover.

Although it was only two double-sided pages, I loved my
program. I loved the stylized waves I used as a graphic motif. I loved the fact that working on it allowed me to shrug
off the thundering silence that continued to greet my job
queries. And I loved that it gave me an excuse to avoid
working on Nettie.

I'd memorized the few dozen lines I had. And the lyrics
to my songs. But ever since my heart-to-heart with Rowan,
I'd shied away from looking too deeply into her character.

This from the woman who urged everyone else to play the "list thing." My avoidance was starting to verge on the pathological and it was a lot easier to distract myself with the program than to seek an explanation.

Like a proud parent, I showed my program to everyone. I brought the final draft to rehearsal, hugged it to my breast, and whispered, "My precious" in my best Gollum voice. Even *The Lord of the Rings* fans eyed me with misgiving.

Helen proved more receptive. "Oh, it's lovely, dear. What pretty curlicues."

"They're waves."

"Of course they are."

"You know. *The Sea-Wife*. Waves."

"We'll get it printed on blue paper," Helen declared. "Like the sea."

Janet's derisive snort failed to puncture my excitement. I was in the zone, seizing the day, drifting happily in the world of make believe.

Then my mother called.

When I saw the voice mail icon, I prayed it was a prospective employer. When I heard her voice, I panicked, fearing something awful had happened to her or—equally awful—that she'd discovered what had happened to me.

Although our seven o'clock call at the theatre was only minutes away, I Skyped her immediately. She picked up on the second ring.

"What's wrong?" I demanded by way of greeting.

"Nothing's wrong. Why should anything be wrong?"

"You never call during the week."

We'd never had a Hallmark card relationship. Or the kind found in ads for feminine hygiene products where mother and daughter sit in a flower-strewn meadow and the daughter asks about "feeling fresh." I spent Thanksgiving and Christmas in Delaware and usually got down there for a week in the summer. In between, I called every Sunday for a five-minute "touching base" conversation.

"Sue's rented a condo at Rehoboth again. She's invited me down the last week of August. I thought you might want to join us. Get away from the city for awhile."

Vacationing with two sixtyish divorcées whose shared passions included board games and Masterpiece Theater sagas like *I, Claudius*. Not exactly thrilling. But it was still a free week at the beach. The theatre's season would be over by then. The only obstacle I could foresee was the possibility that I might have a job. Administrators tended to frown on employees asking for a week off seconds after they were hired. No one was clamoring for my services now, but—please God—that would change before August.

To buy some time, I said, "I'll have to check vacation schedules at work. Let me get back to you."

"Is everything all right? You sound tense."

"Oh, you know. Everyone's a little on edge. Because of the merger. Trying to impress the new bosses."

"Well, go the extra mile, Maggie. Show them you're a team player. Even if it means skipping Rehoboth."

"Mom . . ."

"But don't get caught flat-footed if they make deeper cuts. Make sure your resume is up to date. And put out some discreet feelers to your friends in the industry."

I forced patience into my voice. "I'm already doing that, Mom." When I wasn't rehearsing one show and performing in another. "There's just not a whole lot out there."

"I'll keep an eye out down here and let you know if I see anything."

I envisioned waking up in my childhood bedroom every morning. Sitting across the dinner table from my mother every night. Playing Scrabble with her and Sue every Saturday.

"That'd be great."

"Oh, and I meant to tell you . . ."

She launched into a story about some upcoming program she was helping to organize for the Delaware Nature Society. Between her job at Barclays, the neighborhood association, Thursday night book club, and volunteering with DNS, it was a wonder she still found time to hound me. When she started talking about another volunteer named Chris, I finally interrupted.

"I'm really sorry, but I have to run." I was already ten minutes late; Reinhard would be on the warpath.

"Oh! Do you have a date?"

"No. Just . . . a picnic. With a couple that moved into the building a few weeks ago."

"A picnic? Isn't it raining in New York? It's pouring buckets here."

My heart rate quadrupled. "It stopped. A little while ago. But we may end up going to a restaurant for dinner instead."

"I should hope so. Sitting in a soggy park? You'll catch pneumonia."

My mother was a firm believer that dampness—outside of a bathtub—inevitably resulted in a life-threatening illness. How she ever became a volunteer guide at the Nature Society was beyond me. Try as I might, I could not envision her leading screaming schoolchildren through the marshlands.

"I'll let you go," she said. "Just . . . watch yourself. At work."

"What?"

"You know how you can be."

"No. How?"

"Just be careful what you say to people. Especially in e-mails."

"Mother . . ."

"And don't use the F-word every two minutes."

"Jesus, Mom . . ."

"See? There you go. I try to be helpful—"

"I appreciate that. What I don't appreciate is that you seem to think I'm a complete idiot."

"I don't think—" Her sigh blew through the phone like a sirocco. "Have a good time tonight. I'll talk to you Sunday."

I said the F-word about forty times in the three minutes it took me to drive to the theatre. So I'd had a string of jobs. But I'd done well at HelpLink. Until they fired me. Would it have killed her to acknowledge that?

And why was it I could teach other people all about active listening skills and telephone etiquette, but as soon as I got on the phone with my mother, I reverted to a whiny teenager?

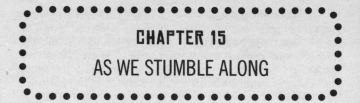
ALTHOUGH I FAILED TO RECAPTURE THE JOY of drifting, I succeeded in banishing my mother by closing night of *Brigadoon*. Twenty minutes after basking in the glow of a standing ovation, we were back on stage in work clothes to strike the set, deafened by hammering instead of the cheers and applause of the audience. After little more than an hour, all that remained of our enchanted village was a pile of lumber.

Rowan stopped by the cast party and—standing at the edge of the patio—thanked us for our hard work. He also took the time to speak privately with everyone leaving the company.

The staff left shortly after he did; they had to be at the theatre first thing in the morning to load in the set of *The Sea-Wife*. Their departure was the signal for the drinking to begin in earnest. By one A.M., everyone was sloppily sentimental, hugging those who were leaving and swearing eternal friendship.

Nancy and I escaped to the sunroom where I asked, "So what have you learned, Dorothy?"

"Maybe just that my life needed a little shaking up. I'd gotten into a rut. Work. Eat dinner with my mother. Play with the cat. Don't get me wrong. I love my mother. And my cat. But I was starting to live out the Marian the Librarian stereotype." She smiled. "Do I get bonus points for that musical theatre reference?"

"Triple bonus points."

"I'll be back next weekend," Nancy promised. "For *The Sea-Wife* and the Follies."

We stared mournfully at each other. When I first met Nancy, I'd dismissed her as dull, failing to perceive her quiet strength and common sense. A bad habit, making assumptions. It had taken Bernie only a few days to realize that. I'd needed weeks. Maybe that was the lesson Rowan wanted me to learn this summer.

From the living room, we heard Lou bellowing the lyrics to "I'll Go Home with Bonnie Jean."

Others joined in. A moment later, a very un-Scottish conga line danced past the doorway.

Nancy nudged me. I smiled. Tears averted, we hurried out of the sunroom to join them.

<hr>

Early the next afternoon, the cast straggled back to the theatre. I was nursing a small hangover, but some of the others looked like they were auditioning for *Night of the Living Dead*.

"How late were you up?" I whispered to Lou.

He groaned and shook his head.

"I think we saw the sunrise," Bobbie said, her voice ragged. "But maybe that was just the rosy glow of Hallee's."

Most of our new village was painted on the backdrop, but the theatre had scraped together sufficient funds for two real buildings. Well, part of two real buildings. The corner of the Craigie cottage jutted from the stage right wings, the schoolhouse from stage left. Both sets had been built atop wheeled platforms that could be turned by the stage crew for the interior scenes. It would have been a lot simpler with revolves, but the theatre's technology was mired in the last century.

Unlike the stylized set of *Brigadoon*, this one was starkly realistic, a symphony of grays and whites and browns. Only the beach scenes offered hints of the fantastic, courtesy of Lee's lighting design that included a blazing sunset, a ghostly dawn, and a star-studded night sky dominated by an enormous golden moon.

"Which cottage do you suppose is ours?" Sarah asked as she studied Hal's backdrop.

"Probably the one with the hole in the roof," I said.

"I'm a pauper," Bernie protested. "What do you want?"

"I vote we move to that ruined fortress on the hill," Kalma said.

Brittany grimaced. "It's in worse shape than our cottage."

"Yeah, but at least we can look down our noses at everyone."

Buoyed by indignation and family spirit, we joined the others drifting onto the stage to receive Reinhard's marching orders.

Having survived one Hell Week, I expected the run-through to be a little ragged. I failed to anticipate just how deadly the combination of too little sleep, too much partying, and a new set could be.

Our first number was a train wreck. Cast members tripped over the cottage sets. Gary's suitcase—roughly the size of a steamer trunk—became a lethal battering ram. Fishing nets ensnared anything and anyone that came within reach.

Janet fetched another suitcase from storage. Hal hung and rehung the nets. Rowan joked that he should simply give us tridents and turn the opening number into a gladiatorial contest. After an hour, the jokes ceased.

We soldiered grimly on. It took three minutes and ten guys to turn the Craigie set. The schoolhouse set refused to turn at all. Catherine was practically in tears. Reinhard's hair stood on end. Finally, Rowan shot to his feet and yelled, "Stop!"

We all froze.

"Take ten minutes."

Silence descended as he strode out of the house. A few cast members exchanged nervous jokes about the sheer magnitude of our awfulness, but most of us just shot each other guilty glances. Then Reinhard walked onto the stage, footsteps thudding ominously in the silence.

"I do not even know what to say. You stay up half the night partying. And this show, you treat like an afterthought."

We shifted uneasily at his accurate assessment. Maybe—as Romaine claimed—success had made us cocky.

Or perhaps the entire cast unconsciously expected Rowan to pull everything together. The "magic" went both ways, he had told me. Clearly, today, we had failed to hold up our end of the bargain.

Reinhard shook his head, his expression more sorrowful than angry. "Those two men spent a year of their lives on this show. They poured their hearts and their souls and their talent into it. If that were not enough, they have spent these last weeks nurturing *your* talents, *your* souls. And you repay them with . . . I will not even call that a performance. And to laugh about it afterward . . ." His reproachful gaze traveled around the stage. "Shame on you." With that, he plodded into the wings.

Lou broke the silence with a heartfelt "Jesus." For once, Romaine and Albertha didn't chide him for taking the Lord's name in vain.

Bernie thumped his cane on the floor. "You heard the man. Ten minutes."

"And when we come back," Kalma added, "let's get our heads out of our asses."

Maya slipped off stage left. Catherine crawled around the schoolhouse set, adjusting wheels. Gary slumped onto the Craigie platform, head between his hands. As the rest continued to mill around in various states of shock, I made my way over to Gary and sat beside him.

"Well, maybe you were slumming," he said, "but I just sucked. And no. I don't need to make a list of my strengths and weaknesses. They're all too apparent."

"The character's strengths and weaknesses. Not yours."

"They're pretty much the same. That's the trouble."

Many directors would urge him to let his personal pain inform his performance. While that sounded good on paper, it just felt too cold-blooded. Like his troubled marriage was merely fodder for his acting.

"You could be over-thinking it," I suggested.

"My life or my role?"

"I don't know. But Rowan said something the other day. About pushing too hard. He told me I should just drift. Or as we actors like to say, be in the moment." I nudged Gary with my shoulder and got a bleak smile in response.

It faded as a rectangle of light appeared at the back of

the house. The staff filed into the theatre. Instead of taking his seat, Rowan continued down the aisle and mounted the steps to the stage. His expression was serious, but I found no hint of anger or disappointment, although he had to be feeling both after watching us mangle his creation.

"You all earned the right to celebrate last night. But now I need you to focus on this show. Remember the passion you brought to your role-play. Feel the emotion behind the words. The emotion of Alex's beautiful music. And above all, listen to each other."

We picked it up at the scene where the schoolteacher and selkie-woman finally connect. As Reinhard called, "Places!" I gave Gary a thumbs-up and hurried into the house to watch.

"Always the Sea" was Maya's only musical number in Act One, the first time the audience hears her voice. During last week's run-through, she'd been as nervous and tentative as Gary, neither able to get past their awkwardness to capture the potential power of the scene.

But from the moment Maya drifted onstage, she was the selkie-woman. Maybe wearing her costume—a loose-flowing shift—helped her make the transformation. Her movements were slow and a little uncertain, as if she was still adjusting to her new body, her voice soft and husky, as if she seldom used it.

The verses of the song expressed the loneliness of her captivity, the chorus her longing for the sea. Alex's music—slow and rhythmic and melancholy—captured the ebb and flow of the tide. The gentle swaying of Maya's body conjured seaweed floating on the waves, foam dissolving on a rocky shore.

She began to dance—a love ballet with the sea as her partner. She splashed through the shallows with childlike joy. Cupped imaginary water in her hands and let it trickle over her face. Then, as if she could not bear the restriction of her shift, she pulled it over her head and flung it away.

For one jaw-dropping moment, I thought she was naked. Judging from the collective gasp that filled the theatre, so did everyone else. Then I realized she was wearing a unitard so sheer I could see the outline of her ribs, the taut swell of her nipples, even the faint triangle of dark hair between her legs.

The music became more passionate, her movements that of a wild creature making love to wind and water and sky. My breath came faster, as if I were the one engaged in that elemental lovemaking. When the music slowed again, I could feel my body relaxing into the languor that follows climax, relishing both the release and the strange sadness that accompanies it.

She sang the last verse on her knees, a prisoner of the land again. On the final note, her arms reached toward us, toward her lost home. That was Gary's cue to leave his hiding place where he had been spying on her. But Gary seemed as spellbound as we were. When he finally picked up her discarded shift, he clutched it to his chest instead of draping it around Maya's shoulders, as if afraid to come too close to her.

Maya's head came up, tangled hair falling back from her face. Her smile was both wary and tender. She plucked the shift from Gary's fingers and let it fall over her body. Then she led him into the dance, guiding first his steps, then his hands, drawing them down over her hips, then up to cup her waist, her breasts, her face.

Her fingertips brushed Gary's cheek. He closed his eyes and drew a long, shuddering breath. Their expressions conveyed both wonder and profound sorrow, both characters realizing that their happiness would be as fleeting as the kiss they shared.

When the scene ended, there was utter silence in the theatre. Then we all leaped to our feet, cheering and applauding

Rowan and Mei-Yin hurried onstage. I saw Gary shake his head as he addressed Mei-Yin. Probably apologizing for blowing the choreography. When she swatted him across the shoulder, his grimace became a grin. Rowan cupped the back of Gary's neck with his right hand and kissed Maya's cheek. The smile he bestowed on them was as tender as the one they had exchanged during their scene.

"I think we all need to catch our breath after that," he said. "Let's take five minutes."

I joined the rush onstage to congratulate Gary and Maya. Then I noticed Rowan leaning against the proscenium arch, watching the proceedings with a strange smile.

When I walked over, he asked, "Do you know how extraordinary that was?"

I nodded. That kind of chemistry was hard to achieve during a performance, never mind a rehearsal.

"It was perfect," he said. "One of those rare moments when everything comes together to create . . ."

"Magic?"

"Can you think of a better word?"

I shook my head.

"And the extraordinary part is . . . I didn't do anything. I just watched it happen. Like everyone else."

Another man might have felt jealousy or resentment. Or pointed out that his direction had allowed the moment to occur. Rowan's expression held only wonderment and pride.

This was what he was trying to do at the theatre. Guide us into the forest, but allow us to choose the path through it, always nearby to help us if we stumbled, but never insisting that the path he saw was the only one worth traveling.

"Perfect," he repeated softly. "Two people completely attuned to each other, completely caught up in the magic. Have you ever felt that?"

"Not onstage."

"But off?"

I replayed the usual moments with Michael during college. Reluctantly added a few from my childhood involving my father. And even more reluctantly acknowledged the quiet communion I'd shared with Rowan as we watched the clouds drift over the hills and the helpless laughter that had left us rolling in the leaves under the beech.

"Yeah. I've felt it." I hesitated a moment, then asked, "Have you?"

"Oh, yes," he replied, still watching Gary and Maya. "But only a few times. A few precious times."

His wistful expression made me wish that one of those times had been with me.

That extraordinary performance launched us into a gloriously trouble-free Hell Week. We even got time off to enjoy

Dale's Fourth of July parade. So I was surprised to catch Rowan's worried expression as he dismissed us after dress rehearsal.

Instead of heading to the parking lot, I slipped up the stairs to his apartment. After knocking a few times and getting no answer, I figured he wanted to be alone. I retraced my steps, ignoring Reinhard's curious look, and hurried out the stage door.

The air was still thick and heavy from the thunderstorm that had blown through, but the sky was clearing and the haze-shrouded moon was full and fat and mysterious. As I murmured a brief prayer for good weather on opening night, I glimpsed something moving down by the pond.

I had to wait for the moon to emerge from behind a cloud to determine it was Rowan. I watched him circle the pond, moving in and out of moonlight and shadow. Then I dropped my bag and picked my way carefully over the uneven ground of the meadow, guided only by the mercurial moon.

The night chorus of insects ebbed and flowed with my passage. Damp grass brushed my bare legs, sending delicious shivers through my body. Another coursed through me when I discovered that Rowan was standing quite still, staring in my direction.

I promptly skidded on a wet patch of grass and fell on my ass. By the time I recovered from the shock, he was reaching down to pull me to my feet.

"Are you all right?" he asked.

"I feel like an oaf, but otherwise, I'm fine. You must think I'm the clumsiest woman in the world."

"Not at all," he replied gallantly.

The moon slipped behind a cloud. I took advantage of its absence to rub my butt. Then I asked, "Are *you* all right? You looked weird when you left the theatre."

"Did I?"

"I thought the show went really well."

"Yes," he replied with a noticeable lack of enthusiasm.

"Oh, come on. Just because the old superstition says a bad dress rehearsal predicts a good show doesn't mean the reverse is true."

I attempted to pat him on the forearm, but the darkness threw off my aim. His stomach muscles quivered, and I quickly withdrew my hand.

"I just don't want people to get overconfident," he said.

"They won't."

"Or sloppy."

"They won't!"

My second attempt was more successful. Having smacked one shoulder, I groped for the other and shook him. "It's going to be great. You're not the only one with powers, you know. I can see the future."

"Really?" His voice hinted at a smile. The emerging moon confirmed it.

"I see crowds thronging the theatre. Women sniffling and dabbing their eyes. Men pretending to have head colds so they can sniffle, too."

"Sounds like an awful lot of sniffling."

"And laughter. In all the right places. And at the end . . ." I stepped back and threw out my arms. "Tumultuous applause and cries of 'Author! Author!'"

"At which point, I will quickly vacate the premises."

"And in your wake, the critics will acclaim you—"

"Critics?" he demanded in a panicked voice. "There are critics coming?"

"Nah, I was just fucking with you."

His fingers found my throat and squeezed gently. "Maggie Graham . . ."

"Strangle away. I hope they do come. Did I mention that the show's going to be great?"

"I believe you said something to that effect."

His fingers slid down my throat to my shoulders, trailing warmth and a little shiver of excitement in their wake. Then he guided my hand to the crook of his elbow.

"I'm escorting you back to civilization. Lest you end up in the grass again."

His words conjured a very different image of me in the grass—one that involved him lying with me. I kept up a stream of inconsequential chatter to distract me, but I was far too aware of the muscularity of his forearm and the warmth of his hand atop mine.

When we reached the walkway, he gently eased away. "Well. It's late."

I clasped my hands behind my back. "Yeah."

"Thanks for talking."

"Sure. See you tomorrow."

I retrieved my carryall, but as I was heading toward the parking lot, I glanced back. He was still standing on the walkway, watching me. The light of the wrought iron lamps revealed his troubled expression. Clearly, he was still worrying about the show.

"It's a great script, Rowan."

My words seemed to startle him. As I walked toward him, I saw him stiffen.

"I mean it. It breaks your heart. You keep hoping for a happy ending, even though you know there can't be one. She has to return to her home. And he has to let her go. When I first listened to it at the read-through, I thought the ending was kind of ... bleak. But now ... even though the ending is sad, it's not depressing. Because he's changed. He's learned to believe in the impossible. To hope again. And to love. And even though he's lost her, you know that—now that his heart and his mind are open—he'll find someone else. Someday."

Emotions flitted across his face as I spoke. Wariness. Doubt. A pained sort of longing.

"That's what I hoped for. What I tried to accomplish. I just wasn't sure I managed it." A smile pulled up one corner of his mouth. "Ever the neurotic artist."

"Well, as long as you don't cut off an ear or anything."

He chuckled. "You always make me laugh. More than anyone I've ever known."

"That's me. Your favorite comic relief."

His smile vanished. "You're much more than that." His hand cupped my left cheek. His lips brushed my right. "Good night, Maggie. And thank you again. For everything."

On the drive back to the hotel, I puzzled over that kiss, mostly because of what didn't happen. I didn't get all goosey with excitement. Or feel any dizzying blast of power that indicated Rowan was particularly goosey, either.

Maybe we were becoming friends. And maybe, as Reinhard had suggested, that was a good thing. The fact that I was leaving in six weeks gave him the freedom to confide in me. And it afforded me the same freedom. I was too smart to get involved with my director. He was too conscientious to allow it to happen. Those boundaries would protect us both.

I went to bed, congratulating myself on my maturity and wisdom.

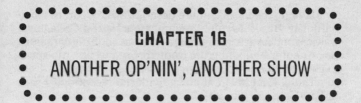

CHAPTER 16
ANOTHER OP'NIN', ANOTHER SHOW

THE NEXT MORNING, WE REHEARSED the opening number one last time. Then Rowan announced that he was giving us the rest of the day off. He interrupted the cheering to remind us about the dangers of overconfidence and insisted that we use our time to relax.

I had no intention of relaxing until I ensured that "Operation Sea-Wife" was on target. Helen had called a secret luncheon meeting at the Bates mansion. The plan was for her to distract Rowan so I could sneak up the hill undetected.

I loitered in the dressing room until everyone took off for the hotel, then crept up to the lobby. I nearly had a heart attack when Helen flew out of the box office, her expression so wild that I feared Rowan had discovered everything.

"Oh, Maggie, Maggie, Maggie!" She waved the newspaper she was clutching.

"What is it? What's happened?"

"I just got off the phone. A critic from *The Bennington Banner* is coming tonight!"

"Oh, my God!"

We hugged each other, hopping up and down like demented bunnies. Then I seized Helen's shoulders. "You can't tell Rowan."

"Are you mad?" Helen demanded, breathless. "When he's already so nervous? Oh, I never dreamed that a big city critic would come."

I suppressed a smile at the description of Bennington as a big city. But it *was* the home of Bennington College, renowned for its arts programs, as well as an Equity theatre. So any entertainment critic would bring a wealth of experience to the job.

"Thank God we went ahead with the reception," I said. "That'll impress the critic."

"The show will impress the critic," Helen said firmly.

"Yeah. But free food and liquor can't hurt."

"Oh, and look!" She brandished her copy of *The Hillandale Bee*. "'Local Playwright and Composer Debut Original Musical.'" Helen read the words slowly, savoring each one. Then her head jerked up and she spun around.

Rowan stopped short as he came through the house door, then hurried toward us. "Helen? Are you all right?"

"Of course, I'm all right. Look!" She thrust the newspaper in Rowan's face.

Rowan glanced at the headline and nodded. "*The Bee* usually puts in something."

"A few lines," Helen said scornfully. "Not a big long article. They printed every word of Maggie's press release. Isn't that wonderful?"

Rowan studied Helen. Then his gaze snapped to me. I tried to look excited and happy and very, very innocent.

"What's going on?"

"Nothing!" I protested.

He rounded on Helen. "There's more to it than this press release. Out with it."

"Well ..." Helen bit her lip. "We ... the staff ... and Maggie, of course ..."

"Of course." That narrow-eyed gaze shifted back to me, and I smiled brightly.

"We're planning a little reception."

Rowan's breath huffed out in a pained exhalation. "A reception?"

"After the show. We're serving traditional Scottish fare. Smoked salmon and cold lobster salad and—"

"Helen! We can't afford—"

"I'm paying for it. And I don't want to hear another word about it. We've already bought the food. And told the cast. It's all settled."

Rowan's frown deepened. "So everyone knew. Except me."

"It was supposed to be a surprise."

"I hate surprises!"

Helen slapped the rolled-up newspaper against her thigh. I sincerely hoped she would whack him over the head with it.

Rowan took a deep breath and slowly let it out. "I'm sorry. I didn't mean to sound . . ."

"Ungracious?" Helen prompted.

"Unkind?" I suggested.

Rowan glared at me. "You keep quiet! This is all your fault. Putting these publicity ideas in Helen's head."

Helen swatted his arm with the newspaper. "So I'm too simpleminded to think up a publicity idea on my own. Is that it?"

"You know I didn't mean . . ." Rowan scowled. "You've been spending entirely too much time with Maggie. You're starting to act like her."

"Good! I was getting tired of being Little Mary Sunshine."

Rowan shoved his fists into his pockets. "I liked Little Mary Sunshine."

"Oh! I almost forgot." Helen darted into the box office and emerged with blue papers in her hands.

"My program!" I exclaimed, snatching one away from her.

"Isn't it lovely, Rowan?"

"It's blue."

"To symbolize the sea," Helen explained. "The little curlicues are waves."

"Ah." When Helen nudged him, he quickly added, "Very nice." Then he winced.

"What?" I demanded. "Is it a typo?"

"No. It's the director's notes."

I skimmed the paragraph quickly. "It's the same text I showed you."

"It's different seeing it in black and white. Black and blue. I sound like a pretentious ass."

"You sound warm and lovely." Helen flashed a mischievous smile. "No doubt that was Maggie's doing."

"See? You're even starting to talk like her."

"Nonsense. I've been putting you in your place for years." Helen patted his cheek. "Now. Maggie and I have some business to attend to."

"More plotting?"

"Yes. A secret meeting to discuss the surprise reception. Tell Maggie how lovely her program looks so we can go."

"The program's lovely, Maggie. Really. I appreciate all your hard work. But if you have any more surprises up your sleeve—"

"Gotta run! See you tonight!"

Helen and I made it to the parking lot before we began giggling like naughty schoolgirls. "What do you think he'll do when he sees the banner?" I asked.

"We'll just tell Javier not to hang it until 7:00. By then, it'll be too late to do anything."

"And when do we tell him about the critic?"

"After the curtain comes down."

"Doesn't give him much time to prepare."

"Rowan's very good at thinking on his feet. And with so many people around, he'll have to be charming."

I grinned. "Then we're sure to get a five-star review."

❧❧

When I pointed out the banner on our way to the theatre that evening, everyone in my car burst into simultaneous exclamations of pleasure. It was very gratifying.

The dark blue banner hung on the central gable, right below the star. White letters proclaimed, "World Premiere: *The Sea-Wife*." The two lines underneath gave the show's dates and the phone number to call for tickets. I'd wanted to include Rowan's name and Alex's, but Hal said it would look too cluttered. He did include my stylized waves, though, under the show's title.

"It's beautiful," Brittany said.

"Just like a real theatre," Sarah added.

"Did Rowan approve it?" Bernie asked.

"He will," I said, forcing confidence into my voice. "When he sees it."

The usual pre-opening frenzy reigned in both dressing

rooms. Unlike our *Brigadoon* opening, however, everyone was more excited than nervous.

Hal popped into the women's dressing room, garbed in a turquoise shirt, and told us to break a leg. Alex wore his usual tuxedo, but he had tucked a midnight blue handkerchief in the breast pocket. Even Reinhard had added a navy pocket square to his usual black ensemble. Janet eclipsed them all in an aquamarine cocktail dress. Clearly, the entire staff had taken our sea motif to heart.

"You look terrific," I told Janet.

"My new fundraising strategy. I'm going to flash my cleavage at wealthy widowers."

"Let's hope they don't keel over."

Janet shrugged. "That's one way of culling the herd."

The door to the green room creaked open. All conversation ceased as Rowan stepped inside. He was dressed in his usual beige and black, but the shirt was silk and the pants were leather. In addition to the chain he always wore, he sported a pair of silver cufflinks.

"Looking hot, boss!" Lou bellowed.

To my amazement, color flooded Rowan's face. The enthusiastic cheers from the rest of the cast made it deepen.

"Yes. Well. Let's settle down and form our circle, please."

I quickly discovered why Janet and Reinhard joined our pre-show ritual. Although Rowan's voice was as quiet as ever, the energy zinging around our circle testified to his nervousness. I heard Sarah gasp and squeezed her hand. This was the first time she had ever stood in our circle and it was nothing like I had promised her.

My nerves were still jangling when I took my place onstage. I tried to focus during Janet's announcement about the reception, but I gripped my basket so tightly that errant strands of braided straw dug painfully into my palms.

The lights went down. The curtain rustled open. Ocean waves sighed over the loudspeakers. A seagull cried. Then the seals began to call, their voices sampled by Alex and augmented by strings to create an otherworldly effect that made me shiver.

As the recorded sounds faded, a pale blue wash came up on the scrim. A single violin sounded the opening notes of "Always the Sea." A second offered a wistful counterpoint.

The lights changed, revealing the chorus in still life behind the scrim: women carrying market baskets and hanging out laundry, men repairing fishing nets. A bodhran tapped out an impatient rhythm. Flutes and fiddles joined in. As the band launched into "Stranger from the Sea," the scrim rose and we came to life.

The number was supposed to offer a musical snapshot of the village: the envy arising from the Craigie's newfound prosperity, the speculation surrounding the strange woman who had joined their household, and the gossip about the schoolteacher who was arriving from the mainland. But our tentative voices undermined the tension of the music and the situation.

A jolt of energy made me catch my breath. A moment later, Hector swaggered onstage and began to sing. His boastfulness and disdain fed us as surely as Rowan's power. Lou pushed past Hector with deliberate brusqueness. Romaine turned her back on him in the middle of a lyric. Kevin pretended to spit in his direction, then quickly lowered his head over his fishing net.

I was exhilarated and terrified. None of this had ever happened in rehearsal. The improvisation fueled my performance, but I recognized that this could get out of hand if Rowan's power continued to rage so fiercely.

Just as my anxiety peaked, the energy receded. Maggie the character shrugged off her resentment, recognizing that the changeable winds of fortune might bless her family next. Maggie the actress realized that Rowan had timed his intervention perfectly. By the end of the number, the community had united to welcome the schoolteacher and the cast had come together to perform.

❧❧

When the finale ended and the lights faded to black, there was a terrifying silence. Then the applause began. The chorus quickly assembled for our bow. The applause surged as the curtains parted. When Maya and Gary came out, the audience rose to its feet.

We all did the standard "hand to the music director" bit.

I heard a man shout, "Author!" and wondered if it was Hal. Gary gestured toward the center section aisle seat where Rowan always sat. One of Lee's crew members swiveled the spotlight in that direction. Rowan rose, lifted one hand in acknowledgment, and quickly sat again.

Lou bellowed, "Speech!" The cast took up the cry, then the audience. Helen nudged Rowan, who shook his head, but when the commotion continued, he rose again and started down the aisle.

I thought his expression seemed strained, but maybe the harsh glare of the spotlight created that illusion. Certainly, he was smiling as he stepped onto the stage, although he shook his fist at Lou in mock anger.

A hush fell as he turned to the audience.

"I see a lot of familiar faces tonight. It's good to know that the friends and neighbors who have supported us for so long enjoyed the show tonight."

He paused to clear his throat. "This might have been my first original script, but Alex Ross has written and arranged the music for our adaptations for many years. He's a gifted musician and a lovely man and I am honored to work with him."

For a moment, Alex stared up at Rowan. Then his face crumpled and he ducked his head.

After thanking the rest of the staff, Rowan acknowledged the cast, adding, "As most of you know, they are not professional actors. They've left homes and families and jobs to come here. To learn about theatre, about acting, and about themselves. If you want to cheer someone, cheer them. They're the ones who create the magic night after night."

He retreated to the far side of the stage, his arm sweeping across us, his gaze embracing us. As the applause diminished, he said, "Forgive me for talking so long. I know most of you have to work tomorrow. But don't even think of slipping away without stopping by our reception. Helen's spent a fortune on the food and she's even put out the good china." He blew a kiss to Helen, waved to the audience, and strode offstage amid laughter and applause.

After the curtain closed, the cast indulged in a lot of hugging and kissing, then raced to the dressing rooms to change.

I donned my kicky sundress and joined the others streaming toward the breezeway, but kept a wary eye out for
Rowan; I didn't want to be anywhere in the vicinity when
he met the critic.

Luminarias glowed along the walkway. Paper lanterns
hanging from the breezeway's ceiling shed pools of colored
light on the faces of the crowd. Lace tablecloths covered the
buffet tables. Helen had raided the Bates mansion for serving trays, ice buckets, and candlesticks as well as the good
china. The silver gleamed softly in the flickering light of the
pale blue candles.

By the time I managed to snag a glass of champagne, I
realized Rowan was conspicuously absent. Spying Helen in
earnest conversation with a teenaged boy, I made my way
over to her.

"Maggie!" she exclaimed. "You have to meet Tom An-
derson, the critic from *The Bennington Banner.*"

I glanced around before I realized Helen was referring
to the teenager.

Tom grinned. "I know. Not exactly Addison DeWitt."

Points for knowing *All About Eve*, the all-time greatest
movie about the theatre.

"I'm a summer intern. When I read your press release, I
volunteered to review the show."

"What school do you go to?"

"Amherst." The grin returned. "Everybody says I look
young for my age."

"But you live in Bennington?"

"All my life. And I never even knew there was a theatre
in Dale." He scanned his program quickly. "Now you
played . . . ?"

"Nobody important. You should talk with Maya and Gary."

"Already did. And Alex Ross. I was really hoping to get
a chance to talk with the director, but . . ."

Helen managed a bright smile. "Let's see if we can find
him."

As they made their way toward the buffet tables, I
scanned the crowd again. When I spotted Lee and Hal, I
began edging toward them, hoping they might have seen
Rowan. Before I could reach them, a man with a mane of
white hair blocked my way.

"Why, hello there. And who are you?"

His voice sounded too deep and mellifluous to be genuine.

"Maggie Graham."

"Longford Martindale. Most people call me Long."

He just managed to avoid leering. His face was as unnatural as his voice, so conspicuously unlined that he had to be either a prematurely white-haired jerk or a generously Botoxed one.

"I don't remember seeing you around town," I said.

"I live in Hill. I'm the owner and editor of *The Bee*."

I quickly plastered an admiring smile on my face. "Really!"

"Among other things."

"Such as . . ."

"Real estate. Banking. The Board of Selectmen."

"My! What a busy life."

"Never too busy to while away the evening with a beautiful woman."

Who said things like that outside of cheesy movies?

"Are you enjoying your stay in Vermont?" he asked.

"It's lovely. Such a change from New York City."

"You're from New York!" He moved closer, allowing his arm to brush against my breast as if by accident. "Well." With one word, he managed to convey approval, lust, and the impression that all women from New York were nymphomaniacs. "You must come over to Hill. I'd be delighted to take you to lunch. Show you the sights."

I took a step back and bumped into someone. My eyes widened when I discovered it was Rowan.

Long appeared surprised as well. "Ah, the elusive Mr. Mackenzie. Longford Martindale. Owner and editor of *The Bee*. Astonishing that both of us have lived here so long without ever meeting."

"Astonishing," Rowan agreed.

"I was just urging Maggie to visit my little town."

"Alas, I lock up my actors when they're not performing. Keeps them out of mischief. Isn't that right, Maggie?" Rowan's arm settled casually across my shoulders.

The touch of his warm fingers on my bare skin brought a flush to my face. Hoping both men would believe it came from the rose-colored lantern hanging overhead, I said, "He's a slave driver, Long. You have no idea."

"Long! There you are!"

Janet sailed toward us. Well, as much as her tight-fitting sheath would allow. She favored Long with a brilliant smile, but he was more interested in her cleavage.

"I was hoping you'd come," she said.

"Well," he drawled as his gaze rose slowly to her face, "the night is still young."

Janet chucked him under the chin. "You old rogue. Come on. I'll let you ply me with champagne and practice some of your other pickup lines."

Long's astonished laugh was the first genuine thing about him. "Ah, Janet. Why do you always take the wind out of my sails? When you know I'm devoted to you."

"Like a fox is devoted to hens."

He laughed again and allowed her to guide him toward the bar. "A pleasure to finally meet you, Mr. Mackenzie," he called over his shoulder. "And you, Maggie. That invitation to lunch is always open."

I waggled my fingers in farewell. Rowan removed his arm from my shoulders.

"Old lecher," he growled.

"He's harmless."

"Show you the sights, indeed. I know exactly what sight he wants to show you."

"Another natural wonder of Vermont?"

Rowan glared at me. "It might be natural, but I doubt it's a wonder. No matter what his nickname is. And you encouraged him!"

"Oh, come on. I just flirted with him. I flirt with a lot of guys. It doesn't mean anything."

Just like that, the mask slipped over his face. "Of course. Forgive me."

I watched in astonishment as he strode off, then scampered after him, lurching a bit in my heels.

"Wait a minute," I said, grabbing his arm. "You're really pissed."

"Don't be ridiculous."

"Jeez, Rowan, you're acting like—"

"Like what?" he demanded.

He was acting like a jealous lover. But I stopped myself from blurting that out and said, "You're acting like an over-protective father."

"A father!"

"Director," I substituted, aghast at his reaction.

"Just because I'm concerned about the welfare of my cast—"

"I did it for you, damn it! For the theatre. So he'd give us a good review."

The mask slowly slipped off. "Yes. Well. You've done quite enough for one night. I suppose that banner was your idea."

I nodded.

"And that cub reporter?"

"He called Helen out of the blue," I protested.

Rowan muttered something under his breath.

"Come on. All this publicity will be great."

"I hope so."

His expression was so serious that I touched his arm lightly. "Hey. You're supposed to be celebrating. You can start worrying tomorrow."

"When we begin *Carousel* rehearsals." A slow smile curved his mouth. "And then, Maggie Graham—Helping Professional, Publicity Hound, and Outrageous Flirt—then, I'll give *you* something to worry about."

CHAPTER 17
I'M THE GREATEST STAR

CAROUSEL.

A seriously dysfunctional romance. A too-little, too-late redemption for its "hero," who dies in the middle of Act Two, leaving me to cheer up his pregnant wife by reminding her that "You'll Never Walk Alone." Plus a scene in heaven. And a real nice clambake.

As Bernie would say, "Oy."

Even the glowing review in *The Bennington Banner* ("New Musical Hits All the Right Notes") and a favorable one in *The Hillandale Bee* ("Crossroads Theatre Reaches High") failed to avert my sense of imminent doom. Nor did Rowan's speech at our read-through.

"Some of you may have seen the movie version of *Carousel*. You might have heard the song 'You'll Never Walk Alone' and found it naïve and sentimental."

His gaze lingered on me, stern teacher lecturing his most recalcitrant pupil.

"*Carousel* is neither naïve nor sentimental. It is a story of haves and have-nots. Of conformity vs. disobedience, Puritan values vs. the primal forces of sex and violence. At its heart is the carousel—this marvelous, almost otherworldly creation that brings color and light and glamour into a hardscrabble world of black and white and gray."

Not a schoolmaster, but a preacher. Or a labor organizer uniting the workers.

"Julie is not a dewy-eyed virgin, nor is Billy a soulless

194

lout. At its best, their love exalts them. As opposed to Carrie whose exuberance drains away under the yoke of a man who begins as ambitious and colorful, and ends as a hypocrite and a bigot."

The four leads reacted in distinctly different ways to those capsule characterizations. Kalma looked relieved, Nick, wary, and Brittany, a little scared. J.T. merely nodded thoughtfully and jotted down Rowan's comments about Enoch Snow.

"These are not trite, sentimental issues, but universal ones about the human condition. I ask you to remember that as we begin exploring this show together."

I felt a little ashamed of my refusal to look more deeply into the characters. I was even more ashamed of my lousy performance during the read-through. Too hearty at some moments, artificially warm in others.

During our first chorus rehearsal, I fell back on all my old theatre tricks to get through "June Is Bustin' Out All Over." So far, the only good thing I'd discovered about Nettie was that she never had to dance. Still, these were early days, and as I joined Rowan in the Smokehouse for our first private meeting, I felt sure he would acknowledge that.

He scrutinized me in silence, then said, "Take out your notebook."

I unearthed it from my carryall.

"Turn to a blank page."

Once again, I obeyed, pencil poised to scribble down his brilliant suggestions.

"Draw a line down the middle of the page."

Without waiting for further direction, I wrote "Strengths" at the head of the left-hand column and "Weaknesses" atop the right one.

"Fill it out. We'll talk tomorrow."

After my next lackluster rehearsal, he signaled me to remain. As I slumped onto my chair, he held out his hand. Reluctantly, I gave him my list.

Under "Strengths," I'd written "Strong" and "People like her." I had a somewhat longer list of "Weaknesses" that included "Bossy cow" and "Mouths platitudes to comfort Julie seconds after Billy dies."

Rowan read the list silently and handed it back to me.

"You have the day off Monday. That should give you plenty of time to write Nettie's life story."

"Oh, come on."

He regarded me coolly. "Is there a problem?"

"It's like some assignment from first-year acting class."

"Did you ever take an acting class?"

"No, but—"

"Then you should find this useful."

"You don't give anyone else homework," I grumbled.

"How do you know?"

"Because we talk about you behind your back!" Which was true, but not the best possible response. "Just about show stuff," I added, lest he think I had blabbed about some of our private conversations. "Nobody else mentioned homework."

"Nobody else requires homework."

Which was pretty damn cold. And insulting. I was the only member of the cast who'd ever acted professionally. And I got homework.

To cap my humiliation, he added, "Ask Kevin to help you. He's very good at inventing backstory."

"Great. So you have no objection if I quietly masturbate among the lobster traps during 'June Is Bustin' Out All Over.'"

"Try it and see."

I picked up my bag, but paused at the doorway of the Smokehouse to ask, "Are you doing this because you're still pissed about me flirting with Long?"

Rowan slowly closed his script. "Whatever disagreements we have had, whatever confidences we have shared, in this room I am your director. And I will do whatever is necessary to drag a good performance out of you."

"What about helping me discover what I need to learn? And guiding me on my journey?"

His expression softened. "When you start digging deeper, Maggie, I'll be right beside you."

"And until then, you'll be standing behind me, kicking me in the ass."

His silence was eloquent.

Nancy was waiting in our room. She'd come down the night before to see *The Sea-Wife* and was staying over for the Follies. I slammed the door behind me, flung my bag on the bed, and declared, "I think you made up all that stuff about how warm and supportive Rowan is."

Nancy calmly looked up from her book and said, "He *was* warm and supportive."

"With you, maybe."

"Because he knew I needed reassurance. If he's tough on you, it just proves that he respects your acting abilities." Nancy hesitated, then added, "And he knows you sometimes need a push instead of a hug."

Recognizing the truth of her words—and his—didn't make them any easier to accept. This was only Act One. If I couldn't make June bust out believably, how could I convince an audience it was a real nice clambake? Or comfort anyone with "You'll Never Walk Alone?"

I'd never liked the song. The music was nice, very soaring and goose bumpy when the company sang the reprise at the end of the show. It was the sentiment that stuck in my craw. And the high G.

"I'll never hit it," I moaned during my first rehearsal with Alex.

I might have had a chance if I was singing a nice open vowel like "ah" or "oh." But no. I had to sing a high G on "nev." As in "never walk alone." Or never hit the note.

"Not with that attitude," Alex replied. "Let's try it from the top."

We tried it. Halfway through, he stopped me.

"I know. I sound awful."

"It's not the sound that concerns me. You don't believe a word you're singing. And you look about as hopeful as a woman heading to her execution."

I attacked the last half of the song, but broke off when I heard the unearthly wail emanating from my throat.

"Oh, my God, I sound like a dying seagull."

Alex laughed. "You do not sound like a dying seagull." At my skeptical look, he added, "A wounded one, maybe."

I offered my most winning smile. "You took Lou's songs down a fifth."

"You'll sound like you're singing 'Ol' Man River.'"

"Better than sounding like a dying seagull. Please, Alex. Couldn't you drop it a third?"

"I could." He raised eyes and hand to heaven to placate the shade of Richard Rodgers. "But we're not going to surrender just yet."

At that moment, surrender would have felt like victory.

"Have you been doing the exercises I gave you?"

I nodded miserably, envisioning more late-night vocal sessions in the laundry room. The first time, I'd heard Iolanthe yowling from the floor above. By the time we opened, all the cats in Dale would be caroling outside the Bough.

"Don't strain. Sing from your diaphragm. Not your throat."

"I know, I know."

I did know. But it was hard to resist the panicked urge to throw back my head and screech out that high G.

"Now that you've got the notes—"

"All except one."

"Let's talk about the spirit of the song."

The spirit of the song was obvious: if you soldier on through the dark times and never lose hope, you'll never walk alone. As a philosophy of life, it was right up there with "every cloud has a silver lining" and "always look on the bright side." Sure, you'll never walk alone. You'll be surrounded by other misguided fools, all with hope in their hearts and the same stupid smiles on their faces.

I just couldn't buy it. But that's what being an actress was all about. Making sure the audience buys it even if you didn't.

Maybe I could channel the nun from *The Sound of Music*. "Climb Every Mountain." "You'll Never Walk Alone." Same difference. I could ask Hal if he had a copy of the film. And a set of rosary beads.

"Maggie?"

"Spirit of the song. Yep. Got it."

But of course, I didn't.

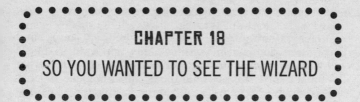

CHAPTER 18
SO YOU WANTED TO SEE THE WIZARD

THANK GOD FOR THE FOLLIES. We all needed a break after Hell Week, the opening of *The Sea-Wife*, and the start of *Carousel* rehearsals. And I definitely needed a break from Nettie.

The weather had been unsettled all day and ominous clouds scudded overhead when we arrived at the theatre. A painted backdrop of an austerely sepia Kansas hung from the two maple trees that flanked the Smokehouse. Lee had cobbled together rudimentary lighting trees by lashing lights to two A-frame ladders. As we ventured closer to inspect them, the black-clad crew members securing the cables waved us away and sternly warned us that anyone caught lurking around the Smokehouse would be summarily ejected.

After chowing down on pizza, we spread blankets and quilts on the grass and waited impatiently for the show to begin. Frannie and Bea made a final pass through the audience to collect ballots and last-minute bets. A few minutes later, the lights came up on the backdrop and the brooding music of the movie's overture crackled through the unseen speakers. We all joined the recorded chorus for that eerie "Oooo-oww-ohh," then burst into spontaneous applause.

A new wave erupted when we spotted gingham-clad Catherine running down the walkway. She cooed endearments to her stuffed Toto, then unceremoniously dumped the doll on the ground and dragged it after her on its leash.

The sight of the poor thing rolling head over paws evoked the first laugh of the evening.

Helen's entrance as Auntie Em drew applause, but I heard worried whispers when Alex appeared as Uncle Henry. We knew the staff had to double up in roles, but when the show skipped over the farmhands' scene and segued right into "Somewhere Over the Rainbow," we realized we'd have to wait a little longer to discover whether Alex would play the Tin Man as most of us predicted.

Tension mounted as we heard the familiar Miss Gulch theme. The entire cast had been waiting nearly two weeks to find out whether Janet or Mei-Yin would play the role.

A long-skirted figure on a bicycle careened down the walkway. My spirits sank as it approached; surely only Mei-Yin could pedal that maniacally. Then the bicycle rider zoomed into the lights and the entire audience erupted into screams of laughter.

Rowan had to circle the picnic area twice before the uproar subsided. He'd augmented his angular features with a jutting nose and long chin, making the resemblance to Margaret Hamilton positively uncanny. And he captured her screechy voice so perfectly that it set us all off again.

Reinhard's avuncular Professor Marvel was eclipsed by Hal's entrance in full Glinda drag. But the staff's performances as Munchkins left us gaping. Mei-Yin tiptoed on to represent the Lullabye League, then somehow managed a lightning-fast change to return as the Mayor. Lollipop Guild members Javier and Lee twitched like they had St. Vitus' dance. Helen showed up again as the Coroner, Reinhard and Alex as soldiers. And all of them—except Mei-Yin—played their roles on their knees, wearing boots and floppy shoes and—I hoped—a lot of padding.

We all gasped when a flash pot went off and smoke obscured the acting area. Then gasped again when it cleared to reveal a green-faced Rowan in black gown and pointy hat.

We alternately booed and applauded during his shameless hamming and sang along as Catherine skipped down the yellow brick road. When the stage crew flipped over the cornfield backdrop and pushed on Alex—crucified on his scarecrow pole—I tore up my ballot and just sat back to enjoy the spectacle.

Alex revealed some impressive dance moves as the Scarecrow, Lee camped it up as a terrifically gay Tin Man, and Javier hammed even more shamelessly than Rowan as the Cowardly Lion. Mei-Yin continued to astonish us in the roles of flying monkey, Oz resident, and guard in the witch's castle. Janet filled the latter two roles as well, but enjoyed playing the grumpy tree far more, lobbing apples at cast and audience alike with murderous accuracy.

The most incredible moment came when Catherine threw the bucket of water on Rowan. The lights went out. A strobe flashed, its stop-motion effect made even eerier by the sickly green gel Lee must have taped over the light. As Rowan writhed in his death throes, he really seemed to be melting into the grass. Then the strobe went out. I was still marveling at his incredible contortions when the lights came up again to reveal his pointy hat atop a puddled black dress.

There was stunned silence. Then a wild explosion of cheers. Of course, Rowan must have slipped behind the backdrop in that brief moment of darkness while a crew member placed his hat atop a heap of black fabric. Even he couldn't just vanish before our eyes.

The farewells in Oz brought another surprise. When Hal asked Catherine what she had learned, she delivered pretty much the same rant I had made to Rowan during our walk in the woods. Everyone onstage looked nonplussed; clearly, Rowan and Catherine had cooked this up without telling the rest of the staff. Hal twiddled his wand and finally demanded, "Look, sweetie, do you want to go home or not?" When Catherine meekly nodded, he said, "Then click your heels together and let's get on with it."

When the lights went out on the final tableau, we all leaped to our feet. They saved Rowan's curtain call for last. He raced out from behind the backdrop, pulled his long dress up to his knees, and executed a sprightly jig. Then he swept off his witch's hat and sketched a bow worthy of a Renaissance courtier.

I'd seen glimmers of his childlike side before, but it was hard to believe this was the same man who had lectured us so sternly about *Carousel* and sung in the woods with such passionate longing. He was a prism with so many facets that

I'd never discover them all. Yet each time a new one was revealed, it left me eager to try.

Unlike the rest of the audience, I knew we were responding as much to the power he could not quite contain as to the joy that caused it. But I cheered and applauded as wildly as the rest, caught up in the contagious excitement.

We were all in love with him. And for once, he permitted it. But only for a moment. Then he motioned the stage crew forward to accept our applause. By the time the entire company bowed, the untamed joy had leached away, leaving us with a breathless but far more ordinary happiness.

❦❦

While the staff retired to the dressing rooms to change, we gathered in the breezeway to exclaim over the desserts Frannie and Bea set out. Helen had baked two enormous cakes, one in the shape of a broomstick with *The Wizard of Oz* emblazoned on the handle in green icing, and the other, a red-frosted ruby slipper complete with iridescent sprinkles.

Hal returned, still wearing his enormous Glinda crown, and acknowledged the applause and laughter with a regal wave. When I made my way over to him, he demanded, "Was I to die for or was I to die for?"

"You were incredibly to die for. And so were you," I assured Lee. "Although poor Jack Haley must be rolling in his grave."

"If there's a bigger queen than Jack Haley, I'd like to see him," Lee replied, prompting Hal's hand to shoot up in the air.

"I totally lost out on the pool. But it was worth it to see the many faces of Mei-Yin."

"And Alex dancing up a storm," Lee said.

"And Rowan," we exclaimed in unison.

We simply had to look for the largest cluster of people to discover him at its center. His head turned, as if he felt our gazes, and he smiled.

"He was on fire this year," Lee said.

"And what about this naughty girl?" Hal snagged Catherine's arm as she passed by. "Little Miss Ad Lib."

"Totally scripted," she assured him.

Again, we turned toward Rowan. This time, he excused himself from his swarm of admirers and began making his way toward us.

"Why the big secret?" Lee asked.

Catherine shrugged. "That's what he wanted."

"This from the man who doesn't like surprises." I deliberately raised my voice so Rowan would hear. He just smiled, looking like the proverbial cat that had lapped up a bowl of cream.

"You know," I ventured, "I've always thought that looking for your heart's desire in your own backyard is overrated."

"But sometimes," Rowan replied, "that's where you find it."

In the silence that followed his quiet pronouncement, I became aware that everyone in our little group was watching us with avid interest.

I flashed a quick smile at Hal. "Good thing, you didn't try that. You'd still be in California. And Lee would be a lonely tech director."

"Maybe. Maybe not." Lee skipped aside, laughing, as Hal tried to swat him.

"Settle down," Rowan warned. "Janet's about to announce the winner of the pool."

As the hubbub on the breezeway faded to excited whispers, Janet said, "Yes, it's that time. As I added up the votes, I couldn't help noting how many people lost because they predicted that either Mei-Yin or I would play the Wicked Witch. Imagine."

"THAT'LL teach 'em!" the erstwhile Mayor of Munchkin City crowed.

"But we do have a winner. And that person will receive a grand total of ... $520." Amid the astonished cries, she called out, "Rowan! This is your cast. And your Follies. Why don't you present the prize?"

Rowan looked so startled that I knew he hadn't been expecting it. Janet handed him a folded slip of paper and graciously stepped aside. He opened it and smiled.

"By virtue of a highly superior brain, our winner is ... Nancy!"

The initial groans gave way to good-natured applause as Nancy edged forward to accept her winnings.

"That's a sizable chunk of money," Janet observed. "What will you do with it?"

Nancy stared at the bulging envelope in Rowan's hand. Then she closed his fingers around it and announced, "I'd like to donate it to the theatre."

If Rowan had been startled by Janet's gesture, he was clearly stunned by Nancy's. As a new wave of cheers and applause erupted, he whispered something to her. When she nodded, he leaned forward and kissed her firmly on the mouth.

Nancy's face had been glowing. When Rowan stepped back, it was scarlet.

"I'd like to donate to the theatre, too!" Bobbie shouted.

"Me, too!" Brittany exclaimed.

"Me, three!" Hal said.

Laughing, Rowan waved them away.

"Now there's a fundraising idea," I said. "Twenty dollars a kiss!"

"Is that all?" Rowan demanded.

"You can get a hundred easy," Nancy said, sparking more laughter and winning an affectionate hug from Rowan.

A gust of wind eddied through the breezeway, scattering napkins and paper plates and eliciting cries of "It's a twister! A twister!"

"Not a twister," Rowan said, "but definitely a storm. Those of you who are driving any distance might want to make a quick getaway. The rest of you better collect your things. Lee . . ."

"I'm on it," Lee replied and raced toward the meadow.

I lingered long enough to congratulate Nancy and tease her about the kiss. Then I joined the cast members snatching up their belongings and helping the crew move set pieces and lights into the Smokehouse. By the time we returned, the rest of the staff had opened the back doors of the barn and moved the tables inside. People groaned when they spotted Bea and Frannie packing up the food, but Helen assured them the party was simply moving to the Bough.

"Why not the green room?" I asked.

"It was Rowan's suggestion." Helen pursed her lips in obvious disapproval.

"He should be with us," I protested. "Not sitting up in his apartment all alone."

Helen went still, her gaze moving past me.

"He's right behind me, isn't he?"

"Listening to every word," Rowan replied.

He took my arm and maneuvered me away from the stream of cast members hurrying toward the parking lot with supplies.

I batted a paper lantern in disgust. "We could squeeze into the green room."

"Not with the crew. And mountains of food. Stop fretting, Maggie. I've had a wonderful evening. And two parties in one week is more than I'm used to."

Before I could argue, I heard Janet calling my name.

"Good," she said as she strode out of the theatre. "You're still here. You can drive Helen back to the Bough. She insists on going to the party. Just make sure she goes to bed early," she added quietly. "She's had enough excitement for one night. And so have I," she said in her usual strident tone. "I've got to get home before the storm hits. I left every window up in the house."

A rumble of thunder punctuated her exit. The rest of the staff wandered out of the theatre, looking tired but happy.

"A magnificent success," Reinhard said.

"Naturally." Alex wriggled as he scratched his thigh and back simultaneously. "But I'm going to be picking straw out of my pants for the next week."

"At least you didn't have to lug around a hundred pounds of fur," Javier said. "No wonder everyone was so excited when I volunteered to play the Cowardly Lion."

"I must have sweated off ten pounds in my tin can," Lee said.

"If I hear one more complaint about my costumes . . ."

Lee slung his arm around Hal's waist. "I'm just saying that I can't wait for a nice, cool shower."

"For two," Hal replied with a leer.

"But you're coming to the Bough later?" When Lee shrugged, I glanced at the others. Mei-Yin said she was leaving for Saratoga Springs to visit an old friend. The rest just shook their heads.

"What a bunch of party poopers," I complained. "Good thing I've got Helen. Where is she, anyway?"

"She wanted to tidy up," Hal said.

Rowan sighed, then cocked his head, listening to another rumble of thunder. "Go home—all of you—and get some well-deserved rest. I'll take down the lanterns while Maggie rousts Helen out."

I found her in the green room, washing out the punch bowl. As I picked up a towel, she smiled. "Oh, Maggie. Wasn't it fun?"

"Even more fun than I imagined."

"I love the Follies. They make me feel like a girl again. I was the very first Dorothy, you know."

"No, I didn't. That must have been . . ."

"A long, long time ago."

I lifted the punch bowl out of the sink, grunting with the effort. "This thing weighs a ton. You shouldn't have been carrying it."

"Now, don't you start. It's bad enough Janet treats me like an invalid." She wiped her hands on the end of my towel and surveyed the small pile of dishes on the drying rack. "There. Everything is spick and span. We'll take the punch bowl with us and leave the rest to dry."

I hefted the bowl and followed her to the barn doors. When Rowan saw me, he hopped off the ladder, took the punch bowl from me, and set it down on one of the tables.

"We can't leave it there," Helen protested.

"It'll be fine for one night. Javier can bring it up to the house tomorrow."

A violent gust of wind sent two lanterns careening around the breezeway. Rowan and I chased after them and stowed them inside the theatre. I snatched up my bag from under one of the tables and hurried back outside. Without seeming to strain, Rowan slid the huge doors closed.

"Come on," he urged. "Let's get you two to the car."

As we rounded the corner of the barn, the wind's fury stopped us in our tracks. A jagged bolt of lightning lit up the meadow. A moment later, a loud crack of thunder made me jump.

"Isn't it glorious!" Helen exclaimed. "I love thunderstorms."

She skipped down the walkway singing, "Follow the red brick path." Rowan and I hurried after her, took her arms, and slowed her pace to a brisk walk.

The first raindrops pattered onto us as we reached the parking lot. I got Helen into the car and raced around to slide into my seat. Damp and breathless, I turned the ignition and rolled down my window.

"You better get inside," I warned Rowan.

"You haven't said a word about the show."

"I loved the show! I told everyone a hundred—"

"Everyone except me."

Although his manner was as easy as his smile, I felt an immediate stab of guilt.

"The show was incredible. I don't think I've ever laughed so much in my life."

The rain was coming down harder now, but he merely stepped closer. Shoving his hands in his pockets, he bent down to peer at me. A drop of water rolled down his nose and splattered on my arm.

"You better tell him how wonderful he was," Helen said. "Because he's going to stay there until you do."

"Oh, good grief! You were impossibly wonderful, okay? And a shameless scene stealer."

"Ouch."

"I don't know how you did that whole melting thing . . ."

"Trade secret."

"But when you came zooming down the path on that bicycle . . ."

"Yes?"

"I very nearly peed my panties."

His breath huffed out in a soft chuckle. I breathed in the faint aroma of fruit punch.

"Now that kind of compliment is worth waiting for."

"Get inside, you idiot!"

He grinned and darted down the walkway. A bolt of lightning illuminated him as he paused by the stage door to lift his hand in farewell. By the time I flicked on my headlights, he was gone.

"He's such a child," Helen mused fondly.

"An exceedingly wet child."

I turned the wipers on high, but they barely managed to clear the water before the downpour obscured the windshield again.

"You'd better wait until it lets up a bit."

The violent tattoo of rain on the roof made conversation impossible, so we just watched the brilliant light show. After five minutes, the storm was as wild as ever, and I grumbled aloud that we were going to be stuck here all night. When Helen didn't reply, I glanced over at her.

"Helen? Are you okay?"

"Just tired. Maybe I *should* skip the party."

"Do you want me to drive you up to the house?"

"No, no. The hotel."

Without waiting for the rain to slacken, I backed the car out and eased cautiously up the lane. Helen gasped as the car jolted into a rut. I muttered an apology and turned my high beams on, but they merely reflected back the fury of the rain.

When Helen gasped again, I said, "Hang on. We're almost at the road." Then I realized that her gasps were too regular, almost as if she were panting.

"Helen?"

I stopped the car.

"Helen!"

"Call Reinhard," she whispered.

I shoved the car into park, punched the release on my seat belt, and twisted around, groping for my bag.

"Use my phone."

I tugged her purse off her arm and snapped it open. Feeling nothing that resembled a cell phone, I cursed and snapped on the overhead light. Helen's eyes were closed, her jaw clenched in a rictus of pain.

Frantically, I dug through her purse. Wallet, Kleenex, datebook, brush. Finally, I found her cell phone in a side pocket. I was still fumbling for the on button when Helen's door flew open.

Rowan fell to his knees beside the car. Rain streamed down his face and plastered his unbuttoned shirt against his body. He folded his left hand around Helen's fist and pressed his right under her breasts.

"Breathe with me, sweetheart."

He shook his wet hair out of his face. Droplets of water spangled Helen's silk dress and dripped down her cheeks like tears.

"Call Reinhard," Rowan said.

"I'm calling 911!"

"Call Reinhard, Maggie."

My hands shook so badly, it took me three tries before I managed to turn the phone on. I scrolled through Helen's contact list, found Reinhard's name, and punched send.

No fucking signal.

I leaped out of the car, stumbled to the head of the lane, and bit back a sob when the call went through and Reinhard picked up. I tried to mimic Rowan's calm, but I could hear the incipient hysteria in my voice.

"Is Rowan there?" Reinhard demanded.

"Yes."

"Good. He knows what to do. Try to stay calm. I'll call 911 and be there in less than five minutes."

"What should I do?"

Receiving no answer, I peered at the display and realized Reinhard had already disconnected. Shoving my dripping hair out of my face, I hurried back to the car. As I slid inside, Rowan said, "Everything will be all right."

I wasn't sure if he was talking to me or to Helen. I tried to control my desperate desire to do something, anything, and simply took a deep breath and slowly let it out. For the first time, Rowan glanced at me and gave a quick, approving nod.

After that, I just breathed in unison with them and listened to the ebb and flow of Rowan's voice. Although the rain had begun to slacken, he spoke so softly that I caught only occasional words of that gentle litany. But my breathing grew as slow and regular as Helen's, my fears easing along with the tension in her face.

Her eyes fluttered open. As they focused on Rowan, she smiled. "You're always here when I need you."

His answering smile was as tender as hers. "No talking," he scolded. "Just nice, deep breaths. That's my girl."

Her hand stirred beneath his. He raised it to his lips, then laced his fingers between hers and returned their joined hands to her lap. Then he stiffened and cocked his head.

Helen sighed. "Oh, dear."

"Hush."

"She'll make a fuss."

"I'll handle her."

Only then did I hear someone screaming Helen's name. If I hadn't realized by then that they must be talking about Janet, I would never have recognized her voice.

There was a blur of movement behind Rowan, hands clawing at him, pulling his shirt off his shoulder.

"Janet! You're not helping matters!"

The scrabbling fingers froze, still clenched in the fabric of Rowan's shirt. Keeping his right hand firmly atop Helen's rib cage, he eased back against the doorframe, wincing as Janet squeezed in beside him.

She slid awkwardly to her knees, sodden negligee clinging to her body. Without her customary makeup, she looked old and unbearably fragile.

Helen's hand came up to stroke her cheek, and Janet's breath caught on a ragged sob. She seized Helen's hand and kissed it.

"Hush, dear," Helen whispered. "Everything's all right."

"You always do too much. You never listen to me."

"Not now," Rowan warned.

"You should never have let her perform tonight. I told you she wasn't up to it."

"Not now!"

Janet's head snapped back and thudded into the closed car window. I flung open my door and ran around the front of the car, stumbling twice on the slick gravel. As I bent over Janet, she flung out her arm wildly, striking Rowan across the face.

"Janet! Come around to the driver's side and sit with Helen."

I had to repeat the words before they finally registered. Then she allowed me to help her to her feet and guide her around the car.

"I know you're frightened," I told her, "but you have to be calm. For Helen's sake."

I waited long enough to ensure that she would follow my advice, then hurried back to check on Rowan. Before I reached him, the white glare of headlights blinded me.

The SUV careened onto the grass next to my car. Reinhard leaped out, his face invisible under the hood of his rain jacket. He paused long enough to squeeze my shoulder, then strode toward Rowan, a small black bag clutched in his hand. I hung back, afraid I would only get in the way.

For a long while, the two men knelt together beside the car. Thunder grumbled off to the east and the rain subsided to a drizzle, but I shivered uncontrollably, chilled by the faint breeze and even more by shock.

Suddenly, Rowan lurched to his feet and bent over, retching. I started toward him, but he waved me away. His head jerked up. A moment later, I heard the faint wail of a siren.

It seemed like an hour before the ambulance arrived, but it was probably less than a minute. The paramedics quickly lifted Helen onto a stretcher. I heard her call my name and rushed over.

"Stay with Rowan," she said.

"Don't be ridiculous!" Janet snapped.

Helen's hand groped for mine. "Please, Maggie . . ."

"Of course," I said, squeezing her hand hard. "Whatever you want."

"Promise me."

"I promise. Please, Helen. Don't worry."

"Ma'am," one of the paramedics interrupted. "We need to go."

I stumbled back as they slid her stretcher into the back of the ambulance. Janet tried to scramble in after it, but Reinhard seized her arm. As the paramedics slammed the doors, I turned, searching for Rowan, and spied Javier helping a sobbing Catherine into Reinhard's SUV. As Janet climbed in after her, Reinhard threw back his rain hood and slowly turned toward me.

"Is Helen going to be all right?" I asked.

"Yes. I think so."

"Was it—is it her heart?"

"Rheumatic fever. As a child. The damage was not detected until years later." With an obvious effort, he dragged his gaze from the ambulance and forced a smile. "You did everything right."

"I didn't do anything." Again, I searched for Rowan. In the twin beams of my headlights, I saw him leaning over the stone wall, watching the ambulance pull into the road.

"Go back to the hotel." Reinhard raised his voice to be heard over the siren's wail. "Get out of those wet clothes."

"I have to stay with Rowan."

"What?"

"I promised Helen."

Reinhard grabbed my shoulders. "You cannot stay with him! Not tonight!"

His ferocious expression made me quail. He must have noticed because he relaxed his punishing grip. "Rowan is too upset."

"He seemed . . . okay. Considering."

"That was for Helen. Trust me when I tell you that he is very upset."

"All the more reason I should stay, then."

"You don't understand! When he's like this, he can become . . . unpredictable."

"His power, you mean."

Reinhard's hands slid off my shoulders.

"He told me about it. How it sometimes . . . gets away from him."

"Then you should realize—"

"I promised Helen!"

Reinhard glared at me. "All right! You will stay. But not alone." He paced restlessly, muttering to himself. "Alex will already be on the way to the hospital. And Mei-Yin is halfway to Saratoga Springs by now. But Lee, maybe. Yes. Lee."

"You think Rowan might . . . hurt me?" I asked in a small voice.

Reinhard's head jerked toward me. "Never! But all the same, I will call Lee. And until he gets here, you will wait in your car."

"Reinhard!" Javier called. "Can we go? Catherine's a wreck and Janet's even—"

"Coming!" Reinhard seized my shoulders again. "You will wait in the car, yes?"

"Yes."

His stern expression softened. "Try not to worry. Helen is in good hands. I will call as soon as I have news."

I watched him carefully turn his SUV, then thunder back up the lane. The red glow of his taillights receded, then disappeared as he turned into the road. His headlights raked the stone wall, but Rowan was gone.

The rain had stopped, but drops of water slid off my car and spattered onto the gravel. It was about as soothing as Chinese water torture.

I got in the car and drove to the top of the lane where I poked my head out the window and called Rowan's name. Getting no response, I made a slow U-turn, scanning the grounds for any sign of him, then drove back to the parking lot.

The stage door hung ajar. Either he'd left it open in his headlong flight to Helen's side or on his despondent return. Clearly, he'd sensed something was wrong. And just as clearly, Janet shared that uncanny knack. Maybe they all did. That would explain why they had been waiting in the meadow after my tumble in the woods, why they had arrived so quickly at Midsummer.

I thrust aside those speculations and tried to do the same with my fears for Helen. As Reinhard had said, she was in good hands. But God only knew how long it would take to get to a hospital. Could the paramedics do more for her than Rowan? Obviously, his power wasn't strong enough to heal her or he would have done so years ago. But just calming her wasn't enough to avert a heart attack. Or maybe it was. Maybe that's why he'd gotten sick.

I shook my head impatiently. There was nothing I could do for Helen now except honor the promise I'd made. Even if it meant breaking the implicit one I had given Reinhard.

I opened the glove compartment, took out the pack of batteries I'd bought after Midsummer, and popped them into my flashlight. Then I set off in search of Rowan.

CHAPTER 19
IT'S A CHEMICAL REACTION, THAT'S ALL

WHEN I REACHED THE APARTMENT, I understood Reinhard's reluctance to let me stay behind. Rowan had flung the door open with such force that the hinges were nearly ripped out of the doorframe. Papers were strewn across the floor of the office. His wooden desk chair lay on its side amid a jumbled heap of books.

I hesitated on the landing and called Rowan's name. Then I cautiously went inside.

The bedroom was empty. So was the enormous living area I discovered through the other door in the office. At another time, I might have lingered to admire it. Instead, I headed back down the stairs.

I made a quick inspection of the theatre, although I doubted I would find him there. At Midsummer, he had sought the comfort of the woods. Likely, he had done so again. But I searched the outbuildings and the grounds, calling his name as I crisscrossed the meadow and circled the pond.

I hesitated at the trailhead before reluctantly admitting that I'd never be able to find my way to the cottage. I shouted his name once more; the only answer I received was the plaintive sigh of the wind through the trees.

Soaked and shivering, I trudged back toward the theatre. I kept recalling my last glimpse of him, straining against the stone wall as if he wanted to leap over it and race after the ambulance.

I froze, then started to run.

I was breathless by the time I reached the big maple at the corner of the property. Panting, I swept the flashlight's beam across the wall. A soft whimper escaped me. I'd been so certain I would find him here, as close to Helen as he could manage.

I edged closer, wincing as wet stones scraped my thigh. The flashlight picked up something pale. Half-hidden by the tree. Bracing my left hand on the maple's trunk, I peered behind it.

Rowan had wedged himself into the small space between the roots of the maple and the corner of the wall. His back rested against the tree, knees pulled tight against his chest. Torn between relief and anger, I opened my mouth to berate him for refusing to answer my calls. I closed it again when I saw that he was rocking back and forth, his expression utterly blank.

"Rowan?"

I crouched by the tree, squeezed my hand past the trunk, and touched his arm. No reaction. He didn't even blink when I shone the beam of the flashlight in his eyes.

I curled my fingers around his and flinched when I felt their chill. I pleaded with him to respond. Assured him that Helen was going to be all right. Begged him to come back with me to the theatre. Threatened to smack him if he didn't.

His blank expression terrified me. This wasn't the controlled mask I had seen before. It was the face of madness.

My breath caught on a sob. "Please, Rowan. Don't do this. You're scaring me."

The incessant rocking stopped for just a moment, then resumed.

Was that the way to reach him? By reminding him of his responsibility to a member of his cast? It had brought him back to us after Midsummer. Maybe it could bring him back to me now.

"Rowan. Please. I need you."

Again, the rocking stopped. Slowly, his head turned toward me. I dropped the flashlight and seized his face, trapping it before he could turn away again.

"I need you to come back to the theatre with me."

Without waiting for a response, I grabbed his hand, then the flashlight, and tugged him to his feet. He lurched forward, knocking me against the wall, and I bit back a cry.

I pulled his arm around my waist and draped mine around his. Just as he had that day in the woods. Reeling like two drunks coming home from a bender, we staggered toward the theatre.

The chill from his body radiated through mine. I was shivering so hard I could barely keep up my stream of soothing chatter. When I realized I was babbling the same sort of platitudes I sang about in "You'll Never Walk Alone," I shut up.

I considered retrieving my bag from my car, but decided it was more important to get Rowan warm. I could always use his phone to call Reinhard. By now, I was pretty sure I needed backup. Short of repeating my mantra about needing him, I had no idea how to reach Rowan.

Only when we arrived at his apartment did I realize he was barefoot. I winced, imagining the gravel lacerating his feet. I picked a path through the papers strewn across the floor. He just marched across them, leaving what I hoped were mud stains on the pages.

I poked my head into the bathroom. It was surprisingly large with a stall shower in one corner and a claw-footed tub tucked under the eaves. While a shower might be easier, a bath would be more soothing. I turned the water on, making it as hot as I dared, and turned to fetch Rowan.

He was gone. Before I could panic, I found him sinking onto the bed.

"Rowan. You need to get out of those wet clothes."

He looked up without a glimmer of recognition.

"Please, Rowan. I need you to get up."

Obediently, he rose. By dint of a lot of tugging, I managed to remove his sodden shirt. His skin was as white as a marble statue and almost as cold.

I fumbled with the buttons on his jeans. The material was so heavy and wet that I had to slip my fingers inside his pants and use both hands to work the buttons free. Each time the back of my hand brushed the bare flesh of his belly, he flinched. By the time I finally managed to shove his pants

down around his ankles, a constant shudder rippled through
his body.

I left on his white boxers. He'd just have to deal with
those himself. But I couldn't help noting that his legs were
as smooth and hairless as his chest and arms.

I rushed to the bathroom to avert a flood. As I turned off
the water, I heard knocking and raced out again, desperately glad that Lee and Hal had finally arrived. Instead, I
found Rowan curled up on the bed, his shivers so violent
that the wooden headboard beat a steady tattoo against the
wall.

I cried out when I saw the soles of his feet, scraped raw
by the gravel and still oozing blood. I seized the lamb's wool
throw hanging on the footboard and threw it over him.
Then I hurried through the office, averting my gaze from
the bloody Rorschach blotches on the papers.

I pulled open cabinets in the kitchen and grabbed the
first pot I could find, a porcelain enamel saucepan. When I
spotted a bottle of whisky on the sideboard, I grabbed that,
too.

Back to the bathroom to fill the pan with water and
gather additional supplies: a box of Band-Aids, a tube of
Neosporin ointment, towels. As gently as I could, I washed
and dried his feet. He might have flinched as I bandaged the
worst cuts, but his shivering made it hard to tell.

In the armoire next to the sliding glass doors, I found
soft lamb's wool socks. In the chest tucked under the eaves,
a heavy wool blanket. I took out a cashmere sweater, too,
but doubting I could wrestle him into it, I stripped off my
wet T-shirt and pulled on the sweater.

I paused long enough to yank the stopper out of the
bottle of Laphroaig and take a deep swig. Then I sat down
on the bed and held out the bottle.

Rowan made a sound deep in his throat. His hand darted
out and wrenched the bottle from my grasp. The sudden-
ness of the movement startled me, but mostly, I was relieved
that he had responded. God bless Laphroaig.

I leaned toward him to help him sit up, but he just tilted
the bottle toward his mouth. Whisky slopped over his chin
and neck to drip onto the quilt. When I tried to steady the

bottle, he scrambled over the pillows to crouch against the headboard. Clutching the bottle in both hands, he drained the whisky in a few deep gulps.

A shudder coursed through him. The empty bottle slipped from his fingers. I gasped when I saw his right hand, the scars on his palm and fingers bright red, as if he'd burned them today instead of years ago.

"Rowan, I'm going to put the bottle on the nightstand. Okay?"

I kept my eyes on him in case he made another sudden move, but he simply watched me.

"Now I'm going to put some ointment on those burns."

He snatched his hand away and cradled it protectively against his chest.

"Okay. No ointment. But at least, let me clean you off."

I retrieved a towel from the pile beside the bed. Moving very slowly, I leaned forward and wiped the dregs of the whisky from his face and chest. As I sat back, two small furrows appeared between his brows. His lips moved, but no sound emerged. He squeezed his eyes shut, then opened them.

"Maggie?"

I was so happy I flung out my arms. He shrank back against the headboard.

"I'm sorry. I won't touch you," I said.

A new wave of shivering overcame him. He fumbled for the blankets that lay in a tangled heap at the foot of the bed. As I reached out to help him, he shook his head wildly.

"Go," he grated between clenched teeth.

"I just want to—"

"Go!"

"I promised Helen I'd stay with you."

He moaned, a soft, terrible sound. The temperature in the apartment suddenly plummeted, and I glanced at the sliding glass doors to see if they were open.

A wave of nausea made my stomach clench. Bile rose in my throat. Gagging, I slid off the bed and stumbled toward the bathroom, only to draw up short as rage flooded my body. I gripped the doorframe, fighting the urge to beat my fist against it, but I couldn't contain the furious scream that tore free from my throat. I was still standing there, panting, when grief overcame me. A sense of loss and despair so profound that I slid to the floor and huddled there, whimpering.

By then I realized that Rowan's power had burst free, that I was being inundated by his emotions, but all I could do was crouch there like a terrified animal. Even more terrifying were the answering emotions his power summoned from the hidden corners of my spirit where shame and guilt crouched, where childish anger yearned to leap into rage, where confusion and doubt and despair lurked just beneath the thin veneer of confidence.

Fear engulfed me. An icicle that seared flesh and bone, mind and spirit. A remorseless knife that shredded my pitiful barriers. A merciless fire that illuminated the shadowy places of memory.

I no longer knew where his pain ended and mine began. I was the boy, helplessly clawing at the cold fire burning his neck. I was the child, battering her fists against the windowpane as her father drove away. The young man, howling his despair to the forest. The young girl, muffling hers in a pillow.

Pain gripped my throat, choking off hope as well as breath. And then strong arms encircled me, lifted me, cradled me. Gentle hands smoothed my hair. A soft voice whispered my name, calling me back.

The mindless fear ebbed. The pain receded to a dull throb that shuddered inside of me with each breath. He soothed me with the calming tones I knew so well, but his voice shook as helplessly as his body and his teeth chattered as he told me not to cry.

His damp hair brushed my forehead. His racing heartbeat thudded under my hand. Goose bumps crawled up my legs. Dully, I noted that I was sitting on his lap, the chill of his thighs seeping into mine. Yet the fingers that wiped away my tears were warm. He must be making them warm. Drawing on his power to chase away the cold as surely as he had used it to drive the demons back to their dark places.

As I groped feebly for the blankets, he seized the lamb's wool throw and wrapped it around my shoulders. For a moment, I simply basked in the warmth and softness. Then I reached for the wool blanket. He tried to wrap that around me, too, but I batted his hands away. Together, we managed to drag it over our legs.

I leaned back into the curve of his shoulder and he rocked me gently, murmuring words too soft to understand. His hand stroked my back, up and down, up and down, the rhythm as soothing as the soft flow of words. Then he fell silent and I just rested against him, breathing in the sweet aroma of honeysuckle and the rain-washed scent of his flesh.

"I'm sorry," he whispered. "I never meant—"

I pressed my fingertips to his lips and felt him catch his breath. Then he let it out in a shaky sigh.

I cupped my hand against the curve of his jaw and traced the outline of his mouth with my thumb. His lips parted. He captured my thumb between his teeth and bit down just hard enough to still its movement.

Molten heat coiled between my legs. Delicate pinpricks of desire tightened my nipples.

Suddenly, the room was stifling. Sweat beaded my forehead and trickled down my sides. I kicked the blankets off, but if anything, the air grew hotter.

Rowan groaned. His tongue scraped against my thumb, sandpaper-rough like a cat's. Before I could do more than register the sensation, another wave of heat seared me. I pressed my thighs together, seeking to contain it, control it, and moaned when I felt the hard ridge of his erection. The waves came faster as I rocked against it, a relentless crescendo of desire I could neither contain nor control.

Rowan shifted beneath me. I dug my fingers into his shoulders, clinging to him. Iron bands closed around my wrists. And then I was tumbling off of him, falling back onto the mattress, my hands still reaching for him, my voice crying out his name as I climaxed.

As my cry dwindled to hoarse pants, another wave shook me, arching my body upward, then slamming me back onto the mattress as it peaked. I clawed at the blanket, seeking something, anything to anchor me.

Strong hands grasped mine. I gripped them hard as another spasm shook me. For a moment I hung there, suspended, every muscle quivering and taut. Then the relentless wave began to ebb, echoes of desire shooting through me like minnows darting through a pool. The minnows grew smaller and slower until there was only the liquid warmth between my legs and an incredible languor suffusing my body that made me slump, exhausted, onto the bed.

Rowan's hands wrenched free. I didn't have the strength to cling to them. I didn't even have the strength to open my eyes. I heard him moving around the bedroom. Drawers opening and closing. The soft slide of fabric against flesh. The rattle of wooden blinds.

A cool breeze wafted over me. I opened my eyes to discover Rowan staring out into the night. He was fully dressed, his hands clasped behind his back. His head moved as I struggled to sit up, then turned back to survey the darkness.

"I'm sorry," he said.

The same words he had spoken earlier. Only now his tone was stiff, almost curt.

Shame flushed my body with damp heat. All I could think of was how ridiculous I must have looked, thrashing about on his bed like a landed fish. Then anger replaced the shame. Yes, I had initiated it by touching him. But that was to comfort him, to demonstrate that I didn't blame him for his earlier loss of control.

Okay, maybe there had been a moment when desire intruded on the tenderness. But it was his arousal that had propelled me into the world's fastest orgasm. Too bad it wasn't an Olympic event; I'd have won a gold medal.

Maybe he sensed my anger. At any rate, he faced me. He'd obviously had time to control whatever he was feeling and plaster the blank mask on his face. He probably kept a supply in his armoire for uncomfortable occasions like this.

I scanned the floor for my T-shirt. When I found it folded neatly atop the low chest, I shoved myself to the edge of the bed. My legs felt as boneless as amoebas. Willpower alone kept me on my feet as I wobbled forward, snatched up my shirt, and headed to the bathroom. I wasn't about to strip off his sweater under his No-Need-to-Thank-Me-You-Know-Your-Way-Out gaze.

"Maggie . . ."

I slammed the bathroom door behind me, ripped off his

sweater, and flung it onto the tiles. Then I picked it up, folded it just as carefully as he had folded my shirt, and set it on the toilet seat. Fitting somehow.

As I wriggled into my damp shirt, he called my name again. I took a moment to gaze into the mirror over the sink, relieved that I looked perfectly normal except for the tangled hair, red-rimmed eyes, smudged mascara, and swollen lower lip. I touched it lightly with my tongue and winced; I must have bitten it during my Olympic orgasm.

I smoothed my hair, then muttered, "Fuck it" and flung open the door. I marched past Rowan without looking at him.

"Maggie, wait."

I kept walking.

"Maggie!"

His shout echoed through the room. Then I realized it wasn't an echo. Someone else was calling my name. Lee.

"Sweetie? Are you here?"

And Hal. The cavalry had finally arrived.

"What are they doing here?" Rowan demanded.

"Reinhard called them. He said . . ."

"What?"

"He didn't want me to be alone with you."

Rowan's mouth tightened into a hard line. "We have to talk."

"There's no—"

He crossed the length of the office in a blur of movement. His fingers bit cruelly into my biceps, and I gasped. He relaxed his hands, but refused to let me go.

"Listen to me," he said, his voice soft but urgent. "It was an accident. I was upset."

Footsteps pounded up the stairs.

"I didn't mean to hurt you. You've got to believe that."

"You're hurting me now!"

And that—naturally—was how Lee and Hal found us. Rowan shaking me, me struggling to break free.

Rowan backed away, the mask slipping into place. Lee stared at him through narrowed eyes. Hal peeked over Lee's shoulder, his gaze darting from the damaged door to the bloodstained papers to me.

Lee stepped into the office, as wary as a man approaching a dangerous animal. "What happened here?"

"Nothing," I said. "Nothing happened."

"The door's off its fucking hinges." His voice was very quiet, but his eyes were hard, his body taut with tension.

"That happened earlier. When Rowan ran out to help Helen."

"Did you hurt her?"

Rowan made the fatal mistake of hesitating. When I saw Lee's hands clench into fists, I quickly stepped between them.

"I'm fine, Lee."

For the first time, he looked at me. "You're shaking, Maggie. And you've been crying." His accusing gaze shot back to Rowan. "What did you do to her?"

"He was upset. And his emotions got . . . out of hand." I grabbed Lee's arm to keep him from pushing past me. "It was a little scary, okay? But everything's all right now."

I flashed what I hoped was a reassuring smile, but I could have murdered Rowan for leaving me to leap to his defense.

"I think we should go," Hal said.

As I babbled agreement, Rowan said, "I need to speak with Maggie."

"I don't care what you need," Lee replied. "We're taking Maggie back to the hotel. Now."

"I warn you, Lee—"

"For God's sake!" I exclaimed. "Would you both dial down the fucking testosterone?"

For a guy who claimed to know exactly which part an actor needed, Rowan was astonishingly clueless about how to handle this situation. Or maybe, after everything that had happened this evening, his control was simply shot. The air in the office curdled with tension, as thick and unsettled as if another thunderstorm approached. That had to be Rowan's power leaking through once again. And once again, it was Maggie Graham, Helping Professional, who had to defuse the crisis before a fistfight erupted.

"Lee. Hal. Would you wait for me downstairs?"

"I'm not leaving you—"

"Lee! Please."

He hesitated, then nodded brusquely. "Two minutes."

With that, he stomped off. Hal lingered long enough to shoot me an anxious glance before following him.

"Okay," I said. "You've got two minutes."

"I don't like ultimatums. From Lee or from you."

"I don't give a shit. You said you wanted to talk. If you've changed your mind, I'll go."

"I can't talk with you when you're like this."

As I turned away, he strode past me and blocked the doorway. "I'm trying to explain."

"What's to explain? You lost control. I came."

He grimaced. His fingers slipped under the silver necklace to knead the scar around his throat. "You have every right to be angry. I can only tell you again how sorry I am. I didn't mean it to happen. Any of it. I was just . . ." He looked away, his fingers obsessively rubbing his throat. "I was upset. Over Helen. And you were so kind . . . afterward . . ."

"You thought you'd return the favor?"

He glared at me. "I told you to go!"

"So now it's my fault?"

"No!" He stalked away, kicking papers out of his way. His shoulders rose and fell as he took a deep breath. "It's been a long time. Since I've held a woman. Any woman."

I took a moment to digest that, then muttered, "Gee, thanks."

He turned back to me. His puzzled frown only fed my shame and anger.

"What?" he asked. "I just told you that—"

"You just told me it didn't matter who was with you. My grandmother could have given you a hard-on!"

"That's not—damn it, Maggie, stop twisting my words!"

"Maggie?" Lee shouted.

"I'm coming!" I called. Then winced at that infelicitous choice of words.

As I headed to the door, Rowan said, "I wanted *you*. Not any woman. You."

I paused and gripped the doorframe.

"Blame me for losing control. For failing to shield you from my emotions. For letting you feel things you should never have felt. But don't blame me for wanting you."

I slowly turned to him. "I don't blame you for any of those things."

The taut lines of his face relaxed and his fingers slipped away from his neck.

"I blame you for turning your back on me. You left me lying there on the bed, trying to make sense of what had just happened. And when you looked at me . . ." I bit my lip and winced. "You made me feel stupid and ugly and ashamed."

His hand had risen to his throat again as I spoke, his expression changing from guilt to shock to pain.

Lee shouted up to me. The urgency in his voice made me obey. I heard Rowan call my name, but I just bolted down the stairs and let the boys hustle me out to the parking lot.

CHAPTER 20
STRONG WOMAN NUMBER

LEE INSISTED I SPEND THE NIGHT WITH THEM. I was too tired to argue.

Hal drove my car back to the hotel, while I rode with Lee in his pickup. Other than asking me if I was all right, we made the drive in silence.

That was easier to deal with than Hal's nervous stream of conversation. While I threw a few clothes into my carryall, he apologized for the length of their shower and their failure to check messages as soon as they emerged, voiced his concern for Helen, and described their anxious drive to the theatre.

"When we saw the door hanging off its hinges ... and Rowan shaking you ... and your scared little face ..."

"I wasn't scared."

Then. But now I was shaking.

"Lee's got this protective thing. And you do not want to fuck with him when it clicks on. He gets quiet. Scary quiet. And when he got scary quiet tonight, I was sure he and Rowan were going to kill each other. I'm awful in those situations. I just stand there like a deer in the headlights. But you! My God. You were like ... Bette Davis. Or Susan Hayward. Or—is that all you're taking?"

"It's only one night, Hal."

When I followed them into their small bungalow a few miles out of town, I almost smiled. The simple but elegant furnishings of the living room reflected Lee's tastes. The

mink stole draped atop one of the bookcases clearly reflected Hal's—as did the curio cabinet crammed with personal photographs, candles, small vases of dried flowers,
music boxes, two silver goblets, and assorted figurines of
naked male gods.

I excused myself to take a shower, explaining that I
wanted to get out of my damp clothes. The dampness that
bothered me most was the one in my panties. I didn't need
that little memento of the evening.

Yet in spite of my Olympic orgasm, I was more troubled
by the Vulcan mind meld that had preceded it and Rowan's
Spock-like coldness afterward. The roller coaster of emotions had left me numb, but whenever I recalled that awful
flood of memories, I started shaking again. Anger might
have provided a safe refuge, but it required too much energy.

So did the effort to keep up a good front for the boys.
Hal plied me with food and wine and more nervous conversation. Lee just watched me. It was hard to say which was
more unnerving. After a half hour, I pleaded exhaustion
and escaped into the spare room. I'd just crawled into bed
when I heard a soft knock at the door.

Stifling a groan, I called out, "Come in."

Lee walked in, one hand covering the mouthpiece of his
portable phone. "It's Reinhard. For you."

I shrank deeper into the bedding.

"Just let him know you're okay."

Reluctantly, I accepted the phone. Lee walked out, closing the door behind him.

"Reinhard? How's Helen?"

"Stable. She's sleeping now."

"Are they going to operate or . . .?"

"Her cardiologist wants to see how she responds to the
medication first. What happened with Rowan?"

"Nothing."

Silence. Then: "I'll be there in half an hour."

"Reinhard, I'm fine. Just really tired. And I know you
must be, too. Can't the post mortem wait until tomorrow?"

Another silence, longer than the first. "All right." After a
brief hesitation, Reinhard added, "How is he?"

I had to take a deep breath before I trusted my voice.

"He's okay. Now. But he was practically catatonic at first. He wouldn't talk. He didn't even recognize me. And then ..."

I broke off, damning my shaking voice.

"He did not hurt you?" Reinhard demanded. "The door, yes. But Lee said—"

"He didn't hurt me." I touched my arm and winced; I'd have bruises tomorrow.

"I should have known better than to leave you there. To expect you to stay in your car. I am a foolish old man. And you! You are a foolish, stubborn, softhearted young woman." He sighed. "But. It is done. Are you really all right?"

"I'm really all right."

"I have office hours in the morning. I will meet you at the hotel at one o'clock. And if you are not there—"

"You'll hunt me down and kill me."

"Kill you, no. But a tongue-lashing? Yes! That I will give you."

I shivered, recalling the rough scrape of Rowan's tongue against my thumb. Or had I imagined that?

"Maggie?"

"How's Janet?" I asked quickly.

"I gave her enough sedatives to knock out an elephant. Alex is staying with her tonight. Are you sure you don't want me to come over?"

"I'm sure."

"Then sleep, *liebchen*. Things will look brighter tomorrow."

My throat closed. I made some inarticulate sound of agreement and hurriedly ended the call.

Moments later, there was another soft knock at the door. I opened it, handed the phone to Lee, and said, "I'm meeting him for lunch tomorrow."

Lee smiled for the first time since taking me under his wing. He was too nice a guy to be relieved at the prospect of passing me off to someone else. Likely, he was convinced that Reinhard would get the whole story out of me and ensure that I was as fine as I claimed to be.

I crawled back into bed. Listened to the low murmur of conversation from the other room. Heard Hal shuffle off to

bed. Waited for Lee to follow. The narrow rectangle of light
beneath my door told me he was still sitting in the living
room. I wondered if he was sleepless, too, or keeping vigil
until he was certain I had drifted off.

I'd never had so many men looking after me. Reinhard.
Hal. Lee.

And then there was Rowan. But I wasn't going to think
about him.

Yeah. Right.

Hal prepared an enormous breakfast and urged me to
spend the morning with him, but I begged off. I'd been
restless and edgy from the moment I had awakened and
doubted I'd be very good company. Besides, I had a million
chores to do.

But once Lee dropped me off at the hotel, I couldn't
seem to concentrate on any of them. Instead of responding
to online job postings, I played around with the *Carousel*
program. Instead of pondering Nettie's strengths and weaknesses, I helped Brittany and J.T. create lists for Carrie and
Mr. Snow. I started drafting a press release and put it aside.
I even jogged up and down the stairs of the hotel, which left
me with aching muscles, but failed to alleviate my restlessness.

By the time I headed downstairs to meet Reinhard, I had
little more to show for my morning than a pile of clean
laundry and the suspicion that I was using hands-on helping
as a way to avoid my problems both onstage and off.

I was still feeling a little antsy when we reached our destination, a rambling, ski lodgey-type inn in Hill. Reinhard
must have noticed because he ordered a bottle of white
wine to go with lunch. The first glass helped dispel the lingering restlessness. Reinhard had the grace to wait until I
polished off another, along with my salad, before folding his
hands atop the tablecloth.

"So."

I gave him the edited version of last night's events. He
probably suspected that I was holding something back, but
I knew he would not press me.

When I finished, he sighed. "I'm sorry, Maggie. Sorry you

had to cope with that alone and sorry that you had to feel Rowan's grief and fear. It is a measure of his love for Helen that he lost control that way. And a measure of your forbearance that you do not seem to blame him."

I shook my head, eyes on my plate.

"He must trust you very much. To tell you about his power. Can you still trust him? After last night?"

I reached for my wine glass, then let my hand fall to my lap. "I trust him as my director. I trust him to try and keep his feelings under lock and key. But if he gets upset, it could happen again. To me or someone else."

"To you, perhaps. But to another cast member? I don't think so. For better or worse, you have a special relationship with Rowan."

"It's not a *relationship* relationship," I protested.

"It's not strictly professional, either," he replied. "And has not been since you went on that picnic."

Had Janet seen us going into the woods together? Or maybe Catherine had spilled the beans; she'd picked up the food and had to realize it couldn't all be for Rowan.

"Nothing happened. We just talked. And ate. He showed me the beech. And the view from the plateau where he . . ."

Reinhard paused in the act of refilling his wine glass and slowly lowered the bottle.

". . . sings," I concluded lamely. "He's never taken anyone else there, has he?"

"Not since I've worked at the theatre."

I felt my face flush and tried to convince myself it was the wine.

"And that, I think, settles the issue of whether or not you have a special relationship," Reinhard said dryly. Any hint of humor vanished as he leaned forward. "The particulars of that relationship are none of my business. But the theatre is. And your welfare as a member of my cast. You'll have to work closely with Rowan during *Carousel*. Can you do that?"

"I think so."

"Do you *want* to?"

Unexpected emotion tightened my throat. Whether I wanted to work with Rowan or simply dreaded the idea of failing at yet another job, I knew I couldn't leave the Crossroads yet.

I raised my gaze from the glassy eyes of my grilled trout and met Reinhard's keen blue ones. "I want to stay, Reinhard. I want to make it work."

He studied me for a long moment, then nodded. "All right. Enough talking. Eat. You're as thin as a rail."

On our way back to Dale, the now-familiar antsiness returned. It was so strong that I squirmed in my seat, hands clenched in my lap.

Reinhard's head snapped toward me. "What's wrong?"

"I don't know. I've been restless all day. Maybe I'm just feeling the aftereffects of last night. Or I'm nervous about seeing Rowan tomorrow."

Reinhard gave a noncommittal grunt, but he stepped on the gas and only slowed when we reached the outskirts of town.

As we walked into the hotel, Bobbie hurried toward me and exclaimed, "There you are."

"What?"

She rolled her eyes. "'Bustin' Out' rehearsal? Three o'clock?" When I continued to stare at her blankly, she pointed toward the message board. "I posted it this morning."

"Sorry. I totally forgot to check. I'll be there in a minute." As Bobbie marched to the lounge, I turned to Reinhard. "Thank you for lunch. And for talking. And . . . everything."

"You can always talk to me, Maggie. Any time. Day or night."

Before I could thank him again, he strode briskly out of the hotel.

I ran upstairs, grabbed my vocal book, and hurried to the lounge. For once, playing Nettie had an up side. As I launched into the introduction of "June Is Bustin' Out All Over," the antsiness that had plagued me all day abruptly vanished.

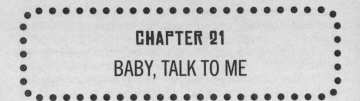

EINHARD BROKE THE NEWS ABOUT HELEN at our company meeting and quickly allayed everyone's fears by assuring them she was doing fine and should return home on Thursday. For the next few days, his daughter Bea would hold down the fort. The relieved smiles faded when he announced that Janet would assume charge of the hotel after that.

The schedule called for Reinhard to work with the chorus that morning, so it was easy to avoid Rowan. But when we broke for lunch, I found him waiting by the stage door. As soon as he caught sight of me, the mask slid smoothly into place.

"May I speak with you, please?"

Reluctantly, I nodded.

Rowan suddenly scowled and snapped, "In private."

I glanced over my shoulder and found Reinhard hovering behind me.

"You can talk in the Smokehouse," Reinhard said. "I'll wait outside."

"We'll talk by the pond," Rowan retorted. "That way, you can watch."

As he strode off, I muttered, "Well, this oughta go well."

"Maybe now is not the best time for this conversation," Reinhard said.

"Better to get it over with."

I walked slowly after Rowan. That gave me a precious

minute to take some very deep breaths. Halfway to the pond, he glanced back, frowned, and waited for me to catch up. As I drew abreast of him, he started walking again, but this time, he matched his pace to mine.

"I wanted to have this conversation yesterday," he said. "Before rehearsals began again. Unfortunately, that didn't happen."

My steps slowed. Stopped.

"It was you. Yesterday. Your power that I felt."

Rowan opened his mouth, closed it, and finally said, "Yes."

Recalling its abrupt cessation, I realized something else. "Reinhard told you to stop."

He nodded brusquely. A muscle jumped in his jaw.

"I should have realized . . ." And then the full implications of what he had done hit me. "You tried to force me to come to the theatre."

"If I'd forced you, you would have come." He grimaced. "To the theatre."

His clumsiness only fed my anger. "Couldn't you sense that I didn't want to?"

"Yes, but—"

"And you deliberately used your power to try and make me do it anyway?"

"We needed to talk. I thought that was important enough to warrant my . . . interference."

"Interference? Jesus. You went ballistic when I poked my head inside your door. But when you spend half the day poking at me with your power, that's just interference?"

"It was a mistake."

"It was more than a mistake, Rowan. It was an abuse of your power. Don't you see that?"

"Fine! It was wrong. I apologize. What do you want me to do, Maggie? Grovel?"

I turned on my heel and strode back toward the theatre. I half-expected him to use his power to stop me. If he had, I would have walked away from the Crossroads and never returned.

"Maggie. Wait."

I kept walking. I heard him curse as he hurried after me. "What I did was wrong. I admit that. But I kept thinking about what you said. How I'd made you feel stupid and ugly and ashamed. I couldn't bear . . . I couldn't let you feel that way. Or believe that I had deliberately tried to hurt you."

I stopped, but kept my gaze on Reinhard, standing guard by the Smokehouse.

"I thought I was doing the right thing after . . . afterward. If I had touched you or comforted you or even spoken to you . . . I was afraid! All right? Afraid of losing what little control I had left. So I . . . retreated."

I heard him sigh and dared a glance at him. He was staring off toward the pond, the fingers of his right hand kneading the scar around his neck.

"I thought I was helping you. Protecting you. Instead, I made things worse. But I never meant to hurt you. If that counts for anything."

"Yes," I finally said. "It counts."

His shoulders rose and fell. "I'll understand if you can't forgive me."

His manner was stiff and formal again, the mask firmly in place. I'd felt only the briefest flash of emotion from him during his speech, a hot wash of shame and anxiety that convinced me that he was telling the truth.

"But if you can't trust me . . . if you want to go home . . ."

"I don't have anything to go home to."

"That's not a good enough reason to stay."

"No. But I've failed at pretty much every job I've ever had. I don't want to fail at this one, too. And I still haven't learned what I'm supposed to. About myself." I hesitated a moment before asking, "Do you want me to stay?"

"Yes! Yes. But we have to be able to work together. If we let the events of the last two days interfere with that, we won't be able to accomplish anything."

"Well, we *are* grown-ups," I reminded him with some asperity. "And professionals." Then I realized what he was really concerned about. "Don't worry. I'm not going to start trailing after you, all moony-eyed."

Instead of looking relieved, the mask slipped back into place. "Of course not." He stared at the barn, clearly eager to end the conversation.

"Okay, then," I said. "We'll behave like grown-ups and make this work. Yet another addendum to our pact."

I thrust out my hand. He stared down at it, hesitating, and I tried to decipher his expression. Finally, his hand rose to clasp mine very lightly. As his fingers started to slide free, I tightened my grip, and felt him start.

"You have to promise me something."

He gave a wary nod.

"I want your word that you'll never deliberately use your power to make me do something I don't want to do."

He gripped my hand hard. "You have it."

Everyone loves a fresh start. This one made me believe that there might be something to those sappy lyrics of "You'll Never Walk Alone." My life had been storm-tossed these last two days. But I'd kept my chin up. I'd warded off fear. And as Rowan and I walked back to the theatre, I felt almost hopeful.

That lasted about a day.

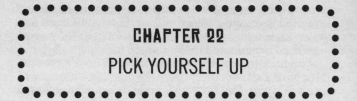

CHAPTER 22
PICK YOURSELF UP

I EXPECTED TO FEEL UNCOMFORTABLE during our pre-show circle. I didn't expect a full-blown panic attack.

As soon as Rowan's power touched me, my body was gripped by the same paralyzing fear I had felt in his apartment. My heart rate tripled. My mouth went dry. My hand gripped Sarah's so convulsively that she squeaked.

Reinhard finally eased me out of the circle, guided my tottering steps down the hall, and steered me into the cluttered production office. I collapsed on the swivel chair behind the desk and put my head between my knees.

The black dots swarming my vision melted away. The roaring in my ears subsided. My racing heartbeat slowed.

I felt something pressing against my wrist and sat up to discover Reinhard silently assessing my pulse rate. "Better now, yes?"

I nodded and started to get up. Reinhard firmly pressed me back into the chair.

"The curtain's going up any minute," I protested.

"It does not go up until I say so."

He suddenly glanced over his shoulder. A moment later, Rowan appeared in the doorway.

"I'm sorry," I said. "That was stupid. I knew nothing bad was going to happen, but—"

"My fault. I should have anticipated how you might react. Are you all right now?"

"I think she should lie down," Reinhard said.

"You mean . . . miss the show?" I asked.

"Do you really think you can perform?"

A minute ago, I would have said, "No." But I refused to screw up the show for everyone. "I may not be the greatest straw plaiter that ever came down the pike, but I'll be okay."

Rowan studied me for a long moment before nodding to Reinhard. "It's Maggie's call."

As predicted, I wasn't the greatest straw plaiter that night. Nor was it the best show we had ever put on. The rest of the cast attributed their disappointing performances to their concern about Helen and the usual bumps that followed a break in the schedule. I knew Rowan had deliberately refrained from using his power to help us, no doubt fearing my reaction.

My pre-show panic attacks abated as the week wore on, but I never completely relaxed into the energy connecting us. As a result, I felt anxious and adrift during performances.

Helen's return from the hospital cheered everyone up, but without her nighttime blessings, I tossed and turned until exhaustion finally claimed me. Instead of escape, sleep brought troubled dreams I could not remember in the morning or sex dreams about Rowan that I recalled with alarming clarity.

Worse still—if that were possible—I found myself resenting Rowan's easy give-and-take with other cast members. I'd watch him laugh at something Brittany said or joke with Bernie or offer gentle encouragement to Sarah, and I'd bristle like an indignant cat.

It was ridiculous. And appalling. I was behaving like a jealous teenager in the throes of her first crush.

Janet had warned me about the dangers. Foolishly, I had considered myself immune. Knowing I'd be safely back in Brooklyn in a month should have reassured me. Instead, the prospect made me alternately depressed and irritable.

Although I did my best to hide my turmoil, the discreet inquiries of my cast mates made it clear I was failing miserably. I was letting everyone down by my inability to master my emotions and my role. After a particularly wooden performance in our Act One run-through of *Carousel*, Rowan took me aside and scheduled our long overdue discussion of Nettie's life history for Sunday morning.

With everything else that had happened in the last week, I'd completely forgotten about the assignment and had to throw something together. Her father, the hard-working foreman at Bascombe's Mill who died tragically in a fire. Her mother who scraped together a living by opening a luncheon shack on the wharf—the precursor of the Spa that Nettie runs in *Carousel*. I decided that Nettie had taken over the Spa after her mother's untimely death in a baking accident. And although she never married, she enjoyed the universal love and admiration of her neighbors.

I perched nervously on my chair in the Smokehouse and watched Rowan's expression as he read. His head remained bent over the page for much longer than the three paragraphs demanded.

Finally, I said, "I know it's not there yet . . ."

"It's a good start."

My initial relief quickly faded. It was a mediocre start. We both knew that. At the very least, he should have chastised me for the blatant steal from *Into the Woods*.

"The luncheon shack is a nice touch."

I'd thought so, too. But for Rowan to single that out was nearly as bad as my attempt to bolster Nancy's confidence by praising her for knowing her lines.

A small part of me was angry that he was treating me like an emotional cripple. A much, much bigger part was relieved. We had never discussed those shared glimpses into each other's pain. When I tried to recall the images that had flooded my mind, they slipped away, as impossible to grasp as mist. I could no longer say with certainty what memories I had dredged up from my past. Only the pain they evoked remained real. If turning in a fabulous performance as Nettie required me to revisit that pain, I was more than happy to be coddled.

Even more unprofessional was my response to being alone with him. I watched those long fingers smoothing the paper and remembered them stroking my back. I studied the sharp angles of his face and recalled how desire had softened them. When his tongue flicked out to wet his lips, it was all I could do to keep from dragging him off his chair, shoving him onto the floor, and riding him like a bucking bronco.

Rowan cleared his throat. "I think you can do better."

For one horrifying moment, I thought he was referring to the bucking bronc scenario. Then I realized he was critiquing what I had written. I babbled agreement and fled.

As I reached the top of the lane, my cell phone erupted into the screeching strings of the *Psycho* ringtone. Groaning, I dug it out of my bag.

"Hey, Mom. I meant to call you earlier, but—"

"What's wrong?"

"Nothing's wrong. Why should anything be wrong?"

"You sound strange."

"It must be the phone. It's been conking out a lot lately. What's up?"

"I was wondering if you'd had a chance to check on those dates." As I sat there in clueless bewilderment, she added, "Maggie? Are you still there?"

"Yeah."

"You're breaking up."

In more ways than one.

As I got out of the car, she said, "Oh, that's better. Anyway. About the beach . . ."

I silently cursed. "I'm working on it."

"If you don't want to go . . ."

"I do! It's just hard working around everybody's schedules."

"Because if you don't, you can just say so."

"I'll pin them down this week."

"I wouldn't pester you except Sue's daughter—Leila? The flaky one? She just told Sue she's getting married. And naturally, she's chosen the week we're at Rehoboth. So Sue won't be able to come down at all now."

"Leila's getting married in a month and she springs it on her mother now?"

"It gets better. She met her fiancé in June."

I'd met Rowan in May. It seemed like two years ago instead of two months.

"At this retreat center near Seattle. Or Sedona. I forget."

Not that we were getting married. We weren't even lovers. Technically. The Olympic orgasm didn't really count.

"They were there for some wacky Midsummer ritual."

Leila and I should compare notes. I was pretty sure the

Dance of the Fireflies trumped anything in Seattle. Or Sedona.

"And get this: she's decided to become a shaman. Can you imagine?"

Actually, I could. Since coming to the Crossroads, my concept of what was possible had changed a lot.

"They're holding the wedding in a field. A three-day celebration. With everyone camping out in tents. Naturally, Sue's booked a room at the Hyatt."

Weren't shamans supposed to be able to summon elemental energy? I wasn't sure about summoning free-floating orgasms, but Leila might have some insights into Rowan's power and my reaction to it. Maybe that's all that had been going on this week—the residue of his power niggling at me. That would be a relief.

"Do you have Leila's e-mail address?" I asked.

"I could get it from Sue. Why?"

"I just thought I'd write and congratulate her."

"You don't even like Leila."

"Well. It would be a nice gesture."

There was a long silence. I could practically see the wheels turning in my mother's head.

"Maggie. You haven't gotten caught up in that New Agey stuff, have you?"

"No, I just want to—"

"Because a lot of those groups are practically cults."

"I'm not joining a cult, Mom."

"That's what those Manson Family girls probably said."

"Mother . . ."

"And the ones who drank the poisoned Kool-Aid."

"I am not—"

"That's what they do. Those cult leaders. Prey on susceptible people and fill their heads with nonsense and shovel drugs into them. And then . . ."

And then I realized what was behind this.

"I'm not Daddy."

Another long silence greeted my pronouncement. Then a sigh gusted over the phone. "I know. You've always been level-headed. Except for the theatre thing."

I winced.

"Which—thank God—you got over."

"Right. So. I'll let you know about the beach, but I've got to run now."

"Do you have a date?"

"No, Mom. Still no date. Just meeting some friends for brunch. I'll talk to you soon."

When I got back to the hotel and booted up my laptop, I found an e-mail from her with Leila's contact information. I added a fresh load of guilt to the ever-accumulating pile, shot off a quick thank you, and crafted a message to Leila that I immediately deleted. Whatever had happened with Rowan, flaky Leila wasn't the one to help me make sense of it.

I spent Monday morning working on Nettie's life history. When I went out onto the porch to check my phone for messages, I discovered two, both from New York area codes. One turned out to be from the United Way, the other from a victims' assistance center in the Bronx where I'd applied as supervisor of their hotline.

Stunned by the sudden change in my employment prospects, I Skyped them both and tried to sound professional and intelligent and not completely desperate. Then I discovered they were scheduling interviews the following week. Hell Week and the opening of *Carousel*.

I pleaded a family emergency to one, an out-of-town conference to the other. No dice. It was next week or never. In two months, these were the only places that had shown a glimmer of interest. I couldn't blow them off.

I tentatively scheduled interviews for Monday, then called Reinhard. He was less than thrilled that I'd miss part of Sunday's rehearsal and most of Monday's, but he agreed that I had to take the interviews. Since I couldn't very well oust the woman subletting my apartment, I called a Help-Link colleague who lived in Riverdale and arranged to stay with her Sunday night.

I gave up any attempt at figuring out Nettie's life and concentrated on mine. I did some additional research on both organizations and worked up a set of questions to ask during my interviews. Then, flash drive in hand, I hurried downstairs to ask Bea to let me into the office to use the printer. My steps slowed when I saw Janet behind the front desk.

I hadn't seen her since Helen's heart attack. She was as impeccably dressed as ever, but the dark circles under her eyes testified to the stress of the last week.

I hadn't seen Helen, either. Janet had left firm instructions that she was to have no visits or calls until next week, so I'd made do with handing get well cards to Helen's home health aide. The staff was clearly exempt from Janet's restrictions; at every lunch and dinner break, they made pilgrimages up the hill. Except Rowan. I hated to think he would allow that ancient feud to keep him from seeing Helen. Maybe he just preferred visiting when no one was around.

I put on a bright smile as I approached the desk and asked, "How's Helen?"

"She had breakfast on the patio this morning."

"That's great!"

"She'll be as weak as a kitten for the rest of the day. If she cajoles that goddamn aide into letting her walk in the garden, I'll kill them both."

Janet lifted one end of the inbox, unceremoniously dumping Iolanthe onto the desk. The cat shot her an irritable green-eyed glare and began repairing her ruffled dignity. As I watched the small pink tongue lapping against her fur, unwelcome heat suffused my body.

Finding Janet's gaze on me, I quickly asked, "So how are you holding up?"

"I always hold up. That's my role in life."

Abandoning any further attempt to play Helping Professional, I said, "I wrote up a press release for *Carousel*. And drafted a program. I still need Rowan's director's notes, though."

"I'll remind him at our staff meeting."

"Thanks. I'll print out the current draft for you. And if you wouldn't mind, I wondered if I could print out some personal stuff. I've got two interviews next week—"

"You're going on interviews during Hell Week?"

"I couldn't put them off."

"Have you told Rowan?"

"I told Reinhard."

Janet studied me, then brusquely beckoned me into the office. To my dismay, she followed me inside and closed the door.

The small office was filled with little Helen touches: the flowered wallpaper, the botanical prints, the bulletin board littered with cards and photos and cheerful sayings. Janet seated herself on the wooden Windsor chair in front of the file cabinet and lit a cigarette. I worked as fast as I could, conscious of her eyes watching me through the haze of smoke.

"I hear you had an eventful week, too," she remarked. As I babbled something about rehearsals, she added, "I was referring to Sunday night."

I took a deep breath. "Well, Rowan was in bad shape when I found him. But I got him inside and he came out of his daze and then—"

"You had sex with him."

My jaws closed and opened and closed again like a broken nutcracker. I stared up at a little card on the bulletin board that read, "Though time be fleet and I and thou are half a life asunder, Thy loving smile will surely hail the love-gift of a fairy tale." At that moment, I felt as thunderstruck as poor Alice after her little trip through the looking glass.

I forced myself to meet Janet's gaze. To my surprise, I found sympathy there instead of scornful satisfaction.

"'Lord, what fools these mortals be.'"

"You were the one who tried to shove me into his bed!"

"And I was the one who warned you to keep out of it unless you could avoid emotional entanglements."

"Yes. You did."

"And you didn't."

"It's . . . complicated."

"I bet. So? Now what?"

"I'll get a grip."

"Pick yourself up, dust yourself off—"

"Do you have a better suggestion?"

"If it's just a sexual itch, you could go on sleeping with him."

"I told him we should behave like professionals."

Janet snorted. "Professionals sleep with each other all the time. And it might—"

"Do me good?"

"Calm you down, anyway. You're as jumpy as the proverbial cat on a hot tin roof."

"Sleeping with him would only make the roof hotter."

"Possibly." She took a deep drag on her cigarette and blew a plume of smoke toward the ceiling. "You didn't tell Reinhard about that part of the evening, did you?"

I shook my head. "Do you think he knows?"

"Probably. Reinhard's very perceptive. But he'll keep his mouth shut. And so will I. Just don't tell Helen."

"God, no! I wouldn't dream of upsetting her."

"She'd probably be pleased. You know what a hopeless romantic she is. But she doesn't need any added excitement right now."

"Neither do I," I muttered.

Janet stabbed out her cigarette and rose. "Forget about that 'road not taken' crap. Make a choice, stick to it, and don't look back. The longer you dither, the harder you'll make it for yourself. And him."

❦❦

I presented Nettie's revised life history to Rowan the next morning. He studied this version even longer than the first. Then he folded the paper in half and handed it back to me.

"Try again. And lose the baking accident."

"You thought it was implausible?"

"I thought it was a direct steal from *Into the Woods*."

I waited for the smile. Instead, he rose, obviously dismissing me.

That was the day he blocked the clambake scene in Act Two. Thankfully, Alex had cut my first solo, which consisted of listing the ingredients in the codfish chowder. So other than a brief recitation about lobsters, I had little to do except lounge onstage and remind the audience over and over again that it had been a real nice clambake.

And Rowan wondered why I didn't connect to the character.

On Wednesday, he staged Act Two, Scene 2: the bungled robbery, Billy's death, and "You'll Never Walk Alone." I didn't have much in the way of blocking in that number, either. Hug Julie. Gaze at her with determination. Face front and sing. Kalma did her best to act comforted, but when I screeched out the high G, she winced.

Rowan called a break. Then called me over to the edge

of the stage. Alex gazed up mournfully from the pit. Rowan gazed at the floor.

"The song's too high for me," I said.

"You think that's the problem with the number?" Rowan asked quietly. "That it's too high?"

"Not the only problem. But if I can't sing it—"

"Why can't you sing it?"

"How could anyone mouth platitudes about keeping your chin up to a woman whose husband just died in her arms?"

Rowan's head came up. "Did it ever occur to you that she's using the only vocabulary a working class woman of that time possesses? That by investing the words with genuine emotion you could lift them above what you insist on calling platitudes? How can Julie believe anything Nettie says if you don't? How can an audience? On paper, you fill this woman's life with tragedy, but none of it shows onstage."

That stung me into defensiveness. "I worked hard on those life histories."

"A baking accident?" Rowan demanded.

"Okay, that was silly, but—"

"You need to consider how events have shaped her, how she developed the strength to go on, the strength that she shares at this crisis in Julie's life. You can't keep skimming the surface, Maggie. That's partially my fault. I allowed you to get away with it. But that ends now. You asked me to be professional and I will. *Carousel* opens one week from today. And if I have to push and pull and drag a meaningful performance out of you, I will."

Clearly, the happy coddling phase was over. And so was our special relationship. Grimly, I recalled Janet's Robert Frost reference. While I hesitated at the fork in the road, Rowan had chosen the safer route for us to follow. Only time would tell whether that would make all the difference.

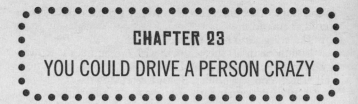

FOR TWO DAYS, HE PUSHED AND I PULLED. He told me to connect with my feelings. I avoided them like the plague. He claimed I wanted to learn about myself, but only if it was easy. I told him nothing about this was easy. He called me a coward. I called him an arrogant prick with a God complex.

That startled him into momentary silence. "You think I'm enjoying this?" he demanded.

"You sure as hell seem to be!"

A hot blast of air eddied around me as he shoved back his chair. I was terrified and delighted that I had broken his iron control.

"Is that what you really think of me?"

He looked so genuinely distressed that I shook my head. "No. I was just mad."

Rowan sighed. "Sometimes, I forget how young you are."

"You're not exactly Methuselah."

"Not quite. Although some days . . ." He shook his head. "What do you want from me, Maggie?"

He'd asked me that at the *Brigadoon* cast party, too. And I still didn't have a good answer. I wanted a breakthrough on Nettie without putting in the effort required to achieve it. I wanted the special relationship we had built up over the last month without any of the risks that might entail. I wanted the indescribable pleasure he had given me without the terror his power evoked. I wanted him to be warm and caring. I wanted him to keep his distance. I wanted to prove I could succeed at something. I wanted to drive away from this place and never return.

"I don't know."

He nodded as if I'd confirmed what he already knew. "How can I help you?"

Tell me I'm getting there. Tell me to stop making excuses. Treat me like a professional. Take me to bed. Coddle me. Demand the best from me. Do it all. Do the impossible.

"I don't know," I repeated.

"Neither do I."

Once Janet permitted the cast to visit Helen, I started going up to the house almost every day. We chatted in the sunroom or strolled through the garden. She never pushed or pried and rarely even brought up Rowan's name. I always came away calm and refreshed, but those feelings evaporated by the time I reached the bottom of the hill.

Knowing Friday was my last chance for a quiet chat before I headed to New York, I bolted a quick dinner and headed over to the house. The front door was open. Peering through the screen, I could make out little, but the house was quiet. Had her aide left early? If so, she'd be looking for another position by morning. Janet would fire her for leaving Helen alone.

No one on the patio. Or in the garden. I told myself Helen was probably napping, but my anxiety spiked as I crept into the house. I was halfway up the stairs when I heard the muffled sound of a man's voice coming from Helen's bedroom. Relieved that she was simply entertaining another visitor, I hesitated, wondering if I should wait on the porch.

The door to her room banged open. Rowan strode to the top of the stairs, his eyes wild.

"Oh, my God!" I cried. "What's happened?"

I raced up the stairs and flew into Helen's bedroom. She smiled calmly at me from her rocking chair.

"Are you okay?" I demanded.

"Yes, of course."

I whirled around and stalked toward the doorway, only to stop short when Rowan's figure loomed in front of me.

"You nearly gave me a heart attack!" I winced at my choice of words and muttered an apology to Helen. Then punched Rowan in the chest. "Don't scare me like that!" I raised my fist to punch him again, then slowly lowered it. "You came into the house."

"Of course," Helen said. "He's visited every day since I came home."

I was instantly ashamed of my earlier suspicions that his ridiculous vow meant more to him than her welfare. The wildness had left his eyes, but he looked distinctly uncomfortable. Maybe he had hoped to keep his visits secret.

"That's a really big deal," I said.

"I just wanted to see Helen," he mumbled.

"But ... are you okay? I mean ... before ... you looked—"

"I'm fine. Helen, I have to go."

She leaned forward, gripping the arms of the rocker. "I wish you'd stay."

"I can't. I can't! Forgive me."

And with that, he bolted.

Mystified, I turned to Helen. "What the hell was that all about?"

She patted the stool next to her rocker. Rowan must have dragged it over; usually, it sat in front of her dressing table. The ruffled cushion was still warm from his body. I tried not to squirm at that unexpected intimacy.

"Things haven't been going too well, have they?"

"Oh, God. He was talking about me." My head drooped, then jerked up again. "What exactly did he tell you?"

"Nothing more than you told Reinhard," Helen replied. "Who was the first to tell me what happened the night of my heart attack. Then Hal came by ... and Lee ..."

I groaned.

"Today was the first time Rowan spoke of it. And everything that's happened since."

"No wonder he couldn't wait to escape."

She held out her hand, and I clasped it. "I was the one who asked you to look after him that night. And now I'm

going to ask for another favor. Be patient with him. He's
used to being able to handle every situation that confronts
him. And he doesn't know how to handle this one."

"Handle me, you mean. If anyone needs patience, it's
Rowan. I'm a disaster. This fuck   sorry   this stupid role . . .
I just can't get it. He called me a coward the other day."

"Yes, he told me that. He mentioned your response as
well." Her mouth quirked in an unexpected smile. "People
rarely talk to him like that."

"It was completely unprofessional. And childish. I don't
know what—"

"Can I ask you something, Maggie? And feel free to tell
me it's none of my business."

I nodded warily.

"Are you in love with Rowan?"

"No! God. Please. I don't even know Rowan! I'm just . . .
confused. By his moods. And all his damn secrets. And his
power."

I slid off the stool and began pacing. "I can't think
straight. About him. Or the show. Or stupid Nettie. I'm
afraid of this role and I don't know why and Rowan doesn't
know how to help me. He can't even stand to be in the same
room with me! And now I've got these interviews and my
mind's in a million places and I'm supposed to be a helping
professional and the one person I can't help is me! I just
want . . ."

"What, dear?"

"To get out of here! To get some perspective. I can't eat.
I can't sleep. I can't concentrate. It's exhausting."

I slumped into the armchair by the window and closed
my eyes. That outburst had been exhausting, too. If cathar-
tic. But the last thing I should have done was pour out my
woes to Helen. Janet would kill me.

Fingertips brushed my hand, and I started; I hadn't even
heard Helen approach. To my relief, she didn't seem upset.
Just as Janet had predicted, she looked pleased.

She opened her arms, and I leaped to my feet. Her embrace enfolded me with warmth and calm. When she released me, I stepped back and forced a smile.

"See? That's the problem. You haven't been around to

bless me at night or give me hugs on demand. No wonder I'm a wreck."

"You're too hard on yourself," she scolded. "And on Rowan. This isn't easy for him, either."

"You won't tell him what I said? He already thinks I'm a basket case. I don't want him to think I'm turning into a stalker, too."

"Maybe the two of you need to go on another picnic."

"Oh, God! Did Reinhard tell you?"

"Goodness, no. I knew as soon as Catherine told me about all the food he'd ordered." Helen gazed out the window, her expression tender, almost wistful.

"He's taken you there, too," I said slowly. "To the beech."

"A long time ago."

Why had Reinhard lied? No. He hadn't lied. He'd just said that Rowan had never taken anyone there since he had joined the staff.

I hesitated, then decided to take the plunge. "Can I ask you something, Helen? And feel free to tell me it's none of my business."

Helen's smile embraced me. "Yes, Maggie. I was once in love with Rowan. And many years ago, we had a very sweet, very brief love affair."

When I'd first considered the possibility that they might have been lovers, the gap in their ages had made me squirm. It was easy to imagine any woman falling under Rowan's spell, but knowing Helen's sweet, caring nature—and imagining how beautiful she must have been when she and Rowan first met—I could understand how he might have fallen under hers as well.

"Isn't it hard? Being around him every day? And not being . . . with him?"

"We're much happier as loving friends. We each hold a special place in the other's heart, but we discovered very quickly that I wasn't the right woman for him."

"I'm not sure there is a right woman for Rowan."

"Of course there is. I don't know if it's you, Maggie, but if you could make each other happy—even for the few short weeks left in the season—that would be something."

"Yeah. A miracle."

"Miracles can happen," Helen said firmly. "Just look at *Brigadoon*."

"That's a musical, Helen. Miracles always happen in musicals."

"Because they're a reflection of life. With all its impossible possibilities."

MISERY LOVES COMPANY. FOR the last week, Kalma and I had ended every evening sitting together in the lounge, bitching about the show. That night was no exception.

"Look at him." Kalma glared at Nick who was bellowing with laughter at something Lou had just said and slopping beer over Maya in the process. "Asshole."

That pretty much summed up my impression of Nick, too. Which made it hard for me to play Helping Professional and suggest she search for his wounded inner child. Ashley and Richard might have been able to overcome their differences, but for Kalma and Nick, working together had only deepened their mutual dislike.

"Did you know he has a kid?" Kalma demanded.

"I didn't even know he was married."

"He's not. But he has a baby daughter. Bobbie told me. You can guess what kind of a father he is."

And why Rowan had cast him as Billy.

"I keep telling myself to forget Nick and sing to Billy," Kalma continued. "Julie recognizes that all the macho crap is just a defense mechanism. But then I start singing 'If I Loved You' and there's Nick smirking at me and I just want to puke."

"Please tell me it's not that bad when I sing 'You'll Never Walk Alone.'"

"God, no!" Kalma exclaimed. "But I'm just so glad he's dead that I'm probably not a good judge."

"Maybe that's how we should play the scene. You laughing gleefully, me singing a cheery version of 'You'll Never Walk Alone' . . ."

"And we skip off arm in arm into the sunset." Kalma grinned. "It'd be worth it to see Rowan's face."

"He'd kill us."

Her grin vanished. "He might kill me anyway. During rehearsals, I'll nod and smile when Sarah asks whether someone can hit you and not hurt you, but I will not do it on opening night." She leaned closer and whispered, "I've written something else."

"I don't want to know about it. I'm already on Rowan's shit list."

"How many life histories are you up to now?"

"Don't ask. At least, he's stopped suggesting I get Kevin to help me."

Kalma glowered. "As if you need a man to help you understand Nettie. All you have to do is look at the two pairs of women. There's Julie and Carrie, who both need a man to feel complete. And Mrs. Mullin and Nettie who are managing just fine without one."

"Mrs. Mullin still wants Billy," I pointed out.

"Because he's good for business."

"And in bed."

"Okay, maybe. But she'll find another guy to fill her bed. Whereas Nettie—"

"Probably snuggles up to a lobster pot at night."

"Whereas Nettie," Kalma repeated sternly, "is independent. An Athena."

"So now I'm a Greek goddess?"

Kalma rolled her eyes. "It's an archetype, Maggie."

"And that helps me create her life story . . . how?"

Kalma's mug thudded onto the bar. "Because she's seen enough bad marriages that she chooses to remain single."

Her vehemence made me wonder if she was talking about Nettie's life or hers.

"Of course," Kalma continued, "a woman usually has the qualities of several archetypes. If Nettie has a strong strain of Aphrodite, there's always the chance that she chose to go for love like Julie and it blew up in her face. Or maybe she let the guy go and regretted it later."

I slowly lowered my mug of ale.

"Either of those scenarios could work," Kalma said. "It might be cool. That way, when Nettie sings 'You'll Never Walk Alone,' she's speaking from experience. Trying to help Julie survive like she has. I mean, it's pretty obvious when you think about it."

"It should have been," I replied.

⚓

Inspired by Kalma, I decided to have another go at Nettie's life history. I even took the Goddess Wheel quiz in one of the books she insisted on giving me. Once for Nettie and once for me.

It was profoundly depressing to discover that a fictional character's life was more in balance than mine. With a twenty-point spread between my top and bottom scores, my Goddess Wheel was decidedly wobbly.

My self-esteem took a second hit as I flipped through another of Kalma's books. My Goddess Wheel score suggested I had issues surrounding motherhood and my place in the community. Now it seemed I also had trust issues, a fear of rejection, and an inability to form meaningful relationships with women. The Aphrodite in me sought men who were complex, creative, and emotional; the Athena chose companions, heroes, or father figures.

I slammed the book shut. Told myself it was all bullshit. Reluctantly admitted that I did have trust issues, no female friends until I came here, and a string of personal and professional rejections. And I was currently attracted to a man who was complex, creative, emotional, often companionable, occasionally heroic, and intermittently fatherly. And a good cook.

"Shit."

I studied my responses again, lingering over my low Demeter score. My stomach lurched as I realized that I'd never called my mother back about the beach. It was far too late to call her now, but I hurried onto the porch to check for messages.

Her first just asked me to call. Her second reminded me that I'd promised her an answer this week and the week was nearly over. Her third had come in at 4:30. All she said was,

"Maggie. Call me. We need to talk." Her voice sounded strained rather than angry. As if she were holding back some unwanted emotion. That was nothing new, but it didn't bode well for our conversation, especially since I couldn't give her a definite answer until I learned the results of my interviews.

I turned off the phone and the clamor of my inner goddesses. As I walked out of the sitting room, I nearly collided with Sarah. I let out a startled gasp and chuckled at our mishap. Then I took in her swollen eyes and red nose. Before I could say anything, she burst into tears.

I hustled her to my room. Eyeing the mess of papers and books on my bed, I pulled her down onto Nancy's and hugged her hard, murmuring the kind of soothing inanities people always murmur at such moments: "Let it all out. I'm right here. Don't be afraid. Everything will be all right."

Abruptly, I realized that I was mouthing Nettie-ish platitudes, just as I had that night with Rowan. To my astonishment, though, Sarah's sobs dwindled. I released her long enough to retrieve the trusty Kleenex box. She blew her nose and stared miserably at the floor.

"Is this about the ballet?" I asked.

She got out the words "I'm so awful" before succumbing to tears once more.

"No, you're not," I assured her.

But I understood why she felt that way. After stumbling over a bit of choreography during today's run-through, Sarah had gotten flustered and the ballet went rapidly downhill. As soon as it was over, she fled the theatre with Rowan in hot pursuit.

They returned ten minutes later. Sarah was calm by then. It was Rowan who looked upset. Maybe that was the reason for his odd behavior at Helen's. I wasn't the only performer who was struggling or the only one that Rowan was struggling to help. But I'd made it all about me and babbled that wild confession to Helen.

Thrusting aside that embarrassing memory, I flung my arm around Sarah's shoulders and said, "You did fine the other afternoon. When you and Ronnie were rehearsing in the Smokehouse with Mei-Yin."

"You watched us?"

"Bernie and I peeked through the windows. The ballet looked good."

"You're just saying that."

"No, I'm not. You were nervous today. Performing in front of everybody for the first time."

"If I can't dance in front of the cast, I'll never be able to perform in front of an audience."

"You've been performing *The Sea-Wife* for three weeks."

"I don't have to do anything in that. But the ballet ... everyone will be watching *me*. And if I make a fool of myself—"

"Rowan would never let that happen."

Sarah's head came up. "That's what he said."

"See?"

"I didn't believe him."

"Well, you should. God knows I'm counting on him to help me hit that damn high G."

That wrested a tiny smile from her. It quickly faded. "I've watched the movie about a hundred times and—"

"Well, there's your problem. You can't compare yourself to a professionally trained dancer. Besides, I hate that Louise. She's so fakey dramatic. You're a much better actress."

Sarah's smile transformed her face. She looked luminous, almost beautiful.

"Stay just like that," I commanded.

I dragged her off the bed to the full-length mirror on the back of the door. "See how your face shines? How sweet and hopeful you look? That's Louise. Right there."

For an instant, I thought she saw it, too. Then she frowned and wiped her wet cheeks. "I'm just shiny because I've been crying."

"Trust me. I saw it." As she flopped back on the bed, I added, "You're miles ahead of me. I don't believe half the stuff Nettie says. And it shows. But in your ballet and your scene with Julie, every emotion feels real. You *are* Louise."

"Rowan said that, too." She peered at me suspiciously. "Did he talk to you about me?"

"Rowan barely talks to me about me."

"Because he knows you'll come through."

"From your lips to God's ears," I said in my broadest Bernie accent.

Sarah giggled, then sighed. "Poor Grandpa. He was so worried today."

I nodded. While Rowan was outside with Sarah, I'd sat in the green room with Bernie. He'd questioned his decision to let Sarah audition, blamed himself for failing her—and invoked Rowan's name like a mantra: Rowan will know what to do, Rowan will help her, Rowan will convince her she can be wonderful.

For a little while, Rowan had. Then—as Nancy and I had discovered that first week—Sarah's newfound confidence had leached away.

I wished Helen were here; Sarah could use a blessing. Instead, I offered a poor substitute.

"We're going to make a pact," I told her. "If one of us sees the other getting down on herself, she has to say, 'Knock it off. Believe what you're doing and you're going to be great.' Okay?"

"Okay."

We bumped fists. As I walked her to her room, I whispered, "Things will be better tomorrow. We just have to keep plugging away. And—"

"Keep our chins up?"

God, I was doing it again.

"It sounds stupid, but it's true," Sarah assured me solemnly. "Things *will* look better in the morning. And if we don't lose heart and keep our chins up and trust Rowan—"

"And ourselves."

Sarah struck a pose and softly sang, "We'll never walk alone."

"Out of the mouths of fucking babes," I muttered.

Sarah did a little shimmy, breasts and booty shaking. "No one's ever called me a babe before."

I cuffed her across the back of the head. "Go to bed, Babe."

CHAPTER 25

TAKING A CHANCE ON LOVE

AFTER A BLISSFULLY DREAMLESS NIGHT, I awoke refreshed and clearheaded. I ate breakfast with the gang, all of whom commented on my newfound cheerfulness. I called my mother, carefully choosing the hour when I knew she'd be grocery shopping, and left a message on the home phone, apologizing for not calling sooner, offering the interviews as an excuse, and promising to call Monday to let her know how they went. Then I returned to my room and started scribbling Nettie's life history. Again.

I trimmed twenty years off her age. Decided that men enjoyed her humor and women admired her common sense. I made her father a whaler who left on a voyage and never returned, and concluded that his stories of faraway places fueled Nettie's imagination and dreams of a better life. I kept the luncheon shack, added a ne'er-do-well boyfriend who dumped her for a rich girl, and killed off her mother with a bout of pneumonia that forced Nettie to pick up the reins of the business at sixteen.

Before I could second-guess myself, I drove to the theatre, slid the pages under Rowan's door, and raced back to the hotel. Almost immediately, I succumbed to a fit of nerves, wondering what he'd think of my efforts. I distracted myself by ironing my business suit and tidying up the room in anticipation of Nancy's arrival for the closing night of *The Sea-Wife*. I tried to review Nettie's scenes with fresh eyes, but realizing I'd never be able to concentrate until I'd talked with Rowan, I slung my gear into the car and drove to the theatre.

As I pulled into the parking lot, I saw him sitting at one of the picnic tables. He immediately rose and strode down the walkway, my life history fluttering in his hand.

I slid out of the car and started toward him, feeling like a Death Row inmate walking the green mile to the electric chair. I told myself I was acting ridiculous, but when I saw his serious expression, my heart sank.

"You hated it." My voice sounded as forlorn as a little kid's whose crayon drawing was about to be consigned to the garbage can instead of proudly displayed on the refrigerator.

"What did *you* think of it?" Rowan asked.

"It's more me than Nettie," I admitted.

"Possibly." A slow smile blossomed on his face. "But it was real. And it was good."

The wave of relief left me giddy. Then I swung my carryall at him and shouted, "You big faker!"

He scampered backward, laughing. I pursued him, still swinging my bag. He danced out of the way of one blow, ducked under another, and neatly snatched the bag from my hands. When he lifted it over his head, I charged in for the kill. He backpedaled, using the bag to deflect my punches. Not that they would have done much damage; I was laughing too hard at his gyrations. He looked like an absurd combination of Rocky Balboa and the Lucky Charms leprechaun.

He backed into the wall of the barn with a sudden "oof" that choked off his laughter. It was still in his eyes, though, and in the smile that replaced his momentary look of surprise. I smacked my palms on his shoulders, pinning him against the barn, and demanded, "Give up?"

His smile fled. He clutched my bag to his chest. His tongue flicked out to wet his lips.

"Maggie . . ."

I leaned forward and pressed my mouth to his.

I felt his quick intake of breath, the rise and fall of the bag trapped between our bodies. But he remained utterly still, his lips unresponsive.

I stepped back, stunned by my impulsive act and by his

reaction. Tiny sparks flashed in his eyes, like sunbeams dancing off damp leaves. I watched them, mesmerized, wondering if he was as unsure as I was about the wisdom of taking this any further. Maybe he was angry that it had taken me so long to act. Maybe he didn't want me anymore.

His chest rose and fell with his quickened breathing. The heavy canvas of my carryall shuddered in his trembling hands. He was fighting for control, I realized, struggling to keep his power leashed. Honoring his promise never to use it to force me to do something I didn't want.

"Yes," I whispered.

He tossed my carryall to the ground and pulled me into his arms. His mouth was as hard as the fingers knotted in my hair. Then it softened, clinging to mine, demanding more. His tongue slipped between my lips, smooth as satin one moment, and the next, rough as sandpaper. When I let mine tease against it, his power burst free, flooding me with a desire so intense that my knees buckled.

His hands slid over my bottom, and he lifted me. I tried to wrap my legs around him, but after one feeble attempt, I just hung there, dangling in the air like a rag doll.

Suddenly, his body stiffened and his head jerked toward the parking lot. Frustration stabbed me; I couldn't tell if it was his or mine or both.

Very carefully, he set me on my feet. For a moment, his hands lingered on my waist, steadying me. Then he stepped back, a grimace twisting his mouth.

"The crew."

Seconds later, I heard the faint crunch of gravel. Reinhard's SUV pulled into the lot, followed moments later by Lee's pickup.

I fought the urge to seize his hand and drag him up the stairs to his apartment. Unsatisfied desire warred with the realization that the staff would sense our lovemaking, that Rowan's power could fill the entire theatre with his passion—and the very practical consideration that I wasn't on any form of birth control and had no condoms.

I managed a shaky smile. "Bad timing."

"Very."

"Rain check?"

A dizzying wave of desire washed over me. "Tonight," he whispered. "After strike."

I nodded.

"After all this time, what's another . . . eleven hours?"

"An eternity."

He cocked his head. "There's always the dinner break."

"With everyone at the picnic tables listening to my screams of pleasure wafting through the skylights?"

"I could stuff a sock in your mouth," he volunteered.

"It's sweet of you to offer."

We grinned at each other. As he pressed my bag into my hands, his fingertips caressed mine, a teasing promise of future pleasure. Then he shook his finger with mock severity.

"We leave the cast party at the stroke of midnight. Understood?"

"Yes, Cinderella."

CHAPTER 26
THE PARTY'S OVER

I DIDN'T REMEMBER MUCH OF THAT MATINEE; I probably floated through it with a goofy smile on my face. After I changed, I gobbled a few mouthfuls of Chinese food and hurried to the parking lot, fending off questions by explaining I had a quick errand to run.

Dale's only pharmacy carried a surprising variety of condoms, considering the town's size. Nothing like New York, of course, where I would have had a choice of flavors, colors, and graphic designs. I grabbed an assortment of Trojans: ribbed, lubricated, non, ultra thin, extra large. Faced with the prospect of presenting all those boxes to a cashier who looked about twelve, I put them back on the shelf and purchased a convenient pleasure pack instead. And the box of Magnums. Hope springs eternal.

On the way back to the theatre, I stopped in at the hotel to ensure that my mother had received my earlier message. She had. And left three increasingly terse ones for me. The last simply said, "Maggie. Call me. Today."

I found it incredible—and incredibly annoying—that she could turn a proposed week at the beach into a crisis. I checked the time and reluctantly booted up my laptop to Skype her.

I barely got out, "Hey, Mom," before she said, "I called you yesterday."

"Yeah, I know. I'm sorry I—"

"At HelpLink."

My stomach churned, a sickening whirl of chicken with snow peas and bile.

"Oh."

"That's it? 'Oh?'"

"Look, I "

"A strange woman picked up your extension. She didn't even recognize your name."

"Probably new," I mumbled.

"She put me on hold, and I sat there for ages. Ages! Not knowing whether she was just an idiot or whether something had happened to you."

"I was going to—"

"And when the supervisor finally picked up, she told me that you'd been fired in—"

"Let go," I corrected.

"In May! When were you going to tell me? Were you *ever* going to tell me?"

"I didn't want to worry you."

"I was already worried! You've been acting strange all summer. Nervous and evasive. I'm not an idiot, Maggie."

No, I was. I should have foreseen this possibility. She'd never called me at HelpLink before, but then, she'd never needed to. If I'd just agreed to go to the beach when she'd first suggested it, I could have avoided this debacle.

As I started to apologize, she said, "You're not even in New York, are you?"

For just a second, I hesitated. But that was enough.

"Oh, God. I was right. You've joined some New Age cult. Like Lella."

"I have not joined a cult. I swear."

Another silence. Clearly, she was waiting for me to tell her what I *was* doing. As I frantically debated coming clean or concocting another lie, she said, "No. Of course not." Her voice sounded flat now, and weary. "You're doing theatre again."

I mustered my courage and said, "Yes."

"Where?"

"Up in Vermont. At this little theatre—"

"Not the Crossroads?"

For a moment, I was too shocked to respond.

"The Crossroads?" I repeated to buy myself time. Time

to think, to make sense of the impossibility that my mother had heard of a theatre few people in southern Vermont knew existed—and sounded terrified by the prospect that I was working there.

"Why would you think I'd be at some theatre called the Crossroads?"

This time, the silence lasted so long that I thought she wasn't going to answer. Finally, she said, "Because your father worked there."

I found myself staring up at a spiderweb in the corner of the ceiling, admiring its intricate construction. Beautiful, really, except for the dead fly trapped in its sticky strands.

"Daddy? Did summer stock in Vermont?"

Could she feel the effort required to keep my voice calm? To give it just the right blend of puzzlement and curiosity? To judge from her impatient, "He did summer stock all over," she had no idea I was turning in a Tony Award-winning performance.

"But this was later," she continued. "After he'd been working at A.I. for three years."

A.I. DuPont, the high school where he had worked as an English teacher.

"I thought he'd gotten acting out of his system. Then he suddenly decided to go to Vermont for the weekend. To visit a college friend, he said. And when he came home, he told me he'd been offered a job at the Crossroads Theatre for the summer."

I pictured him driving slowly past the barn. Stopping for coffee at the Chatterbox. Waving to a waitress who called, "Break a leg!" as he hurried off to audition.

"Well, you can imagine how I felt. He'd finally settled down in a real job—a job he liked and was good at—and then . . ." My mother sighed. "In the end, he agreed to finish out the school year and only go up for the second and third shows. And after that, no more acting except in local productions."

"What happened?"

"He went. And when we drove up to see him—"

"Wait. I saw him? At the theatre?"

"Don't you remember? Well, you were only six or seven. And you were doped up on Dramamine because you always got carsick and I wasn't about to drive seven hours with you throwing up the whole way. You slept through most of the show. But you loved the theatre. Especially the big star on the side of the barn."

I squeezed my eyes shut and took a deep breath. "But . . . I still don't understand. You sounded so panicked when you thought I was working at that place."

"It's just . . . it's completely irrational. He was fine when he came home. Happier than he'd been in years. But later . . . things got bad. You know." Her sigh was heavier this time. "Maybe it would have happened anyway. But I always sort of blamed that place. If he hadn't gone there, if it hadn't been such a great experience . . . God, he was always talking about it. The cast. The staff. That damn director."

"What . . . what was wrong with the director?"

"Oh, he was nice enough. And the show was good. Remarkably good, for such a hole-in-the-wall place. But for the next six months, all I heard was 'Rowan this' and 'Rowan that.'"

I clamped my lips together and swallowed down a burning surge of bile. It was possible—just possible—that Rowan could have directed my father. It might have been his first season. Fresh out of college. Or wherever.

I managed a weak laugh. "Maybe I should look this guy up. See if he remembers Daddy."

"I don't want you going anywhere near that place!"

"You said yourself you were irrational about it."

"I don't care! Humor me. Besides, he's probably retired by now."

I took a careful breath. "Retired?"

"Well, he had to have been forty when I met him. And that was—what? Twenty-five years ago?"

My stomach muscles clenched as I fought another wave of nausea.

"But even if he's still there . . . stay out of it, Maggie. Please. There's no point digging up the past. You'll only get hurt."

"Yes."

"I knew I shouldn't have told you."

"No. I'm glad you did."

"I just wanted you to understand why I was so upset."

"I do. It's okay. I'm sorry I didn't tell you sooner. About
HelpLink. I'll call you Monday. Let you know how the interviews go."

"You really have interviews? I thought . . . I was afraid
you were just making those up."

"No. That was true."

It was everything else about my summer that was a lie.

❦❦

A few women—Kalma, Brit, Bobbie—noticed my distraction and commiserated with me when I explained that my
mother had found out that I'd lost my job. Sarah squeezed
my hand and whispered, "Things'll look better tomorrow."

I trudged up the stairs to the green room, groping for
logical explanations, trying to understand how my mother
could have met a man of forty who still looked that age
twenty-five years later. I told myself that her memory was
faulty, that it had been dark when they met, that Rowan's
natural self-assurance made him seem older than he was.
But I didn't believe any of it.

Rowan bounded into the green room, full of energy and
high spirits. Then his head snapped toward me, an expression of profound shock banishing his excitement. I gripped
the back of the battered armchair, fighting for control, but
when the pre-show circle formed, I slipped out of the green
room and hurried down the hall to the production office.
Hearing footsteps behind me, I whirled around and discovered Reinhard.

"Stay away from me!"

He must have heard the hysteria in my voice. Or maybe
he could sense it. He was part of this. The secret of the
Crossroads. They all were.

Had my father stumbled on that secret? Had they tried
to brainwash him the same way they had brainwashed
Caren? Only in his case—and mine—it didn't stick. Once he
left, the power wore off—and he drifted away.

I'd go crazy if I thought about that, if I allowed wild
speculations to carry me into Helen's realm of "impossible
possibilities." There was no time for these questions, no
time to process the answers. In five minutes, the curtain

would go up. And suddenly, I was pathetically grateful for that.

"I'll be fine," I told Reinhard. "Just some personal stuff I have to work out."

I eased past him and returned to the green room. I didn't trust myself to look at Rowan. As soon as Reinhard called places, I joined the stream of cast members hurrying back-stage. Safely screened from Rowan by their bodies, I escaped into the world of *The Sea-Wife*.

I turned my resentment against the swaggering Craigies. Directed my suspicions toward the strange woman who had joined their household. Took out my anger on the new schoolteacher who thought he was so much wiser than the rest of us. Channeled my roiling fear about my family's past into concern for my stage family.

Back in the dressing room after the show, my fierceness evaporated. I felt completely disengaged from the closing night high, the good-natured moaning about strike, the hugs and tears and congratulations. Every action felt slow, as I if were moving underwater. I was still hanging up my costume when the rest of the women were removing their makeup, pulling on my street clothes as they hurried upstairs for strike.

When their voices faded, loneliness threatened to choke me. Then I heard footsteps in the hallway. I let out my breath a moment later as Nancy peeked into the dressing room. I leaped out of my chair. My eyes closed as I hugged her. When I opened them again, I found Rowan standing in the doorway.

Nancy must have felt me tense. She reared back, then noticed the direction of my gaze.

"Hi, Rowan." She eased free from my embrace, but I clung to her hand like a frightened child.

"Hello, Nancy," Rowan replied, his gaze fixed on me. "Maggie, I think we need to talk."

"I have strike."

"One pair of hands won't be missed."

Nancy squeezed my hand. "Do you want to talk now? Or do you need some time?"

Rowan's mouth tightened. He wasn't used to the staff

questioning him, never mind a cast member. But if Nancy felt his flash of annoyance, she gave no indication.

Knowing that no amount of time would be enough, I said, "It's okay. But would you wait for me? At the hotel?"

"Of course." She hesitated at the doorway and turned to Rowan. "I don't know what's happened, but I think you should be very careful what you say and do in the next few minutes."

He regarded her with open astonishment, then nodded stiffly. With a final glance at me, Nancy walked out.

"Not here," I said before Rowan could speak.

Cast and crew swarmed over the stage. Ignoring Reinhard's worried gaze, I strode through the chaos, threw open the stage door, and walked to the picnic area without looking back to see if Rowan was following. I chose the table closest to the theatre, the bench facing the woods. I wanted him to sit where the light from the walkway lamps would shine on his face.

As he slid onto the bench opposite me, I laced my fingers tightly together atop the table. His hands moved toward mine, stopped, then retreated.

"What happened, Maggie?"

The kindness in his voice made me ache. I hated that.

I stared down at my hands, listening to the low buzz of conversation wafting through the back doors of the theatre, the rapid thud of hammers, and Lee's voice calling out occasional directions to the crew. Then I forced myself to look up.

The lamplight revealed the concern on his face. And something else I couldn't identify.

"You were so happy this afternoon. And now it's gone."

Then I recognized the emotion I had not been able to name. Sadness. So deep it verged on grief. I didn't know whether it stemmed from his emotions or his perception of mine. But I refused to let it sway me from seeking the answers I needed.

"There are some things I have to ask you. And I need you to tell me the truth."

"I've always told you . . . as much of the truth as I could."

"Do you know a man named Jack Sinclair?"

The lines between his brows deepened, but he seemed puzzled rather than shocked. "He worked here. Years ago."

"And you were his director?"

His nod destroyed my ridiculous hope that his father had preceded him here, that Rowan Mackenzie, Sr. had been the man my mother had met.

"What does Jack Sinclair have to do with ?"

"Did you know he was married?"

"Yes. And he had a child, I think. A little—" His eyes flew wide as he stared at me. "You're Jack's daughter?"

I nodded. "My mother changed our names. After the divorce."

"Why didn't you tell me?"

"I never knew he worked here. Until a few hours ago."

"Your mother?"

"She found out I'd lost my job. And when I confessed that I was doing theatre again, the first thing out of her mouth was, 'You're not at the Crossroads, are you?'"

Rowan's gaze slid away.

"The thing that scared me was how panicked she sounded. She tried to explain it away. Said she was irrational about this place. Because of everything that happened afterward."

"What?" he demanded. "What happened?"

I described that last year with my father. The happy family reunion. His determination to make things work. And then the slow unraveling of a marriage and a life: the dreams that haunted him, the obsessive research into New Age religion and mysticism, the arguments that alternated with the ominous silences.

I described the drinking and the drug use, the first to keep the dreams at bay, the second to encourage them. The days he missed work. The weekends he raced up to Philly or New York to do research in the libraries there. The weekends he simply disappeared with no explanation at all. Losing his job at the high school. Bouncing from one job to another, each paying less than the last, each lasting a shorter while, until he simply stopped working altogether.

That was the worst time. When he had no job to anchor him and very little family life to cling to. When he locked himself in the basement with his precious books. Or vanished for a week, two weeks, a month, returning elated at some new discovery or utterly dejected. Running through the bank account and credit cards until my mother cut him off. Running through the therapists she couldn't afford, the meds he wouldn't take. And through it all, his increasingly frantic assertions that he wasn't losing his mind, that everyone was just too narrow-minded to look beyond conventional religion and medicine and wisdom to seek the ancient beliefs and exalted experiences that would lead—must surely lead—to enlightenment.

I told him everything I had gleaned from my mother over the years, my voice as calm as if I were talking about a stranger. Which is what Daddy had been and still was. I didn't offer my memories of those final years; they were too clouded by confusion and unhappiness to be reliable. Perhaps my mother's were as well. Certainly they were tainted by her sense of betrayal, her anger and frustration and fear. But she was the only witness I had.

Except for the man sitting opposite me. The man who had known my father during his last summer of happiness. Who might possess the missing piece of the puzzle. Who sat unmoving, unspeaking throughout my recitation, staring down at his clasped hands.

When I finished, I waited for him to say something. When he didn't, I asked, "What are the odds? Me showing up at the same theatre my father worked at."

"Better than you'd think." He looked up then, his expression grave but calm. "I call to them, you see. Just like I called to you after Helen's heart attack. And they come here."

"Who?"

"The Mackenzies. Descendants of the original family who owned this farm."

When I picked up that bed and breakfast guide, when I chose the turn to Dale, when I slowed down to examine the barn—each time, I'd thought instinct had prompted my decisions. Just as I'd believed my love of the theatre—my desire to return to that happy period of my life—had prompted me to audition. But it had been Rowan all along. Calling me—calling all of us—who were bound to him by virtue of a blood tie I hadn't even known existed.

With as much calm as I could muster, I asked, "So we're related? You and I?"

"No! I merely . . . took the name."

Again, I waited for an explanation. When none was forthcoming, I asked, "But why do you call them? If the owners of the farm and your folk were enemies."

"Because I am cursed."

His expression was too serious for it to be a joke. But my nerves betrayed me and I blurted out, "You violated some ancient Indian burial ground or something?"

"No. I violated a girl's innocence."

His calm gaze never wavered as he uttered that damning statement. I tried to square the man I knew—the man I thought I knew—with the one sitting across from me who had just admitted to raping a girl. Then I realized he might be speaking metaphorically. I prayed he was.

"I can't believe you would commit rape."

He looked down at his hands again and cleared his throat. "Thank you for that." Then his head came up and his eyes seared me. "But I don't deserve your good opinion. I used my power to seduce her. To overcome her fear and her reluctance. And no matter how willingly she came to me, how many times she sought me out and enjoyed what I gave her, the fact remains that I abused my power—and her innocence—simply because I wanted her."

My hands had come up to clutch my arms, shielding myself from his words, from his act, from the revulsion that shuddered through my body.

"I told you—the day of our picnic—that my arrogance and selfishness had led me to hurt people when I was young. She was one of them. There were others, of course. Who suffered because I could not offer them the friendship—the love—that they wanted. Needed."

I thought of Janet's blistering accusations about Rowan's inability to love, of the sadness and tenderness on Helen's face when she described their brief affair.

"The consequences of my crime against that girl were very heavy. For her and for me. I left her, you see. At summer's end. And when I returned, I learned that she had borne a child. And that both had died during the birth."

I studied him, hoping for some sign of distress. All I found was weariness. And although I knew his ability to hide his emotions, I exclaimed, "Did you feel anything at all about what had happened? About what you'd done?"

"She asked me that, too. Her mother."

He never spoke the girl's name. Did he even remember it? Or did he refuse to say it because that would bring the tragedy too close?

"I told her that I . . . regretted the deaths."

"Two people were dead and you were regretful?"

"You asked for the truth, Maggie, and that's what I'm trying to give you."

Although his voice was still calm, I glimpsed genuine grief on his face. He looked down at his clasped hands. When he raised his head again, all traces of emotion had been banished.

"I felt regret," he said without inflection. "But if not for what happened afterward, I would have walked away and forgotten about them."

I shook my head, unable to believe what I was hearing.

"That's the kind of . . . creature I was. But I am not like that now. I have lived with the sorrow and the guilt and the shame of my actions for many years."

Janet's voice and Helen's warred in my mind, Janet's claiming that he was incapable of change, Helen's affirming that he was.

"I did not—could not—feel such things then. Perhaps if I had . . ." His mouth twisted in a bitter smile. "'Perhaps' holds no weight. And regrets cannot change the past. I was responsible for their deaths and I was cursed. By her mother. You probably don't believe in curses—or in the witches who cast them—but they exist, Maggie. I know. That girl was the heart of their family, a being of light and music and joy. When I stole her from them, I stole those things as well. And brought them grief and sorrow."

His gaze had become distant, his voice an eerie singsong, as if he were repeating the actual words of this "curse."

"What I stole, I must return. What I brought, I must take away. What I had never felt—"

He broke off abruptly. Then he said, "Her curse bound me to the Mackenzies. To this farm. To this theatre."

I could not accept that a witch had cursed him. But I could believe that the words of a distraught mother had awakened his sense of responsibility and guilt, that an imaginative mind like his could have played those words over and over, twisting and distorting them, until he was convinced that he could neither leave this place nor abandon the work that was—for him—both punishment and penance.

Whether or not I believed in the curse, he surely did. It explained his anger at being held hostage to this place. It explained why I never saw him in town, why he cast people according to need rather than talent, why he took so seriously his responsibility to his cast. But it didn't explain why my mother feared this place and blamed it for my father's breakdown.

Rowan nodded, as if I had voiced those thoughts aloud. But again, he forced me to ask.

"Did something happen to my father that summer?"

He let out his breath as if he had been bracing himself for that question. "Yes. Something similar to Caren's experience at Midsummer. But I helped him recover. And—"

"You brainwashed him?"

He grimaced. "I helped him forget. And Helen kept in touch with him for months afterward. To make sure he was all right."

"Helen? Not you?"

"I had to use a great deal of power to help Jack. And I knew that could create a bond between us. So I thought it best to . . . keep my distance. But I thought . . . Helen said he sounded . . . fine."

"He was an actor! Didn't it ever occur to you that he was lying?"

Rowan's hesitation gave me the answer he refused to speak.

"How could you just abandon him?"

"If I had known what was happening—if I knew where he was today . . ."

"It's too late," I whispered. "He's lost."

"He was already lost, Maggie."

I shook my head.

"Your father was an unhappy man. Unhappy with himself and unhappy with his life. I know it hurts you to hear that, but it's true. He thought he'd found his purpose, his joy in the theatre, but it wasn't enough. Nothing was ever enough. Not his family, not his work. He was always seeking something more. Even he didn't know what that was. I tried to ease that restlessness, to show him all the good things he had, but—"

"But that wasn't just to help him. You were protecting yourself. Covering up whatever he had seen, whatever secrets he'd exposed."

"He should never have been in the forest that night!"

Rowan rose with such violence that the bench tumbled over. I shrank back, buffeted by the cold blast of his anger and the ragged desperation in his voice.

"What did he see?" I whispered.

As suddenly as it had surfaced, all the violence left him. He stood quite still, his gaze resting on me with an expression that was almost tender.

"He saw what Caren would have seen if I had not stopped her. He saw my folk."

He carefully righted the bench and seated himself, clasping his hands atop the table once more. For a moment longer, he hesitated. Then he raised his eyes to mine.

"We have always been among you. Slipping between moonlight and shadow. Wandering woodland groves and darkened streets. In the Old World and the New. Forever linked by curiosity and envy, by wonder and fear. By blood."

His voice had taken on the lilting cadences of a storyteller. Like my father's when he wove one of his tales about pirate gold or gnomes living under tree roots. And although his expression was as gentle as his voice, a chill spread through my flesh. I wanted to make him stop, to tell him that some secrets should never be revealed.

"We are all around you, but you rarely see us. It's safer that way. For when our paths cross, it is your folk who invariably suffer."

He leaned forward, but somehow, the movement only reinforced my sense that he was far away from me, separated by miles instead of the narrow width of the table.

"Over the centuries, you have called us by many names. The Still Folk. The Blessed Ones. The Prowlies and the People of Peace. The Daoine Sidhe and the Fey. Mostly, though, your folk refer to us as Faeries."

I stared at him. A burble of incredulous laughter escaped

me, and I shoved my fist against my mouth. Finally, I whispered, "That's impossible."

"Yes. But it's still true." When I shook my head, he said, "Think, Maggie. Look back on everything you've experienced this summer. Then find another explanation."

His surprising strength. The beauty of his voice. The grace of his movements. The sudden playfulness and the terrifying mask that hid every emotion. His ability to transform a group of rank amateurs into a company of real actors, to transform a mediocre show into something magical.

All those I could explain away. Somehow. Even his strange power to beguile humans and fireflies alike. But to believe that power stemmed from an otherworldly source—that *he* was otherworldly . . . not even human . . .

"No."

I'd seen his wild mood swings. And the scars on his wrists. Maybe he had tried to kill himself after learning of the death of the girl and his child. And failing to do so, sought refuge in this impossible delusion.

And then my carefully constructed arguments collapsed. No matter how hard I tried, I could not explain away the fact that he still looked like the man of forty my mother had met twenty-five years ago.

I shook my head, unable to accept that everything I knew about the world had changed, still seeking refuge in logic and reason even though they could no longer serve me. It was as if I had spent months struggling to complete a jigsaw puzzle, picking up one piece and discarding it for another, trying to force others together when I knew they wouldn't connect, and only now discovered the essential piece that allowed me to see how all the others fit together.

"I'm still the same person I was a minute ago," he said gently. "With the same flaws, the same strengths. I'm still . . . me."

But he wasn't. He was something new and frightening.

His expression grew remote. "I only told you about myself so that you would understand what happened to your father. May I tell you about that night? Or are you too upset to listen?"

I wasn't sure any of it would make sense, but I had gone too far to stop now.

"From the earliest days of the theatre, we've always taken precautions to ensure that the cast is occupied at Midsummer. The staff realized Jack was not at the restaurant with the others, but his roommate told them that he'd decided to take a drive. Jack was a bit of a loner. It seemed . . . reasonable. But he never made it past the theatre. Maybe he decided to take a walk instead. I don't know. By the time I sensed his presence in the woods . . ."

His brows drew together, and he looked away. With a visible effort, he forced himself to meet my gaze.

"To chance upon one of our kind is dangerous enough for a human. To chance upon an entire clan . . . at Midsummer . . ."

Again, he looked away. And again, he mastered his momentary weakness.

"Eventually, I got him away."

"Eventually?"

"Please listen. Please try to understand. My clan has dozens of members. Most far older and more powerful than I was. Than I am. If I had tried to snatch him away, they might have retaliated. I had to wait. Until they . . . lost interest."

"What did they do to him?" I demanded, my voice shaking.

"At first, they were angry. Because he had intruded on their revels. But soon—"

"They were the intruders! Sneaking into our world and—"

"It was our world first, Maggie. Humans drove us from it. That's one of the reasons there has always been friction between your folk and mine. Why there are rules to discourage . . . fraternization. Which only increases our mutual fascination. That's why their anger faded so quickly. They began . . . playing with him. Petting him. Teasing him. Heightening their glamour to enthrall him."

My arms ached. I realized they were wrapped around my body again as if to shield me from their cruelty. I remembered my headlong flight through the woods when I heard Rowan singing, the physical sensations that had rocked me in his apartment. And he hadn't even been trying to enthrall me.

My poor father. He hadn't had a chance.

"When they tired of their game—"

"Their game?" I repeated, stung into speech. "Is that what you call it?"

Rowan shook his head wearily. "No. But that's how they viewed it. They left after that. To enjoy their revels elsewhere. When he tried to follow, I restrained him." Rowan hesitated. "He wept. Like a brokenhearted child."

My breath hissed in.

"It gives me no pleasure to tell you these things. But—"

"Go on."

"I carried him to my apartment and lulled him to sleep. For a night and a day and another night, I sat with him, using my power to get him to eat, to drink. To forget."

"Two days?"

"He didn't want to forget, you see. He had found that . . . something more that he'd always been looking for. Forcing him to give it up would have shattered his mind. I had to be careful. And gentle. Coax him into accepting a new reality. Much like the one the staff gave to Caren."

"They're . . . they're faeries, too?"

"No. But they carry the blood. I'm not the only one of my kind who has trespassed in this world."

My mind told me that was only reasonable. But it sickened me to know that these creatures regularly invaded our world, playing with us, seducing us, then discarding us like unwanted toys when they became bored.

"Blood calls to blood. That's how the staff found this place. How the cast does, too."

"But . . . you said it was the Mackenzie blood, that we weren't related . . ."

"The first Mackenzies carried the blood."

My stomach heaved.

"It was strong in the witch. Only three or four generations removed. It's strong in some of the staff as well."

Janet. Reinhard. Helen.

"In the end, Jack accepted the new reality I gave him. If he had been pretending, if he had felt any doubt, I would have sensed it. But still, we watched him carefully. All summer. He was a different person. Relaxed and happy. Mingling with the rest of the cast where before he had been aloof. He even helped them with their roles. Like you did."

Hot tears burned my eyes. I blinked them back.

"And when he left us at the end of the summer, he was eager to go home. To start over again. He was healed. And whole. For the first time in his life."

I could only stare at him, stunned at his monumental arrogance in assuming he had made my father into something better.

"I should have foreseen the possibility that the memories might come back. Realized that he loved them so much that—"

"He didn't love them! If he thought he did, it was because they made him."

"He ran to them with open arms, Maggie."

"I ran to you that day in the woods. That didn't mean I loved you."

Rowan flinched. Then his expression hardened. "I know how to use my power to seduce a human. There's fascination, yes. And excitement. But always, there is fear. And reluctance. Not with Jack. He wanted them. More than he had ever wanted anything in his life."

I pushed myself up, but I had to lean on the table for fear my shaking legs would betray me. "You have no idea what my father wanted from life. And he never had a chance to find out. He was as much a victim as that poor girl you raped."

The mask slipped smoothly into place. This was the true face of Faerie. This blank-faced stranger who knew nothing of kindness or compassion or love. Janet was right. No matter how long Rowan lived among us, he would never be like us.

"You allowed a sensitive man to be tormented and call it caution."

The mask slipped, and I was savagely glad.

"You watched his life and his world crumbling and blame him for it. You manipulated his memories and call it healing. You twisted him into something new and congratulate yourself on making him whole. And then you sent him away and regret that you didn't foresee what might happen to him. To us."

"Should I have abandoned him in the forest?" Rowan demanded. "Stood by while his mind cracked under the weight of that experience? Allowed him to go with them knowing they might toss him aside in the end and leave him even more miserable?"

"You should never have called him here in the first place!"

Rowan shook his head. "He needed me. You all need me. You're unhappy—"

"Maybe we are! But we have the right to try and heal ourselves. The right to choose our own paths, even if we choose the wrong ones. To make mistakes and try to correct them. That's what being human is all about."

"I've helped hundreds of people. Thousands."

"Just because you have the ability to change people doesn't mean you have the right to. It's an abuse of your power."

"No."

"You're the puppet master and we're the puppets who dance and sing—and spread our legs—when you pull the strings."

"No!"

"You cloak it all in colored lights and pretty scenery and kind words. But in the end, you're only using us to expiate your guilt."

His wave of fury sent me stumbling backward. I sat down hard. As he stalked toward me, I slid off the bench, wincing as splinters scraped my thighs.

"You're being completely unfair! And unreasonable." His features twisted in an ugly sneer. "You want to know the truth about your father, but only if it reinforces what you already believe. You want to discover the truth about yourself, but only if it's comfortable. You want me to be your lover and you want me to keep my distance. Well, you can't have it both ways, Maggie! Life isn't that neat. You have to take chances. You have to risk being hurt. Risk being honest. Until you do, you'll never find what you're looking for."

I whirled around and raced for the parking lot.

"That's right. Run away," he called after me, his voice rich with the scorn and arrogance and cruelty of his kind. "That's what you always do. It's a lot easier than facing the truth."

I stopped and slowly turned back to him.

"Try facing the truth about yourself, Rowan. About why you started this theatre. About what *you're* looking for. About your pathetic attempt to act human without bothering to understand us or care about us. It's easy to stand back and play God. Well, take a good, hard look at your life, pal. Maybe then you'll earn the right to lecture me about mine."

I turned my back on him. And the Crossroads Theatre.

ENTR'ACTE
THE JOURNAL OF ROWAN MACKENZIE

Miserable, irrational, ungrateful, self-centered bitch.

Why am I surprised?

It doesn't matter how long you live among them, how well you think you know them. Give them truth and they shudder in revulsion. Heal their pain and they spit in your face.

And they call us capricious.

Jack Sinclair's daughter. What a colossal irony. The old witch must be laughing.

Two hours before I trusted myself to go to the cast party. To smile and hug them and tell them how wonderful they were. They *were* wonderful. I mustn't blame them for her failings. She would only point to that as further evidence of mine.

At least they recognize my achievements. Our achievements. They understand what I'm trying to do here. What I have been doing for one hundred and fifty years.

One hundred and fifty years repudiated in five minutes.

What gives her the right to judge me? She doesn't know me. She has no conception of what it's like to spend centuries among strangers.

Jamie never thought of it as interference. He encouraged me to do this. Yes, it was a penance. An unwelcome one in the beginning. But what choice did I have? To remain aloof and give up all hope of returning home?

Maybe I should talk with Helen. Ask her if someone might misinterpret my work. No. I've already burdened her too much. And the rest of the staff is as gossipy as old women. I've spent half the summer ignoring their speculative glances. And—in Reinhard's case—his outright defiance.

She's a bad influence. On them. And on me.

Now Nancy, there's a woman to admire. Strong. Solid. Reliable. And a far better actor than I ever gave her credit for. That story about the phone call from Mother Graham that left her dear roommate too upset to attend the cast party? Brilliant. And brilliantly underplayed. Within minutes, the whole company was sighing over poor, poor Maggie.

If poor, poor Maggie were here now, I'd cheerfully strangle her. Or fuck her until she screamed. She wouldn't call me a pathetic imitation of a man after that.

Gods. I'm ranting. How humiliating. Did I do that with her? No wonder she walked out.

She'll be back, though. If only to disprove what I said about running away.

The break will do us both good. Give us time to think. Let our tempers cool. When she's calmer, she'll accept the truth. Right now, she's too blinded by what happened to her father. And what happened to her as a result.

Stupid to taunt her. To allow anger and hurt to provoke me. I should have remained calm. Pointed out his flaws. Set her on the path to forgiving him for his neglect. Instead, I gave her the perfect excuse to blame me for her unhappiness and bestow upon him the title of helpless victim.

Jack Sinclair. Now there's a pathetic imitation of a man. A trickster. Like the Jacks in the old tales. Thieves. Giant slayers. Charming, yes. And clever. About everything except himself. But completely self-absorbed. And arrogant and superior. Always making excuses for his failures. Always standing apart, judging

I am not like that.

What happened to Jack was unfortunate, yes. But it doesn't outweigh all the successes. The thousands I have helped over the years. Unless everything they learned here just leached away, too.

No. His was a special case. I did help the others. I am helping them. Look at the letters and e-mails Helen gets. The hundreds of Christmas cards people send every year. I should have told her about them.

And my folk. I should have made her understand just how powerful they are. Even the young ones. Their power burns brighter every year, while mine remains stunted.

And the agony of the iron searing my flesh, my spirit. Feeling my life and my power drain away week after helpless week until they finally removed the collar and bound my wrists and nursed me back to health. Not out of compassion, of course. They simply refused to let me escape so easily.

Would she have listened if I had told her that? Would she have felt a shred of sympathy or pity? Likely, she would have accused me of making excuses and detested me even more.

There are always mistakes. Blunders. Things you regret. People you fail to reach. But my intentions were good. Can't she at least credit me with that?

If I failed Jack

I failed Jack. I saw his neediness, and I turned away. I recognized his fragility, and I didn't protect him. I observed his desperation to grasp the impossible, and I stood by while they ripped apart his soul.

I failed Jack and I've failed his daughter. She is as lost to me now as he is

But there are others who still need me: Kalma, who is so afraid of showing her vulnerability; Sarah, who cannot recognize her beauty; and Nick, who refuses to acknowledge his feelings or his responsibility to his family.

I cannot allow this incident to blind me to *my* responsibilities. And I cannot keep wondering if she might have been the one to finally lift the curse.

How could I have been so foolish? To imagine that I could love her.

Love makes you soar. Like Alex's music. It provides a refuge when you're tired and disheartened. Like Helen. It's built upon friendship and trust and the knowledge that in the vast emptiness of this world, there is one person who sees you with all your flaws and still accepts you. Like Jamie.

She doesn't accept me. She's never a refuge. And the only thing that soars around her is my blood pressure.

Who could love a woman who scorns your beliefs, your work, your very existence?

Who delights in pointing out your flaws and holding you up to her impossibly rigorous standard of right and wrong.

Who pushes and pushes, but turns on you in a fury when you push back.

Whose anger burns you like iron.

Whose tenderness makes you ache.

Whose laughter is the last thing you conjure before falling asleep and whose face is the first thing you long to see when you open your eyes in

Oh, gods.

ACT THREE

WHERE DO I GO FROM HERE?

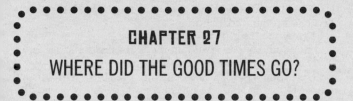

CHAPTER 27
WHERE DID THE GOOD TIMES GO?

I DON'T KNOW WHAT I WOULD HAVE DONE without Nancy. After covering for me at the cast party, she sat up with me half the night. I told her that my mother had discovered I was doing theatre again. I even talked about my father's breakdown. Of course, I didn't tell her the rest. How do you tell someone, "My father had a close encounter with a bunch of faeries? And guess what? Rowan's one of them!"

Each time I burst into tears, she held me until I calmed. If her embrace failed to flood me with peace as Helen's did, her strong, skinny arms were a comforting shield against fear and grief. And they were real. She was real. Real and natural and normal.

When I finally cried myself out, she helped me undress and tucked me into bed. And when I woke the next morning, she assured me that I wasn't losing my mind, that anyone would have been overwrought after the events of the last few days, and that I would feel much better after breakfast.

I did feel better—until I walked back into the Bough and found Reinhard in the lobby. The condition of his hair and the worried expression on his face told me he already knew about my confrontation with Rowan.

Nancy stoutly volunteered to hang around as long as I needed her. I hugged her hard and reluctantly urged her to go home. Then I followed Reinhard into the deserted

287

lounge. He motioned me toward a table, but I shook my head and remained standing.

"Are you all right?"

I nodded, my gaze fixed on the worn floorboards.

"But you cannot bear to look at me."

The sadness in his voice made my eyes burn with unshed tears. "Don't do that. It's not fair."

"Maggie . . ."

"No!" I met his gaze and felt a reluctant pang of sympathy when I took in the heavy bags under his eyes. But I kept my voice firm as I said, "Just say what you have to say."

Reinhard sighed. "In light of . . . last night's events, Rowan suggested that you might wish to skip rehearsal and drive to New York this morning."

Rowan might be too cowardly to face me, but I was made of stronger stuff.

"I'll leave as planned. At the dinner break."

"If you are this upset, you will gain nothing from rehearsal. And your anger will affect the rest of the cast. And Rowan."

He was right, of course, but I was damned if I was going to run away. Not after the taunts Rowan had thrown at me last night.

"This is not a competition between you and Rowan to prove who is stronger."

"He's a faery. Pretty hard for a measly human to compete with that."

"He still has feelings, Maggie. You are not the only one who is hurting."

"Good!"

Reinhard drew himself up, as stiff and formal as the day I met him. "If this is your attitude, I cannot permit you to attend rehearsal. I have the welfare of the entire cast to consider."

"Rowan might sense how I'm feeling, but no one in the cast will."

Reinhard shook his head. "You are very bad at hiding your feelings."

"Just watch me."

Rowan was sitting in the house when I walked into the theatre. His gaze burned into me as I marched down the aisle. When I passed his row without speaking, I heard the creak of his seat, the muffled thud of his footsteps.

"Maggie."

Calling upon my inner Meryl Streep, I summoned an expectant expression and turned toward him. I don't know why I thought I'd find some evidence of strain; unlike me, he was adept at hiding his feelings. But his air of mild puzzlement infuriated me.

"Didn't Reinhard speak with you? About—"

"I told him I'd leave at the dinner break. Is that a problem?"

Rowan studied me. "That remains to be seen."

"Was there anything else?"

He shook his head. But as I reached the steps to the stage, he asked, "Will you be coming back?"

"I have a contract, don't I?"

"That's not a good enough reason," he replied, just as he had that day in the meadow when I told him I had nothing to go home for.

"I'll be back." My shaking voice undermined the Terminator effect.

"If you can't bear to be near me . . ."

The slight tremor in his voice gave me the will to master mine.

"I'll be back," I repeated.

"Fine." His voice was cool now, and as remote as his expression. "If you change your mind, please call Reinhard. We'll need to choose another actress to play Nettie."

I strode into the wings where I glanced around to ensure I was alone before beating my fist against the wall. Then I took a number of deep breaths and got ready to turn in the performance of a lifetime.

I succeeded in convincing my cast mates that I'd recovered from my argument with my mother. But my performance in "June Is Bustin' Out All Over" was so manic that it felt like I was welcoming the storm of the century rather than the onset of summer.

"You'll Never Walk Alone" was worse. Big surprise. Any Julie hearing my words of comfort would have impaled herself on the nearest harpoon. By the third time we ran it, I sounded about as hopeful as the Grim Reaper. Rather than screech out the high G and shatter Kalma's eardrums yet again, I dropped an octave for the final line, surprising Alex so much that he gawked at me from the pit.

Without waiting for Rowan's notes or the dinner break, I fled as soon as the scene ended. Reinhard watched me go without comment.

I bombed at my interviews.

Only minutes after each began, flop sweat erupted from every pore. My manner veered from stiff formality to syrupy warmth and finally to a desperation as palpable as the waves of heat rising from the city streets.

I felt none of the relief I'd expected at being back on helping professional home turf. The office milieu felt alien, as if I'd been absent for years instead of months. The corporate-cubicle vibe at the United Way made my skin crawl, the "one heartbeat from closing our doors" shabbiness of the victims' assistance center depressed me. And as Reinhard had pointed out, I was very bad at hiding my feelings.

When I reluctantly reported back to my mother, I braced myself for a gusty sigh or a disappointed silence. Instead, she said, "Neither of them sounds like a good match for you. Wait for the right opportunity. It may seem pretty bleak right now, but you'll see the light at the end of the tunnel eventually."

Which was so reminiscent of the lyric in "You'll Never Walk Alone" about the golden light at the end of the storm that I might have laughed if I hadn't been so close to tears. Again. All I needed was a reminder to keep my chin up and walk on with hope in my heart.

"Something else will come along," Mom said. "Keep your chin up."

At which point I hurriedly signed off.

Yet I felt better. Not because she'd said anything profound, but simply because she'd offered support instead of criticism. Clearly, platitudes worked on me as well as they'd worked on Sarah. And just as clearly, Rowan had been right to take me to task for looking down my nose at them—and at Nettie. Hard to say whether his crystalline perception stemmed from his directorial skill or his faery power.

On the long drive back to Dale, I realized that what Rowan *was* mattered less than what he had done—to my father, to me, to everyone who had ever been dragged, unsuspecting, to the theatre. Reluctantly, I admitted that he *was* helping some of my cast mates. But they might just as easily have discovered what they needed without his interference.

Perhaps my father's dreadful experience was an isolated incident. But if there were others who had suffered lasting damage because of the Crossroads Theatre, I had to find out about them and make Rowan acknowledge the harm he was doing.

But what could I do if he refused? Go to the police? Write a blog? Find an exorcist?

Think about it tomorrow, Scarlett.

There were three weeks left in the season. I had stayed this long because I had nothing to go home to, because I was too intrigued by the many mysteries of the Crossroads Theatre, and—in the wake of Saturday's confrontation—because I was determined to refute Rowan's accusation that I was always running away. Now, I had a more compelling reason to stay. Maybe I wouldn't figure out what the hell I was supposed to do with my life, but if I could prevent Rowan Mackenzie from ever hurting anyone the way he had hurt my father, I would have accomplished something this summer.

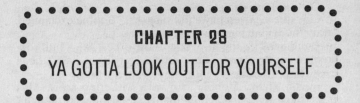

CHAPTER 28
YA GOTTA LOOK OUT FOR YOURSELF

ARRIVED BACK IN DALE to find my cast mates streaming out of the Bough. A chorus of voices eagerly inquired about my interviews. When I gave them the bad news, there were a lot of sympathetic groans and a few assurances that I'd done better than I imagined. Sarah said, "Don't get down on yourself." Lou loudly asserted that my interviewers were assholes.

"I'm okay. Really. But how come you're out so early? Dinner break's at six."

"Rowan let us go so he could run 'Soliloquy' with Nick," Lou said.

I glanced around the circle of glum faces and sighed. Nick had always been able to capture Billy's swagger, but the rare moments of tenderness and vulnerability seemed beyond him. At best, he was wooden. At worst, petulant and insincere. But who was I to point fingers?

"Look, the song just cuts a little too close to home," Lou said.

"I'll say." Bobbie shook her head in obvious disgust. "He gets his girlfriend pregnant. Dumps her. And hasn't seen his daughter since she was born."

"She's probably better off," Kalma muttered.

Lou's face had gotten redder and redder, but all he said was, "Come on ..."

Kalma turned on him in a fury. "How can you defend him?"

"I just think—"

"He doesn't even pay child support!" Bobbie exclaimed. "Are you telling me you think that's okay?"

Lou's head swung from one to the other, like a bull confronted by twin matadors. "I'm just saying it hasn't been easy for him, either."

"Yeah, right," Bobbie said with withering scorn. "It's hard to screw around and then walk when things get tough."

"That's not—"

"Well, if you're all right with that, Lou Mancini, you are not the man for me!"

Bobbie stormed off. Lou hurried after her, crying, "Baby, wait! Listen!"

Kalma watched them go, then surveyed Gary and Bernie through narrowed eyes. "Typical. You guys always stick together."

"Hey!" Gary protested. "I'm the one who got dumped, remember?"

"And I was married for fifty-two years!"

"Yeah. Well. You're the exceptions."

"Let's eat," I suggested.

We headed for Duck Inn. Although Lou and Bobbie seemed to have patched up their quarrel, Lou remained glum throughout dinner. The rest of us avoided any mention of Nick.

When we arrived at the theatre, I noticed Rowan standing in the doorway, watching the line of cars ease down the lane. As mine passed, he turned and walked inside, leaving me to wonder if he'd been anxiously awaiting my return or was simply relieved that he didn't have to get somebody else up to speed on Nettie.

For days, we'd been bracing for this tech rehearsal. The design relied mostly on painted backdrops, a few set pieces to suggest location, and shifts in lighting to establish mood. But then there was the carousel. Lacking a turntable in the floor, the actors had to roll out the "pulpit" where Billy drums up business and the six painted horses on their stands, then connect the stands and lock each to the hub of Billy's pulpit. After which the skinniest women in the cast mounted the horses and the men gripped the handlebars sprouting from the hub to turn the carousel.

Rowan claimed the do-it-yourself carousel reinforced the theme of community, but it seemed more like a desperate attempt to get around the theatre's limited technology. Even with the glowing umbrella of colored lights that descended from the flies to shimmer above the carousel, Rowan would have to use all the magic he possessed to create the glamour the opening number required.

Javier and the stage crew had spent the afternoon putting the chorus grunts through their paces. But once we added the other performers into the mix, plus lighting and sound cues—and the necessity of timing our actions precisely to the music—mistakes were inevitable.

It took two hours of stopping and starting to get everything running smoothly. After that, thank God, there were only the usual glitches: set changes that took too long, lighting cues that got screwed up, avalanches of lobster pots.

It was after midnight when Billy marched back to heaven, leaving the rest of us in a glassy-eyed final tableau. Rowan thanked us for our patience and called a workthrough of the problematic numbers the next afternoon, followed by a full dress rehearsal that night.

After driving nine hours in the last twenty-four and enduring two excruciating interviews, I thought I'd be too exhausted to obsess about Nettie or Daddy or the existence of faeries. Instead, I tossed and turned, reliving my confrontation with Rowan and every dreadful moment that had followed. Including the way he had avoided me at tech rehearsal.

The staff adopted the same guarded formality, clearly closing ranks behind him. I shouldn't have been surprised; it was their theatre at risk as much as Rowan's—and their secret. But it still hurt when Hal watched me with obvious anxiety, but avoided me just as assiduously as the others.

The last thing I expected was for Janet to wave me into the office the following morning. "It just gets better and better," she muttered as she lit a cigarette.

"At least you're talking to me. That's more than the others will do."

"Oh, grow up!" As I opened my mouth to protest, she added, "If Reinhard or Alex made their usual solicitous inquiries, you'd have either cried or bitten their heads off. You want us to comfort you *and* stay the hell away from you. Well, you can't have it both ways."

I suppressed a wince; Rowan had flung those same words at me Saturday night.

"Cut them a break, Maggie."

"Cut *them* a break?"

"Now that Rowan's spilled the beans, nobody knows what you'll do. So we're worried. Not just about ourselves, but about the show and the theatre. And believe it or not, we're worried about you, too."

Her manner was as brusque as ever, but her unexpected concern brought a now-familiar tightness to my throat.

"If you cry, I'll strangle you."

I managed a shaky laugh instead. "That would certainly solve all your problems."

"I've done a lot to preserve this secret, but I haven't stooped to murder. Yet." Janet took a deep drag on her cigarette. "Look. I know this business about your father is a shock. But you have to let it go—at least for the next couple of days—and concentrate on this damn show. There'll be plenty of time after we open to obsess about your life."

She was right, of course. I owed it to my cast mates to turn in my best performance. But I couldn't help asking, "Do you believe in what he does? Calling people here? Pushing them to discover what he thinks they need?"

Janet studied the glowing tip of her cigarette. "Rowan has a more exalted opinion of his work than I do. By putting on successful shows, the actors accomplish something they never dreamed they could. And leave with a lot more self confidence than they had when they arrived. Maybe that's all it takes to change your life. The belief that it's possible." She shrugged. "There are always some who experience the kind of breakthrough Rowan longs for. People like Gary and Bernie. Lou and Bobbie. But there are probably an equal number who'll return to their lives, relatively un-changed by this summer."

"And then there are those like my father."

"That was a unique experience, thank God."

"But there must be others. People who resist change. Who resent Rowan's pushing."

"Like you?"

I glared at her. "You don't think there's anything inherently wrong in calling people here against their wills? In tinkering with their lives?"

"You could have refused the call, Maggie. Or gone home after auditions. You can still go home now. As far as tinkering with people's lives, how is Rowan's technique any different from method acting? That encourages actors to draw upon their emotions and memories."

I considered reminding her that method acting was a far cry from faery magic. Or brainwashing. Instead, I just said, "I never thought I'd hear you defend him."

"My issues with Rowan have nothing to do with his directing."

"Just the affair with Helen."

"Just? He knew before he began it that she wasn't the one. Worse, he knew she was vulnerable. If not for him, she might have married again. Instead of wasting her life pining after a man who could never love her. A man who isn't even a man."

"So it's true? He really is a . . ."

"We're not in church, Maggie. You don't have to whisper."

"This might be a joke to you—"

"It's not a joke. I've just had a lot longer to come to terms with the truth."

"Still, it must have been a shock. When he told you."

Janet rolled her eyes. "I knew what he was—and what I was—long before I met Rowan Mackenzie. I grew up with the stories. So did Alex and Helen. Most of the others found out about their faery blood after they joined the staff. Some were understandably skeptical. Others took it in stride. Hal, of course, was thrilled—until he found out he has no more faery blood than you do. It's rich, isn't it? The biggest fairy on staff is the one with the weakest bloodline."

"But you all have the same . . . powers."

"More or less," Janet replied. "The gift weakens with each generation as the faery blood gets more diluted. And of course, each of us has developed various aspects of the power. Helen's green thumb, for example. Alex's extraordinary musical gifts."

"And you?"

"I can sense what people are thinking and feeling. A useful gift. And I can make them do what I want. If I choose. Also useful."

"Couldn't that just be a testament to your strong personality?"

Janet laughed. "Well, there's that, too. But if it's proof you're looking for, I could always show you my birth certificate. The real one." She took a deep drag on her cigarette and chuckled as she exhaled. "I was born in 1850."

I just stared at her. I had thought a lot about the powers faery blood might bestow, but never made the leap to longevity.

"Rowan looks . . . what? Forty?" Janet speculated. "Even he doesn't know how old he is. Faeries, apparently, don't keep track of time the way we do. His best guess is that they can live up to a thousand years. So the offspring of a faery and a human might live four or five hundred years. The next generation . . . well, you can do the math."

"Then Helen must be . . ." I shook my head, unable to imagine her real age.

Janet frowned. "You still don't get it, do you?"

"Well, she's older than you are, obviously, so—"

"Helen only looks older. Because the faery blood is thinner." Janet leaned forward. "Helen is my daughter, Maggie."

Again, I could only stare at her. Lee had told me . . . no. I'd said they were mother and daughter and he had agreed. I'd jumped to the obvious—and completely incorrect—conclusion.

"Naturally, everyone assumes I'm her daughter. It's easy to encourage that misperception." She crushed out her cigarette. "A lot easier than watching your children age faster than you do."

I quelled the impulse to comfort her; Janet wouldn't welcome any display of emotion. And what words could comfort a woman who knew her child would die long before she did? Who had never known the luxury of growing old with a man she loved?

All summer, I'd noticed the way Janet scolded Helen, fussed over her, set limits on her behavior. My mother had morphed from child to parent during Nana's final years; I'd just assumed Janet had, too.

Then I realized something.

"You said . . . children."

"Helen had a brother. He died in a car accident. Nearly sixty years ago."

Her voice was completely matter-of-fact. But like Rowan, she had the ability to hide her emotions.

"Helen and Robbie were too young to remember their father. He fell at Verdun."

I felt my head nodding, but I was numbed by the realization that her husband had died during World War I.

"When I remarried, I was reluctant to have another baby, knowing I would outlive any child I brought into the world. But accidents happen." Her bleak expression softened. "That's how I got my Alex."

Details clicked into place. Their similarity in coloring. Their mutual affection. Reinhard's assumption—puzzling at the time—that Alex would rush to the hospital after Helen's heart attack. Catherine's equally puzzling hysteria that night. I'd assumed they were all bound by friendship, by their shared commitment to the theatre. I never dreamed they were family.

"We're an incestuous little group." Janet's voice held the familiar brittle sarcasm, but her shifting expressions hinted at other emotions: bitterness, tenderness, love.

"Why are you telling me all this?"

She shrugged. "No use hiding it, is there?"

But this was Janet who always had an ulterior motive. As I continued staring at her, she acknowledged my unspoken suspicions with a tight smile.

"Rowan entrusted you with a secret that has never been shared with anyone beyond our little circle. I want to ensure that it will go no further. And the best way to do that is for you to know who we are as well as what we are. All our lives, we've had to protect ourselves. Explain away the impossible. Disappear from time to time and return with new names, new identities."

"And no one in Dale suspects?"

"Probably. But most of the people hereabouts can trace their roots back to the original Mackenzies. We're family as well as neighbors. We look out for one another. We don't make trouble. And we don't welcome those who do."

"Are you . . . threatening me?"

"Don't be silly." The coldness of her eyes belied her smile. "I know you're angry about what happened to your father. But destroying us is not going to change that."

"I don't want to destroy anyone! I just don't want some-one else to get hurt."

Janet studied me for a long moment before nodding briskly. "Then we understand each other. As long as my family isn't hurt, I don't much care if Rowan Mackenzie takes a fall."

She'd probably relish it. What better way to get back at him for his affair with Helen?

"You're the only one who might be able to do it. Because he cares about you. That makes him vulnerable—and gives you power. Use it right and you might shut down his pre-cious theatre. And stop him from ever hurting anyone the way he hurt your father."

Janet's speculative gaze disturbed me. Was that really what she wanted or was she just testing me to discover how far I would go? I didn't want to shut the theatre down, just stop Rowan from interfering in people's lives. He could still direct shows. Put on his original musicals. Run the Cross-roads like an ordinary theatre.

But he wouldn't, I realized. As long as he believed that the theatre was the key to lifting the curse, he would call the Mackenzies every spring, try to heal them every summer. If I tried to make him stop, he could remain an exile forever. And I'd be interfering in his life as surely as he'd interfered in mine.

Everything had seemed so much clearer in New York. Now I wondered if my desire to prevent Rowan from hurt-ing people was just a way to exact vengeance for my father.

I hurried out of the hotel, my mind churning. I was too close to all this, too confused to be objective. Every day, another impossible revelation battered at my understand-ing of what was right and normal and real. By the time I reached the theatre, I couldn't wait to slip out of my head and into Nettie's.

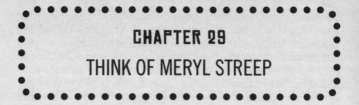

CHAPTER 29
THINK OF MERYL STREEP

MY NUMBERS FEATURED PROMINENTLY in the afternoon's work-through. So did Nick's.

While Mei-Yin rehearsed the ballet in the theatre, Rowan ran Kalma and Nick through "If I Loved You." Judging from Kalma's stormy expression as she left the Smokehouse, it had not gone well. And judging from the shouts we could hear during the rehearsal of "Soliloquy," Nick continued to resist—loudly—Rowan's efforts to help him discover Billy Bigelow's softer side.

By the time the chorus began work on "June Is Bustin' Out All Over," Reinhard's hair was in full porcupine mode. Rowan appeared calm, but his grim expression indicated that he was feeling the strain as well.

Alex joined us onstage, but instead of giving us specific notes, he talked about the community of *Carousel*.

"Remember how in *Brigadoon* I wanted the miracle of the village's return to explode into the excitement of 'Mac-Connachy Square'? That's what's missing from this number. These people have shivered through six long months of snow and ice and rain. Now—finally—summer's arrived! And their joy and excitement and relief overwhelm their New England stoicism and make them all a little punch drunk. That's what I want to see onstage."

We all nodded wearily; he and Rowan had told us this during the early days of rehearsals. But we just couldn't bring it to life onstage.

Alex suddenly swung around and pointed his finger at me. "You're the one who has to set it up, Maggie. The anticipation of the intro and then the release of that first chorus. Forget about the blocking Rowan gave you at the top of the number. Just do what feels right."

I glanced at Rowan, sitting in his usual aisle seat in the house, but he remained silent. Maybe he thought I wouldn't accept his direction any longer.

I thrust the thought aside as I began the intro. The events of the last week made it hard to summon Nettie's confidence that the long, dreary days were ending. But then the men responded, their choral line as insistent as the beat of a tom-tom. When the girls chimed in and the music grew more impatient, I recalled the giddy elation of my audition, the excitement of opening nights, and—in spite of everything that had happened—the relief I had felt leaving the helping professional world behind and returning to this one.

And just like that, the number popped and June finally busted out. The boys and girls were flirty and foolish, each singer trying to top the preceding one to come up with the perfect image of June. I egged them on in the choruses and allowed Nettie's memories to infuse the slower bridges with a dreamy wistfulness.

At one point, I heard Alex shout from the pit, "That's what I'm talking about!" And when Rowan walked onstage after the number, he wore the first smile I'd seen in days.

It was Alex who helped us find the heart of the fucking clambake song as well. And once again, he did it by reminding us of the bonds of community, as critical to this small town's survival as the bounty of the sea.

Maybe we were simply buoyed by the success of our last number, but for once, it *was* a real nice clambake, bloated with good food and good feeling. I gazed at my cast mates, recalling that warren of cubicles at the United Way and that shabby, desperate office in the Bronx, and felt newly grateful for the community I'd found here.

Yet when it came time to perform "You'll Never Walk Alone," my confidence evaporated. Although I understood the emotions I wanted to pour into it, the song felt as flat as if I were still spouting meaningless platitudes. And the high G still sounded like a dying seagull.

"It's much better," Alex assured me. "Don't you think so, Rowan?"

Rowan nodded.

"You're still worrying about the high note, though, and it's throwing you off."

I nodded.

"Maybe we *should* take the song down a third. What do you think?"

I shrugged. Rowan shrugged. Alex's head swiveled back and forth. Then he flung up his hands. "For God's sake! Would you just talk to each other?"

I started. Rowan frowned. We stared at each other. We looked away.

"Fine! If you want to take the goddamn song down, just let me know before the goddamn show opens." Alex disappeared into the bowels of the pit, muttering about some people's stubbornness and other people's blindness and he wasn't going to get caught in the middle and he was way too old for this crap.

Rowan cleared his throat. "You did good work today."

"Not on this number."

"It's a lot closer." He glanced around the theatre as if searching for the nearest exit.

"Why can't I get it?" I blurted.

For the first time, he looked at me. "Stop thinking about the number so much and just feel it, Maggie. Then it will come alive. Like the others did."

"You make it sound easy."

"It's easy to tell someone else what to do. A lot harder to do it yourself. To let go. And allow your heart to carry you. Especially when you don't know where you're going to end up."

For a moment, I forgot what he was, what he had done. I just saw the weariness of his eyes, the wistfulness of his expression. And I wished we could go back. Not to the hectic sexual excitement we had known for those few minutes outside the theatre, but to the unrestrained laughter under the beech, the quiet joy of the plateau, the brief tenderness we had shared in his apartment.

I took a step back. His half-smile vanished.

"I'll see you at seven," he said. And hurried out of the theatre.

* * *

Our final dress rehearsal got off to a promising start. The chorus hit their marks, the carousel turned, and if the overall effect was not as glamorous as I'd dreamed, neither was it as hokey as I'd feared.

Brittany struck all the right notes in her scene with Kalma. Kalma embodied Julie's combination of strength and vulnerability in "If I Loved You." And for the first time, Nick managed to capture some of the fear lurking beneath Billy's bravado. If their kiss was stiff rather than gentle, an audience might still believe they had fallen in love.

So when Kalma hurried past me in the wings to make her costume change, her angry expression shocked me.

"The son of a bitch has been drinking," she said in a furious whisper.

Bobbie and I turned toward Lou, who held up his hands in protest. "One beer at dinner."

"And how many more in your room?" Bobbie demanded.

"None. I swear to God. Look, he was nervous about tonight. Rowan's been riding him hard. He thought a beer might loosen him up."

There was no time for more. Lou had to make his entrance.

Nick did fine in his exchanges with Mrs. Mullin and Jigger, but he just couldn't summon up the proper balance of concern and tenderness when Julie tells him she's pregnant. Then the "Soliloquy" rolled around. We'd caught snatches of the song during rehearsals and heard Nick arguing with Rowan earlier in the day, but this was our first opportunity to see the number.

Maybe that was partly responsible for what happened. He had to know we were clustered in the wings, watching him. Maybe he thought we wanted him to fail, when all we really wanted was the breakthrough Rowan had been pushing him toward for weeks.

The swagger was evident during the "My Boy, Bill" section, but there was also a strange, manic quality. I doubted the beer was responsible; I'd seen Nick put away a six-pack after a show and just get boisterous. More likely, he was afraid of what was coming next. Like me with the high G.

The music returned to the darker, more reflective theme of the opening. As Billy imagined a daughter who would be a smaller version of her mother, a sneer entered Nick's voice. And as he began to sing about the sweet attributes of his little girl, his expression alternated between sullen and truculent.

"Stop!"

All of us watching caught our breaths in a collective gasp. Rowan had interrupted numbers when technical snafus threatened to disrupt them completely, but he had never stopped a dress rehearsal.

"Go back. Take it from the dialogue into the bridge."

Alex hastily flipped pages in his score and whispered the measure number to the musicians. The slow minor vamp began. Nick spoke the lines where Billy wonders aloud what he could possibly do with—and for—a daughter. Then he began to sing.

Rowan stopped him at the end of the first chorus.

"Go back. Same place."

I saw Alex's head turn toward Rowan. Then he obediently signaled the musicians.

This time, Rowan stopped Nick as he launched into the first chorus.

"Go back. Same place."

Nick began again. And again, Rowan stopped him and ordered the music to start over.

Alex hesitated. "Rowan, I'm not sure this is—"

"Same place."

Alex shook his head, but raised his hand. The music began. Nick just stood there, staring at Rowan in his aisle seat.

"Say the lines."

I could see the tendons standing out on Nick's neck, hear the labored sound of his breathing.

"Say the fucking lines!"

Another gasp from the cast, this one louder than the first.

Nick spat out the words. Rowan rose from his seat and

stalked down the aisle. Alex swiveled around on his piano bench. The music faltered, then fell silent.

"Play."

"Rowan . . ."

"Play!"

Rowan stopped in front of the stage, his gaze locked with Nick's. "Say the lines."

Nick obeyed.

"Now sing."

Hands fisted at his side, Nick sang. I couldn't tell if it was anger that choked his voice or some other emotion.

"Go back."

"Jesus," I heard someone whisper.

I'd seen directors push actors to their limits to get to the truth of a performance. But never at a dress rehearsal and never in front of the entire company. It was like stripping an actor bare, forcing him to go to the dark places he was trying so desperately to avoid and then shining a spotlight on his shame and fear.

Rowan didn't need to do that. All he had to do was sprinkle a little faery dust and Nick would turn in a great performance. But clearly, he wanted Nick to do it himself.

And the worst of it was, Nick had already learned the lesson Rowan was trying to cram down his throat. It was obvious from his trembling body, his angry grimace, the way he broke off, unable to sing the line about being a faithful dad.

Nick knew what this song was about. He understood the parallels to his own life, to his failures as a partner, as a father. He was just too proud or too scared or too ashamed to offer them up for Rowan Mackenzie's approval.

"Again," Rowan said in that same steely monotone.

Rowan talked about standing beside his actors, helping them on their journeys of discovery. This wasn't helping. This was just cruel. As cruel as the faeries tormenting my father.

"Again!"

As I strode out of the wings, the hot blast of Rowan's frustration buffeted me.

"Get off the stage, Maggie."

Rowan's voice was low, but there was no mistaking the

warning in it. I continued toward Nick, who had turned up-stage, one hand shielding his face.

"Get off my stage. Now!"

"You have no right to do this!"

"Don't tell me how to direct."

"You're not directing. You're bullying him!"

I heard the muffled thud of his footsteps on the carpet, then the louder clatter as he ran up the steps to the stage. But I was already reaching for Nick, murmuring words of reassurance, of compassion, of caring.

Nick whirled around, smacking aside my hand with such force that I staggered.

"I don't need your help, you fucking cunt!"

For a moment, there was utter silence in the theatre. Then I became dimly aware of voices shouting, floorboards shaking as people stampeded from the wings. But all I saw was Nick's face twisted in a grotesque mask of anger. A single tear winked in the lights before it slipped, unheeded, down his cheek. His right hand clenched into a fist that grew larger and larger as he rushed toward me.

Suddenly, Nick froze, staring at his fist suspended a mere foot from my face. I shrank back, so stunned by his sudden fury and so relieved that he had reined it in that I barely noticed the blur of movement to my right.

Rowan's arm slid around my waist, steadying me. He thrust out his right hand, warding Nick away.

"Touch her again and I'll kill you."

Even more shocking than the words was the quiet savagery in his voice.

And then I understood Nick's stupefied expression. He hadn't quelled the urge to hit me. Rowan had used his magic to hold him at bay until he could reach my side.

Nick stumbled backward, his eyes wild. Everyone else remained frozen, watching us. I wondered if Rowan was holding them at bay, too, or if they were simply too stunned to move.

Rowan's arm slid free, and I turned toward him. Instead of the menace I expected to find, his expression was eager, his lips drawn back over his teeth in a feral smile. Blood lust rose from him like a malevolent fog.

A shiver raced up my back. Saliva filled my mouth. I swallowed it down, terrified and disgusted and excited.

A smile blossomed on Nick's face. His hands bunched into fists. And I knew we were both under the sway of Rowan's emotions, Rowan's power.

They wanted this fight. And so did I.

I wanted to hear the meaty smack of fist on flesh, the hollow crack of shattering bones. I wanted to feel the impact of a punch shuddering up my arm, the warm spray of blood oozing over my fist. The smell of it in my nostrils, the salty-sweet taste filling my mouth. The wild elation as my opponent reeled, the thud of his body as he crashed to the floor, the echoes of his defeat racing through the boards, through my feet, resonating throughout my body, as hot and fierce as any climax.

"Rowan."

Reinhard's voice, very close. I wanted him to go away; he'd ruin everything.

"Rowan!"

The blood lust spiked, and I bit back a moan. Then frustration stabbed me, and I did moan.

The surge of adrenaline ebbed. In its wake, I began to tremble. Firm hands gripped my shoulders. It must be Reinhard; Rowan was still beside me, panting like a winded animal.

The tension drained from Nick's body. Lou hurried over to him, softly urging him to be cool, to let it go. Nick shook off Lou's hand impatiently. His face darkened to the color of fresh liver. His gaze snapped to me.

"Fuck you. And fuck you, too." He glared at Rowan, then hawked a gob of phlegm onto the floor. "Fuck you and your whole fucking theatre!"

He pushed Lou aside, shoved his way through the crowd, and thudded down the steps. As he ran up the aisle, Rowan spun toward me.

"You had to interfere!"

Before I could reply, he took off after Nick.

"Everyone stay where you are!" Reinhard instructed.

Still shaking, I allowed him to guide me toward the collection of bales and baskets and crates that comprised the wharf set. He eased me onto a wooden box and gently probed my wrist and fingers.

"Any pain?"

My wrist ached, but I just shook my head.

"Bobbie! Would you please fetch a cold pack from the freezer in the green room?"

Bobbie raced off, probably glad to have a mission; everyone else just milled around, watching me uncomfortably and conversing in whispers.

"I just wanted to . . ."

Stop Rowan. Help Nick. Do something.

"I know."

Reinhard's voice was kind, but his frown indicated that he shared Rowan's belief that I had interfered. Maybe I had. But there were limits to what a man should have to endure.

"I couldn't just stand there—"

"But it wasn't about you, Maggie. Or what you needed."

I recalled Nick's furious expression and shuddered.

Reinhard patted my shoulder. "It is done. We move on."

Before I could ask how, an unearthly scream filled the theatre. A woman's scream. Coming through the open doors to the lobby.

"*Gott im Himmel*, what now?" Reinhard demanded. "Stay here!" he shouted to the cast as he raced for the stairs.

But no power—faery or human—could have kept us on that stage. We stampeded after him and poured up the aisles like a flood of lemmings.

The lobby was empty. Craning my neck to see past those in front of me, I made out a woman standing in the open doorway. The fingers of her right hand curled like claws over the doorframe as she stared out into the deepening twilight.

Reinhard's steps slowed as he approached her. "Madam? Are you all right?"

She started at the sound of his voice and spun around. And I found myself staring into my mother's terrified face.

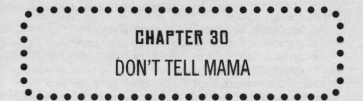

CHAPTER 30
DON'T TELL MAMA

"MOM!"

Her gaze darted around the lobby, frantically searching for me. I flung up my hand and began pushing toward her. When she spotted me, she threw out her arms, a drowning woman reaching for a life preserver.

She clung to me for a moment, then swung me away, shielding me from the crowd. Only then did I realize how mistaken my initial impression had been. She might be terrified, but this was no drowning woman; this was a lioness defending her cub.

As ferociously as Rowan had protected me from Nick.

"Are you all right?" she demanded.

"I'm fine," I replied automatically.

But my world was teetering on its axis again. I tried to square this wild-eyed stranger with the mother I knew. The mother I thought I knew. The woman who offered brisk advice instead of hugs. Who lectured me on how to get ahead in the business world. Who greeted me on every trip home with a quick perusal of my appearance and a resigned sigh. The shirt-waist dress from Talbots was the only thing that was familiar.

Without relinquishing her painful grip on my arms, she turned to keep her wary gaze on the crowd. "I saw him," she whispered. "That man. That director. He looked the same, Maggie. Exactly the same as he did twenty-five years ago!"

I had to do something, say something before everyone heard her accusations.

"If I may."

My mother's head jerked toward Reinhard. She eyed him suspiciously, but without any hint of recognition.

"Forgive me for interrupting. I am Reinhard Genz, the stage manager."

Only Reinhard could perform a brisk little Teutonic bow at such a moment.

"I could not help but overhear. You seem to have mistaken our current director for his father. It happens often. The resemblance, I am told, is quite striking."

My mother shook her head. "I saw him, Maggie. It was the same man."

I couldn't bring myself to lie to her. Again. I could only ask the logical question and allow her to reach the logical — and incorrect—conclusion. Just as I'd done all summer.

"How could it be the same man, Mom?"

"An easy mistake," Reinhard said. "Especially if you only caught a glimpse of him, yes?"

She was still shaking her head, but her expression held doubt now. Her gaze darted from me to Reinhard and back to me. Like Caren when the staff first began their brainwashing. But this time, I was on their side.

My stomach lurched on a wave of nausea.

"Maggie, perhaps you should accompany your mother to the hotel. She must be tired after her long drive." Reinhard still wore a benign smile, but his underlying warning was clear: "Get her out of here."

"No! I want to see that man. I want to talk to him. Tonight!"

"Mom, it's dress rehearsal."

Her gaze traveled over me, belatedly taking in the heavy theatrical makeup, my prim bun, the high-necked blouse and billowing skirt.

"Things are a bit hectic tonight," Reinhard interjected, "but tomorrow, I am sure Rowan will be happy to—"

"Rowan? His name's Rowan?" Panic returned to my mother's face.

"He was named after his father," Reinhard lied smoothly.

I squeezed her hand. "Come on, Mom. We can talk about it back at the hotel."

"But what about your dress rehearsal?" she asked, unexpectedly reverting to maddening practicality.

Reinhard dismissed the necessity of my presence with a nonchalant wave. "Get your mother settled in, Maggie. You can always come back later. If time permits." Subtext: "Once you've locked her up for the night."

As I led her, still protesting, out of the barn, Reinhard shouted, "Everyone! Back into the theatre, please."

I glanced back. Through the open doors, I saw the staff huddled together, watching us.

We took her car; I abandoned my gear in the dressing room, unwilling to leave her for fear of another meltdown. To forestall more questions that I didn't want to answer, I asked, "What are you doing here? How did you even know—?"

"The only number I could find for this place was an answering machine that wouldn't let me leave a message. So I called every theatre in Vermont. When you weren't at any of them. . . ." She shrugged.

I considered reminding her that she could have asked me. But after all the lies I'd told her this summer, she probably doubted she'd get a truthful answer.

"So you drove all the way up here."

She shot me an exasperated look. "Obviously."

She must have left work after lunch. If she'd even gone in today; God only knew how long it had taken her to track down every theatre in Vermont.

"But . . . why?"

"Oh, for God's sake! Why do you think?"

Because I'd been depressed as hell when I called her after my interviews. Because even though she knew it was irrational, she couldn't shake her concerns about this place. Because she had to see for herself that I was okay. Because she was my mom.

I found myself recalling all the times she had dragged herself to my performances. From my debut as a spinning top in kindergarten to my shows in college—including that dreadful original one-act where I'd played an hermaphrodite with a pair of socks stuffed in my leotard. Only once—after I'd taken the HelpLink job—had she ever revealed her fear that acting would leave me as disappointed and disillusioned as my father.

Ever since I was a kid, I'd resented what I considered her coldness, always comparing her to my father who was so free with his hugs and his kisses, who would tuck me into bed at night and play dress-up with me on the weekends. And pretend fireflies were faeries.

But my affectionate, imaginative, volatile father had left. And she was here. As reluctant as ever to talk about feelings. Maybe she thought she didn't need to. She showed them in everything she did, everything she'd ever done—feeding me, clothing me, keeping a roof over our heads, squirreling away money so we could afford a vacation every summer, so I could take piano lessons and art classes and go to an expensive private college. Offering sensible advice that I invariably rejected and keeping her mouth shut about her concerns.

Only Maggie Graham, Helping Professional, had been too stupid—or too stubborn—to see that.

I shifted in my seat to look at her. "I'm glad you're here," I said in a small voice. And in spite of the havoc it might wreak, I was.

"Are you sure you're all right? You looked . . . stressed out. In the theatre."

The understatement of the year. I was still reeling from everything that had happened and finding it hard to think straight, to know what to say, what to avoid saying.

"It's our final dress rehearsal," I said. "Everybody's stressed out."

"Touch her again and I'll kill you."

"Not that Rainer or Rupert or—"

"Reinhard. He's a doctor. He has to be calm."

"I thought he was the stage manager."

"He is. But he's also a pediatrician."

"I don't like him."

"He's really very—"

"And I don't like that theatre. There's something strange about it. I noticed it the first time I was here. Everyone was so happy. It wasn't natural."

Only my mother could observe happiness and conclude it was unnatural. Then again—given the life she'd led with my father—it probably was.

"Like that movie," she added. "The one where they replace the wives with robots."

I smiled, recalling my first impression of Dale.

"And just look at this town!" she exclaimed as she cautiously eased her Audi through the empty roundabout. "Nothing's changed! Except for that . . . pink nightmare." She waved her hand at Hallee's, awash in neon.

"It's a small town, Mom. I doubt it's changed much in the last century. The Bough's just up here on the right."

She pulled into a parking space and ducked her head to stare at the hotel through the windshield. "We stayed here last time."

"Of course we did! It's the only hotel in town. Come on. I'll help you with your stuff."

That proved easy. All she had was a small overnight bag.

Frannie was behind the front desk. She and Bea were spelling each other until Janet could hire a regular night manager. She hurried forward when she saw us.

"Reinhard called and said you'd be coming over. I'm Frannie. You must be Maggie's mom."

"Alison Graham," my mother replied, surveying the empty lobby. "It's just the same," she added with a pointed glance at me.

Frannie clucked. "Lord, yes. Those drapes will probably fall off the rods before someone replaces them. And the upholstery on the chairs is so shiny you can practically see your face. Come on over to the desk and we'll get you settled in, hon."

My mother visibly started at the "hon," but followed Frannie to the reception desk.

"Now," Frannie said briskly. "I can give you your own room for the next two nights, but after that, you'll have to bunk with Maggie. We're full up 'cause of the show."

My mother and I exchanged glances.

"Or I can put you in with Maggie from the get-go. That way, you girls can have a little slumber party."

Another furtive exchange of glances, each of us waiting for the other to make the choice.

"My room doesn't have a bathroom," I ventured. "We share the ones in the hall. But if you don't mind that—"

"No, of course not."

I tried and failed to imagine my mother trotting back and forth to the john with the women in the cast.

"All righty, then!" Frannie plucked a key off the board. "You must have had a long drive, Alison. All the way from New York City."

"Delaware."

Frannie gasped. Her admiring glance suggested my mother was akin to a pioneer woman who had just crossed the limitless prairie. "Lord love you, you must be beat. But I could open up the lounge if you'd like a cocktail before bed."

"Yes!" my mother and I exclaimed in unison. Then Mom frowned. "Or do you have to get back to dress rehearsal?"

I couldn't just desert her. And we could both use a drink. Maybe a few vodka tonics would help her forget the shock of seeing Rowan—and her desire to talk with him tomorrow.

"They'll manage without me."

Frannie beamed and fished a ring of keys out from under the counter. "Best part of being night manager. I got the keys to the kingdom."

Jingling all the way, she led us to the lounge, unlocked the door, and ushered us inside. "Just help yourselves. First one's on the house. After that, just sign the notepad on the bar. You can square up later." Noting Mom's shocked expression, she chuckled. "You're in Dale now, hon. Things are different here."

"Yes," Mom replied, shooting another glance at me. "They certainly are."

I nursed my mug of ale, refilled her glass, and kept the conversation focused on the bloodbath at HelpLink, my interviews, Leila's wedding—anything and everything except the theatre and Rowan. Three vodka tonics and an hour later, we mounted the stairs to my room. I waited until she returned from the bathroom, freshly scrubbed and attired in a lacy blue nightgown, to announce, "I'm going to run back to the theatre."

Mom yawned and crawled into Nancy's bed. "Won't they be finished by now?"

"Probably. But I need to pick up my stuff. It'll only take a few minutes."

"Take my car." She nodded vaguely in the direction of her purse, then bolted upright in bed. "And tell that man I want to talk to him."

That, of course, was my real reason for going to the theatre. In different circumstances, I might have appreciated the irony of urging Rowan to come up with a believable life history. But I was more concerned that he'd never be able to invent one that could allay her suspicions.

As I reached the lobby, the cast began filing into the hotel. Lou paused only long enough to pat my shoulder before pounding upstairs to the room he shared with Nick. Others clustered around me, asking if everything was okay. I told them Mom had been worried about me after my interviews, that she'd decided to surprise me by coming up for the show, that she'd been spooked when Nick bolted past her in the dark.

By the time I reached the theatre, the events of the evening came crashing down on me. The sight of the staff gathered around one of the picnic tables gave me a much-needed jolt of adrenaline. They turned as I approached and I glimpsed Rowan slumped on the bench, cradling his forehead in his hands.

Hal rushed forward and blurted, "Is she all right? Are you all right? God, what a night! I think I've aged ten years."

Lee's hand descended on his shoulder, and Hal fell silent.

"Mom's . . . okay. But she wants to talk with you tomorrow, Rowan."

He lowered his hands and nodded. Then he slowly rose, his gaze sweeping the staff. "There's nothing more we can do tonight. I suggest we all try to get a good night's sleep. We'll have a long day tomorrow."

Reinhard silently handed me my carryall. He hesitated, as if he wanted to say something, then joined the others trudging to the parking lot.

"What did you tell her?" Janet demanded.

"Nothing," I said, not bothering to disguise the bitterness in my voice. "I just backed up Reinhard's story."

"And she believed that?"

"It's the only explanation that makes sense."

Janet rounded on Rowan. "We need to make sure—"

"Yes, Janet. Thank you. You should go back to the house. Helen will be worried."

Of course. She would have sensed the uproar at the theatre, just as Janet had.

Rowan beckoned me to the bench opposite his. I slid onto it, all too aware that we had been sitting in these same positions only three nights ago. Just as he had done then, he folded his hands together and stared down at them.

"I'm sorry I upset your mother."

"It's not your fault."

His head came up at that. "What do you want me to do?"

"Obviously, you have to make her believe Reinhard's story."

"Is that what you *want*?"

"What I want doesn't matter!"

"It does to me."

I was the one to look away. "Do I want you to brainwash my mother? No! But I don't want her obsessing about this. She's already paranoid about you. And this theatre. If she starts asking questions, she'll never stop. You wouldn't believe how stubborn she is."

A tired smile lightened his expression. Then it vanished. "All right. Bring her to my apartment tomorrow morning at nine."

I nodded and started to rise, then sank back down on the bench. "She'll ask about my father. We didn't discuss him, but . . ."

"I'll tell her as much of the truth as I can."

"And . . . she'll be okay? Afterward?"

"I swear to you on everything and everyone I hold dear."

That comforted me a little; if he could swear on Helen's life, I knew he'd ensure that Mom came through this unharmed.

CHAPTER 31

RAZZLE DAZZLE

PROMPTLY AT NINE O'CLOCK, I knocked on the door of Rowan's apartment, noting with relief that it had been repaired. It swung open a moment later.

"Maggie. Mrs. Graham. Please come in."

I just gaped at him. He'd chopped off his hair. The loose waves that normally fell to his shoulders now brushed his jaw. Even more astonishing was his short-sleeved shirt. Some designer's misguided idea of a Hawaiian theme. Black and white fish swam in an aqua ocean studded with pink and yellow seaweed. Already unnerved by the prospect of this meeting, I needed every ounce of self-control to keep from bursting into hysterical laughter.

As I stepped inside, my desire to laugh vanished, replaced by the uncomfortable realization that this was the first time, I had ventured here, since. . . . that night. His office was immaculate now. I resolutely avoided glancing toward the bedroom. My mother was far less circumspect, head swiveling this way and that to take in his abode. As she'd called it during breakfast.

Her eyes widened slightly as he led us into the living area. So did mine. The night of Helen's heart attack, I'd merely noted its size and its blend of comfort and elegance. Now I studied it, as I had so often studied the man who lived here.

I took in the thick rugs scattered across the floor, their tangle of vines and flowers echoing those painted on the

317

wooden sideboard. The L-shaped sofa of deep forest green. Easy chairs in a paler shade of misty gray-green. A spray of bare branches in a tall porcelain vase. It was almost as if he wanted to re-create the forest here.

Ceiling fans whirred softly, stirring the faint breeze that wafted through the windows nestled under the eaves on the eastern side of the room. I hadn't noticed them on my previous visit. Nor the small, antique melodeon that stood near the baby grand piano. The battered wooden trunk that served as a coffee table was a startling contrast to the other furniture; perhaps—like the melodeon—it was a treasure preserved from his early days in this world. Certainly, there were few other personal items in the room, unless you counted the leather-bound volumes that filled the bookcases and the floor-to-ceiling collection of record albums.

Hazy sunshine filtered through the skylights, but Rowan had turned on the lamps that flanked the sofa, as well as the track lights near the impressive bank of stereo equipment and the hanging lamp over the circular dining table. The overall effect was one of warmth and openness. My mother's expression conveyed just the opposite, but Rowan pretended not to notice as he waved us toward the sofa.

"May I get you something to drink? Coffee? Tea? Water?"

"No. Thank you." My mother gave him the quelling look that always drove away officious waiters.

I sat in the middle of the long L of the sofa and anxiously kneaded the soft velvet. Rowan waited for my mother to seat herself at the end closest to the door, then perched on the easy chair near her. I heard the soft scrape of her sandals on the hardwood floor as she ostentatiously moved her feet away from his.

Rowan leaned back in his chair, shifted position, then leaned forward again, clearly uncomfortable. My mother observed him, silent and unsmiling.

"I'm sorry for startling you last night," he finally said. "I can't imagine what you must have thought when I came racing out of the theatre like that."

"I thought you were the same man I'd met twenty-five years ago," she replied with devastating bluntness.

"Yes. Maggie told me." A quick smile. An awkward shrug.

"I get that a lot. I've never been able to see the resemblance. Maybe I just didn't want to." His smile faded, then reasserted itself with obvious effort. "My father was taller, of course. Not half so skinny. And his eyes were green."

I fought to conceal my shock when I realized that his eyes were a muddy hazel. Almost brown. I'd been so blinded by his shirt that I hadn't even noticed.

"But mostly," Rowan continued, "it was his air of confidence. He was so much more distinguished. In every way." Another smile, tinged with bitterness this time. A helpless flutter of his hands. Somehow, he'd managed to make the scars less visible, too.

Belatedly, I realized I was watching a carefully orchestrated performance. The stupid shirt. The "aw, shucks" manner. The subtle changes to his physical appearance. He even looked younger—or maybe his self-conscious gestures made him appear so.

And it was working. My mother's frown had deepened, obviously contrasting this awkward young man with the self-assured director she had met. So much more distinguished in every way.

Even I found it difficult to believe this was the same man I had worked with all summer. Was he using faery glamour to create these effects? Or were his acting skills just as uncanny?

"Forgive me," Rowan said. "I'm monopolizing the conversation. Maggie said you wanted to talk about . . . my father?"

"I wanted to talk *to* your father."

"That won't be . . . he moved. Out of the country."

I let out the breath I hadn't realized I was holding. Too easy for her to check the obituaries if Rowan claimed he had died.

"When was this?"

Rowan considered. "Ten years ago?" He frowned. "No, eleven now."

"Rather young to retire, wasn't he?"

"Yes. Everyone called it a tragedy." His tone made it clear he didn't share that opinion. I found myself wondering what had caused the rift between them before I remembered that this was an imaginary relationship with an equally imaginary father.

"Would you mind giving me his phone number? Or e-mail address?"

Rowan regarded his hands. A hot blush stole up his throat to fill his cheeks with color. "We don't keep in touch. But I'd be happy to ask some of the older folks in town."

My mother studied him, clearly curious. But all she said was, "There was a woman—Helen?—who called our house a number of times. A member of the staff, she claimed."

Part of me was relieved to know Rowan had told the truth about Helen checking in on Daddy. But there was something unsettling about the way Mom emphasized "claimed." Why would she think Helen had lied?

"Is she still with the theatre? Or has she retired and left the country as well?"

"She lives in Dale," Rowan replied, ignoring the barb. "But she's not in the best of health."

"She just had a heart attack," I added.

Mom's frosty smile suggested Helen had arranged it just to avoid speaking with her. "It's not important. I just wanted to ask a few questions about my ex-husband."

"I can try and answer them."

"You knew Jack?" she asked sharply.

"Not well. I was only an intern that summer. On the stage crew. We didn't mix much with the cast. I never even realized he was Maggie's father until a few days ago. But I do remember his performance."

"He did two shows."

Rowan's eager expression faded, as if crushed by his forgetfulness. "I'm sorry. I just remember the one."

"Yes?" Mom's fingers dug into the nap of the velvet, belying her indifferent tone.

Rowan's expression grew soft, almost dreamy. "He was very good. Amazing, really. He brought a sort of . . . lost boy quality to Billy. He had the toughness and the swagger, but he made you realize—"

"Wait!" I interrupted. "Are you saying . . . did Daddy play Billy Bigelow?"

Rowan and Mom turned to me, identical expressions of surprise on their faces.

"Yes, of course," Mom said. "Didn't I mention that?"

I shook my head.

"I'm sorry, Maggie." Rowan's voice was very gentle. "I thought you knew."

"That's the show we're doing," I told her.

She blew out her breath and muttered, "Christ on a crumpet."

Rowan started. I'd heard her use that expression countless times and just nodded.

"What are the odds?" she demanded. "Not only that you'd stumble on the same theatre but star in the same show?"

I felt an unexpected rush of pride that she assumed I'd have a starring role. Along with the shock of realizing I'd been so successful in steering our conversation away from the theatre last night that I hadn't told her anything about my season at the Crossroads.

"It *is* pretty incredible that both of them would end up doing the same show," Rowan admitted. "But we've had generations of families coming here. Parents tell their children about the theatre. Years later, their kids audition."

"I never talked about this place with Maggie. And if her father did, she was too young to remember. She didn't even remember coming here." My mother's head snapped toward me. "Unless . . ."

Unless I'd been lying about that along with everything else.

"The barn looked familiar. But when I drove into Dale, I was just looking for a bed and breakfast. And then somehow . . ."

My mother sighed.

Anxious to avoid dwelling on the incredible "coincidence" of Daddy and I stumbling upon the theatre, I asked her, "*Was* Daddy good? As Billy?"

I had another motive, of course. She rarely talked about my father and this seemed as good an opportunity as any to try and learn more.

Her expression softened, just as Rowan's had. "He was amazing. Just like you said." A grudging nod to Rowan. "Maybe it was the role. Or the direction. But it was the best thing he'd ever done. And I saw most of his shows."

"You did?"

"Well, not the ones where he was a chorus boy or a spear

carrier. But the important ones. I traipsed all over the country. Even after you were born. I don't know how many hole-in-the-wall theatres I dragged you to. Then he got the teaching job and I thought we were finished with all that." She shot an accusing look at Rowan before asking, "Do you remember anything else about that summer? What he was like? His friends?"

"He didn't seem to have many friends," Rowan replied with obvious reluctance.

"He rarely did." Mom's voice was crisp. "Probably because he looked down his nose at the rest of the cast."

Rowan's head drooped in silent agreement.

"Jack always thought he was the best actor onstage."

"Was he?" I asked.

"Yes. But that was no great feat given the places he performed."

I inwardly cringed, wondering if she'd felt the same watching me—the best of a mediocre bunch.

"He seemed to get along with everyone," Rowan said. "I don't remember any problems, anyway. With his cast mates."

Neatly skirting his problems with faeries.

"And with your father?" Mom asked.

Rowan hesitated. "My father wouldn't have spent much time with Jack. He was rather . . . aloof."

"Well. Thank you for your time, Mr. Mackenzie. I'll be going now."

As Mom prepared to rise, Rowan's hand came down upon hers. She recoiled, then sank back onto the sofa.

Now it would begin. Already, she would be feeling that power flowing through her, the desire to stay, to hear what this man wanted to tell her. In a few moments, her head would be bobbing as she mindlessly accepted any lie he chose to offer. I wanted to close my eyes and blot out what was happening, but I was part of it. And I owed it to my mother to witness everything.

Rowan released her hand, but remained leaning forward, his knees almost touching hers.

"Maggie told me what happened to Jack. Afterward. I just want to tell you how sorry I am."

My mother nodded stiffly.

"I can understand why you blame this theatre. Suspect

that we made things worse by stirring up feelings that had lain dormant. But I swear to you, when he left here, he was happy. Eager to go home and start over. If any of us had known what was happening, we would have done everything in our power to help."

Mom nodded again, more slowly this time. She didn't have that glazed look I'd seen on Caren's face. She merely looked . . . thoughtful.

"That's kind of you, Mr. Mackenzie."

"It's not kind!"

His vehemence made us both start.

"I feel responsible," he said more calmly.

"Why? You were just a boy at the time."

"Because as long as I've been a part of this theatre, we've made it our job not just to put on good shows, but to help people. And we didn't help Jack."

"I'm not sure anyone could have, Mr. Mackenzie. Jack was always a . . . what did you call him? A lost boy? It was part of his attraction." Her mouth twisted as she grimaced. "Of course, there's a big difference between being attracted to a lost boy and building a life with one."

Rowan's gaze drifted to the windows. "You always wonder, don't you? If you could have done more. If you made the right decisions. If there was a certain crossroads where you might have changed everything simply by choosing another path. Whether that might have led to greater happiness or greater tragedy. Or simply taken you to the same place in the end."

My mother was watching him with open curiosity. I was barely breathing, knowing he was speaking as much about his past as hers.

"In the end, all we can do is live with our choices and learn from them. And move on."

"Is that what you've done, Mr. Mackenzie?"

Rowan acknowledged her question with a small smile. "No. I dwell in the past. And advise others not to." Abruptly, his smile vanished. "Maybe that's why I'm a successful director. I sit in the shadows, moving people about on a stage. Observing their successes, their failures, their lives. Much easier than shining a spotlight on mine."

Mom observed him silently. Then she said, "I think you

should call your father, Mr. Mackenzie. Life is too short to spend it dwelling on the past."

"You're a very perceptive woman," Rowan said. "Your daughter takes after you."

"Do you think so?"

"Well, she called me an arrogant prick with a God complex."

There was a moment of appalled silence. Then my mother burst out laughing. When I glared at Rowan, she laughed even harder.

"Maggie does tend to be . . . plainspoken."

"A trait we share," I reminded her tartly.

"One of many," Rowan remarked. "You may have gotten your imagination and your love of the theatre from your father, Maggie, but your strength, your stubbornness, your common sense . . . those you get from your mother. You even look like her."

Mom and I exchanged frowns. I saw a small-boned, perfectly groomed woman with hair that was still black (thanks to her hair stylist Paul), a milkmaid complexion (thanks to her genes and Olay Regenerist) and arresting blue eyes. She undoubtedly saw her slightly overweight, inadequately groomed daughter, auburn hair in a messy ponytail, a sprinkling of freckles on her cheeks, a budding zit on her chin, and eyes of some indeterminate color between blue and green.

"The coloring's different, of course," Rowan said. "But you've got the same jawline, the straight nose. The way you thrust your chin out when you're angry. And flash that scornful look that makes a man want to slink away. And the same wonderful bellow of laughter." Catching our astonished stares, he cleared his throat. "The kind of things anyone might notice."

My mother regarded him for a long moment before turning her speculative gaze on me. "This has been an interesting morning. But I won't take up any more of your time, Mr. Mackenzie. You must have a great deal to do today."

"More than you can imagine. Our Billy Bigelow walked out last night."

"He'll be back," I assured her. I glanced at Rowan for confirmation. "He *will* be back?"

"I'm not sure. Lou called last night after he got back to their room. Nick's things were gone."

I'd thought the staff had looked despondent because of my mother's untimely arrival. Now I realized they'd been reeling from the shock of Lou's call as well.

"What sort of an actor walks out on a show?" Mom demanded.

"It was my fault," Rowan replied. "I pushed him."

"That's what directors are supposed to do."

Rowan shook his head. "I pushed too hard. I was frustrated with his performance, yes. But there were . . . other frustrations. And I took it out on Nick. It was inexcusable."

I was the "other frustration," of course. Our blowup. His concern about what I'd do with my newfound knowledge. But I found it hard to believe that could have overridden his sense of responsibility to Nick.

"I think you're being a bit hard on yourself," Mom said. "After all, you're only human."

Rowan looked away.

"And you're still dwelling on the past."

This time, he nodded slowly. "It's been a pleasure speaking with you, Mrs. Graham."

"Likewise, Mr. Mackenzie. I look forward to seeing the show tonight."

Mom headed for the door. When she realized I wasn't following, she glanced over her shoulder.

"I'll be down in a minute."

Her gaze darted from me to Rowan. Then she nodded and strode out of the room, closing the front door firmly behind her.

"What an extraordinary woman," Rowan mused.

"You seem to have won her over."

His expression grew hard. "Well, that was my job, wasn't it?"

I was suddenly aware that the light in his apartment seemed harsh and unforgiving, accentuating the lines around his eyes. His green eyes. But of course, he didn't need to create illusions for me.

"I know you used your power to change yourself. But you didn't . . ."

"Brainwash her? No." Seeing my puzzlement, he made

an impatient gesture. "I owed it to her to be honest. As honest as I could. To try and make up for the harm I'd done. And help her move on."

She wasn't even one of his Mackenzie chicks. But once she entered his world, she became his responsibility.

"Maybe this visit is a gift, Maggie. For her and for you."

I wondered if that was the reason I had come here. If so, it was an extraordinarily roundabout way to reconnect with my mother.

"Not much of a gift for you," I noted. "Or the rest of the staff."

"Neither Reinhard nor Alex was on staff that summer. Janet and Helen are the only ones she might remember. I'll just make sure they're seated in the balcony tonight."

"Helen's coming?"

"You think anything would keep her away?"

He wandered over to the piano. The score of *Carousel* rested on the music stand. The open script lay facedown on the bench.

"You don't think Nick's coming back, do you?"

"No."

Firm. Final. And devoid of emotion.

"You're going on as Billy."

"If I have to."

He had created the blocking. He knew the songs. Hell, he probably knew every line of dialogue. And if he could alter his appearance for my mother, surely he could perform in the show and work his necessary magic at the same time.

I hesitated, then said, "Last night . . . what you said to me about interfering . . ."

"I said a lot of things last night. I let my emotions rule me. That was a mistake."

"I thought we were supposed to let our emotions carry us."

He looked away. "I was talking about a song."

"But if I hadn't—"

"It's done, Maggie. And we just discussed the futility of dwelling on the past." He picked up the *Carousel* score and flipped through it. "I've scheduled a company meeting at ten. After that, you'll have the rest of the day off. I'm just going to rehearse Billy's big scenes today."

As I walked to the front door, I heard him tapping out the first few notes of "If I Loved You" on the piano. He stopped in mid-phrase.

I closed the door on his silent apartment. As I reached the bottom of the stairs, my mother hurried toward me. "I was so charmed by Mr. Mackenzie that I forgot my purse." She rolled her eyes and started up the stairs. "I'll be back in a sec."

I sank onto the bottom step. The meeting had gone better than I could have hoped. Mom seemed satisfied. Rowan had assumed responsibility for last night's fiasco—and for what had happened to my father. If Nick didn't return, he would be brilliant as Billy. And he'd assured me often enough that I could shine as Nettie.

So why did I feel so depressed?

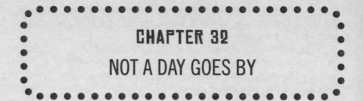

CHAPTER 32

NOT A DAY GOES BY

ROWAN APPEARED AT THE COMPANY MEETING in his regulation linen shirt. His shorn hair caused a greater sensation than his announcement about Nick; clearly, word had already spread. And his calm statement that he would be stepping into the role evoked more relief than surprise.

Mom and I headed off to spend the day in Bennington. Instead of commenting on our meeting with Rowan, she remarked on the scenery, the steep hills, a Moose Crossing sign. It was half an hour before she said, "You avoided talking about your summer last night."

"You were already upset."

She twisted around in her seat to look at me. "Has it been that bad?"

"No. It's been . . . pretty great, actually."

I waited for the inevitable warning about getting caught up in the false glamour, the reminder that it was a brutal business, that I'd never make any money, that I was too old to be bouncing from one second-rate theatre to another. But all she said was, "Tell me about it."

I talked about the shows, about the cast. I talked about Rowan, too, careful to avoid praising him to the skies as Daddy had done. Her expression grew thoughtful when I described his philosophy of casting people in roles that would force them to dig deep and learn something about themselves.

"I never even asked who you were playing in *Carousel.* I just assumed it was that perky best friend. But from what you just said . . ."

"I'm the inspiring anthem singer."

"The 'You'll Never Walk Alone' woman?"

"That's the one."

She digested that in silence. Then said, "I've never liked that song. It's fine at the end of the show. Quite moving, actually. Much as I hate to admit it. But if anyone told me to keep my chin up while my husband was lying dead at my feet, I would have killed her."

I laughed. "That was pretty much my reaction, too. At first."

I felt more than saw her head turn toward me. "And now?"

I told her about my struggle to find meaning in the platitudes, to construct a life history for Nettie, to make the character real. I even shared my Goddess Wheel experience.

"A tie between Athena and Aphrodite? That doesn't bode well."

"No. But it pretty much sums up my experience with men." I hesitated a moment before adding, "Maybe you should take the quiz when we get back to the hotel."

"Oh, that should be fun," she replied, her dry tone indicating just the opposite.

We strolled through Bennington, popping in and out of shops. Mom sprang for an unbelievably expensive serving platter at Bennington Potters. I settled for a mug on the seconds rack. We visited the Bennington Center for the Arts, where we lingered at the Covered Bridge Museum and I tried—in vain—to get a peek at the space where the Oldcastle Theatre Company performed. After a late lunch at the packed Blue Benn Diner, we hopped back in the car to scope out three nearby covered bridges, exclaiming over each like typical city mice.

Our covered bridge tour sparked memories of other vacations: the trip to Mystic Seaport, where I threw up; the trip to Williamsburg, where she got a massive sinus infection; our many pilgrimages to Rehoboth.

"You *will* come?" she asked. "The season will be over by then."

"Unless—by some miracle—I have a job."

"Just tell them you can't possibly start until after Labor Day. If they want you badly enough, they'll wait."

"Right now, nobody wants me at all."

"They will," she said firmly.

By the time we reached Dale, the afternoon was waning. I knew I should go to the hotel and relax before the show, but the memories we had shared—and the rare confidences—encouraged me to keep driving.

As I pulled into the empty parking lot at the theatre, I said, "I thought we could sit by the pond for a bit. It's a lot cooler than my room."

We walked in silence to the pond. Sat on a bench. Stared at the upside-down trees reflected in the calm surface of the water.

Suddenly, she turned toward me. "Look. If you love this . . ." She gestured brusquely toward the theatre. ". . . then that's what you should be doing. I'm not going to pretend I'm happy about it. But you're a grown woman."

Caught off-guard, I just stared at her. Then I admitted, "I *do* love it."

There were times during these last few days that I'd forgotten that. The joy of stepping out of the everyday world, of sloughing off Maggie to become someone else, of inhabiting that person, that world for a few hours. The sudden tension as the house lights dimmed, an excitement born of uncertainty, of knowing that in live theatre you could never predict exactly what might happen. The symbiotic relationship between performer and audience, each charging the other emotionally.

Every actor experienced that. But this summer, I'd come to value the sense of community as I never had before. Maybe because I'd usually been a jobber, coming in to do a couple of shows, then moving on to another round of auditions, another home away from home, another set of cast mates who were quickly forgotten. I'd found unexpected friendships here and unexpected support on and off the stage.

And in spite of all my difficulties with Nettie, there was a certain satisfaction in proving that I could go the extra mile, explore more deeply than I wanted, relinquish my inhibitions and trust my director and my cast mates to help me. And an even greater satisfaction in knowing that I could help them on their circuitous paths of discovery.

Even Rowan. If he'd pushed me to look into my dark places, I'd pushed him just as hard. And if I still wasn't sure what this summer was supposed to teach me, I had discovered one thing, perhaps some time ago, although I only realized it now.

"I love acting," I said. "But I don't think that's what I should be doing with my life."

Mom let out her breath in obvious relief. Then demanded, "Well, what *is*? You're thirty-two years old, Maggie. Don't you have any idea what you want to be when you grow up?"

"I'm working on it, okay?"

We glared at each other, the earlier camaraderie evaporating.

Still a little shaken by my realization, I said, "That's not what I wanted to talk about."

She nodded so wearily that I almost let it go. But this conversation had been postponed for too many years. And I needed to have it before I walked onstage tonight.

"Tell me about Daddy."

My father would have turned it into a grand tragedy. Told in my mother's measured voice, it was the largely expressionless recounting of a relationship that began in college and ended sixteen years later in divorce.

I knew the broad outlines: that he had gone off to New York after graduation hoping for his big break, that he had worked in a series of non-Equity theatres while she got her graduate degree in business administration and her first job in banking. I didn't know that she had performed in college as well. Or realize how many times they had broken up and gotten back together again.

She talked about the early years of their marriage, Daddy stealing a few days at home when he was working nearby, more often gone for months. The pain of being left behind morphing into a strange contentment at organizing her days as she pleased. The excitement of their reunions that made her feel like a newlywed. But there were also the months without work, the inevitable quarrels over money, over the future, over other women.

I gaped at her. "Daddy cheated on you?"

"He was faithful to me when he was home. As to what might have happened when he was away . . ." She shrugged.

Her stoical acceptance shocked me almost as much as the idea that he might have been unfaithful. Now I understood why she'd been suspicious about Helen's calls. Maybe Helen had been one of a long line of women calling Jack Sinclair after the season ended.

"That lost boy quality . . . it drew a lot of people to him. Including me. I thought I could make him happy, give him what he needed, make everything right. Of course, I couldn't. No one could. Which is why I never worried that much about what he was doing when he was away. It hurt my pride more than anything else."

"Your father was an unhappy man. Unhappy with himself and unhappy with his life."

Reluctant to press her about Daddy's possible infidelities, I just listened as she described the move to Wilmington, the months when it looked like the marriage would founder, the discovery that she was pregnant. All in that same expressionless voice.

When she described how Daddy had exchanged acting for grad school, I just stared at the upside-down trees. I'd always feared I'd broken up their marriage. Now I realized that I had stolen his dreams as well.

Mom seized my arm. "Nobody could make Jack Sinclair do anything he didn't want to do. If he gave up acting, it was because he was ready to. Your arrival just gave him the graceful exit he needed."

I nodded, only half-believing it. Then I recalled how he had fought Rowan's attempts to brainwash him for two days before finally surrendering.

"Those were good years, Maggie. The best we'd had since college. You gave us a common bond. And he adored you."

Saturday evenings, falling asleep to the sound of his guitar. Sunday mornings, curled up in bed with him while he read me the funnies. Clapping and laughing as he sang along to an MTV video. Coming down the stairs Christmas Day to find the letter he had helped me write to Santa, now marked with comments in red or green ink: "In stock" next to my request for a light-up wand; "Moondancer" next to my urgent plea for a unicorn My Little Pony. And at the bottom, the name and badge number of the elf who had filled the order. By the time I realized that "Everett" and "Ernie" and "Ellsworth" were all Jack Sinclair, he had already left.

Mom released my arm and sighed. "And of course, you adored him. That's why I let things drag on as long as I did. It might have been kinder for all of us if I'd made the break sooner."

He'd always let her make the tough decisions. He indulged my whims and fed my imagination. She gave me time-outs and made me eat my vegetables.

I'd spent the first half of my life blaming her for driving him away, and the second half blaming him for abandoning us. But I'd never stopped longing for him.

You want to know the truth about your father, but only if it reinforces what you already believe.

I wasn't sure who my father was anymore. Or what to believe.

"Do you ever think about him?" I asked.

Her smile was infinitely weary. "Every day."

"You still love him."

"No. But I can't help worrying about him. Wondering where he is. If he's even alive."

He was always seeking something more.

I almost wished that he had found what he was looking for. Then I could imagine him frolicking in Faerie, drinking nectar from a golden cup or whatever the hell they did.

Should I have allowed him to go with them knowing they might toss him aside and leave him even more miserable?

Rowan couldn't have done that any more than my mother could have ended the marriage sooner. Both of them had tried to redeem Jack Sinclair, to save him from himself, to reconcile him to this world. Neither had dreamed their failure would condemn him to endlessly seek the elusive portal to another.

"Does it help?" Mom asked. "Knowing any of that?"

"Yes."

I had a few more pieces of the puzzle, but I would never have them all. The lost boy was lost to me forever.

THE AIR IN THE DUNGEON CRACKLED with nervous tension that night. Hal flew around making last-minute adjustments to Rowan's costumes. Catherine had a small nervous breakdown when she discovered a wheel had come off one of the carousel horses. Javier had a small nervous breakdown watching Catherine's. Reinhard's hair grew progressively higher.

I observed it all without being touched by any of it. I felt numb, my senses muffled as if I were swaddled in cotton. Even when Alex told me he had dropped "You'll Never Walk Alone" a third, I just nodded and obediently ran through the key change with him.

The man of the hour was conspicuously absent, which sent the cast into a brief frenzy until Reinhard explained that Rowan would be dressing in his apartment.

"That's a relief," Kalma said. "The guys would have freaked. Imagine seeing Rowan in his tighty-whities."

"Mmmm," Albertha purred. "I'm imagining it right now."

For the first time that evening, I smiled, picturing their reactions if I told them he wore boxers.

By the time we gathered in the green room, the anticipation of witnessing Rowan's transformation had risen to a fever pitch. When the door swung open, there was a moment of slack-jawed silence. Part of it was the novelty of seeing him in a blood-red sweater, black leather vest, and red-and-black checkered pants. But it was more than his costume or the stage makeup that lent a ruddy glow to his complexion. He exuded that explosive combination of danger and sexuality that was the very essence of Billy Bigelow.

His sudden grin dispelled that impression. "If you like this, you should see my tropical fish shirt."

As the laughter ebbed, his expression grew serious. "The last few days have been difficult for all of us. I'd like to thank you for your patience and your hard work and your belief in me." His gaze lingered a moment on me before he added, "This is the first time I've ever performed on this stage. And to be honest, I'm a little nervous. But we have a fine show and a splendid cast and I'm honored to be part of it."

We formed our usual pre-show circle. Ever since learning what Rowan was, I'd been dreading this moment, but instead of flinching when his power touched me, I felt strangely awed to recognize its source. In spite of his claim of nervousness, the energy flowing around our circle felt perfectly controlled.

When Reinhard called places, Rowan allowed us to precede him backstage. As each person passed, his hand gripped a shoulder, patted an arm, shook a hand. Like a priest blessing his congregation.

When it was my turn, he just stared at me. The black liner made his eyes look enormous and brilliantly green; I hoped he would remember to tone down the color if he ran into my mother after the show.

His hand rose. A long forefinger gently tapped my breastbone.

"Stop thinking about the number and just feel it."

I waited in the wings while the mill girls and fishermen eased in front of the scrim. Across the stage, Reinhard perched like Bob Cratchit on his stage manager's stool. His head came up as Rowan and Albertha took their positions. Then he slid off the stool and disappeared into the darkness of the stage right wings. A few moments later, the murmur of conversation in the house ceased.

Reinhard cleared his throat. "Ladies and gentlemen. Welcome to the Crossroads Theatre's production of *Carousel.* For tonight's performance, the role of Billy Bigelow will be played by Rowan Mackenzie."

Even through the thick velvet curtain, I could hear the audience's whispers. As they rose to an excited babble, Reinhard slipped back onto his stool and pulled on his headset. The work light winked out, leaving only the faint glow from Reinhard's desk lamp, shining down on his open notebook of cues.

The audience grew quiet, and a shiver of anticipation rippled through me. I groped for Bobbie's hand in the darkness. Felt fingertips brushing my left wrist, a hand gripping my shoulder. Knew the same thing was happening in the stage right wings, in front of the scrim, in the lobby where others waited to make their entrance down the aisles. Clusters of performers, scattered throughout the theatre, yet linked together. Waiting.

The jolt of Rowan's power made me catch my breath. Clearly, he *was* a little nervous. But within moments, the energy subsided to a slow, steady pulse.

The curtain whispered open. The lights came up behind the scrim, twilight blues and lavenders as soft and mysterious as the music that rose from the pit. In front of the scrim, two pools of pale light illuminated the mill girls sweeping their brooms stage right and the fishermen repairing their nets stage left, their movements as dreamlike as the music, as steady as the pulse of Rowan's power.

The sweet dissonance of the piccolos. A shivering ripple of energy through our bodies. Alex and Rowan, twin conductors, perfectly attuned to each other.

Shafts of misty blue light revealed the roustabouts emerging from the wings, otherworldly figures half-visible through the scrim as they wheeled on the pieces of the carousel and paraded slowly around Billy's pulpit.

Horns called mournfully, their sound fading with each repetition. Rowan's power faded as well, only to swell again as the strings came in, lush and sweeping, to release the workers from their drudgery. As the carousel began its first slow revolution, the girls ripped kerchiefs from their heads, the men snatched up coats and hats. My body quivered with the same urgency.

The music grew faster, Rowan's power more palpable. No longer a current passing through me to Bobbie, but a web connecting all of us. A shimmering web of power as brilliant as the umbrella of multi-colored lights suspended over the carousel. It carried us along with the frenzied rush of music, the frenzied rush of the townsfolk spilling down the aisles. Then it slowed, hovering like the music on the brink of resolution, hovering like the crowd at the edge of the fairgrounds, savoring the anticipation for one final moment before the scrim rose and the music exploded into the joyous waltz and Rowan leaped onto Billy's pulpit to sweep cast and audience alike into the lights and spectacle and swirling motion of the carousel.

I caught only glimpses of him during the opening number: exhorting the crowd from his pulpit; lifting Kalma effortlessly onto her carousel horse; leaning casually against its pole, smiling at her.

Then it was over and I was hurrying to the dressing rooms with the other chorus members. Brittany's voice crackled through the ancient speakers as she sang about "Mister Snow." Tomorrow night, I promised silently, I would watch her scene with Kalma. But tonight—like everyone else—I rushed through my costume change so I could get back to the wings in time for "If I Loved You."

When Rowan began to sing, I felt both relief and disappointment because he sounded so ... ordinary. He drew me in slowly, his voice sometimes rough with frustration, other times faltering with uncertainty, only to soar, clear and strong and sure when he reached the main theme. His quicksilver mood changes captured Billy's struggle to remain aloof from Julie and the reluctant fascination that pulled him relentlessly toward her, his vain attempt to laugh off his attraction, only to fall, helpless as the blossoms drifting down from the trees, and surrender with a kiss so sweet and gentle it made me ache.

His "Soliloquy" explored all of Billy's shifting emotions: the concern of an expectant father; pride in his son and confidence in the infinite possibilities that await him; the shock of realizing he might have a daughter; disappointment turning to tenderness as he pictured her; and finally the panicked determination to do anything to ensure her welfare.

The applause continued through the lighting change and Rowan's cross to stage right. It was still going strong when

he glanced over his shoulder to where I was waiting in the
stage left wings. I obediently made my entrance, but I still
had to ad lib a few lines until the tumult subsided enough
to move on with the scene.

That was one of the few moments when I was aware of
my performance. The rest of my scenes passed in a sort of
blur. Even "June" and "Clambake."

Suddenly, I found myself walking toward Kalma and
Rowan, walking toward the number I had dreaded since the
day I was cast.

Rowan was so still I could almost believe he was dead.
Kalma was on her knees beside him, her long wig masking
her face. I knew I should be watching Billy and Julie, but I
just stared at the man who had pushed me so hard, at the
woman who had given me the key to unlocking Nettie's
character. I observed the tension in Kalma's narrow shoulders, Rowan's hand lying palm-up on the floor, those long,
slender fingers far too beautiful to belong to Billy. Noting
little details like a reporter at a crime scene.

I knew then that I was going to fail.

A soft cry escaped me, covered by Kalma's line. Then it
was my turn to speak, to respond to her desperate plea, to
tell her what she must do.

The silence stretched. Still on her knees, Kalma twisted
around. For a moment, her tear-streaked face went blank.
Then she shook her head, suddenly fierce.

"Nettie. Please!"

I realized my hand was covering my mouth. I let it fall.

And then I felt him, his touch as reassuring as if he cradled me in his arms. And something else, very faint, a
feather brushing against my consciousness.

Alex stood in front of his piano bench, facing the stage.
His eyes were closed, his face a grimace of concentration.

Rowan and Alex would not let me fail. Not on opening
night. Not in front of my mother.

Kalma's features blurred as tears welled in my eyes. I
squeezed them shut. Opened them.

I am standing at the top of the stairs, staring down into
the basement. Daddy is stretched out on the carpet. Mom is
kneeling beside him. Her long hair hides her face. I smell
throw-up. My stomach heaves.

I wonder if he's sleeping. I wonder if he's dead.

I'm so scared.

Mom raises her head. Tangled black hair. Angry white face. Is she angry with me for peeking? Or at Daddy again?

Her face smoothes out. "Everything's all right, Maggie. Go on up to bed now."

Her blue eyes darkening to Kalma's brown. His unshaven face changing to Rowan's smooth one. Rowan and Alex bringing me back, urging me to speak. And out there in the darkness, my mother. Waiting.

I heard my shaking voice urging Julie to keep on living, to recall the song she used to sing in school. The harplike arpeggio flowing from Alex's piano. Kalma's voice, splintering with grief. A silence broken only by her sobs. And then Alex again, accompanied by the hushed sostenuto of the strings.

I tottered downstage and knelt beside Kalma. Her head jerked up in surprise, but when I opened my arms, she flung herself into them.

I cradled Julie in my arms, but I sang to my mother. To the thirty-five-year-old woman in the basement and the sixty-year-old one sitting in Row G, Seat 114. To the stark-faced woman who had tried so hard to keep her family together and when she realized she could not, had torn it apart so that the two of us could survive. To the wild-eyed woman who had stormed the theatre to protect me. To the mother who would always push and pull and nag and worry and love me.

I sang my fear of the dark memories. My yearning for that promised golden sky. My doubt of ever finding it. I let hope swell my voice as I sang my determination that we would make the journey together. But the upwelling of sorrow for all we had lost made it dwindle to a whisper as I sang that final word.

". . . alone."

It seemed only moments later that we were lining up for curtain calls. The applause swelled for Brittany and J.T. and became deafening as Rowan and Kalma entered from opposite sides of the stage and met at the center.

They bowed together. Before he could gesture to her to

take a separate call, she stepped back, leaving him alone as the audience rose to its feet. He acknowledged their ovation with a quick nod, then pulled Kalma forward for her bow. She thrust her free hand toward the pit. A final company bow. Then the curtains closed.

Reinhard opened them twice more in deference to the storm of applause. After our third bow, Rowan made a slashing motion with his hand and the work lights snapped on.

All that was left were the hugs and the kisses, the squeals of excitement, the relieved laughter. I said all the right things, but my face felt like it would crack as I smiled. Exhaustion shattered my numbness, bringing with it the recognition of everything I had done wrong in "You'll Never Walk Alone." When I caught Rowan watching me, I flinched, then raced downstairs to the dressing room.

I lingered in the shower, the cool spray stinging my skin without refreshing me. Returned to the empty dressing room to dry my hair, apply a fresh coat of makeup, and put on the inevitable kicky sundress. Then I fixed an unconvincing smile on my face and headed upstairs.

Mom was waiting outside the stage door. She stopped pacing when she saw me and exclaimed, "What took so long?"

I burst into tears.

She stared at me, aghast. Then hurried forward, fumbling in her purse. "Don't cry. Your mascara will run."

It was so typically Mom that a cracked laugh broke through my sobs. "It's waterproof."

She thrust out a wadded tissue. I started when I felt its dampness.

"You'll have to make do. I used up all my Kleenex."

I could feel my cheeks stretch as I smiled. "A whole pack?"

"Yes. Blow your nose."

I blew my nose and accepted a somewhat soggier tissue to dab my eyes.

"I'll never be able to listen to that song now." Her glare made my smile grow broader. "It was so . . . it was like you were singing to . . . oh, damn!" She fished another crumpled tissue out of her purse and blew her nose with a resounding snort. Then she sighed. "I'm exhausted."

"Me, too."

Laughter and noisy conversation emanated from the breezeway where cast and audience were enjoying the opening night reception that Helen had insisted we hold because it was now "a tradition."

"Want to skip it?" I asked.

"Yes. But I should congratulate your friends. And Mr. Mackenzie."

"No one calls him Mr. Mackenzie, Mom."

"I do."

As we edged toward the refreshment table, people kept stopping us to congratulate me, which was nice considering how I'd mangled my big number. Each time I introduced Mom to someone, she found exactly the right thing to say. Not some generic "you were wonderful" compliment, but specific words of praise about a specific moment in the show. With others, she astonished me by remembering the stories I had told her that afternoon, confiding to Lou and Bobbie that she had heard terrific things about their performances in *Brigadoon*, telling Maya that she so wished she had seen her dance in "Always the Sea," asking Caren about her recent redecorating.

Then Hal pushed through the mob and swept me up in an embrace. "Oh. My. God." He stepped back and pressed his palm to his chest. "Shattered. Shattered! I had to borrow Kleenex to make it through the end of the show."

Lee shook Mom's hand. "I'm Lee. Tech director. The shattered one is Hal. Costumes and set design."

Hal embraced Mom with his usual fervor. I watched her eyes widen as she gazed at me over his shoulder. When he released her, she said, "Hal and Lee? Are you two . . . that shop? Hallee's?"

Hal beamed. "I am. Lee's just a lawyer."

Lee rolled his eyes.

"You have to stop by while you're in town. I just got in a satin bed jacket—the same misty blue as your dress, well, maybe the tiniest bit darker. It would look fabulous on you. And then you can persuade Maggie to buy the emerald green sarong I've been holding for her all summer." Hal glanced at my kicky sundress. "You know I love you in that, but every party?"

It was the first time I could remember anyone rendering my mother speechless. She blinked a couple times and glanced at me, but her gaze returned to Hal as if mesmerized.

Lee broke the spell by inquiring, "How long will you be in town?"

"Only a day or two."

The stab of disappointment surprised me. "I thought . . . I just assumed you'd stay through the weekend."

"Well, I wouldn't see very much of you with two shows Saturday and another on Sunday. Besides, your friend's coming. Nancy. No, I'll leave Friday morning. We'll have a whole week together at the beach."

Hal moaned ecstatically. "I love the beach! But my skin's so fair, I have to sit under an umbrella in a caftan. With a hat. Like Nathan Lane in *The Birdcage*."

"Well, well, well," boomed a familiar voice behind me. "The woman of the hour!"

"That would be Kalma," I replied, suppressing a sigh. "Mom, this is Longford Martindale."

"Your mother? No, I won't believe it. Your older sister, perhaps."

"Alison Graham," my mother responded with a frosty smile.

"He prefers to be called Long," I added.

My mother pursed her lips. "Most men do."

I gasped. Hal shrieked. Long just waggled his eyebrows.

"Long publishes *The Hillandale Bee*," Lee said. "He's also our local theatre critic."

Mom's smile grew noticeably warmer. "Really? Well, I hope you enjoyed the show as much as I did."

"Don't fish for compliments," I muttered.

"A beautiful woman need never fish for compliments," Long replied.

Mom shook her head, still smiling. "Maggie warned me that you were a charmer." I watched in astonishment as she rested her fingers on his bicep and stared up at him, blue eyes wide. "Would you be a dear? I'm absolutely parched and there's such a crowd at the drinks table . . ."

In spite of the press of bodies, Long actually managed a bow. "Your servant, dear lady."

As he maneuvered through the crowd, Lee began to applaud. Mom grinned and said, "I did a bit of acting myself in my younger days." Then she sighed. "It's been lovely talking with you, but I'd better beat a hasty retreat before he returns."

"I'll come with you," I volunteered. Rowan seemed to have skipped this reception just like the last one, but I was eager to escape the celebration.

"Don't be silly. The party's just beginning."

"I'll walk you to the car," I insisted.

As we headed toward the parking lot, a figure emerged from the shadows of the picnic area. Mom followed my gaze, her eyes narrowed in a nearsighted squint. Then she recognized the Hawaiian shirt.

"Why, Mr. Mackenzie," she said. "I was wondering where you were hiding."

"I'm not much for parties."

"Nonsense. You should enjoy your success. You were quite brilliant tonight."

"Thank you, Mrs. Graham. I hope . . . was it very difficult? Watching the show again?"

How typical of Rowan to recognize that. And how typical of me to overlook it. I was so caught up in my performance that I forgot she had to contend with the memory of Daddy's as well.

"It *was* difficult," she admitted. "But mostly, because your performance was so moving. And Maggie's, of course." She smiled at me, then nodded toward the breezeway. "Go back to the party. Both of you. Congratulations on a wonderful show, Mr. Mackenzie. And, Maggie, be sure and make my excuses to that man."

"What man?" Rowan inquired.

"The long one." Mom shuddered. "Be nice, Maggie. We want a good review, after all."

Before I could scurry back to the breezeway, Rowan caught my arm. "You have to stay," he reminded me. "And make excuses."

Clearly, he wasn't referring to any apology I would offer to Long. My performance tonight might have made Hal and Mom weep, but it could only have disappointed Rowan.

He steered me into the theatre, flicked on a light, and demanded, "What's wrong?"

"What do you think? I screwed up! I butchered your blocking. Nearly blew the whole scene. I wobbled through the beginning of the song and sang the rest as Maggie Graham instead of Nettie Fowler. And I'm sorry, okay? I don't know what happened. I was just standing there, watching myself blow it, and I couldn't do anything!"

Rowan frowned. "Didn't anyone tell you what they thought of your performance?"

"Everyone said I was great. And it was nice of them to try and make me feel better. But I knew I'd let you down."

He cocked his head, his frown deepening. "Don't you have any idea how good you were? How powerful that scene was?"

"I . . . it felt right for me. But I couldn't tell what the audience thought. Or Kalma or—"

"It was right. For everyone."

I shook my head, still unable to believe what I was hearing. "If you and Alex hadn't been there . . ."

"We just gave you a little push."

"That vision of my mother wasn't exactly a little push."

"What are talking about?"

"My mother. In the basement. With . . . that wasn't you?"

Rowan shook his head.

Had I been so aware of my mother's presence that I'd simply replaced Kalma's face with hers? Or tapped into some long-forgotten memory?

I started shaking. Rowan's hands grasped my shoulders, steadying me. "It's all right. Whatever happened, it's all right."

"It was so real," I whispered, recalling the cool tiles under my bare feet, the sour stink of vomit.

"Visions can be like that. Do you want to tell me about it? Sometimes that helps."

I let him ease me onto Reinhard's stage-manager stool. It seemed like the most natural thing in the world to rest my cheek against his chest, to feel his palm smoothing my hair. Yet only four days ago, we had flung horrible accusations at each other.

His heartbeat thudded in my ear with the steady pulse of his magic at the beginning of "The Carousel Waltz," the same slow rhythm I had noted during our very first encounter. I'd been more certain of everything then.

I tried to describe what had happened, what I'd felt when I became my seven-year-old self. I told him about the strange sensation of floating through the show, never fully inhabiting my own skin. Or Nettie's. I told him about my conversation with Mom by the pond. And when I finished, I said, "I feel so slow."

"You're tired."

"Not just tired slow. Stupid slow. Like it's all right there, but I can't see it."

"See what?"

"Nettie. My mother. My father. My life. And . . . you."

His chest rose and fell as he sighed.

"Mom asked when I would figure out what I was going to be when I grew up."

"What did you tell her?"

"That I was working on it."

"Good for you."

"I'm sick of working on it."

"I know."

"I'm so confused. I hate being confused."

"I know."

"You know everything," I grumbled.

"No. I'm confused, too."

My head came up. "About what?"

"My life. My work." He hesitated. "You."

I searched his face and found only kindness and concern. My head drooped. He took a step back.

"You don't have to be afraid of me, Maggie."

"I'm more afraid of myself," I whispered.

His hand rose, then fell back to his side. "It's been a long day. You'll feel stronger in the morning."

"You're supposed to say 'better.' Don't you know anything about platitudes?"

That made him smile. "I defer to your expertise." He thrust out his hands and pulled me to my feet. "Come on. I'll walk you to your car."

We detoured to the dressing room so I could pick up my stuff. As we walked through the lobby, I noticed a box of programs. The goldenrod paper was nice. A reflection of the lyric about the golden sky in "You'll Never Walk Alone," maybe.

As we walked outside, I said, "You were great tonight."

"So were you."

"I watched all your songs."

"I know."

"I just wish ..."

"What?"

"I wanted to hear you sing 'If I Loved You' the way you sang 'The Mist-Covered Mountains.' I know you couldn't, but ..." I shrugged.

Rowan gazed at the woods, the outline of the trees barely visible against the backdrop of the sky. "Maybe I'll sing it that way. Just once. Before the summer's over."

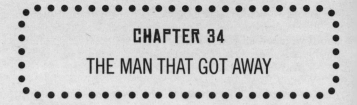
MOM AND I PLAYED TOURIST IN BRATTLEBORO. I caught her sneaking glances at me all day. Maybe I looked as distracted as I felt.

She insisted on stopping at Hallee's when we got back to Dale. Hal swept her up in his arms, exclaiming, "I thought you'd forgotten me."

"That would be very difficult," Mom said dryly. But her smile was affectionate.

She tried on the bed jacket and—as Hal had predicted—she looked fabulous. To my surprise, he didn't even have to coax her into buying it. She also sprang for the emerald-green sarong. It was actually various shades of green. With a bamboo design. I looked like a slightly overweight wood nymph on vacation in Bali. Or that chick from *South Pacific*.

When I mentioned that, Hal promptly burst into "Younger than Springtime." If I hadn't felt older than Moses, I would have laughed.

Mom skipped the show that night. Said she just wasn't up to it. Neither was I. A great actress could have conjured the vision of opening night and tapped into the emotions it had evoked. I managed to tap into Nettie. Her strength and endurance comforted me, but after the show, Kalma seemed a little disappointed; I guess she wanted another meltdown. I couldn't tell what Rowan wanted.

The next morning, as I walked Mom to her car, she asked, "Is everything all right?"

"It's just been a really long week."

She examined me critically, then said, "Don't obsess about your father. Mr. Mackenzie was right about dwelling on the past. You have to put it behind you and move on."

"The way you have?"

"Yes."

"Oh, come on! You haven't had a serious relationship since Daddy left."

"I've had several, in fact."

"Who?"

"Adam Peterson."

I vaguely remembered him. She'd brought him to one of my junior high school plays and I'd instantly decided I loathed him.

"And then there was Joe Laurence."

"That skinny, bald guy who looked like Ichabod Crane?"

"He looked like James Taylor," she corrected. "And recently, I've been seeing Chris."

I stared at her blankly.

"He volunteers with me. At the Nature Society?" Impatiently, she added, "I told you all this weeks ago, Maggie."

I vaguely recalled someone named Chris. But she'd definitely skipped the part about dating. For that matter, I was pretty sure she'd skipped the part about Chris being a man. When I mentioned that, she had the grace to look abashed.

"So? What's he like?"

"Please. Whenever I tell you about one of the men I'm seeing, you either take an immediate dislike to him or act like we're a pair of puppies rolling around on the floor."

"You roll around on the floor with this guy?"

To my astonishment, her cheeks turned pink. I nodded thoughtfully. "Now I understand why you were so eager to buy that bed jacket."

"I'm leaving."

"Without telling me anything about Chris?"

She smiled sweetly. "I'll tell you all about him. When you come to the beach."

We stood there, suddenly awkward; neither of us had ever mastered the art of the fond farewell.

"I'm glad you came up."

"So am I." She hugged me quickly and stepped back. "And I'm glad I met your friends. They're really very nice." She sounded mildly surprised. "Hal's sweet. I wish you could find a man like him."

"I did. Michael."

"Michael . . ." She sighed. "He was a love."

"Just not my love."

She opened the car door, hesitated, then turned toward me. "Be careful, Maggie."

"What?"

"He's very charming. And sensitive. And talented. But there's something . . . strange about him. Mysterious is fine in novels, but it usually spells trouble in real life."

"We're just . . . we just work together."

"Any man who can sum up all our similarities after knowing me for fifteen minutes has to have studied you for a good, long while."

"He studies everyone! He's a . . . studier."

"Just be careful." She slid into her car, then rolled down the window. "You were wonderful in the show, Maggie. Really."

Before I could reply, the window slid up and she backed out of her parking space. Typical Mom. Say something from the heart and make a quick getaway to avoid the emotional fallout.

I paid some bills. Browsed some jobs. Considered the irony that my mother's love life was more robust than mine. Recalled her comment about Rowan studying me, the comforting warmth of his arms on opening night. Then I thrust the memories aside and tried to get on with my life.

❧❧

Nancy joined us in the lounge after that night's show. I made her laugh with the tale of my mother storming the theatre. But when everyone began vying with each other to describe Rowan's showdown with Nick, her eyes grew wide.

"I've never seen anyone move that fast in my life," Bernie said. "One minute he was on the steps and the next, he was standing beside Maggie."

"Like a vampire," Kalma said. "You know how they always move in this incredible blur in the movies?"

Anxious to steer the conversation away from such otherworldly speculations, I said, "The whole thing was pretty much a blur."

"If you could have seen his face . . ." Brittany shuddered. "I thought he'd kill Nick."

"He called."

Every head at our table swiveled toward Lou.

"Nick? When?" Bobbie demanded.

"During the show." Lou scowled. "When he knew I wouldn't be around to pick up."

"Did he leave a message?" I asked.

"Yeah. He said, 'Leave me the . . . eff . . . alone.'"

"You can say fuck," Sarah assured him. "I've heard it before." She darted a wary glance at her grandfather, but Bernie just waved his hand dismissively.

"I called back and left *him* a message. Told him he was acting like a fucking crybaby and Rowan was right to push 'cause he was doing a shitty job and if he didn't visit that kid of his, I was writing him off as a bum."

Bobbie squeezed his hand. Kalma nodded approval. I said, "I guess that means we won't be seeing Nick again."

"Good riddance," Kalma said. "He *is* a bum!"

"Rowan didn't think so," I said. "Or he wouldn't have cast him."

Any chance of a breakthrough was lost now. And although Rowan had assumed the blame, I knew I bore part of the responsibility, too.

"Do you think I should tell Rowan about the call?" Lou asked.

"No!" Brittany and Bobbie exclaimed in unison. "It'll only upset him," Brittany added. "He's been so down lately."

"He has?"

Bobbie rolled her eyes. "I love you, babe. But sometimes . . ." She shook her head.

"Haven't you noticed how quiet he's been?" Kalma demanded.

Bernie stared morosely into his beer. "This Nick thing has really thrown him."

"He hardly smiles at all anymore," Sarah said. "And when he does . . ."

Brittany sighed. "It just about breaks your heart."

"Wait a minute!" Lou demanded, still staring at Bobbie. "You love me?"

Everybody laughed. Even I had to smile.

"Of course I do, you big ape." Bobbie punched Lou's shoulder. Lou just shook his head, a dazed smile on his face.

Nancy was unusually quiet for the rest of the night. Several times, I caught her studying me. Rowan, Mom, Nancy. Everybody was eyeing me these days. Did I look that fragile?

As we were climbing into our beds, Nancy said, "It's not Nick."

"What?"

"Rowan may be upset about him leaving, but that's not the reason he's been down."

I stared at the quilt, unable—unwilling—to answer.

"He won't make the first move. You know that, too."

"It's not like that, Nance." I gave her an edited version of my father's summer at the Crossroads that roughly paralleled Nick's.

"Maggie, your father didn't go off the deep end because of some blowup with Rowan."

"I know. But we're both better off keeping our distance."

She regarded me with a mixture of fondness and exasperation. "I love you to death," she said, "but sometimes, you're a dope."

❧❧

I'd had no time to visit Helen since my return from New York. So after Nancy left Sunday morning, I drove over to the Bates mansion.

Janet answered my knock. She gave me a long, considering look, then said, "If you're going to get all weepy . . ."

"Cut me a break," I snapped. "It's been a shitty week."

"Well, just don't—"

"I won't upset Helen!"

"Good. She's in the sunroom."

Helen must have heard our voices; she was already on her feet when I walked in.

"Oh, Maggie! I'm so glad to see you." Her embrace enfolded me with love and concern. "Come sit down and tell me everything."

"First, tell me how *you're* doing," I said. I thought she looked pale, but the wooden blinds were down, rendering the sunroom rather shadowy.

Helen waved away my concern. "I'm fine. Just feeling cut off from everyone. Momma should have been a prison guard instead of a producer."

"I heard that!" Janet called from another part of the house.

It was a shock to hear her refer to Janet as "Momma." But there was no longer any need to pretend for me, no secrets left to hide.

"I put my foot down opening night. I refused to miss that." Helen clasped her hands. "I cried through your whole number."

"You cried through the whole damn show." Janet appeared in the doorway, holding a silver tray with a pitcher of lemonade and glasses.

"I did not! I laughed at all the right spots." Helen eyed the two glasses on the tray. "Don't you want to join us?" she asked Janet.

"I thought I'd let you girls have a *tête-à-tête*. So you can talk about me behind my back."

"Oh, Momma. Don't be such a grumpy puss."

Helen pressed Janet's hand to her cheek. The hard angles of Janet's face softened as she smiled. Then she frowned and said, "Don't drink the lemonade too fast. You'll get a headache."

I watched her walk out of the sunroom and continued staring after her for so long that Helen asked, "Maggie? What is it?"

"I just realized who she reminds me of."

The same brusqueness. The same dislike of emotional displays. The same immaculate grooming and self-assurance. God, my mother had even handled Long with the same ease as Janet. Mom was a little less outspoken, a little more gracious. But I'd seen both of them at moments of crisis, their careful facades shattered as they rushed to the aid of their daughters.

It made me a little queasy to reflect upon my dislike for a woman who shared so many of my mother's qualities. Only now could I admit that I usually valued Janet's frankness—even when it made me squirm—and that she used that brusque manner to hide her vulnerability. The same way I used humor as a shield. Or tried to. Lately, I seemed incapable of shielding any of my emotions.

Helen was watching me with a small smile. "It's your mother, isn't it?"

"Yeah."

"You sang to her opening night."

I nodded.

"So it was a good visit."

"A long overdue one in a lot of ways."

"I'm sorry I didn't have a chance to talk with her. Although I doubt she would have welcomed that. She seemed so ... formidable."

"When you met her before?"

"I don't remember that visit very well. If anything, she seemed more frightened than formidable. But of course, she didn't want Jack to be here, did she? No, this was later. When I called. She was polite at first. But after a few months, she told me to stop calling."

I closed my eyes. Clearly, Mom *had* viewed Helen as a threat. If not a rival for her husband's affections then a reminder of his wonderful summer. But if she had just let Helen talk with him ...

"I'm so sorry, Maggie." Helen's voice was little more than a whisper. "Rowan told me what happened to poor Jack. I thought ... when you stopped visiting ... I thought you blamed me.

"And no wonder. If I had just kept in touch with him, I would have realized something was wrong. And then maybe ..."

"It's not your fault, Helen. Or Mom's." I hesitated, then said, "Or Rowan's."

"Have you told him that?"

"I think I just realized it."

I realized something else, too. And wondered why it had taken me so long.

At that afternoon's show, I sang to my father. To the playmate who had fed my imagination and my dreams. To the
reassuring presence at my bedside. To the lost boy he had
been and the lost man he had become.

I sang reassurance for his dark fears and clouded memories. I sang understanding for his restless nature that drove
him to search for the impossible. I sang the hope that his
solitary journey would lead him to a calm harbor. But I also
sang my sorrow—for what we had shared and lost, for what
we had never had, for all the years that we had both walked
alone.

I forgave him for leaving us and asked his forgiveness for
failing to cherish the gifts he had given me. And then I said
good-bye.

When the curtain swung shut after our final bow, there
was the usual Sunday rush for the dressing rooms. Rowan
and I were two islands in the stream of bodies flowing
around us.

Our gazes met. I needed neither words nor the touch of
his power to realize that he had understood my song. And
that this was why he had called me to the Crossroads.

His smile held quiet joy and an extraordinary sense of
peace. But Brittany was right; it did break my heart.

CHAPTER 35
MAYBE THIS TIME

WITHOUT REHEARSALS TO FILL OUR DAYS, I joined my cast mates on day trips. Instead of enjoying the incredible vista from the Mt. Olga lookout, I found myself recalling the one from the plateau. When we picnicked in Woodford State Park and sunbathed on the minuscule beach, I closed my eyes and envisioned another picnic and a very different beech. Each excursion outside of Dale reminded me that Rowan was trapped on those twenty acres and might remain a hostage for centuries more.

On show nights, I tried to lose myself in Nettie's world. But Rowan was part of that world, too, onstage and off. He still gave his little blessing as we filed past him for places, but I received only an encouraging smile rather than the touch he offered everyone else.

I worked with Helen in the garden when it was nice. Went out to lunch with Alex, Catherine, and Javier. Out to dinner with Hal and Lee. I had the strange feeling I was being vetted for a club I wasn't sure I wanted to join.

The staff was much more relaxed now, finally able to talk about themselves and their reactions to discovering the source of their powers. Whenever Rowan's name came up, they shared anecdotes about him eagerly—almost too eagerly—but deflected my questions about the curse, the "witch," anything that touched on the reason he was trapped in this world and the ways we might help free him.

Reinhard remained aloof from the camaraderie. He

would listen if I needed to talk, but he would not press me to do so. Nor would Rowan. As Nancy observed, he would never make the first move. And I couldn't decide if I wanted to.

Time hurtled past in a headlong race toward season's end. After Sunday's matinee, I returned to the hotel, painfully aware that in one week, I would be back in Brooklyn.

I showered and changed, then headed down to the lounge where people had started to gather for a special Sunday movie night; Kander and Ebb were on the docket— *Cabaret* and *Chicago*. When I made an abrupt U-turn in the lobby, Lou called out, "Hey, Brooklyn! You're going the wrong way!" I walked out the front door and down the street to my car, hoping I was finally going the right way.

The light rain that had been falling all afternoon had stopped. As I pulled into the theatre parking lot, a watery sun peeked out between the breaks in the clouds. A good omen, I concluded. As I started down the walkway, the stage door opened. Rowan hesitated on the threshold.

"Maggie?"

I'd spent the last week wondering if I would ever reach this moment, but I'd neglected to think about what I was going to say if I did.

"Is something wrong?"

Was it nervousness that sharpened his tone or merely concern? I'd be concerned, too, if a woman showed up at my home and walked toward me as silently as a goddamn zombie.

"Maggie!"

"You know when I went home after you cast me?"

An understandable silence greeted that question. Then he nodded.

"I made a list of pros and cons. To help me decide if I should come back. I filled a whole column with reasons why I shouldn't. But I just wrote one thing in the other column: I want to."

Another silence, longer than the first. "Yes. Well . . ."

"I spent the last week putting together a similar list in my head. About you. And me. And I came up with the same answer."

His hand gripped the doorframe. "I don't think this is a good idea."

"You thought it was two weeks ago."

"That was before I knew you were Jack Sinclair's daughter."

"Does that matter?"

"It does to me. I hurt him. I don't want to hurt you. I've thought about this a lot, too. I'm happy that we're friends again. But it would be best if we left it there. That would be the wise course. The safe course. For both of us."

"What happened to taking chances?" I asked quietly. "That's what you said the night we quarreled. That I had to risk being hurt. Being honest."

"I was—please don't come any closer!"

The hoarse rasp of his breathing filled the silence. His fingers tightened on the doorframe until the tendons stood out on the back of his hand. Yet in spite of those outward signs of turbulence, he still had his power under tight control.

"I was angry that night," he said more calmly. "And I said things I shouldn't have. What you should remember—what you must remember—is the danger for any human who gets too close to my kind."

"You also told me to stop thinking. And let my heart carry me."

"I was talking about the song!"

His power lashed me, but the sensation faded immediately.

"One week, Maggie. We just have to be sensible for one more week."

In that brief instant when he'd lost control, I'd felt desperation, anger, desire. He was just as conflicted as I was. As I had been. If he truly wanted me to leave, all he had to do was shut the door in my face. Instead, he hovered on the threshold, heart and head battling for supremacy as mine had for so much of the summer.

I took another step, and heard his breath hiss in. Touch had unleashed his emotions before. If I could just get close enough to touch him, I could break through his rigid self-control.

"I understand the risks. And I know that, a week from now, we'll say good-bye and we'll probably never see each other again. But I don't want to be sixty years old and wonder what might have happened if we had just taken this chance."

I never saw his hand move. One moment I was reaching for his face and the next, my wrist was snared by his imprisoning fingers.

"So you want me to fuck you, is that it?"

His face was as expressionless as his voice; he might have been discussing the weather.

"You want it the way I gave it to you after the Follies? Or would you prefer a human fuck? Either way, you'll come hard and fast. They always do."

Stung by the studied cruelty of his words, I wrenched my hand free and whirled around. Then I froze, finally recognizing what he was doing and why.

He had promised never to use his power against me. He might use words to drive me away, but even now, he was honoring that promise.

I slowly turned toward him, and the mask slipped. His hand moved suddenly to his throat, slipping under the silver chain to knead the scar around his neck.

"It's okay," I told him. "I'm scared, too."

His eyes flew wide. Then he stumbled backward, the first time I'd ever seen him move gracelessly.

I followed him into the theatre and found him sitting on the stairs. When I touched his hair, he flinched. I stroked it gently, just as he had stroked mine during the reception, then pulled his drooping head to my breast. He made a strangled sound that might have been a laugh or a sob or a muffled protest. Then he flung his arms around my waist and buried his face between my breasts.

I felt the bone-deep ache of his loneliness. A tremulous longing. A shiver of desire. And a relief so palpable that I sighed. So many emotions pouring over and through me like waves crashing against the shore. But none threatened to overwhelm me. Even now, he was holding them back, trying to protect me.

I let my hands speak for me, one smoothing his hair, the other stroking his back. We swayed gently, drifting with the flow of our emotions. The arms squeezing my waist gradually relaxed. His cheek rested against my breast like a sleeping child's.

I had felt this peace before—the afternoon I drove into Dale, the moment I stepped into the theatre, the day of our picnic when we had stood hand in hand on the plateau with the world stretching out before us. Then and now, it felt like coming home.

His head came up and I found peace in his face as well. I took his hand and led him up the stairs. He pushed the door open, but hesitated on the landing.

"I haven't done this in a long while."

"Neither have I," I assured him.

"A really long while."

"It's okay."

"You were probably in diapers."

Laughter had been lost to us, but we rediscovered it then and I knew everything would be all right.

⋙⋘

I expected a mad scramble to rip off our clothes, the same wild rush of sensation, the same cataclysmic results. Instead, he kept a tight rein on his power, clearly wanting to savor every moment. The simple act of unbuttoning each other's shirts seemed to take forever because his hands were trembling even more than mine.

My shorts were easier. Thank God for drawstring waistbands. When they lay in a puddle around my ankles, he stepped back, his gaze drifting over my body.

I could feel my face growing warm and fought the urge to snatch up my clothes, suddenly conscious of every extra pound, every tiny mole, every imperfection. I took refuge in desperate humor. "I guess after thirty years any woman looks good, huh?"

His gaze returned to my face. "But only you would look so beautiful."

It was impossibly sweet. Of course, I didn't believe a word of it. But it gave me the courage to unhook my bra and let it fall to the floor.

He sighed. Then slowly knelt before me.

He explored me with his eyes, his hands, his mouth. There was such wonder in his gaze, such reverence in his touch—as if my body were a precious gift, as if I were truly

Aphrodite and he, the worshipper at my shrine. I felt humbled and powerful and just as beautiful as he had claimed.

He skimmed off my panties and sank back on his haunches. Then he looked up, an astonished grin stretching his mouth wide.

"It's so . . . red! Redder, I mean. Than your hair. On your head. Like the sun just after it's been born in the morning. Or just before it dies at night."

I had to laugh. Never in my life had a man composed an ode to my pubic hair.

He twisted a few curls between his thumb and forefinger, then rubbed his cheek against them. His hands slid up my thighs to grasp my bottom and pull me closer. He nuzzled me like an overeager puppy, and I laughed again. Then his tongue flicked out, satiny smooth, teasing deeper, and the laughter caught in my throat.

The temperature in the bedroom suddenly soared. Sweat popped out on my forehead, under my arms, my breasts. Desire curdled between my trembling legs. I dug my fingers into the smooth, bare skin of his shoulders to keep from sinking onto the floor.

He rose swiftly, and I breathed in the thick, sweet aroma of honeysuckle. Not cologne. His scent. The scent of desire. And beneath it, another: wilder, gamy, an animal musk.

Golden sparks glittered in his eyes. His features seemed sharp, his expression almost feral. And suddenly, I was afraid.

He sensed the shift in my mood immediately and drew back. The golden sparks still flashed in the depths of those green eyes, but the feral avidity had vanished, replaced by concern and then frustration.

"This is what I am, Maggie."

"I know."

"If you're afraid of me—"

I groped for his hand and raised it to my mouth. The clenched fingers slowly uncurled. I pressed my lips to his palm, to his fingertips, and finally to the jagged scar on his wrist. His left hand shook as I lifted it and performed the same ritual. Then I leaned forward, lifted the chain off his neck, and kissed the red ridge of the scar. It tasted strangely bitter.

His throat moved under my mouth as he swallowed. His groan rumbled against my lips. I raised my head, and he captured my mouth. A starving man who had finally reached the feast table. His tongue rasped against my lips, sandpaper-rough now. The cat's tongue I remembered from that rainy night of the Follies.

We stumbled backward, awkward in our urgency, and I tumbled onto the bed with a startled grunt. He sprawled beside me, but when I reached for the buttons on his jeans, he seized my hands.

"Later."

"I want you inside me."

His power leaped, making me shudder with pleasure. He licked his lips and regarded me through heavy-lidded eyes.

"Later," he repeated a bit less firmly.

My hand moved over his chest, his belly. Then slid lower.

His head fell back and he stretched, languorous as a cat, while I stroked him. Then he suddenly twisted and pinned my hand to the mattress.

"If I can wait thirty years, you can wait thirty minutes."

He teased me with his mouth, his hands, his power, by turns sweet and tender and rough. Once, he murmured, "Slippery as seaweed." And later: "You even taste like the sea." I opened my eyes and discovered him sucking his fingers, his expression rapt.

I wondered briefly how he knew what seaweed felt like, what the sea tasted like. Before I could ask, impatient hands grasped my hips and swung me around until my legs dangled over the side of the bed. He stood before me, his green eyes enormous and glittering. Strands of hair clung to his damp cheeks. Sweat streaked his face and pooled at the base of his throat where a pulse throbbed with the same inexorable rhythm of his power.

His fingers closed around my knees and parted them, exposing me to his avid eyes. He sensed the exact moment I realized what he intended. His lazy smile flushed my body with a fresh wave of heat.

He knelt between my legs, still smiling. His fingertips slid lightly up my thighs, trailing tingling sensation in their wake. His mouth followed the same path, pressing damp kisses to my skin, nipping me gently with his teeth. Anticipation clenched my thigh muscles tighter. His breath eased out on a shaky groan.

"I've dreamed your scent."

When his cat's tongue rasped against my sensitive flesh, I shot halfway across the bed. He leaped up and bent over me, his expression anxious.

"Did I hurt you?"

"No. Just . . . that tongue."

"I'm sorry. It gets like that. When I'm . . ."

"Yeah."

"Should I stop?"

"No! Just . . . go easy."

He slid off the bed again and took a series of deep breaths. God help me, all I could picture was Shelley Winters, getting ready for her epic underwater swim in *The Poseidon Adventure*.

"Stop giggling. I'm trying to concentrate."

Which made me giggle even more. Then he lowered his head and I stopped.

For several delicious minutes, he went easy. Then his groan vibrated through my flesh and his fingers tightened on my thighs. The satiny texture of his tongue grew rough, his mouth more demanding. He licked me, kissed me, teased me with tongue and lips and teeth. I fought to escape, even while my fingers tangled in his hair, pulling his head closer, wanting more.

Too much. Not enough. Excruciating tension twisting inside me, harder, tighter. The relentless throb of his power, a wild tattoo that carried me along with the same frenzied rush of excitement that I had felt during "The Carousel Waltz," the same momentary hesitation at the brink of fulfillment, a note held, aching with anticipation. Then it shattered and I shattered with it.

I surfaced slowly, feeling bruised and tender and swollen. My legs oozed off the bed like the melting clock in that painting by Salvador Dali. A heavy weight rested against my thigh. My hand stirred feebly and ascertained that it was Rowan's head. He raised it with a damp squelch of flesh parting from flesh and kissed me lightly on the knee.

I stroked his hair; it was as wet as if he'd just emerged from the shower. Mercifully, the stifling heat in the bedroom had faded along with his power. I even shivered a little as a breeze wafted over me.

He rose then and pulled the lamb's wool throw over me before sliding onto the bed. We lay there, side by side, staring into each other's eyes.

"Are you . . . is everything . . .?"

I smiled. "I am. And it is. You?"

Spiky lashes veiled his eyes. "I've never tasted a woman before," he confessed.

"Did you . . . like it?"

"You were delicious." A shiver of power rippled through me. "Can we do it again?"

"Oh, Lord . . ." I moaned.

"Not right away."

"Thank you."

"After dinner, maybe. Are you hungry?"

"Starving."

"I'll cook for you." He smiled, happy as a child at the prospect. Then his smile faded and he cleared his throat. "First, though, I need to use the bathroom."

I studied him, wondering why he seemed embarrassed. "Okay."

He slid off the bed and walked stiff-legged toward the bathroom. And suddenly I understood. Sloughing off my lethargy, I forced myself upright.

"I'm sorry. I've been completely selfish."

He turned back to me, frowning. "What?"

"You did all the work and got nothing in return."

His frown deepened. "That's not true."

"Look, that's got to be uncomfortable. Come back to bed and let me take care of it."

He opened his mouth, closed it, ran his fingers through his damp hair, and finally said, "It's already . . . taken care of. Now I have to take care of the aftermath."

The light finally dawned.

"But I didn't even touch you!" I exclaimed.

"If you had, I'd never have lasted as long as I did."

A wave of tenderness filled me. And with it, an incredible sense of feminine power. I'd never made a guy come in his pants before. And although I realized that had a lot more to do with his long years of celibacy than anything I had done, I felt like I'd out-Aphrodited Aphrodite.

"It's so . . . great!"

His surprise gave way to a rueful smile. "It was at the time. Now, it's just . . . soggy."

"Sorry. It's just . . . I feel like I have faery magic, too."

He leaned down and kissed me on the nose. "Your own magic is quite powerful enough."

As he straightened, I asked, "Want some company? In the shower?"

His gaze slid away. "I'm a little . . . shy."

"After what we just did?"

"Not about your body. Just mine."

"What are you talking about? You have a beautiful body."

He grimaced, so clearly uncomfortable that I let it go.

After he had showered, I treated myself to a cool soak in the tub. It was like bathing in a forest glade: pale green tiles and wooden beams and the last golden rays of the sun slanting through the skylight. But my pleasure faded as I recalled Rowan's discomfort and wondered who could have made him so self-conscious about his body.

A woman's ethereal voice interrupted my thoughts. As other voices joined hers, I recognized the haunting tune of "The Mist-Covered Mountains." I quickly dressed and hurried toward the living area, only to draw up short on the threshold.

Candles glowed in the silver candelabra on the sideboard, the silver candlesticks on the dining table. Votives in dozens of glass containers created shimmering pools of green, blue, and gold. Rowan walked toward me, a stately shadow moving in and out of the flickering light.

He wore the leather pants and silk shirt I'd seen at the opening of *The Sea-Wife*. I felt hopelessly underdressed in my shorts and blouse, but his eyes assured me that I was beautiful.

"I'm afraid dinner's pretty simple," he said as he led me to the table.

By his standards it was: lollipop lamb chops with morel sauce, asparagus spears, and a crusty baguette. The first sip of wine made me shiver with pleasure. I lifted the bottle and inspected the label. Chateauneuf du Pape. Then I saw the date and gasped.

"Rowan, this bottle of wine is older than I am."

"I was saving it. For a special occasion."

The warmth that suffused my body owed little to the wine.

We shared stories as we ate. Rowan told me about his early years in this world when the land was still a wilderness. And he described the genesis of the theatre: the first musicale he attended where he used his magic to comfort the families grieving for their loved ones who had fallen at the battle of Gettysburg; the first shows he had staged— Gilbert and Sullivan, Victor Herbert; the leap to "professional" productions when charging two bits for admission seemed like an impossible gamble; the first call to the Mackenzie descendants and the astonishment of seeing them arrive on foot, horseback, and bicycle, and a few in their spanking new automobiles.

My descriptions of acting in school plays and stumbling through my first piano recital seemed impossibly dull by comparison, yet he listened as if fascinated. He seemed to find our family vacations even more fascinating, but of course, his only glimpses of the world had come from photos in newspapers and books and—much later—images on television and computer.

I was surprised to learn he even owned a television. He laughed and said he no longer did; there was little need when you could stream video on a computer. But when Helen purchased one for him back in the 1950s, he had spent entire days in front of it, enthralled.

"And when color television arrived . . . that was simply extraordinary. As magical as anything in Faerie."

I hesitated a moment, then asked, "What's Faerie like?"

His gaze drifted to the windows under the eaves as if Faerie lay just beyond. "What I remember most is the clarity. Of the light. The air. The colors. Everything so perfect and pure. As if the world were freshly made each morning."

"Why would anyone leave, then?"

"Because it's also . . . muted. Insubstantial. This world is so raw. Sometimes beautiful, often ugly, but always real. The rain stinging your face. The earth pressing against your feet. Flavors bursting in your mouth. And so many emotions slicing through you, filling you up. For all its beauty, Faerie lacks passion."

"You don't."

"Maybe passion is the wrong word. Humans are as raw and real as their world. Burning with such intensity. Maybe that's why your lives are so short. We're drawn to that heat. The Fae burn as well, but it's a cold fire. Like ice."

For a moment, his expression clouded. Then he smiled. "That's what makes this theatre so extraordinary. The crystalline perfection of Faerie translated into something even more powerful through the intensity of the human experience."

He might have been describing himself—that combination of cold and heat, aloofness and intensity.

As if I'd spoken aloud, he said, "This world has rubbed off on me. Because I've lived here so long. One of the reasons my power is weak."

"Weak?"

"Compared to the rest of my clan. Imagine any adolescent—a mass of raging hormones. Well, it's worse for us. Fae children age much like human ones until puberty. Then our power just . . . explodes. And the aging process begins to slow. I was roughly fifteen when I was trapped here. My power was still developing. The iron collar drained much of its strength, but—"

"The iron . . .?" My horrified gaze snapped to the scar at his throat. I swallowed hard, tasting that metallic tang again.

"Crude, but extraordinarily effective." His shudder belied his dismissive words.

"Does it . . . does it still burn?"

"No." His tender smile faded. "But when I hurt someone, it throbs." He drained his wine and quickly refilled his glass.

How many times this summer had I seen him kneading the scar? And the burns on his fingers—he must have gotten those while clawing at the collar, trying to rip it off.

I suddenly understood what had happened the night of Helen's heart attack. Steel burning his fingers as he wrenched open the door, steel surrounding him—sickening him—as he leaned inside the car. Yet he had ignored the pain, remaining at Helen's side until Reinhard arrived.

"And your power never recovered?"

He shook his head. "The best I can do is maintain what was left to me after they removed the collar. Being in nature helps. I spend part of every year at the cottage. Longer during one of my periodic . . . absences. But without Faerie to nourish it, my power will always remain stunted. And so will my ability to control it."

I understood how that lack of control must frustrate him. Yet, somehow that very helplessness made him seem more human.

"Why didn't your folk help you?" I demanded. "How does a single witch trump an entire clan of faeries?"

"After I was . . . lost, they avoided these woods. Nearly a century passed before they returned. A few wanted vengeance for what the Mackenzies had done. But by then, of course, the witch and her brood were dead." His mouth twisted. "Most, though, made it clear that if I was too weak to overcome a human curse, I didn't deserve their help."

"But you were one of them!"

"And I had broken the rules. Worse, I'd been stupid enough to get caught. If it had happened to another, I would have laughed and thought he deserved his punishment. Then."

"So they just . . . abandoned you?"

"They've returned more frequently this last century. They even seem happy to see me. But our chief declared it was too risky for anyone in the clan to help me break the curse."

"And they accepted that?"

"The chief is the final arbiter. There's no court of higher appeal. No Faerie Queen in spite of what the legends say. And to be fair, I doubt they could have helped me. The heart of the curse is beyond the power of Faerie to comprehend."

"They could have tried! I would have. So would your staff. We wouldn't have laughed or shrugged it off or washed our hands of you."

"Because you're human, Maggie. And humans have an infinite capacity to change. To forgive. To . . . love."

"Well, fuck them! Cruel, unfeeling little fuckers."

He regarded me with a small smile. "Pity the poor Fae who comes up against the wrath of Maggie Graham."

"You've come up against it often enough."

"And I pitied myself every time."

"How can you joke about this? More than two hundred years of your life!"

"Because it *has* been more than two hundred years, Maggie. I've learned a lot in that time. Including patience."

"But why go back? I don't care how beautiful it is. You don't belong with them."

"I wonder if I belong in either world. Sometimes I feel I'm neither Fae nor human, but some monstrous amalgam of both."

I shoved back my chair. "Don't you ever say that! You are not a monster."

"You thought I was. Not so very long ago."

"I was wrong! I was angry and hurt and wrong. You're not perfect. You can be arrogant and dictatorial and stubborn and blind and standoffish and temperamental and impossible to understand and a major pain in the ass . . ."

"Please tell me it gets better soon."

"But you're also perceptive and clever and amazingly talented. And tender. And kind. And you try to help your cast, even if you don't always succeed. And sometimes, you're so sweet that it breaks my heart."

He bowed his head. "I'm not . . . you're the one who's kind."

"Shut up."

He watched, wide-eyed, as I marched around the table.

"I don't know what the hell kind of faery you are, but you're a good man, Rowan Mackenzie. Got it?"

His breath eased out in a shaky sigh. "Got it."

"Good."

CHAPTER 36
SECRET SOUL

ROWAN DIDN'T URGE ME TO STAY. Maybe he sensed that I needed to be alone. Maybe he needed that, too. Sleeping beside another person was a greater act of trust than making love; in sleep, you were truly naked, incapable of maintaining the barriers around your soul.

His kiss was tender, but doubt shadowed his face when he asked, "Will you come back tomorrow?" When I nodded, relief chased away his doubts.

Mine remained. There was so much I didn't understand about him, so many shadows I could not penetrate.

I slept restlessly and woke to the warbling of a mockingbird. The Bough awoke more slowly, a sporadic symphony of trilling alarm clocks and squeaky springs, thudding footsteps and groaning pipes.

The aromas of coffee and frying bacon lured me to the Chatterbox, where I invented excuses for missing movie night and skipping today's planned trip to Bennington. After everyone departed, I threw some things into my carryall and drove back to the theatre.

Rowan was waiting in the picnic area. A huge smile filled his face as he hurried toward me, and I felt an answering one blossom on mine. He swung me off my feet and kissed me, apparently unconcerned that the residents of the Bates mansion and the Mill might see us.

"What should we do today?" he asked as he set me down.

"You choose," I replied, caught by his boyish enthusiasm.

"Let's go on another picnic."

"I just ate breakfast!"

"Well, we don't have to eat right away. Not food, any way." He offered a leer as convincing as Long's and laughed when I smacked him. Then suddenly asked, "You haven't told your mother about us?" When I shook my head, he muttered, "That's a relief."

"Oh, come on. She's not that bad."

"The day you brought her to my apartment. Remember how she came back afterward?"

"Oh, God. What did she do?"

"She picked up her purse, smiled very sweetly, and told me if I hurt you, she would geld me with a spoon."

When I stopped laughing, I repeated, "A spoon?"

"Maggie. The implement she chooses is not my prime concern here."

"Oh, she'd never . . ." I considered the matter further and shook my head. "No. She might murder you, but I doubt she'd waste time gelding you first."

"Well. That's a relief," he repeated, far less fervently than before.

We took a more roundabout route to the beech. Just as Reinhard had declared after Midsummer, Rowan knew every inch of the woods. And every inch seemed to have a story. The little pool where he had bathed in the summer. The clearing where he had brought down his first deer with bow and arrow. The shallow grotto beneath a rock formation where he had lived—a dark, dank hole so small that his head would have brushed the ceiling when he sat, so cramped he would have been unable to stretch out full-length when he slept.

"Fifty years?" I whispered. "You lived in . . . that . . . for fifty years?"

"I lived in the woods. I only slept there."

"But fifty years . . ."

"They brought me blankets that first winter. And food. They even left me weapons so I could hunt. And were solicitous enough to fashion the knife blade and arrowheads from flint instead of iron. They wanted me to live, you see.

And when I tried to escape . . ." He shoved back the sleeve of his shirt and stared at the jagged scar on his wrist. ". . . they nursed me back to health. They wanted me to live a long, long time."

"You still hate them, don't you?"

He turned to me, clearly shocked by my question. "They stole my life, Maggie! They didn't just drain my power and bind me to this world. They drained my very essence. I might have lived a thousand years in Faerie. But because of that collar, I'll be lucky to live half that long. Five centuries may seem endless to you, but I can never recapture all the years they stole. Not even if I return to Faerie one day."

I took his hand, torn between my horror at the terrible price he had paid and my reluctant understanding of the motives of those who had exacted it.

"I'm not trying to excuse what they did. It was horrible. But they were frightened of you, and angry and grieving and—"

"I never set out to harm her."

"No. You set out to seduce her. And succeeded. Are you telling me you didn't know the risks she might face?"

Cold air buffeted me as he wrenched his hand free and stalked away. Then he faced me and sighed. "No. I just didn't care enough to protect her."

Cautiously, I took his hand again. "What they did was incredibly cruel. But their hatred is easier for me to understand than your own folk abandoning you."

"It wasn't just hatred, Maggie. The witch loved her daughter. They all loved her. Hatred, my folk have always understood. But love . . . love is the most powerful, most human of all emotions. And it is alien to us."

"To them, maybe. Not to you."

"How do you know?" he demanded.

"I've seen how much you care about your cast. About Helen."

"Caring is not the same as loving."

"No, of course not, but—"

"I've never loved anyone."

His voice was as expressionless as his face, yet the air around us crackled with tension. Was this some kind of a test to see if I would abandon him as his folk had? Or was he warning me that—whatever else we shared this week—it was not, could not be love?

"Maybe you just haven't found the right person," I finally said.

"Or maybe I'm incapable of love."

I shook my head. "I don't believe that."

I couldn't tell if he was relieved or disappointed.

We visited the beech and picnicked on the plateau. Rowan's mood slowly improved, but the weather deteriorated. Scudding gray clouds and ominous rumbles of thunder soon had us scrambling to pack our supplies. We reached the hut as the first fat drops of rain gave way to a pelting downpour.

Even with the top half of the Dutch door open, it was gloomy inside. The table and benches looked as worn and battered as the narrow bed. The cold fireplace resembled a gaping maw, its stones blackened from centuries of smoke. Although it was a huge improvement over that awful hole he had lived in, I couldn't imagine spending months in this one small room.

Then I noticed the candlesticks and crockery in the tall wooden hutch, the frayed rag rugs, the small cross-stitched sampler carefully preserved under glass. And suddenly, the hut became a home, his first refuge in this world. Isolated, perhaps, but not entirely lonely. There had been people nearby who had cared about him, friends who had woven that rug, stitched that sampler, brought him those bowls.

I found him watching me and asked, "Were you happy here?"

"Yes," he replied, sounding faintly surprised. "Mostly. It was good to have a real home. And as much as I enjoy the comforts of my apartment, this is the place I always come back to. Maybe because Jamie and I built this cottage. And everything in it."

Rowan had mentioned Jamie Mackenzie last night—the great-grandson of the woman who had cursed him, the man who had dragged him out of the shadows and urged him to create the theatre.

"He was my first friend—my only friend for many years. The first of the witch's clan to speak to me. Forty years without hearing the sound of any voice save those of the birds and the animals. By then, I was as wild as they were. And then a ten-year-old child walked into this glade and said he thought it was fitting we should meet face-to-face. Being neighbors and all."

A fond smile filled Rowan's face. "One of the first gifts he ever brought me was a jug of milk and a basket of strawberries."

I could only gape at him.

"So now you understand why your gift took me aback."

Rowan caressed the smooth wood of the table. I pictured him sitting there with Jamie, sharing food and drink and laughter. Just as we had last night.

Jealousy stabbed me, so startling and unexpected that my stomach churned. I realized he had begun speaking again and forced myself to focus on his words.

". . . and when Jamie insisted that I become a part of the community, the easiest thing was to pass me off as a distant Mackenzie cousin."

"People believed that?"

"The witch had seven sons. There were plenty of distant cousins to go around," he said dryly. "I chose my first name. Pretty much on the spur of the moment when I met Jamie. Rowan is a sacred tree—to humans and faeries alike. The Scots thought it provided protection against witches."

"That's appropriate."

"And faeries."

His grin made me shake my head. "You have a strange sense of humor."

"More of a gift for appreciating irony. I've had a lot of names over the years. But Rowan Mackenzie is still my favorite."

As he smoothed the faded quilt atop the bed, the fond smile returned. And jealousy pierced me again. Stupid to be jealous of a man who had been dead for more than a century. Yet I couldn't help wondering if Rowan had led Jamie to the bed they had built together, had loved him with the same passion and tenderness and ferocity he had shown me last night.

Rowan's smile faded as he studied me. "We were never lovers, Maggie."

I shook my head. "It's none of my business."

"I *have* slept with men. It was . . . simpler. No risk of pregnancy, of course. But also less chance of any romantic entanglements."

"I've known plenty of gay men who've gotten romantically entangled."

"Yes, of course. But I chose my partners carefully. Men who wanted pleasure, not love. Men like . . ."

"Your folk."

With a curt nod, he walked to the door and stared out at the rain. "The Fae rarely have sex as you know it. There's little need when you can give and receive pleasure without even touching."

"But you must . . . they must . . . reproduce."

"Occasionally. To replenish the clan. And introduce new bloodlines."

It sounded as cold and clinical as I'd expect from beings that could taunt my father and abandon one of their own without a backward glance.

"That's why children are such a gift," Rowan continued in the same flat voice. "There's rarely more than one birth every few decades. We don't know our parents. The whole clan raises the child. And he is spoiled and pampered and doted upon."

And grows into the kind of arrogant, self-centered creature Rowan had once been.

"And then another child is born. And becomes the center of our world."

Maybe that was why he had trespassed in this one, why they were all drawn here. Not just to sample the intensity of human experience, but to recapture—if briefly—that time when they were the center of the world.

"The rain is letting up," he said. "We should be able to leave soon."

I walked over to him, slipped my arms around his waist, and rested my cheek against his back. His body was as unyielding as a tree trunk. Then his hand came up to clasp mine.

We walked back to the theatre in silence. The whole way, he seemed to be undergoing some silent, internal struggle. For once, I didn't press him.

As soon as we reached the apartment, he excused him-

self and disappeared into the office. I unpacked his knapsack, washed the empty food containers, and wandered
through the living area, scanning the books on his shelves.
Leather-bound classics and modern fiction and collections
of poetry. Art books. Travel books. The King James Bible,
the Koran, the Tao te Ching. An eleven-volume history entitled *The Story of Civilization*. A dozen books by and
about explorer John Muir. Other than an edition of Shakespeare's plays, there were no books on the theatre, no scripts
or scores; maybe he kept those in his office.

On one shelf, I discovered a black-and-white photograph
in a silver frame. As I picked it up, Rowan walked back into
the room, a small sheaf of papers in his hands.

He nodded at the photograph and said, "That's Jamie
and his family. His wife, Jeannie. Duncan, Andrew, Wee
James, Meg, and little Jennet. She's the one who made the
sampler you saw in the cottage."

It was one of those stern-faced family portraits so typical
of the Victorian age. Jamie wore a frock coat, Jeannie a long,
black gown. She looked far more fearsome; even with a
mustache and beard, I could see the hint of a smile curving
his mouth.

"Was Jamie a redhead?"

"Yes. Wee James and Jennet got his coloring. The rest
were dark, like Jeannie."

"Was she as terrifying as she looks?"

"Almost. She was the disciplinarian in the family. Jamie
was . . . its heart."

Suddenly, he thrust the papers at me. I read the heading
on the first page and started. "*By Iron, Bound?* This is . . .
your story?"

He nodded. "These scenes are from Act One. I thought
they might . . . explain things."

"You don't have to—"

"I know. But I'd like you to understand. Not just about
me and Jamie, but . . ." He shrugged. "I'll take a walk. Be
back in half an hour."

Before I could respond, he strode out of the apartment.
A little flustered, I sank onto the sofa.

As I read the first scene, I understood why he had entitled it "Simple Gifts." Three times, the character of Young

James brought food and drink to Ash, stubbornly refusing to be deterred by his coldness. I smiled a little to discover Rowan had chosen yet another tree name for his character. But it was hard to smile at the stage directions that described Ash as a barefoot creature in tattered clothes who seizes a half-eaten bone from his campfire and gnaws at it.

Scene two skipped forward fifteen years. Jamie was now a man on the verge of marriage, full of dreams and hopes for the future. I bit my lip as he attempted to describe love to a being who had never known it, cringed as Ash coldly rejected his attempt to forge a true friendship. But when Ash turned his power against Jamie to drive him away, I had to put the manuscript down until I grew calmer.

At least with me, Rowan's power had simply escaped his control; he had deliberately used it to hurt Jamie and shame him. And still, Jamie left the gifts he had brought, including the *McGuffey Reader* from which Ash—Rowan—learned to read and write. And when Jamie returned months later, he forgave Ash for his cruelty.

The man's sweetness flowed through the ensuing scenes: when he calmed Ash's nerves before that first musicale, when he urged him to find a nice level-headed widow to spark, when he brokenly confessed that he was in danger of losing the farm.

I gasped when Ash presented him with a gift of faery gold that saved both their homes—a necklace intended for the girl who had died. Smiled as Ash wrangled with Jamie's wife—as tough a cookie as she looked in the photograph. She was the one who brought the news of Jamie's passing—along with a forged birth certificate and Jamie's bequest of five acres, including "the parcel with that big beech you love so much."

Jamie's letter to Ash was almost too painful to read. It was filled with such love and humor and kindness, the words of a man who had lived a full life and a happy one, yet even on his deathbed, worried about the future of his friend. The final scene showed Ash singing at Jamie's wake. The words of "Amazing Grace" had never seemed so powerful: "Through many dangers, toils and snares/I have already come; 'Tis grace that brought me safe thus far/And grace will lead me home." When Ash stared front at the end of the

act "into a future filled with uncertainty, but also possibility," I broke down.

I was almost as shaken as the night Rowan confessed his
otherworldly origins to me. It wasn't just that I understood
Jamie. It was that my experiences with Rowan so closely
paralleled his. In a weird way, I *was* Jamie.

But that was nonsense. The man in the play was sweeter,
kinder, and far more forgiving than I was. Whether or not
Rowan acknowledged it, his love for Jamie filled every
page. Who could ever mean as much to him? Fill that void
in his life, in his heart? Even Helen had failed.

I had tried to accept this week as an unexpected gift and
resolutely avoided speculating about our future. Only now
could I admit that we had none.

CHAPTER 37
WHAT'S THE USE OF WOND'RIN'

NEITHER ROWAN NOR I SPOKE about our inevitable parting. Nor did we offer comforting lies about seeing each other after the season ended. We both realized it would be better to make a clean break.

Knowing he was still in love with a man who had died more than a century ago made that decision a little easier. Otherwise, I doubted I could simply walk away. Yet when I told him I understood why he had loved Jamie, Rowan looked startled. As if he had never realized it. And then he shook his head and said, "Not enough."

I hated to think that he would spend another century grieving. Jamie wouldn't want that. "Go out into the world," he had exhorted Ash. "Seek the happiness you deserve. And the love. Surely, then, you will find your way home." Although Rowan had joined the human world, he still hovered on its periphery. He might have found happiness, but he had not discovered the way home. And I was powerless to help him.

Afraid of betraying my turbulent emotions, I avoided talking with my mother. Instead, I left a message, claiming that I was already going through withdrawal and would probably be a complete mope at Rehoboth. I must have sounded convincing because her return message assured me that it was better to mope on a beach than swelter in Brooklyn.

It would be impossible to fool Nancy so easily. When she

came up for the final cast party, she'd discover I was sleeping elsewhere. I worked up the courage to tell her that I'd made the first move after all, but got off the phone fast when she started making plans to see me when I came up to Vermont in the fall.

I found the greatest peace with Helen. Mostly, we just sat on the patio, sipping lemonade and chatting about unimportant things. On Thursday, she greeted me with a basket over her arm and we walked down to the garden to harvest lavender. Only the snip of our shears, the hum of the bees, and the gentle splash of the fountain broke the heavy stillness of the August morning.

But as we walked up the stone steps to the house, she said, "I'm so happy you found each other, Maggie."

I realized then that she knew Rowan and I were lovers, that the entire staff probably knew. I felt as if I had stolen something precious from her. Recalling the staff's bird-dog-on-point sensitivity to Rowan, I was struck by the horrifying possibility that Helen had felt his emotions, that all of them had shared the heat of his desire, the shuddering release of his climax.

Helen rested tentative fingers on my arm. "Are *you* happy?"

"I'm . . . all over the place."

She nodded as if this was only to be expected. "You've given him a great gift, Maggie."

I felt like I was the one who had been given a gift. And in three days, it would be snatched away from me.

"Has he talked about . . . going home?"

I nodded.

"Does he seem . . . happy?"

"More like confused. He doesn't seem to know where he belongs. He even said that he's not sure whether he's faery or human any longer."

Helen surprised me by smiling. "You know, Saturday will be so busy with the two shows and the cast party. Let's have a little farewell lunch here tomorrow."

I was startled by the sudden shift in the conversation, but happily agreed. When I suggested that Rowan join us, Helen said, "I think we should make it just us."

"Just us" took on a new meaning the next day when Janet answered my knock. Her appraising look confirmed my fears that she knew exactly what had been going on in Rowan's apartment this past week. But for once, she held her peace and simply ushered me inside.

I followed her to the dining room and drew up short when I saw the entire staff seated around the table. I shot Helen a pointed look, and she flushed.

"This is not a farewell lunch," I said.

"As a matter of fact, it is," Janet replied. "Only it's Rowan's farewell we're concerned about."

I stared blankly at her. "What are you talking about?"

It was her turn to look blank. Glancing around the table, I saw her expression reflected on the faces of all the staff members.

"We believe he intends to return to Faerie," Reinhard said. "As soon as the season ends."

"But . . . the curse . . ."

"Maggie, dear." Helen squeezed my hand. "The curse is lifted."

"Didn't you know that?" Janet asked.

I shook my head, dazed. I was vaguely aware of Reinhard rising, guiding me to the empty chair, easing me onto it.

"When? How?"

There was another exchange of glances. This time, it was Helen who answered.

"I'm not sure exactly when it happened. Certainly by that first weekend of *Carousel*. As to how . . ." Helen smiled. "Why, that was you, Maggie."

I heard Janet demanding, "Didn't he tell you?" Helen replying, "That's not his way." And Alex pleading with everyone to stop talking and let me take it all in.

But it was happening too fast and there was too much to take in. I looked up at Reinhard, as if he might provide the answer, but his face held the same concern and confusion as the others. Only Helen seemed . . . peaceful. But she was probably the first to realize what had happened.

I sifted through her words again. The first weekend of *Carousel* I had sung to my father. Perhaps, my ability to forgive him and to forgive myself had been the keys to

Rowan's breakthrough as well as mine. The first step in my healing, the final act of his.

I realized how many clues he had given me. His determined efforts to drive me away, pleading with me to be sensible for just one more week. His pain at losing Jamie, so visceral in the pages of his play. The terrible knowledge that he would have to relive that pain over and over again with each parting, each death. The way he had clung to me these last few days. I thought he was sad because I was leaving, never realizing that he intended to make that final, irrevocable break.

Back to the muted world of Faerie, where partings were so much more infrequent, so much less painful. Where everyone shared the same long lifetimes, and pleasure came without the risk of love or loss.

They were all watching me, their expressions ranging from concern to pity to affection. Oddly, Janet seemed angry. I would have expected her to be pleased that Rowan was leaving.

I finally managed to say, "You should be happy for him. I am."

"Then why are you crying?" Hal asked.

I glared at him and swiped at my cheeks. "It's what he's wanted. For hundreds of years."

"He's changed," Helen said.

Mei-Yin thumped the table with her fist. "THIS is his home."

Alex nodded. "And you're the only one who can convince him of that."

I wondered why they thought I possessed such power over Rowan. Yes, I had pushed him into making changes. But it was one thing to demand that he attend a cast party, quite another to demand that he abandon his world and his folk and—possibly—his only hope for peace.

"Even if I had the power to convince him to stay, I wouldn't use it. That would be holding him hostage as surely as the Mackenzies did."

"Would you rather lose him?" Catherine asked. "Forever?"

"I'd still lose him. He'd hate me for doing that. Just as he hated them."

I pushed my chair back. I had to lean on the table to ensure that my trembling legs would support me, clear my throat to ensure that my voice wouldn't break again when I spoke.

"This is Rowan's choice. And we have to let him make it."

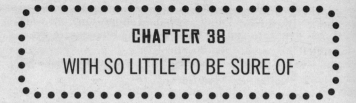

CHAPTER 38
WITH SO LITTLE TO BE SURE OF

SATURDAY ARRIVED, REEKING OF ENDINGS: the last matinee, our last company dinner, our final performance of *Carousel*. I felt strangely calm; I wasn't sure if it was because I had accepted what was going to happen or because it still seemed unreal.

I shook off my daze for the evening show. This performance was my gift to Rowan. I wanted it to be one we could both recall with pride.

The exuberance of June burst inside of me with the remembered giddiness of our shared laughter under the beech and his undisguised delight in my body. The repletion of the clambake suffused me with the same languorous afterglow of our lovemaking.

He offered me the same gift: his boyish enthusiasm as he sang about his son, his protectiveness as he imagined his daughter, his fierce attempt to resist his attraction to Julie, only to surrender with impossible tenderness.

You are all these things to me, we told each other in every song. The gentle emotions and the angry ones. The push and pull of dissension and the melding of minds and bodies into oneness. The fears and the doubts one tries to hide and the shelter the other offers when darkness threatens to suffocate the light.

When I saw him lying on the stage in Kalma's arms, all those emotions tumbled in upon me. I listened to the vamp repeat once, twice, three times. I felt Alex watching me, and Kalma. But I waited until I found my voice.

And then I sang to Rowan. To the director who had pushed me so hard. To the friend who had comforted me when I felt lost. To the lover who had delighted me with his tenderness and his wonder.

I sang the marvelous impossibility of his existence and the sorrow that it carried. I sang healing for his pain, and the recognition of the centuries of healing he had shared with the wounded souls of this world. I sang forgiveness for what had happened to my father and asked his forgiveness for doubting that his intentions were honest and good and true. I sang my gratitude for all that he had helped me discover, the pain of losing him, the fear that I would never know his equal. The joy of sharing his life—however briefly—strengthened my trembling voice so that I could sing the hope that his journey would be safe, that his life would be happy, that his spirit would find peace.

For a moment, I found peace as well, but it shattered during the reprise of "If I Loved You." It was impossible to hear the lyrics about Billy leaving this world forever without recognizing that Rowan would soon do the same.

While he was still singing to Kalma, his gaze shifted to where I huddled in the wings. He offered me a gift to ease my pain, the gift I had longed for since I first heard him sing "If I Loved You." For just a moment, he freed his power. And it infused his voice with such passion and longing and regret that tears spilled down my face.

His gift gave me the strength to master my emotions and sing to him one last time. In the number that ended the show and our season, I assured him that he would never walk alone, that the love and respect of each member of his cast—of all his casts—would follow him. That we would always remember the lessons of the Crossroads. And that I would always hold him in my heart.

When the curtain swung shut after our bows, we were all strangely silent, recognizing the end of an extraordinary chapter in our lives. Everyone turned to Rowan, like flowers seeking the sun, and his power embraced us with love and encouragement and the reassurance that this was a beginning rather than an ending.

Our pent-up emotions burst free in tears and hugs just like any other closing night. I glanced around the stage, knowing I was unlikely to encounter most of these people again. But some would always be part of my life. Lou and Bobbie. Bernie and Sarah. Kalma and Brittany. Gary. I might have to let Rowan go, but these few I would hold onto twice as hard. And Nancy, of course. They were as great a gift as any of the others I'd received this summer.

Lee shattered the tremulous emotion by yelling at us to change and get our asses back for strike. As everyone rushed to the dressing rooms, I discovered Rowan in the stage right wings, hovering between shadow and light.

I closed my eyes, imprinting that picture on my memory. Somehow, it captured all the contradictions of his nature and the dichotomy of his existence. When I opened them, I found him striding toward me. In the harsh glare of the work lights with the crew swarming over the set, he took me in his arms.

"It's all right," I whispered. "Everything will be all right."

He pulled back and regarded me with a bleak smile. "Maggie Graham, you're the worst liar in this world or the other."

"Points for trying?"

"Always."

He kissed me gently, and I heard someone gasp. Only then did I realize that the pounding of hammers and the shouts of the crew had ceased.

Rowan scowled at the rapt crew. "Don't you have a set to strike?"

Lee was the first to recover. "Yeah. And maybe if you two would stop making out center stage, we could actually strike it."

"You know nothing of romance," Javier complained. He grabbed Lee— hammer and all—and dragged him into a waltz, singing "Love Makes the World Go Round." Then Catherine cut in and spun Javier away, warbling "I'm in Love with a Wonderful Guy." Within moments, the entire crew was dancing around the stage.

Rowan shouted, "You've all lost your minds!" But he was smiling. We both were. And for a moment, at least, the fear retreated.

The cast seemed more shocked by Rowan's presence inside Janet's house than the fact that his arm was around me. Brittany and Ashley sighed. Kalma nodded wisely and whispered, "Aphrodite. I knew it all the time." Nancy beamed like a Jewish yenta, while Lou pounded Rowan on the back and said, "Love, man. There's nothing greater."

My pained smile drew understanding looks; it was, after all, a night filled with an equal measure of celebratory joy and the sadness of incipient partings. Rowan handled it much better than I did. Only during the obligatory end-of-the-season speech did his facade crack. But practically everyone was weeping by then; if he had to pause to compose himself, it was merely proof that this summer had meant as much to him as it had to us.

I seized his hand before he slipped away and blurted, "You'll ... wait up, right?"

"Yes. I'll wait."

"I can leave now—"

"No. Stay. You have other good byes to say."

So I lingered. I'd already exchanged e-mail addresses and phone numbers with everyone I was determined to keep in touch with, but there were a few last minute additions, including Caren, who seemed so unhappy at the prospect of leaving and so desperately relieved when I invited her to visit me in Brooklyn.

It was nearly 2:00 A.M. when I finally turned to Nancy and asked, "Did you ever think we would become friends? When all this started?"

"I thought we'd loathe each other. You seemed so smart and confident and funny. I was ... well ... me."

"I'd never have made it through without you. You know that."

"Same here." She hesitated, then asked, "You're ending it, aren't you?"

I nodded, unable to speak.

"Are you sure, Maggie? The two of you ... you're so good together."

I nodded again.

"I can hang around tomorrow if you need me. And if you don't want to drive home, you can spend a few days with me."

I clutched her desperately, then forced a smile. "I might take you up on that." Then I bolted for the front door.

The staff was gathered on the porch. Janet stopped pacing when she saw me.

"When are you leaving?" she demanded.

"Tomorrow morning. Early." Drawing out our farewells would be far too painful.

"Have you thought any more about . . . what we talked about?" Alex asked.

"I can't do it, Alex. It's not that I want him to go, but . . ."

"Enough!" Reinhard rounded on the others. "Maggie has made her decision. It is not fair to try and bully her into changing her mind."

"I wasn't bullying!" Alex protested.

"No. But this discussion is over." Reinhard gave me a brief, hard hug and quickly stepped back. "We are always here. You know that."

I swallowed down the lump in my throat and nodded.

One by one, I hugged them. Tears welled in my eyes when I reached Hal. They overflowed when I came to Helen.

She dabbed at my cheeks with her handkerchief. "No matter what happens tomorrow, Rowan will always carry you in his heart. We all will. Remember that, my dear. And know that you will always have a home at the Crossroads."

❦

I mounted the stairs to his apartment for the last time. Each step carried the memory of other visits, other emotions. If the stairs could do more than creak, they could tell the whole story of our relationship.

The door swung open, and he appeared above me, surrounded by light. He held out his hands and smiled. "I never even told you how pretty you look in your new dress."

"Sarong," I corrected. "Please don't break into 'Younger than Springtime.'"

"'Some Enchanted Evening' is your song, as I recall."

What I recalled was the closing wisdom of that song: once you had found your true love, you should never let her go. But I wasn't Rowan's true love. And I had to let him go.

Our loving was tender and slow, yet it was still over too soon. And in spite of my resolve to remain awake all night, to share every minute with him, I dozed off.

When I rolled over sometime later and found him gone, I bolted upright in bed, my heart pounding. A moment later, I heard the scrape of a chair from the office, the quick slap of his feet on the floorboards. The door flew open, and I blinked as light streamed into the bedroom.

The mattress sagged as he gathered me in his arms and whispered, "I'm here."

Before I could stop myself, I said, "Until morning."

His silence was answer enough.

I pulled away and took a deep breath. "I'm not going to make a scene. Or ruin these last hours. I just . . . are you sure, Rowan? About going back?"

"Yes, Maggie. I'm sure." His voice was as calm and steady as his gaze. "How long have you known?"

"Just since yesterday."

"You know it's the right choice. Don't you?" His eyes pleaded with me to agree.

"THIS is his home."

"You're the only one who can convince him . . ."

"You've given Rowan a great gift."

And now I had the opportunity to give him another.

"Yes. It's the right choice. The only choice. It's just . . . hard."

"For me, too. I never expected . . . any of this."

He hesitated as if he wished to say more, then strode toward the balcony where he stared out into the night. Then he turned.

"I want you to see me. As I really am."

He'd never allowed me to see him naked. During the day, he loved me with his hands and his mouth. At night, he slipped into the bathroom to put on a condom, then came to me in darkness. By now, I'd concluded that it was more than shyness that prompted his behavior. But his discomfort only fed mine, and I shook my head.

"Rowan. You don't have to—"

"I know. But I'm tired of hiding in the shadows."

He walked toward me and turned on the lamp on the nightstand. Then he stepped back. His hands rose to his waist. For a moment, he hesitated. Then he untied the sash and shrugged off his dressing gown. It slid to the floor with a soft hiss of silk. And he stood naked before me.

I had expected him to be hairless. But none of my imaginings prepared me for the soft white folds of flesh between his legs.

I felt neither shock nor revulsion, only a deep sense of confusion. He looked completely sexless, neither male nor female. Yet I had felt him inside my body. Could he have created that illusion with his magic?

His face was expressionless, all emotion hidden behind that unblinking mask. I had to say something to reassure him. He had offered me the great gift of his trust. Every moment I hesitated would only deepen his conviction that I was unworthy of it.

As I groped for the right words, he snatched up his dressing gown. "Now you know why I've never allowed anyone to see me like this."

That drove me to my feet. "You're beautiful, Rowan."

He flinched as if I'd told him he was hideous.

"Everything about you is beautiful and strange and impossible. And I want to make love with you."

I tugged the dressing gown from his hands and led him to the bed where I kissed and caressed him until the tension drained away, replaced by his growing desire. My fingertips brushed the smooth expanse of his chest. My gaze swept over his body. I gave a strangled squeak.

A pink rosebud of a penis peeped out of the folds of flesh between his legs.

Rowan cleared his throat. "It . . . does that."

"What else does it do?"

"The usual things."

I dragged my gaze from the rosebud and regarded him with exasperation. "Then why in God's name did you make such a fuss about it?"

"Because it's . . . well, look at me! I'm not like . . . I'm different."

"I figured that out the first day I met you, you big goof."

I silenced his protest with a very thorough kiss. When we came up for air, he offered the sweet smile I loved so much. "You always astonish me."

"I don't know why. I'm the least astonishing person I know. Whereas you are—oh."

The rosebud had ... bloomed. Was blooming. The kind of astonishing growth spurt you see in time-lapse photography on a nature show. Or a cartoon.

Without thinking, I murmured, "Hello, Pinocchio."

I clapped my hand over my mouth, horrified at the words that had just popped out of it. Rowan's expression underwent a series of changes ranging from shock to disbelief to embarrassment. Then he burst out laughing. My babbled apologies made him laugh harder.

Finally, he subsided into a succession of long, wheezing sighs.

"Maggie Graham. You are the only person in the world who could make me laugh at such a moment." Suddenly, he glanced down. "'Look what you've done!'" he screeched. "'I'm melting, melting ...'"

Once we regained some measure of control, I set myself to the task of reviving his drooping rose. It recovered far faster than we did. We were giddy and breathless, surprised by our unexpected laughter, by the ease with which we had coped with this secret. Playfulness quickly shifted to tenderness, and tenderness to desire.

When his body covered mine, I felt as if I were filled with light and heat. I pulled him closer, my urgency tinged with the painful awareness that I could never bring him close enough.

The hoarse rasp of his breath, the rhythm of his movements, the honeysuckle musk of his body ... they pierced me with the same silvery music I had heard at Midsummer. It vibrated with his power, striking an answering chord in me that blossomed into fullness, harmonizing with his and building to a fierce crescendo until we lost ourselves in helpless dissolution.

Only afterward, as we lay in each other's arms, did the sadness set in. For no matter how close we had become or how many barriers had fallen, the ending would remain the same.

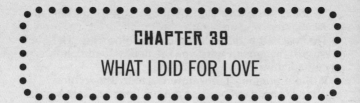

WHEN THE FIRST HINT OF BLUE APPEARED in the skylights, I slipped out from between the sheets and hurried into the bathroom with my clothes. I left the door open so I wouldn't be tempted to cry. I washed my face, brushed my teeth. I didn't wash my body, though; I wanted his scent on me—the sweet, musky smell of him. That, at least, I could keep for a while.

By the time I returned to the bedroom, he had dressed. I wore last night's finery, feeling anything but fine.

He took my hands and said, "I want to give you something. In return for all you've given me this summer."

Before I could protest that he had already given me so much, he leaned close and whispered in my ear. When I began to repeat the words, he pressed his fingertips to my lips.

"My true name. The one I chose as a boy. In the wrong hands, it could be used to bind me. Or steal my power."

"You mean if I had said it just now, something awful would have happened?"

He smiled. "No. I'm just superstitious. To harm me, you'd have to use it in a spell. If the witch had known it, she could have bound me to this world without the iron. And there are those who still practice the old ways who could use it against me. Including my folk." His expression became very serious. "No one knows that name, Maggie. Not in this world or in Faerie."

If I had been humbled by his trust last night, I was stunned now. To entrust such a gift to me who was forever blurting out the wrong thing at the wrong moment. I vowed to safeguard his name and speak it only in my mind. For me, of course, he would always be Rowan.

"Thank you. For telling me. For trusting me."

He kissed me gently. For a moment, we clung to each other. Then I eased free.

"Let's go down to the stage," he said.

That's where it had begun, after all. It seemed only fitting that it should end there as well.

I followed him through the living area and into the kitchen. My puzzlement grew as he opened a door that I had assumed was some sort of pantry. Instead of shelves of dry goods, I saw a dark stairway. He flipped on a light switch and led me down the stairs.

I waited outside the cramped lighting booth while he bent over the control board. Moments later, a pool of golden light illuminated the stage.

Hand in hand, we walked down the stairs from the balcony, followed the aisle through the orchestra section, and slowly mounted the steps to the stage. Rowan switched off the ghost light and together, we stared out at the darkened house.

"The last audition of the day," he said. "I heard you trotting down the aisle after Reinhard . . ."

"Bitching and moaning the whole way."

"What made you choose 'Some Enchanted Evening?'"

"I heard Bernie singing it. To Nancy."

"The whole of our summer in the way you performed that song," he mused. "So flip and sarcastic in the beginning. And then—halfway through—you sang. Really sang. With so much passion and hope that I knew you had to be Nettie." He smiled. "And I knew what an uphill battle I'd have on my hands to help you discover her. I just never imagined how much I would discover, too."

His face suddenly went blank. Then he whirled around, his gaze raking the wings.

One by one, the staff emerged from the shadows. I wondered why Rowan had failed to sense their presence earlier; perhaps he'd been concentrating so hard on restraining his emotions.

"What are you doing here?" Rowan asked.

I'd expected anger at their interruption. Instead, I felt confusion and a cold shudder of fear, quickly banished as he regained control.

"We didn't know when you were leaving," Helen said. "Or if you intended to say good-bye."

"I would never have left without . . . I was going to come up to the house. Later."

"And the rest of us?" Lee asked.

"I . . . I wrote letters."

"Jesus, Rowan." Alex looked shocked. "I've known you my whole life. Worked with you for forty years. And you were going to leave me a letter?"

"Oh, for God's sake, Alex!" Janet glared at her son. "He was trying to spare us—and himself—from exactly that kind of grotesque emotional outburst. An instinct I approve of as much as I disapprove of this melodramatic intervention. It's like the ending of some goddamn Agatha Christie mystery."

"Then why are you doing it?" I demanded.

Janet just shot me the same exasperated look she had given Alex. Of course, she was doing this for Helen. But I couldn't help saying, "It's unfair to mount this last-ditch effort to convince him to stay."

"That's what this is?" Rowan asked.

"They wanted me to do it. But I said it was your decision."

"There are things you need to know," Helen said, "that might affect that decision."

Rowan's expression grew wary. "What do you mean?"

"You think of us as your colleagues," Helen said. "And in some cases, your friends. But we're your family, too."

"I understand that, Helen. But it doesn't change—"

"No, you *don't* understand," Janet interrupted. "You've never understood." For a moment, she hesitated, regarding Rowan with a frown. Then she said, "Marsali Mackenzie died in childbirth. Just as her mother told you. But the child—your child—lived."

Rowan's shock broke over me with such force that I gasped. He backed away, shaking his head. "No. That's not . . . the witch said—"

"She told you the child was taken," Helen said, her face full of pity. "You preserved her words in your play, remember?"

Rowan's memories assailed my mind: a forest glade; a circle of men, red hair glinting in the shafts of sunlight; a gray-haired woman, hatchet-faced like Janet, clutching something that hung on a chain around her neck.

"They named her Margaret," Helen said quietly, glancing at me.

A girl running toward him through sunlight and shadow, her laughter as joyous as birdsong. Not Margaret, of course. Her mother, Marsali.

"She was raised by one of the Mackenzie brothers," Janet said. "A blacksmith in Dale." Her voice was as flat as if she were narrating some dull piece of local history. "Later, of course, they had to move to another town. To protect Margaret and avoid arousing suspicion."

"Where is she?" Rowan demanded.

"She died," Helen said. "In 1854."

Rowan's hand came up to shield his face.

"She killed herself," Janet said. "Family legend claims it was because her faery blood drove her mad."

"We don't know that!" Helen added quickly. "Not for sure."

Wave after wave of shock and misery pummeled me. I flung my arm around Rowan's waist to support myself as much as him.

I couldn't believe Helen would allow Janet to concoct such a monstrous lie. Easier to believe that Janet had convinced her it was the truth and was using it to exact vengeance against Rowan for becoming Helen's lover. But nothing in Janet's manner conveyed satisfaction or pleasure. She looked tired, almost pained, as if she just wanted to get this over with.

"Before Margaret died," Janet continued, "she gave birth to twin daughters. I was one of them."

"It's a lie!"

Even Janet took a step back in the face of Rowan's fury.

"You're making this up! All of it! You've always hated me. Even before Helen."

"Yes, I hated you. Your lust killed my grandmother. Your

blood drove my mother mad. Your selfishness ruined Helen's life. You couldn't even leave me Alex. His life revolves around you as much as Helen's does. And because they were determined to remain here, I was bound to this place as surely as you were."

Suddenly, Janet's passion evaporated and she shook her head wearily. "I've spent most of my life hating you. But after Helen's heart attack, I didn't have the energy for it. It never changed anything. And left me with . . . ashes. Ironic, isn't it? I've finally made my peace with you and you want to leave."

Rowan's gaze swept the faces of the staff. "Why didn't you tell me, Helen? Why didn't any of you ever tell me?"

"It was my secret," Janet said. "My precious secret. I held onto it for years, waiting for the right moment to use that knowledge. To wound you. When I realized that Helen was falling in love with you, I told her, thinking that would keep her from you." Janet's smile was bitter. "But my little plan backfired. So I'm as much to blame as you for ruining Helen's life."

"No one ruined my life," Helen said. "I wanted to be the one who opened the gateway for you. I knew you'd never allow yourself to love me if you knew the truth. Later, I was afraid you'd be angry that I had kept it from you. Please try to understand. And forgive me."

Rowan had his power under control again, his emotions carefully hidden. Only the tremors coursing through his body betrayed his shock.

"I was afraid, too," Alex said. "Afraid we wouldn't be able to work together. And the work was what kept me going after Annie died. That and Catherine, of course."

Rowan's gaze moved from his face to Catherine's to Helen's. "So you're all . . . family."

"And so am I," Reinhard said.

Rowan's breath hissed in. His hands came up as if to hold back another assault.

"Janet's sister, Isobel," Reinhard said quietly. "She was my mother."

"And my grandmother," Lee added.

"Lee is my sister's son," Reinhard said. "She and I were . . . estranged for years. I never even knew she had married. Or had a child. Until Lee came here. He looks . . . very like her."

Rowan was shaking, his hoarse pants loud in my ear. As if he had been running for miles, a stag pursued by baying hounds.

"There was also my son from my first marriage," Janet said. "Robert. He settled in California after World War II."

Rowan's gaze snapped to Mei-Yin and Javier.

"I'm his grandson," Javier said.

"I'm his daughter. A BASTARD. Big surprise, huh? Which makes Reinhard my second half cousin or something." Mei-Yin smiled up at Reinhard. "Doesn't change ANYTHING for us."

"Or us," Catherine said, squeezing Javier's hand. "Dad told us when we started dating."

"I, of course, didn't know anything about anyone until yesterday." Hal shot a reproachful glance at Lee. "I'm just . . . me. No relation to anybody." He sounded forlorn.

"Dearest, I know how hard this is for you," Helen said. "And please forgive us for breaking it to you like this. We hoped you would stay because of Maggie. If you had, we would have told you then. But when we realized you were going back . . . it was my decision I thought you had to know that you would not only be leaving the woman you love, but your family, too."

"Wait," I said. "No. You're . . . you don't understand. Rowan isn't in love with me."

Nine blank faces stared back at me.

"But that's how the curse was broken," Helen said. "I thought . . . we all thought you understood that."

I turned to Rowan, but he was staring at the floor.

"The curse was about music and light and healing. There was nothing about love."

Janet's mirthless laugh broke the silence. Alex shook his head. Reinhard glared at Rowan and said, "You never told her."

My desperate gaze returned to Helen.

"There were three parts to the curse, Maggie. To return light and music to the world. To use his power to heal the Mackenzies' grief. And to feel the one emotion he had never known."

*"What I stole, I must return. What I brought, I must take
away. What I had never felt—"*

"But it's not . . . it can't be me. It's Jamie. Rowan finally
realized that he loved Jamie."

Again, I looked at Rowan for confirmation, but he refused to meet my gaze.

"For God's sake, say something!" Alex exclaimed.

Helen sighed. "Oh, Rowan. How could you leave without telling Maggie the truth?"

"Maybe he left her a letter," Lee said.

"Enough!" The word burst from Rowan on a blaze of anger. Then he turned to me and seized my arms. "I wanted to
tell you. A hundred times this past week. But I thought you
knew how I felt. After everything that happened, all the
things we've shared—things I've never shared with anyone. I
thought you were trying to make it easier for us. Just as I
was."

The words reached me, without bringing the sense of
them any closer. I took them apart and attempted to put
them together again, a child struggling with a puzzle far too
complex for her inadequate brain and fumbling fingers. Apparently, he had given me the last piece of that puzzle, but
still, I could not determine its proper setting.

I searched his face and found desperation there, and
concern, and the fear that he had wounded me. His power
fluctuated wildly with those same emotions. But not love.

Then his hands came up to cup my face. And his love
poured over me. Not the turbulent stream I had imagined,
but the deep, still waters of a lake. Not the rock I had battered against for so many weeks, but one I could lean on for
strength and support. No longer a shadowy sensation, half-
sensed but always dismissed as fancy, but the strong, clear
sunlight flooding the plateau.

"But if you love me . . . ?"

"It doesn't change anything," he said gently.

"It does for me."

"If I asked you right now if you loved me, you'd say yes.
You'd always say yes, Maggie. Because you will always feel
my power—my emotions for you."

I shook my head, but I couldn't help recalling all the
times his power had left me giddy and breathless, when his

emotions had swamped mine and carried me along, helpless as a leaf in a stream.

His smile was filled with sadness and understanding. "Even if you were certain of your feelings, I'd still have to go." He regarded his silent staff. "You came here to convince me to stay. Instead, you gave me the best reason to leave."

He took my hands, his expression still sad but determined now. "You deserve a man who can share your life without forever looking over his shoulder, hiding his real self from the world. A man who can give you a child without fearing that his tainted blood would destroy it. A man who can grow old with you. I can't give you any of those gifts, Maggie. And I'd rather lose you forever than stand by helplessly and watch you die."

I doubted I could bear that either. To watch him transform from a lover into a caretaker. To see him struggling to control his emotions lest they add to my grief. I had tried not to consider a future beyond this week, and when rebellious daydreams intruded, they extended only to next week, next month, next year, never twenty years from now or fifty. I had imagined the anticipation of seeing him, our combustible reunion, its drowsy aftermath. Walks in the woods and picnics on the plateau. Although I had known he would no longer be chained to this small parcel of land, I'd never even envisioned him beyond its borders.

Someday, I might laugh at the bitter irony that a faery made me realize what a completely impossible fairy tale I had created. Now, as his grief stabbed me, I became calm.

I had to help him, lend him the strength he needed to walk away. Time enough later for me to fall apart. Right now, he needed Maggie Graham, Helping Professional.

I watched him bid farewell to his staff, offering a handshake to some, a quick embrace to others. He held Helen for a long moment. I saw his lips move as he whispered something. She was weeping when he finally stepped back.

"Forgive me if I've seemed cold. Or if I ever gave the impression that your friendship was unimportant. It was. It is." His gaze lingered on Alex, then Reinhard. "I had hoped to avoid a painful farewell. Even though I knew it was wrong to slink away. But you'll have to forgive me if I leave now. Before —"

His voice caught. Blindly, he flung out his hand and I stumbled forward to grasp it. He led me quickly toward the stage right wings, but paused there to look back.

"May the gods bless you all. And keep you ever safe."

We hurried out the stage door and into the picnic area. His words flowed at the same breathless pace.

"The letters to the staff are in my desk. There are two for Reinhard. Make sure he reads the first one before you leave. There's also a copy of *By Iron, Bound* for you. Act Two is a mess. I couldn't capture you. Foolish to try."

Like a dying man, dictating his last will and testament, disposing of his possessions, tying up the threads of his life.

He halted abruptly at the edge of the meadow. "I'm going to the cottage. I'll cross at sunset. Don't wait. It will be harder if I feel you here. Will you do that for me?"

I nodded, unwilling to trust my voice.

His hands fumbled at the back of his neck. The silver chain slipped free. He thrust it out. When I just stared at it, he seized my hand and dropped it into my palm, the metal warm from his skin. He closed my fingers around it. Immediately, he released my hand and stepped back.

I studied his face, just as I had the day I met him.

Remember everything about this moment. Those wild-winged eyebrows drawn together in a frown. The hard line of his mouth. The golden sparks, shining like tears in his eyes. Remember.

One final time, I held him.

Remember how his breath comes short and hard. How his fingers dig into your back. How those antler tine buttons dig into your breastbone. The thud of his heart against yours. The softness of his hair against your cheek. The sweet aroma of honeysuckle filling your nose.

And then I let him go.

Remember his eyes, soft and green as moss.

His hand came up to touch my cheek.

Remember the scars on his fingertips, on his palms. The slide of them against your flesh.

His mouth came down on mine.

Remember his lips, hard and bruising. The scrape of his tongue. The warmth of his breath.

"You are my heart."

His voice, shuddering through you like his power. Raw and harsh, in spite of the tenderness of his words. Remember the contradiction. All his contradictions.

He turned away and started walking toward the woods.

Remember his long, purposeful stride. His fingers knotted into fists. Remember how the grass bends before him. How his hair gleams in the early morning sunlight, shiny and black as a raven's wing.

Remember how he lurches to a halt at the very edge of the pond, as if he forgot it was there, then stumbles around it, a blur of beige and black against the green of the grass, the pewter of the water.

Remember the liquid song of a robin in one of the maples.

Remember the breeze caressing your face, the sun warming your back.

Remember the creak of the weather vane atop the barn. How you heard it that first day.

At the edge of the woods, he paused and turned back.

Remember how small he looks, dwarfed by the trees. Small and alone and vulnerable.

His hand came up.

Remember his fingers, long and slender as a girl's. Remember the scars on his wrists. Is he smiling or weeping? Weeping. His power tells you that. But remember his smile, remember all of his smiles, but especially the one that surprised you so much with its unexpected sweetness.

I raised my hand, still clenched around his silver chain.

Remember that he loves you, that you are his heart, that he will carry you with him all the days and nights of his long life. Remember how much you love him, that it's not merely an echo of his feelings, but as real as the sun on your back and the tears on your face.

His hand came down. He turned away. In three strides, he was lost among the trees.

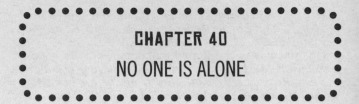

CHAPTER 40
NO ONE IS ALONE

THE NEXT THING I REMEMBERED was the absence of warmth and sunlight. That seemed fitting, somehow. Then I realized I was inside a building. Janet's house, cool and shadowy.

Hands guided me up the stairs, led me into a room, urged me onto something soft. A bed. I was sitting on a bed. Hands stroked my hair, my back, my arms. Voices murmured quiet words that lapped against me, warm and soothing as bathwater.

"No! Don't take it away! Don't make me forget!"

A hand squeezing mine. Helen's face, blotchy from crying. "No, dear. Never. Just a blessing. For strength."

He was still here. In the woods. He probably hadn't even reached the cottage yet.

I lurched to my feet, pushing past the clustered bodies, the restraining hands. "There's still time!" If I called his secret name, if I asked the staff to help me ... together, we could find some way to stop him from leaving.

Reinhard's hands grasping my shoulders. Reinhard's eyes looking down into mine. "Is that what you want?"

"Yes!"

But that was not what he wanted, not what he had asked of me.

"It will be harder if I feel you here."

"I have to go home."

"Rest a bit first," Reinhard urged.

402

I let him guide me back to the bed, ease me onto it.

"Why don't you lie down?" Helen suggested.

I shook my head. There was something important I was supposed to do. Instructions to pass along. I recited them to Reinhard, surprised that my voice sounded so calm.

"I will take care of everything," he assured me.

What else? What else was I forgetting?

"Nancy. She's waiting at the hotel."

"She's probably still asleep," Helen said. "It's not even seven. Are you sure you won't lie down, dear? Just for an hour."

He wouldn't be sleeping. How could I?

Helen sat beside me and clasped my hand. "He would want you to be peaceful, Maggie. He would want us to give you that peace."

"I have to do something."

"What?"

"Something. Anything."

"Fine." Janet pushed through the crowd. "You can help me make breakfast."

Reinhard shook his head impatiently, but I said, "Yes. All right."

Janet gave me a brisk nod of approval. "Helen can show you where everything is. Alex, Lee—help Reinhard at the apartment. Javier, gas up Maggie's car. Catherine, Mei-Yin—go to the hotel. Pack Maggie's things. Bring them here. And Nancy, too. Just tell her Maggie and Rowan have broken up and Maggie needs her support. Not the rest."

"You think I'm an IDIOT?" Mei-Yin exclaimed.

"What about me?" Hal asked. "What can I do?"

He looked so miserable that I lowered the fist I'd been pressing against my breastbone and uncurled my clenched fingers. "You can help me with this."

He stared at the silver chain coiled in my palm, and his face crumpled.

"If you're going to cry," Janet said, "go out on the porch."

Hal threw back his head and glared at her. "I can do this. I'm a costume designer!"

I surrendered the chain and rose. Cold fingers fumbled at the nape of my neck. How unlike Hal to be clumsy. The chain nestled atop my collarbone. I caressed the braided

silver with trembling fingers and glanced over my shoulder
at Hal.

He gave me a wobbly smile. "It's beautiful. Now. We'll go
to the bathroom and I'll help you fix your pretty face. We'll
both feel better after that."

I looked better, but I felt just as numb. That was a good
thing, Hal assured me. When the numbness wore off, I'd
be a mess. Which is why, he insisted, I should stay with him
and Lee.

Everyone seemed to have the same idea. As they trickled back to the house, I was inundated by invitations, surrounded by worried faces. When Janet herded us all into the
dining room, I picked at my eggs for a few minutes. Then I
put down my fork and said, "I have to go." Ignoring the
storm of protest that ensued, I added, "The longer I stay, the
harder it'll be. For both of us."

"Yes," Reinhard agreed. "But we will all worry if you
drive alone. So. I will drive you in your car. Wait. Listen. I
will not pester you with questions. I will not talk at all if you
prefer. But it will ease my mind if you allow me to do this.
Lee will follow in his truck and bring me home."

I nodded wearily. It was easier to agree than to argue.

"Good. Then say good-bye. And we will go."

I hugged Catherine and Javier. Received a rib-bruising
embrace from Mei-Yin, a tender one from Alex. And with
Janet's brisk hug, the stern advice to cry my eyes out for a
day and then get on with my life.

Nancy's hug was every bit as bruising as Mei-Yin's. "I'll
call you tomorrow. And I'll come down to Brooklyn next
weekend if you want me to. Any weekend."

I felt like Dorothy leaving Oz. I wished for a Glinda who
could magically transport me . . . somewhere. Not over the
rainbow. Or to Brooklyn; it had never felt much like home.

When I reached for Hal, he stepped back, his expression
fierce. "I'm coming with Lee. Don't even think of trying to
stop me."

Helen enfolded me in her arms. When she'd welcomed
me to the Crossroads that first day, I had thought she was a
fairy godmother, little realizing the truth behind that fanci-

ful impression. She had offered blessings to lull me to sleep, a kind and open heart when I needed advice, a maternal embrace when I needed solace. Even now, I felt comfort and peace flowing from her. And I hated to think how little I had given her in return.

"Hush," she whispered. "You made me feel young again, and hopeful. And you gave me the greatest gift I could ever wish for—to see him happy. You must be happy, too, Maggie. He'd want that. And don't ever regret loving him."

Reinhard guided me down the path, a strong arm around my waist. Lee and Hal followed behind, like official mourners. Reinhard was speaking. Something about Rowan's journals. I tried to focus, but it was difficult.

"He wanted you to have them. It was in his letter to me."

Yes. I remembered the letter. The one he was supposed to read before I left.

"There were more than we expected. They filled five boxes."

"Five boxes?"

Reinhard smiled. "It would seem he was always a writer. The first journal was written in 1838. I've packed it—and this year's—in a separate box as Rowan requested. With his play and the other things. The rest of his journals I will store. Or ship to you when you are ready. Yes?"

I nodded, too dazed to inquire about the "other things" Reinhard had packed.

When we reached my car, I rubbed my streaming eyes, ruining all of Hal's efforts. My gaze moved from the cluster of people on the front porch to the deep green of the woods.

Can you feel me? Do you know I'm about to leave? If you know that, you must feel my love as well. Carry it with you to that other world. And I will carry yours with me.

I raised my hand in farewell—to my friends on the porch, to the man in the woods. Then I collapsed into the passenger seat.

I stared straight ahead as we drove up the lane and out into the road. Only when we started up the hill did I twist around. Through my tears, the Crossroads Theatre was little more than a pale blob floating between green grass and blue sky. Then we crested the hill and it disappeared.

It was still early afternoon when we arrived in Brooklyn.
Reinhard expressed cautious approval of tree-lined Eastern Parkway with its rows of brownstones, but seemed
surprised by the diversity of the neighborhood where
black-coated Hasidim shared the sidewalks with weekend
soccer leagues, yuppie couples pushing strollers, teenagers
calling to each other in Spanish and Creole, and formally
dressed African-American families heading home from
church.

Sweltering heat and reggae music blasted me as I threw
open the car door. My apartment was an oven, but at least
my tenant had left it clean. The three men tried unsuccess-
fully to conceal their shock at its size; if I had told them the
rent I paid, they would have been even more shocked.

Reinhard gazed around the room and announced that
we were going out to lunch. I took them to Tom's Restaurant. It was a bit of a hike, but we all needed to stretch our
legs after the long drive. Even if they didn't want to try the
out-of-sight egg creams, they'd find something familiar on
the menu; I wasn't sure how Reinhard would fare at the
West Indian places near me.

Afterward, we trudged back to the apartment, heavy
with food and heat. Lee and Hal hesitated at the steps to
my building, looking at Reinhard for guidance.

"We could stay a while," he told me.

Their presence would be a bulwark against the inevitable pain that sunset would bring, but I shook my head. They
had already done more than I could have asked—today and
throughout the summer. These three men—all so different—
who had leaped to my aid so many times. Lee, fiercely protective the night of the Follies. Hal, whose sweet, open
nature had been apparent from the very first day.

And Reinhard. Two months ago, I could never have
imagined that the man who had bullied me into auditioning
would become my staunchest ally. I had cast Alex as my
surrogate father, but it was Reinhard who had stepped into
the role. Never obtrusive, never pushing me for confidences
I was unwilling to share, but always there, guarding my back
and ensuring my welfare, hiding his affection and concern

beneath a gruff veneer, never realizing that the state of his hair always revealed his emotions.

It was in full porcupine mode now. I resisted the urge to smooth it and simply hugged them one by one. Hal wept. Lee kicked the step of my brownstone. Reinhard frowned.

"You will be all right. You have our numbers. You will call if you need us."

"I'll call even if you don't," Hal said.

I shoved a napkin into Reinhard's hand with scrawled directions to the Whitestone Bridge. Waited on the steps, smiling and waving until Lee's truck rounded the corner. Then my smile faded, my arm fell to my side, and I walked slowly up the stairs to my apartment.

I cranked the A/C up another notch. Washed my face. Exchanged my sarong for a T-shirt and shorts. Stared at the cardboard "Store-All" box sitting under my front windows and decided I wasn't ready to tackle it.

I unpacked my carryall and my suitcase. Put fresh sheets on the futon, hung fresh towels in the bathroom. Scoured the tub and the sink. Picked up some supplies at Food Town. Each task distracted me, kept me calm, allowed me to focus on the immediate problem confronting me. French baguette or seeded Italian loaf? Cottonelle or Charmin?

I called Jorge and thanked him for doing such a great job on the bathroom ceiling. Called my mother to let her know I was home. Pleaded exhaustion to avoid a long conversation and promised to call tomorrow. Only then, as afternoon was sliding into evening, did I sit down beside the box.

I took a deep breath and removed the lid.

I saw the envelope first. With some surprise, I realized I had never seen his handwriting before. I studied the small, precise letters of my name, then set the envelope aside.

The first leather-bound journal I picked up was the size of a notebook. The other was more like a diary, the leather cracked with age and torn at the corners. Those, I set aside as well. And the script of *By Iron, Bound* that he had placed inside a large manila envelope.

I found his script and score of *Carousel*, both filled with tiny, penciled notations. A battered copy of the 1836 edition of the *McGuffey Reader*. A CD entitled *The Rankin Family*.

I studied the back cover and caught my breath when I saw a track entitled "Chì mi na mórbheanna." The Gaelic title of the song I knew as the "The Mist-Covered Mountains." I put the CD on my player, skipped ahead to the track, and sank onto the floor again as the sweet, unearthly female voice I had heard in his apartment filled mine.

I pulled out the soft lamb's wool throw, the knapsack he had carried on our picnics. Inside I found a bottle of Chateauneuf du Pape. And—carefully wrapped in a linen napkin—a faded beech leaf.

I had to pause then and wait until I collected myself before opening the second manila envelope. It was larger than the one that held his script, softer and lumpy. And the handwriting on the outside belonged to someone else.

Maggie. This was not on Rowan's list. But I thought you would wish to have it. Forgive me if I presume too much.

I opened the clasp. My fingers brushed the nubbiness of linen. And something hard and pointy.

I held the wrinkled shirt to my face, the shirt he had worn only yesterday, and breathed in his animal musk and his honeysuckle sweetness and the faint tang of his sweat. I wept for the loss of the man I loved, but also in gratitude to the one who had given me this gift. Reinhard had guessed rightly that the memories it evoked and the sheer physical closeness of Rowan would far outweigh the pain.

Reluctantly, I let the shirt fall to my lap while I examined the last item. A rectangular wooden box, roughly the size and shape of a box of tissues. The painted green vines on its cover and sides were so faded with age that I had to squint in the dying light to make them out.

I raised the lid and gasped.

Hundred dollar bills in ten neat bundles, each secured with a rubber band. My hands shook as I counted.

Fifty thousand dollars.

"My salary doesn't allow me many luxuries, but it does put clothes on my back and food on my table."

Long summer days blocking the shows, exhorting his casts, helping them discover what was lacking in their lives. Long winter evenings collaborating with Alex, shaping and reshaping their newest creation. A century of directing and writing. A century of savings. Tucked away in a wooden box. And given to me.

It was far more than a gift of money. It would give me time to decide what I wanted to do with my life. With my unemployment, I could live on half that money for a year. Longer if I moved out of New York.

And the balance? That would go back to the Crossroads. To give the staff the time it needed to create a plan for the theatre's future. And to take care of some of the immediate necessities: augmenting those wretched salaries, painting that tired-looking lobby. New chairs—comfortable ones— for the Smokehouse. And furniture for the green room to replace the chairs and tables that were literally falling to pieces. Maybe there would even be enough left over for Hal to splurge on some snazzy costumes next year.

For the first time in days, I was excited, looking forward to the future. And I blessed him for that gift, too, amazed that I could feel those emotions when the light filtering through my windows told me it must be close to sunset.

I wondered if his power was strong enough to touch me here. He had reached me before; I'd been looking through travel books then. But he had been calling all of us. Maybe it was harder to call one person. Maybe he would prefer to slip away. Spare us both that final pain.

Then I realized he *was* calling me. Not with his magic, but with his words.

I slipped my arms through the sleeves of his shirt. Carried his play, his journals, and his letter to the futon. Grabbed a Mike's Hard Lemonade from the fridge; the Chateauneuf du Pape was meant to be shared.

I would not sit and watch the light fade, wondering when he chose to make his crossing. I would let his words bridge that moment, fill the hole left in the world, fill me with his thoughts, his hopes, his fears, his love.

My dearest Maggie,

Before I can write the words of my heart, I must say a few words about the things I have instructed Reinhard to pack for you. Most are sentimental in nature. Not—I hope—maudlin. You will have to judge.

The journals are a window into my life, my thoughts, my heart. I should warn you: some of the sections from this summer are ugly. I reread the worst passages while you slept and winced. I was angry when I wrote them. And hurt. I worry that you'll feel the same after you've read them. But I am through hiding in the shadows.

Other sections are—I don't know, maybe you'll wince at those, too. Because they're so graphic. Not pornographic. I hope. Your body is such a wonder to me. I go on at embarrassing length about it. I will not do so here.

There is money in the wooden box. Not much for more than a century's labor. But it is free of all encumbrances, including those imposed by the government. I have never had a bank account or an Internet account, a credit card or a phone. There are inconveniences in having no identity—I used Helen's Internet account to purchase my clothes, did I ever tell you that?—but there are advantages as well. So keep the money in the box as I did, so that you can benefit from it rather than Uncle Sam.

I suspect your first reaction will be to give it to the theatre. I beg you to keep some of it for yourself. It will give you time to consider what you will do next. Take that time, my love. Allow yourself to drift and dream as I urged on our first picnic. Trust yourself to find your true path. And when you do, don't be afraid to take it.

I have just reread what I've written. I sound more like a lawyer than a lover. Except for the remarks about your body. Were I a lawyer, I'd be disbarred for those.

Are you smiling? I hope so. I am. Almost.

I'm procrastinating. Because when I finish writing this letter, all that's left is the waiting. For morning. For our farewells. I pray I'll have the strength. I know you will. You're much stronger than I am.

Know that I will always love you. For making me laugh. For making me doubt. For making me change. I love your kindness and your stubbornness and your courage. Your great bellow of a laugh. Your quick wit. Your blush. The sight and the smell and the taste of you.

Loving you is the most impossible thing that has ever happened to me. And the most humbling. I never expected love to bring equal measures of joy and sorrow, delight and fear. And those unexpected moments of peace. I imagine this is what it must be like to shoot the rapids in a leaky canoe and then emerge from heart-stopping tumult into a quiet pool.

You will be with me every day, every night. My shield against loneliness. The bright, pure flame that burns at the core of my being. And if there is an afterworld where humans and faeries meet, we will find each other again and our spirits will dwell together until the world's end.

My love. My heart. My beautiful girl. Be well. Be happy.

Yours,
Rowan

CHAPTER 41
THERE'S NO CURE LIKE TRAVEL

I FILLED MONDAY MORNING BY PICKING UP MY MAIL at the post office, running a load of wash at the Laundromat, dusting, vacuuming. When I ran out of tasks, I called Mom at work and asked if I could come down to Delaware a little early.

Three hours later, I was sitting on her horribly uncomfortable settee, calmly explaining that I had been involved with Rowan Mackenzie but we both realized it wouldn't work out and we had gone our separate ways and I was fine, really, not really fine, but okay, would be okay, I just needed a little time, and could we please not talk about it any more.

Her gaze rested on the silver chain around my neck, but all she said was, "All right. Would you like to go to Domaine Hudson for dinner?"

I spent much of that week just wandering along the Brandywine. Sometimes, I sat by the river reading Rowan's journals and his play. I thought a lot about *The Sea-Wife*. The parallels to our situation were obvious. The selkie who had to return to her home. The lover who had to let her go. I'd told Rowan that the schoolteacher would find love again because he had learned to hope, to change, to embrace the impossible. I wanted to believe that was true for me, too. But Rowan had left the ending ambiguous. And that's how my future felt.

Mom did her best to distract me in the evenings, taking me to a concert at the Riverfront, a concert at Longwood

412

Gardens, a concert at the Chadds Ford Winery. "Thank God we're going to Rehoboth," she said near the end of the week. "I'm running out of concerts."

She studiously avoided taking me to the theatre—and talking about Chris. Finally, I asked if I was ever going to meet the mystery man.

"I wasn't sure . . . I thought it might be . . . difficult."

"Well, as long as you don't make out in front of me or anything."

"Maggie!"

After extracting a promise to say nothing that might embarrass her, she invited Chris to dinner on Friday night. He turned out to be a lawyer with a neatly trimmed gray beard, an earnest expression and—after two glasses of wine—a wicked sense of humor. We took turns embarrassing my mother, who blushed and protested and enjoyed it immensely. As happy as I was for her, it was hard to suppress the feelings of regret and longing and envy that filled me each time she and Chris exchanged smiles.

Rehoboth was crowded and noisy—your typical beach town in August. Maybe because it held fewer memories than Wilmington, it was easier for me to relax there. I still woke to the pain of Rowan's absence and went to sleep with that pain at night, but in between I tried to drift as he had urged, to live in the moment, to enjoy the cool slap of the waves, the tackiness of the boardwalk, and the quaint shops in nearby Lewes.

By the end of our week, Mom had stopped studying me for signs of a nervous breakdown and allowed me to take solitary walks on the beach in the evening without fearing I would swim out to sea and drown myself. I could even talk about the summer—at least parts of it—without the threat of tears. To Mom and to the astonishing number of people who called.

After inundating me with calls those first few days in Wilmington, Helen and Hal apparently decided to give me time off during my week at Rehoboth. But Nancy called every couple of days. Although I was happy to hear from her, I was reluctant to talk about Rowan; it just brought everything crashing down on me again.

Chatting with Kalma and Brittany was easier, sighing

over the annoyances of the "real" world and speculating about what the next few months would bring. Bernie called to complain about the boring old people at the senior center, Sarah to complain about her mother. Gary called to make sure I was okay. Caren wanted to know how soon she could visit Brooklyn. Bobbie wanted to do the "list thing" over the phone to help her weigh the pros and cons of moving in with Lou.

"You certainly have a lot of friends," Mom remarked after I hung up with Kevin, who called to invite me to a gig in Queens.

I smiled; three months ago, I couldn't name one friend I could comfortably call on for help. Now I could name dozens.

Two weeks after leaving the Crossroads, I was back in Wilmington, packing yet again—this time for my return to New York. I was no closer to discovering my path in life than when I'd arrived in Delaware, and the prospect of returning to that empty apartment left me anxious and depressed.

When my phone broke into the "People" ringtone I'd programmed to identify Hal, my spirits revived a little.

"Maggie?"

Hearing the quaver in his voice, I immediately assured him I was okay.

There was a brief silence. Then something that sounded like a sob.

"Hal. What is it? What's wrong? Is it Lee?"

"No. It's Helen."

CHAPTER 42
I BELONG HERE

FIVE DAYS LATER, I WAS BACK IN DALE, still hearing Hal's tearful voice, still struggling to cope with this new loss. According to Hal, she had died quietly in her sleep—how like Helen—and Janet had discovered her the next morning.

She had lived more than a century, but even her faery blood could not protect her from the rheumatic fever that stole her strength. What a terrible irony that it should be Helen's heart that betrayed her.

I'd railed at Hal for failing to call me sooner, then felt horribly guilty when he burst into tears. "Janet wouldn't let me call anyone," he said when the storm subsided. "She insisted on a small, private funeral. Not even an obituary."

"But after the funeral? Why didn't you call me then?"

"That was Reinhard. He said you needed your vacation. And since we'd convinced Janet to hold a memorial service, I thought . . . oh, I knew I should have called! I don't know why I let people talk me into doing things I don't want to do. Now you'll hate me forever."

I assured Hal I wouldn't hate him, didn't hate him. I even volunteered to call my cast mates and let them know about the memorial service.

Helen had touched so many lives; people would want the chance to say good-bye. But I could understand Janet's desire to keep things private. What if some octogenarian former cast member arrived? How did you explain that

415

Helen—middle-aged when he had worked at the Cross-roads fifty years ago—had lived so long? Or the seemingly ageless appearance of Reinhard and Alex and Janet?

Reinhard provided the answers when I called him to get phone numbers for some of my cast mates. "We will only be contacting those who worked at the theatre in the last ten years," he told me, his voice heavy with grief. "After the memorial, we will notify the others. It is a pity. There are many who would want to attend. But the dangers are simply too great."

Most of our cast was making the trip back to Dale. Some, including the Rastas, couldn't afford the airfare. Others, like Kevin, had weekend jobs. Nick never returned my call, but I'd expected that.

Even those who had been forced to seek accommodations in neighboring towns showed up at the Bough Friday evening. There had to be close to two hundred people, spilling out of the lounge into the lobby, clustering on the stairs and porches. Although many had decided to speak at the memorial service the next day, we held an unofficial one that night, sharing stories about Helen, about the theatre—and about Rowan.

Everyone had a similar account of his patience, his insight, his mysterious gift for pulling astonishing performances from his cast. And many shared personal stories about how their lives had changed after their season at the Crossroads. Like the young guy I'd seen around town who told me that playing little Winthrop in *The Music Man* had helped him overcome his shyness. And the woman who explained that her role as Louise in *Gypsy* had convinced her to attempt a reconciliation with her mother.

Late that night, I pulled out Rowan's final journal and jotted the stories down. A sort of memorial for him and a testament to the effects of his healing on so many lives.

Reinhard had prepped me about the party line on Rowan's absence. He had gone home to Scotland. He had no plans to return. They had not even notified him of Helen's death yet. My job was to convince my cast mates that our failed relationship had been partly responsible for his decision. I would also have to convince them that I had only learned of his departure in the last few days; otherwise, close friends like Nancy and Kalma would surely wonder why I'd said nothing earlier.

Yet another unforeseen acting job. But if I could manage to let him go, I could surely lie about where he had gone.

The happy memories of the summer helped offset some of the sadness that flooded me when I entered the theatre the next day. Reinhard directed the memorial service with a firm voice and a ravaged face. He expressed the staff's love for Helen and their gratitude for all she had done for them and for the theatre. Then he invited others to share.

The tributes lasted more than three hours. So many stories, all citing Helen's generosity and kindness, her unfailing cheerfulness and warmth. When the last person finished, Reinhard returned to the stage and read Rowan's farewell letter to Helen. He skipped over any passages that hinted at the intimate relationship they had shared, but even with those omissions, Rowan's letter was filled with humor and tenderness, with his gratitude and his love, his sorrow to be leaving her and his joy that she had been part of his life for so many years. And hearing his words, picturing him as he struggled to write them—to write all those letters—I wondered how he could ever have imagined that I was the strong one.

I was walking out of the theatre when I glimpsed someone talking to Lou and Bobbie. When I realized who it was, my mouth fell open. I hesitated, wondering if he'd want to talk to me. When he nodded brusquely, I decided to chance it.

"How are you, Nick?"

"Okay. You?"

"Okay."

I glanced at the skinny blonde beside him, teetering on the gravel in her spike heels, a squirming infant in her arms.

"This is Deb. Maggie."

"Nice to meet ya," Deb said. "Nicky, I gotta put Angie down for a nap."

"Okay." He nodded to us awkwardly. "Good to see you guys."

"Janet's having a reception at the house," I said. "Why don't you come for a little while?"

Nick shrugged. "We only got the one car."

"So I'll give you a lift after," Lou said.

"We're staying out of town."

Lou punched Nick's shoulder. "So I'll still give you a lift, asshole."

Nick grinned. Then glanced doubtfully at Deb. "You came all this way," she said. "You should spend time with your friends. I'll see ya at the motel."

"Come back after Angie's had her nap," Bobbie urged. "Janet puts out a great spread. You should spend time with Nick's friends, too."

This time it was Deb who glanced doubtfully at Nick.

"That's a great idea," Lou said. "Isn't it, Nick?"

Nick muttered agreement. Deb smiled wanly, then tottered off in search of their car.

"It'll never last," Bobbie muttered as we followed Lou and Nick up the path.

"Probably not," I agreed. "But at least, he's making an effort."

"Damn, I wish Rowan could've seen this."

"Yeah. Me, too."

❧❧

Janet was conspicuously absent from the reception, but the rest of the staff was there. Alex put up a brave front, but I knew how hard it must be to pretend that Helen was merely a good friend, not his sister. At one point, I saw him sitting on a bench in the garden and made my way down to him. For a long while, I just sat with him, listening to his childhood memories of Helen; even then she had been as much mother as sister to him.

"How's Janet?" I asked.

Alex shook his head. "You know Momma. She keeps everything inside. Even with me. Especially with me."

Her only child now.

He squeezed my hand. "How are *you* doing?"

"You know. A wreck some days. Other days, okay."

"It's like he died, too."

I bit back my protest. In the space of a week, Alex had lost two people who had been part of his life for more than seventy years. But I could not—would not—think of Rowan as dead. For me, it was more like when my father went away. A sort of limbo.

As afternoon turned to evening, people began drifting away. I was walking to the door with Nancy when Lee stopped me.

"Would you mind hanging around, Maggie? There's some stuff we need to discuss. About Helen."

"That sounds mysterious," Nancy said as Lee walked off.

"Maybe she left me a letter or something."

An hour later, I found myself seated at the dining room table, trying to banish memories of the last time I had been there. Janet walked in and greeted me with, "Good. You're here. Let's get started." Which did little to relieve my growing anxiety.

"If this is about the money Rowan left me, I've already decided to give half of it to the theatre. I didn't think today was a good time ... I mean ..."

My voice trailed off as I took in their expressions. Only Reinhard seemed unsurprised; clearly, Rowan must have told him about the money in his letter.

"This meeting is about Helen's bequests," Reinhard said. "Not Rowan's."

"I don't know whether you realized this," Lee said, "but I was—am—Helen's lawyer. A couple of weeks ago, she called us together to discuss some changes she wanted to make to her will. Make sure we were okay with them. Her new will leaves you two specific bequests to you. The first is what she called her Recipe Book."

What I had called her book of spells.

"But that's an heirloom," I protested. "It should stay in the family. With you," I added, looking across the table at Catherine.

"There are two herbals," Janet said. "Helen left Catherine the original written in the Gaelic."

"I have such a black thumb it wouldn't matter if it was in English," Catherine replied with a small smile. "Besides, you're a Mackenzie, too. That makes you family."

"The other," Janet continued, "is a copy my great-grandmother transcribed in English near the end of her life."

"But—"

"Helen wanted you to have it," Janet said, putting an end to further argument.

She placed a worn leather volume on the table. I opened it and peered at the spidery handwriting on the first page, the ink faded to tan.

The Herbal of Mairead Mackenzie. 1817.

The paper crackled as I carefully turned the pages. There were remedies for chilblains and "joint-ill," insect bites and green fractures, "costiveness" and quinsy. Directions for preparing ointments and poultices. Rituals to observe when harvesting plants. Incantations and charms to soothe the heart and the bowels, to attract a lover or repel one, to curse an enemy or bless a loved one. Talismans to protect the wearer from witches and faeries.

A treasury of folklore and knowledge and superstition— and a gift of love from the woman who had hesitantly told me about her nighttime blessings.

I blinked back tears and whispered, "This belongs in a museum."

"Probably," Lee agreed. "But Helen's instructions are very specific. By accepting this bequest, you agree to pass it on only to a blood descendant of Mairead Mackenzie. Do you accept that proviso?"

I nodded, still a bit overwhelmed.

"The other bequest is a little . . . bigger," Lee said.

I glanced at the sideboard. One of the lovely Chinese vases, maybe? Or Helen's candlesticks? I was still trying to decide which she might have chosen when Lee announced, "Helen left you the Golden Bough."

"Yeah. Right." I glanced around the table; no one was laughing. "You can't be serious!"

Lee nodded.

"But that's yours!" I exclaimed to Janet.

"I transferred ownership to Helen decades ago."

"But it's still yours."

"No, Maggie. It's yours. If you want it."

"What am I going to do with a hotel?" I blurted.

"It was Helen's hope that you would run it," Lee said.

"But I don't know anything about running a hotel!"

"I do," Janet said. "I can teach you. And then I can wash my hands of that old rattletrap."

"It's a lovely example of the Greek Revival style," Hal retorted. "It just needs sprucing up. Especially that lobby. The furniture's ancient and the moths are devouring those draperies. And those horrible portieres might have been fine for Scarlett O'Hara but—"

"Hal," Lee interrupted. "You're jumping the gun a bit. Obviously, this isn't a decision you can make in five minutes, Maggie. I'll go over all the documents with you: recent capital improvements, profit and loss statements—"

"Mostly loss," Janet muttered, prompting Alex to demand, "Do you want her to stay or not?"

"Is that what this is about?" I asked. "God. First Rowan, now me. Trust me, you'd be better off hiring me to direct the shows rather than run the hotel."

A furtive exchange of glances greeted that statement.

"I was joking. You knew that, right?"

"Suppose we finish up with the hotel first," Lee suggested.

"I haven't directed since college. And that wasn't even—"

"The hotel? Please?"

I didn't follow half of what Lee said. Finally Reinhard interrupted.

"I know this is a lot to take in. But Lee will help you understand the legal and financial ramifications. You should also know why Helen left you the property."

"That's in the letter," Lee said.

"Which you have not mentioned," Reinhard pointed out.

"I was getting to it! If everybody would just let me talk." Lee took a deep breath and blew it out. "Okay. Here's the deal. Helen dreamed of this theatre becoming a nonprofit. An educational facility that would not only present plays and musicals, but offer classes in acting and dance and directing. Children's programming. Summer internships for college students. Maybe even a residence hall for actors. Obviously, it'll take years to accomplish all that. But Helen thought—we all thought—that you were the right person to run that organization. To be its executive director."

My heart was beating so hard I was having trouble breathing. I managed to say, "I've never run a nonprofit. Or done a lot of fundraising."

"Well, you could learn, couldn't you?" Janet demanded.

"Of course! But this a huge step. For you, I mean. You need someone experienced."

"We want someone we know," Alex replied. "Someone who knows *us*."

"Someone we TRUST," Mei-Yin added.

"And not just because Rowan left," Hal said. "Because he would have been awful. I mean, he's brilliant and everything, but he's an artist. You are, too," he added hastily. "But you're practical. You can handle the details. And you get along with everybody. Even Janet. I mean . . . well . . . sorry."

"But what does that have to do with the hotel?"

Lee glanced uneasily at Reinhard, who said, "That bequest was a subject of some discussion. Some of us—myself included—felt it was too soon for you to return. That you needed time to . . . heal. And consider your options."

"But Helen was afraid you'd find another job," Alex said. "That by the time we were ready for you, you would have moved on."

"We need you NOW. We want you in on the PLAN-NING. The VISION. The DREAM."

"She never saw managing the Bough as a permanent gig," Javier said. "Just a way to tide you over while we were getting the new and improved Crossroads Theatre going."

"But more than that," Reinhard said, "Helen wanted you to have something of your own."

"Know that you will always have a home at the Cross-roads."

"At the time, none of us knew about Rowan's bequest," Alex said. "That might affect your decision."

"It's not about money," Hal said. "It's what you want to do with your life, who you want to be."

"You're thirty-two years old, Maggie. Don't you have any idea what you want to be when you grow up?"

"No matter what you decide, you're going to need Rowan's bequest," Lee said. "For the first couple of years, you'll be making the same kind of crap salary we get. So. The Golden Bough."

I glanced around the table. My gaze lingered on Janet. "If I do this, you and I are going to have to work together pretty closely. Managing the hotel. Getting the new Crossroads Theatre up and running. Can you do that? Do you *want* to do that?"

Janet smiled. For a moment, I saw Helen in her.

"Yes, Maggie. I want to do that. You're smart and you're tough. And you've got a good heart. I don't know if I'll be able to call back the Mackenzie descendants without Rowan. So—"

"You helped him?" I interrupted.

"Well, it was my blood that he used." As I was digesting that astonishing statement, she added, "Because I'm the eldest." As if that explained everything.

"The point is, the Crossroads Theatre is at . . . a crossroads. It has to change and grow if it's going to survive. And if you could get Rowan Mackenzie to change, you can surely do the same for this theatre. And that rickety old hotel."

"The more the theatre is in the spotlight, the more dangerous it could be for you."

"Alex and Reinhard and I discussed that. And we all agreed that it's worth the risk to realize Helen's vision."

Janet would risk almost anything for that.

"I . . . I don't know what to say."

"You will say nothing now," Reinhard replied. "You will talk with Lee. You will think about it. And then you will tell us what you've decided."

"Never mind all the legal stuff," Hal said. "You *want* to stay, don't you?"

I looked at the circle of expectant faces and swallowed hard.

"Oh, yes, Hal. I want that more than I've ever wanted anything in my life."

Except Rowan.

FINALE AND
CURTAIN CALLS

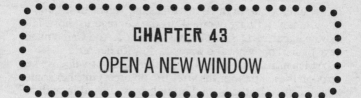

CHAPTER 43

OPEN A NEW WINDOW

I WAKE WITH THE BIRDS, INSTANTLY ALERT although I've probably slept a grand total of fifteen minutes. The floorboards creak as I hurry toward the kitchen. I gulp my first cup of coffee at the sink, pour another, and begin sifting through the papers and folders and notebooks that I pored over for hours last night.

I force myself to stop. I'm as ready as I'll ever be.

Radiators clang as the heat comes on. It sounds like the Seven Dwarfs and their extended family are performing a demented version of "The Anvil Chorus." Iolanthe's head jerks up. The tip of her pink tongue curls as she yawns. After a minute or two, the dwarfs settle down and, after kneading the sofa cushion into submission, so does Iolanthe.

Shower. Dress. Another cup of coffee. A magnet on the fridge reminds me: "I will not obsess! I will not obsess! I will not obsess!"

I head into the office to check e-mail and glance at the little card on the cluttered bulletin board: "Though time be fleet and I and thou are half a life asunder, Thy loving smile will surely hail the love-gift of a fairy tale." Although it's unsigned, I know Rowan must have given it to Helen. Janet urged me to redecorate when I moved in, but I like feeling Helen's presence in these rooms. And Rowan's. To feel they're both watching over me as I work.

Besides, Caren will be moving in after Memorial Day. God only knows where I'll be living after that. I may take Janet up on her offer to stay at the Bates mansion. Maybe by the end of the summer, I'll have worked up the courage to move into Rowan's apartment. Or at least walk inside. And Caren might have figured out what she wants to do with her life.

At least, managing the Bough this summer will ease her through these first months after the divorce. Give her something positive to focus on. She's already started in with re-decorating ideas. Thank God, Hal approves her suggestions, although he describes her taste as "fussy." This from the man whose current window display features a jungle theme with feather boas and garter belts hanging like snakes from the artificial foliage, and mannequins wearing bras and panties with leopard spots and tiger stripes.

And if Caren works out . . . if she becomes the permanent manager . . .

Think about it tomorrow, Scarlett.

I answer the flood of "break a leg" messages in my inbox. Nothing in the hotel's mailbox that can't wait until tomorrow.

I pour another cup of coffee and cross to the wooden milk crates that hold my father's record collection—Pull out *The Fantasticks* and place it on the turntable—one of the few personal purchases I made with Rowan's money. Wait for the crashing chords of the overture to segue into the gentle intro of "Try to Remember." Then I remove Rowan's journal from the bookcase Catherine made me.

Last-of-the-Mohicans-Menswear.com, indeed. She'll be a tough nut to crack. It will be interesting to see what happens if she comes back . . .

Naturally, she had to be the one to hear me sing. And see the scars. Her concern moved me. I must tread carefully . . .

She's puzzled by my distance. And hurt. I need to find some middle ground where we are both comfortable . . .

Only she can decide how much to risk, how far to travel. My job is to keep her safe on the journey. To let her choose her own path, but remain close enough to support her . . .

When he wrote those words, neither of us could have imagined how far we would travel or how many twists and turns our paths would take. And if there were times that summer when I felt he had failed me, I understand now; his journey was far more difficult than mine.

I glance at my watch and gasp. Grabbing my briefcase and travel mug, I race for the door.

As I burst into the lobby, Bea calls, "Break a leg!" from the front desk. Thank God, she's holding down the fort today. I just pray the fort needs holding down. That the ritual Reinhard, Alex, and Janet have been performing for the past month works. Reinhard assured me there was very little blood involved. And that the Mackenzies will come. God, I hope so. I hate turning away guests to hold rooms for actors who may not even appear.

I console myself with memories of our brisk business over the winter. And bless the Rastas for designing our new Website. I still feel guilty about letting them do it for nothing; their business is still new and needs all the support it can get. When it's time to design a Website for the theatre, they're getting paid for every hour.

I dart into the Chatterbox and smile as patrons call out greetings and good wishes. As I slump onto a stool at the counter, Frannie clucks sympathetically. "Long night, huh?"

"Very."

"The usual?" She reaches for the pot, then scrutinizes me. "Or maybe decaf today."

"Definitely decaf."

"Be ready in a jiff. Help yourself to a muffin."

"I'm too nervous to eat."

"Save it for later, then. It'll taste even better after auditions."

She fills my travel mug, adds a dollop of cream, and snaps the lid on. Then lifts the glass dome over the muffins. I sigh and select one.

"Didn't think to see you so early."

"I'm stopping by to visit Helen first."

Her plump hand comes down atop mine. "She'd be real proud of you, hon. They both would."

My throat tightens and I lose any desire to nibble at the muffin. Although everybody in town talks freely about Helen, Frannie is one of the few who mentions Rowan. He was much more a part of the community back in Jamie's day. Now they remember the work, not the man.

As I slide off the stool, Frannie flings back the counter's

bridge and follows me to the door. "Now don't worry. You'll do fine. And your hair looks terrific. All tousled."

"Probably because I spent most of last night pulling it out in handfuls."

"It'll be fun. You'll see."

She follows me outside. So do most of the patrons. Mr. Hamilton in his John Deere cap. Sally and Trish, two of the waitresses at Duck Inn. Gina and Tony from Nonna's. Mr. Banerjee from the pharmacy. They wave as I ease my car into the street. Frannie shouts, "Break a leg, hon!"

"From your lips to God's ears," I mutter.

Everyone refers to Maple Lawn Cemetery simply as the new cemetery to distinguish it from the old one where Mairead and Marsali Mackenzie are buried and the second one nearby where Jamie and Jeannie lie. The oldest headstones here date only from the beginning of the twentieth century. The surnames speak to the growing diversity of Dale, but there are still a lot of Mackenzies.

I pick my way carefully through the wet grass, avoiding the muddy spots left by last night's storm. I pass the headstone for Reinhard's first wife, Greta. One row over is Victor Ross, Janet's second husband. Annie Ross, Alex's wife. And Helen.

I brush away the damp leaves clinging to the top of the headstone. Pluck out those that are tangled in the heather Janet and I planted. Read the five words etched into the stone: "Helen Mackenzie O'Mara. Always beloved."

"Well, here I am. Ready or not for my big day. This time a year ago, I was in Brooklyn, packing up for a getaway weekend. Who knew? Maybe you did. Maybe you knew from the beginning how it would end."

I glance reluctantly at my watch. Nine-thirty already.

"I can't stay long. I just wanted to thank you for everything. Again. You must be getting sick of hearing that. I say your blessing every night—when we have guests, that is. Hopefully, we'll have a lot tonight. I'll come back tomorrow and let you know how everything went. And if you know a blessing for a first-time director, say it for me. I need all the help I can get."

A breeze gusts through the leaves of a nearby maple, spattering drops of water onto my head and neck. I smile, imagining Helen scolding me for my doubts.

Everyone on staff seems convinced that I can do this. "We'll help," they keep telling me. "We'll lend you our magic. We'll make it work."

So now I'm about to plunge into *The Fantasticks*. A small show—only eight actors. A good way to get my feet wet. I have Rowan's script and score with his neatly penciled notes. And Alex and Reinhard at my back. I can't go too wrong.

Except for sloshing through a giant mud puddle. Not what I had in mind in terms of getting my feet wet. I slow my pace to avoid slipping. Muddy shoes, I can hide. Muddy ass, not so much.

As I reach the parking lot, my phone breaks into "I'm Still Here."

"Hey, Mom."

"Has anyone shown up yet?"

"I'm not at the theatre."

"It's nine forty-five, Maggie."

"I'm on my way."

"You don't want to be late for—"

"Mom! I won't be late."

A silence. "No, of course not. I'm just nervous. Call me when you get a break. Let me know how it's going."

I pull onto the road and smile as I spy the giant banner on the side of the barn that screams "The Crossroads Theatre—Auditions Today!" My smile fades when I discover that the only cars in the lot belong to the staff.

You are not going to cry. There are still ten minutes before auditions begin. Someone has to show up.

Thank God I sent out those press releases. Some of the staff members weren't wild about the idea, claiming we'd get a bunch of "strangers," professional actors only looking for their next job. I assured them few professional actors would traipse out to Dale to audition, especially for a hundred dollars a week. And if they did, they probably needed healing as much as any Mackenzie.

My smile returns as Hal races out of the theatre, warbling "Everything's Coming Up Roses." We link arms and march into the lobby. It still smells of fresh paint.

"I finished the stencils last night," he tells me.

I survey the intertwining vines twisting along the tops of the walls. "They look terrific."

So does Bernie, although it gives me a brief pang to see him sitting in Helen's place. Still, it's great to have him handling the box office this summer. He even took a computer class so he could help with the programs. And came a week early to reorganize the production office.

"How about those posters Hal framed for us?" Bernie asks.

More than a dozen line the walls of the lobby, including the one from last year's production of *Carousel*. I swallow down the lump in my throat and say, "They're gorgeous, Hal. Very professional."

The bulletin board studded with flyers from local businesses looks less professional, but it's comforting to see the bright pink one advertising Hallee's "Spring into Summer" Sale. And to know that—once again—all corsets are twenty-five percent off.

The house door swings open. Reinhard emerges, clipboard in hand. Mei-Yin and Janet trail behind him.

"So," Reinhard announces. "We are ready."

I can't help blurting out, "No one's here!"

"They will come."

"And if they don't," Mei-Yin says, "WE'LL put on *The Fantasticks*. I'll play the MUTE! HA!"

"Last year, the first people didn't show up until ten-fifteen," Janet assures me. But in spite of her confident words, she looks worried, too.

Hal takes up his post at the front door. The rest of us troop into the house.

The air of hushed anticipation is even thicker than the dust motes floating in the pool of light center stage. Alex's head peeps over the rim of the orchestra pit. In the center section of the house, I spot the dark silhouettes of Lee, Javier, and Catherine. Everyone's here to offer their support and their insights into casting.

My stomach goes into freefall. Then I straighten my slumping shoulders and try to walk down the aisle as if I own it.

Lee's laid a piece of plywood across several rows of seats. A surface for scripts, notebooks, scenes, and coffee mugs. I slide into a seat. Janet and Mei-Yin position themselves on either side of me. Reinhard checks his watch before edging sideways down the row of seats behind me where the others are sitting.

His hand comes down on my shoulder. Other hands pat my back, squeeze my hands. Warmth and calm and affection flow through me. "The cousins," Hal calls them. Mine now, too.

A door opens, admitting a shaft of light from the lobby.

"A car just pulled in!" Hal exclaims.

As the light vanishes, a jolt of energy makes me catch my breath. There is no single battery charging us any longer. We all charge each other. I've begun to recognize the subtle differences in their power: the zinging spikes of Mei-Yin's, the steady throb of Reinhard's. Janet's is just as steady but more intense.

Another shaft of light. "Two more are coming down the lane. The first one has out-of-state license plates!"

I feel their relief and confidence filling me. And a quick thrill of excitement. It is time.

As Reinhard heads to the lobby, Hal slips into the row behind me, whispering that more cars are coming, that he always knew it would work, that this is going to be our best season ever.

I close my eyes. I can almost feel him. That calm presence. That soothing voice.

"You are my heart."

The door behind us opens. Reinhard marches down the aisle. A middle-aged man walks hesitantly onto the stage. His bulky green sweater makes him look heavier than his thin, worried face suggests. He blinks as he steps into the light. Pulls off his Irish tweed cap and smoothes his thinning hair. Kneads the soft cap between nervous fingers and peers out into the house.

I caress the silver chain at my throat.

"Welcome to the Crossroads."

SPELLCROSSED

ACKNOWLEDGMENTS

Thanks to everyone who helped in the creation of *Spellcrossed*:

My writing friends who provided feedback and critiques: Michele Korri, Michael Samerdyke, Susan Sielinski, and the NOVA critique group.

My friends and colleagues in the theatre who offered scripts, suggestions, and memories of past productions: Jeanne McCabe, Nellie O'Brien, and Steven Silverstein.

Ellie Miller who gave me the title.

My sister, Cathy Klenk, who confirmed and corrected details of Wilmington (and even traipsed out after a snowstorm to reconnoiter the Brandywine Zoo).

My editor, Sheila Gilbert, whose insights and suggestions were—as usual—invaluable.

And my husband, David Lofink—my first reader and my best friend. His encouragement has nurtured my writing career and his love has nurtured me since we starred opposite each other on the stage of the Southbury Playhouse. As always, this one's for him.

OVERTURE

I AM DANCING WITH FIREFLIES.

Part of me knows that this is only a dream, that I must wake up and resume my responsibilities as director of the Crossroads Theatre. But for now, I dance in their golden light.

I am a child, chasing fireflies with her father. I am a woman, hearing Rowan Mackenzie laugh as fireflies swarm around him on Midsummer's Eve.

The light flickers uncertainly, as if my fireflies understand the mingled joy and sorrow those memories evoke.

I sense the others before I see them, the family that I found at the Crossroads. My family in blood as well as spirit. They hover at the edge of the glade, half-seen among the shadows.

Hal rushes forward and embraces me. He is dressed in a flowing gown of green. He, too, wears many faces tonight: costume designer, lingerie shop owner, and Titania, queen of the faeries. That must make Lee his Oberon, although he wears his usual T-shirt and jeans. The light grows brighter as Lee crosses the glade, as if he were bringing up the house lights in the theatre.

Javier waves his hand, and the fireflies obediently move to the far edge of the glade like members of his stage crew. Catherine waves hers, and they construct a glowing pyramid of light. The pyramid dissolves into a dance again as Mei-Yin stalks forward; even fireflies know better than to defy their choreographer. Alex raises his hands, the conductor cueing his orchestra, and the erratic flashes of light become a single steady pulse. On. Off. On. Off.

Reinhard jots a note on his ubiquitous clipboard, checking off fireflies like cast members reporting for their seven o'clock call. Janet rolls her eyes. Hard to believe I once considered her my enemy. But I knew so little about her—about all of them—during that first summer at the Crossroads.

They begin to dance—Lee with Hal, Javier with Catherine, Reinhard with Mei-Yin. Husbands and wives, partners and lovers. Janet pulls Alex into the dance. The widow and her widowed son. Alone in life, but in this dream, they are partners. In this dream, everyone has a partner.

Everyone except me.

Sadness touches me again. And then Bernie rolls his walker forward, observing the dance with wonder, as if he finally understands the secret of the Crossroads Theatre.

"Faery magic," the fireflies whisper.

Bernie cannot hear them, but he casts his walker aside and dances with me. We all dance, caught up in the spell of the fireflies and the spell of the Crossroads.

Only the one who created the spell is missing. My faery lover who was the heart and soul of the Crossroads Theatre— and my heart and soul as well.

"Rowan will always carry you in his heart. Remember that, my dear. And know that you will always have a home at the Crossroads."

I search the shadows, but I cannot see Helen. Yet I know she is here, taking her bow with the others.

This is not the time for curtain calls; the season is just beginning.

There is work to do.

I must stop dreaming.

I must wake up.

I must forget Rowan Mackenzie.

ACT ONE

SOMETHING'S COMING

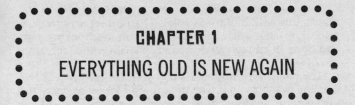

CHAPTER 1

EVERYTHING OLD IS NEW AGAIN

THERE IS NO UPSIDE to losing your lover—especially in Dale, which is not exactly the singles capital of Vermont. But having a faery for a lover does teach you to accept the impossible and cope with anything that life throws at you.

Since Rowan Mackenzie returned to Faerie one year, eight months, and twenty-two days ago, life had thrown me a lot of new and unusual experiences. I had helped judge the watermelon seed spitting contest at the Farmers Day Fair and frozen my ass off collecting buckets of sap during the Maple Sugar Festival. I had enjoyed fishing with Reinhard, Christmas caroling with Alex, and a romantic Valentine's Day sleigh ride. With Janet.

As manager of the ramshackle Golden Bough Hotel, I had dealt with a flooded basement, a kitchen fire, and the mysteries of ancient plumbing. As executive director of the newly nonprofit Crossroads Theatre, I had learned to write successful grant proposals and appeal letters. As the theatre's interim artistic director, I had staged three small musicals and plucked out twice that many long gray hairs.

After all that, auditioning dogs was a breeze.

As the latest contender shuffled across the stage, I heard soft chuckles from the seats behind me, quickly converted into coughs. Naturally, the entire staff had turned out this morning, eager to see Maggie Graham, Dog Director, in action.

It was my own damn fault. I'd pitched the idea of doing a show with children's roles. The perfect way to draw attention—and warm bodies—to our after-school program and bring in enough money to keep it alive after the grant ran out.

The board was thrilled, visions of ticket-buying relatives dancing in their heads. The next thing I knew, we were doing an entire season featuring young performers, and I was auditioning dogs to play Annie's adorable sidekick Sandy.

The lugubrious click of toenails ceased as Arthur finally made it to center stage. At a hand signal from his owner, his arthritic hindquarters drooped onto the floorboards. Doreen kissed his shaggy head. She looked exactly like the handlers I'd seen during my infrequent viewings of the Westminster Dog Show—portly, middle-aged, and tweedy.

She straightened and peered into the darkened house, awaiting my reaction.

"He's very obedient," I said.

"Arthur's a pro."

Which was true; his resume was more impressive than mine.

"And he's played Sandy twice before," she noted.

Judging from his age, he'd probably starred in the original Broadway production of *Annie*.

"He's very . . . calm, isn't he?"

"Oh, nothing upsets Arthur."

The entire set could fall down, and he'd just sit there. But he was sweet-tempered and scruffy if not exactly adorable. Who cared if he was a little long in the tooth?

"Play dead, Arthur."

Frankly, it wasn't much of a stretch. I watched him anxiously until the rise and fall of his rib cage assured me he was merely playing. Then I smiled brightly.

"I'm sold. Arthur's our Sandy."

"Oh, that's wonderful! Isn't that wonderful, Arthur?"

Arthur's tail thumped the floorboards once.

"I hope Fifi won't be too crushed," I said.

"Her time will come," Doreen assured me.

She coaxed Arthur to his feet and released Fifi from her "stay" position. Fifi shot across the stage and jumped up on her stubby legs to lick Arthur's face. He appeared unmoved by her display of affection, but clearly, wagging his tail was a monumental effort. He hobbled down the five steps from the stage, and slowly—very slowly—made his way toward the back of the house with Fifi literally running circles around him.

I kept my smile in place until the lobby door clicked shut behind them.

"Oh. My. GOD!" Mei-Yin exploded.

I swung around in my seat. "Not another sound until they're out of the theatre."

"Better give them five more minutes," Janet advised. "It'll take Old Yeller that long to reach the front door."

"Oh, hush. He was better than the hyperactive Border collie. Or that ugly pit bull."

Or Fifi who appeared to be the unfortunate offspring of a golden retriever bitch and a very determined toy poodle.

"You're as picky about dogs as you are about men," Hal complained. "I don't know how many hours I've wasted setting you up with eligible bachelors."

"Bachelors, yes. Eligible, not so much."

"What about Mitch?" Hal demanded.

"The cross-dresser?"

"He was straight."

"Which is more than you can say about Rafael."

"Rafael is bi!"

"With a decided preference for your team. As we discovered at the cast party of *The Fantasticks* when he went home with my date."

I shot a pointed look at Javier, who sighed. "Yeah. I kind of missed the mark on Tad."

"Kind of?"

Catherine poked her husband's arm. "I told you he was gay."

"But he likes basketball. And fixing up old cars."

"So do I," Lee pointed out as he leaned over to kiss Hal's cheek.

"I rest my case," Catherine said.

"Well, what was so wrong with Don?" Alex asked, jumping into the fray.

"The real estate guy who never shut up?"

"That was Ron! Don! The English teacher."

Janet groaned. "He spent the entire date crying about his ex-wife."

"How do *you* know?" Alex demanded.

"I insist on hearing about all of Maggie's awful dates. Much more gratifying than charging her rent. For what it's worth," Janet added, "I'd have given Mitch the Cross-Dresser another shot. His fashion sense was impeccable."

Hal nodded solemnly. "And there are very few men his size who look elegant in a strapless gown."

"And that," I announced, "ends this discussion."

Shadowy figures rose and began drifting up the aisle toward the lobby: Hal to his lingerie shop, Lee to his law office, Javier to his antiques store, and Catherine back to the Mill to finish constructing the Warbucks mansion set. I felt a pang of regret; last year, everyone had sat through auditions to lend me moral support.

But I was a big girl now. And I had Mei-Yin, Reinhard, Alex, and Janet to get me through the rest of the day. If I could survive dogs, how bad could children be?

"Shoot me NOW," Mei-Yin whispered. "Just put a GUN to my head and SHOOT me."

As yet another Annie wannabe stuck out her chin and grinned and warbled that the sun would come out tomorrow, I was sorely tempted to grant Mei-Yin's request and then turn the gun on myself.

Instead, I envisioned a sold-out house and a big, fat program filled with "break a leg" ads placed by adoring parents. And the opportunity to mount two shows that had never been staged at the Crossroads Theatre, a thought that filled me with enough excitement to weather a hundred renditions of "Tomorrow."

The blonde girl onstage gulped a breath of air and belted out that final "aaa-waaay." Alex pounded out a succession of triumphal chords on the piano. Janet and Mei-Yin heaved simultaneous sighs of relief.

Then the applause started.

"Brava, my dear," the mellifluous voice called. "Brava!"

Mei-Yin leaned close to whisper, "When did HE sneak in?"

I gave a dispirited shrug. It was harder to shrug off the

déjà vu that shivered through me as I recalled Hal bursting into spontaneous applause after my ever-so-reluctant audition.

Rowan had quelled Hal's ebullience with a single glance. I had to swivel around in my seat, clear my throat, and call Long's name twice before the applause died.

I swung back to face the stage. "Very nice . . ." Quick glance at the resume. ". . . Chelsea."

"I know all the songs," Chelsea informed me. "I played Molly when our community theatre did *Annie* four years ago."

"Yes, I see that."

"If you'd like to hear something else . . ."

Mei-Yin's fingernails dug into my forearm.

"That won't be necessary. We'll be in touch next week to let you know our casting decisions."

Chelsea nodded briskly. "My home number and e-mail address are on my resume. But the best way to reach me is my iPhone. It's always on."

Instantly, I morphed from vital thirty-four-year-old to doddering crone. When I was eleven, I'd been thrilled to have a Princess Phone in my bedroom. Cell phones and e-mail didn't even exist back in those dark ages.

Cronehood receded as Janet began humming "Thank God, I'm Old" from *Barnum*; when she was eleven, the telephone hadn't even been invented.

"Thanks for coming in, Chelsea."

From stage left, Reinhard effortlessly picked up his cue and announced, "Please follow me to the lobby." He marched out of the house, leaving Chelsea to scamper after him.

Janet rose and stretched. "Thank God that's over."

Long's laughter shattered the peace. "Why so gloomy?" he chided. "That little charmer was born to play Annie."

For the gazillionth time, I wondered why I had listened to Janet. After she agreed to join the board, she'd urged me to invite Longford "Call Me Long" Martindale to serve as president, citing the benefits of his wealth and influence. So far, the only benefit I'd discovered was a newfound ability to curb my temper.

A shaft of light signaled the reopening of the lobby door.

I glanced around, hoping Long had slipped out. Instead, I found Reinhard striding down the aisle with Long hard on his heels.

I made a big deal of stuffing papers into my briefcase. Unlike Reinhard, Long failed to pick up his cue and planted himself at the end of my row. His meticulously coiffed mane of white hair gleamed dully in the light from the stage. When he smiled, I caught the fainter gleam of white teeth.

"Thanks for stopping by, Long."

"No trouble at all. I just wanted to pop in and see how auditions went."

He was always popping in: to observe the after-school program and the green room renovations, to check on the progress of a grant proposal, to offer a few "humble" suggestions and his usual leer. At first—like a good little executive director—I'd welcomed his interest, but lately, he always seemed to be underfoot.

I mustered what I hoped was a convincing smile. "Actually, there is something we should discuss."

His face rearranged itself into a pontifical expression.

"We saw close to forty kids today. I'd like to use them all this season."

"Are you NUTS?" Mei-Yin exclaimed.

"We have to double cast the principal children's roles, anyway. What's a few more orphans?"

"A lot more WORK!"

"You and Alex could still teach choreography and music to the whole group. But when I block scenes, I thought we could break the orphans into teams. Each headed by one of the Annies. And rehearse each team separately to avoid competition and build camaraderie." I shot a pleading look at Reinhard. "I know that'll make things tougher on you. And me. So if you think it's impossible . . ."

"Impossible, no. But to hold separate rehearsals . . . and work around their school schedules until Hell Week . . ."

"Okay. Bad idea."

"We will discuss it tonight at casting. Extra children mean extra costumes. We cannot make that decision without Hal's input."

"Extra costumes mean extra money," Janet noted.

"Oh, I don't think we need to worry about that," Long

said with an airy wave. "The week we've added to *Annie*'s run will easily offset the cost. And with all those children in the show ..." His eyes gleamed as he mentally calculated the additional ticket sales.

"So you're green-lighting this?" I asked him. "If the staff goes for it?"

"Absolutely, my dear. And if you'd like me to sit in on casting—"

"Oh, no," Janet said. "You just want the phone numbers of all the pretty women."

Long heaved a sigh. "Janet, Janet, Janet. Why do you always ascribe the basest motives to me?"

"Long, Long, Long. Because you're a bigger hound than any of the dogs we saw today."

Long chuckled and threw up his hands in surrender.

Ten more minutes crawled by before he finally left us in peace. By then, Reinhard had brought up the house lights and Alex had emerged from the orchestra pit to join us.

I sighed. "We're going to have to cast Chelsea as Annie, aren't we?"

"Why not?" Alex asked. "She's perfect."

"Revolting, but perfect," Janet agreed.

Against my will, I pictured Rowan trying to suppress a smile as I questioned the wisdom of casting me as the middle-aged, anthem-singing, clambake-loving Nettie in *Carousel*.

"I cast people in the roles they need, not necessarily the ones they'd be good at. I know it sounds crazy, but it's worked for a very long time."

And it *had* worked—for me and most of my cast mates. Only later did I learn that Rowan had called us all to the Crossroads, the far-flung descendants of the Mackenzie clan who had bound him to this world in the eighteenth century. He forced us to dig deep and let down our defenses. And that season at the Crossroads changed many lives, especially mine.

Even with the support of a staff with some pretty impressive Fae bloodlines, I would never be able to accomplish what Rowan had. But I still yearned to offer our actors the same opportunity for healing that I had discovered here.

Once a helping professional, always a helping professional.

A hand descended on my shoulder, startling me from my reverie. Reinhard frowned down at me—my stage manager, my mentor, my rock.

"We all agreed that this season we would adopt more . . . traditional casting methods."

"We shouldn't even have called the Mackenzies," Janet muttered.

"It's not the Crossroads without them," Alex protested. "Besides, it wasn't much of a call."

But it had been strong enough to interrupt my dinner with Hal and Lee. Lee possessed enough Fae power to block its effects. Hal and I—who had about five drops of Fae blood between us—became totally antsy. Even Lee couldn't calm us down. Finally, we grabbed two bottles of wine and drove to the theatre.

As soon as we stepped inside, the antsiness vanished, replaced by the reassuring sense of coming home that had embraced me the first time I entered the old white barn. By the time we polished off the wine, a troupe of faeries could have been calling and we wouldn't have noticed.

"Calling the Mackenzies is a tradition," Reinhard said.

"A tradition that's going to have to change," Janet replied. "We're a professional theatre now. Well. Almost. We can't keep living in the past."

The pointed look she directed at me made it clear she wasn't referring to calling the Mackenzies.

❧❧

With an hour to spare before our dinner meeting, Mei-Yin raced off to torment the staff of the Mandarin Chalet, "Vermont's only restaurant specializing in fine Chinese and Swiss cuisine." I shooed the rest off to the Bates mansion and promised to join them after I'd collected all the resumes.

I smiled as I mounted the steps to the stage. Alex had been taken aback to learn my moniker for his childhood home, a stately Victorian perched on the hill near the theatre. Janet—whose sense of humor was as twisted as her family tree—loved it. At last year's Halloween party, she had donned a gray wig and black dress and greeted us by brandishing a butcher knife. The feathers on Hal's evening gown very nearly carried him aloft.

I paused to straighten the drooping metal cage of the ghost light and made a mental note to ask Lee to add another layer of duct tape to the ancient mic stand. It would be a lot easier to use a standing lamp with a bare bulb to ward off specters, but Reinhard insisted we cobble ours together from backstage detritus. A Crossroads tradition as time-honored as calling the Mackenzies.

I flung open the green room door and paused again to admire the new furnishings. Hal might shudder at the green-and-blue plaid upholstery and the "chunky-clunky" tables, but even he admitted they were a huge improvement over the dilapidated furniture that had graced this room during my season as an actress.

Best of all, they were free, donated by one of our theatre "Angels" when she redecorated her den. As were the stove (which had four working burners instead of one) and the kitchen cabinetry (which had doors that actually opened and closed without falling off their hinges). Even the paint had been donated, although Mr. Hamilton at the General Store had to special order it because Hal insisted on a shade of pale green called "Crocodile Tears."

The production office down the hall was still a work-in-progress. One day, I hoped it would live up to the shiny brass nameplate on the door that Hal had given me last Christmas—"Margaret Graham, Executive Director & Goddess."

I plopped my briefcase on the desk and began transferring resumes and info sheets from my inbox. The towering stack said as much about the desperation of the actors as my PR brilliance, but it was still very satisfying.

Thirty professional actors had shown up at our Bennington audition, a pitifully small turnout for any other theatre, but a cornucopia of talent for the Crossroads. With the community theatre actors we'd auditioned yesterday, we would have an experienced company this season. Except, of course, for the fourteen bewildered Mackenzies.

Nearly eighty performers in all. Which posed a dilemma. In its long history, the Crossroads had never turned away an actor. A tradition that seemed destined to change.

Rowan would hate it. But it wasn't his theatre any longer. No matter how wistful I felt about my season here, the Crossroads had to move on. And so did I.

My fingers caressed the silver chain around my throat. Rowan's chain. He had thrust it into my hand the morning he left me to return to Faerie. Since then, I had worn it every day, waking and sleeping. Maybe it was time for that tradition to change, too.

I reached for the clasp, then let my hands fall. Talk about empty gestures. If I really wanted to make a break with the past, I knew exactly what I needed to do.

The ghost light provided just enough illumination to mount the stairs to his apartment. There was no lock on the door. When Rowan lived here, no one would have dreamed of invading his privacy. Except me, of course.

The staff tactfully refrained from reminding me that I'd passed up two opportunities to move in: last spring when Caren agreed to manage the Golden Bough and again in the fall, when she began a graduate course in interior design in New York City and I hired Frannie to replace her. If they thought I was out of my mind to accept Janet's invitation to move into the Bates mansion, only Hal voiced his reservations.

Clutching the arm of one of the scantily clad mannequins that graced his lingerie shop, he'd said, "You and Janet? Living together?"

"It's better than a cheap walk-up in town."

Which was all I could afford on my meager salary. I was saving the money Rowan had left me to refurbish the Bough.

"It's like something out of *The Children's Hour*. Or *Little Women*."

"Trust me, I don't harbor repressed lesbian desires for Janet. And the day I call her Marmee, I'll move out."

Eight months later, I was still living there. Funny, how I kept filling the spaces that Helen had once occupied: her apartment in the Bough, her bedroom in the Bates mansion. Janet and I surprised everyone—including ourselves—by adapting easily to the arrangement. Maybe because we were both lonely: she had lost her daughter, I'd lost the man I loved. At any rate, it was nice to hear her puttering around downstairs while I worked on a grant, to take out my frustrations on the weeds in Helen's garden and share my little victories over dinner.

"I just don't want to see you turning into Helen," Hal had told me. I sure as hell didn't want that, either. I loved Helen. Missed her every day since her untimely passing. But I was not going to live with Janet forever— or spend the rest of my life dreaming of the man who got away.

My thumb traced the ornate whorls and grooves of the wooden latch. Then I took a deep breath and pushed the door open.

The office was neater than I remembered; the staff must have tidied up when they packed Rowan's journals and the other items he'd set aside for me, including the painted wooden box containing $50,000—everything he had saved after more than a century at the Crossroads.

As I stepped inside, I realized I was holding my breath. An unnecessary precaution. The air smelled a bit musty, but it held no trace of honeysuckle sweetness and animal musk, that peculiar scent of Fae desire.

Golden shafts of sunlight streamed through the three skylights on the western side of the steep roof. Instead of making the room more cheerful, the dust motes only underscored the emptiness.

I walked through the office to the large living area. Everywhere, there were reminders of Rowan: the extensive collection of books and records; the baby grand piano and the antique melodeon; the table where we had shared candlelit dinners and stories from our pasts. Yet, oddly, the room felt less like Rowan's home than a photo in one of those free real estate booklets: "For rent or lease. Sunny artist's loft. Soaring ceilings. Hardwood floors. Recently renovated to remove faery magic."

Unexpected tears burned my eyes. I'd heard that old buildings retained the energy of their former occupants. Sometimes, I swore I could feel Helen's comforting presence in the Bough and smell the faint whiff of lavender from the sachets that had scented her clothes. But I could feel nothing of Rowan here. The apartment was just a dusty shrine to the past.

Someday, these rooms might house the theatre's artistic director—if we ever scraped together the funds to hire one. A stranger could be happy here, but not me.

I returned to the office and stared at the desk where he

had written his farewell letters. Then I turned toward the final doorway, steeling myself to enter the bedroom.

Warmth embraced me. Something soft caressed my cheek.

I gasped and whirled around, but of course, no one was there.

I gripped the doorframe hard and waited for my heartbeat to slow, for reason to conquer imagination. A shaft of sunlight had warmed me. And the touch ... a cobweb, perhaps, or a draft from the open door. Stupid to allow my longing to conjure phantoms.

Rowan was gone.

I pulled the front door closed behind me. I silently blessed the man who had once inhabited this apartment and this world. And then I said good-bye.

CHAPTER 2
LITTLE GIRLS

THE NEXT WEEK WAS YOUR BASIC FRENZY of activity. Alex made up music files. Reinhard sent out scripts and vocal books, schedules, and parental consent forms. I scrambled to fill roles when some of the professionals refused the ones they were offered. Bitched about prima donnas. Shot off a final batch of grant proposals. And sent exuberant e-mails to the board urging them to sell, sell, sell those tickets for the opening weekend fundraiser.

My horde of orphans arrived a week later. Mei-Yin had grumbled that casting every young hopeful encouraged the hopelessly untalented, but she had voted with the others to include every kid who had auditioned in one of our shows.

The prospect of coordinating thirty orphans ranging in age from seven to thirteen was daunting, even with the assistance of my Orphan Wranglers. Frannie had corralled one of her Chatterbox cronies and I'd roped in Janet by promising full disclosure on any and all awful dates I went on for the rest of my life.

Janet took one look at the throng onstage and muttered, "You better go on a lot of awful dates." Frannie's chum Eleanor just shrugged. "This is nothing. Try hosting a birthday party with nineteen six-year-olds and a drunk magician."

Fortunately, my magicians were sober. Reinhard's power rippled through me, calm and authoritative. To my surprise,

Janet's held a hint of banked excitement—that "We've got a barn, let's do a show!" vibe.

When I announced that we'd play the Name Game by way of introductions, Chelsea rolled her eyes, but even she seemed amused when Reinhard joined us. In terms of ice-breakers, it's hard to beat a heavyset, frowning man sitting cross-legged in a circle of little girls and declaring, "R my name is Reinhard and I like rohwurst."

I asked the girls playing the secondary orphans to choose names for their characters; nothing says "You're part of the huddled masses" more than playing some nameless part in the chorus. An endless discussion ensued with all the girls weighing in. By the time the last girl settled on the nickname "Marbles," Reinhard's gray crew cut was standing on end in full porcupine mode and I had only ten minutes left for my Red Light-Green Light version of Stage Directions 101. Although that evoked more eye rolling from Chelsea, the rest got into it, and I was pleased to see the older girls helping the little ones sort out upstage from down.

The wranglers and I escorted the girls over to the Smokehouse. Chelsea shot a dismissive glance around the rehearsal studio, but the others seemed impressed by the recently framed posters of past shows that lined the wall above the dance barre.

Alex led them through the same exercises I had performed during my season at the Crossroads. The girls hissed like snakes to practice breath control and giggled their way through the bubble blowing that was supposed to relax their lips. They giggled even more at the tongue twisters like "unique New York" and "fluffy, floppy puppy." They yodeled and chanted and followed Alex up and down the scale. By the end of the hour, even Chelsea seemed to be having fun, a tribute to Alex's charm as much as his magic.

In subsequent rehearsals, I introduced other games, including the ever-popular Mirror Exercise, where each girl had to mimic her partner's movements, and the Emotion Party, where they had to "catch" the feelings of each arriving guest. That one left me totally strung out. I asked for sad and got Greek tragedy. I asked for scared and got *A Nightmare on Elm Street*. But at least they grasped the idea of committing to the emotional moment.

When we plunged into the real work, the girls proved themselves more prepared than most of the professionals I'd worked with during my years in summer stock. Even the little ones knew their songs and their lines. They threw themselves into learning their choreography with such fervor that Mei-Yin exclaimed, "Give me kids ANY day. When THEY fall over their feet, it's CUTE!"

Staging their scenes proved more challenging. Blocking adults is dull. Blocking restless children is about as rewarding as herding cats. It required the concentration of a traffic cop and the energy of a cheerleader on crack.

By the end of the second week, I wished I had three more wranglers and a lot more time. Two weeks of "orphans only" rehearsals worked out to less than thirty hours to teach them their staging, music, and dance numbers before the adults arrived.

I was also beginning to worry about my two Annies. Chelsea had all the nuance of a police siren. When called upon to dry Molly's tears in the opening scene, she seemed impatient rather than comforting, and her rendition of "Maybe" shattered eardrums instead of capturing hearts. It was Amanda who discovered the bittersweet longing of the song during the rare moments I could actually hear her.

Chelsea's "damn the torpedoes, full steam ahead" approach served her better in "Hard Knock Life." Her team of orphans turned in a spirited performance while Amanda's were as tentative as she was.

The Cheshire Cat and the Dormouse; if I could roll them together, I'd have an Annie who would break your heart and make you cheer, all in the same scene.

I tried to bolster Amanda's confidence and tone down Chelsea's. Amanda nodded and looked miserable. Chelsea nodded and looked bored.

It was Alex who filled me in on what lay behind Chelsea's tough facade. Divorced parents. Mom in banking. Father living overseas somewhere and hadn't seen his kid in more than a year. No wonder she reminded me a lot of . . . well . . . me.

"Can you help her?" I asked Alex. "Everything I try meets with a shrug or a grimace."

"Same here," he replied. "We'll just have to keep trying."

Rowan would have known what to do. But it seemed my rehearsals could only provide a distraction instead of the healing I hoped she would find at the Crossroads.

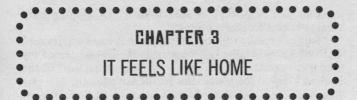

CHAPTER 3

IT FEELS LIKE HOME

SOME PEOPLE CLAIM SUMMER BEGINS Memorial Day weekend. Traditionalists hold out for the solstice. For the citizens of Dale, summer officially began with the annual migration of actors to the Golden Bough.

Last year's migration had consisted of seven Mackenzies and one semi-pro actor trickling into town for *The Fantasticks*. This year, the line of cars crawling around the village green and clogging Main Street evoked approving nods and relieved smiles from the citizenry.

"Now it feels like summer," Frannie remarked during check-in. The professionals seemed surprised to find me behind the front desk. The Mackenzies were too busy trying to figure out what *they* were doing here to wonder why their director was doubling as a hotel clerk.

When I heard the quavering strains of "When the Swallows Come Back to Capistrano" wafting through the windows, I raced through the lobby and flung open the front door. Now it felt like summer to me. Bernie Cohen—friend, volunteer, and board member—had returned.

My smile faded as Reinhard unloaded Bernie's walker from his SUV. Naturally, Bernie noticed. Seventy-plus he might be, blind he wasn't.

"These old hips stiffen up over the winter, but a couple weeks back at the Crossroads and I'll be doing a Highland reel. Just seeing the old barn again was a tonic."

A "tonic" he had first experienced during our season of

459

summer stock and had accepted ever since without questioning how it worked.

"Boy, it's good to be back. Leah was driving me crazy. If she had her way, I'd spend my life playing canasta at the senior center. The whole time I'm packing she says, 'Don't overdo, Dad.' I say, 'How can I overdo? I'll be living with Reinhard and Mei-Yin. He's a doctor. She's a terror.' How're your teeth?"

"Once a dentist, always a dentist." But I bared my teeth for his inspection.

Bernie tsked. "Floss more. It's the secret to good health. Look at Long."

"Must I?"

"Okay, he's a putz. But such teeth. How's ticket sales?"

"We can discuss this at the barbecue," Reinhard said.

"What's the deal with that?" Bernie asked. "Some new Crossroads tradition?"

"My secret weapon. With half the cast living off-site, I wanted everyone to get to know each other before rehearsals started."

"Smart. Did you get Long to pay for it?"

"You bet."

"Very smart."

"Bernie claims to have a secret weapon, too," Reinhard said. "One that will sell ads like pancakes."

"Hotcakes," Bernie corrected. "I got a bet with Reinhard that I can sell a thousand bucks of ads for *Annie*. You want in?"

"Absolutely."

"Loser treats the winner to dinner at the Bough."

"Deal. But it'll be like taking candy from a baby. Even you can't sell that many ads."

"Just you wait, girlie."

The barbecue broke up around ten o'clock, but it was well after midnight when Janet and I crept into the Golden Bough to carry out a far older tradition.

During my season, Helen had performed her blessing every night until her heart attack confined her to the Bates man-

sion. When I moved into the Bough, I carried on the tradition
in her memory. Once I was no longer managing the hotel, I
made do with a furtive blessing when each new wave of cast
members arrived. This season, I'd decided to enlist Janet's help
to back up the blessing with some genuine Fae power.

As we tiptoed up the stairs, I caressed the worn leather
cover of Helen's book of spells. Although I knew the words
of the blessing by heart, just holding the book brought me
a small measure of the comfort and reassurance that Helen
had always provided.

I knew the words on the cover page as well: "The Herbal
of Mairead Mackenzie. 1817." The woman whom Rowan had
called a witch. The woman who had cursed him and bound
him to this world. The woman whose collection of remedies,
charms, and talismans had been passed down through generations of Mackenzie women before coming to me in Hel-
en's will.

Janet rested her palm against the first door. I held the
book to my breast and silently repeated the words of the
blessing:

> *Deep peace of the running wave to you.*
> *Deep peace of the flowing air to you.*
> *Deep peace of the quiet earth to you.*
> *Deep peace of the shining stars to you.*

Janet and I repeated the ritual at each door, bound by
our love for Helen and our blood tie to Mairead Mackenzie.
Maybe that was why the blessing seemed so potent, why I
felt like I was participating in an ancient rite rather than
one that Helen had invented, a rite that signaled the beginning of our summer stock season.

By the time we had bestowed our final blessing, peace
flowed through me as surely as it flowed through the sleeping inhabitants of the Bough. Janet seemed to feel it, too, a
rare smile curving her mouth. Then she rolled her eyes and
whispered, "Let's get the hell home and go to bed." And the
spell was broken.

Helen's peace and Janet's sarcasm. Somehow, they
summed up all the contradictions of the new Crossroads

Theatre: a board of directors unknowingly leading a Fae-powered staff; a cast composed of professionals, community theatre actors, and bewildered Mackenzies; and a director who fervently hoped she could keep her head above water while balancing all those disparate elements.

CHAPTER 4
YOU'RE NEVER FULLY DRESSED WITHOUT A SMILE

WHEN REHEARSALS BEGAN, I found myself dog-paddling furiously to keep afloat. As excited as I was to work with professional actors, I was painfully conscious of my lack of directing experience. Last season, the small casts had made staging easy, but this production of *Annie* was the musical theatre equivalent of *The Ten Commandments*. And I sure as hell was no Cecil B. DeMille.

I'd resorted to a graph paper floor plan of the stage and moved tiny paper cutouts of actors around it like an interior designer planning the layout of a room. Naturally, Hal discovered my shameful secret. Reinhard put a stop to his teasing with the stern admonishment, "Every director works differently. If this technique helps Maggie, why should she not use paper dolls?"

Which wasn't exactly the boost I needed.

In the mornings, I blocked scenes with the principals, leaving the chorus to the tender mercies of Reinhard and Mei-Yin. Then I gobbled lunch in the production office, fielded questions from the staff, and tried to ensure that the fund-raiser was on track. More scene work in the afternoon, then over to the Golden Bough to check in with Frannie. A quick dinner at the house, then back to the theatre to work the big musical numbers in the evening. By the time I trudged up the hill to the Bates mansion, I was too wired to sleep and spent an hour sending out e-mails and prepping for the next day's rehearsal. While the hectic pace left me jazzed, I worried that I'd be as lively as Arthur by opening night.

The staff was putting in the same killer hours. Every afternoon, Alex raced over from the high school for music rehearsals. Mei-Yin juggled choreography and the Mandarin Chalet. Reinhard somehow managed to maintain his medical practice during his few hours off. On the days his antique store was closed, Javier helped Catherine with set construction. And although we had rented some of the principals' costumes, Hal had to construct the rest and enlist volunteers to alter the Depression-era drag he had scoured from area thrift stores.

Bernie flung himself into selling ads for the program, visiting shop owners in the morning and waylaying parents every afternoon as they dropped off their daughters. He alternated between the fast-talking salesmanship of Harold Hill in *The Music Man* and the sad-eyed pleading of Puss from the *Shrek* series. Throw in "little old man in a walker" and even the most tight-fisted parents caved, convinced their daughters would suffer lifelong damage if they failed to buy an ad.

"What a con artist," I told him, watching yet another mother walk to her car, paperwork in hand.

"It's called salesmanship," he retorted, morphing from sad-eyed Puss to keen-eyed retiree. "Know how much I've sold so far, Miss Smarty Pants? Five hundred and fifty bucks!"

"Are you fucking kidding me?" I glanced around and hastily lowered my voice. "In four days? How the hell did you do it?"

I scanned the papers he thrust at me. A full-page ad—lavishly adorned with stars—screamed, "Some families are dripping with diamonds. Some families are dripping with pearls. Lucky us! Lucky us! Look at what we're dripping with! A fabulous little girl!" Another proclaimed "To a little orphan with a big heart and the talent to match! We love you!!" And yet another: "Our FILL IN YOUR CHILD'S ROLE shines like the top of the Chrysler Building!" "Break a leg!" and "We're so proud!" messages adorned other—significantly smaller—ads.

"It's brilliant, Bernie."

Tacky, but definitely brilliant.

"It was Sarah's idea. That granddaughter of mine is gonna be a millionaire someday."

"If this keeps up . . ." I glanced around, frantically seeking wood to knock on, and settled for his sheaf of papers; they'd been trees once, after all.

"From your lips to God's ears." Bernie executed a jig—quite a feat for a little old man with a walker. "Better up the credit limit on your MasterCard, girlie. I'm gonna order the most expensive dinner at the Bough!"

"I can't think of anyone I'd rather dine with."

Bernie cocked his head in the characteristic gesture that always brought to mind a bright-eyed—if balding—sparrow.

"You sure about that?"

I found myself remembering a gourmet meal, a bottle of wine older than I was, and Rowan sitting across the table, angular features soft in the flickering candlelight. And as usual, everything I was thinking and feeling must have shown on my face because Bernie sighed and patted my hand.

"Time to exchange 'Some Enchanted Evening' for 'I'm Gonna Wash that Man Right Out-a My Hair,'" he scolded gently.

I managed a smile. "From your lips to God's ears."

❦

My crazy schedule left me little time to moon over Rowan Mackenzie or wash my hair. I was lucky to squeeze in a weekly call to my mother and to my Crossroads roommate Nancy. I kept those conversations upbeat, but sometimes found myself venting to Frannie. She possessed Helen's boundless optimism and handled every crisis with a firm hand and a cheerful smile. My eyes and ears at the Golden Bough, she alerted me to the rift developing among the cast.

"They're clumping," she confided. "Mackenzies huddled in one corner of the lounge. Professionals in another."

So much for the "getting to know you" barbecue. And my strategy of giving each Mackenzie a pro for a roommate to encourage mingling.

"What about the locals?" I asked.

"Mostly, they head home after rehearsal. The ones who stop by hang out with the pros." Frannie clucked. "Not like the old days, is it, hon?"

No. Our cast had been a family. An occasionally fractious, somewhat dysfunctional family, but a family nonetheless. Of course, we were all in the same boat: separated from our families, desperately trying to cope with the murderous schedule, and—except for me—woefully inexperienced.

"Let's see if movie night helps."

Hal shattered that hope when he stormed into the production office and declared, "Only half the cast showed up! And most of them just came for the pizza. There's something wrong when theatre people can't bond over Judy Garland films."

"I can't require them to attend, Hal. Most of the locals are holding down day jobs. Monday's the one night they can spend with their families."

Working around their schedules made rehearsals incredibly frustrating. Every evening, we had to get the strays up to speed. They felt clumsy, the pros got impatient, and the Mackenzies shot anxious looks at both groups and clumped together even more fiercely. Mei-Yin and I began reserving the first hour of the evening rehearsal to work through the big numbers with the locals and the Mackenzies, so they could perform confidently—and competently—when the pros arrived.

Naturally, that came back to bite me in the ass.

"The professionals are griping," Frannie reported. "They say you don't give them as much attention as the others."

"They don't need as much attention!"

"I'm just saying."

For the next few days, I gave the pros "extra attention." End result . . .

"They say you don't trust them," Frannie told me. "That you're treating them like amateurs."

"I'd like to treat them to a swift kick in the ass."

Instead, I set my sights on Debra, the most experienced actor in the company. If I could win her over, the rest would fall in line.

I knew it wouldn't be easy. Debra was big, brassy, and ballsy—and completely set in her ways. She'd played the wicked orphanage director Miss Hannigan before and saw no reason to do anything differently this time.

I considered it a good sign that she arrived right on time for our first one-on-one in the Smokehouse. Then she blew a hank of brown hair off her forehead, plopped onto a chair, and folded her arms across her chest. As her gaze drifted around the room, I wondered if she was studying the posters on the wall behind me, each emblazoned with the words "Directed by Rowan Mackenzie" in letters as dark and forbidding as Debra's eyes.

I forced a smile and praised her work in rehearsals. She nodded absently and glanced at her watch. So I cut to the chase and earnestly suggested that she consider Hannigan's backstory and find moments to let her genuine desperation shine through—without, of course, losing the humor.

Debra frowned. Then she burst out laughing. "Oh, God. You really had me going. For a minute, I thought you were serious." Her smile abruptly vanished. "You're not serious, are you?"

"I'm not asking for *Long Day's Journey Into Night*. Just pick a few moments—"

"It's *Annie*! A musical based on a comic strip! You work the laughs, try not to walk into the furniture, and accept the fact that the kids or the dog will always upstage you." She heaved a long-suffering sigh. "Let me guess—first season directing?"

"No! My second."

"You'll learn."

After favoring me with a pitying smile, she waltzed out of the Smokehouse.

Way to win her over, Graham. Now she thinks you're an artsy-fartsy novice.

I glowered at the posters, but I had only myself to blame. I'd been so desperate to leave my mark on the show that I'd tried to play Rowan Mackenzie.

Stupid.

Had I delved into Ado Annie when I'd played the role? No. I'd learned the lines, worked the comic bits, and enjoyed a vacation in the country. Which was what Debra wanted to do.

Stupid, stupid, stupid.

And even more stupid to waste time fine-tuning a perfectly acceptable performance when I had much bigger
headaches.

Like Paul, the earnest Mackenzie playing cheesy, breezy
Bert Healy. He was about as breezy as one of Hal's mannequins and sounded more like a soloist in the Mormon
Tabernacle Choir than a radio show host. If you're never
fully dressed without a smile, Paul was half-naked.

Then there was Bill, the community theatre actor playing Warbucks' butler. You could drive a bus through his
pauses. A simple "Everything is in order" required a glance
heavenward, a considering frown, and a thoughtful nod before he delivered the line. His entrances and exits added a
minute to every scene he was in.

"Could he walk any slower?" I fumed to Reinhard after
the Scene 5 work-through. "I swear to God, Lurch was live-
lier."

"Lurch?"

"*The Addams Family.*"

"Ah, yes," Reinhard replied. And followed up with
Lurch's deep, shuddering groan.

"I can't wait until he brings Arthur in at the end of the
show. Talk about the slow leading the slow."

"You are the director. You cannot allow him to control
the pace. Or the scene."

"I've given him the same notes after every fucking rehearsal!"

Reinhard winced a bit at my profanity. "You still want to
be a helping professional. With some, you must be a dictatorial director."

"Couldn't you just clout him with your clipboard?"

"No. Although it is tempting. Do not worry. You will find
a way to get through to him." Reinhard sighed. "Now, if only
we can do something with poor Otis."

The entire staff had taken to calling him "poor Otis." A
sweet-natured bear of a man with a brown moon face and a
gleaming bald pate, I'd known from the moment he stepped
onstage at auditions that he had to play Oliver Warbucks.
But while he had all the warmth of the Daddy Warbucks
who emerges late in Act One, he couldn't capture the self-
important, multitasking tycoon we meet at the outset.

Maybe because he was cowed by Chelsea and Kimberlee, the actress playing Warbucks' long-suffering but faithful secretary. The more he rehearsed with them, the more flustered he became. Lines and lyrics went out the window. By the time he finished butchering the lyrics to "N.Y.C.," we were both streaming flop sweat.

I tried role-play, my old reliable "list thing," and just talking with him, but the only thing that seemed to help was working with Amanda. Since that boosted her confidence as well as his, I gave them more rehearsals together, even if it meant reducing his time with Chelsea.

I resisted the urge to ask Alex to give him a magical nudge. Even Rowan had used his magic sparingly during rehearsals and then, mostly to reassure us.

When I tried out the reassuring voice I'd used on Help-Link calls, Otis asked if I was coming down with a cold. So I packed it away in mothballs and resumed my performance as The Calm Director Who Had Everything Under Control, even though I felt more like Chicken Little.

❧❧

The sky didn't fall during our Act One run-through. Just a lot of props. As the orphans bewailed their "Hard Knock Life," wash buckets and mops flew around the stage as if bespelled by the sorcerer's apprentice. A wheel fell off at the top of Scene 2, literally upsetting the apple cart. In "I Think I'm Gonna Like It Here," the efficiency of Warbucks' army of servants was belied by the clang of dropped platters, an inner tube zigzagging across the stage, a cascade of gift boxes, and an avalanche of linens. Alex got bonus points for fielding the tennis ball that bounced into the pit with his left hand, while his right soldiered on with the tune.

Two hours later, Chelsea warbled the reprise of "Maybe" and mercifully ended things. Then we had to go through it all again on Sunday with Amanda's team.

I quelled my fear that the show would run longer than *The Ten Commandments* and *Ben-Hur* combined and focused on the positives. As the brainless Lily, Nora proved you could chew gum and sing at the same time. Steven made a deliciously oily Rooster, winning laughs with just an artful flip of his fedora. Debra's "Little Girls" was a comic masterpiece of defiance and disgust, her scenes with Lily and Rooster, a triumph of sleaziness.

I knew I'd had little to do with their success; I pretty much stayed out of their way and let them strut their stuff.

Unfortunately, Long didn't do the same with me. After our second Act One run-through, he trailed me to the production office, shaking his head.

"That Otis fellow. He's not very good, is he?"

"It's a demanding role."

"Pity you didn't cast a professional." When I bristled like an angry cat, he hastily added, "I'm sure you had your reasons. But he's dragging down the whole show."

"He'll get it."

Long turned on his megawatt smile. "Of course he will. But you understand my concern. There's a lot riding on this show."

My reputation. And the theatre's. The board was counting on a crowd pleaser. Now, I had to deliver.

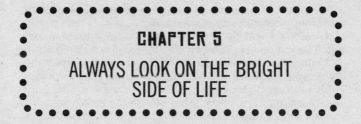

CHAPTER 5

ALWAYS LOOK ON THE BRIGHT SIDE OF LIFE

ACT TWO WAS MERCIFULLY SHORTER and the run-through mercifully smoother. I fretted that I should have trimmed the Cabinet scene more ruthlessly as well as the dreadful finale: "A New Deal for Christmas." Was it me or was there something creepy about the President of the United States pretending to whip his reindeer orphans?

After three weeks of giving Bill notes about pace and chiding Kimberlee for her impatience with Otis, I took Reinhard's advice and told Bill he was failing to capture Drake's brisk efficiency and warned Kimberlee to knock off the snide remarks. Mr. Method Actor looked stricken. Ms. Bitch looked stunned. But Bill walked marginally faster and Kimberlee kept her mouth shut—at least in front of me.

I saved my hugs for my girls who were working their little tails off and for my Mackenzies. Paul was evolving from choirboy to radio singer. The others were holding their own in various chorus roles. Even Chelsea thawed once I abandoned my attempts to play helping professional and settled for theatre professional instead. If her emotional moments failed to resonate like Amanda's, they were less relentlessly upbeat.

Working with Otis had nudged Amanda from a waifish Dickensian orphan to an almost-plucky comic strip one. An admittedly silly session of scream therapy had helped, too. At first, Amanda regarded me like I had lost my mind, but

471

after a couple of minutes—and a lot of prodding—her timid squeak became a full-fledged shout. Amanda—who barely spoke above a whisper onstage and off. She looked nearly as astonished as I felt. Minutes later, we were both screeching with such abandon that Reinhard stormed into the Smokehouse, fearful that someone was being murdered.

Otis remained my biggest hurdle. During our final one-on-one before Hell Week, I led him to the picnic area for one last try at helping him discover his inner Donald Trump. He sat down opposite me, clearly dreading another scintillating discussion about his performance. When I asked why he'd come to the Crossroads, his expression shifted to surprise.

"Tell the truth, I don't know. Just felt the urge to take a trip and somehow ended up here. Why did you cast me?"

"Because I knew you had the heart to play Daddy Warbucks."

"Takes more than heart," he said, his face gloomy.

"Come on, you're a natural for this role. You started out poor like he did. And you made a good life for—"

"I'm nothing like him! All high and mighty. Buying up fancy art and big houses and looking down his nose at all the folks he'd grown up with."

Nothing in the script indicated Warbucks looked down his nose at people. He was pretty much oblivious to everyone at the beginning of the show. Did Otis still feel the sting of growing up poor even though he was the self-proclaimed "Plumbing King of Canarsie?" He'd been married for nearly thirty years and clearly adored his wife. But he rarely spoke of his daughter, the law student, and his son, the accountant. Were they ashamed of their father's humble beginnings? Or worse, did they make Otis feel ashamed?

Reluctant to pry, I just said, "But Warbucks changes. He realizes that—"

"'Something Was Missing.' I know." Otis' voice was quiet again, his shoulders slumped. "It doesn't always happen in real life the way it does in the theatre, Maggie."

"It can."

He regarded me for a long moment. "Happened to you like that, did it?"

I nodded.

"Here?"

I nodded again, embarrassed to feel my throat tighten.

Otis reached across the table to cover my hands with his. Big, strong hands, but as gentle as the man himself.

"Don't you worry about me. I'll do a good job for you."

"I knew that the day you auditioned. I just . . . I wanted you to find something here that would help *you*. The way it helped me."

"Found you, didn't I? And little Amanda. And some of the folks in the chorus."

"And Kimberlee. And Bill."

Otis waved them away. "Gotta pick and choose, child. Like fishing. Keep the good ones and throw the crappy little ones back."

That astonished a laugh from me. And for the first time in days, Otis laughed, too.

As we rose to return to the theatre, I casually asked, "Are your kids coming up to see the show?"

Otis studied me. "You're one smart lady, Maggie Graham."

"If I was all that smart, I would have been less obvious."

"The kids have their own lives. But Viola's coming up. And a good thing, too. Haven't been apart from her this long since we were married."

"I can't wait to meet her."

As soon as his car pulled out of the parking lot, I made a beeline for the production office. I dug Otis' contact information out of the file cabinet and dialed his home number. Viola picked up on the third ring.

It took less than a minute to discover we were both on the same wavelength. Ten minutes later, there was a knock on the door. I reluctantly ended the call, but I was so buoyed by our conversation that I greeted Bill with a smile.

"What's up?"

He glanced around the office, shuffled his feet, and cleared his throat. Realizing that the preliminaries could take another ten minutes, I tried to curb my impatience.

After enduring his solicitous concern about burdening me, his stirring endorsement of my directing, an even longer declaration of his work ethic, and an avowal of enthusiasm for his roles in the next two shows, he finally said the magic words: "I've been offered the role of Henry Higgins in our community theatre production of *My Fair Lady*."

Shoot me now.

"You know what an incredible opportunity that is. A role any actor would kill for."

Just put a gun to my head and . . .

"Well, long story short . . ."

SHOOT ME!

"How could I turn it down?"

As this was clearly a rhetorical question, I just stared at him.

"Naturally, I wouldn't dream of leaving you in the lurch for *Annie*. But I've only got a small part in *The Secret Garden*. You won't have any trouble filling that. I hate to miss out on *Into the Woods*, but . . ." He heaved a sigh. "What could I do?"

Tell them you were already committed for the summer? That you had signed a contract to that effect and had to honor it?

I rummaged through my collection of smiles and found a very sweet one. "That's great, Bill. Congratulations! Just be sure to notify Reinhard. He'll need to dock your salary for backing out of *The Secret Garden* rehearsals with less than a week's notice."

Still smiling sweetly, I ushered him out of the office, closed the door, and waited until the sound of his footsteps receded before pounding my fist on the wall. Then I yanked open the file cabinet drawer and pulled out my stack of resumes.

Thus beginneth Hell Week.

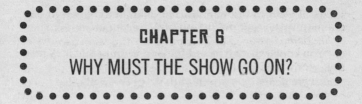

TECH REHEARSAL WAS AS TEDIOUS as I'd expected. Yes, it was exciting to see the neon lights on Times Square, but there were only so many times I could watch those lights come up before I wanted to slit my wrists.

Hal's set design relied largely on a series of backdrops that evoked the comic strip origin of *Annie*: the orphanage sketched in shades of black and gray; sepia brownstones and shanties for the street scenes and Hooverville; a brightly colored Times Square. The only fixed set was the upstage Warbucks mansion, a stylized Art Deco confection with a central staircase and two landings.

With so little moving scenery, I figured we were on Easy Street.

Naturally, I figured wrong.

Warbucks' servants tripped up and down the stairs. Chorus members jostling for position sent shudders rippling through the painted streets of New York. The orphans' metal bunk beds clanked and screeched as if Marley's Ghost plodded across the stage, dragging the chains he forged in life. The crash of furniture and thudding footsteps of the unseen crew members would have worked like gangbusters in the final scene of *The Diary of Anne Frank*, but made it sound like the Warbucks mansion was under construction.

By contrast, our first dress rehearsal was a breeze. If Javier's crew didn't display ninja-like stealth, neither did they

sound like storm troopers. The pit band only drowned out
the performers half the time. The nearsighted actress playing the housekeeper only tripped on the staircase twice.
Only one platter and two gift boxes dropped during "I
Think I'm Gonna Like It Here." And Bill's entrances and
exits were nearly as smooth as those of the well-oiled bunk
beds.

As the company launched into "A New Deal for Christmas," I glanced at my scrawled notes and wondered why I
had bothered. I'd reached the "Que Será, Será" stage of
directing when I had to trust my actors to carry the show.
Well, maybe a few reminders about pace, especially in that
endless fucking Cabinet scene.

Let it go, Graham.

It was a good production. As good as I could make it,
anyway. Otis was still fumbling his lyrics in "N.Y.C.," but
he'd found his inner tycoon. Kimberlee might still be a bitch
offstage, but when Otis dropped the ball, she picked it up
and kept their scenes moving. The audience would be too
busy admiring Chelsea's pipes to notice her lack of nuance.

Stupid to look for shades of gray in cartoon characters. Or
yearn for the healing magic that Rowan Mackenzie could
have brought all the actors instead of the handful I'd been
able to reach. We were in the business of theatre, not healing.
And *Annie* would do good business.

Long seemed to think so; I could hear him clapping in
time to the music.

In a minute, Bill would lead Arthur onstage. Applause.
Quick rehearsal of the curtain calls. A rousing speech by
yours truly. Then up the hill to the Bates mansion for a very
long bath and a very large tumbler of single malt whisky.

The cue for Bill's entrance came and went. The cast
forged ahead, but some shot surreptitious glances stage left.

Just when I was starting to worry, Arthur tottered on
with Bill. I gritted my teeth as I watched them. Glaciers
moved more swiftly. The cast appeared mesmerized, every
pair of eyes monitoring the duo's infinitesimal progress toward center stage.

Arthur stopped. Bill tugged his leash. Arthur obediently
trudged forward and stopped again. Bill gave another tug.
Arthur stood there.

At which point, Chelsea apparently relinquished any hope that Arthur would reach her before the end of the number and skipped toward him. The chorus' triumphant "this year" was still hanging in the air when Arthur collapsed.

Alex's hands froze, still upraised from cueing the cutoff to the cast and pit band. A high keening shattered the stillness. Doreen burst out of the stage left wings. Reinhard strode on from stage right, shouting, "Stay in your places!"

But by then, I was already running down the aisle.

As I pounded up the steps to the stage, two of the younger orphans burst into tears. I paused long enough to squeeze a shoulder and pat a cheek before hurrying over to Doreen.

She had flung herself to the floor next to Arthur and pulled his head onto her lap. My desperate hope that he was merely worn out vanished when I saw that his rheumy brown eyes had begun to glaze over.

And still, stupid Bill kept tugging at his leash. As I shot him a furious look, Javier and Reinhard's daughter Bea pushed through the crowd. In their black stage crew garb, they looked like mourners at a funeral.

Javier's fingers closed around Bill's wrist. Bill regarded him with bewilderment. Then the leash slithered onto the floor.

As I stared helplessly around the stage, a hand came down on my shoulder. The steadying throb of Reinhard's power pulsed through me. My galloping heartbeat slowed. My anguish receded a little—just enough for me to collect myself.

Janet and Alex drifted among the huddled orphans, pausing as I had to pat a trembling shoulder, to stroke a drooping head. Lee must have raced down from the lighting booth, because he and Mei-Yin were offering the same fleeting gestures of comfort to the adults, their magic easing grief and fear and uncertainty.

Bea sat beside Doreen, one hand resting lightly on her arm. It was the first time I'd ever seen her use the power she had inherited from Reinhard, but it was clearly working. Although Doreen's face was streaked with tears, she seemed more stunned now than heartbroken.

A strange lassitude settled over me, like the calm that had descended during the staff's "brainwashing" after Caren nearly stumbled on Rowan's Fae kin. With a start, I realized that tomorrow was Midsummer's Eve. This year, disaster had struck a day early.

Reinhard released my shoulder, and my languor dissipated. I shot him a grateful glance and asked him and Mei-Yin to take the cast to the green room.

As they began herding everyone into the wings, Hal moaned, "Poor Arthur."

Doreen's head came up. "It was just his time. And this is how he would have wanted to go. Not lying in his doggie bed, but performing in a show he loved. Arthur was a professional."

All of us onstage nodded solemnly.

"I should have known he didn't have the strength for another show. But he was so excited at auditions."

Excited? He could barely shuffle across the stage.

Guilt swamped me at that traitorous thought. When I recalled how Arthur had obediently played dead, I winced.

"I'm so sorry, Doreen. If there's anything we can do . . ."

"I'll be all right. But this will be so hard on the girls. They loved Arthur."

Well, the little ones did. They treated him like a combination furry futon and living doll, alternately sprawling atop him and tying bows around his tail. Arthur tolerated it with only an occasional twitch. But Chelsea eyed him with ill-disguised impatience and some of the older girls took their cue from her. I might have done a better job at hiding my emotions, but I'd certainly shared their frustration.

"Don't worry about the girls," Janet said. "We'll make sure they're okay."

I was the only one likely to become hysterical. How was I going to find another Sandy and get him up to speed before opening night?

The thought provoked a fresh wave of guilt. Poor Arthur wasn't even cold and I was worrying about his replacement. But I was the director. I had to worry.

Right now, though, I had more immediate concerns, including a grief-stricken owner, a nervous cast, and a lot of unhappy children.

"We could hold a memorial service," I suggested. "So we can all say good-bye."

A tremulous smile lit Doreen's face. "Oh, that's so sweet."

"Tomorrow," Hal declared. "Before the second dress rehearsal."

I exchanged a quick look with Long. "I'm not sure there will be a second dress rehearsal."

Doreen gasped. "You're not thinking of postponing the opening?"

"We may not have a choice," Long said.

"Oh, but you can't! Arthur would want the show to go on."

Fumbling for a solution, I said, "I could rewrite Scene 2. And cut Sandy's—"

"Nonsense! Fifi will play the role."

Unwillingly, I pictured the unholy product of mixed breeding that was Fifi. The stumpy legs. The too-broad chest. The pom-pom tail and curly fur. Granted the fur was sandy-colored, but the audience would be too busy gawking at her bizarre physique to notice Annie.

"You didn't think I'd let Arthur take on the role without an understudy?"

No. Only the director would do that.

"I worked with her at home. She knows the blocking and the cues. And she watched Arthur from the wings."

Until Javier banished her for piddling all over the floor in excitement.

"All she needs is one rehearsal with Chelsea and Amanda and she'll be ready."

"Maybe we should talk about that tomorrow."

"After the memorial service," Hal said firmly.

Janet cleared her throat. "I'm not sure it would help the girls to see Arthur being . . . laid to rest. That is, if you're going to . . ."

"Of course!" Doreen regarded Janet with astonishment. "I don't believe in cremation. All those jars on the mantel. It's ghoulish. Besides, Arthur would want to rest with the others."

Another unwilling picture, this one of Stephen King's *Pet Sematary*.

Now who's being ghoulish?

"We could have a little gathering in the picnic area," I ventured.

"But this is a formal occasion," Hal protested.

Before I could suggest an alternative, Doreen said, "We'll hold the service at my house."

Praying we could fit a funeral into our overcrowded schedule, I nodded.

❧❧

I left Janet and Long to break the bad news to the parents who were beginning to filter into the theatre while I hurried to the green room to speak to the cast. As soon as I opened the door, the murmur of conversation ceased. I couldn't help noting that the pros clustered together on the far side of the room, while the Mackenzies huddled near the kitchenette with the orphans. The community theatre actors were in the middle, squeezed onto the sofa and chairs and crowded around the central table.

Even in grief, my cast remained divided.

As I searched for inspirational words to recognize Arthur's loss, address their concerns, and pull this cast together, Kimberlee demanded, "Are we postponing the opening?"

Thrown off stride, I fumbled to get back on script. "While Arthur's death is a terrible loss, we will still open as planned. Fifi will be taking over the role of Sandy."

"Are you kidding?" Bill exclaimed.

"Well, who else is there?" Debra demanded.

Heartened by her support, I flashed a grateful smile. Then she added, "Even if she is a weird little mutt and pees at the drop of a hat."

I silenced the titters with a stern look. "I know it's been a long night, but there's one more thing before I let you go. We're holding a memorial service for Arthur at Doreen's house. Tomorrow at eleven o'clock."

Most of the children brightened. Otis nodded. Bill said, "But we're not expected to go or anything, right?"

I'd merely planned to encourage a good turnout, but Bill's look of disbelief pissed me off.

"Arthur was a member of this cast. I realize that the

commuters may have scheduling conflicts, but I hope you'll make every effort to attend. I expect all cast members living at the Bough to be there to support Doreen and show your respect for Arthur. Reinhard will e-mail directions tomorrow morning. Frannie will have copies at the Bough. Those who'd like to carpool, please meet at the theatre at 10:30. Are there any more questions?"

Silence greeted my speech. And no wonder. The moment had called for warm and supportive and I'd given them cold and bitchy. Hoping to mend things, I groped for the inspirational words that had eluded me earlier.

"Arthur's death has been a shock. But we have a terrific show and if we pull together, we'll have a wonderful opening night. One that will make us—and Arthur—proud."

Chelsea heaved a dramatic sigh. Kimberlee muttered something to Bill. Debra stifled a yawn.

So much for inspiration. Before Arthur's death, I had a divided cast. Now, I had a divided, resentful cast.

Maggie Graham. Hapless Professional.

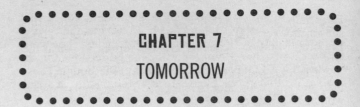

CHAPTER 7
TOMORROW

I SPENT THE NEXT MORNING checking in with Doreen, touching base with the staff on funeral arrangements, helping Janet organize the luncheon we'd decided to hold at the Bates mansion, and fielding a gazillion phone calls from parents and board members. After my third conversation with Long, I dialed my mother's number.

"Are you serious?" she exclaimed after I told her about Arthur. "He just dropped dead? Onstage? In front of the entire cast?"

"I'm very serious."

There was a long silence. Then: "It could be worse. It could have happened opening night."

"That's the silver lining?"

"You said yourself he was a thousand years old!"

"I know, but—"

"How are you handling it?"

When I told her about the funeral and my dreadful "be there or else" ultimatum, she sighed.

"I know. I screwed up."

"You were upset. And that . . . whatever his name is . . . Lurch. He's an idiot."

"Please tell me I'm going to live through this."

"Of course you will. You're a survivor."

"Yeah. And tomorrow night, I'll find out if I'm going to be voted off the tribe."

"Don't be silly. Who could they find to replace you?

Especially for that pittance they call a salary. When this season is over, Maggie, you put your foot down. Hard. Preferably on Long's neck. Chris will represent you at the trial."

"When are you going to stop shacking up with that nice man and accept his offer to make you a respectable married woman?"

"When you stop referring to an adult relationship as 'shacking up.' Now go to your funeral. And call me afterward and let me know how it went."

Janet and I waited at the theatre until 10:45. When no one showed up, we got into my car and drove in silence to Doreen's house.

It turned out to be a rambling country cottage that looked like it had last been painted during the Nixon administration. But there were about a dozen cars out front. At least, some of the cast had shown up.

Janet and I hurried to the backyard where the service would be held. As we rounded the corner of the house, I stopped short.

Dozens of people milled about on the lawn. Sixty . . . seventy . . . too many to count. Children and adults, board and staff, cast members and strangers.

I gratefully accepted the tissue Janet brandished and followed her through the maze of dog poop that littered the patchy grass. A chorus of howls, yips, and barks accompanied us, along with the occasional clang of metal as a dog hurled itself against the wire mesh of its run.

"Maybe they don't like strangers," I said, nervously assessing the sturdiness of the mesh.

"Maybe she's breeding a pack of Cujos."

Reminded of the pet cemetery, I scanned the lawn. Failing to find any gravestones, I concluded her other animals must be buried somewhere in the field behind the house.

The focal point of the gathering was a rickety, octagonal gazebo that was decidedly off-kilter. A good gust of wind would knock it down. Which might not be a bad thing since Long was standing inside it.

I wormed my way through the crowd, but stopped a few feet from the Leaning Tower of Zebo. "I thought we agreed that Reinhard would lead the service."

Frowning at a hole in the roof, Long said, "I'm just going to make a few introductory remarks."

I resisted the urge to tell him to keep it short, nodded to Bernie, Frannie, and Bea, who were representing the board, and made my way toward the staff.

"Shouldn't you be standing with the board?" I asked Janet.

"No. I want to be able to yawn inconspicuously if Long gets windy."

The faces of some of the professional actors were as sullen as the sky, but they were all there. So were the Mackenzies, of course, and most of the commuters, looking harried but dutiful. Plus a few parents who had obviously ferried carloads of kids. Only the men on my staff were missing.

"Where are the guys?" I whispered.

"Pallbearers," Janet whispered back.

"Pallbearers?"

"Well, SOMEONE has to carry the coffin!" As always, Mei-Yin's whisper was loud enough to make heads swivel in our direction.

Long waved his hands and called, "May I have everyone's attention?" A wave of shushing ensued until the crowd fell silent.

"For those of you whom I have not met, my name is Longford Martindale, president of the board of directors of the Crossroads Theatre. I just wanted to thank you for coming this morning. Especially the actors. I know how hard you've all been working and to sacrifice even an hour of free time shows how deeply you cared about Arthur and how much you wanted to support Doreen. I have been impressed by your performances in rehearsals, but today, I am moved by your compassion and generosity of spirit."

Several actors preened—naturally, those who'd been conspicuously short on compassion and generosity last night. I had to hand it to Long; he might be a pain in the ass, but he had struck just the right tone—something I'd completely failed to do during my address.

A loud, nasal wheeze interrupted my thoughts. I spun around to discover Mr. Hamilton in full Scottish regalia. With measured tread, the treasurer of my board and owner

of Dale's General Store advanced toward the gazebo, bag-
pipes blaring "Loch Lomond."

Reinhard carefully descended the three rickety porch
steps and extended his hand to Doreen. The rest of the staff
followed, Lee and Hal supporting one side of the small coffin, Alex and Javier the other. Like Reinhard, they were
wearing suits—with white carnations in their buttonholes.

The little procession marched toward us. Reinhard escorted Doreen to a folding chair. Mr. Hamilton walked
slowly around the gazebo while Reinhard took his place
inside. The pallbearers laid the coffin at his feet and broke
into pairs on either side of the gazebo. Long produced a
floral wreath from somewhere and laid it atop the coffin,
then stepped back to join the other board members.

Catherine must have labored all night on the coffin. Instead of the simple pine box I'd expected, she had stained
the wood a soft honey color and varnished it to a high
sheen. Two sets of shiny brass handles adorned the sides.
Between the handles, Hal had painted a line of dark, multi-
petaled flowers. Poppies, perhaps.

No, not poppies, I realized as I peered more closely. Paw
prints. And the stain that I had initially thought of as honey-
colored was—of course—sandy.

I swallowed hard to dislodge the giant lump in my throat.
Glancing around, I noticed cast members fumbling in pockets and purses for tissues.

I had hesitated before asking Reinhard to deliver the
eulogy, knowing it would conjure memories of Helen's memorial service. But even Janet agreed that someone on the
staff should speak, and since I was a basket case, Reinhard
was the logical choice.

His eulogy combined gentle warmth with humor as he
described Arthur's adoption from the shelter, his performances in other shows, and the companionship he had offered Doreen for so many years. At his invitation, a
succession of people stepped forward to share their memories. I stopped sniffling long enough to talk about his unfailing patience and even temperament. A neighbor described
how Arthur used to give piggyback rides to her kids. Tori—
who played little Molly—won smiles by saying, "He never

minded when I painted his toenails purple. And he didn't smell all doggy."

After the final tribute, Doreen rose and stammered something about how grateful she was. Then she lowered her head onto Reinhard's shoulder and began to cry. Long stepped forward and awkwardly patted her back. The mourners cast uncertain glances at each other, clearly wondering what was supposed to happen next.

From somewhere off to my right, a thin voice began singing "Tomorrow."

People craned their necks, trying to identify the singer. I didn't need to. I recognized Amanda's voice—quavering with emotion, but louder than I'd ever heard her sing onstage.

I promptly burst into tears.

I'd never been an *Annie* fanatic like so many little girls. But after my father left, "Tomorrow" came to epitomize everything I hated about the show: the too-easy sentiment, the happiest of happy endings, the cheeriest of cheery orphans who overcame every obstacle with a smile and a song. What I hated, of course, was the way everything worked out so neatly onstage when our lives were falling apart.

For weeks, I'd been pushing Chelsea to discover the heart behind those sappy lyrics, the shadows as well as the sunshine. Amanda had gotten it from our very first rehearsal. An old soul, that one. But only now did she capture that perfect blend of hope and longing and doubt—the same emotions Rowan had pushed me to discover when I sang "You'll Never Walk Alone."

I'd seen my younger self in Chelsea without suspecting that she might have been resisting the message of her song just as I had resisted the truths of mine. How could I have been so damn blind?

Amanda's voice cracked. Otis slipped in behind her. Resting his hands on her narrow shoulders, he began to sing. To my surprise, Debra joined in, her strong voice and Otis' mellow one lending Amanda support.

A few of my orphans chimed in. And then some of the adults. In moments, the whole crowd was singing—

professionals and Mackenzies, parents and children. Even
Chelsea.

I'd spent weeks trying to create the tribal bond of community that had sustained me during my season at the
Crossroads. In the end, a shy waif and an ancient dog had
succeeded where I had failed.

Bless you both for bringing us together.

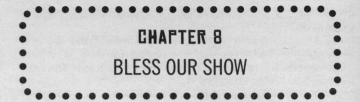

CHAPTER 8

BLESS OUR SHOW

AT 5:30 THE FOLLOWING EVENING, I perched on the stool before Helen's dressing table while Hal put the finishing touches on my makeup.

"Stop fidgeting!" he commanded. "We're at the critical stage." Flourishing the 3-in-1 lip wand he had insisted I purchase, he bent over me again. "A little liner . . . a little color . . . a touch of gloss. Perfect!"

He swung me around to face the mirror. I looked like a perfectly made up zombie. Considering I'd survived Arthur's funeral, the luncheon, two rehearsals with Fifi and the Annies, plus our final dress rehearsal, it was a miracle my head wasn't spinning like Linda Blair's in *The Exorcist*.

Little wonder Midsummer had passed unnoticed. No dance of the fireflies. No mysterious lights in the woods. No unexpected visits from the Fae.

I cursed the sudden burning in my eyes and blinked rapidly.

"What? Did you get mascara in your eye?"

"I'm just PMSing."

Hal snatched a tissue from the box on the dressing table and watched anxiously as I blew my nose. "Tonight's going to be wonderful. Now get into your dress. We've only got a few minutes before call."

For the run of *Annie*, we had changed curtain time to seven o'clock instead of our usual eight, hoping to bring in more families and ensure that our orphans got to bed at a decent hour. We'd also eschewed the traditional "opening of the season" cast party in favor of two small receptions so both teams of orphans could share the celebration. God knows, they needed one.

Hal ducked outside while I changed. He'd helped me pick out my dress, an apricot-colored halter that complimented my auburn hair. According to him, the flared skirt said flirty and fun. My catatonic expression suggested otherwise, but maybe people would listen to the dress instead.

"I'm dying, Egypt!"

I had to smile. Ever since we'd done *The Fantasticks*, Hal had used the phrase to cover a gamut of emotions from impatience to shock to despair.

"Prepare to be dazzled!" I called.

He froze in the doorway, hands clasped over his heart. "God, I have wonderful taste. Pivot. Yes! Flirty, fun, fabulous! If I were straight, I'd ravish you this instant." He seized my hand. "Come on. We just have time to show Janet before I dash."

I snatched up my purse and allowed him to drag me through the house. After calling Janet's name for five minutes, we finally discovered her on the lower patio, staring out at the woods while she smoked a cigarette.

"Damn!" Hal exclaimed. "I have no time to revel in her reaction. As we speak, Clumsy Cow Kimberlee is probably putting her foot through her hem." He took my hands, his expression solemn. "You're beautiful. The show's beautiful. And the audience is going to love it." He hugged me quickly, careful to avoid tousling my carefully tousled hair. "See you down there!"

As I descended the steps to the patio, Janet turned.

"What do you think?" I asked, striking a pose.

"Very nice." She took a long drag on her cigarette, her gaze drawn again to the woods.

"Anything wrong?"

"No." She flicked the cigarette away and ground it out. "Just enjoying some peace and quiet." Before I could question her further, she started up the steps to the house.

It *was* peaceful here. Summer flowers filled Helen's garden with color: purple iris, orange poppies, blue delphiniums, multicolored spikes of foxgloves. Early evening sunlight turned the field gold and burnished the treetops to a glossy green that looked positively unreal—like the plastic flowers in Munchkinland.

Still, Janet's manner seemed odd. I studied the woods, already bathed in gloom although sunset was two hours away.

"Are you coming?" Janet called.

Shaking off my disquiet, I hurried to join her.

～◆◆～

After checking in with the staff to ensure that there had been no last-minute catastrophes, I hustled down to the Dungeon. Voices echoed in the empty corridor—the normal, excited dressing room chatter you'd hear before any opening, thank God.

A chorus of greetings welcomed me to the women's dressing room. Orphans and principals lined three banks of tables cluttered with theatrical makeup, combs and brushes, wig stands and good luck totems. The long mirrors reflected multiple images of their painted faces, making the dressing room seem even more crowded. In order to accommodate the large cast, we'd had to turn Hal's sewing room into a makeshift dressing room for the chorus women. Not the best solution—for Hal or for them—but the best we could do.

I told them all to break a leg and murmured a few words to each of the principals. After going through the same routine in the other dressing rooms, I hurried upstairs.

6:40. Right on schedule.

I pulled the bottle of champagne from the green room fridge and wrestled the cork free. One of the few traditions I'd inaugurated at the Crossroads. Reinhard had disapproved, equating it with the bad luck that came from giving an actor flowers before a performance. I assured him we weren't celebrating the success of the show, but the hard work that had gone into it.

One by one they filtered in: Reinhard, Javier, and Lee dressed in black; Alex in his tuxedo; the rest in summer stock casual. Hal wore a scarlet shirt in honor of Annie's trademark dress.

As they picked up their plastic glasses, I said, "If I start listing all the ways you've helped me during these last few weeks, the curtain won't go up until midnight. And besides, I'll start crying and Janet will strangle me. So I'll just say thank you. And I love you all." I raised my glass. "To us! And the start of another season together."

"To us!" they chorused.

We savored the moment for about three seconds. Then Alex took off for the Dungeon to warm up the cast and musicians, Lee headed up to the lighting booth, and the rest went to their seats in the house or their positions backstage.

To the accompaniment of muffled voices singing "Tomorrow," I poured the last of the champagne into my glass and raised it again, this time to absent friends.

Rowan. Helen. Nancy. Mom. Nancy and Mom had called, of course. And I'd see them this weekend. Some of my old cast mates—Lou and Bobbie, Gary and Kalma, Caren and Brittany—had sent "break a leg" e-mails. But I still felt a little wistful and envied the shared excitement that was coursing through the cast.

The speaker on the wall crackled, ending my moment of self-pity. Reinhard's disembodied voice announced, "This is your ten minute call. All cast members to the green room, please."

I hastily cleared the empty glasses and champagne bottle. Took the pitcher of lemonade out of the fridge and set it on the table between the plate of orange slices and the bowl of herb tea bags. Straightened the banner that read, "You're Gonna Shine like the Top of the Chrysler Building."

Footsteps thudded up the stairs as the cast converged on the green room. The backstage door eased open. Janet and Reinhard slipped inside. Reinhard gave me an encouraging nod. I took a deep breath and surveyed my cast.

"I want to thank you. For your hard work. For your professionalism. And for believing in me and in each other. These last few days haven't been easy, but tonight, we're going to give the audience a terrific show."

My gaze swept across every face, just as Rowan's had on opening night of *Brigadoon*. And, like Rowan, I asked everyone to take the hands of the people standing beside them and close their eyes.

My voice guided them, but it was Janet's power and Reinhard's that filled the green room. As many times as we had performed this ritual last season, I was still surprised by the exhilaration that filled me—as if I were the one who possessed faery magic.

My hands trembled as their energy flowed into me, Janet's strong and commanding, Reinhard's steady and calming. I urged the cast to let that energy move up through their arms, and as I spoke, the power rippled through mine, leaving goose bumps in its wake. I summoned it into my legs, and a rush of sensation shivered down my thighs and calves. As it circled back to fill my belly and my lungs, my heart and my throat, I felt like a medium, filled by the spirits she channeled.

The energy raced around the circle, linking us as surely as our joined hands, building in intensity and excitement until I could not contain it a moment longer.

"Let it go!"

The power burst free to the accompaniment of muffled groans and sighs and a couple of squeaks from my orphans. None of them had known the giddy excitement Rowan conjured or felt that uniquely powerful current zinging through every cell, raising them to a fever pitch before returning them safely to earth. And I would never experience it again.

But what we had was strong and satisfying. It was enough.

"You're gonna shine like the top of the Chrysler building. Break a leg, everybody!"

Although I knew the show was sold out, I still shivered when I saw that packed house. I took the aisle seat that Rowan used to occupy. As usual, Janet sat beside me; I needed her calming presence on opening nights. Mei-Yin and Hal sat behind us with Catherine and Bernie.

As the lights faded to half and Reinhard's recorded voice reminded the audience to silence their phones and refrain from flash photography, Janet handed me a copy of the program. I glanced at the piece of paper inserted into it by our volunteers—a brief paragraph I'd written honoring Arthur and announcing that the role of Sandy would be played by Fifi.

The house lights went out. A spot picked up an Armani-clad Long strolling onto the stage, white mane and teeth gleaming. His voice was particularly mellifluous as he introduced himself and welcomed the audience. As he rambled on about the theatre, the show, and the fund-raiser, I fidgeted impatiently. Finally, he flung out his arms and said, "And now, I give you Alex Ross and the overture to ... *Annie!*"

"Good God," Janet whispered. "It's the Greatest Show on Earth."

Alex briefly acknowledged the applause, then raised his hands to cue the musicians — and, apparently, my stomach, which fluttered in nervous anticipation.

A solo trumpet sounded the opening notes of "Tomorrow." A trombone offered a soft counterpoint. They climbed slowly to the high note and held it for a breathless moment. Then the trumpet skittered down the scale, the trombone slid up, and with a crash of snare drums, the band launched into the jaunty melody of "Hard Knock Life."

I took a series of deep breaths to control the butterflies in my stomach, but by the time the triumphal restatement of "Tomorrow" neared its conclusion, the linguine I'd had for supper had tied itself into knots.

Alex's hands sliced the air. The final sforzando chord was greeted by polite applause. Then the red velvet curtains swished open.

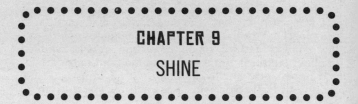

CHAPTER 9
SHINE

MY ORPHANS BARRELED THROUGH the opening dialogue, but the pace settled down as the initial burst of nerves calmed. I suppressed a sigh as Chelsea blared out "Maybe." So much for getting in touch with Annie's softer side. But the audience creamed over her voice, chuckled at Debra's grumpiness, and cheered the orphans' spirited rendition of "Hard Knock Life." When Fifi made her entrance in Scene 2 and I heard that collective "Aww . . ." I knew we were going to be okay.

Suddenly, Fifi's legs wobbled, and she lurched sideways.

"It could be worse. It could have happened opening night."

Before I could do more than recall my mother's words, Fifi regained her balance and began crawling on her belly toward Chelsea.

I slumped back in my seat, drenched by a wave of flop sweat. Maybe Fifi had stepped on something or gotten a cramp in one of her stumpy legs. It didn't matter. She was fine now.

But Chelsea wasn't. Instead of speaking the lead-in lines to "Tomorrow," she just crouched there, staring at Fifi.

I'd run this scene half a dozen times with both girls. Amanda had broken down the first time Fifi appeared instead of Arthur. If Chelsea had been shaken, she'd hidden it well.

But she was clearly rattled now. She took a series of deep

breaths before she finally began to speak. Her voice was so high and quavering I barely recognized it. When she broke off, unable to say the line about taking care of Sandy, my fingers closed convulsively on Janet's arm. She shook me off impatiently, her face screwed up in a frown of concentration.

Alex signaled the band to begin the intro to "Tomorrow." They repeated the vamp once. Twice. A third time.

Oh God, oh God, oh God . . .

Chelsea's head jerked up. For a moment, she stared out at the audience. Then her dazed eyes focused on Fifi. She flung her arms around the dog's neck and began to sing.

Her voice was halting and uncertain at first. When she scrambled to her feet for the bridge, Fifi yipped once as if to encourage her. Chelsea nodded firmly and sailed through the rest of the verse with confidence.

"Good old Sandy" hit every cue during the dialogue interlude, crossing to Chelsea when called, jumping up to place her small front paws on Chelsea's thighs, wagging her tail as Lieutenant Ward strolled off, and obediently trotting downstage for the repeat of the bridge.

Chelsea ruffled the curly fur on Fifi's head. Then she stuck out her chin and grinned and belted the bejesus out of the D flat.

Goose bumps rippled up my arms. The audience broke into spontaneous applause. They quieted down immediately so they could hear the rest of the song. But when Chelsea hit the final note, they began to cheer and kept on cheering long after the music ended.

As soon as the lights came up for intermission, I rushed to the women's dressing room and drew Chelsea into the corridor.

"Are you okay?"

She stared at the scuffed linoleum floor and nodded. "I'm sorry I screwed up."

"You didn't. The song was wonderful. The best you've ever done it."

Her head came up. "Really?"

"Really."

"It was just . . . when Fifi stumbled . . . all I could think of was . . ."

"Me, too. But you kept going. That's the important thing."

"It was funny. All of a sudden, I felt . . ."

"What?"

"It's stupid."

"Tell me."

"It was kind of like . . . an arm around my shoulders. Not a real arm. Just something telling me that everything would be okay. I know that sounds totally lame—"

"No. That happened to me once."

Rowan's touch before "You'll Never Walk Alone," as reassuring as if he cradled me in his arms.

"Maybe it was knowing there were so many people rooting for you."

"Maybe," she said, clearly unconvinced.

"Well, whatever happened, you were a pro out there. I'm really proud of you."

Her expression grew thoughtful. "You were right. About the song. I always thought it was stupid. But when I sang it tonight, it felt . . . real."

"I had a song like that. In *Carousel*."

Chelsea grimaced. "That 'when you walk through a storm' song?"

"You got it."

When I grimaced, too, she surprised me by laughing. I tried to remember if I'd ever heard her laugh before. It made her seem less of a world-weary adolescent and more like . . . a kid.

"Watch it," I warned her. "Or thirty years from now, you'll be back on this stage singing about clambakes and June bustin' out all over. Unless, of course, you're on Broadway. In which case, I expect you to tell everyone that working at the Crossroads changed your life."

She laughed again, and I sent her back to the dressing room to prepare for Act Two. As I turned toward the men's dressing room, I discovered Debra standing outside one of the bathrooms. I raised my eyebrows in silent inquiry.

"Not bad," she admitted. "Maybe there's something to

all this touchy-feely crap you and Alex have been dishing out. For the kids, anyway."

It was as close to a compliment as I was as likely to get from Debra, and I acknowledged it with a smile.

Janet's seat remained vacant after the house lights went down for the "Entr'acte." When she finally appeared, the stage lights were coming up for The Oxydent Hour of Smiles radio show, giving me no opportunity to ask about her role in averting Chelsea's meltdown.

Both versions of "Fully Dressed" worked like a charm. Less charming was the interminable Cabinet meeting, but Otis won the restless audience back with "Something Was Missing." His slow waltz with Chelsea standing on the toes of his wingtip shoes provoked sighs. So did Chelsea's reprise of "Maybe" which had all the bittersweet longing I could desire.

When the Secret Service agents led off Rooster, Lily, and Hannigan, the audience cheered. They even clapped along to the horrible reindeer number. And when it was all over, they gave Chelsea a standing ovation. Of course, Annie *always* got a standing ovation. I was more relieved to see the cast smiling and clowning during their curtain calls.

Maybe I would never be able to heal the wounds of the Mackenzies or help people find their paths in life or create the ineffable magic that held an audience spellbound. But I had helped Chelsea and Amanda and Otis. And with the staff's talent and dedication and just a dash of magic, the new Crossroads Theatre would be a success.

After the house lights came up, I was surrounded by board members and neighbors and parents. I made the kind of gracious remarks every director offers at such moments: "I'm so glad you enjoyed it." "The credit really goes to the cast." "Yes, they were wonderful." It was more professional than screeching, "We pulled off a fucking miracle!"

After a brief detour to the Dungeon to congratulate my cast, I headed to the breezeway to make the rounds of newspaper critics and theatre "Angels" and indulge in hugs with my staff. I kept an eye on the stage door, waiting for the cast to appear, eager to see the reaction of their relatives.

Chelsea looked embarrassed but proud when her mom burst into tears. Paul and his wife broke into an impromptu duet of "Fully Dressed." Otis' face lit up when he spied Viola, then went utterly blank when he saw his children standing behind her.

As he covered his face with his hands, the trio made their way over to him. Otis' son awkwardly patted his shoulder. His daughter hugged him. Viola's gaze met mine and we shared a conspiratorial smile. I didn't know how much persuasion—or bullying—it had required, but she had gotten them up here. I just hoped that sharing their father's triumph would help them see him with new eyes.

"Was that your doing?"

I turned to find Lee watching the family reunion, too.

"Not really. Viola and I both had the same idea."

"I remember when my mom came up to see me in *West Side Story*. It was the first time she and Reinhard had spoken in . . . God . . . forty years? And when Hal's mom dragged his dad from California to see the first show he designed."

And when Mom broke down after listening to me sing "You'll Never Walk Alone."

"This is what the Crossroads is all about," Lee said. "What it has to be about. For everyone who comes here— not just the Mackenzies."

I nodded. We might be in the business of theatre, but there had to be more than just putting on good shows. The board would never understand, but the staff did. We had all been changed by our seasons at the Crossroads.

The reception broke up quickly, the adult performers eager to get to some real drinking and the parents vainly hoping to bring their kids down from the combined highs of opening night and sugary cake.

The board volunteered to handle cleanup. Instead of pitching in, Long motioned the staff to the far end of the breezeway. Acknowledging us with a pontifical nod, he said, "We can be proud—very proud. An excellent start to our season."

"Thanks, Long. I'm glad you were pleased."

"Weren't you?"

I shrugged. "You know how it is with the director. She sees every little mistake."

"Well, I thought most of the actors did quite well tonight. Even that Otis fellow. But next season, we really must get some higher caliber performers."

"Then we need to start paying higher caliber salaries," Janet noted dryly.

"Rowan Mackenzie used nonprofessionals and look what he accomplished."

Well, duh. He's a faery!

"Naturally, I wouldn't dream of comparing your efforts to his, Maggie. You're still a novice."

I bit back my retort. He was right, after all. But I really didn't need to hear this tonight.

A sudden gust of cold air made me shiver. Long used that as an excuse to wrap his arm around my bare shoulders.

"I don't want you to be discouraged if the production fell a bit short."

From "an excellent start" to falling short in fifteen seconds or less.

As I eased free of Long's arm, another blast of cold air swirled around us. Long glanced skyward, frowning. Bernie was examining the skies as well, but the rest of the staff regarded Long with stony expressions.

I had felt the chilly blast of Rowan's anger often enough to recognize what was happening. The staff was pissed — and some of them were unable to rein in their power.

"Do you suppose a storm's blowing in?" Long asked, oblivious to the one that was brewing on the breezeway. "Ah, well. It's like Twain said: 'If you don't like the weather in New England, just wait a few minutes.'" He chuckled. "Don't worry about the show, Maggie. You'll reach Mr. Mackenzie's level of excellence one day. You're like a fine wine that only grows more—"

"That's enough!" Alex thundered.

"You're damn right!" Lee exclaimed.

I had expected Lee's outburst. But I had never seen Alex lose his temper.

"Do you really think we need to hear remarks like that on our opening night?" Catherine was literally shaking with anger. Like her father, still waters clearly ran deep.

"Maggie worked her ass off for this show," Javier said, his expression nearly as threatening as Lee's.

"We ALL did," Mei-Yin added.

"And for you to say such things is so . . . so . . ." Hal's face got redder and redder as he struggled to find the words. "It's just wrong!"

My throat tightened. How many times had they warned me to curb my temper around our not-so-beloved board president? Now they were ignoring their own advice to leap to my defense.

God, I love these people.

"The members of this staff are fully aware of how talented Rowan was," Reinhard said with icy deliberation. "But Maggie is our director now. And she deserves your support."

"But I *do* support her."

"You got a funny way of showing it," Bernie said.

Long's gaze darted from face to face before coming to rest on mine. "I didn't mean . . . you seemed dissatisfied with the show and I thought . . . why, you've worked wonders this past year. I've told you so a hundred—oh, no, please . . ."

As he fumbled in his breast pocket for a hanky, I swiped at my cheeks, furious at my unprofessional behavior. "Sorry. It's been a long week."

Janet took Long's arm. "I'll walk you to the parking lot."

Instead of picking up his cue, he thrust his hanky into my hand. "Forgive me, my dear. I wouldn't hurt your feelings for the world. Or ruin this night for you."

Which turned on the waterworks again quite effectively.

"Parking lot," Janet said. "Now."

As she pulled him down the walkway, I groaned. "I'm such an idiot."

"HE'S the idiot!" Mei-Yin hissed. "If the Archangel GABRIEL had touched down on that stage tonight, he'd complain that it wasn't Jesus CHRIST."

"Everything he said was true. I *am* a novice. The show *did* fall short."

"We don't think so," Alex said quietly.

"I just mean that Rowan—"

"Was *Brigadoon* perfect?" Reinhard demanded. "Or *The Sea-Wife*? Or *Carousel*? No! And neither was *Annie.*

But we put on a show that none of us had ever attempted. We pulled good performances out of amateurs and excellent ones out of professionals. We gave children an opportunity to work in the theatre and experience the thrill of hearing an audience laugh with them and cry with them and cheer their performances. Is that not cause for celebration?"

I smiled up into his worried face and nodded.

"Good! Now. We will go up to the house and toast our accomplishments."

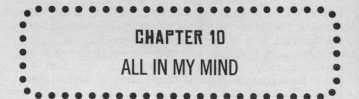

CHAPTER 10
ALL IN MY MIND

IT WAS A RELIEF TO LET THE BUSINESS of theatre slide and just enjoy the company of good friends. Unfortunately, the opening night high wore off in a hurry. Catherine and Javier made their exit only a half hour after their entrance. I followed them to the front door, my yawns almost as huge as Catherine's.

As I reached for the switch to turn on the porch lantern, Javier said, "Save the electricity. We don't need it." He grinned. "Faery eyesight," he added in a whisper. "Great for running around backstage during a blackout. And for late-night strolls."

Hand in hand, they started down the hill. After they disappeared into the darkness, I leaned on the railing to stare up at the sky. There was no moon, just a million stars splashed across the heavens. I closed my eyes, breathing in the pine-scented air. Then opened them again when I heard the faint sound of Catherine's laughter. The lights in the parking lot provided just enough illumination to show her running down the walkway by the barn with Javier in pursuit. Then they both vanished into the shadows. A moment later, a light flicked on in the Mill.

Married more than two years and they still acted like newlyweds. I suppressed an envious sigh and turned to go inside.

A faint flash made me glance back. At first, I thought it must be another lamp going on in the Mill. But when I walked to the end of the porch and peered into the darkness, I realized the narrow sliver of light was coming from the theatre.

It was the ghost light, shining through the open stage door.

A shadowy form darted through the light and into the theatre. Then the door closed.

Maybe Catherine or Javier had gone back for something. But if I could see the ghost light shining through the stage door, I would have noticed the front door of the Mill opening.

There was only one explanation: someone was breaking into my goddamn theatre on my goddamn opening night.

I flung open the screen door and strode into the foyer, narrowly avoiding a collision with Reinhard, who was emerging from the powder room. "Someone's broken into the theatre," I told him. Then I hurried into the library. With shaking fingers, I dialed 911.

"Hillandale Police Department," a woman's voice said.

"Becky?"

"No, it's April. Becky was feeling a little under the weather so I—"

"April, it's Maggie Graham. At the Cross—"

"Oh, hi, Maggie! Heard the show was a big hit. Burt and I are bringing the kids Saturday."

Only in Dale can you call 911 for a cozy chat.

"That's great, April. But we have a problem. There's an intruder in the theatre."

"An intruder?"

"Or intruders."

"In the theatre?"

"I saw someone breaking in through the stage door." I glanced up as Reinhard walked in. "It's okay," I whispered. "I'm talking to the police now."

"The police!"

I waved my hand to shush him. "What was that, April?"

"I asked if you were in the theatre now."

"No, I'm at Janet's. I spotted the ... uh ... perpetrator from the porch."

"Maggie ..." Reinhard began.

"Sure it wasn't one of the staff?"

"The staff's at Janet's, too."

April chuckled. "You theatre folk sure keep late hours."

"Maggie, give me the phone."

"Wait! No, not you, April. Look, there was something distinctly furtive about the perpetrator's manner."

"Furtive, huh."

"Nobody has keys to the theatre except the staff. And Reinhard always locks up . . . you locked up, right?"

Instead of answering, Reinhard wrested the phone from my grip. "Hello? This is Reinhard—yes . . . yes, we were very pleased with the show. April, I think Maggie might be over-reacting."

"I am *not* overreacting!"

"I am sure it was only Catherine or Javier. They left a few minutes ago."

"It wasn't—"

"Yes, she *is* from New York."

"That has nothing to do with it!"

"I will go to the theatre now. But I am certain there is nothing to worry about."

"Reinhard, would you please—?"

"And I shall look forward to seeing you then, too, April. Good night."

"Are you crazy?" I demanded as he hung up the phone.

"Maggie. We do not call the police. Ever."

"This isn't some Fae thing," I whispered, conscious that Bernie was in the house. "This is a burglar!"

"I very much doubt it. Please calm down. And let me handle this my way."

Still protesting, I followed him to the living room. In a few terse sentences, he told the rest of the staff what had happened. Hal and Mei-Yin and Bernie all began talking at once. Janet and Alex exchanged glances.

"It was probably Javier," Reinhard said. "Or a youngster who wanted to poke around backstage. I will go down now and find out."

"I'm coming with you."

"No, Maggie. You are not."

"Let her go," Janet said.

Alex's head jerked toward her.

"Short of tying her up, she won't stay here." Janet shoved herself off the sofa. "Let's just find out what's going on."

❦

Bernie pleaded his hip and stayed behind. Mei-Yin pleaded four glasses of whisky and stayed with him. The rest of us marched off.

All the way down the hill, I tried to make sense of Reinhard's behavior. I knew the staff had an aversion to dealing with the authorities, but surely, in a case like this it was warranted. What disturbed me most were the looks that had passed between Reinhard and Alex and Janet—almost like they knew something was up.

Maybe it was some kind of practical joke. Catherine and Javier had been sent ahead to oversee the final preparations. And when I walked in, everybody would shout, "Surprise!" But the last thing I needed after the past few days was yet another surprise.

By the time we reached the parking lot, I was beginning to wonder if I'd imagined the whole thing. I almost hoped there *was* a burglar. If we walked in on Catherine and Javier having a quickie on one of the orphans' beds, I'd feel like an idiot.

Reinhard held up his hand. "Lee and Alex and I will go in. The rest of you wait outside."

"Why do I always have to wait with the women?" Hal complained.

Before anyone could answer, the wrought iron lamps along the walkway flared to life. For a moment, we just stood there, gaping. Then Janet gripped my hand and Reinhard flung his arm around my waist. I looked from one to the other, suddenly scared. Whatever this was, it wasn't a practical joke.

As they guided me toward the nearest picnic bench, I heard a protesting creak of hinges. My head jerked toward the stage door. Hal gasped. Alex whispered, "It's okay, honey."

No sneaky little sliver of light this time, but a big, bold rectangle that cut a shining swath across the brick walkway.

A figure stepped out of the shadows. With the light behind him, I could make out little more than his dark pants and pale shirt and the gleam of glossy, black hair.

A shiver crawled up my spine. Cold sweat broke out under my arms.

Janet's fingers closed convulsively around mine. Reinhard squeezed my waist. Alex gripped both shoulders. Calming energy flowed through me, but it wasn't enough. Not by a long shot.

Slowly, he walked toward us. The light from the lampposts confirmed what I already knew but still couldn't believe. Then he hesitated, his gaze fixed on me, a frown carving two furrows between his brows.

"Don't be afraid," Rowan Mackenzie said. "It's only me."

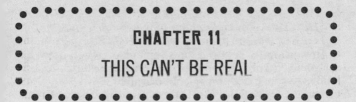

CHAPTER 11

THIS CAN'T BE REAL

THE WORLD HASN'T STOPPED REVOLVING. You haven't stopped breathing. You haven't entered The Twilight Zone. *Those are Janet's fingernails digging into your hand. That's Hal whispering, "Oh, my God, oh, my God." This must be real. He* must *be real.*

Rowan is here. He's here!

His hair's longer. He looks so tired. And his clothes look like he's slept in them. Has he been wearing the same clothes all this time? Didn't the goddamn faeries give him some goddamn clothes?

Focus, Maggie. Janet's saying something. He's saying something. Apologizing for causing an uproar.

I'm moving. Good. But I'm going the wrong way. Why am I—?

Something hard. Picnic bench. Okay. Sitting works.

Why is he just standing there? Hovering on the walkway like it's some kind of DMZ? The middle ground between light and shadow, between—

Forget the fucking Twilight Zone! *Focus. Breathe.*

In. Out. Slow. Deep.

Calm . . .

Janet. She's keeping me calm. And Reinhard and Alex. I can't feel Rowan at all. Why can't I feel him?

Get a grip. Everyone's staring at you. Everyone's waiting for you to say something.

Say something!

507

"Hi."

"Hi?" You've thought about him every day since he left and the best you can come up with is "Hi?"

Rowan smiled, but the lines remained etched between his brows. "I know this must be a shock for all of you, but I'd like to speak with Maggie. In private."

"No," I whispered. When I saw Rowan's shock, I realized he'd misunderstood me. "They knew. They had to. They always know when you're nearby." Anger surged, a welcome relief from the numbness that had enveloped me. Dragging my gaze from Rowan, I turned to Janet.

"I . . . suspected," she said.

"Why didn't you—?"

"Because you had opening night to deal with! And I wasn't sure. Even after you told us someone was breaking into the theatre."

Rowan frowned. "I didn't break in. I used the keys I always kept at the cottage."

He kept keys at the cottage?

Who cares? Focus!

"So you were the one who helped Chelsea," I said.

His frown deepened. "Chelsea?"

"No," Janet said. "Reinhard and I did."

"Then why did you suspect—?"

"I felt . . . something . . . at Midsummer. That was when you crossed over."

Rowan nodded.

Midsummer? That was yesterday! Why didn't he come to the theatre then? Why was he sneaking around tonight?

Maybe he didn't want to see me. Maybe he just came back for a change of clothes. Maybe . . .

Don't be stupid, Maggie. Pay attention. Javier's asking Janet something.

When did Javier show up?

"It didn't feel like Rowan's power," Janet said to Javier. "Just . . . a Fae presence. And it was gone so quickly, I couldn't be sure." She regarded Rowan thoughtfully. "You learned a few things during your sojourn in Faerie."

Maybe that was why I still detected no hint of his emotions. He'd always been able to mask his expression; now, he could disguise his power just as easily.

"Pity you couldn't have timed your entrance a little better," Janet remarked.

"This wasn't . . . I didn't intend to have this conversation tonight."

"Then you shouldn't have been sneaking around the theatre at midnight," she snapped.

"I wanted to shower! And change. Make myself . . . presentable."

Rowan smoothed his wrinkled shirt. His gaze swept over me, from my carefully tousled hair to my carefully painted toenails. It rose more slowly, but stopped short of my eyes. It took me a moment to realize he was staring at the silver chain around my throat.

As always, his sweet smile made my breath catch. His face blurred as I smiled back. Probably the goofy smile that made me look like a pole-axed heifer, but I didn't care. For the first time, he looked like my Rowan.

"Can we talk, Maggie?"

I nodded. He watched me expectantly. I realized I'd missed my cue. I was supposed to stand up. I made it halfway and sank back down on the bench.

"Maybe this should wait until tomorrow," Reinhard said.

"I'm fine," I insisted.

"You can't even stand up!" Lee said. "If you want to talk, talk here."

Rowan stiffened. "I played out my farewells in front of an audience. I have no intention of playing out my homecoming in front of one, too."

"And you shouldn't have to!" Hal exclaimed. "Neither should Maggie. They just need ten minutes of private time."

"They need a lot more than ten minutes," Janet muttered.

"Maybe so," Alex said, his voice sharp. "But Hal's right. Let's all go back to the house."

"I will wait in the Smokehouse," Reinhard said. "And escort Maggie back after she and Rowan have finished talking."

Hal tugged Lee's arm. When Lee hesitated, I summoned a reassuring smile. His frown deepened. Clearly, I didn't have a good grip on my inventory of smiles—or much of anything else except Janet's cold hand.

"I'm okay. Really."

As okay as anyone could be who had just faced an opening night, a mixed review from her boss, and the return of her long-lost faery lover.

Javier nodded to Rowan and walked back to the Mill, glancing over his shoulder several times as if to assure himself that Rowan hadn't vanished into thin air. Alex paused to shake Rowan's hand, but his expression was troubled. Janet just marched off into the darkness.

Hal tugged Lee's arm again. As they started up the walkway, he suddenly whirled around. "I didn't even say welcome back! Welcome back!"

Rowan smiled. "Thank you, Hal."

"It's so romantic! Like the end of *My Fair Lady*. Or *Gigi*. Or *The Ghost and Mrs. Muir* except Maggie didn't have to die first. Oh, I wish Helen—" Hal's hand flew to his mouth.

"It's all right," Rowan said, his smile gone. "I know about Helen."

"I'm sorry," Hal whispered. "I didn't mean . . . oh, I've ruined everything!"

Lee pulled him into his arms and murmured something. Then, one arm around Hal's waist, he guided him toward the parking lot.

"When did it happen?" Rowan asked.

"A week after you left," Reinhard replied. "How did you know?"

"I couldn't feel her. When I crossed." Rowan's gaze returned to me. "Instead, I felt you. I had prepared myself for the possibility that Helen might be . . . gone, but I never imagined . . . I thought someone on staff would know where to find you. But clearly, you found a home here. Just as I did."

"Is that why you have come back?" Reinhard asked. When Rowan hesitated, he shook his head impatiently. "Forgive me. You asked for privacy."

"No, stay a moment. You deserve an answer. I simply resented Lee's attempt to bully me into a public confession."

"Lee is—"

"An alpha male defending his pack from the intruder."

"You're not an intruder!" I exclaimed.

"No?" Rowan's smile was bleak.

"No," Reinhard said firmly. "But it is only natural that we should have questions. And concerns. When you left—"

"I thought I was going home. But when I got to Faerie, I realized this was my home."

Those impossibly green eyes looked deep into mine.

"*You* are my home."

I drew in a shaking breath and let it out. I knew I should speak, should tell him I had come to the same realization. Only mine had occurred before he'd even left this world.

Reinhard squeezed my shoulder and walked away. Rowan waited for the Smokehouse door to close. His expression was as calm as a teacher about to lecture his pupil. Only the trembling of the antler tine buttons on his shirt-front attested to his quickened breathing.

"Leaving you was the hardest thing I've ever done. I thought it was the right choice—the only choice—for both of us. I didn't want you to lead the sort of shadow existence I must to safeguard my secret. I was afraid of watching you grow old and dying centuries before me. Most of all, I was afraid that my love—my power—would always overcome any doubts you might have about choosing a life with me."

"But ..."

"Wait. Please. I know all those arguments are just as valid today as they were the morning I left you. I tried to stay away. To lose myself in Faerie and enjoy the world I barely remembered. But without you ..." He glanced around the picnic area, as if the words he was seeking were hidden in the darkness. "... it was empty. Perfect and passionless and empty."

He shrugged helplessly. "I was as much of an outsider there as I had ever been in this world. Maybe I had changed too much. A better man would have stayed there. But I'm a selfish creature like all the Fae. I wanted you and this place and the chance to build a life together."

He waited for me to speak. But everything was happening too fast. The earth was spinning wildly out of orbit, the ground beneath my espadrilles shifting like quicksand. Only a few minutes ago, Rowan Mackenzie had been part of my past. Now, he wanted to build a future with me. If I'd never stopped longing for him or dreaming of him, I had accepted that he was as unreachable as the moon. Now, the moon had tumbled out of the sky.

I wanted to cry, "Yes! I want those same things!" But how could anyone hold the moon in her hands?

"I know things have changed," he said. "I saw a program in the green room." His mouth quirked in a brief smile. "Margaret Graham, Artistic Director."

"That's just temporary. I'm really the executive director. We're a nonprofit now. But we couldn't afford—"

"A nonprofit? Already?"

"It's been nearly two years, Rowan."

His eyes widened. Then he nodded slowly. "Of course. Time moves differently there."

"Funny how the Fae always know when it's Midsummer, though."

"What are you saying?"

"Nothing. I'm just . . . I don't want to be the consolation prize because Faerie wasn't all it was cracked up to be."

"Good gods, Maggie! Do you really think I would turn your life upside down just because I was having trouble adjusting to Faerie?"

"No! But it still hurts. It took me about a minute to realize how much I loved you, how much I wanted you in my life. And for you to need two years . . ."

"I didn't need two years, Maggie. Or two months or two days."

Finally, he walked forward. But instead of sitting beside me, he slumped onto the far end of the bench and rested his forearms on his knees.

"There was something I had to do. I'll tell you about that tomorrow. For now, please believe that I love you. That it took all the self-control I possess to keep from running to you as soon as I realized you were here. That I could never regard you as a consolation prize."

His face, sculpted by the lamplight, was as calm as his voice. His long tapering fingers, knotted tightly together, provided more trustworthy evidence of his emotions.

"If you don't want me . . . if there's someone else . . ."

"Would I be wearing your chain if there were? I've never taken it off since the day you gave it to me."

A tremor rippled through his linen shirt.

"You're a pretty hard act to follow."

"So are you," he replied.

Which was the part I still didn't get. He'd listed all his reasons for loving me in his farewell letter, but when you can have any woman in the world, why choose me?

"Why do you always doubt yourself?" he asked.

I wondered if he'd added mind reading to his lists of talents, but decided he was merely reading my expression. Never a tough task.

"Why are you always so sure of everything?" I countered.

"Because I'm centuries older and infinitely wiser."

"And incredibly humble."

He chuckled. "Someone once described me as an arrogant prick with a God complex."

"Someone once described me as a pit bull. And a coward. And—"

"Beautiful."

His gaze roamed over me, as intimate as a caress. Heat flushed my body and traveled rapidly faceward.

"Someone needs faery spectacles," I said a bit breathlessly.

"Someone needs—" He leaned away from me and shook his head. "If we give in to that temptation, neither of us will be able to think clearly. And we must."

I had a million questions, a million concerns—about us, about where he would fit in at the new Crossroads Theatre. But those could wait. Right now, there was only one thing I needed.

"I really want to touch you."

His breath caught.

"The picnic table won't spontaneously combust or anything?"

"No. But I might."

"Let's both go down in flames, then."

As I slid closer, he tensed, wary as a wild creature. My fingertips touched his hair. His eyes closed, and he took a deep, shuddering breath.

I traced the wild-winged brows, the sloping cheekbones, the ridge of that beautiful, beaky nose. Like a sculptor, I molded the boyishly smooth cheeks, the line of his jaw, the curve of his chin.

My fingers trembled as I fumbled with the antler tine. Then I pushed it through the buttonhole and parted the collar of his shirt to reveal the thick red weal at the base of his throat.

He shuddered again as my fingertips caressed the mark of the iron collar that the vengeful Mackenzies had forced upon him more than two hundred years ago. He would always bear the scar—and the deeper scars of memory: the agony of the iron burning his flesh, the slow but inexorable draining of his power, the long years of exile and isolation and loneliness.

So much pain burned into his flesh and his soul. And so little I could do to relieve it.

His eyes opened, soft and green as moss. And for the first time, he allowed his power to touch me. Just a whisper of his love, gone in an instant, but as tender as his expression, as warming as single malt whisky.

To my questing fingers, it seemed that the grooves around his mouth were deeper. But the soft lips were the same. And his scent, honeysuckle sweetness and animal musk.

Heat flooded my body, his desire feeding mine. He groaned and shook his head. Before he could slide away, I captured his face between my palms and pressed my lips to his.

For a moment, he remained perfectly still. Then his lips parted. His tongue rasped again mine, sandpaper-rough like a cat's, and the heat ramped up to mildly volcanic.

He slid to the far end of the picnic bench, breathing hard, and held up his hand as I began inching after him.

"Any closer and I will throw you to the ground and ravish you."

"It's the dress. Hal swore he'd do the same thing if he were straight."

Rowan's smile froze.

"What?"

He was beside me in a blur of movement, his hands gripping mine. "Do you trust me?"

"Yes, of—"

"Then don't say anything. And try to forgive me. Stay with her," he added as he strode toward the stage door. Only then did I notice Reinhard hurrying toward me.

"What is it?" he asked. "What is wrong?"

Still trying to make sense of Rowan's sudden change in mood, I just shook my head.

From inside the barn, a muffled voice called Rowan's name.

"I'm right here," Rowan replied.

"Maybe there really *was* an intruder," I whispered.

"Then it is one Rowan knows."

A head peeped around the doorframe. All I could make out was a tangle of long, white hair before it ducked out of sight again. For one unreasoning moment, I thought it was Helen. Then logic kicked in. Rowan Mackenzie might possess extraordinary powers, but resurrecting the dead wasn't one of them.

"Come out," Rowan urged. "These are friends."

Seconds ticked by while his hand hung suspended in the air. Then another reached out of the shadows to grasp it.

A figure shuffled into the light. Not Helen, but Rip Van Winkle. A skinny scarecrow of a man whose knobby knees protruded from the frayed holes in his jeans. Those had faded to so pale a blue that they looked almost as white as his long hair and beard. The right sleeve of his shirt was neatly buttoned at the wrist; the left hung in tatters from his elbow.

He darted frantic glances at us as Rowan coaxed him forward, his right arm around the man's waist, his left hand resting lightly on his bicep. In spite of the soothing murmur of Rowan's voice and the calming power that must be flowing into him, the old man held his battered guitar before him like a shield.

There was nothing about him to suggest that he was a faery; maybe they came in different varieties, like humans. But faery or human, there could only be one reason why Rowan had brought him here: if anyone needed the kind of healing to be found at the Crossroads, this poor, terrified creature did.

The lamplight revealed a face far younger than his hair suggested. The skin of his forehead and nose was roughened by exposure to sun and wind. Judging from the freckles, he must have been a redhead in his youth.

"My name's Maggie. What's yours?"

For a long moment, he just stared at me. Then he flashed a smile and I saw the little gap between his front teeth and the ground slipped out from under my feet once more.

The dark blob on the front of the guitar. All that remained of the Gibson's teardrop-shaped pickguard.

The bright splash of yellow on the guitar strap. Barely visible as it curved over his shoulder, but I knew it was the sun. A smiling sun whose features I had traced countless times.

Those huge, frightened eyes, the same indeterminate shade of blue-green as mine.

I wanted to tell him I was sorry, that I hadn't meant to frighten him, that I was just as scared as he was. But all I could manage was a single, whispered word:

"Daddy?"

CHAPTER 12
SEEING IS BELIEVING

ROWAN GRIPPED MY ARMS HARD. The black dots swarming around the edge of my vision receded. Calm washed through me, stilling my chattering teeth and slowing my frantic heartbeat.

Then I heard Daddy whimper, and it all crashed down on me again. Not just the moon this time. The whole fucking universe.

My father was alive. The playmate of my childhood. The obsessed stranger, searching through his mountain of books for something that would explain his haunted memories. The broken man who had walked out of my life, leaving my mother to pick up the pieces.

How many years had he wandered through this world seeking a portal to the other? And dear God, what had happened to him after he found it? For he must have found it. He was the mysterious "something" that had kept Rowan in Faerie.

"They began playing with him. Petting him. Teasing him. Heightening their glamour to enthrall him."

That chance encounter with Rowan's clan had nearly destroyed him. What was left of him now, after spending years in that place?

Rowan's hands cupped my cheeks. Rowan's voice whispered my name.

"I need you to listen to me."

I nodded, obedient as a child.

"He's lost twenty years of his life. He has no idea how much time has passed. If you tell him you're his daughter, the reality will shatter him."

I was eight when he left. Ten when we received that final postcard. Twenty-four years without knowing whether he was alive or dead. And now I had to pretend he was a stranger?

"I know what I'm asking. But while he's so fragile, I don't think we have a choice."

Rowan's calm pulsed through me, as steady as Reinhard's arm around my waist. Reinhard who always reminded me that I was very bad at hiding my feelings.

"Maggie?"

But I didn't have to hide them. Only the fact that I was his daughter.

Only . . .

"Maggie."

Three times, Rowan had spoken my name. Three times for a charm, Mairead Mackenzie had written. Maybe the charm worked for I heard myself say, "I can do this."

Rowan pressed a quick kiss to my forehead and hurried back to Daddy.

To Jack.

The whimpering was constant now, high-pitched and terrified like a wounded animal. His fingers plucked anxiously at Rowan's sleeve. "I'm sorry. I didn't mean to make her cry. Please don't send me back there!"

A sob caught in my throat. Reinhard's hand tightened around my waist. Rowan shot me a warning glance, all the while murmuring, "No one will send you back. Maggie's all right. You just startled her."

"I'm so sorry." My voice trembled as much as my father's. I swallowed hard and tried again. "You reminded me of . . . an old friend."

"Who are they?" my father whispered.

"I told you about Maggie, remember?"

He shook his head wildly. "No. No! I don't remember!"

"Think, Jack."

As Rowan stroked his arm, he grew calm again. His eyes widened with recollection and he flashed that gap-toothed smile. "Yes! Yes, she's your girlfriend."

"That's right. And this is Reinhard. He's my friend, too."

"You have a girlfriend *and* a boyfriend?"

My laugh was too close to a sob, and I pressed my lips together.

"I am the theatre's stage manager."

Daddy's smile faded. "I don't remember you."

"I joined the staff after you performed here."

Daddy suddenly straightened. "You wouldn't think it to look at me now, but I played Billy Bigelow in *Carousel*. My 'Soliloquy?' The applause went on for three minutes. Remember, Rowan? And the standing ovation at the end? God, they loved me."

Suddenly, he was my father again, flipping through his album of reviews, pointing himself out to me in photos, boasting about his performances.

"Maggie was in *Carousel* during her season here," Rowan said.

"Julie or Carrie?" my father demanded.

"Nettie," I replied.

"Nettie! You're way too young for that role."

"That's what I said."

"Rowan and his crazy casting."

I managed a weak laugh, still stunned by his transformation. "Somehow, he pulls it off."

"Well, sure. He's a faery." He cringed and shot a frightened glance at Rowan. "I'm sorry! I didn't mean to tell. Please don't send me back there!"

And just like that, my father was gone. Numbly, I watched Rowan soothe him, watched the terror leach away yet again.

"Why don't we all go up to the apartment?" Rowan suggested.

Daddy shook his head. "I don't like it up there. I like the little house in the woods."

"Yes, but you can take a bath and—"

"No! I don't like it!"

"And finish the rest of your cake."

Daddy's face lit up. He strummed a chord on his guitar and marched into the theatre, singing, "There is nothing like a cake. Nothing in the world!"

If someone else had transposed the words of a song from

South Pacific into an elegy on cake, I might have smiled. But my father wasn't trying to be clever; he was clinging to sanity using the only lifeline he knew.

Rowan took my hands. "He's frightened, Maggie. And confused. He'd just settled into the cottage when I moved him here." He glanced over his shoulder. "Let's go inside. He gets nervous if I leave him alone too long."

One by one, we filed up the stairs. The door to the apartment hung open, but it was dark inside. Years of experience had taught Rowan to find his way around, but I groped for the light switch and flicked it on.

Something crashed to the floor, followed by the sharper sound of shattering china.

"Turn it off!" my father shrieked. "The eyes! The eyes!"

I quickly switched off the light and slumped against the doorframe. Reinhard squeezed my shoulders and whispered, "Steady, *liebchen*."

The quick tattoo of Rowan's boots on the hardwood floor. The muffled thud as he crossed the rugs. The murmur of his voice. My father's sobs, ebbing to sniffles.

Then Rowan's footsteps again, slower now. A drawer opening. The harsh rasp of a match.

Light blossomed in the doorway of the living area. When Daddy cried out, Rowan said, "It's all right. They can't find you here. You're safe here."

Another flare of light. Then Rowan's footsteps coming toward us.

He opened his arms and I stumbled into them. Our first embrace. Not the one we would have exchanged a mere ten minutes ago. The only desire now was to comfort and be comforted.

"Eyes?" Reinhard inquired softly.

"The skylights."

Rowan leaned back to study me. When I nodded, he took my hand and led me into the living area.

The two candles on the sideboard provided barely enough illumination to make out the shadowy outlines of the furniture. I couldn't see my father at all.

"Jack. I'm going to turn on some lights."

The soft moan made me shudder.

"I'll keep them low. And I won't turn on any in the kitchen. But you can't expect our guests to sit in the dark."

"They'll see . . ."

"No, Jack, they won't. They can't. They're in the Borderlands. And you're here—in my apartment in the theatre."

The Borderlands?

"I like the little house. They can't see me there."

"They can't see you here, either. You know why?"

A long silence. "Because they're in the Borderlands?"

"That's right. Now wouldn't you like to come out and have some cake with Maggie and Reinhard?"

"No. I'll eat my cake here."

"After I turn on the lights."

"I want it now!"

"Jack!" For the first time, Rowan's voice was sharp. It drew another whimper from my unseen father.

"For God's sake, just give him the cake," I said.

"Let me handle this, Maggie."

Unwanted memories assailed me.

"Get off my stage. Now!"

"You have no right to do this!"

"Don't tell me how to direct."

"You're not directing. You're bullying him!"

Rushing to Nick's defense had helped bring about the confrontation that had made him walk out of *Carousel*. But it required all of my self-control—and Reinhard's firm grip on my shoulders—to keep me from rushing to my father.

Rowan turned the dimmer switch and the track lights above the bank of stereo equipment bloomed with soft golden light, enough to make out the kitchen: Daddy's guitar resting against the refrigerator; a beat-up red backpack beside it; a chair, lying on the floor; clumps of cake strewn among the shards of china. And my father, huddled under the dining table.

"Cake?" he prompted hopefully as Rowan walked toward the kitchen.

"After I clean up this mess."

"I'll do it," I volunteered, eager for some task that might distract me.

"I'm already filthy. Why don't you clear off some space on the table? Sit, Reinhard. You've had a long night."

"We all have," Reinhard replied as he sank heavily onto a chair.

Rowan had clearly raided the green room fridge. A half-empty bottle of lemonade sat on the table, along with an unopened bottle of iced tea and plastic containers filled with leftover cookies and veggie sticks. The slab of sheet cake bore a legend in red piping gel that read "ulations, Cast of An."

I moved everything to the counter and pulled plates and glasses out of the cabinets. Reinhard refused food, but accepted iced tea. I poured three glasses of lemonade; the only iced tea Daddy would ever drink was Mom's. Steeped for hours in that chipped brown pitcher. He'd always teased her that only a weightlifter could pick it up.

I set the plates down a little harder than I'd intended.

"Cake?" a plaintive voice inquired.

"In a minute," Rowan replied.

As he dumped the mess in the garbage can, I grabbed a chocolate chip cookie and thrust it under the table. I heard a startled squeak. Then the cookie was snatched out of my fingers.

"Cookie!" my father crowed in Cookie Monster's gravelly voice.

Another flood of memories: Daddy sitting on the floor, growling, "Cookie, cookie, cookie!" while I danced around him, holding it just out of reach. His arms waving futilely, then suddenly pulling me into his lap. My delighted laughter. His unintelligible words as he shoved the cookie into his mouth. My mother protesting that he was getting crumbs everywhere.

"Me want another cookie!"

"Me want a bottle of Laphroaig," Rowan muttered, slumping onto the chair opposite Reinhard.

"Cookie, cookie, cookie!"

"Jack . . ." Rowan said, a warning note in his voice.

A pause. Then: "Cake?"

Rowan lowered his head onto his hands. Reinhard frowned. I laughed—a little hysterically judging from their concerned looks.

"You have had enough sugar," Reinhard said. "But you may have some vegetable sticks."

"Vegetables?" my father wailed.

I laughed again. I really *had* entered *The Twilight Zone*. With Rowan and Reinhard serving as stand-ins for my parents and my father reverting to the role of child—easily frightened, often entertaining, and difficult to pacify. Leaving me the thankless role of the daughter who could not be acknowledged, the helping professional who didn't know how to help.

My laughter caught in my throat. Rowan gripped my left arm. Reinhard clamped down on my right. I pressed my lips together and clenched my fists in my lap.

Something tugged at the hem of my dress. A moment later, a tentative hand patted my knee.

"It's all right," my father whispered. "You don't have to eat the vegetables if you don't want to."

I sat there, shaking silently, until their power calmed me. And all the while, my father's gentle fingers patted my knee.

The first time I had felt his touch since I was eight years old.

I seized a napkin and blew my nose. Reinhard pushed back his chair and announced, "I think it is time for us to go home."

Daddy's fingers gripped the hem of my dress. "You go. Maggie can stay."

"I'll be back tomorrow," I promised. "With breakfast."

"Breakfast!"

"Eggs and bacon and English muffins and orange juice," I said, reciting our traditional Sunday morning menu.

"Thomas'. Not the store brand."

"Of course Thomas'. The store brand never has the good—"

"Nooks and crannies."

How many times had he lectured my poor mother about that when she was just trying to save a buck by buying the cheaper brand?

"So is it okay if I go now? I *am* pretty tired." The understatement of the year. "And you must be, too."

The fingers relaxed their grip. Regretfully, I pushed back my chair.

"Are you going to come out," Rowan asked, "and say good night to Maggie and Reinhard?"

"I can say good night from here."

"Well, you have to come out eventually."

"Why?"

"You can't sleep under the table."

"They'll never think to look for me here."

Rowan crouched down. "Jack. They're not looking for you."

"Just in case."

I crouched beside Rowan and said, "We could put cushions on the floor. And bring a pillow and a quilt."

Daddy surveyed his prospective sleeping quarters with a frown. "My feet'll stick out. If they see them—"

"We'll drape a sheet over the table. Like—"

"A tent!" he exclaimed. "I used to do that with my little girl. Her name's Maggie, too. But I call her Magpie 'cause she talks a blue streak."

Unwilling to trust my voice, I simply nodded.

"We used the dining room table. It was much bigger than this," he informed Rowan loftily. "We'd crawl inside with books and toys . . . and sometimes, a plate of cookies." He flashed a beguiling smile.

"You are *not* going to wheedle more cookies out of me," Rowan replied, unbeguiled.

"Rowan and Reinhard will make up the tent. I'll show you where the bathroom is."

Daddy craned his neck to peer up at the skylights. "But what if they see me?"

"They won't if we run."

"They won't see you at all!" Rowan exclaimed. "They can't find you here!"

"Not if we run quick like a bunny!" Daddy said.

"Quick like a bunny, Magpie. That way, the gnomes'll never catch us!"

"We'll let Rowan go first so he can put a candle in the bathroom. When he gives us the signal, we'll run. Okay?"

Daddy nodded. Rowan sighed and stalked off.

Long minutes ticked by. Daddy grew increasingly restive, his questions more panicked. Finally, I hurried into the bedroom and found Rowan standing before his armoire, barely visible in the flickering candlelight.

"What is it? He's getting nervous."

Rowan slowly closed the doors to the armoire. "No toothbrushes, I'm afraid."

"I'll pick up whatever you need tomorrow."

Rowan nodded and walked over to the small chest under the eaves. When he just stood there, staring down at it, I edged around him, yanked open the top, and unearthed a neat pile of bedding and a pillow.

"Put the candle in the bathroom, okay?" I hesitated, trying to make sense of his queer expression. "Is something wrong?"

"Just very tired all of sudden."

I pressed a quick kiss to his cheek and hurried back to my father.

"Ready?" I held out my hand and smiled as he clasped it. "On the count of three. One. Two. Three!"

Hand in hand, we sprinted through the apartment. Daddy scurried into the bathroom and slammed the door behind him. I paced the bedroom until the door eased open again. We shared another ten seconds of handholding during our return sprint. Then he scrambled under the sheet.

"A pillow . . ." he sighed.

How long since he'd rested his head on one?

"Will you wait for me downstairs?" Rowan asked quietly. "It won't take me long to get him to sleep."

With a final longing glance at the tent, I followed Reinhard out of the apartment.

We slowly descended the stairs. As the uncomfortable silence lengthened, I said, "He'll be fine. After he settles in."

"He needs a doctor's care, Maggie."

"A doctor would lock him in a psych ward, pump him full of meds, and spend years trying to convince him that he'd imagined all of this. Maybe he's confused and frightened, but he's not delusional."

"I know you love him, child. And I know you believe Rowan is a miracle worker. But there are some miracles even Rowan cannot achieve."

"How do we know until we try? We have to try! Doesn't he deserve the chance to lead a normal life?"

"Locked up in that apartment with Rowan for months? For years, perhaps? This is the kind of life you want for him? For both of them?"

"He'll get better."

"But he will never be as he was. That man is gone, Maggie. Can you accept that?"

Rowan's arrival spared me from answering.

"He's asleep?" I asked.

Rowan nodded. "He's exhausted."

"So are you," Reinhard said. "When did you last eat?"

"Yesterday. I think. Jack finished the last of the food this morning. That's why I had to bring him here tonight. Helen . . . we always kept snacks in the green room refrigerator."

"Cake and cookies," Reinhard said with a disapproving frown.

"I know. But after all he's been through . . ."

"Tell me," I said.

"Let it wait, Maggie. Just until tomorrow."

"Rowan is right. Your father is alive. He is safe. As for what happens next . . ."

"I won't let you send him away!"

"Our return affects everyone on staff," Rowan said. "And everyone deserves a say in . . . what happens next."

"I will call a meeting. For eleven o'clock tomorrow morning." Reinhard frowned. "Bernie cannot be there. We cannot speak openly—"

"Bernie?" Rowan interrupted. "Bernie Cohen?"

"He has taken on Helen's jobs—publicity and program."

"Bernie Cohen . . . back at the Crossroads . . ."

"Yes. Well. I will deal with Bernie. Somehow. Can you leave Jack alone for an hour?"

"If we hold the meeting in the green room or the Smokehouse. Somewhere close where I can feel him if he needs me."

"The Smokehouse, then. I will stop by before the meeting. I would like to examine him. He seems remarkably healthy, but—"

"Would you stop arranging things?" I exclaimed. "I need to know what happened to him. Nothing you tell me will be as bad as what I imagine. Please."

Rowan and Reinhard exchanged glances. Then Reinhard sighed and nodded. Rowan led me over to Reinhard's stage manager stool and eased me onto it.

"I don't know how long I searched for him in Faerie. Months, probably. None of the clans I visited had heard of any human who'd been adopted. And I couldn't feel Jack's energy. At first, I thought he might be too far away for me to sense. Then I realized I'd stupidly overlooked the obvious."

"The obvious?"

"The older Fae can always sense when a human has breached the borders of Faerie. But none of the elders I spoke to had detected such an intrusion. That's when I thought of the Borderlands. It's a place between the worlds. A sort of . . . buffer zone."

His grim expression made me ask, "Is it . . . awful?"

"Some of it is as beautiful as Faerie. But its magic is wilder. You can be walking through a darkened thicket at moonrise and suddenly find yourself on the brink of a sunlit precipice. Even time seems to follow no rules. That's why it seemed that only a few months had passed while I was searching for him."

He hesitated, clearly reluctant to say more. Then he took a deep breath.

"The Borderlands draw the darkest elements of Faerie. Guardians, we call them, for they keep out hapless trespassers from both worlds. But some use their power to lure the innocent and the foolish. Once inside the Borderlands, few manage to escape."

Until now, I'd been terrified about the ordeals my father must have undergone. Rowan's haunted expression made me wonder what he'd had to endure in order to find him.

"These . . . creatures," Reinhard said. "Could they have followed you back here?"

"No. I sealed the portal behind us and warded it against intruders."

"And Daddy?" I prompted. "How did he survive there for so long?"

"Jack was no hapless trespasser. He had prepared for his crossing. He brought extra clothing, a medical kit, cooking utensils, a tarp—anything and everything he could fit into that backpack."

Mom protesting that we were only going away for the weekend and couldn't possibly need everything he was stuff-

ing into suitcases and carryalls and shopping bags. Daddy invariably responding, "Be prepared. That's the Boy Scout motto."

"Once his food ran out, he hunted and fished. Gathered fruits and nuts and berries. Much as I did during my early years in this world. He hid from the dangers as best he could. And when he discovered that the magic was wilder in some places than others, he sought out the pockets of relative safety. Most of all, he clung to his memories. He read—and reread—the few books he'd brought. Recited his old theatre monologues. Sang show tunes. In spite of everything, I think he was relieved to find the Borderlands. To know that the things that had happened to him here were real. That he wasn't crazy."

Lying in bed, listening to the muffled shouting. Cringing when I made out his words: "I am not losing my mind! I'm finally beginning to see things clearly!" Pretending to be fast asleep when Mom eased open my bedroom door to check on me.

"I couldn't leave him in the Borderlands. My clan would never accept a . . . damaged human. And if I'd taken him to Faerie, I knew I'd never convince him to leave."

No. He had sacrificed everything and everyone he loved in his search for Faerie. Once he found it, he would never give it up.

"So I have thrust both of us upon you. I hope you can forgive me."

"Forgive you?" I echoed. "You came back to me. You brought my father back. Nothing is more important than that."

Rowan's sweet smile faded when he noticed Reinhard's dubious expression.

"Nothing," I repeated firmly, "is more important than that."

ENTR'ACTE
THE JOURNAL OF ROWAN MACKENZIE

"Nothing is more important than that."

She loves me. After all this time, she still loves me. She is still my Maggie. As long as I have her, I can accept the rest. Even the loss of my theatre.

Of course, no one expected me to return. Those empty wooden hangers in my armoire brought that home far more powerfully than their incredulous looks.

At least they didn't throw out the contents of my desk. I'll have to ask Maggie to buy me a new journal. For tonight, I will make do with blank paper.

If only my mind were equally blank.

A nonprofit. Had I remained here, it could never have happened. Helen would not have allowed it. She knew I could play no role in a theatre where accountants issue paychecks to employees with Social Security numbers.

Foolish to have expected everything to remain the same, to imagine that I could simply pick up the threads of my life again. Places change. People change. Even Maggie. She is stronger now, more confident about herself and her place in the world.

What a colossal irony that she has taken my place.

How could I have ever imagined that she would be content to be my assistant? But that was the play I wrote in my head. I would direct the shows. She would work with the actors, doing her list thing, helping them with their music. We'd work together and live together and love each other. We would give Jack a home and he would grow strong in mind and body.

A pipe dream. The kind of happy ever after found in musicals.

She is still my Maggie. But I am not the same Rowan Mackenzie. Can she really love a penniless beggar with nothing but the clothes on his back? A man as ill equipped to deal with this world as her poor damaged father?

If only I had never left.

If only I had given up the search sooner.

I could have returned months ago. And faced Maggie without shame and told her without lying that I could not feel his presence in Faerie. I would still have my theatre and my life.

My first completely unselfish act and look how it turned out.

I mustn't blame Jack. It was my choice to leave, my choice to search for him. He would not have been there in the first place had I protected him all those years ago.

I failed him then. I will not do so now.

The staff will let us stay. Maggie will insist on it. And when Maggie Graham digs in her heels, she is as immovable as the Green Mountains.

And then?

I must help Jack heal.

I must help Maggie succeed.

I must find a new purpose, a new life, a new place in this world, just as I did more than two hundred years ago.

And never allow Maggie to suspect how much that prospect terrifies me.

ACT TWO

LIVING IN THE SHADOWS

CHAPTER 13
WHO ARE YOU NOW?

AS I STAGGERED FROM THE PARKING LOT with
the first four bags of groceries, the stage door banged
open and my father poked his head out. He surveyed the
picnic area, the Smokehouse, and finally craned his neck to
study the sky. Then he bounded out of the barn and sprinted
toward me.

I felt like I'd stumbled into *The Twilight Zone* again. Although his clothes were still ragged, the terrified Rip Van
Winkle was gone, replaced by a smiling stranger, white hair
secured at the nape of his neck, white beard and mustache
neatly—if inexpertly—trimmed.

My delight faded as he wrested a bag from my hand and
began rummaging through it.

*So he's more excited about the groceries than you. Just be
grateful he isn't cowering under the table.*

"Jack!" Rowan called as he hurried toward us. "We'll unpack the groceries upstairs."

"There's more in the car," I said.

"I'll get them!" Daddy replied.

I watched him race toward the parking lot, still shocked
by his transformation. If Rowan could accomplish so much
in a single night, I'd have my father back before the end of
the season.

As I turned to thank Rowan, his gaze rose abruptly from
my legs to my face. I wished I'd worn something flirty, fun,
and fabulous instead of throwing on shorts and a T-shirt.

Then his desire flashed through me, and I decided that shorts and a T-shirt were just fine.

His lips brushed my cheek. I heard his deep intake of breath. Then he suddenly recoiled.

"Did you cut yourself?" he demanded.

I shook my head before I remembered. "I nicked myself shaving. How did you—?"

"The iron. In the blood."

"You can smell it?"

"I just wasn't prepared."

In spite of his reassuring smile, his face was even paler than usual, and he kept swallowing as if he might vomit.

"But people cut themselves all the time. And women . . ." Heat burned my cheeks. "Women . . . bleed. Every month. Not old women, but . . ."

"I understand the female reproductive cycle, Maggie."

I envisioned him retreating to the cottage every time a woman got her period. But if he'd done that during my season, he never would have gotten around to directing.

Rowan cleared his throat. "I'm usually careful to keep up my . . . shields."

Now all I could envision was some *Star Trek* character shouting, "Red alert! Shields up!" And menstruating women bouncing off them like ping-pong balls.

What is wrong with you? Focus!

Which wasn't easy on two hours of sleep and five cups of coffee.

"So you left your shields in the apartment today?"

"Not exactly."

I tugged my ear. "Sounds like . . . ? Three syllables?"

"I wanted to smell you."

Six rather surprising syllables.

"I know that sounds disgusting, but—"

"It's sweet," I replied and smiled at his astonishment. "Did I smell okay? Other than the blood?"

"You smelled wonderful." He closed his eyes, his expression dreamy. "Something ambiguously herbal in your hair. The dusty fragrance of lavender permeating your shirt. Lemongrass soap. A salty hint of sweat. A sweet whiff of baby powder . . ."

"All that? In one breath?"

He regarded me through heavy-lidded eyes. "The musk between your legs. And your scent. Sweet and spicy. Like ginger."

"My perfume," I managed.

"Yes. But it's also you. Your essence."

I took a shaky breath and let it out. So did Rowan. Then he said, "We'd better help Jack."

We found Daddy bent over the open trunk of my car. He straightened as we approached, a guilty expression on his face as well as a great many crumbs.

"I said we'd unpack upstairs," Rowan reminded him.

Daddy muttered a protest, spewing crumbs everywhere. "It's Entenmann's crumb cake. My favorite!"

"Mine, too," I said.

"But you bought English muffins, right?"

"And new clothes."

"Good thing. I'm a regular Raggedy Andy. I hope you bought clothes for Rowan, too."

Belatedly, I realized that he was still dressed in the stained and wrinkled clothing I'd seen last night.

"Mine seem to be . . . missing," Rowan said.

"Missing?"

"Along with my toiletries. Jack and I showered with Joy this morning. The dishwashing liquid, not our state of being."

"You don't have any clothes?"

"I imagine Janet or Reinhard cleaned everything out."

"And left the fucking dishwashing liquid?"

Daddy hooted. "That's what I said!"

I scowled and heaved two bags out of the trunk. "Let's get this stuff inside."

As we headed back to the theatre, I said, "I can't believe they gave away your clothes. I mean, I can. But still . . . what a shitty homecoming. Well, I have one of your shirts. I'll be able to find the manufacturer's name and—"

"You have one of my shirts?"

"Reinhard packed it for me. With your other things." Another embarrassing wave of heat suffused my cheeks as I recalled the times I had pressed it to my face and breathed in the faint scent of him that clung to it. "Anyway, I can order more. I'll run out and pick up some other stuff to tide you over."

"Naturally, I intend to pay for the clothes. And the groceries."

"Don't be silly."

"I don't have any money, but—"

"You have the money you gave to me."

"That's yours."

"Well, you're back now. That makes it *your* money."

"I don't *want* the money!"

"Please don't fight," Daddy whispered.

That silenced us. After an awkward exchange of glances, we both began apologizing, then broke off. Finally, Rowan said, "Suppose we wrangle about finances tomorrow."

"Okay. But I'm paying you back everything I spent on the hotel."

"The hotel?"

"The Bough. I spent most of your money fixing it up."

"Why would you—?"

"I own it."

"You *own* the Golden Bough?"

"Helen left it to me."

"But I thought Janet—"

"I'm hungry," Daddy complained. "And I want to try on my new—"

His head jerked toward the Smokehouse. Then he dropped his bag and shrieked, "Run!"

I was too stunned to do anything except watch him bolt down the walkway and disappear into the barn.

"It's the crow," Rowan said, easing his bags to the ground. "In the maple tree. There were shapeshifters in the Borderlands who took that form."

"Shapeshifters?"

But he was already hurrying after Daddy.

A shudder rippled through me. Were the shapeshifters the mysterious "they" that Daddy feared? Or were there other creatures—even more terrifying—in that awful place?

Unwillingly, I pictured giant crows gorging on carrion. Or maybe they looked like ordinary humans with feathers instead of hair, talons instead of fingers, and cruel, hooked beaks that they used to tear the flesh of their victims.

I tried to banish the disturbing images as I walked toward the theatre. Rowan crouched in the stage doorway. Daddy was hidden in the shadows, but I heard him exclaim, "Get Maggie! Before the Crow-Man does." After that, there was only the murmur of their voices.

I felt utterly useless. It was Rowan my father needed, Rowan whose power could calm him. All I could do was buy groceries and clothes.

I glared at the small black form, half hidden among the branches of the maple.

"Scat!"

Daddy's anguished cry made me glance over my shoulder. He was peering around the doorframe, frantically beckoning out to me.

"Don't do that! They're worse if they're angry."

"Yeah? Well, so am I!"

I ran toward the tree, waving my arms like a crazy woman and shouting, "Scat! Shoo! Get out of here, bird!" I wrenched a clod of dirt from the ground and hurled it at the little fucker with all my might. I missed the tree completely, but the crow gave an irritable caw and flew off.

Absurdly elated at my victory, I dusted off my hands and walked back to my men.

"You're very brave," Daddy said. "But you've got to be more careful. Those Crow-Men'll rip you to pieces. I'm starving! Let's eat."

And he clattered up the stairs.

Stupid to imagine that he'd been magically cured overnight. Or to see him venture outdoors and believe that he was no longer haunted by his experiences in the Borderlands.

One day at a time, Graham.

"We need to wash your clothes," I told Rowan. "And Daddy's."

Clearly taken aback, Rowan nodded. "I'll borrow something from Jack for now."

"We can use the machines in the Dungeon."

"Why don't I unpack the groceries while you start the laundry?"

It was a perfectly reasonable suggestion. But all I could hear was Hal's voice: "I just don't want to see you turning into Helen."

One day at a time, remember? He'll learn to do his own laundry. And his own grocery shopping. Just wash his damn clothes so he has something to wear for the staff meeting!

"Maggie?"

"Sounds like a plan."

⚞⚟

They were still unpacking the groceries when I returned from the Dungeon. I admired Daddy in his khaki shorts and "I L♥VERMONT" T-shirt, then burst out laughing when I saw Rowan. The droopy shorts were funny enough. The T-shirt was adorned with two bizarre cartoon creatures. Each had the body of a cow and the head of a moose. In between the pair were the words "It's different in Vermont."

"It's so you," I said.

"Another remark like that," Rowan warned, "and you get dry toast for breakfast."

We settled Daddy at the table with a slab of crumb cake while we finished putting away the groceries. When Rowan unearthed the fresh strawberries and vanilla ice cream, his mouth curved in that sweet smile. For a moment, we just gazed at each other. Then Daddy exclaimed, "Don't just stand there! Cook!"

Rowan cooked. I brought him up to speed on my life. I downplayed the financial problems the theatre still faced; I didn't want him to think I was incompetent. Rowan smiled and nodded and told me how proud he was. Over and over again. Like he was putting on a performance—or we were strangers trying to find some common ground.

Stop reading into everything! He's feeling his way just like you are. You'll have plenty of time to get to know him again. To get to know both of them.

He was astonished to learn that I was living with Janet and even more astonished to discover that I was enjoying it. But he studiously avoided asking about my personal life, and when I started telling him about my awful dates, he changed the subject.

I'd expected him to laugh. What had *he* expected? That I would sit at home, staring tearfully into space and clutching his journal to my bosom? Okay, I *had* done that. For a while. But he acted like I'd spent my winters sprawled on a bearskin rug with a succession of naked strangers, and my summers sunbathing beside hunky bronzed Vikings in Speedos.

Reinhard's arrival rescued us.

"What's in the box?" I asked as he set it atop the battered wooden trunk that Rowan used as a coffee table.

"Rowan's wines."

"You stored his wine?"

"It would have been ruined if I left it here. You know how cold the barn gets in the winter. And in the summer, with all the sunlight pouring in . . ." Reinhard shook his head. "I also stored some of your books, Rowan. The first editions. You'll have to apply to Maggie for your journals."

"I don't suppose you've got his clothes, too?"

"They are in my SUV."

"You're kidding!"

"You cannot be too careful with moths. The clothes are clean, of course, but after so long in storage, I would recommended laundering them." Reinhard's mouth quirked in a brief smile as he surveyed Rowan's attire. "I suppose you will have to wear that to the staff meeting."

"I'm doing a load of wash now," I said.

"Pity. I would have liked to have seen Janet's face. Now, Jack, if you will accompany me into the bedroom . . ."

"Why?" Rowan asked.

Reinhard frowned. "If you prefer that I conduct his physical examination here—"

"Why did you store my clothes?" He seemed more stunned than pleased by Reinhard's revelations. "The books, the wine, those are valuable. But my clothes . . ."

"I thought you would return."

"You never told me that!" I exclaimed.

"And if I was wrong?" Reinhard demanded. "Should I build up your hopes for nothing?" He smoothed his crew cut and added, "As it turns out, I was right. And now Janet owes me a very expensive bottle of wine."

Rowan silently walked over to the trunk and withdrew a bottle from the box. After examining it, he put it back and chose another, which he held out to Reinhard.

"Now you can enjoy two bottles of wine."

Reinhard glanced at the label and shook his head. "Too expensive."

"Not nearly expensive enough after what you've done. Please. I would be honored if you'd accept it."

Reinhard gave one of his little bows. Then he led my protesting father into the bedroom. Rowan followed, still looking a little dazed.

Between sprints to the Dungeon, I hovered anxiously outside the bedroom, listening to Daddy's complaints and Rowan's soothing murmur. I returned from my final trip in time to hear Reinhard pronounce Daddy remarkably healthy.

"I could have told you that before you started poking me," Daddy grumbled.

"Does the wrist bother you much?"

"What's wrong with his wrist?" I asked, hastily depositing my armful of clothes on the bed.

"An old fracture," Reinhard replied.

"It aches sometimes. But I did a good job setting it, didn't I? One-handed, too! The good ol' *Field Guide to Wilderness Medicine*. Never travel without it."

"And the earlier problems?" Reinhard inquired as he closed his bag.

"What problems?"

"I understood there was a history of alcohol and drug abuse."

Daddy shot an anxious look at Rowan. "Was there? Did I tell you that? I don't remember. So many missing pieces . . ."

As he began to tremble, Rowan's hand descended on his shoulder.

"Perhaps we should postpone the meeting," Reinhard said.

"Why don't you and Maggie go ahead?" Rowan suggested. "Jack and I will be there soon."

When Reinhard frowned, I said, "I thought Jack should meet the staff."

"Then they should meet him as he is. Not under the influence of Rowan's power."

Rowan stiffened, but his hand slid from Daddy's shoulder. "Give me a few minutes to talk with him."

"I'm right here, you know!"

Daddy's querulous voice made me grimace. If they met this Jack Sinclair—or the onc who'd run shrieking from the crow—would they really allow him to stay?

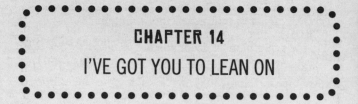

CHAPTER 14

I'VE GOT YOU TO LEAN ON

A S SOON AS I WALKED INTO THE Smokehouse, Hal hurried over and swept me into a hug.

"I didn't sleep a wink last night." He reared back to examine my face and sighed. "Clearly, you didn't, either. And no wonder, poor lamb. First Rowan, then . . . but don't worry. Everything will be fine."

"From your lips . . ." I glanced around and breathed a sigh of relief when I discovered Bernie was absent. "What did you tell Bernie?" I asked Reinhard.

He, too, was surveying the room. "Nothing. I just dropped him off in town to wheedle more ads out of the merchants. Javier, is Catherine coming?"

Before Javier could reply, Reinhard's head jerked toward the Smokehouse door. Right on cue, the rest of the staff went into their familiar bird-dog-on-point attitude. Either Rowan's control was shaky or he was deliberately warning us of his arrival.

There was a breathless pause. Then a soft knock.

It just killed me to imagine Rowan standing outside, humbly awaiting permission to enter the rehearsal studio that had once been his. But when he walked inside, he seemed as self-assured as that morning he'd welcomed our cast to the Crossroads.

Daddy's gaze darted from face to face. When I gave his arm a reassuring squeeze, he regarded me blankly—as if he'd never seen me before in his life.

"This is the staff of the theatre," Rowan told him.

"I don't know these people," Daddy said in a loud whisper.

"Most of them began working here after your season, but they've all heard about your performance as Billy Bigelow."

Once again, those words proved to be the mental health equivalent of "Abracadabra!" Flashing his gap-toothed grin, Daddy strode toward Alex and thrust out his hand. "Hi. Jack Sinclair. Great to meet you." Leaving a startled Alex to stammer, "Ah. Yes. Alex Ross. Music director."

Daddy worked the room like a politician at a rally—or an actor who had been well coached by his director. The staff exchanged glances, obviously trying to square this confident man with the one Reinhard must have described.

Daddy's smile slipped as Janet introduced herself. Then his troubled expression cleared. "I remember now! You're Helen's daughter. How come she's not here?"

"I'm afraid Helen passed away," Janet said.

Daddy's mouth began to tremble. Then he slumped onto a chair and covered his face with his hands. Rowan reached for his shoulder, then let his hand fall.

"I'm sorry," he said to Janet. "I know how hard it must have been for you."

Janet nodded brusquely.

"I wish I had been here."

"I doubt even you could have saved her."

Daddy leaped up from his chair, his face twisted in horror. "Was it the Crow-Men?"

"There are no Crow-Men here," Rowan said. "Helen just had a bad heart."

"She did not! Helen had the best heart of anyone I ever knew!"

"Rowan meant she had a heart attack," I said, desperate to avoid another meltdown. "But her passing was very peaceful. She died in her sleep."

Daddy let out a shaky sigh. "Thank God. Not that she died! That it was peaceful. I couldn't bear the thought of those awful Crow-Men tearing poor Helen to pieces and then gobbling her up like—"

"I think it's time to go back to the apartment," Rowan said.

"Did I do something wrong? I didn't mean to. Please, don't send me—"

"It's okay," I assured him, all too aware of the shell-shocked expressions of the staff. "I need you to try on the rest of your new clothes. And make up a list of anything else you need."

"More crumb cake! And shoes. And underwear. Briefs, not boxers. Only Rowan wears boxers."

That revelation caused a mild sensation among the staff.

Rowan took Daddy's arm and marched him to the door. Daddy shook off his restraining hand and turned to face the staff. "It was a pleasure to meet you. I look forward to seeing you again very soon."

Head high, he made his exit, leaving Rowan to trail after him.

Every head immediately swiveled toward me.

"The Crow-Men ... he wasn't making that up. They're shapeshifters. In the Borderlands. The place where Rowan found him."

Hal shuddered. "I don't even want to imagine. And meeting a bunch of strangers his first day back ... and learning about Helen ... I wouldn't have managed half so well!"

"I expected him to be worse," Javier said cautiously. "After what Reinhard told us."

"What exactly *did* you tell them?" I asked.

"The truth, Maggie. As I saw it."

Before I could press him for details, Catherine eased through the half-open door. She looked drawn and pale. I hoped she hadn't caught some sort of stomach bug.

"Have they left already?" she asked.

"Rowan will be back in a minute," I said. "After we finish talking, I'll introduce you to ... Jack."

"How are you doing?"

"It's all so ... surreal. I keep waiting for someone to pinch me."

Mei-Yin obligingly gave my arm a brief but brutal pinch. I was still glaring at her when Rowan strode into the Smokehouse. He checked when he saw Catherine, then hurried over to her, his smile of greeting shifting to a frown.

"What is it? Are you ill?"

"No, no . . ."

He seized her hands and became very still. "Something's . . . changed."

Catherine shot a quick look at Javier. A huge grin blossomed on his face as he put his arm around her.

"We were going to make the official announcement later, but you can't keep anything a secret around this place. We're going to have a baby!"

Rowan's astonishment crackled through the Smokehouse like heat lightning. A dizzying array of emotions inundated me: wonder, affection, joy—and a longing so palpable it made me ache.

Everyone was so shocked by his reaction that it took us a moment before we remembered to congratulate Catherine and Javier. I was the only one who seemed genuinely surprised. The staff must have picked up on some change in her energy just as Rowan had. Even Hal had heard, undoubtedly from Lee. For a moment, I felt as much of an outsider as Rowan.

"We just found out last week," Catherine told me, her expression anxious. "I didn't want to give you anything more to worry about during Hell Week."

"Are you kidding? It's wonderful news! Although I don't know where you found the time or the energy."

"Where there's a will, there's a way," Javier said.

"I know it's not the best timing in the world," Catherine added. "But I won't let you down. I promise."

"Just promise you won't push yourself too hard. We can always scrounge up some volunteers to help with set construction."

"Already on it," Javier said.

"I was sure you'd guessed," Catherine told Rowan.

He gave a helpless shrug. "Your energy felt different, but I didn't . . . I've never been around a woman who was expecting a child." His gaze flicked toward Janet, and the mask descended.

Had she left Dale during her pregnancies? Or had she remained here and shunned all contact with Rowan?

His smile returned so quickly that I wondered if I was imagining things.

"You're the only baby I've ever known. And you were

already a toddler when Alex and Annie brought you here."
His left hand came up to cup Catherine's cheek. His right
clasped Javier's shoulder. "What a blessing for you. For everyone. To have a child at the theatre again."

He had told me that there was rarely more than one
birth every few decades in his clan. Little wonder the Fae
considered children such a gift. But his words hadn't prepared me for the storm of emotions that had escaped him
after Javier's revelation—or for the worshipful way he was
gazing at Catherine.

Hal's hand was over his heart. Lee looked shocked.
Clearly, neither had seen this side of Rowan Mackenzie.
And just as clearly, the others had. Alex and Mei-Yin were
smiling. Even Reinhard's expression had softened. Janet
just studied Rowan through narrowed eyes.

"Forgive me," Rowan said. "I'm holding up the meeting.
And we have a lot to discuss."

"No, we don't!" Hal declared. "You're back. So is Maggie's father. End of discussion."

"We are all happy that Rowan has returned," Reinhard
said, although his frown suggested just the opposite. "And
that he rescued Jack. But we cannot allow emotion to cloud
the issues."

"Why NOT?" Mei-Yin demanded.

"We've always followed our emotions when it came to
running this theatre," Alex said.

"Which explains why it never made a profit," Janet muttered.

"But we do not run the theatre any longer," Reinhard
pointed out. "The board of directors does."

"Everybody on the board knows Rowan," Catherine
said. "And they'll get to know Jack."

"In time, perhaps. But right now, he needs a doctor's
care."

"What are YOU? A PLUMBER?"

"I am a pediatrician, Mei-Yin! Not a psychiatrist."

"And Rowan's a FAERY! Are you telling me the TWO
of you can't do more for him than a SHRINK?"

Reinhard dragged his fingers through his hair. "How can
I know this? Even Rowan cannot promise that he can help
Jack to heal."

"Who's asking for PROMISES? I'm asking you to TRY. Maybe it'll work. Maybe it won't. How the hell should I know? You think I got a crystal BALL up my ASS?"

"They're family," Lee stated firmly. "A lot may have changed at the Crossroads, but we don't turn away family."

Rowan had been observing the give-and-take calmly, but Lee's comment startled him. Whatever misgivings our resident alpha male may have had last night, Lee had obviously decided that Rowan and Daddy were members of our pack.

"So you are all agreed?" Reinhard asked.

"Did you really expect us to show Rowan Mackenzie the door?" Janet said.

"Would you like to?" Rowan asked.

Janet hesitated, then shook her head. "Lee's right. Like it or not, we are family. And we've always protected our own." As I let out my breath in a relieved sigh, she added, "And speaking of family, I trust you haven't forgotten your mother is arriving tomorrow."

"Your mother?" Rowan echoed.

In other circumstances, I might have found the trace of panic on his face amusing. But I'd lain awake half the night, thinking about what I would—could—say to her.

"I can't tell her about Daddy." Not until he bore some resemblance to the man she had once loved. "Or you," I added, shooting a pleading glance at Rowan. "She'll storm your apartment."

"Armed with a spoon," Janet mused.

There were a few fleeting smiles; everyone had heard the story of how my mother had threatened to geld Rowan if he hurt me.

Rowan, however, was frowning. "I hate to think of you keeping secrets from her again."

So did I. And not only because she always managed to sniff out the truth. We'd worked too hard to develop a good relationship to jeopardize it now. But if I was hiding Daddy, I could keep Rowan a secret, too. Just until she was safely back in Delaware.

"You're sure?" Rowan asked. When I nodded, he said, "Then I'll take Jack back to the cottage for a few days. He likes it there. And it might be better for us to be alone. While we start working on his recovery."

"How do we explain Jack to everybody else?" Hal asked. "He can't stay locked up in your apartment. Or hidden in the woods." He shuddered; Hal's idea of roughing it was when the hot water didn't come on immediately.

"Keep as close to the truth as possible," Rowan advised. "Jack's an old friend of mine. An actor who's fallen on hard times. And I invited him to stay for the summer."

"That explains how Jack fits in around here," Janet said. "What about you?"

"I've come back to be with Maggie. To work out our relationship."

"And what about your relationship to the theatre?"

"I can't think that far ahead."

"But surely, you *want* to be a part of things," Alex protested.

"Of course I do!"

After his calm acceptance of all the changes at the theatre, Rowan's vehemence startled me. Why hadn't he shared his true feelings with me?

"Maggie is the artistic director now," he said more quietly. "And I don't intend to usurp her authority. As long as I possess no official identity, I couldn't even if I wanted to. Perhaps one day, I'll direct again. I don't know. Any more than I know whether I can help Jack heal or whether Maggie and I can make this relationship work."

Green eyes pierced me.

"I can only promise that I'll try. I will not walk away again. From you or your father or this theatre. That is my pledge."

His fierce gaze swept over the staff, lingering longest on Janet and Reinhard.

"My pledge to all of you."

CHAPTER 15

TAKE IT ON THE CHIN

NOTHING SCREAMS WEEKEND FUN like losing the two men you love most in the world yet again.

I bundled Rowan and Daddy off to the cottage with enough food in Daddy's backpack to last a week, enough clothes in Rowan's old knapsack to weather anything short of a blizzard, and enough toilet paper to withstand the most virulent attack of enteric diarrhea.

Rowan paused at the edge of the trees to wave farewell, just as he had two years ago. I firmly reminded myself that I would see them Sunday evening, that it was foolish to interpret Daddy's delight at returning to the "little house" as a personal rejection. Then I cried for ten minutes, blew my nose, and hurried to the Smokehouse for my "getting to know you" rehearsal with the two sets of kids playing Colin and Mary in *The Secret Garden*.

Yet another show about orphans. Belligerent Mary who erected walls to hide the pain of losing her parents in a cholera epidemic. Bedridden Colin who was an orphan in all but name since his hunchbacked father was lost in grief over the death of his wife.

Not exactly a laugh riot.

As the kids and I discussed the characters, I wondered if I was out of my mind to stage such a dark musical. Yes, there was a happy ending—eventually. And ghosts and magic and redemption and love. Kind of like *Carousel* without the clambakes.

Maybe that's what had convinced me that the show could be another four-hanky success story. But it suddenly struck me that I'd ended up with an entire season of shows about characters in search of a family. A therapist would have a field day.

The four kids seemed undaunted by the show's darkness or the difficult gamut of emotions they would have to convey. Their determination made me ashamed of my earlier weepiness, and we broke for the day on a wave of enthusiasm.

After which I changed my clothes and mentally prepared myself for the "lying to my mother" phase of my festive weekend.

When I walked into the Golden Bough, a little shiver of excitement zinged through me. Tourists wandered through the lobby. The muted hum of voices emanated from the lounge. And—be still my heart!—a young guy was working in our new Media Center. Okay, "Media Center" was just a fancy term for a cubicle with a computer, printer, and landline phone, but someone was actually using it.

During my first year as owner, I'd been too busy working for the theatre to do more than learn the ropes and discuss redecorating with Hal and Caren. Frannie took over as manager a week before the flood. Although many neighboring towns were inundated, Dale escaped with only soggy basements. When I breathlessly asked Janet if faery wards had averted disaster, she rolled her eyes and assured me that our salvation was due to geography; short of a Biblical flood, the Dale "River" was too small and too far from town to do much damage.

We had to close the hotel for a few days to deal with the basement. Frannie was the one who suggested we close again during March and April to dive into renovations. It made perfect sense; southern Vermont drew more black flies than tourists in early spring.

After we reopened, I obsessively checked bookings, fearful that we'd go under before the Fourth of July. But the trickle of tourists had turned into a babbling brook, if not a flood, and we were pretty much booked through early October. Even the fact that a third of our rooms went to cast members failed to diminish my satisfaction.

The secret to our success looked up from the guest book and beamed as I approached the reception desk. Iolanthe—lounging in the inbox as usual—raised her head to allow me to rub her behind the ears before resuming her twenty-two-hour-a-day catnap. Even Janet had no idea how old Iolanthe was; I'd begun to suspect the cat was Fae.

"Have they checked in yet?" I asked Frannie.

"No. But traffic on the interstate can be murder on a Friday. Don't you worry, hon."

We discussed the ongoing maid shortage and accommodations for the handful of professional actors arriving Sunday to begin rehearsals for *The Secret Garden*. Every time the bell over the front door tinkled, my head jerked up, hoping to see Mom and Chris. In the middle of perusing the horrifying estimates to install a new boiler, the bell jangled again and my mother staggered through the door.

"I thought we'd never get here," she said by way of greeting. "The entire Eastern seaboard was fleeing north. I feel like something the cat dragged in."

Naturally, she looked anything but. Black hair perfectly coiffed, barely a wrinkle marring her pale blue shirtdress. Martians could level Wilmington and the woman would emerge from the rubble looking chic.

She gave me a quick hug, then stepped back, frowning. "You look nice."

"Want to try that line reading again? Without the surprise?"

"I'm used to seeing you in shorts and a T-shirt."

"I'm dressed for dinner. I'm even skipping tonight's show so we can have a relaxing one. God knows we won't have much time to talk tomorrow."

The cornflower blue eyes narrowed. "What's wrong? You seem tense."

Great. She's here five seconds and already picking up bad vibes.

"Of course, I'm tense! I've got a fund-raiser tomorrow, and I thought my mother was road kill."

"We nearly were. This giant wolf lumbered across the road—"

"It was a German shepherd," Chris remarked as he edged through the doorway with their luggage.

"It was a wolf," my mother declared.

"It was a wolf," he agreed. "That looked remarkably like a German shepherd."

He dropped their bags and gave me a warm hug. He was a great hugger. One of the many things I liked about him. Along with his brown eyes that could look soulful one moment and devilish the next. And the way he teased my mother, whose pursed lips had curved into a reluctant smile.

Her eyes widened as she finally registered the new and improved lobby. Hardwood floors gleamed. The dark oak paneling had been stripped and restained a lighter shade. Overstuffed couches and armchairs in deep forest green and green-and-white gingham graced the seating areas. In place of the ancient draperies that had shrouded the lobby in gloom, wooden shutters allowed morning sunlight to pour through the top half of the tall windows. Ferns and peace lilies nestled atop plant stands. And scattered throughout, a collection of funky lamps that Hal and I had scavenged from flea markets.

I'd deliberately refrained from sending her pictures and my uncommon restraint was rewarded by her look of pleasure. Needy child that I was, I couldn't resist asking, "You like it?"

"It's what a Vermont country inn should look like."

"It'll never be as elegant as the Four Chimneys . . ."

"It's cheerful and homey. Like Dale. And it doesn't cost an arm and a leg to stay here. You should have seen it before, Chris. Like something out of the Victorian age."

"Those old draperies probably were," Frannie called, waggling her fingers in greeting.

Mom hurried over to the reception desk. "I was so busy gawking I didn't even say hello. How are you?"

"Just great, hon."

"And your mother? Is the arthritis still troubling her?"

"Oh, you know. Good days and bad. But she's as feisty as ever."

Mom introduced Chris, then gazed around the lobby again. "You and Maggie have worked wonders."

"Wait'll you see your room." Frannie winked. "Maggie put you in the Honeymoon Suite."

"You have a Honeymoon Suite?"

"The Rose Garden Room." I struck a pose and quoted from the Web page: " 'The romantic rose-colored décor is highlighted by a wall of windows and French doors leading out to a balcony overlooking the Green Mountains and the quaint shops of Main Street.' Come on. I'll walk you up."

As we mounted the wide stairs, I said, "Your room is the only one we've fixed up. The rest of the second floor just got new bedspreads and curtains and paint slapped on the walls."

"One step at a time," Chris said.

"Yeah. That's my new mantra." I paused outside their room, my palm a little damp as I gripped the brass door-knob. Then I flung open the door. "Welcome to your private rose garden."

Mom drifted through the "suite," making more gratifying noises as she admired the canopy bed, the floral draperies and bedspread, the bouquet of pink roses on the table in the sitting area, and the claw foot tub in the bathroom that had cost me a fucking fortune.

"It's beautiful, Maggie. When you called it the Rose Garden Room, I was afraid it would be . . ."

"Too girly?"

"Too flowery. You know. Flowered curtains and bed-spreads and pillows and wallpaper." Mom shuddered. "Who can relax in a room with flowered wallpaper? It gives me a headache."

"It gives me the creeps. Like I'm staying in Sleeping Beauty's castle and the vines will eventually strangle me."

Chris stroked his beard thoughtfully. "Now there's an idea. An inn where every room is decorated in a different fairy-tale theme. The Sleeping Beauty Room. The Snow White Room."

"With a glass coffin instead of a bed," I suggested.

"The Hansel and Gretel Room with its charming wood-burning stove—ideal for incinerating unwanted guests."

Mom rolled her eyes. "The pair of you."

She used to say that when Daddy and I embarked on one of our flights of fancy. But her voice held affection now instead of the exasperation I remembered from childhood.

"Maggie? You've got that tense look again."

"I forgot to order flowers for the fund-raiser," I lied.

Mom continued to study me during dinner, but Chris, God love him, kept refilling the wineglasses. By the time we said good night, Mom was pleasantly tipsy and too tired to study anything other than the inside of her eyelids.

The next morning brought a final frenzy of cleaning before the fund-raiser. Amanda did a terrific job at the matinee, but I was glad Chelsea was on the docket at night; her performance was the kind of big bang donors expected for their bucks.

After the matinee, Hal accompanied me up the hill to oversee my toilette. Naturally, he'd helped me pick out tonight's dress, too.

"What do you think?" I asked Janet as I descended the stairs.

"I told her the jade silk brings out the green in her eyes," Hal prompted, "and the Chinese style evokes an air of exotic mystery."

"The plunging neckline should bring in some last-minute donations," Janet remarked.

"You don't think I look like the lone Caucasian cast member of *Flower Drum Song*?"

Janet examined me critically. Then began singing "You are Beautiful." From *Flower* fucking *Drum Song*.

"I hate you."

"At least it doesn't have dragons on it like Mei-Yin's."

"Mei-Yin's wearing her dragon dress?" I demanded, turning on Hal.

"How was I to know? She didn't consult me!"

"Maybe later, the two of you can put chopsticks in your hair and treat us to a rousing rendition of 'Fan Tan Fannie.'"

"I'm changing."

The doorbell chimed and Janet grinned. "Too late now."

Within half an hour, nearly a hundred guests were milling around the Bates mansion, the front porch, and the patios and garden. We'd kept prices modest, but the dozen "Angels" who'd popped for the five hundred dollar tickets ensured that the evening would be a financial success.

Three minutes with Bernie's daughter Leah made me wonder yet again how he survived the off-season. He endured her fussing with a resigned sigh, but Sarah finally said, "Lighten up, Mom," and began talking about her recent graduation.

Hard to equate this self-assured young woman with the plump, awkward girl who had been my cast mate. I'd grown so accustomed to the agelessness of the older staff that it was Sarah's transformation that seemed unnatural. Maybe by the time I was eligible for Social Security, Janet might have sprouted a few gray hairs, but Rowan would look exactly the same.

You knew that going in, Graham. Deal with it!

I could only spend a few minutes with Sarah before resuming my duties. I was so busy chatting up patrons that I merely waved to Mom and Chris. When I finally caught up with them, I found her working the room just as hard, praising past productions and the dedication of the staff and board.

"They should have appointed you executive director," I noted.

"Actually, I hate these affairs. I just put on my game face and play the devoted patron of the arts."

"The devoted and fabulous patron of the arts." Hal paused in the sunroom doorway to fling open his arms, then hurried over to envelop Mom in a hug. "You look gorgeous as always. What I wouldn't give for that complexion! Please tell Maggie she doesn't look like a Caucasian cast member of *Flower Drum Song*. She's been obsessing all evening. You must be Chris. I can't believe it's taken this long to lure you up here."

"And you must be Hal," Chris said, smiling. "Alison's told me so much about you, I feel like I know you."

"I hope she's been equally kind in her description of me," Long boomed, edging into our circle. "Alison, Alison. Don't break my heart and tell me that this is your inamorato."

"Call your cardiologist," Chris advised as he held out his hand. "Chris Thompson, Inamorato. You must be Long Martindale, Impresario."

"I have the good fortune to be the president of the board of directors. But if you've won the heart of the fair Alison, then you are the fortunate one."

"We have swords in the prop room," I noted. "If you want to fight a duel on the front lawn."

"Behave," my mother said. "And you, too," she added, eyeing Long sternly. "Honestly, I think you'd flirt with any female between seven and seventy."

"My cut-off is eighty," Long whispered. "But I might have to revise my limit. I see a very rich, very elderly widow who's in need of company."

After he excused himself, Chris remarked, "You know, he may not be as much of an ass as you suspect. It's hard to tell with theatre people. They're good at playing roles off-stage, too."

"Some are." My mother favored me with a speculative glance.

I took that as my cue to beat a hasty retreat. When I spied Nancy talking with Bernie, Bea, and Frannie, I wobbled out to the patio as fast as my spiky heels would allow.

When Nancy smiled, I realized just how much the events of the last few days had been weighing on me. She had kept me sane during our season and we'd shared a lot of ups and downs since, including my struggles to steer a course for the theatre and hers to survive the budget cuts at the library. And while she knew nothing about the secret of the Crossroads, she understood more about my relationship with Rowan than anyone. I could always count on her for sensible advice and a sympathetic ear. At that moment, I longed for both and wished I could drag her off to a quiet corner and blurt out everything.

Instead, I just hugged her. When I stepped back, everyone eyed me uneasily; clearly, my hug had been a tad desperate.

"Everything okay?" Nancy asked.

"Great!" I snagged two glasses of champagne from a passing waiter and downed the first in a few deep swallows.

"You just thirsty or trying to drown your sorrows?" Bernie asked.

"Thirsty. I've been yapping with donors nonstop."

"Well, save the second for a toast," Bea said. "Here's to a successful fund-raiser."

As we clinked glasses, Frannie giggled. "I hope we do this every year. It's fun getting all dolled up."

Bea, of course, always looked gorgeous, a statuesque blonde easily mistaken for one of Wagner's Rhinemaidens. Put her in a slinky sheath dress and she could set the Rhine on fire. Nancy looked businesslike in her tailored navy suit. Frannie's flowered silk dress made her look like a stocky nymph transplanted from the Rose Garden Room. Judging from her fuchsia fingernails and newly brown hair, she'd stopped in at Bea's Hive of Beauty.

I glanced nervously at my watch. "Should I start rousting people out? It'll take forever to get them all seated."

"I'll give Janet the high sign," Bernie said. "If anyone can get 'em moving, she can."

"Great. I'll talk to the caterers and—"

"Frannie and I are sticking around to make sure everything's packed up," Bea said.

"Sorry. I'm anal. And you guys are the best. You totally busted your asses for this."

"We're going make a fortune!" Bernie gloated. "Who knows? Maybe we'll be able to afford some new lighting equipment. Or a turntable for the stage."

"Or a weekend of inpatient mental health care." My comment elicited more uneasy glances. "Lighten up, I'm joking!"

Bea and Frannie departed to supervise the caterers. Bernie followed, cautiously navigating through the crowd leaning on the same cane he'd used during *Brigadoon*.

"Okay, they're gone," Nancy said. "So do you want to tell me what's bothering you?"

Evening sunlight glinted off her glasses, making it seem that her eyes were shooting fire. As I pleaded Arthur's death, the opening, and the fund-raiser, she shook her head impatiently. "This is me, Maggie. I know you. Is it your mom? Did she—? Oh, Lord. She's coming."

In an instant, her expression shifted to one of apparent delight. It always amazed me. I was the actress with a face that gave everything away, while Nancy—the most sincere person in the world—could convince a sunbathing meteorologist that it was going to snow.

I just prayed she could snow my mother.

"I was lecturing Maggie about working too hard," Nancy said. "Right lecture, wrong time. You should already be at the theatre," she scolded. "You've got to warm up the cast."

"Warm-ups can wait," my mother said. "What's going on, Maggie? You've been as jumpy as a cat ever since I arrived."

"Hey, it's been a tough week and—"

"It's more than that and you know it. More to the point, I know it. You're acting evasive. Just like you were that first summer here."

"Maybe this should wait until after the show," Nancy suggested.

"I thought we were through with that," my mother continued, as relentless as the pit bull Rowan had once called me. "The secrets. The lies. I can't do that again, Maggie. I *won't* do it. If something's bothering you, then for God's sake, just come out and—"

"Rowan's back."

My mother's eyes widened. Then her lips compressed into a hard line.

"Rowan?" Nancy said. "Came back?"

I nodded, all my attention focused on Mom. "Look, I'm sorry I didn't tell you right away, but I know you've always had . . . reservations about him. And I wanted us to have a good time this weekend."

"I can't believe it," Nancy said.

"Imagine how I—"

"Who does he think he is?"

Nancy's vehemence left me speechless; I thought she would be on my side.

"You haven't heard boo from him since he left and now he waltzes back into your life?"

"He needed time. To figure things out. And be sure of his feelings."

"What about *your* feelings?"

"He loves me, Nance."

Her expression softened. "I knew that two years ago. But he still left."

"It all happened too fast. We weren't ready."

"And now you are?"

"Yes."

The quiet certainty in my voice silenced her. Mom's face was blank—as if she'd borrowed Rowan's expressionless mask.

"Say something!"

"What do you want me to say? You know how I feel about that man."

"Give him a chance, Mom."

"To do what? Break your heart a second time?"

"That won't happen."

She gave a harsh, brittle laugh. "You know who you sound like? Me. Thirty years ago."

"It's nothing like—"

"Enough. I'm not going to change your mind about Rowan Mackenzie and you're certainly not going to change mine about him."

"Will you at least talk with him? Will you do that much for me?"

She opened her mouth, closed it again, then snapped, "Fine."

With that, she stalked into the house. I just stood there, already regretting the impulse that had led me to suggest that she and Rowan meet. But I couldn't let her go home without trying to convince her of his sincerity.

Aware of Nancy's concerned gaze, I managed an unconvincing laugh. "That went well."

"She'll come around."

"In another ten or fifteen years."

I'd worry about winning her over later. First, I had a show to deal with.

Then I realized I had an even more pressing need.

"Do me a favor, Nance? I've got to talk with Janet. Could you go to the theatre and tell Reinhard I'll be down in five minutes?"

"If you want me to wait for you . . ."

"No. Thanks. Just keep Reinhard from pulling out all his hair."

I didn't have to search for Janet. Seconds after Nancy disappeared into the house, she strode onto the patio and demanded, "What happened?"

"I spilled the beans. About Rowan. I had to! Mom and Nancy knew something was up and Mom was going nuts and—"

"Just once, I wish you were as good an actress offstage as you are on."

"Tell me about it."

"How's Alison?"

"Tickled pink." I dropped the sarcasm and gave Janet the highlights, adding, "I'll have to go to the cottage tomorrow morning and fetch Rowan. Unless . . . could you call him?"

"Call him?"

"You know. The way you . . . communicate with each other."

"On our magic faery phones?"

"Well, I don't know how it works!"

"Not like that."

"Then I'll go—"

"No. I will. Someone has to stay with Jack."

"Right. God. I'm sorry I made a mess of things."

"Please. This barely rates a "three" in the long list of Crossroads Theatre crises. Come on. Reinhard's hair will be standing on end."

As we hurried down the hill, I admitted, "I know this wasn't what we planned, but I'm glad it's all out in the open with Mom."

"Except the part about her traumatized ex-husband camping out in the woods with your faery lover who rescued him from shapeshifters in the Borderlands."

"Yeah. Except that part."

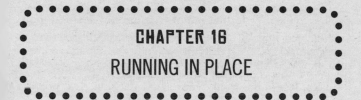

CHAPTER 16
RUNNING IN PLACE

THE NEXT MORNING, ROWAN WAS WAITING for us in the picnic area. He must have ducked into the apartment for a quick shower, because his hair was still damp. As my mother scrutinized him, I realized that his eyes were their usual green instead of the muddy hazel his Fae glamour had made them appear at their first meeting.

Did he think she'd be too pissed off to notice? Or hope that the passage of time had dimmed her memory? He could always claim that he'd gotten contact lenses, but it wasn't like him to be so careless. He must have wanted her to see him as he truly was.

As they nodded to each other, I jumped in to introduce Chris, adding, "He's a lawyer. And Mom's ... um ... gentleman friend."

"I trust you're not here in a professional capacity," Rowan said, shaking Chris' hand.

"I think I'm the designated referee."

"Don't be silly," I lied. "You're practically a member of the family."

"A position I have not yet achieved," Rowan said.

"No," my mother replied. "Since Chris has been part of our lives for the last two years, while you were—"

"In absentia. Yes. Shall we sit?" Rowan gestured to a picnic table. "Or we can go up to my apartment if you prefer."

"No. Let's just get this over with."

"Mom ..."

"Maggie says she loves you, Mr. Mackenzie. And that you love her. While that might reassure her, it's not good enough for me. You hurt her deeply when you left. More deeply than I think you realize."

"It was a painful decision. For both of us."

"And now you realize it was a mistake?"

"No. It was the right decision. At the time. But people change, Mrs. Graham."

"Some do. Others suffer disappointments and scurry back to familiar places—and familiar people."

Rowan stiffened. "If you're implying that I came back because I was afraid no one else would have me—"

"I'm saying that if you're not in this for the long haul, it would be kinder to walk away now, instead of putting Maggie through that pain again."

"You're asking for guarantees that neither Maggie nor I can give you. I can only tell you what I told the staff: I love Maggie. I want to build a life with her. And I will do everything in my power to make her happy."

"It takes more than love to keep a relationship going. It takes hard work and commitment. If you're going to run at the first sign of trouble—"

"I am not Jack Sinclair."

Mom's breath hissed in.

"When I make a commitment, I stick to it. And I'm sticking to Maggie. I realize I've given you little reason to trust me. And I'll do my best to change that. But please understand that neither your distrust nor your lectures will drive me away. They will only create a deeper rift between us and make your daughter miserable. So I suggest we keep a respectful distance and allow Maggie to decide if I am the right man for her."

Their eyes locked in a challenging stare. Chris and I watched them anxiously, heads swiveling back and forth like spectators at a particularly lethal tennis match.

"Fine," Mom snapped. "Is there anything else?"

"Just this."

Rowan reached into the back pocket of his jeans and held out a silver spoon.

My mother's face underwent several rapid changes of expression before settling back into a frown.

"A teaspoon?" she inquired. "After that speech, I expected a gravy ladle."

"I didn't want to appear boastful."

Instead of smiling, she merely plucked the spoon from his fingers.

"The entire staff is looking out for Maggie. And if I screw this up, they'll all be lining up for a piece of me. But I promise you'll get first crack."

"I'll hold you to that." She favored me with a radiant smile. "It was a wonderful show, Maggie. No one could have done a better job."

With that final dig at Rowan, she turned on her heel and marched toward the parking lot.

"Hang in there," Chris said as he shook Rowan's hand. "Graham women are a tough sell."

"I know. I'm in love with one, too."

Mom's hug was longer than usual, but all she said was, "If you need anything, call."

I waved until the car crested the lane, then walked back to Rowan.

"I'm beginning to feel I should pin a sign on my chest: 'Did not come back to hurt Maggie.'"

"The staff never said—"

"No. But they're as worried as your mother. And with the exception of Hal and Catherine, they've allowed me to stay out of a sense of duty—and because they love you too much to turn me away."

"That's not true," I protested.

"Do you think I'll hurt you again? Or walk out?"

"You promised you wouldn't walk out. That's good enough for me. As for being afraid you'll hurt me ... it's more of a generalized terror."

"Well, now I feel better."

"Hey, it's hard enough for humans to build a lasting relationship, never mind a human and a Fae. And I've never been good at the 'one day at a time' thing. I want to fast forward to the happy ever after."

"You want the Act One finale of *Into the Woods*."

"Who wouldn't? Happy ending. Journey over. Yadda, yadda."

"The journey's never over," Rowan assured me solemnly.

"I know. It's one of the more annoying things about life. And if you give me any crap about what a wonderful adventure it is, I'm going to punch you."

"How about the discoveries we can make about ourselves along the way?"

I punched him. He grinned. I grinned back. Then I noticed his bulging knapsack sitting atop one of the picnic tables.

As I struggled to quell the blind rush of panic, Rowan said, "I think Jack and I need a few more days at the cottage. He's too easily distracted here. When he heard the pit band Thursday night, it was all I could do to keep him from running down to the stage."

"But after today's matinee, there won't be a show again until Wednesday. If you bring him back this evening—"

"It will be less distracting for me, too," he said with a smile.

For a moment, I basked in my distracting Aphrodite sensuality. Then my inner Athena yanked me down to earth.

"You don't want me around while you're brainwashing Daddy."

"I hate that word."

"So do I! But whether we call it brainwashing or helping Daddy heal, it still amounts to wiping out his memories."

"I might be able to banish some of his memories, but not years of his life. Even if my power were strong enough, I wouldn't risk it. I might damage him forever."

"Then what are you going to do?"

"After he encountered my clan, I took the memories from him, as much to protect myself as him. This time, he deserves to choose. And to understand the role he'll have to play if he's going to live with his memories. Maybe it will help him to think of it that way—preparing for yet another role. But his performance will have to be believable enough to convince everyone. Especially your mother."

"Maybe he just wants to forget the Borderlands."

"The bad experiences, perhaps. But some of it was beautiful. And all of it was magical. He spent half his life looking for that magic. Do you really think he'll give it up?"

"Why can't he be content with *this* world?"

I sounded like a petulant child. Next I'd be exclaiming, "I want my Daddy back!" But I *did* want my Daddy back, even though I knew that was impossible.

"He's a restless soul, Maggie. I can't change his nature."

"I know. I just want . . ."

Everything to be the way it was when I was a child.

"Tell me," Rowan urged.

I sighed. "I want you to blow some fairy dust on him and make everything perfect. And then we can all fly away to Never Never Land."

When Rowan's lips puckered, I thought he really *might* blow fairy dust over me. Instead, he kissed me gently on the forehead, then drew me into his arms.

Calm washed over me and with it, his reassurance that even if he couldn't make everything perfect, we would face whatever happened together.

"Better?" he asked as he stepped back.

"Better. But . . ."

"What?"

"How's Daddy supposed to find his place in the world if he's hiding out in the woods?"

"It's only for a week."

"Squatting in the leaves. Living off roots and berries."

"I'd hardly describe cold chicken and endive salad as living off roots and berries."

"You can't keep food fresh for a week out in the wilderness."

"It's two miles away! And we have plenty of packaged food to—"

"Cold, fresh milk," I crooned. "Red, ripe strawberries."

"Get thee behind me, Satan."

I offered a winsome, satanic smile. Rowan threw up his hands in surrender. Then he held up a warning finger. "You have to promise to give us a few days alone."

"Absolutely."

"No popping up after rehearsal or dropping in for dinner."

"What about 'absolutely' didn't you understand?"

"I know you."

"Oh, please. I barge into your apartment one time—"

"Maggie . . ."

"I won't pop or drop. Promise."

We shook hands as we used to do to solemnize one of our pacts. And I resigned myself to spending more time apart from the men I loved.

CHAPTER 17

IT'S A HELLUVA WAY TO RUN A LOVE AFFAIR

ON THE PLUS SIDE, MY PERIOD ARRIVED the day they went into seclusion. That would spare us a reprise of the icky blood thing for another month. And give me time to pick up a box of condoms.

Like we're really going to make love when my father's in the next room listening to me yowl like a cat in heat.

I thrust that depressing thought aside and focused on more immediate concerns.

On Sunday evening, Frannie and I hosted a reception at the Bough so that the newly arrived cast members could meet the rest of the company before rehearsals for *The Secret Garden* began. To our relief, everybody seemed to have a good time and the reception was relatively clump-free.

I remained cautiously optimistic after Monday's read-through. Gregory might look more like a linebacker than my idealized version of tormented Archibald Craven, but he had angst up the wazoo. And as Reinhard sternly reminded me, "There is no rule that says you must be gaunt to be grief-stricken."

Or to play a ghost. Hal was still grumbling about casting a zaftig Mackenzie descendant as Lily. I sternly reminded him that while Michaela might not be ethereal, her lovely soprano was. But she was shy and awkward, lacking the serenity that Lily required, and I was glad to see Otis reassuring her during the break.

In the largely thankless role of Neville Craven, Roger

was a tad too queeny to convince anyone that he had ever pined for his brother's wife, but if toning him down was the biggest battle I faced during the next three weeks, I'd be a happy camper.

The supporting cast—largely locals and Mackenzies—had a pretty good grasp on their characters and a decidedly shaky one on their accents. A few managed a decent "stage British," but it was hard to keep a straight face when the rest trotted out their "Yorkshire" accents.

"I don't know why I bothered making those damn recordings," Janet fumed.

"I'm sure they helped," I said. "How did *you* master the Yorkshire accent?"

"I listened to the goddamn CD! Maybe they should try it."

I refrained from mentioning that they had. As for the sections in Hindi, I just prayed they wouldn't sound ridiculous, a tall order with lyrics like "mantra, tantra, yantra."

Otis had agreed to take on the role Bill had abandoned. He played one of the Dreamers—the ghosts who drift in and out to comment on the past and try to help those in the present. Debra was back to torment a fresh crop of children as the stern housekeeper Mrs. Medlock.

"It's my Wicked Witch summer," she commented after the read-through.

Since her third role was the Witch in *Into the Woods*, there seemed little point in denying it. "Don't take it personally."

"Are you kidding? It's a helluva lot more fun playing nasty than nice. I had a ball when I played the Stepmother in *Into the Woods* a few years ago."

"Who wouldn't enjoy sawing off bits of her daughters' feet so they would fit into the golden slipper?"

"Exactly."

"If we ever put on *Psycho: The Musical*, I'll know who to call."

"Now *that's* what you should do to bring in money during the off-season. Not *Psycho*. One of those murder mystery dinners." She jerked her thumb toward the Bates mansion. "You've already got the House on Haunted Hill."

It would be perfect for Halloween. If the board would

approve it. If Janet would go for yet another event in her
home. And if I could pull it together, run the after-school
program, and prepare for our Christmas production.

Think about it tomorrow, Scarlett.

I concentrated on blocking the Act One scenes with the
principals and left the chorus in Alex's capable hands. He
got dibs on the kids as well. Although Sallie and Natasha
were veterans of various school productions, Mary's songs
were difficult emotionally and vocally, often requiring the
actress to hold her melody line against two or three com-
peting voices. Colin's material was easier, but neither of my
ten-year-old actors were great singers. Having only an hour
a day to block the children's scenes made me anxious, but
the extra week in *Annie*'s run meant an extra week of rehearsals, so I tried to avoid obsessing.

My "one day at a time" mantra did little to quell my
anxiety about what was happening in Rowan's apartment.
The two men were as ghostly as Dreamers. Not even a foot-
step overhead betrayed their presence.

I was true to my promise. I didn't pop or drop. I just
lurked.

I took casual strolls around the barn during my breaks,
craning my neck for a glimpse of their figures through the
windows. I dropped off groceries and hovered at the door,
hoping to detect some sound from inside.

"You must have patience," Reinhard ordered.

"You've got to let Rowan do his thing," Lee advised.

"You're creeping me out," Hal complained. "Maggie
Graham, Stalker."

Rowan's letter put a stop to my not-so-clandestine surveillance. He must have slipped it under the front door because Janet handed it to me when I came down for breakfast
Thursday morning. I tore open the envelope with trembling
fingers.

"I know you're anxious," he began without preamble,
"but we are both fine and the work is going well. And although I can think of no one I would rather have pressing
an ear to my door, you are hereby forbidden to lurk. I love
you."

Not quite as romantic as the first letter he had written
me, but it left me with a warm glow that survived Neil's

disappointingly stilted performance as Dickon and Roger's inability to keep his hands off Gregory during the library scene.

Then we blocked the opening. Exit warm glow. Enter queasiness.

The music was difficult enough, but the staging was a bitch. It had to take the audience from India to a train platform to the door of Misselthwaite Manor to Mary's room to the gallery where Mary searches for the source of the mysterious crying while her uncle prowls around looking for the ghost of his dead wife. And like all the scenes with the Dreamers, the action had to flow seamlessly—song fragments interwoven with dialogue, Dreamers drifting in and out, past incidents mingling with those in the present.

I'd recognized early on that I would need Mei-Yin's help to stage the Dreamers' scenes. When she cheerfully agreed, I was surprised and excited. I was equally surprised—but far less excited—when she stormed into my office last February, brandishing a rolled-up script in one meaty fist, and demanded, "Where are the DANCE numbers?"

"There's a lot of dancing," I'd protested. "The opening is a—"

"A CHOLERA epidemic! With people passing around a red HANDKERCHIEF."

"It's a metaphor."

"I KNOW it's a metaphor! I'm not STUPID! And it's NOT a DANCE."

"Well, if you think about it, all the scenes with the Dreamers are like a ritualized—"

"I mean REAL dances."

"There's the waltz in the ballroom. And 'Come Spirit, Come Charm.'"

"With actors chanting HINDI? I TOLD you we should do *Gypsy*. THAT has kids. THAT has a STRIPTEASE. THAT I can choreograph."

"Mei-Yin. Did you . . . read the script?"

"Of COURSE I did! I read it last NIGHT!"

"I mean before we chose the show."

"It was ROWAN'S job to choose the shows! And HE chose NORMAL ones where the chorus sings a big SONG, the actors WITHOUT two left feet break into a big

DANCE, and the audience breaks into big APPLAUSE! THIS ..." She flung the script across the room. "I don't know WHAT this is."

Moments after she marched out of the office, Reinhard scuttled in.

"She will be fine," he assured me in a hoarse whisper. "Trust me. She will view the show as a challenge. It will excite her artistic sensibilities."

"Any idea how long that'll take?"

"A day. Maybe two. No more than a week. In the meantime ..."

"I'll stay out of her way."

Three days later, Mei-Yin breezed into the staff meeting and announced, "Sometimes, I'm so good, it's SCARY! I got it all figured out. Even the goddamn STORM sequences." She stabbed her forefinger at Hal. "I'll need a KICKASS set. And some KICKASS lighting, too!" she added, redirecting the forefinger to Lee. "So you boys better put on your THINKING caps."

Hal contented himself with an offended sniff. Lee just nodded wearily. Reinhard beamed. "Now the work can begin!"

To Mei-Yin's credit, her staging *was* good. Better than anything I could have dreamed up. Since I'd endured her rants when I was an actress and her regular pleas to shoot her since I'd become a director, I remained undaunted by the prospect of working cheek by jowl with her.

I woefully miscalculated the discomfort of having my cheek adjacent to Mei-Yin's jowl. Hence, the queasiness that shuddered through my stomach as we staged the opening.

"You're GHOSTS!" she shouted after our first walkthrough. "Not CONSTRUCTION workers! WAFT more, CLOMP less!"

"WAFT!" she shrieked after the second walk-through. "Not MINCE! You're GHOSTS, not CHORUS queens!"

She stormed out of the Smokehouse with Reinhard in hot pursuit. I hastily called a break. After peering outside to make sure Mei-Yin had left the vicinity, the actors dispersed.

Through the open windows, I heard someone ask, "Is she always like that?"

I couldn't identify the hushed voice, but it obviously belonged to one of the new members of the company.

"She's just getting warmed up," Debra replied.

"You should've heard her when she was teaching me to waltz," Otis said. " 'ONE-two-three. ONE-two . . . LEFT foot! LEFT! How many left feet you GOT?' "

"Does she get . . . nicer?" asked another unfamiliar voice.

"Not much," Debra replied cheerfully. "But you'll get used to her. Eventually."

Someone groaned. "I hope I live that long."

I trudged over to the piano where Alex was trying to keep a straight face.

"Easy for you," I grumbled. "She's not shouting in your ear."

"You just haven't seen her in action since you began directing."

Actually, I had. I'd made damn sure to sit in on her first rehearsals with the orphans. She wasn't exactly warm and fuzzy, but she *had* been encouraging. The strain of storing up so much unused bile was clearly showing now.

"Maybe it bugs you that you need her help with the staging," Alex said. "But you know what? She's having the time of her life. I can't remember when she's been this excited. And it's because you've given her more of an opportunity to shape this show than she's ever had before. Mind you, she'll never admit that. And you'll probably be deaf by opening night. But it's true."

I leaned down to kiss his forehead. "You know I'm crazy about you, right?"

"No, but if you hum a few bars . . ."

Reinhard appeared in the doorway, smoothing his troubled hair. He shot us a quick glance and nodded.

As the actors filtered in, Alex whispered, "I give her two more minutes. Then she'll sail into the Smokehouse—"

"And be sweet as pie."

Right on both counts. After the actors stumbled through the scene a third time, she regarded them with a maternal smile and purred, "Now that wasn't so hard, was it?"

Debra nudged Otis. He grinned. I made a mental note to

pick up a very large bottle of antacids on my next shopping trip.

❧❧

The Dreamers clomped, minced, and wafted. Mei-Yin ranted, raved, and purred. I gobbled Rolaids like breath mints and slipped a note under Rowan's door that accentuated the positive and pointed out that note-slipping didn't technically qualify as lurking. He slipped a note under Janet's door that assured me of his love and remarked that if I ever changed careers, I should consider becoming a lawyer.

"This is turning into Abelard and Heloise," Janet muttered.

"Don't be silly," I replied. Then rushed upstairs to search Wikipedia for Abelard and Heloise. I remembered their passionate correspondence. I'd forgotten the parts where he got her pregnant, her father castrated him, and they were both consigned to religious orders.

Given our enforced chastity and my mother's penchant for threatening Rowan's testicles, the similarities were depressing. I didn't even have erotic letters to fall back on. Rowan's latest note had included a brief protestation of love and a much longer list of grocery items. It's hard to whip up sexual fantasies with ingredients like lamb chops and orzo.

Since there was no immediate prospect of fulfilling any sexual fantasies, maybe that was a good thing. But I felt adrift and blue. A loverless lover, a fatherless daughter, and—in spite of Alex's pep talk—a rudderless director who needed help staging her show.

Hal was sympathetic, Janet, practical. My mother avoided any mention of Rowan during our usual Sunday morning phone chat. By contrast, Nancy called three times that week to see how things were going. On Sunday evening, I broke down and told her about my father.

She said, "Oh, my God!" about twenty times. In between, she asked how I was, how Daddy was, and then added, "How did Rowan ever find him?"

Let the lying begin.

"Daddy wrote a letter. To Rowan's father."

The imaginary one we made up two summers ago.

"It took awhile for the letter to reach Rowan."

You know how unreliable the Faerie postal service is.

"By then, Daddy had moved on and it took forever to track him down."

Since those pesky maps of the Borderlands shift as often as the landscape.

"And Rowan didn't want to tell you he was looking for him," Nancy said. "And raise your hopes. Is he going to be okay? Your dad?"

"He's getting better every day."

"He must have been so excited to see you."

I hesitated.

"Well, wasn't he?"

"I haven't told him that I'm his daughter. I want to give him time to settle in."

"What did your mom say?" When I hesitated again, Nancy's sigh gusted through the phone. "Oh, Maggie . . ."

"I'm going to tell her. When he's more like his old self."

"Oh, Maggie . . ."

"Stop saying, 'Oh, Maggie!' "

"Look how fast she figured out something was wrong at the fund-raiser. Never mind tracking you down two summers ago. The woman's a bloodhound!"

"I know, I know . . ."

By the time I hung up the phone, I'd hit the trifecta of guilt, depression, and loneliness. I slipped out of the house and wandered down to the pond. Too far from the theatre to qualify as lurking, but close enough to feel connected to the men inside.

The pale rectangles of light on the barn's roof cheered me; at least Daddy was no longer hiding from "the eyes." I sat on one of the benches, imagining them finishing their lamb chops and orzo, enjoying ice cream and strawberries, relaxing on the sofa.

As twilight faded into dusk, the skylights deepened to gold. As if to complement them, tiny flashes of light drifted through the meadow—the fireflies beginning their mating dance. I half-expected the staff to emerge from the trees as they always did in my dream. Instead, the breeze freshened, carrying the scent of rain, and I reluctantly rose.

As I reached the picnic area, I caught the faint notes of a piano and the answering strum of a guitar. When I recognized the melody, I sank down on a picnic bench.

I had heard "Try to Remember" dozens of times last season. Tonight, the song seemed even more poignant and bittersweet, the simple words evoking thoughts of my father's youth when he was as green and tender as the grass, and love was just beginning to blossom.

At first, Daddy merely echoed "Follow, follow, follow" in a sweet but tentative baritone. But on the final verse, he took the melody, his voice gaining power as he sang of wounded hearts that could be healed and cold Decembers warmed by memories.

In the long silence after the song ended, I wondered if he was recalling the bright promise of his youth or his lost dreams and lost family. Could Rowan heal the wounds that had gnawed at his heart and spirit for so many years? Could I?

Still aching from their song, I was shocked by the sound of Daddy's laughter. A moment later, Rowan launched into "You're Getting to Be a Habit with Me." Daddy interrupted him halfway through the first verse with "You Do Something to Me."

The singing quickly escalated into a contest. Rowan sang "You Could Drive a Person Crazy." Daddy broke in with "Let's Call the Whole Thing Off." Rowan advised Daddy to "Take It on the Chin" and Daddy demanded that he "Put On a Happy Face." They "lahdle-ahdle-ahdled" their way through "Friendship" and "doodle-oodle-oodled" their way through "A Bushel and a Peck." Then Rowan warbled "We Are Dainty Little Fairies" and the contest ended in exuberant laughter.

My father sounded so happy, so . . . normal. No longer babbling show tunes in an effort to cling to sanity, but singing and clowning for the sheer joy of it. If only I could find a way to sustain that happiness.

And then I thought of the Follies. Why not invite Rowan and Daddy to join our annual evening of staff silliness? It would ease them both into the world of the Crossroads and give them something fun to anticipate.

I was so excited that I failed to notice that Rowan had begun playing again. When I recognized "Some Enchanted Evening," I smiled. And when Rowan imitated my mocking delivery from auditions, I knew he was singing to me.

I should have realized he would sense my presence; maybe he had even called me from the house, knowing that sharing my father's happiness would ease my anxieties more than any note. Now he was offering another gift: the song we had shared at our first meeting.

As he continued singing, the mockery vanished, replaced by the quiet surprise of hearing laughter across a crowded room, the unexpected joy of discovering that same laughter in his dreams, the wonder of realizing that something impossible was happening.

His voice resonated with the passion we had shared, the pain of our separation, and the love that had brought him back to me. Our whole relationship captured in a song I had chosen on the spur of the moment, a song I had once dismissed as overblown and sappy, a song that became a reaffirmation of his vow never to leave me.

The final note faded. One by one, the golden rectangles of light winked out. A rumble of thunder urged me back to the house, but still, I lingered.

I felt more than saw him on the balcony outside his bedroom. His power embraced me and offered yet another promise: that tomorrow, we would be together again.

Ignoring the raindrops spattering my face, I skipped along the walkway singing "A Wonderful Guy." Rowan's affection and amusement bubbled through me like champagne.

So what if it wasn't the moon-happy night of Oscar Hammerstein's lyrics? I still had a conventional star in my eye and a definite lump in my throat.

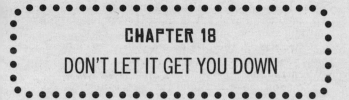

CHAPTER 18
DON'T LET IT GET YOU DOWN

ROWAN WAS WAITING OUTSIDE THE BARN the next morning, his energy zinging with the same excitement I felt. He swept me up in his arms and spun me around. We were both breathless and laughing when he set me on my feet again.

My laughter died when I saw his eyes, a dull gray-green instead of vivid emerald.

"My God, what happened?"

"I had to use more of my power than I'd anticipated. To calm him," he quickly added, "not to brainwash him. He's stronger than he was, but his moods are still . . . unpredictable."

I cupped Rowan's cheeks between my palms, as if I could somehow restore the power that had been drained from him, and was rewarded by a smile.

"Spending the day with you is the best possible medicine."

"But . . . I have rehearsals all day."

His smile vanished. "On a Monday?"

"The *Annie* cast has the day off, but I'm working scenes for *The Secret Garden*."

"Well. There's still lunch."

"Staff meeting. But we could squeeze in a quick dinner."

His smile returned, but I knew how disappointed he must be.

"Why don't I print out a copy of the schedule? That way, we'll be able to make plans for the rest of the week."

577

He followed me into the barn. Every time I glanced back, his smile was firmly in place. I would have preferred if he'd bitched me out.

As we neared the production office, he said, "At least your evenings will be free."

"Some of them. But I have the show most nights."

"You don't have to attend every performance."

I stopped, frowning. "You did."

"I had to be there. In case anything went wrong."

"And I don't?"

He hesitated, clearly searching for the right words.

"Look, I may not have the faery magic to avert a train wreck, but at least I can be there while my cast deals with the derailment. And laugh with them later about how Jeff turned a runaway inner tube into a moment of comic genius. And how two of the Hooverville residents pulled the newspapers out of their shirts to clean up when Fifi took a dump onstage!"

"One of your actors defecated on—?"

"The dog, Rowan! Fifi's the dog!"

"Ah."

"Sometimes humans need to work stuff out for themselves."

"If I didn't realize that, I would have told you why I cast you the first day we met."

"I know! It's just . . . I need to be there. To be part of whatever happens. The way you were part of that day with Maya and Gary."

His expression softened at the memory of that completely human moment of magic that had occurred during a disastrous rehearsal of *The Sea-Wife*.

"I'm afraid you're in love with a selfish pig," he said, "instead of a wonderful guy."

"Shut up and kiss me."

He shut up and kissed me.

When we came up for air, I murmured, "I suppose I could skip one show."

That was all the encouragement he needed. His long, lingering kiss sent a little shock wave of desire rippling through my body.

"Mmm . . . maybe two."

Golden sparks flashed in his eyes. Was it my imagination or were they greener than they had been a few moments ago? He kissed me again and I forgot about his eyes. I forgot about pretty much everything except his teasing tongue and his hands sliding up under my T-shirt and his body molded to mine.

When he suddenly released me, I clung to him, dizzy and dazed. Then I heard Daddy calling Rowan's name. I was still smoothing my shirt when he rounded the corner.

He'd shaved off his scraggly beard and mustache. Without them, his jaw and neck looked pale and oddly vulnerable. But for the first time, he looked like my father.

"Where were you?" he demanded. "I've been calling and calling."

"I told you I was going outside to meet Maggie."

"You were gone a long time." He studied us for a moment, then grinned. "Someone's been making out," he chanted in a singsong voice.

"Someone would have made out much better if you had remained in the apartment," Rowan replied.

"Look at Maggie blush! Her face is as red as a tomato!"

Since the floor showed no inclination to swallow me, I quickly asked, "How are you, Jack?"

Daddy's expression grew solemn. "Well, I won't lie to you. I went through some bad times. Drugs, alcohol, you name it. But a few years ago, I finally got my shit together. Even started acting again. I was—"

"Jack," Rowan interrupted. "Maggie knows the truth. You don't have to put on an act for her."

"But it was a good act, wasn't it?"

"Very good," I assured him, still a little stunned by his recitation. "Very . . . believable."

"I added the part about getting my shit together. It sounded more natural than what Rowan wanted me to say."

"That was an especially nice touch."

"And don't I look good without the beard?"

"You look ten years younger."

"I smell good, too."

He stuck out his chin, and I obediently sniffed. The rush of emotion as I breathed in the familiar scent caught me unprepared.

"Don't you like it?" Daddy asked.

"It's my favorite," I managed.

"See, Rowan? You should have used some."

"I don't shave."

"Yeah, but still . . ." Daddy winked at me and crooned, " 'There's something about an Aqua Velva man.' "

"Yes, there is," I agreed. "I'm so glad you're feeling better. And that you're not worried about 'the eyes' or the Crow-Men or—"

"I don't want to talk about them!"

As I recoiled at his unexpected outburst, Rowan snapped, "Jack! You don't respond to concern with rudeness."

Daddy flinched. "I just . . . I don't like thinking about them."

I nodded, silently cursing myself for spoiling his happy mood.

"Let's talk about something fun," he said. "Like our picnic. Rowan's been cooking all morning . . ." He glanced uncertainly from me to Rowan. "What? Did I blow the surprise?"

No, I did.

"I'm afraid I'll have to skip the picnic. I have a meeting at lunchtime and—"

"Just cancel it," Daddy said with an airy wave of his hand.

"I can't. But we could pack up Rowan's food and take it to the picnic area for dinner."

His crestfallen expression made it clear that was a poor substitute. As I groped for a solution, inspiration struck.

"Why don't we have our picnic on the Fourth of July? The theatre's dark so everyone can go to the fireworks at the high school."

"I love fireworks!" Daddy exclaimed.

Wilmington's display had always been the highlight of the summer, both of us in such a fever of anticipation that we hardly tasted the food my poor mother prepared. I loved the brilliant colors and screamed with excitement at every big "boom." It took me so many hours to calm down afterward that Mom threatened each year would be the last. And each year, he wheedled her into attending again.

"Just think, Rowan. Your first time in town and we'll have fireworks to celebrate. It's perfect!"

His dubious expression suggested otherwise. "Are you sure you're ready for this, Jack?"

"Yes! I'm sick of being stuck in that stuffy old apartment. I want to get out and see things. And eat some real food. Not that fancy-schmancy stuff you cook."

"What is so 'fancy-schmancy' about pepper-crusted grilled tuna with basmati rice and a frisée and pear salad?"

Daddy and I exchanged glances and started laughing.

"Tell you what," I told Daddy. "After I print out the rehearsal schedule for Rowan, we'll set a date for lunch at the Chatterbox Café."

"The Chatterbox is still here? Man, I'd kill for one of their chocolate shakes. And a burger. And fries!"

Smiling at his enthusiasm, I unlocked the office door. As it swung open, I glanced at Rowan to gauge his reaction to the changes. He hadn't said a word about the green room. Could he possibly miss those awful furnishings? Maybe if I'd lived with them for decades, I'd feel nostalgic, too.

His expression was completely neutral as he took in the new desk and the landline phone. Then two small furrows appeared between his brows. I realized he was frowning at the laptop. His laptop.

"I'm sorry. I meant to tell you we were using it. Reinhard found it in your armoire. And since we needed a computer for the office—"

"Of course."

"I'll just use mine. It's no big deal to carry it back and forth from the house."

"No, keep this one. At least until the season's over. I only used it to watch movies."

"What are you talking about?" Daddy demanded.

Frantically, I tried to recall whether we'd had a personal computer when he lived in Wilmington. If so, it would have looked nothing like the laptop. Would he freak out if I showed him its features—or guess that it had required decades to invent them?

"What computer?" Daddy insisted.

I gave the laptop a tentative pat.

"That's a computer? I thought it was a hot plate!"

Relieved by his reaction, I said, "They'll probably add that feature to the next model."

"But where's the screen? And the keyboard?"

I opened the laptop, and he gasped. When the wallpaper came up with its photo of Stonehenge, he gasped again.

"I was there. I saw that. What are all the little pictures around it?"

"You click on them to open the program you want."

"Wait—the stuff at the bottom just disappeared."

"It'll come back if you move the arrow down there."

As I skimmed my fingertip over the touchpad to demonstrate, he said, "Let me try."

Still dazed by his enthusiastic acceptance of all the technological changes, I eased aside. Finally, I could do something for him besides buying clothes and food.

He guided the arrow along the icons at the bottom, crowing with delight each time a descriptor popped up.

I smiled at Rowan. "It might take a little while to print out that schedule."

Rowan tensed. At first, I thought he was upset with me. Then I realized Daddy had fallen silent.

He was staring at the screen. In the bottom right-hand corner I saw a tiny beige pop-up field with the day of the week, the month, the date—and the year.

Oh, God . . .

Rowan gripped Daddy's shoulder. Daddy shook him off impatiently and pointed a trembling forefinger at the screen. "Is that the year? Is that *this* year?"

As I nodded miserably, Rowan steered Daddy over to the wooden chair near the file cabinet and eased him onto it.

"Twenty years," Daddy whispered. "I thought five, maybe. Ten at the most." His gaze slowly focused, and he glared at Rowan. "Why didn't you tell me?"

"I thought it might be . . . unsettling."

"No shit, Sherlock!"

When Rowan's hand settled on his shoulder again, Daddy leaped up with such violence that his chair toppled over. "Stop calming me! Just for once, let me *feel*!"

He backed into the file cabinet. Then the anger left his face and he slowly slid down its smooth wooden side and sank onto the floor.

Stupid, stupid, stupid!

Reinhard and I had gone through the theatre, taking down wall calendars, dated notices, anything that might set Daddy off. The rest of the staff had been warned to keep their organizers and datebooks under wraps. But I had been so eager to prove how knowledgeable I was that I'd forgotten the fucking date popped up when you passed the arrow over the time.

Daddy's shoulders began to shake. Only when he looked up did I realize he was laughing. A hoarse croak of a laugh, but not the tears I had expected.

"Twenty years. And except for that . . ." He nodded at the laptop. ". . . everything looks the same."

"Communications technology changes very quickly," explained Rowan, who didn't even have a phone in his apartment.

"What else has changed?"

This time, Rowan deferred to me. "There are mobile phones now that fit into the palm of your hand. And flat screen TVs. And something called the Internet. It's this big global network . . . thing. You can send messages and watch movies and order stuff from stores and play interactive games and—"

"Show me."

I spent the next hour teaching him the basics and conducting a whirlwind tour of the last twenty years. Daddy hurled questions at me and I fumbled for answers, painfully aware that I knew more about Tony Award winners than the events that had shaped and shaken my world.

"A black dude?" he exclaimed. "Was elected President?"

"Mixed race, but—"

"Next you'll be telling me Arnold Schwarzenegger is Secretary of Defense."

"No. But he *was* Governor of California. And Jesse Ventura—the wrestler? He was Governor of Minnesota."

Daddy burst out laughing. Real laughter this time—the same exuberant bellow I'd heard last night.

"Jeez, when it comes to crazy, this world has the Borderlands beat by a mile."

At some point, Rowan left. I suppressed my guilt at ignoring him and vowed to make up for it at dinner.

With only minutes before rehearsal began, I said, "You know, you can find other things on the Internet. Old TV shows, old friends . . . family . . ."

My heart pounded like a rabbit's as he scrutinized the screen. Then his face lit up and he began to type.

"Over two million results!" he crowed.

He was so absorbed in his findings that he never even noticed when I walked out.

I'd hoped—no, I'd expected him to search for me or Mom. But after so many years apart from us, so many years without even knowing if we were alive, what was he most eager to find?

Ms. fucking Pac-Man.

The best part about working with magical people is that you never have to tell them you're upset. It's also the worst part because you can't hide anything. My little ups and downs generally passed unnoticed, but any major emotional roller coaster drew them like bears to honey.

So naturally, just when I needed to ride out this roller coaster, Rowan, Reinhard, and Alex all converged on me in the stage right wings. And naturally, I took one look at my three bears and burst into tears.

They clustered around me, offering masculine comfort and soothing magic. When I explained what had happened, Alex suggested Daddy might have needed some sort of distraction after the shock of finding out how much time had passed. Reinhard observed that he was unready to deal with the guilt of deserting his family.

Rowan demanded, "So he searches for some woman instead?"

I had to laugh. Alex joined me. Even Reinhard's lips twitched as he enlightened Rowan about arcade games and the true identity of Ms. Pac-Man.

The unexpected laughter eased the pain a little. Blocking Scene 4 forced me to focus on something else. By the time our staff meeting rolled around, I was able to turn the whole incident into an amusing anecdote. I didn't fool anyone, of course. Maybe that was why they agreed to invite Daddy to perform in the Follies.

After the meeting, I pulled the box containing Rowan's keepsakes out of my bedroom closet. It was the first time I had opened it in more than a year.

I set aside his script of *By Iron, Bound*, his battered copy of the 1836 edition of the *McGuffey Reader*, and the equally battered diary in which he'd recorded his first thoughts and feelings. Then I unearthed the slim leather-bound journal he had kept during my season at the Crossroads. I flipped through the pages until I found the passage I was seeking.

"Jack Sinclair. Now there's a pathetic imitation of a man. Charming, yes. And clever. About everything except himself. But completely self-absorbed. And arrogant and superior. Always making excuses for his failures."

Those bitter words filled my mind as I trudged up to Rowan's apartment after rehearsal. Daddy's enthusiastic greeting surprised me. I was even more surprised when he asked about my day.

I glanced at Rowan, wondering if he'd coached him. But Daddy seemed genuinely interested so I started talking about the show. He loved the idea of the magical garden and nodded thoughtfully when I explained its themes of healing and transformation. But he was more interested in the characters. At one point, he exclaimed, "I'd be great for Archibald!" And immediately began reminiscing about some of the roles he had played.

Rowan was very quiet during dinner. But as he walked me to my evening rehearsal, he said, "Be patient, Maggie. And don't expect more than he can give."

I nodded wearily. "Did you tell him to ask about my day?"

Rowan hesitated. "I told him he should have thanked you for teaching him. And that he should think more about other people's feelings."

"So should I."

"What do you mean?"

"I ignored you to show Daddy how to use the Internet. Like father, like daughter."

"Hush."

"I'm sorry."

This time, he hushed me with a kiss. Then he asked, "Did you ever read my journals?"

Surprised by the sudden shift in the conversation, I said, "The one from my year. And the early ones. But once people I knew began showing up ... it just made me uncomfortable."

"Then you never read about your father's season here?"

I shook my head.

"Maybe you should."

I'd deliberately avoided reading that journal. I'd come to terms with my past—and my father—and saw little benefit in picking at those wounds. Daddy's return had pretty much ripped off the Band-Aid. So instead of going straight to my bedroom, I climbed the stairs to the attic.

Each spring, Hal and I sorted through the costumes and set pieces we might want to use during the upcoming season. The only other time I'd ventured there was when I'd helped Reinhard carry up the five boxes containing the rest of Rowan's journals.

I opened the door and groped for the light switch. A single naked bulb blazed to life over my head. I made out the shadowy forms of sheet-draped furniture. Garment bags hung like corpses from the rows of clothes racks. It looked much spookier at night than it had during the day and I was glad I didn't have to rummage around to find Rowan's journals; the boxes were only a few feet from the door, as carefully labeled as the boxes of props nestled under the eaves.

I opened the one on top and easily found the journal from Daddy's season, its first page inscribed with the year in Rowan's neat handwriting. As I straightened, I bashed my head against a slanting roof beam and got a faceful of cobweb.

Not an auspicious beginning.

I retreated to my bedroom, clutching the journal in my left hand and massaging the top of my head with my right. I sank into Helen's rocking chair and turned on the light, wishing for some of her calming energy. Then I took a deep breath and opened the journal.

I knew Daddy had arrived only days before Midsummer to begin rehearsals for the second show. Oddly, neither Rowan nor my mother had ever mentioned that it was *Camelot.* Now, I learned that he had played one of the knights defeated by Lancelot in the joust.

I skimmed the pages, seeking other references to Daddy, and winced when I found them.

"*Jack was quite good at the read-through, but clearly disdainful of his cast mates.*"

"*Jack took me aside to suggest that he take over the role of Arthur. The man has bullocks the size of basketballs and an ego to match. Yet underneath it all, his insecurity throbs like a heartbeat. He is so eager for me to like and respect him, but fails to see that his behavior accomplishes just the opposite. Still, these are early days. And my perceptions are always suspect at Midsummer.*"

I turned the page and braced myself for a description of Daddy's encounter with Rowan's clan. Instead, there was only a hastily scrawled word: "*Disaster.*"

Ragged edges were all that remained of the next three pages. Perhaps Rowan had decided it was too dangerous to leave a record of the incident. The next entry—dated three days after Midsummer—said only: "*It is done. And if we watch him carefully, all may yet be well.*"

Every entry for the rest of the season contained some snippet about my father. Reading between the lines of Rowan's cryptic entries, I pieced together his transformation from the dazed man who had rejoined the company to the hard working one who enjoyed the fellowship of his cast mates and put so much of himself into the character of Billy Bigelow: the fear beneath the bravado; the doubts beneath the swagger; the desire to make amends to his wife and child.

Rowan's last entry for the season read:

"*Met Jack's wife. I had hoped that seeing the show—and seeing how it has changed Jack—might reconcile her to his long absence. But she eyes both of us with suspicion, unable to accept his transformation and unwilling to exonerate me for luring him away.*

Perhaps she's seen Jack's chameleon act too often to trust his latest incarnation. And perhaps she is wise. Whatever else I accomplished, I did not change Jack's nature. Once he leaves, his dissatisfaction with himself and his life might resurface.

I hope I'm wrong. Mostly for the child's sake. Such a pretty little thing, with that shining cap of bright red hair. And clearly

*her father's daughter. She was practically falling over from ex-
haustion until he appeared. Then her face lit up and she cried,
"Daddy!" And from the look on his face and the way he swept
her into his arms and spun around and around with her . . . yes,
I think I'm right to hope.*

*If anyone can save Jack Sinclair from himself, his daugh-
ter can."*

Fat chance. It was Rowan's magic that had brought him
back from the brink of madness; Rowan's coaching that had
helped him create a new persona. So far, all I'd done was
reintroduce him to Ms. Pac-Man and promise him an evening of fireworks.

My father was as much a stranger as ever. He was my
indulgent, imaginative playmate and the haunted, unpredictable stranger locked away in the basement. The "lost
boy" my mother had loved and the restless, unhappy one
that Rowan had known. In the last few days, I'd added new
pieces to the puzzle: the terrified Rip Van Winkle; the impatient, demanding child; the charming Aqua Velva man.

How could I help my father find his place in this world
when I didn't even know who he was?

I undressed and crawled into bed. Tired as I was, sleep
eluded me. I tossed restlessly, beat my pillow into submission, and tossed some more.

I was reaching for the bedside lamp when warmth enfolded me. And with it, the fleeting sensation I'd experienced in Rowan's apartment of something caressing my
cheek.

I breathed in the faint scent of lavender.

"Helen?" I whispered to the darkness.

The only reply was a deep peace that banished my anxiety and eased me gently into sleep.

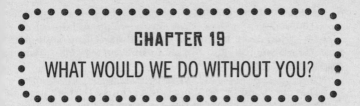

CHAPTER 19

WHAT WOULD WE DO WITHOUT YOU?

A DAY OF LACKLUSTER REHEARSALS—during which Daddy remained glued to the laptop—eroded that peace. So did the prospect of our Act One run-through, which ranked about as high on the "Can't Wait!" meter as a Pap smear.

The kids would be fine. They'd been strong from the beginning and had only grown in confidence. Gregory had cornered the market on inner torment, Michaela on sweetness. But the chorus was having a tough time with the vocals, and in spite of Mei Yin's hectoring, their scenes looked more like a bunch of lost travelers wandering through Grand Central than restless spirits wafting through Misselthwaite Manor.

And then there was Roger.

"He's turning Neville into an incestuous gay stalker," I complained to Hal and Lee as we bolted pizza in the green room before the run-through.

Lee grinned. "Not what you were going for?"

"Not so much."

"That's a relief. I thought it was some radical reinterpretation of the character."

"'Too bad about 'Lily's Eyes,'" Hal said, nibbling a slice of pepperoni.

"The song is the one moment that works!"

"Yes, but if Neville didn't come right out and say he'd been in love with Lily, the incestuous gay love angle might work."

"But it would still be icky."

"True."

Lee tossed aside his pizza crust and picked up another slice. "Have you told him Neville is too repressed for public displays of affection?"

"Yes."

"That everyone in the show is too repressed to—?"

"Yes, yes, yes! The weird thing is, he seems to get it. But once he's onstage, it's like he can't help himself. And now Gregory's started."

"Started what?" Hal asked.

"Touching Roger almost as much as Roger's touching him!"

Hal's face lit up. "Maybe Gregory's coming out of the closet!"

"Great. My father went home after his season, obsessed with faeries. Now Gregory's becoming obsessed with the theatrical kind."

"We have to be supportive," Hal chided. "This is a very difficult and confusing time for him. Oh, I hope he won't get his heart broken. Roger can be such a bitch."

"He's not coming out," Lee said. "I didn't get any of the usual signals."

"Gaydar or Faedar?" I asked.

"Either. There's something else going on."

"As long as it goes on offstage."

"And you call yourself a helping professional," Hal scolded.

"Right now, I'm calling myself a director. If Roger doesn't butch up soon, I'll have to have him play Lily."

"If only," Hal muttered.

"Don't you dare start on Michaela!" I exclaimed.

"I'm not! She's a sweetheart. It's just . . ." Hal sighed.

"I thought you of all people would be more sensitive."

Hal slowly lowered his glass of diet soda. "Why? Because I'm fat, too?"

"You're not—"

"I may have gained a few pounds over the winter—"

"You're not fat!"

"Then why did you say—?"

"Because you know what it's like to get bullied for being

different. And you love dressing up in pretty things like she does. Only when she looks in the mirror, she doesn't see a beautiful woman with sexy curves. She sees a fat chick." I grabbed Hal's arm. "Could you push up her costume fittings? Maybe when she puts on one of those lovely dresses . . ."

"She'll see a fat chick in a lovely dress," Lee said.

"Not if I'm her mirror!" Hal declared. "She'll see in my eyes that she's beautiful. Who wouldn't be in a lavender silk ball gown with silver lace and sequin embroidery?"

Emboldened by his dreamy expression, I threw caution to the wind. "Maybe if she wore it tonight . . ."

"Absolutely not!" Hal exclaimed. "It's the most beautiful costume I've ever made and I'm not having it ruined before opening night."

"The more beautiful she feels, the more ethereal she'll look. Please?"

Hal heaved a dramatic sigh. "It'll have to be the coral chiffon garden dress. That's already been fitted. Or the white cotton-and-lace afternoon dress. No, that'll get filthy."

Still mulling possibilities, he hurried down the stairs to the costume shop. Lee snatched the last slice of pizza and headed for the lighting booth. I played housewife and cleaned up. Fortunately, that just meant rinsing our glasses and tossing out the pizza box.

I wound my way through the maze of *Annie* set pieces in the wings and dodged the first wave of actors hurrying toward the Dungeon to don character shoes, rehearsal skirts, and the few costume pieces Hal permitted them to wear before dress rehearsal. Reinhard—ever unwilling to trust them to sign in—stood guard by the stage left steps, checking off names on the call sheet attached to his clipboard.

His head came up, and he stared past me into the stage right wings. A moment later, I heard Rowan greeting Javier. The butterflies dancing in my stomach morphed into pterodactyls performing loop-de-loops. Of course, I wanted him and Daddy to see my work; I just wished their first exposure to it was a polished performance of *Annie*.

Reinhard gave me a reassuring nod, but the tension in his body betrayed his anxiety. No one on staff had objected to Rowan attending the run-through, but I wondered if they were as nervous as I was about his reaction.

Daddy walked out of the wings and glanced around warily, but if Rowan felt any discomfort at the prospect of seeing Maggie Graham, Director, it was well hidden behind his easy smile.

"We just wanted to wish you good luck," Rowan said.

Daddy stared at him, aghast. "It's bad luck to wish her good luck."

"That only applies to actors."

"No, it doesn't!"

"Just don't let Reinhard hear you," I said. "He'll want to perform a cleansing ritual."

"Hear what?" Reinhard called from across the stage. How he could detect my whispers and fail to hear Rowan speaking in normal tones was beyond me.

Before I could answer, Bernie called, "Rowan! About time you crawled out of that apartment!"

"That's Bernie," I whispered to Daddy as Rowan trotted down the steps. "He's on the board, but he helps out with the box office and program, too. He doesn't know anything about Faerie. We just told him the story you and Rowan came up with. Come on, I'll introduce you."

"Maybe later."

"He's a great guy. You'll like him."

Reluctantly, Daddy followed me into the house. Rowan and Bernie walked down the aisle, Bernie chattering like an excited squirrel and Rowan smiling at him with affection.

"Would it have killed you to age a little? I'm not asking for much. A couple lines around the eyes. A few gray hairs. Something to prove you were miserable without us."

"Trust me, Bernie, I was miserable."

"Good!" He smiled at Daddy. "Bernie Cohen. You must be Jack. How does it feel to be back at the Crossroads?"

"Well, I won't lie to you. I went through some bad times. Drugs, alcohol, you name it. But a few years ago, I finally got my shit together. Even started acting again. I was in between gigs and staying at a friend's cabin in the mountains when I wrote to Rowan's dad, asking if he had anything for me here. And who do you think shows up at the door? Rowan! Hadn't seen him since he was a kid. Well, you could have blown me away with a feather."

Clearly, his monologue was in danger of blowing Bernie

away, too, but he recovered quickly and said, "Well, it's great to have you here. Maggie tells me you're becoming quite the computer expert. If you feel like pitching in with the program, I'd love the help."

Before Daddy could reply, laughter rang out in the house.

"Do my eyes deceive me," Long called, "or is that Rowan Mackenzie?"

"Longford Martindale," I murmured to Daddy. "President of the board."

Daddy straightened. Rowan merely looked resigned. I'd warned him that Long might be here tonight. No matter how many times I begged him to wait until dress rehearsal to see the show, he invariably "popped in" for the runthroughs. The squirming usually began during the first scene, and by the time we were finished, he was convinced we had a disaster on our hands.

"This *is* a pleasure!" Long exclaimed as he shook Rowan's hand. "Although not exactly a surprise. I always suspected there was something between you two. And Maggie's blushes prove that my instincts were correct."

After favoring me with a brief leer, Long turned to Daddy, eyebrows elevated.

"This is Jack Sinclair," I said. "An old friend of Rowan's."

"Long Martindale. Delighted."

"Jack worked here years ago," Rowan said. "He played Billy Bigelow in *Carousel*."

"Why, of course!"

Hard to tell if he remembered or was just turning on the charm, but his enthusiasm made Daddy beam.

"What have you been doing since then, Jack?"

"Well, I won't lie to you. I went through some bad times—"

"But he's turned the corner in the last few years," Rowan interrupted. "Since he was between acting jobs, I invited him to spend a few weeks at the Crossroads."

"Wonderful! And what about you, Rowan? Are you just visiting? Or dare I hope that you'll be staying?"

"I hope to stay a very long while."

Rowan's warm gaze brought another wave of heat to my cheeks.

"Excellent! We must have dinner. We have a great deal

to discuss. Maggie's been filling in as artistic director because of our precarious funding situation, but all that's changing. I'd love to get you back on board and free her up to focus on her responsibilities as executive director."

As he rambled on, my face grew even hotter. Was he actually suggesting that I step aside? In the middle of the fucking season? Maybe Rowan was a hundred times the director I was, but these were *my* shows.

Before I could vent my outrage, Rowan said, "There will be plenty of time to discuss next season after this one's over."

"Naturally, naturally. But you can't blame me for being eager when I see my dream team standing before me."

"Your dream team?" I faltered.

"Why, you and Rowan, of course! Normally, I'd be leery of hiring a couple. So much potential for professional difficulties if personal ones should arise. But the rest of the staff manages just fine. I'm beginning to think this theatre is the crossroads of romance!"

Sweat prickled my forehead as I realized how close I had come to going off the deep end, alienating Long, and making a complete fool of myself.

Long glanced at his watch. "Well, it's almost time. Let's take our seats, shall we?"

As he escorted my reluctant father up the aisle, Bernie whispered, "Don't worry about your dad. He just needs to get his sea legs. And I meant it about helping with the program. Get him involved, that's the ticket!"

I hugged him so hard that Rowan had to grasp his arm to steady him.

"Catherine and I usually sit behind Maggie," Bernie told Rowan. "We're the 'Pat Her Shoulders During the Train Wrecks' Brigade. But if you need me to keep Long out of your hair . . ."

"I'll manage," Rowan replied. "Besides, I'd hate to break up the brigade."

I waited for Bernie to make his way up the aisle before whispering to Rowan, "Thanks for jumping in with Long."

"Did you really believe he wanted to replace you?"

"He thinks I'm a novice."

"Well . . . you are."

"I know! But on opening night of *Annie*, he told me the show fell short of your high standards, so excuse me if I'm a little sensitive."

"Stop bristling."

"I'm not—"

"Yes, you are. And stop comparing yourself to me."

"I'm not—"

"Yes. You are."

I sighed. "Yes. I am."

"Maggie, I have more directing experience than Hal Prince, George Abbott, and Jerome Robbins combined. You could direct for the next fifty years and you'd still be a novice compared to me."

"I know that!"

"Lower your voice. Long's watching." Rowan studied me, frowning. "Why do you do this to yourself?"

"Because I know what it's like to work with you. And I want to give my actors that same magic."

"Well, you can't. You're not a faery. So give them your passion, your determination, your . . . the staff's told you this a hundred times, haven't they?"

"Two hundred, three hundred. I've lost count. I'm just nervous about tonight. I don't want you to be disappointed."

"If it's anything like my run-throughs, the cast will blow their harmonies, drop half their lines and all of their props, and exit through a window instead of a door."

"Well, as long as you have high expectations."

He smiled. "Go do your job. I've got to keep an eye on Jack."

Please God, don't let Daddy say anything damaging in front of Long. And don't let the run-through suck.

———

For about thirty seconds, the run-through was terrific. In her coral chiffon garden dress, Michaela looked as beautiful as she sounded. Then Paul came on for his solo. It took me a few seconds to figure out what was off about his performance: his nighttime role as Oxydent Hour of Smiles host Bert Healy was bleeding into his *Secret Garden* role. The result was a cheesy, breezy Indian Fakir chanting the Hindi equivalent of "you're never fully dressed without a smile."

The Dreamers clomped through the rest of the opening like Clydesdales. During "The House Upon the Hill," Debra managed to shout out her lines over their impossibly loud "Oohs," but Natasha looked like a mime trapped in a glass box.

From somewhere behind me, I heard the ominous squeak of Long's seat. The squirming had begun.

The squeaking became more prolonged after Gregory's entrance. I'd complained to Hal that the first hump he'd created was barely noticeable under the layers of shirt, vest, and frockcoat. No such worries tonight.

"He looks like a goddamn DROMEDARY!" Mei-Yin whispered.

Hal was already hurrying toward the stage. The next time Gregory appeared, he was humpless.

He was also largely unintelligible. It wasn't entirely his fault. "I Heard Someone Crying" was the first of several numbers where each actor sang a different lyrical thread. In the best of all possible worlds, their voices would weave together to create a unified whole. In our world, they created a wall of incomprehensible noise. "It's a Maze" was marginally better, but only because Ben and Natasha kept dropping out, Ben when he lost his melody line and Natasha whenever she tripped over her jump rope.

In spite of my repeated notes, Roger and Gregory were all over each other during the library scene: gripping a shoulder, squeezing a bicep, smoothing a fucking shirtfront. Long before the scene concluded, I wanted to inter them both in "A Bit of Earth."

They redeemed themselves with "Lily's Eyes." And Natasha and Ethan captured all the anger and resentment, humor and pathos I could have wanted in the Scene 7 meeting of Mary and Colin. Even the blocking in the final storm sequence worked—at first. Then the number devolved into yet another wall of noise with Natasha looking more exhausted than terrified and the chorus staggering around like zombies in the final stages of decomposition.

By the time Natasha opened the door to the secret garden and Alex pounded out the final chords on the piano, I was awash in flop sweat. The staff gamely applauded. Bernie and Catherine patted my shoulders. Mei-Yin whispered, "I need a DRINK!"

Although I felt like a condemned prisoner walking the green mile, I put a smile on my face and a bounce in my step as I trotted down the aisle. Alex hoisted himself out of the pit, smiling just as brightly. The cast slumped onstage, grim-faced and silent.

"Come on, people, it wasn't *that* bad. We'll smooth out the staging and the vocals in the big musical numbers over the next few days. Now for the good news. Natasha and Ethan—you both did terrific work tonight."

"Here, here!" Debra said.

The cast applauded. Natasha and Ethan glowed.

Maybe I couldn't create magic for my actors, but I *had* helped create this sense of community. And maybe before the end of this season, my father would be able to share it.

I praised their hard work, "oyed" over some of the mishaps, and promised Gregory that Hal would give him a good hump. Gregory looked startled, I blushed, and the cast began to chuckle. I removed my foot from my mouth and said, "Notes can wait until tomorrow. For now, go home and get a good night's rest."

Alex and I kept our smiles in place until the last actor drifted into the wings. Then we sank down on the stage, our feet dangling over the apron.

"Sorry I let you down," he said.

"You never let me down."

"The group numbers were awful."

"They're hard numbers, Alex! We knew that going in."

As Lee brought up the house lights, the rest of the staff trooped down the aisle toward us. I was dismayed to discover Long heading my way as well—and even more dismayed when I realized Daddy had vanished. Maybe he'd just wanted to escape from Long. Rowan was still sitting quietly in his seat, so nothing too awful could have happened.

I focused my wandering attention on the changes we would have to make in the schedule to accommodate the extra musical rehearsals we clearly needed.

"These local actors and their work schedules are KILL-ING us!" Mei-Yin complained.

"Tell me about it," Alex replied. "Next year—"

"Let's get through this one," I interrupted.

"Next year," Alex repeated, shooting a stern look at Long, "we've either got to cast people who'll commit to attending every rehearsal or hire an assistant vocal coach. Or both."

"We have never had to hire an assistant in the past," Reinhard pointed out.

"Because I always managed to wheedle some poor fool actor into helping out."

I raised my hand. "Poor fool actor. Duly wheedled."

"So wheedle someone NOW!" Mei-Yin demanded.

"The best musicians are in this show," Alex replied. "And they need to concentrate on learning their material, not teaching their cast mates."

Long regarded us with a beneficent smile. "You're overlooking your most valuable resource." When we all stared at him, he called, "Would you mind coming down here, Rowan?"

"I can't ask Rowan to be my assistant," Alex said in a soft but vehement voice.

"Nonsense. I'm sure he'll be happy to help out."

Rowan joined us, his expression carefully neutral. He listened politely to Long and glanced at me before turning to Alex.

"Tell me what you need."

"Four more hands."

"I only have two. But they're yours if you want them."

"Rowan, I can't ask you to plunk out harmonies."

"Why not? You do it. Besides, I can't just be Maggie's personal chef all summer."

Although his voice was light, his longing lanced through me. Long started and glanced around uncertainly. By then, Rowan had tamped down his power and Long's smile returned.

"Thank you, Rowan. A true team player. Now that we've got that settled, I'll—"

"Hold your horses," Bernie said. "If Rowan's going to be on staff, he needs to get paid."

Janet glanced heavenward. I suppressed a sigh. Bernie was just trying to help, after all.

In the old days, Helen had simply handed Rowan an envelope filled with cash. Asking Long to pay him under the table would raise too many questions. And if Rowan refused to accept any of the money he had left me, he would never allow me to give him part of my salary.

As Long hemmed and hawed, Rowan said, "Thank you, Bernie. But if you can volunteer your time to the theatre, so can I."

Long looked genuinely touched. Bernie shook his head. "So be it. But before the end of the year, you're sitting down with the board and hashing out a long-term contract. You and Maggie both! This year-to-year stuff is for the birds. Who can plan a life based on that? Especially a young couple starting out."

I smiled at Rowan and hoped I could disguise my jumble of emotions. He obviously needed something more fulfilling than babysitting Daddy and cooking me dinner. And the actors were blessed to have someone so talented working with them. But a small part of me wanted to prove that we could mount this production without his help.

"Maggie? Alex? Are you okay with this?"

"Are you kidding?" Alex's smile was more convincing than mine, but his voice was just a bit too hearty. "It'll be great working with you again."

CHAPTER 20

THE "YOU-DON'T-WANT-TO-PLAY-WITH-ME" BLUES

I INTRODUCED ROWAN AT THE COMPANY meeting the next morning. Judging from the awed expressions of the locals, they had seen the shows he'd directed. Doubtless, word would spread to the rest of the cast in the time it took to walk to the Smokehouse.

Alex and I left the chorus with Rowan and worked some of the principals' scenes and songs. Then I took Gregory and Roger aside for a little chat.

Lee's instincts were right. Turned out Gregory—a local—was so impressed by Roger that he was simply following his lead. And far from putting the moves on Gregory, Roger was groping—literally—to make his character more sympathetic.

I pointed out that his performance in "Lily's Eyes" accomplished that and suggested he find one or two moments to use gestures to show that Neville wanted to break out of his shell, but couldn't do it. If he indulged in five or six gestures during the subsequent rehearsal, at least he and Gregory kept their hands off each other.

At the break, Alex and I wandered outside for some fresh air. As we reached the picnic area, piano music poured through the open windows of the Smokehouse. The voices of the chorus matched the wildness of the music, but each word was distinct, the harmonies perfect.

I glanced at Alex as the storm of music subsided, but his gaze was riveted on the Smokehouse.

Slowly, the piano built the chord in the bass. One by one, voices took up the chilling "Mistress Mary, Quite Contrary" chant. And then a new vocal thread—"It's a Maze"— offered a solemn counterpoint that built into a relentless round.

More voices joined in, more threads in the musical tapestry, the gorgeous complexity of the number revealed at last: the lament of the Fakir and Ayah a quiet sostenuto; Wright's echo of Mary's skipping song playing off the "Mistress Mary" chant of Shaw and Claire; the fear that shook Alice's soaring soprano; and weaving in and out of all those vocal threads, the sadness of Mary's mother and the growing desperation of her father as he searched for his lost child.

I shivered as their voices united in the dissonant harmonics of "Mistress Mary." And shivered again as the number reached its terrifying climax.

I let out my breath and heard Alex do the same.

"We knew it would be like this," I reminded him.

Alex nodded.

For a few moments, there was only the murmur of Rowan's voice, punctuated by occasional chuckles from the chorus. Then I heard the scrape of chairs and the buzz of conversation.

The Smokehouse door swung open. Rowan emerged, surrounded by a cluster of local actors. Like a king and his courtiers. The Mackenzies trailed behind, wearing the exalted expressions I remembered from my season at the Crossroads. Most of the entourage dispersed when Rowan walked toward our picnic table, but a few lingered by the stage door, whispering and watching.

As Rowan dropped his score on the table and slid onto the bench beside me, Alex regarded him with a rueful smile. "Magic wand's still in good working order, I see."

"A little magic, a lot of hard work. And as soon as they get back onstage, half of what they learned will fly out the window again."

"Maybe. But look how excited they are."

"The cast always left your rehearsals smiling."

"Not lately."

"It's a hard show, Alex."

"But it's perfect for the Crossroads," I said. "Magic and healing and transformation. And the music may be difficult, but it's wonderful."

Rowan shrugged. "Some of it. The songs for the Yorkshire characters."

"What about 'Lily's Eyes'? And 'Where in the World'? And—?"

"I'll grant you 'Lily's Eyes.' But by the time Archibald gets to 'Where in the World,' I'm tired of his endless sorrow and just want him to go home and take care of his son. How can anyone sympathize with a man who abandons his child?"

Rowan's passionate expression froze. Then his mouth twisted in a bitter smile. "I'm a fine one to talk."

"You never knew you had a child," I said.

With a brusque gesture, Rowan dismissed the daughter he had never known, the daughter who had lived long enough to give birth to Janet and her twin sister Isobel— Reinhard's mother.

"My opinion of the score doesn't matter," he said. "The staff clearly loves the show or you wouldn't have chosen it."

Alex's gaze slid away. I nudged his foot under the table. "This is where you're supposed to chime in."

He shifted uncomfortably on the bench. "I'm afraid I have to agree with Rowan."

"Well, why the hell didn't you say that when we were discussing it?"

"Because you were so excited. And the message *is* perfect for the Crossroads." He shrugged helplessly. "That's what I meant about letting you down. And why there haven't been many smiles in my rehearsals. I've been struggling and it shows."

"So we'll find a way to make the problematic numbers work," Rowan said.

He walked around the table and sat beside Alex. At first, Alex merely nodded at Rowan's suggestions, but as they paged through the score, Alex's coppery head bent closer to Rowan's dark one. Within minutes, they were so completely in sync that whenever one started to make a suggestion, the other finished the sentence.

Alex returned to rehearsal, brimming with renewed energy. Afterward, he hurried off to the green room to meet

Rowan for a working lunch. I wandered back to the production office and discovered Bernie and Daddy hunched over the laptop.

I scolded myself for feeling jealous. I was grateful that Bernie had taken Daddy under his wing. Relieved that Rowan and Alex were adapting to their new relationship. But I still felt like the last girl picked at the junior high school dance.

During the next two days, the "king and his courtiers" thing diminished, but at every break, I discovered Rowan deep in conversation with a different actor. I knew he would never coach the cast behind my back, but the situation gnawed at me and I finally decided to address it.

I found him in the Smokehouse with Gregory. As soon as I walked inside, they broke off their conversation and Gregory beat a hasty retreat.

"You're very popular," I noted.

"What do you mean?"

"All these little conclaves with the actors."

"I'd hardly call them conclaves."

"Well, what would you call them?"

"They're curious, Maggie. They want to know where I've been, what I've been doing . . ."

"What suggestions you have for improving their performances?"

"Some of them, yes."

He waited, watching me, until I was forced to ask, "And what do you tell them?"

"I don't tell them anything. I ask them what suggestions their director gave."

I was both relieved and ashamed. I felt even worse when Rowan asked, "Do you really think I would undermine your authority?"

"No! But as you pointed out, you're far more experienced than I am."

"I also pointed out that you had to stop comparing yourself to me."

"Well, it's damn hard to do that when half my cast is flocking to you for advice."

"That's not my fault."

"I didn't say it was!"

"Then stop blaming *me* for their behavior!"

Tension crackled through the Smokehouse, along with a decidedly chilly breeze.

"You're right. I'm sorry."

The temperature grew noticeably warmer. So did Rowan's expression. "And I'm sorry for shouting. Actors are needy creatures. You don't see the Mackenzies asking for my suggestions, do you?"

"They're too cowed by your reputation."

"It doesn't even occur to them. You're the one they need. It's ironic. The ones that came here for healing flock to you and the experienced actors seek me out."

"Because the Mackenzies trust me."

"They all trust you."

"Maybe." When Rowan blew out his breath in exasperation, I added, "Okay, so I'm hopelessly insecure. A few actors ask for a second opinion and I become a basket case."

Rowan took my hands. "That's not true, sweetheart. You've always been a basket case."

I pulled free, but he easily avoided my intended smack.

"I hate you!"

"Then why are you laughing?" he asked from a safe distance.

"Because I have a kind and generous nature."

His teasing smile vanished. "Yes. It's one of the things I love most about you."

"Hey, no fair."

"What?"

"Playing the love card. That trumps everything."

"I hope so."

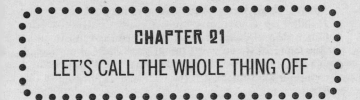

CHAPTER 21

LET'S CALL THE WHOLE THING OFF

THE FOURTH OF JULY BROUGHT BLISTERING heat, but I was too excited to care. I was going out on the town. And I would have my lover and my father all to myself.

I put on my apricot sundress and hurried up the stairs to Rowan's apartment. When the door swung open, I flung my arms around his neck and kissed him soundly.

"Ready?"

"Jack's still dressing."

Deflated by his lack of enthusiasm, I asked, "You don't mind that we're going to the Chatterbox instead of picnicking at the high school? It's just so hot. And I didn't want you stuck in the kitchen, cooking all afternoon."

"It's fine, Maggie."

As he walked into the living area, I noticed something dangling from his back pocket. Before I could ask about it, he paused by the sideboard to pick up a rolled-up napkin.

"Would you put this in your purse?"

"Rowan, the Chatterbox may not be fancy, but they *do* have napkins. Not linen, but—"

"It's the silverware I'm concerned about."

Only then did I realize he'd wrapped his utensils in the napkin.

"Oh, God. I didn't even think . . ."

"I'll be fine if I use my own silverware. And I'm bringing my gloves. Just in case."

605

Gloves. Those were what I'd seen in his pocket.

I called up a mental picture of the Chatterbox. The booths were wooden, the tabletops, Formica, but the milkshakes came in those giant metal containers. You had to pour your shake into a smaller glass to drink it. Well, I could always pour his shake for him if he didn't want to don the gloves.

"Were you planning on driving into town?"

That one I *was* prepared for. I still remembered him retching as he staggered away from my car the night of Helen's heart attack.

"We'll walk. It's only half a mile."

He looked anything but reassured. "Are we likely to encounter any dogs?"

"You don't like dogs?"

"They don't like me. Well, Jamie's didn't. The first time Jamie brought him to the cottage, Blue charged out of the underbrush, baying like the Hound of the Baskervilles. I had to hide in the cottage until Jamie dragged him off."

Jamie Mackenzie—Rowan's first friend in this world. I knew he had arranged for Rowan to get a fake birth certificate and left him five acres of land in his will, but Rowan had not included the incident with Blue in *By Iron, Bound*.

"Why didn't you just use your magic to stop him?"

"I had far less control over my power then. I was afraid I'd kill the damn beast. Maybe Blue was just excited. I didn't stick around to find out. I just ran like hell."

Again, I called up a mental image, this time of Main Street. I went house by house, trying to remember who owned dogs, and came up with one golden retriever, a German shepherd, a dachshund, two pugs, and a couple of those yappy little "mops with feet" dogs.

"At least most of them are small," Rowan said.

"It's weird. I assumed animals loved the Fae."

"Many do. Especially the wild ones. I became quite good at charming birds, rabbits, squirrels. It made them much easier to kill."

"Jesus . . ."

"And Helen's cats adored me."

"I hope you didn't kill them, too."

He scowled. "Of course not. Although at times . . ."

"Rowan!"

"Well, they were always hanging about. It was a source of endless amusement to the staff, particularly when they were in heat. The cats, not the staff. They were so shameless Helen had to keep them locked in the house."

"Maybe Blue was doing the 'alpha male protecting his territory' thing, while Helen's cats—"

"Wanted to mate with me?"

Finally, a smile.

I'd always known travel would be difficult for Rowan. But if dinner in town required this much preparation, how were we ever going to have a normal life?

Think about it tomorrow, Scarlett.

For now, I just prayed that our celebratory evening wouldn't begin and/or end with all the dogs in Dale chasing us down Main Street.

Daddy remained blithely ignorant of Rowan's concerns. He was as excited as a kid about our outing. He might have forgotten his alcohol and drug use, but he seemed to recall every burger joint he'd ever eaten in. Maybe he had simply blocked out the bad memories.

Is that why he never talks about his family? Are we just another bad memory?

I became as silent as Rowan. It was too hot to chat, anyway. Even in my skimpy sundress, I was sweating like a stallion. Rowan looked as grim-faced and sweaty as the day of our first picnic when I'd been terrified he was having a heart attack.

"It'll be better when we reach the road," I assured him.

At least, there might be a breeze from a passing car. And I would have solid asphalt beneath my espadrilles instead of shifting gravel.

My anxiety increased as we trudged along the lane. Daddy's running monologue faltered. His surreptitious glances worried me more—as if he feared something was lurking in the tall grass. He flinched when a jay scolded us and let out a startled yelp when some insect buzzed past.

Maybe we should have driven, even if Rowan had to stick his head out of the car like a dog. Or maybe, as the old song advised, we should just call the whole thing off.

At the top of the lane, Daddy slumped against the low

stone wall that ran along the road. Rowan just stood there, staring at the waves of heat rising from the asphalt. Sweat streamed down his face and plastered his shirt to his body. He closed his eyes and gulped at the hot air like a drowning man.

That decided me. "I'm going back for the car."

Daddy screamed.

I jumped about a mile and came down on the side of my espadrille. Pain stabbed my ankle, and I cried out. Rowan caught me as I staggered, then shouted, "Jack! It was just a chipmunk."

Daddy went ballistic and I broke my ankle over a fucking chipmunk?

Rowan had warned me. Just because Daddy enjoyed surfing the Internet didn't mean he was ready to face the world.

"Let's go back," Daddy begged. "Please?"

"We'll have to," Rowan replied. "Put your arms around my neck, Maggie."

A moment later, he was racing down the lane at the speed of Fae. The world blurred into a dizzying smear of green and blue and gold. Although Rowan was doing a five hundred yard dash carrying 139 pounds of hot, cursing female, he wasn't even breathing hard. But I could feel the tremors coursing through his body as he rushed me up the stairs to the apartment.

By the time Daddy arrived, I was ensconced on the sofa, my ankle swaddled in ice packs, and Rowan had started dinner preparations. Daddy collapsed into an easy chair, winded and sweating and very apologetic.

"We'll go to the Chatterbox another day," I promised. "And we can still watch the fireworks from Rowan's balcony."

Daddy waxed rhapsodic over Rowan's dinner of steak, new potatoes, and salad—his closest approximation of the meal we might have had at the Chatterbox. Not the celebration I had planned, but better than the debacle we had faced an hour earlier.

As darkness fell, Rowan dragged a chair onto the balcony for me and the three of us watched the fireworks explode beneath the fat, full moon. Daddy whooped and I squealed. It was like time had rolled backward and we were once again father and daughter, laughing together and applauding each time another flower of colored light blossomed in the sky.

Minutes after the big finale, Daddy's head began to nod. As he toddled off to the sofa, Rowan leaned on the railing and stared into the darkness.

"I've always experienced this world from a distance. I watched the fireworks from this balcony every July. I saw the first school bus roar past the lane every September. I glimpsed the houses on the outskirts of Dale through the bare-limbed trees of winter. I followed the changes in the town in *The Hillandale Bee*. Heard about Hallee's and the Golden Bough and the Mandarin Chalet from the staff."

His shoulders rose and fell as he sighed.

"Tonight, I hoped I would finally see the world firsthand."

"I'm so sorry," I whispered.

He bent to kiss the top of my head. "It's not your fault."

"Yes, it is. Maggie Graham, Clumsy Professional."

"No. It was . . . it just wasn't meant to be. There will be other nights."

"Not with fireworks."

His lips moved lower, and I breathed in the faint aroma of wine. "Says who?"

CHAPTER 22
ROLE OF A LIFETIME

UNSATISFIED DESIRE DID MORE TO RENDER me sleepless that night than my sore ankle. My desire remained unsatisfied during the ensuing days. Whenever Rowan had a free hour at lunch, I had a meeting. When I was free, he had an extra music rehearsal. We couldn't even sit together during *Annie* for fear Fifi would go berserk. Instead, he and Daddy were exiled to the last row in the balcony.

My worries about Daddy were as hard to subdue as my hormones. He spent his days sequestered in the office and his evenings sequestered with Rowan. Daddy grew moody. Rowan grew irritable. I played peacemaker and wondered if Daddy was picking up Rowan's energy or if the enforced companionship was grating on both of them.

My father had always been the life of the party, the man everyone was drawn to. Had that merely been an act to disguise his insecurities? Or had the Borderlands destroyed his ability to interact with people?

"What did you expect?" Janet demanded. "That he would emerge from Rowan's apartment like a butterfly from its chrysalis?"

"No!" I lied. "But if he won't even mingle with the staff, what's the point of asking him to join us for the Follies?"

"Rowan never mingled."

"But he had contact with people. He was part of things."

Janet heaved a long-suffering sigh. "Fine. I'll host a barbecue after the Sunday matinee. If all goes well, we can invite Jack to perform in the Follies then."

I flung my arms around her. She cuffed me on the back of the head.

My excitement slowly leached away. The barbecue would give him a chance to get to know the staff, but ultimately, it was just one night of fun like the fireworks and the Follies. If he was going to become a part of this world, he needed something more.

That's when I realized the answer had been staring me in the face all along.

I called a staff meeting in the Smokehouse before the matinee. I'd already warned everyone not to breathe a word about the Follies to Rowan; I wanted to surprise him as well as Daddy at the barbecue. But I was reluctant to spring my other surprise without the staff's advice.

Once everyone was seated, I took a deep breath, flashed a winning smile, and said, "I'd like to offer Daddy Bill's role in *Into the Woods*."

For a moment, they just stared at me. Then Mei-Yin exclaimed, "Are you NUTS?" and everyone began talking at once.

"Wait! Listen!" I had to shout to make myself heard. "This is supposed to be a place where people can heal."

"It's supposed to be a professional theatre," Janet remarked.

"And Daddy's a professional actor."

"Was."

"He needs a purpose. And the only thing he knows is acting."

"Wasn't he a teacher?" Alex asked.

"He taught. There's a difference. Look, I know it's a risk. But he needs ... something!"

"What role?" Rowan asked.

"Roles," Reinhard corrected. "The Narrator and the Mysterious Man."

Rowan shook his head. "The Narrator, perhaps. But not the Mysterious Man."

"It's the perfect role for him," I said.

"That's why you can't ask him to play it."

"You always talk about casting people in the roles they need. Well, Daddy needs—"

"Is this about Jack's needs or yours?"

I hesitated. "Both." As Rowan shook his head again, I added, "So leave me out of the equation. Don't *you* think he needs this role?"

"A character who abandons his wife and child? Who runs mad in the woods? Jack may be damaged, but he's not stupid. He won't even discuss his past with me, Maggie. You're asking him to act it out in front of the world."

"You asked Nick to do that in *Carousel*," Bernie noted.

"And look how that turned out," Rowan replied. "Jack's just not ready."

"Why not let *him* decide?" I asked.

"Because just offering him the role will bring up all the issues he wants to avoid. Trust me. It will be victory enough if he can play the Narrator."

It was not what I'd hoped for, but it was better than nothing. And maybe the show would help us connect as father and daughter as well as actor and director.

"It's been a long time since he's performed," Alex said. "Suppose he's not up to it? Or something happens to set him off?"

"I could understudy the part," Bernie said.

"Oh, Bernie, would you?"

"If Bernie understudies the role, he goes on for the matinees," Reinhard declared.

"What are you?" Bernie demanded. "My manager?"

"If you are going to add that to your long list of responsibilities, you deserve the chance to perform."

"You're right," I said. "We can split the role."

"What about the box office?" Javier asked.

"I could work the matinees," Catherine said. "If Bernie handles advance sales."

"You're working way too hard as it is," I replied.

"I can do it," she insisted.

"I'll run the damn box office," Janet said.

I swallowed hard. Everyone was working long hours to make this season a success. And now I was asking them to do more.

"I'm being completely selfish. You all have more than enough to do. The Follies is plenty for Daddy to deal with."

"And when the Follies is over?" Lee asked.

"Lee's right," Catherine said. "Jack needs more. And if we have to work a little harder to give it to him, we can."

It took longer to dislodge the new lump that formed in my throat. For the gazillionth time, I thanked God for giving me this staff.

"Then we are all agreed?" Reinhard asked.

One by one, every head nodded.

"That still leaves us without a Mysterious Man," Hal said. "Bernie can't play both roles. Not with all those quick costume changes."

"I must have made a dozen calls after Bill left," I replied. "The professionals all turned me down. And the locals were already committed to another show or a family vacation or—"

"I'll learn it," Rowan said. "If you find another actor before rehearsals start—"

"Why bother looking?" Hal exclaimed.

"Because it might make Maggie uncomfortable to direct me."

I hesitated, knowing Rowan had directed the show before. But if we could deal with the "king and his courtiers" issue, we could deal with this, too.

"Thank you. It'll be great having you in the show."

"You just want to order me around the stage."

"Well. That, too."

We shared a smile. Then Janet asked, "And what about Alison?"

"She has to find out about Daddy eventually."

"We're not talking eventually. Opening night is a month away. If Jack is too traumatized to consider the role of the Mysterious Man, do you think he'll be ready to see his ex-wife?"

"Who knows what he'll be ready for in a month?"

"I could always go on while she's here," Bernie said.

"But she'll still see Jack's name in the program," Janet noted.

"So I'll pay to have extra programs printed. And just list Bernie's name."

Mei-Yin groaned. "This is a recipe for DISASTER."

I shot a pleading look around the circle.

Reinhard sighed. "We will work it out. Somehow. I would suggest, however, that we avoid the term understudy when we broach this to Jack."

"Tell him I asked for someone to share the role," Bernie suggested. "Because I'm too old and feeble to handle all the performances. Then he'll feel like a hero."

"Feeble, my ass," I said. "*You're* the hero."

CHAPTER 23
A REAL NICE CLAMBAKE

I LEFT THE MATINEE AT INTERMISSION and raced up to the Bates mansion to help with final preparations for the barbecue. There wasn't much to do. Alex and Janet had supplied enough meat to satisfy the most raging carnivore. Bernie, enough beer to float a battleship. Catherine was bringing her Mexican bean salad, Mei-Yin, her German potato salad, and Hal, the fruited Jell-O with mini marshmallows that was a hideous—if hallowed—tradition at our gatherings. All that was left for me to do was throw some leafy green stuff together and set out the silverware and plates. At least Rowan wouldn't have to bring his own utensils; Janet always used real silver, too.

Mei-Yin fired up the grill with such maniacal enthusiasm that we all feared she would go up in flames. Self-immolation narrowly averted, we settled ourselves on the patio with pitchers of lemonade and daiquiris.

The rest of the staff began trickling in shortly after the matinee let out. But still no sign of Rowan or Daddy.

"The invitation was for 6:00," Janet reminded me.

I couldn't help hovering anxiously on the front porch. At 5:58, I saw them marching up the hill.

The screen door creaked, and I turned to find Janet observing me with a sardonic smile.

"What's wrong with being punctual?" I demanded.

"Not a thing."

The two men hesitated at the foot of the steps, then held up their containers.

"We brought dessert," Rowan said.

"Blueberry pie, apple pie, and peach cobbler," Daddy declared. "We baked them ourselves."

I suspected Rowan had done the baking, but I just smiled, happy to see his enthusiasm.

"The faery Betty Crocker," Janet noted.

"No more Fae comments," I whispered. "Bernie's here."

Daddy nodded solemnly, then marched up the steps and peered through the screen door. Rowan just looked up at Janet. She stared back at him for a long moment, then gargled something, which I took to be Gaelic. Rowan gargled something in reply. Her sardonic smile returned, but she merely ushered us inside.

"What was that all about?" I whispered.

"A Scottish tradition," he replied just as softly. "Janet offered me one hundred thousand welcomes. I wished her good health and every good blessing to those under her roof."

"You do this every time you go visiting?"

"Janet's never invited me to her home before."

"What are you talking about? She invited you here today. And to all the cast parties. Which you refused to go to until I dragged you."

"The cast parties don't count. She knew I wouldn't attend. And *you* invited me here today, not Janet."

"But you've been inside the house. After Helen's heart attack. And—"

"This is the first time Janet has ever personally invited me into her home. Asked me to sit at her table and break bread together."

"So it's a really big deal."

"It is to me."

I touched his arm lightly, and he smiled. Then we hurried after Janet and Daddy.

Rowan gazed longingly at the library, but when he entered the enormous country kitchen, his eyes widened.

"Kitchen envy?" Janet inquired.

"Kitchen lust," he admitted, placing his containers on the counter. His fingertips skimmed lightly over the marble while his gaze roamed from the stainless steel appliances to the gleaming white cabinetry to the terracotta floor.

"Pretty ritzy, huh?" Daddy remarked. "Janet must be loaded!"

Rowan grimaced. Janet just laughed. "That's me. The wealthy widow."

"A widow?"

I was appalled to detect a speculative gleam in my father's eyes.

"And determined to remain one," Janet said firmly.

As she led us into the sunroom, Daddy's head came up like an animal scenting the air. "Charcoal!" he exclaimed. Then rushed outside and trotted down the steps to the lower patio.

"The lure of the grill," Janet remarked. "Men can't resist it."

Apparently, Rowan could. He just continued to survey the sunroom: the hanging plants above the white shutters, the flowered upholstery on the love seat, the crockery vase filled with fresh-cut flowers.

"This room reminds me of Helen."

"It was her favorite place," Janet said.

"I can almost feel her here."

"I think I *have* felt her," I said.

I told them what had happened in Rowan's apartment and in my bedroom, the countless times I'd seemed to sense Helen's presence in the Bough. Always, I suddenly realized, when I felt sad or troubled or needed reassurance.

"That's when I feel her, too," Janet said quietly.

"Is it possible?"

"I don't know. I'd like to believe that she's watching over us. Offering us reassurance when we need it. Just as she did in life." Janet blew out her breath impatiently. "First faeries. Now ghosts. Next, we'll have werewolves roaming the woods."

"Helen wouldn't allow that," I said.

"No. She never liked hairy men." Janet's gaze slid over Rowan. Then she strode onto the patio.

I started to follow her, then noticed Rowan's troubled expression. He rarely spoke of Helen, but I knew how much he must miss her. She had been his friend and confidante and—briefly—his lover. The one person on the staff with whom he could let down his guard.

"It must be a comfort," he said. "Living in this beautiful house. Feeling her presence."

I nodded.

"Even if—when—I get a real identity, I'll never be able to give you a home like this."

Dumbstruck, I just stared at him. "Who's asking you to?"

"I know you're not asking, but—"

"I lived in a shoebox in Brooklyn."

"You lived there. It wasn't your home."

"Yes. But the home I grew up in wasn't much bigger than your apartment." I shook my head, still reeling. "Jesus, Rowan. If all I wanted from life was a big house and a fancy car and expensive vacations, I would have set my cap for Long!"

"I just don't want you to be . . . disappointed."

"I *am* disappointed! You say you know me and you still think that I need that kind of stuff to be happy!"

His frustration stabbed me. "Of course, you don't need it. But I need to feel I can take care of you."

I resisted the urge to shout, "I can take care of myself!" This was about his pride, his sense of self. I'd been so consumed with helping Daddy find his place in the world that I'd overlooked Rowan's struggles. And clearly, he *was* struggling, although he had hidden it from me.

"You helped me rediscover my past. You helped me find my path. You gave me my father and $50,000 to start a new life. Most of all, you loved me enough to come back and share that life. From where I stand, you've given me an awful lot."

Some of the tension drained away, but he still looked troubled.

"You've done everything you can to support me when it must kill you to see all the changes at the theatre you built and ran. I can't promise it's going to get easier any time soon. But I swear you won't have to keep hiding in the shadows and watching from the sidelines. You'll direct again. And we'll work together and live together—and take care of each other."

His arms came around me. "You make it sound so easy."

"Hell, no! It'll be hard work. Even you might have a few gray hairs before this is over."

"Well, Bernie would find that reassuring."

I molded my body to his and whispered, "I don't want the house or the car or the vacations. I just want you."

And he obviously wanted me. He might be able to control his power, but the hard ridge in his pants was difficult to disguise.

"Get a ROOM!" Mei-Yin called from the patio.

We jumped apart. Rowan glared at Mei-Yin. As he started toward the patio, I caught his hand.

"I have a room, you know. Maybe we could ... ?"

He hesitated, desire warring with discretion. Then he shook his head. "We'll find a time and a place to make love. For now, we'll just have to enjoy each other from a respectable distance."

❦❦

I had to enjoy Daddy from a distance, too. In true ur-male tradition, he parked himself by the grill with the other men. Judging from the occasional laughter, they were all having a good time and that was the important thing.

Rowan made awkward conversation with the female contingent. At first, I thought he was still troubled by our conversation, but I gradually realized that in all the years he had worked at the Crossroads, he'd never actually socialized with his staff.

I plied him with daiquiris, and by the time we settled in around the picnic tables on the lower patio, he seemed more relaxed. But although he answered pleasantly whenever anyone addressed him, he took little part in the noisy free-for-all conversation.

By contrast, Daddy chatted easily with everyone as we chowed down on burgers, hot dogs, and bratwurst. Rowan and Catherine washed their meals down with milk, drawing a grimace from Daddy, who drained the last of his Long Trail Double Bag Ale in a few deep gulps.

"How many has he had?" I whispered to Reinhard.

"Only one. I was the keeper of the cooler. Now, he has a new reason to dislike me."

"Great BURGERS," Mei-Yin called.

"Thank Jack," Lee said. "The man knows his way around a grill."

Daddy beamed. "It's all in the patties. Most people make them too thin. Three-quarters of an inch—that's my rule. And never flatten them with a spatula. Squeezes out all the juices."

Eager to involve Rowan in the conversation, I asked, "Are you getting all this?"

"Jack just won himself the role of head chef. For our non-fancy-schmancy meals."

When the laughter subsided, Janet said, "We were wondering if you'd like another role, Jack. In the Follies."

Daddy's eyes widened. Rowan slowly lowered his fork and stared at his plate. When he finally raised his head, the blank mask was firmly in place.

Why did Janet have to spoil this by fucking with Rowan? He obviously believed we were excluding him from the invitation.

She ignored my furious look and said, "Usually, it's just the staff that performs. But we're doing *Snow White and the Seven Dwarfs* and the doubling is a nightmare. Which is why we could use your help." Her eyes locked with Rowan's. "And yours. If you're so inclined."

Rowan took a sip of milk, slowly lowered his glass, and patted his lips with his napkin.

"Say something!" I demanded.

"Hush, Maggie," Janet said. "You're spoiling the moment. Rowan's drawing out the tension the way I just did. A fine theatrical tradition."

"And here I thought you were just screwing with me," Rowan remarked. "A fine Janet Mackenzie tradition."

They regarded each other as intently as they had outside the house. Then Rowan smiled and raised his glass of milk as if toasting Janet.

"It's nice to know some things haven't changed."

As I let out my breath, Rowan nudged Daddy. "So what do you think? Would you like to be in the Follies?"

"Of course! I still remember the show from my year. *Hansel and Gretel*. You were the wicked witch."

"Rowan was the wicked witch our year, too!" Bernie exclaimed.

"I'm always the wicked witch," Rowan remarked dryly. "And Catherine always plays the ingénue."

"Not this year," Catherine replied. "My big role is Sleepy. Not much of a stretch."

"I'm GRUMPY," Mei-Yin said. "Not much of a stretch for ME, either."

"I am Happy," Reinhard said, staring glumly into his ale.

"And I," Janet announced, "am the Evil Queen."

"So many comments spring to mind," Rowan murmured. "Try to restrain yourself."

"So who *is* playing Snow White?"

I groaned and raised my hand. "I told them I didn't have the time or the energy or the ditzy soprano voice, but—"

"Weren't you complaining about casting when we met?" Rowan teased and laughed when I stuck out my tongue. "Do Jack and I have to guess our roles or are you going to tell us?"

"I was supposed to play the Prince and Sneezy," Lee said.

Daddy frowned. "But then you wouldn't have the right number of dwarfs at the end."

"Exactly. But now that you're onboard . . ."

"You want me to play the Prince!"

There was a horrifying moment of silence.

"Uh . . . no," Lee said. "We'd like you to play Sneezy."

I watched in agony as the emotions flitted across Daddy's face: disappointment, annoyance, truculence.

Rowan nudged him again. "Come on, Jack. An inveterate scene stealer like you should be able to add five minutes to the show with those sneezes."

A slow smile blossomed on Daddy's face. "Damn straight!"

I clapped my hands like the delighted child I was. "Then it's all settled!"

"No, it's not!" Rowan retorted. "Who am I playing? Let me guess, Janet. Dopey?"

"Tempting. Alas, we need you to play the old crone."

"But . . . that's the Evil Queen."

"The transformation is a bit daunting. We need some of that special Rowan Mackenzie magic to pull it off."

Rowan's face lit up, then creased in a frown of concentration. "I'll need a flash pot," he said, turning to Lee. "And a strobe."

"No problem."

"And I have to die spectacularly."

"Knock yourself out," Janet said.

"No, don't!" I protested.

"The old crone has to plummet to her death from a rocky crag," Rowan said.

"No plummeting. No crags."

Rowan smiled sweetly. His power teased through my body, a coaxing caress that urged me to give in. I glared at him, and it subsided, but his pleading look remained.

"Fine. But if you break your neck . . ."

"Don't be silly. I'm a professional."

And a faery. He could probably plummet from a rocky crag and stick the landing like Mary Lou Retton.

We discussed the Follies over dessert and coffee. Rowan's baking won a lot of compliments, which seemed to surprise and please him. As the shadows deepened, Janet lit the votives on the picnic tables and Mei-Yin turned her pyromaniacal talents to the tiki torches.

The atmosphere encouraged Bernie to serenade me with "Some Enchanted Evening." The staff soon joined in. When they got to the ending with its reminder to "never let her go," everyone seemed to be looking at Rowan.

Maybe that's why he cleared his throat and said, "Well. It's getting late."

I nodded. "But before we go, Jack, there's one more role we wanted to discuss with you."

He grinned, showing blueberry-stained teeth. "I'd make a cute bunny."

"This is a role in *Into the Woods*."

He stared at me blankly.

"You know the show, right?"

You had the cast album. You listened to it a million times. You can probably sing every song in the score.

Daddy's fork clattered onto his plate. "You want me to be in a real show?"

"If *you* want to. One of our actors dropped out. Bernie volunteered to fill in, but . . ."

"It's just too much for me." Bernie took a trembling

breath and morphed into the sad-eyed Puss in Boots. "I'm only good for two matinees a week. So I was hoping you'd play the Narrator at the evening performances."

Daddy frowned. "The Narrator?"

"The one who opens the show," I said. "And . . . narrates the action. Until they throw him to the giant."

I glanced at Rowan, who was frowning, too. Uncertain what was happening, I laughed uneasily and added, "I'm afraid you won't get to die spectacularly. It all happens off—"

"That's a dual role," Daddy said.

"On Broadway, it was. But we're going to—"

"You want me to play the crazy man."

"No! Just the—"

"I get it! Let's cast Jack. It's the perfect role for him. He won't even have to act!"

I babbled out a denial, too horrified by his reaction to put a coherent sentence together.

"I won't do it! You can't make me!"

"Jack!"

Daddy turned on Rowan, his lips curled in a snarl. In that instant, he *did* look crazy.

"No one's asking you to play the Mysterious Man," Rowan said. "Maggie is offering you the role of the Narrator. That's it."

The fury in Daddy's face leached away and his uncertain gaze shifted to me.

"I didn't want to spring it on you as soon as you arrived. But I kept thinking, why should I scrounge up some inexperienced actor when I've got the man who played Billy Bigelow?"

For once, those words failed to work their magic. Daddy just shook his head. "That was a long time ago."

"But you're still an actor."

"I'm not sure what I am anymore."

Suddenly, he looked far older than his sixty-three years. Old and small and unbearably fragile.

"Maybe this role will help you figure it out," Bernie said. "That happens a lot at the Crossroads."

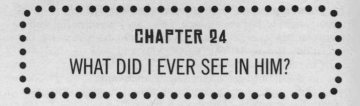

ON MONDAY MORNING, DADDY ACCEPTED the role of the Narrator.

On Monday evening, he had a panic attack and shut himself in Rowan's apartment.

On Tuesday morning, he laughed off the incident and announced that he was fine.

On Wednesday morning, he declared that he was never going to act again.

On Wednesday afternoon, he began giving helpful little suggestions to the actors. Then stormed back to the apartment when I told him he was overstepping his bounds.

On Thursday morning, he was all smiles and penitence, but the cast was eyeing him with misgiving, the staff was shooting me murderous glances, and Reinhard's hair was standing on end. Only the fact that mine was longer prevented it from rising heavenward, too.

Although Rowan appeared as preternaturally calm as ever, he was clearly struggling to control his temper—and his power. His frustration infected everyone. The actors sniped at each other; the younger staff grew moody or snappish. Even Reinhard and Alex couldn't always shield themselves and became increasingly short-tempered. Janet remained immune because she refused to set foot in the theatre.

Something had to change or none of us would live to see opening night. So on Friday, I suggested to Rowan that we have a little chat with Daddy over lunch.

Rowan scowled. "I am sick of chatting with Jack. I spend every waking hour with Jack. The prospect of eating lunch with Jack is about as appealing as eating cast-iron filings out of a cast-iron skillet with cast-iron utensils."

"I'll take that as a no."

"Maggie Graham. Perceptive Professional."

He stomped up the stairs to his apartment in a very un-faery-like manner. I muttered a few unflattering names under my breath, then whisked Daddy into town for lunch.

He marveled at how little Dale had changed, just as Mom had when she visited me for the first time. But where she had been suspicious of the town's timeless quality, Daddy was delighted by it.

"It's exactly the same," he exclaimed as we walked into the Chatterbox.

From the waitresses in their powder blue uniforms to the soda fountain stools at the counter to the jukeboxes in the cramped booths, the Chatterbox evoked a candy-coated past where kids were never more than naughty and parents never less than loving.

We slid into a booth, the wooden seats worn smooth by generations of Dale butts. My father studied the menu. I studied him.

He had talked about me that first night. Recalled the tent we had built, the games we had played. Since then, he had never brought up his family. Did he have to be on the brink of a mental breakdown before he could think about us? Was he avoiding the pain or didn't he feel any?

Look at me. I have the same auburn hair you had as a young man, the same smattering of freckles across my nose. You gave me your pointed chin and your blue-green eyes and your love of theatre. Can't you see any of that?

Obviously not. He just wolfed down his burger and fries, moaned ecstatically over his chocolate milkshake, and flirted outrageously with Dot, our waitress. I picked at my tuna salad and kept the conversation light, unwilling to risk a public meltdown by broaching the subject of his recent mood swings.

Afterward, he insisted on stopping by the Bough. I warned him that it had changed, but I was still shocked when he took one look at the lobby and demanded, "Why can't people leave things alone? The Bough was great. It had character! Now it looks ordinary."

My mother had deemed it perfect. I'd thought so, too. But now I recalled the quirky old furnishings and the moth-eaten draperies and the Victorian gloom and wondered if I'd stolen everything that had made the Bough unique.

"Do *you* like the changes?" Daddy demanded.

"I should. I made them. I own the Bough, remember? I told you and Rowan that your first morning back."

Daddy mumbled, "Oh, shit." Then he shrugged and flashed that charming gap-toothed smile. "Oops."

I turned around and walked out.

His dismissive words had stung. That little "oops" totally pissed me off. Why was I surprised? He'd thrown the the-atre into chaos this week and hadn't apologized for that, either.

"Charming, yes. But completely self-absorbed."

"Maggie!"

"And arrogant and superior."

"Wait!"

"Always standing apart, judging."

I flung open the car door.

"Please!"

I turned to find him standing on the curb, quivering with anxiety.

"It looks nice. Really. It's just ... I loved the Bough the way it was."

"Always making excuses ..."

I slumped against the car, suddenly exhausted. "I loved it, too. But I worked really hard on redoing the lobby and it hurt my feelings when you called it ordinary."

"I'm sorry," he whispered.

"If you'd said that earlier, I wouldn't have gotten mad. An apology goes a lot farther than a shrug and a smile."

He stared at me as if I were chanting Hindi.

"Do you understand?"

"Yes. I was just ... yes."

"Come on. I need to get to rehearsal."

Neither of us spoke on the short drive back, although Daddy kept stealing glances at me. After I parked the car at the theatre, I asked, "Do you want to tell me why you've been so up and down this week?"

His hands tightened on his thighs. I found myself studying them: the loose flesh, the network of ropy blue veins, the tiny spots of dried blood where he'd gnawed his cuticles.

"Are you worried about performing in *Into the Woods*?"

"What if I'm awful?"

"You won't be."

"But what if I am?"

"In all the years you acted, were you ever awful?"

His forehead creased in a thoughtful frown. "Well, I wasn't great in *Natalie Needs A Nightie*. But the material was so bad that—"

"You were actually in a play called *Natalie Needs a Nightie*?"

"In Scranton. Or Wilkes-Barre. Some place like that. I did a lot of dinner theatre. *There's a Girl in My Soup. Right Bed, Wrong Husband. Run for Your Wife*."

"I was in one called *Don't Start Without Me*," I confessed.

He smiled. Then his gaze slid away. "The thing is . . . my memory isn't so hot anymore."

I resisted the urge to pat his hand. I was his director now, not his daughter.

"The lines will come. It just might take awhile to get back in the groove." When my words elicited only a dispirited nod, I added, "I'll do whatever I can to help. Coaching. Running lines with you. But I can't have any more disruptions during rehearsals."

"It's Rowan's fault. He's making everyone nervous."

"Giving notes to my actors? That was Rowan's fault?"

"I was just talking with them."

"You were giving notes, Jack. And I won't have it."

"You're just mad because of what I said about the Bough."

"That's not true."

"And now you're taking it out on me!"

"That is not true!"

He scowled and looked away. I scowled and stared out the windshield.

Had he always been like this? Was I inventing a shared

past as candy-coated as the world conjured by the Chatterbox?

"I want you to play this role, Jack. But if we can't work together . . ."

"We can."

"No more disruptions."

"Okay."

"And no more notes."

"Okay! Jeez . . ."

He slid out of the car. I slumped back in my seat and closed my eyes.

I was tired of pretending I wasn't his daughter, worn down by his apparent lack of interest in his family, and increasingly fearful that Rowan's assessment of his character was accurate. My mother's had been more charitable, but equally gloomy:

"That lost boy quality . . . it drew a lot of people to him. Including me. I thought I could make him happy, give him what he needed, make everything right. Of course, I couldn't. No one could."

But I had to try.

CHAPTER 25

FASTEN YOUR SEAT BELTS

WITH DADDY ON A MORE-OR-LESS EVEN KEEL, I expected Rowan to even out as well. But when I walked into the theatre the next morning, the chill raised goose bumps on my arms.

It grew colder as I made my way through the stage left wings. The green room was empty. So was the hallway outside my office. The air felt noticeably warmer there.

I felt like a kid playing Blind Man's Buff . . . warmer, colder, really cold . . .

Which is how it felt in the Dungeon. Tension crackled like static electricity, raising the hairs atop the goose bumps.

When I heard muffled voices coming from the end of the corridor, I started to run. Fae-powered anger sent a storm of adrenaline pumping through my body. I paused outside the closed door of the men's dressing room long enough to hear Rowan claim that Alex had begged for his help and then resented him when it was offered, and Alex retort that he had never begged Rowan for anything in his life and wasn't about to start now.

At which point I flung open the door and shouted, "Have you completely lost your minds? Stop it! Both of you!"

It wasn't exactly helping professional behavior, but I was too infected by their anger to care. The roiling tension subsided. The temperature rose a good ten degrees. Alex slumped onto a chair. Rowan stalked past the costume rack and leaned his hands upon a table. I studied his reflection in the mirror, but his long hair shielded his face.

Still shaking from the cold and the shock, I demanded, "What started this?"

Alex frowned. Rowan shrugged.

"I swear to God, if one of you doesn't start talking . . ."

"It was my power." Rowan straightened abruptly and turned to face me. "My control has been a bit . . . shaky lately."

"No kidding." When he glared at me, I said, "Sorry. Aftereffects."

Rowan's hand rose to knead the scar at his throat. He'd told me once that when he hurt someone, it throbbed. Judging from both men's expressions, it must be throbbing like hell.

"I apologize, Alex. I said a lot of stupid things I didn't mean."

"That makes two of us. It's so weird—understanding exactly what's happening but feeling helpless to stop it. I've always been bad at shielding myself. When I succeed, I feel like I'm going through life swaddled in cotton. When I don't, I act like a lunatic."

"So are we okay here?" I asked.

After a cautious exchange of glances, Alex nodded. Rowan hesitated, then said, "Alex, you and I have known each other for decades. I've worked with you more closely than anyone on the staff. Our relationship has always been . . . cordial."

Cordial? Jesus. My relationship with the maids at the Golden Bough was cordial.

Rowan's head swung toward me. "I never had the kind of relationship with the staff that you have. I didn't attend birthday parties or holiday dinners—or barbecues. A necessary precaution, I believed. To avoid . . . emotional entanglements. Even with Helen, I never really let down the walls."

"You did for Maggie," Alex said.

"More accurately, Maggie bulldozed the walls and I stood there in the rubble, blinking in shock." Rowan's tentative smile faded. "The point I'm trying to make is that I've never had a truly close friendship with anyone. I'm not even sure that I can. But I've watched all of you these last few weeks—laughing and talking and arguing with each other. Somehow, you manage to maintain that precarious balance between your personal lives and your professional ones. And I . . . envy that."

I wondered if Alex was as shaken as I was by that unexpected confession.

"Friendship's like any other relationship," I said. "It takes two to tango. If you never get out on the dance floor . . ." I grimaced. "Okay, stupid metaphor."

"Actually, it's a very good one," Alex said.

Rowan scrutinized him. "Did you resent my aloofness?"

"When I was younger, I sometimes wished I had the key to unlock the door, but I appreciated the dangers. Even without Momma's warnings—and Helen's example."

"And my power?"

"It always seemed as much a burden as a gift. But there were still times I was damn envious."

Rowan nodded, the blank mask on his face and the firm grip on his power hiding every hint of emotion.

"I always wondered what I might have done with that kind of power. If I could have been a world-class musician or composer instead of a high school teacher."

"You *are* a world-class musician and composer," Rowan said quietly.

Alex bowed his head. "Thank you for that."

I was surprised to hear the tremor in his voice. And more surprised that I was party to this conversation. Maybe I was the safety net Rowan needed to crack open the door.

"But I doubt you'll be recognized as world-class in Dale," Rowan continued. "If you want that . . . if you need that . . ."

"I think about it sometimes, but . . . no. I'm happy in my little corner of the world. And I love teaching. Maybe that's something I inherited from you."

"From me?" Rowan echoed.

"By blood or by example. You're a teacher, too. You just have a different classroom."

Rowan nodded. Then he awkwardly stuck out his hand. Just as awkwardly, Alex rose and shook it.

"For what it's worth, Alex, I envied you, too. What you had with Annie."

Alex smiled, but the ache of his sadness throbbed through me.

"Maybe someday, you'll find—"

"Another Annie?" Alex shook his head.

"Another person to love."

Alex looked startled. Then he ducked his head and mumbled, "Sounds like one of Helen's impossible possibilities."

"I found Maggie. What's more impossible than that?"

Both men gazed at me, Alex with fondness and Rowan with a smoldering intensity that stole my breath. Then he abruptly strode out of the room.

Alex sank onto a dressing table. "In all the years I've known him, he's opened up to me just twice. Once, when Annie died. And again, in the letter he left when he returned to Faerie."

"It won't be easy for him," I warned. "The whole friendship thing."

"You're telling me? Still, he's making great progress."

Helen had said that during the early days of my rocky relationship with Rowan.

"But right now," Alex continued, "we've got to address this . . . situation."

"I thought he'd improve. Once Daddy settled down."

"Jack may get under Rowan's skin, but that's not why he's strung as tight as piano wire. You two haven't had a moment alone since he returned."

That wasn't entirely true. We'd had about forty-five minutes altogether, which had included a few passionate kisses and one interrupted feel.

I could focus during rehearsal. It was afterward—during a break or a hurried lunch—that I found myself watching him like an obsessed schoolgirl. The way his tongue flicked out to retrieve a blot of mayonnaise from his lip. The way his jeans hugged his ass when he walked back to the Smokehouse. Those long fingers cradling a glass of milk.

I came out of my reverie to discover Alex grinning. "And here I thought you were handling it better than he was."

"Yeah. Right. In the middle of my meeting with Catherine about the set for *Into the Woods*, she started giggling. I couldn't figure out why until I saw her staring at the rolled-up script I was holding and realized I was giving it a hand job."

Alex burst out laughing. "I can't believe Catherine didn't tell me."

"She was being kind. And you better be, too. Otherwise, I'll never hear the end of it."

"I promise. But you and Rowan have to carve out some time alone or you'll drive everybody crazy."

"How? Even if we could find a free hour, Daddy's always around."

"Then tell Daddy to take a nice, long walk around the pond."

"He'll know exactly what we're doing."

"So will your staff. If we're in the theatre."

I grimaced, recalling Mei-Yin's "Get a room!" comment.

Alex's expression became stern. "You're going to have to accept that, Maggie. When Rowan's power breaks free, everyone in the vicinity will feel it. I doubt even he can control it at the . . . um . . . height of passion."

"I can't believe I'm having this conversation."

"Then take steps. If Rowan's happy . . ."

"Yeah. I know."

I'd had *that* conversation with Janet two years ago.

"Tomorrow night's the cast party for *Annie*. I'll have Momma drag Jack up to the house as soon as the show's over. I suggest that you and Rowan arrive fashionably late."

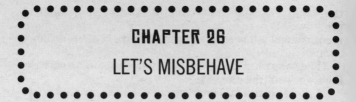

CHAPTER 26
LET'S MISBEHAVE

AFAERY IN THE THROES OF SEXUAL anticipation is no less distracting than one in the throes of sexual frustration. It's just a lot more enjoyable for all involved. And that Saturday afternoon, everyone was involved.

As soon as I walked into the theatre, Rowan's desire raced through me like a brushfire. Reinhard must have anticipated my reaction because he was waiting by the stage door. He seized my arm to steady me, and the power immediately receded. But I was light-headed with longing and even Reinhard had to dab his forehead with a handkerchief.

"This is not good," he said.

"This is not good," I agreed.

"I will speak to . . . *Gott im Himmel!*"

A Category Five hurricane of lust blasted through me. Moments later, Mei-Yin strode through the wings bellowing, "LOVE is in the AIR!" She shoved Reinhard up against the wall and began devouring his mouth like a rapacious tiger.

When she finally came up for air, perspiration was dripping down Reinhard's face and he was wearing a decidedly goofy smile. Then he caught sight of me, frowned, and extricated himself from his wife. The earth resumed its normal rotation and Hurricane Mei-Yin was downgraded to a tropical storm.

"I will definitely speak to—"

As Reinhard broke off, I darted nervous glances around

the theatre, seeking the direction of the next assault. A grim-faced Rowan marched down the stairs from his apartment. Daddy followed, looking as dazed as I felt.

"We're going for a walk," Rowan announced.

He strode out of the theatre, knapsack on his back, leaving Daddy to trail after him.

"I don't get it," I said. "It was never like this before."

"His power is stronger now," Reinhard said.

"And he's not GETTING any!" Mei-Yin leered at Reinhard and waltzed across the stage, singing "Some Day My Prince Will Come."

Reinhard mopped his forehead. "I will speak to the entire staff."

"Why? Rowan's gone."

"But the energy lingers, yes? And if the rest of the staff is like Mei-Yin . . ."

I groaned.

"Exactly. Come. We will round them up."

As we hurried across the stage, Reinhard stopped short and peered up at the balcony. That's when I noticed someone creeping up the stairs to the lighting booth.

"Hal!" Reinhard called.

Hal froze, then slowly turned toward us.

"What are you doing?"

"I just wanted to talk with Lee for a sec."

"You can talk later."

As Hal slunk back down the stairs, Reinhard's head jerked toward the stage right wings. "Where do you think *you* are going?"

Silence. Then: "I . . . forgot something," Javier said. "At the Mill."

Reinhard sighed. "You have twenty minutes."

"We'll only need ten!" Javier called. A moment later, I heard the pounding of footsteps and the slam of the stage door.

"How come they get to have fun and we don't?" Hal shouted from the balcony.

"Because they will be having fun off-site," Reinhard retorted. "If you and Lee cannot exercise a modicum of restraint, I suggest you do the same."

The door to the lighting booth banged open. Lee bolted

down the stairs and grabbed Hal's hand, putting an end to any speculation regarding their capacity for restraint.

"If you are not back by the half-hour call, I will dock you both a month's salary!"

As they sped toward the lobby stairs, I said, "It's an epidemic."

Reinhard handed me his handkerchief. "It will pass."

Ten minutes later, Javier returned to the theatre, whistling a happy tune. Lee and Hal showed up soon afterward, leaving me to suspect they'd gone no farther than the Smokehouse. When I went down to the Dungeon to check on the cast, I heard suspicious moaning coming from the men's bathroom. I cracked open the door and hissed, "There are children here!" After which I fled to the picnic area to allow my raging hormones to subside.

Thankfully, most of the energy had dissipated by curtain time. The overture still sounded like a 33-rpm record played at 78 speed and the girls were a bit manic in the opening scene, but Amanda got us back on track with "Maybe" and after that, the show proceeded normally.

I got a little misty at curtain calls, knowing this was the last time Amanda and her orphans would perform. I also realized Rowan and I needed to get to the cast party on time or I'd miss celebrating with the little ones whose parents would whisk them off after a half hour.

I briefly contemplated squeezing in a quickie during strike. Then I shuddered: Rowan's power plus a distracted cast and crew plus hammers, nails, and large set pieces . . . talk about your recipe for disaster.

Sighing, I shooed the company out to the picnic area for the usual post-matinee meal, courtesy of the Mandarin Chalet. Reinhard led the charge. When I spied him getting into Mei-Yin's car, I realized he wasn't hungry for Chinese food. Before the passenger door was even closed, they were speeding off, trailing dust and the faint sound of Mei-Yin's cackle.

I was still leaning against the stage door, smiling, when Rowan suddenly materialized beside me. Before I could do more than gasp, he grabbed my hand and pulled me up the stairs.

"Rowan! Wait!"

"Can't."

"But the cast is right outside. If they feel—"

"They won't."

"If they hear—"

"They won't!"

"But Daddy—"

"Dinner. Janet's."

"I don't have any condoms!"

"I do."

"Where did you get—?"

"Lee."

"Lee bought you a box of condoms?"

Rowan paused on the threshold of his apartment. "No. Lee bought me six boxes of condoms. Including Magnum Ecstasy, Magnum Fire and Ice, and one with climax control."

I started to giggle.

Rowan glared. "It was bad enough having to ask Janet to invite your father to dinner. I'll never hear the end of The Climax Control Crisis. Now do you want to do this or not?"

"Well, I was kind of looking forward to my shrimp and snow peas ..."

He pulled me inside and kicked the door shut.

If Mei-Yin's uncontrolled power had been a Category Five hurricane, Rowan's was just shy of a nuclear meltdown. The aroma of honeysuckle and animal musk made me dizzy. Creamy warmth curdled between my legs. Molten heat flooded my body, and my knees buckled. Only his body pressing mine against the door kept me on my feet.

His tongue slipped between my lips, the sandpaper-rough cat's tongue I had fantasized about for weeks. I sucked on it, and a low growl rumbled in his throat.

My breasts ached, swollen and heavy in my bra. My kicky sundress rubbed unpleasantly against my shoulders, my ribs, my waist. The very air hurt my oversensitive flesh.

The shock of his fingers on my bare thighs made me gasp. Warm hands slid inside my panties, but as Rowan pushed them down, they got caught somewhere north of my knees.

I shimmied wildly. Rowan cursed.

I heard the sound of ripping fabric, and the pressure

around my knees gave way to the shivery sensation of nylon skimming down my legs and settling atop my feet.

I clawed at his shirt. Rowan batted my hands away and began fumbling with the buttons on his jeans. I moaned, nearly weeping with frustration. He seized the waistband of his pants and gave a mighty tug. Buttons clattered onto the hardwood floor like hailstones.

He dug a packet out of his pocket. Holding one end in his teeth, he ripped it open, then spat the sliver onto the floor.

He seized my hand and turned toward the bedroom.

"No. Here. Hurry!"

His mouth claimed mine again as I fell back against the door. His knuckles brushed my bare belly, sending shock waves of desire through me. I stared into those glittering green eyes, mesmerized by the golden sparks flashing in their depths. Then his hands cupped my bottom and he lifted me as effortlessly as he had torn open his jeans.

I wrapped my legs around his hips. Visions of *The Godfather* danced in my head: Sonny Corleone giving it to the bridesmaid, and—for some unknown reason—fat Clemenza drawling, "Leave the gun. Take the cannoli." Then Rowan's cresting desire swept away all thoughts of Corleone and cannoli and I just hung on for dear life.

It was over in seconds, shattering my previous Olympic orgasm record. My legs oozed off his hips to dangle in the air like a rag doll's. His heart thudded against mine, as rhythmic as the blood pulsing in my ears. Then I made out another sound—just as soft, just as rhythmic—that seemed to be coming from outside the apartment.

Rowan cursed. A moment later, I identified the sound as footsteps pattering up the stairs.

The Olympic judges would have deducted points for my dismount, but I managed to stick the landing. After that, it was all I could do to stagger into the bedroom and collapse on the bed.

The latch rattled once. Twice.

"The door won't open," my father complained.

"No," Rowan said. "It won't."

"I left my script in your knapsack."

"Get it later."

"But Janet's going to run lines with me after dinner."

"I have company, Jack."

There was a long silence. Then a soft chuckle. "Well, why didn't you say so? Hi, Maggie!"

I pulled a pillow over my face. Then threw it aside and called, "Hi, Jack!"

"I thought I felt something weird. Now I know what it was. Hot monkey love!"

Rowan cleared his throat. "I'll get your things."

"Jeez, if you wanted some private time, you should have just asked. Next time, tell me to take a walk around the pond. That'll be the code."

I almost wished Alex was here to share this moment.

Rowan's boots thudded on the floorboards. The front door creaked open.

"Here's your script. And your notebook. And a pen. Enjoy dinner."

"I will. We're having fried chicken and potato salad and—"

The door slammed.

I made a brief effort to sit and gave it up; my limbs felt like they were weighted down with rocks. In spite of the ceiling fan, the bedroom was stifling. That's when I noticed that the door to the balcony was closed. As were the skylights. With any luck, Rowan's precautions had prevented the cast from hearing my final shriek of ecstasy.

The soft sound of footsteps alerted me to his approach. He hesitated in the doorway, then strode through the bedroom and wrenched open the sliding door.

For a moment, he stood there with his back to me. It was unpleasantly reminiscent of his behavior the night of my first Olympic orgasm. But when he turned toward me, he looked so miserable that I struggled into a sitting position.

"If you ever doubted the selfishness of the Fae, you saw ample evidence of it just now. I acted like a stag in rut."

"Well, I acted like a cat in heat, so I guess it all evens out."

"And you're not upset."

A statement, not a question; he could feel that I wasn't.

"A little unnerved, maybe. It was kind of like . . . that first time."

"At least that night, I tried to control my power and failed. Today, I didn't even try. I wanted you and I just . . ."

"Got what you wanted?"

He winced.

"That was supposed to be a joke."

"And you're supposed to be angry!"

"And *you're* angry because I'm not?"

"I just . . . I don't understand! I drag you up the stairs. I pull you into the apartment. I mount you like an animal . . ."

"I could have said no when you were dragging me up the stairs. Or when you asked if I wanted to do this. Your power wasn't influencing me then." I patted the bed, and he sank down beside me. "What happened wasn't exactly what I expected. But I wanted you, Rowan. You must have felt that."

"Yes, but—"

"That's why I'm not mad."

The tension in his body drained away, but his frown remained. "It was supposed to be perfect. Our first time together. I wanted it to be slow and beautiful and romantic. Yet when push came to shove—"

"So to speak."

That won a small smile from him.

I mustered my energy and leaned forward to plant a kiss on the tip of his nose. "So this time we ended up with wham, bam, thank you, ma'am. And Daddy pounding on the door. Next time, we'll do slow and beautiful and romantic. Okay?"

He just stared at me. "I can sense your feelings, your moods. Sometimes, I can even guess what you're thinking. But I'll never be able to understand you, will I? Not completely. Or predict how you'll react."

"Well, how dull would that be?"

"Predictable isn't dull. It's reassuring. And safe. And—"

"Dull. People aren't predictable, Rowan. Life isn't predictable."

"It was. For me. Once. Then I met you."

"You're supposed to smile now and say it was the best thing that ever happened to you."

"It *was* the best thing that ever happened to me. But it was also . . . frightening. It still is. I've never behaved like I did today. Even when I was young and stupid and susceptible to every shift in emotion. Ever since I came back, I feel like I'm walking on quicksand. I'm not even sure who I am anymore."

Did he even realize he was echoing my father's words? I considered assuring him that he, too, would find the answers he needed. Instead, I cupped his face between my hands.

"You're a faery in a human world. A man without an identity. A director who's not directing. And a lover who's spent almost no time with his beloved. If you weren't unsure, you'd be nuts! But it'll get easier."

"Promise?"

I crossed my heart. "And when we're old and gray... well, when I'm old and gray and you're still raven-haired and handsome and we have to pretend you're my son or you have to do the whole glamour thing in order *not* to look like my son because we'd totally creep people out if they saw us together and we were making out ... I forget my point ..."

"We'll laugh about this?"

"Absolutely."

Rowan nodded. But his smile was disturbingly bleak.

BLEAK PRETTY MUCH DESCRIBED HELL WEEK, too. Even with a cue-to-cue Sunday afternoon and a walk-through of the scene changes Sunday evening, Monday's tech rehearsal lasted a brutal five hours.

The set was simple enough—a stepped unit with two playing areas for the children's bedrooms upstage left and right and a larger central area for the other interior scenes. The maze and greenhouse would be created downstage. Hal had also built a painted "frame" around the proscenium arch that looked like elaborately turned wrought iron until the lights came up for the finale to reveal it as a flower-bedecked arbor.

Lee's lighting set the mood: a fiery Indian sky and a cloud-filled one in Yorkshire; the ghostly blues of the storm sequences and the amber pools of light that illuminated the dreary mansion; the silvery moonlight that poured through the door to the secret garden in the final moments of Act One and the brilliant sunlight that flooded the garden at the end of the show. But all those effects required a zillion cues and twice that many stops and starts to ensure that they were coordinated with the music and scene changes.

A few of Hal's design elements had to be raised and lowered from the flies: two crystal chandeliers for the ballroom, large portraits of Lily in the gallery, damask draperies in Archibald's library. Unfortunately, one bank of draperies kept getting stuck in mid-flight, adding a Salvador Daliesque touch to the Yorkshire sky. The portraits were more obedient, but the empty frame in which Michaela was supposed to stand swayed back and forth as if she were on the deck of the *Titanic*.

The other set pieces were placed and cleared by the actors. Most were easy—a garden bench here, a settee there. What they couldn't carry on was supposed to roll smoothly. Given the Crossroads tradition of reluctant rolling, Catherine had been zealous about her casters—a bit overzealous judging from the way Colin's bed whizzed onto the platform, accompanied by the startled shrieks of its occupant.

However, the giant topiaries in the shapes of stylized birds and flowers took top honors in the "Neither Smooth nor Seamless" competition, turning "It's a Maze" into a rousing Edwardian bumper car sequence. Every time an actress brushed against them, her dress clung to the damn things like Velcro. The ghosts spent more time tugging at their skirts than wafting.

And then there was the mist. Our fog machine had been recalcitrant during *Brigadoon* and surly during *The Fantasticks*. Now, it was gleefully bent on world domination. By the end of tech, the atmosphere was more *Jekyll and Hyde* than *The Secret Garden*.

Rowan gave me a magical neck rub. Janet gave me whisky. Between the two, I managed to sleep.

Our first dress rehearsal was rocky. Our second was marginally better. Whatever substance Hal applied to the topiaries mitigated their desire to snatch at the women's clothing. Whatever magic Alex applied to the pit band helped them discover volumes other than fortissimo. The set changes more or less worked. The actors more or less found their pools of light. The Dreamers wafted, menaced, and comforted at most of the right moments. Michaela looked and sounded beautiful, Gregory looked and sounded tormented, and Roger avoided filial fondling. Hal's costumes were flat-out gorgeous. Gregory's worked so well that I serenaded Hal with a non-Lerner-and-Loewe approved version of "I've Grown Accustomed to His Hump."

Daddy skipped both dress rehearsals. He said he wanted to be wowed opening night. I just hoped he—and the rest of the audience—would be.

I approached the opening without my usual blend of hope, terror, and excitement. Even with the staff, the possibility of disaster had always existed. When a faery's got your back, the "anything can happen in live theatre" vibe dissipates—especially since we had discussed the moments that required a little magical boost.

I yearned for my days as an actress when Rowan's magic had been mysterious and thrilling and occasionally unnerving. The whole idea of planned magic felt wrong.

Nancy's "break a leg" phone call lifted my spirits. Having lived through Hell Week of *Brigadoon*, she knew how to transform this one from a hair-whitening disaster into a series of comical misadventures.

By the time my mother called, I was able to greet her with a cheery hello.

"What's wrong?" she demanded.

"Nothing's wrong."

"You sound too cheery."

"I was trying to disguise how exhausted I am."

"Well, you failed. Was Hell Week awful?"

"No more than usual. But the show will be fine. You'll see for yourself on Saturday."

There was a brief silence, then a sigh. "Sue's mother has taken a turn for the worse. The hospice people think it's only a matter of days. Flaky Leila and her husband are doing some shamanic circle thing this weekend. Laura said she'd try to fly in next week. By then, her grandmother will be in the ground."

As her tirade escalated, a shameful feeling of relief washed over me: at least now we wouldn't have to worry about hiding Daddy. I didn't want Sue's poor mother to die or Sue to be grief-stricken or Mom to be worried about her best friend, but I had to admit the timing was terrific—and that I was an awful person for thinking that.

"There's a special circle in Hell for unfeeling daughters," my mother declared.

"I feel bad!"

"I'm talking about Laura and Leila. Anyway, I hate to leave you in the lurch, but . . ."

"Of course, you have to be there for Sue."

"I'll pay for the room. And the tickets."

"We'll fill the room. And sell the tickets. Just let me know when you're coming up and—"

"It'll have to be closing weekend. We have a birthday party for Chris' granddaughter next Saturday."

"I'll put aside two tickets. And if there's no room at the inn—"

"You'll put us up in a stable?"

"Only if you arrive on a donkey. And pregnant."

"Round up some wise men to offer me gold and frankincense and I'll consider it."

"No myrrh?"

"Ancient embalming fluid is not my idea of a hostess gift."

"I'll talk to Janet. I'm sure she'd be happy to put you up."

"*I'll* talk to Janet. You have enough on your plate." There was a brief pause. Then she said, "How are ... things?"

"If you mean Rowan, they're okay."

"Just okay?"

"I've hardly seen him since ..."

He ravished me against the front door.

"... Hell Week started. We'll have more time together during *Into the Woods*."

"Yes. I suppose you will."

Her voice was heavy with disapproval. She'd been openly skeptical about the wisdom of casting Rowan and our ability to work together.

"So the two of you are ...?"

"We're fine, Mom."

"Don't get defensive."

"I wasn't ... okay, I *was* defensive. But I hate that you want this to fail."

"That's not true! I want it to last a lifetime." In the silence that followed, I could practically hear her choosing her words. "I'm just afraid it won't."

I sighed. She sighed. We avoided talking about Rowan. By the time I hung up, my cheery mood had vanished.

"Snap out of it!" Janet ordered. "You've got more important things to worry about than your mother's opinion of Rowan." When I stared at her blankly, she exclaimed, "*The Secret Garden*? Opening night? Ring any bells?"

"I don't have to worry about the show. Rowan will work his magic. Everyone will be awed ..."

"Is that what you've been in such a funk about?"

"I don't know. Maybe. It just feels so ... predictable."

"Theatre? Predictable? You've got to be kidding. And since when has Rowan pulled all the strings? There were plenty of flubs in *Brigadoon* and *The Sea-Wife* and *Carousel*. Rowan's magic is the icing on the cake. And he'll use it as sparingly as he always has."

"But when you know the garden will look real at the end of the show, it kind of kills the anticipation."

"You're on the inside now, Maggie. Knowing how the magic works is never as much fun as watching the magician pull a rabbit out of his hat. It's our job to make the hard work look effortless and the magic seem like a cool special effect or an especially wonderful performance. But we can still marvel at those moments. Because *we* know they're really magical."

CHAPTER 28

IT'S BAD LUCK TO SAY GOOD LUCK
ON OP'NING NIGHT

WHETHER JANET'S WORDS GOT ME OUT OF my
funk or I realized I was being a total drama queen, I was
back in my groove by that evening: the heart racing, cotton-
mouthed, armpit-soaked, stomach-lurching, everything's-
coming-up-roses-unless-we-bomb excitement of opening
night.

I stopped in Rowan's apartment when I arrived at the
theatre. Daddy preened when I complimented him on the
seersucker shirt and chinos I'd bought for him. Then Rowan
walked in from the bedroom.

"Catherine and I did a little online shopping."

The black leather pants were the same ones he'd worn to
The Sea-Wife's opening, but the silk shirt was new. The deep
green made his eyes sparkle like emeralds.

He shrugged, as if his beautiful shirt had suddenly
shrunk two sizes "I just wanted to do you proud on your
opening night."

"You always do me proud. And you look gorgeous."

"So do you."

His gaze traveled over the green sarong that Hal had
insisted I wear. I'd resisted at first; I'd worn it my final night
with Rowan and it carried too many sad memories But Hal
claimed the bamboo pattern was perfect for opening night
of *The Secret Garden*. And the warmth of Rowan's gaze
made me happy I had acquiesced.

"I carried the memory of you in that dress every day we were apart."

I let out a shaky sigh and reluctantly said, "We better get down to the green room."

"Not yet. Jack and I have an opening night gift for you."

Mystified, I followed them into the bedroom. On the bed I discovered a jug of detergent, a bottle of fabric softener—and two stacks of neatly folded clothes.

Most women wouldn't get weepy about grown men doing their own laundry, but for my men, it was a milestone.

"Rowan didn't like touching the machines," Daddy said. "Even with gloves. So I did most of the work."

"You also said that bleach brightens everything," Rowan said. "Fortunately, I insisted on a test run."

He opened the armoire and pulled out the jeans he'd ripped open during our quickie.

"The tie-dyed look'll come back," Daddy declared.

"And I'll be in the fashion vanguard when it does," Rowan replied.

"It's the best present you could have given me."

"Don't worry," Daddy said. "He got you flowers, too. But it's bad luck to give them to you before the show."

I nodded. "And tonight, we don't want anything but good luck."

❧❧

When we gathered in the green room for our toast, I discovered why Hal had been so insistent about my sarong—and why Rowan had taken the unusual step of wearing a green shirt: the entire staff had gone not-so-secret garden. Alex sported a red rose on the lapel of his tuxedo. Reinhard had tucked a green pocket square into the breast pocket of his black suit. Hal had chosen a mauve shirt for the occasion, Lee, a gold one. Janet wore a pale green silk sheath, Catherine, a breezy little flowered number, and Mei-Yin, a scarlet dress with white plum blossoms. As captain of the stage crew, Javier was doomed to wear black, but he sported a goofy circlet of flowers on his head—our ninja Queen of the May.

I got predictably sniffly, Janet predictably rolled her eyes, and even Catherine took a tiny sip of champagne during our toast.

Although Janet and Reinhard flanked me as I led warm-ups, it was the faery lounging against the back wall of the green room who made the magic. As many times as Rowan's power had touched me, I had never deliberately called it forth. As I instructed the cast to close their eyes, I felt like an ancient priestess summoning the elemental forces of the universe.

My toes tingled as his power touched them. My feet grew heavy, as if rooted to the very bedrock of Vermont. A steady vibration rose up through my legs, like sap rising in the spring.

Heat flushed my body as the power flowed up through my belly and chest. My voice fell into a rhythmic chant. My fingers uncurled like new leaves. My body swayed like a sapling, moved by an otherworldly force as ageless as wind and sun and time.

I was caught in the spell yet standing apart, observing its effects. Driven by the growing urgency of the power yet directing it from my little island of calm.

Rowan sensed every shift in my emotions and responded as I framed the words for the cast. We were dancers, our spirits moving together instead of our bodies. We were music, he the song and I the singer. We were separate yet linked by the power flowing between us and through us, between and through the clasped hands of those in our circle.

Twin powers—Fae and human—feeding us and feeding on us, charging us with anticipation and excitement, racing around the circle, pulsing through every body, every mind, every spirit as the song built to a relentless climax.

"Let it go!"

The energy burst free on a wave of cries and groans and sighs. Even the cast members who had performed in *Annie* looked dazed. But they had never experienced a warm-up powered by Rowan Mackenzie.

"Just breathe."

His power retreated on a wave of love that told me more clearly than any words that our brief communion had touched him as deeply as it had me.

Maybe that's why I jettisoned my usual speech and simply said, "Hold on to that power. Bring it to the stage. And we'll make magic here tonight."

The house lights began to dim as Rowan and I slid into our seats. Daddy swiveled around and flashed a grin. "Janet's my date."

Janet gazed heavenward before whispering, "Turn around and behave."

Daddy winked at me and obediently faced the stage. The house lights faded to black. Rowan gave my icy hand a reassuring squeeze. A spot picked up Alex in the orchestra pit. He acknowledged the applause with a quick nod and took his place at the piano.

The rustle of a program. The creak of a nearby seat. The palpable anticipation as if the theatre itself were holding its breath. Then the brass section launched into the "Prelude."

After three short measures of "A Bit of Earth," the strings introduced "Come to My Garden." My heartbeat ignored their serene strains to gallop along with the racing counterpoint of the woodwinds.

The full orchestra took up the melody. The majestic tempo grew slower. My heartbeat sped up. The brass and woodwinds dropped out, leaving only the throb of strings. I took a series of calming breaths as harp and bells shimmered up the scale in the mysterious motif of the "Opening."

A pool of amber light picked up Natasha sitting downstage right, studying a gilt-framed photograph. The motif sounded again and behind the scrim, a cool lavender light picked up the ghostly figure of Lily on the upstage left platform. Michaela's voice made me shiver with pleasure as she sang the gentle lullaby about the flowers she would keep safe in her garden.

As the lights slowly faded on her, the sky behind the scrim glowed orange, revealing the Indian Fakir on the upstage center platform. Thankfully, Paul no longer resembled Bert Healy with a turban. He even managed to avoid teetering when he lifted a foot in the slow, stylized movement Mei-Yin had taught him.

Before I could wonder if she was giving him some magical help, Larry entered and bent to kiss Natasha's hair. My fingers involuntarily tightened on Rowan's, knowing that our first technical hurdle was looming.

Instead of the bed called for in the script, Hal had come up with the idea of using a stylized canopy that would rise from the floor as the Fakir chanted, like a cobra emerging from a snake charmer's basket. After the fly operator raised it to the right height, four actors would install poles and stretch the gauzy fabric out to create an open-sided canopy. While the idea was cool, the effect was usually spoiled by actors juggling poles and fabric.

As Larry lifted Natasha, the scrim rose. A quartet of actors dressed as Indian servants emerged from the wings. As the groups moved slowly toward center, the tent shimmied upward. The servants seized the four corners of the long swath of fabric, slipped their poles into them, and backed away just as Larry gently laid Natasha in her "canopy bed."

There were appreciative murmurs from the audience. I squeezed Rowan's hand in thanks and felt his love warming my fingers.

He used his magic as sparingly as Janet had predicted: to control the mist that snaked obediently around the actors' ankles, to make the topiaries glide smoothly around the stage, to calm Ethan when he dried up in his first scene, and to give Neil the extra nudge he needed to transform "Winter's on the Wing" into a joyous rite of spring.

The "Final Storm" erupted with lightning and thunder, drawing gasps from the audience. The frenzied singing of the Dreamers gave way to the ominous "Mistress Mary, Quite Contrary" round. Natasha appealed to the Dreamers, but they glided past her like living topiaries, brandishing their red handkerchiefs.

Rowan suddenly tensed. I glanced at him, then back at the stage, wondering what had disturbed him. Natasha conveyed Mary's growing terror perfectly as she wove in and out of the maze of Dreamers, desperately searching for her father. Maybe Rowan was concentrating on controlling the mix of voices so that each individual line came through clearly against the choral singing of "It's a Maze."

As the Dreamers slowly circled Natasha, Daddy began shifting in his seat. Was he simply restless or did he have to pee? Well, Act One would be over in a few minutes. He could certainly wait that long.

I forced my attention back to the stage, but I couldn't concentrate because of Daddy's infernal squirming.

Janet's head snapped toward him. She whispered something, but he just rocked back and forth in his seat.

My impatience vanished at his obvious distress. I leaned forward to reassure him, but when I touched his shoulder, he cried out and batted frantically at the air.

Heads turned in our direction, audience members distracted from the action unfolding onstage by the personal drama playing out in the house.

Rowan's forearm thrust me back in my seat. He slid forward to rest his hand on Daddy's right shoulder. Daddy moaned, and I pressed my fist to my mouth to keep from doing the same.

I'd worried that the vivid special effects might frighten some of the children, but my father knew too much about stage magic to be this upset. Had the ghostly Dreamers triggered some awful memory of the Borderlands? Did Mary's futile attempt to escape the maze of Dreamers remind him of his terrified flight from the Crow-Men?

The number built in intensity, the Dreamers' "Mistress Mary" chant underscored by the dissonant blare of horns and the wild twittering of the piccolo and the relentless beat of the timpani. In a few moments, the terrifying music would segue into the soothing melody of "Come to My Garden" and the nightmare would be over. If Daddy could just hold on, if Rowan and Janet could keep him calm for ten more seconds ...

Daddy quivered like a dog straining at its leash. Natasha darted through a pool of light, red hair washed to a pale strawberry blonde by the white light.

Only then did I understand my father's distress. I was too shaken to move. All I could do was sit there as the music reached its frenzied peak.

A single oboe played "Come to My Garden." Natasha flung herself into Larry's arms, father and child reunited at last.

The Dreamers began drifting offstage. I leaned forward to touch my father, to let him know without words that I shared his anguish.

Rowan shoved me back and clambered over me just as Daddy leaped to his feet and shouted, "No!"

There were startled exclamations from the audience. Still frozen in their embrace, Natasha and Larry broke character to stare into the house. The oboe faltered, then picked up the melody once again.

Daddy tottered down the aisle. Tears welled in my eyes as he raised his arms to embrace his lost child.

To embrace me.

My fingers dug into the worn nap of his abandoned seat, still warm from my father's body. Only by gripping the seat hard could I keep from jumping up and running down the aisle and crying, "I'm here, Daddy. I've always been here."

Rowan seized Daddy's left arm. Janet seized his right.

The music swelled, mercifully covering the rising tide of whispers. Soothing magic rippled through the sostenuto of the strings as Alex tried to calm musicians and audience alike. I felt the steadying throb of Reinhard's power and the determined beat of Mei-Yin's, urging everyone to focus on the stage.

As Michaela stepped aside to reveal the door to the secret garden, even those seated around me settled back in their seats. Their soft "Ahh" told me that the door had swung open, silhouetting Natasha in a flood of moonlight.

I didn't see it. I was still watching the shadowy figures escort my struggling father out of the theatre.

CHAPTER 29
HOLD ON

I HAD NO TIME TO DEAL WITH MY EMOTIONS. When the house lights came up a moment later, I had to concentrate on damage control. I delegated my available staff to handle the audience and asked Bernie and Frannie to deal with the board. As Long made a beeline toward me, I beat a hasty retreat to the Dungeon to check on the cast and found Reinhard outside the women's dressing room.

"They are fine," he whispered. "I told them it was Jack and . . ." He shrugged uncomfortably.

They had all witnessed Daddy's outbursts. This was just another crazy Jack moment.

Natasha, God love her, was more concerned about Daddy than the fact that he had spoiled her big moment. Most of the other women were mollified when I told them he had been overcome by their performances, but a few grumbled that he had ruined their opening night.

"Be glad the guy got into it," Debra snapped, "and focus on Act Two."

I shot her a grateful look and continued down the hall to the men's dressing room. Larry still seemed a little nonplussed, but Otis' reassuring presence was calming everyone. I squeezed his arm, got a firm nod in return, and moved on to the musicians' green room.

Trapped in the pit—and assuaged by Alex's magic—they were just puzzled because the underscoring had fallen apart. Alex had his arm around the shoulders of the poor

654

oboe player, clearly bolstering his sagging confidence with Fae magic.

I arrived at the breezeway to find staff and board doing their best to downplay the incident. The audience members who had been sitting near Daddy still seemed shaken, but Mei-Yin and Lee were working them hard. Lee's power pulsed with strength and calm, while Mei-Yin's crackled with humor. The odd combination worked. My racing heartbeat slowed and I felt the urge to laugh the whole thing off—just some poor old guy who'd gotten carried away by the magic of theatre. Things could be worse, I thought, as I raced up to Rowan's apartment.

Then I heard the shouting.

I flung open the door and hurried inside to find Long stalking around the living area and Janet clinging to his arm.

"Jack's asleep in the bedroom," Janet informed me. "Rowan gave him a tranquilizer."

I nodded my understanding of her faeryspeak. Before I could assure Long that everything was under control, he said, "What the hell just happened? What's *wrong* with that man?"

"Nothing's wrong with him," I replied, trying hard to keep my voice level.

"First, those disturbances in rehearsals . . . oh, I heard all about them. Is he mentally unbalanced or—?"

"No! And keep your voice down or you'll wake him up."

"Let's all keep our voices down," Janet advised. "And let's not overreact because Jack got caught up in the show."

"He's an actor, for God's sake! How could he get *that* caught up in the show?"

"He's been through a lot!" I exclaimed. "So cut him a fucking break, Long."

Long's eyes widened, but I was too sick with worry to care.

"Why don't we all sit down?"

I hadn't even noticed Rowan standing in the doorway, his voice and power radiating calm. The tension in the room dissipated. I sank into an easy chair, limp and weak-kneed. Janet and Rowan guided Long to the sofa. They sat on either side of him, Janet clasping his hand, Rowan gripping his forearm.

"The show brought back some painful memories for Jack," Rowan said.

"He just wasn't ready to deal with them," Janet murmured.

"But he'll be fine."

"And so will the show."

"Actors are resilient. They're used to dealing with little bumps during a performance."

"And that's all this was."

"There's nothing to worry about."

"Nothing at all."

Long nodded, soothed by their soft voices and their seductive Fae power. Then he blinked and asked, "Should I make some sort of announcement before Act Two? To reassure the audience?"

Rowan patted Long's arm. "That might draw more attention to the incident. Better to go on as if nothing had happened, don't you think?"

"Yes . . . better to go on . . ."

Janet squeezed Long's hand. "If anyone asks, we'll say that Jack was taken ill."

"Yes . . . that's good . . ."

Brainwashing my board president was *not* good. And observing the way Long's head bobbed obediently made me a little queasy.

Get used to it, Graham. This is what it will be like living with a faery. There will always be suspicions to quell, truths to avoid, lies to invent.

Rowan ushered Long toward the front door, one hand resting lightly on his shoulder. Long hesitated, then eased free.

"I know he's your friend, Rowan. But as president of the board, my first responsibility is to this theatre. No matter how much I may sympathize with Jack's problems, the fact remains that he's a disruptive influence."

"I'll look after Jack. And I give you my word, there will be no more disruptions."

"That's not your job."

"But it *is* my responsibility."

Long shook his head. "The Crossroads Theatre isn't a . . . a halfway house. If this man is as deeply troubled as I suspect, he needs professional care."

"He needs the Crossroads," I said. "He was an actor once. He could be again."

"And when he's ready, I'll be the first to welcome him back."

"Back?" I echoed.

"I'm sorry. Jack has to leave. Tomorrow."

"No!"

Rowan's power lanced through me, an urgent plea for silence. Janet advanced on Long, her cold eyes belying the warmth of her smile.

I couldn't let Long send Daddy away, but neither did I want to watch them break him. And they *would* break him. Long might be less susceptible to their brainwashing, but he would not be able to resist it forever. It would eat away at his resolution, transform his objections into complacency, convince him to do what they wanted—what we wanted. Could I let them do that when his concerns were perfectly valid?

"Stop!" I exclaimed.

Rowan and Janet shot me identical looks of disbelief; it was the first time I had ever noted any resemblance between them. Long merely seemed puzzled.

"You can't send Jack away. I've cast him in *Into the Woods.*" As Long's expression shifted into outrage, I quickly added, "He needs to act again. He needs to find a purpose in life."

"Why is it our responsibility to give him that?" Long demanded. "And why are you so worked up about him? You've only known the man a few weeks."

"He's my father."

Long gaped. Janet sighed. Rowan just watched me.

"My mother divorced him more than twenty years ago. She took her maiden name again and changed mine, too. I got an occasional postcard from him and then . . . nothing. Until Rowan brought him back to me. He didn't recognize me. He doesn't even know I'm his daughter."

My voice broke. Rowan hurried to my side, his arm and his power steadying me.

Long glanced toward the bedroom. "He doesn't know?" he whispered.

Rowan shook his head. "We thought the shock might be too much for him."

"That's why he got so upset tonight. He was seeing *me* on that stage, not Natasha."

Rowan's anxiety flashed through me, then vanished as he tamped down his power. All the time he'd been dealing with Daddy, he must have been worried sick about me.

"He's had a hard life," I told Long. "But he's coping. And he's excited about performing again. The Narrator is only a small part. I've asked Rowan to play the Mysterious Man."

"Rowan!" Long exclaimed.

"You saw him as Billy Bigelow," Janet reminded him. "He can certainly handle the Mysterious Man."

"That's not the point! I should have been informed. About all of this."

"You're right," I agreed. "I'm sorry. But—"

"What happens if Jack can't go on?" Long demanded in a furious whisper. "Or—God forbid—he breaks down on-stage?"

"Bernie is understudying the role. And he'll be playing the matinees."

"Bernie's in on this, too? Good God, what else have you been keeping from me?"

"I'll be with Jack during rehearsals and the show," Rowan said. "I can keep him calm and focused."

"You didn't do a very good job tonight," Long noted.

"No. He caught me ... off guard. That won't happen again."

"I know it's a risk," I said. "But I'm asking you to trust our instincts. To trust *me*." Careful to keep my voice soft, I added, "He may be my father, but I love this theatre. If I thought he couldn't handle the stress—or turn in a good performance—I would never suggest this."

Long frowned. "Letting him stay is one thing, Maggie. But putting him in the show ..."

"Come to the Follies," Rowan urged. "See how he does in that."

"He's in the Follies, too?"

"A kind of dress rehearsal," Rowan said.

"That's hardly the same as performing on the main stage."

"It'll be fun," Janet assured him. "I'll even wager Jack will exceed your expectations. If I win, I'll make you dinner.

If I lose . . ." She flashed a teasing smile. ". . . I'll make you breakfast."

To my astonishment, Long blushed. Then he nodded brusquely. "But if I decide he's not ready to perform in *Into the Woods*, that's the end of it. Agreed?"

I nodded meekly. I even worked up a grateful smile; I only hoped it was half as convincing as Janet's kittenish one.

No matter what happened at the Follies, I would never permit Long to send my father away. Daddy had finally opened the door to his past, and I was going to help him walk through it.

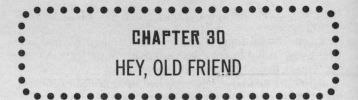

CHAPTER 30
HEY, OLD FRIEND

THANKS TO THE SHITLOAD OF FAE POWER circulating through the theatre, Act Two went off without a hitch. When the lights came up on the final scene, even I gasped when I beheld the brilliant red and gold of the roses, the deep green of the foliage, and the otherworldly blue of the sky. When Archibald embraced Colin and Mary, I sniffled along with the audience, my vision blurred by tears and the shimmering light that suffused the stage.

I wished Daddy could have seen it: the transformation of the garden, the transformation of all those touched by its magic. I wished he could have seen Archibald and Colin reunited. And I wished that life imitated art. I didn't expect that Mom and Daddy and I would ever stand in Helen's sun-drenched garden, all wrongs forgiven, all happiness restored, but for the first time I had real hope that some of those old wounds could be healed.

For the next two days, he remained closeted in Rowan's apartment, emerging only to apologize to the cast for "getting carried away" and to come to Janet's house to run through *Snow White* with the rest of the staff. He seemed so relieved to throw himself into our rehearsal that I gave up any thought of telling him I was his daughter. It was far more important for him to shine during the Follies.

Nancy's arrival offered a welcome respite. Even if I could only escape for a few hours, dinner at the Bough would give me a chance to decompress.

When I invited Frannie to join us for a drink, she shook her head. "I'm waiting for the couple who've booked the Honeymoon Suite to check in."

"So sit where you can see the lobby."

After a brief hesitation, she agreed, and for the next fifteen minutes, I enjoyed the rare treat of talking about ordinary things like the weather, the economy, and the recent coyote incursions in Dale. Then Frannie jumped up and exclaimed, "I think Mr. and Mrs. Louis just came in."

"Maybe I should go out and—"

"No. You gals enjoy your dinner." She winked at Nancy and whispered, "If you get any juicy gossip about Maggie and Rowan, be sure and pass it along."

As soon as Frannie disappeared into the lobby, Nancy pounced.

"Something's happened."

"You and my mother should start a detective agency."

I waited until Beth presented our salads and retreated to the kitchen. Then I plunged into the saga of opening night. Nancy expressed cautious optimism about Daddy's breakthrough, but her expression clouded when I described the aftermath with Long.

"You used the F-word?"

"I was upset. I apologized later. And was very sweet. Well, sweet for me."

"Don't shrug this off!" she exclaimed with rare heat. "Rowan allowed you to talk like that because he loved you. But you can't do it with Long."

The arrival of our dinners saved me from answering. When Beth departed, I said, "I know I should follow Janet's example and smile and coax and cajole. It's just . . ."

"Cajoling isn't your strong suit. But at least treat Long with respect. And when he drives you crazy, count to five before you say anything."

"Not to ten?"

"You'd never make it that far." Nancy picked up her fork and set it down again. "I know you love your father. And you want him to be happy. But you can't sacrifice your future for him."

"It won't come to that. Long will—"

"It's not only Long. There's Rowan to consider. And

Alison. And your staff. I don't want to see you jeopardizing those relationships because you're putting all your time and energy into developing one with your father."

I poked my grilled trout, appetite gone. I was all too aware of how little time I had spent with Rowan, how much extra work I had thrust onto my staff. And every day that I allowed to pass without telling my mother about Daddy seemed a betrayal of the closeness we had forged. I doubted my father would ever give me the kind of love and support I received from them.

And from the woman sitting across the table from me.

"You're absolutely right," I said. "And now, enough about Daddy. Let's talk about you."

She described her added workload at the library in the wake of the budget cuts and her poor mother's case of shingles. In the middle of a story about her cat's ear infection, she broke off abruptly.

"This is about as much fun as discussing your fight with Long."

"Who cares? Sometimes, life is crappy bosses and shingles and ear infections. So what did the vet say about Dante?"

Only when coffee arrived did she casually mention that she'd gone out on two dates with a college professor named Ed.

"Two dates? And I'm only hearing about it now?"

"Well, we just had the second date last night and—"

"Wait. Start at the beginning."

Through a combination of wheedling and relentless interrogation, I got most of the details. Nancy assured me it was "too soon to tell" if anything would develop, but her faint blush and soft expression indicated things were developing pretty fast.

When she said she had a surprise for me at tomorrow's matinee, I was sure she was going to produce Ed. I waited outside the theatre in a fever of anticipation. But Nancy arrived alone.

"No Ed?"

She surveyed the horde of people streaming toward the lobby and suddenly grinned. "I brought someone else. Two someones, actually."

A bass voice bellowed, "Yo, Brooklyn!" And the burly

figure of Lou Mancini waded through the crowd like a T-shirted and tattooed Moses parting the Red Sea.

I managed to squeak, "Yo, Joizey" before Lou engulfed me in a bear hug. Then squeaked again as his girlfriend Bobbie shouldered him aside and treated me to an equally rib-bruising embrace.

"Why didn't you tell me you were coming?"

"We wanted to surprise you," Bobbie said.

"And we sure as shit did," Lou added.

Bobbie punched his shoulder. "It's a kids' show," she informed Lou in an undertone. "So watch your language, ass-hole."

"How long are you up for? Can you stay for the Follies?"

"Hell . . . heck, yes!" Lou said. "That's why we came up this weekend. Got into the Bough last night and—"

"Wait. You're not . . . are you Mr. and Mrs. Louis?"

"That was Frannie's idea. In case you started poking around."

"We nearly had a heart attack when she told us you and Nancy were in the dining room," Bobbie said. "We ran all the way upstairs. And—oh, my God, Maggie—our suite's gorgeous!"

"Yeah. But I kinda miss my crappy old room." Lou nudged Bobbie. "We had some good times up there."

"We know," Nancy said. "Our room was under yours."

Lou's bellow of laughter made several nearby patrons wince and earned him another punch from Bobbie.

"I just can't believe you're here. Rowan will be so happy to see you. Maybe we can all go out for a quick dinner after the show."

Too late, I recalled all the reasons why that would be a really bad idea: mad dogs, special silverware, projectile vomiting.

"Or grab some Mandarin Chalet grub and eat in Rowan's apartment."

Lou and Bobbie exchanged awed glances. "*The* apartment?" Bobbie said.

"Maybe you should check with Rowan first," Nancy suggested.

"We can check with him now," I said as Rowan edged through the crowded lobby.

He kissed Nancy's cheek, squeezed Bobbie's hand, and staggered only a little as Lou enthusiastically pounded his back. But when I mentioned dinner, his smile slipped.

"We don't have to go out," I assured him. "Just take some Chinese food up to your apartment."

"I wish we could, but Alex and I are meeting to discuss music rehearsals for *Into the Woods*."

"What about lunch tomorrow?" I suggested.

"I'm helping with setup for the Follies."

"There's plenty of time for that after the matinee."

"Lee and I are still working out some of the special effects."

"But—"

"It's not a problem," Nancy said, shooting me a quelling glance.

Lou nodded. "A man's gotta do what a man's gotta do."

"We can talk after the Follies," Bobbie said.

But their smiles failed to hide their disappointment.

Rowan's fingers rose to his throat, kneading the scar that was hidden beneath his tightly buttoned collar. "Maggie and I should get backstage. I'll see you after the show."

I smiled brightly and allowed him to take my arm, but as soon as we rounded the side of the barn, I shook off his hand.

"You haven't seen them in two years. Lou and Bobbie came all the way from Jersey! And you couldn't make time to have dinner?"

"In my apartment."

"Where else can we go? You refuse to go out. The cast will be eating in the picnic area."

"So you invited them to my apartment."

"I thought it would be fun!"

"But it's *my* apartment, Maggie. You might have asked whether I wanted guests."

"Okay. Yes. I'm sorry. But—"

"I've never even invited the staff to my apartment. Except Helen, of course."

I knew he'd never socialized with the staff until this summer, but I'd assumed that Alex had been there to work on the shows. Certainly, most of the staff had been inside—Lee and Hal when they stormed the barricades the night of my first Olympic orgasm, the rest to pack up Rowan's things. But none had been invited guests.

Rowan glanced at the milling crowd, then took my arm again and led me into the Smokehouse. He closed the door and regarded me gravely.

"I'm not like you, Maggie. You're at ease with people. You know what to say. How to ... fit in."

"How are you going to learn to fit in if you lock yourself away?"

"I won't always ... I was thinking of hosting a party for the staff after the season is over."

"Why wait? Throw a cocktail party before the Follies."

He stared at me, aghast. "I can't invite guests over on such short notice."

Sometimes, I forgot that he had learned human manners in the nineteenth century.

"Newsflash. You don't need to send engraved invitations. Especially to old friends who are all going to be at the theatre that afternoon."

"But—"

"Ask Nancy and Bobbie and Lou to stop by for the last half hour. That way, the staff will be flattered that they got first dibs, and the others will be flattered that they were included."

"All those people ..."

"Nobody will mind. They'll be having too much fun."

"Maybe *they* will."

I put my arms around his neck. "Say yes."

"That's coercion."

I kissed him. "Say yes."

"Unfair coercion."

I deepened the next kiss and felt his groan rumble against my mouth. "Say yes?"

"I believe the correct term is 'uncle.'"

I slipped free and clapped my hands. "A new Crossroads tradition."

"Dear gods. From a cattle call of a cocktail party to a new Crossroads tradition in ten seconds."

"It's better this way. Get it over with fast. Like pulling off a Band-Aid."

"The perfect analogy."

"Oh, stop being a grumpy old faery. You'll have a great time. Just give me a shopping list and I'll pick up everything you need tomorrow morning. I'll even help with prep."

"You in the kitchen? That almost makes this worth-while."

"I can cook! Some things. And I can certainly chop and peel and do the grunt work."

"Maggie Graham, Sous Chef." He studied me a moment, then said, "You never give up, do you?"

"Maggie Graham, Pit Bull." My smile faded as I took in his serious expression. "This is the easy stuff, Rowan. If we can't do this—"

"We can. I can."

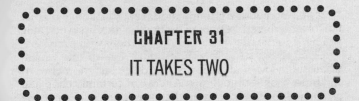

CHAPTER 31

IT TAKES TWO

SHOULD HAVE KNOWN ROWAN WOULDN'T be content with cheese and crackers. It was only by dint of considerable persuasion that I got him to include veggies and dip—or what he called crudités with tarragon aioli.

Daddy fled after the first fifteen minutes. I soldiered on in Hors D'oeuvres Hell.

"The point is having people in," I said as I eviscerated a cucumber. "Not to win an award from *Gourmet* magazine."

"If we're going to do this," he replied, stirring his lemony fennel slaw, "we're going to do it right. The cucumber cups need to be smaller. They're an—"

"If you say amuse bouche one more time, I'm serving up bacon-wrapped faery testicles."

"I'd prefer Graham on the half shell."

Our chuckles died at the same moment. I slowly lowered my knife. He slowly lowered his spoon.

"We're alone," Rowan said. "We have an hour until the actors arrive for the matinee. And we're making hors d'oeuvres. Does that strike you as incongruous?"

"No. It strikes me as crazy."

He took my hand and led me toward the bedroom. En route, he paused by his desk, ripped a page out of his new journal, and scrawled, "Jack. Take a long walk around the pond."

I taped the note to the front door and closed it firmly.

"What's the lady's pleasure?"

My face grew warm.

Rowan grinned. "Graham on the half shell, it is."

❧❧

The first time we had made love, we'd been a little awkward and more than a little desperate for the fulfillment we had postponed for so long. Later, the knowledge of our parting cast a bittersweet shadow over our lovemaking. As for our wham bam quickie, that didn't count as lovemaking at all.

Now, I could simply enjoy him. The otherworldly paleness of his body. The smoothness of his skin. The soft folds of flesh between his thighs, the most alien part of his anatomy and the one he had hidden from me the longest. The pink rosebud of a penis peeking out shyly, then rapidly losing its shyness as it shot skyward.

His hands gliding over my skin. His cheek rubbing against my thigh. That cat's tongue teasing between my legs.

I think I screamed shortly after that. And made some unearthly noises. Rowan didn't seem to mind. After he'd reduced me to a quivering Jell-O woman, he rested his chin on my belly and summed up with a succinct "Yum."

When he reached for the box of condoms, I stayed his hand. "I have a better idea."

I've never been Frieda Fellatio. The preliminaries are fine. It's the inevitable ending that always gives me trouble. Which is why I'd never ventured into this territory with Rowan. But the way his eyes widened when he realized what I intended and his little moan of pleasure when I seized his hips and pulled him toward me encouraged me to take the plunge.

Unfortunately, I didn't factor in the effect of faery power. It's hard to give a guy a hummer when you're gasping and moaning yourself.

I finally raised my head and said, "Rowan. Can you tamp down the power a bit?"

I felt like Santa in the animated *Rudolph the Red-Nosed Reindeer* special asking Rudolph to turn down his nose. But this little experiment was never going to reach a satisfactory conclusion while I was experiencing secondhand arousal.

Rowan stared into space, his eyes glazed with pleasure.

When I tapped his thigh, his gaze finally focused. "I'm not sure . . . it's very difficult . . ."

"Maybe we should give this up and—"

"No! I'll try. Very hard."

There were a couple of dicey moments when his desire flooded my body and I was sure he'd have to finish without my assistance. But Rowan clamped down on his power and I clamped down on Rowan and, apart from the moment when his fingers tightened involuntarily in my hair, the inevitable ending proved oddly satisfying. Oddly for me, that is. He tasted the way he smelled, sweet and musky and warm. I licked up every delicious drop and smiled smugly as he collapsed onto the bed.

"That was amazing," he breathed, giving my not-so-inner Aphrodite an added boost.

"You mean no one's ever—?"

"You know perfectly well you're the only person who's ever seen me naked."

"Well, you don't necessarily have to see the flagpole to polish the chrome."

He gave a startled yelp of laughter. "In my day, it was discreetly called the French way."

"In your day, they didn't have chrome to polish."

"Gods. I wasn't sure I was going to make it."

"A credit to your control."

"A credit to my imagination. I pictured myself going off like an unattended fire hose and—"

It was my turn to yelp.

He propped himself up on his elbow and grinned. "I don't suppose you'd care to polish the chrome again?"

"I'll get lockjaw. Besides, the actors will be arriving soon and you can't possibly . . ."

My eyes widened.

Rowan lay back and folded his hands behind his head. "Faeries have extraordinary recuperative powers."

"Smug bastard."

"Chrome polisher."

I pinned him to the mattress and straddled him, a pretty easy task since he wasn't putting up a fight. Then I kissed him, and he shivered.

"Is that what I taste like?"

"Mmm-hmm."

"Did you ... was it ... ?"

"Yum."

❧❧

I was more aware of the pleasant ache between my legs than the performances at the matinee. Afterward, I raced back up to the apartment and found Daddy perched on the sofa, scowling at the plate of crudités.

"I told him that was all he could have," Rowan called from the kitchen, "until everyone arrives."

Fortunately for Daddy, there was a knock on the door a few minutes later. I hung back to let Rowan greet his guests. The men solemnly shook hands. Mei-Yin clapped him on the shoulder. Catherine gave him a quick peck on the cheek.

Janet brought up the rear. She hesitated on the threshold, just as Rowan had the day of the barbecue. They went through the same Gaelic gargling. Then Janet stepped inside and I let out my breath in relief at surmounting another hurdle.

"No need to stand in the office," Rowan said a little too heartily. "Let's all go into the other room."

Hal let out a soft shriek as he entered the living area; obviously, he'd never seen it. Nor had Bernie, who gave a low whistle and murmured, "Man, oh, Manischewitz, such a hayloft."

Because of the Follies, we were serving nonalcoholic beverages, but I couldn't resist buying two bottles of champagne to mark the occasion. Rowan opened one, splashed a swallow into Catherine's glass, and filled the rest.

"As you probably guessed, this was Maggie's idea. I have to admit I was ..."

"Horrified?" Janet prompted.

"Taken aback," Rowan conceded. "But she assured me it would be fun. So a long overdue welcome. To colleagues. To family. To old friends."

We clinked glasses, all of us savoring this extraordinary moment. Then Daddy said, "Can we eat now?" and we exchanged solemnity for laughter.

Daddy circled the room like a shark as he sampled hors d'oeuvres. The rest of us milled around and exclaimed over Rowan's food.

"You MADE this?" Mei-Yin demanded, examining a basil leaf topped with a tiny ball of pine nut-coated goat cheese.

"Maggie helped."

"Mostly, I gouged out cucumber cups for the salmon mousse."

Hal popped a mango shrimp in his mouth and mumbled, "Yum."

I studiously avoided looking at Rowan.

"I'll never fit into my Follies costume," Hal declared. Then he immediately plucked a puff pastry from Lee's plate. "Ooh! What are these?"

"Lemon parsley gougeres," I informed him.

"Goo-who?" Lee asked.

"Who cares?" Catherine replied. "They're terrific."

Her happy laugh gave me almost as much satisfaction as her heaping plate. Morning sickness seemed to have given way to a rapacious appetite. And although she would probably fall into bed after the Follies, her face—if not exactly glowing—was less drawn.

"I had no idea you were such a good cook," Javier said.

Daddy paused long enough in his circling to note, "There aren't any mini-hot dogs."

"Try a bacon-wrapped date," I advised.

"Try . . . what *are* these, anyway?" Bernie asked.

"I hope you're not kosher," Rowan said.

"Only at Passover."

"Prosciutto crostini with lemony fennel slaw."

Alex laughed. "I never imagined I'd hear those words coming out of your mouth."

"You're as bad as Maggie. I informed her that the miniature quiche is properly called a mushroom pomponnette and—"

This time, everyone laughed. Hal picked up two tiny quiches and exclaimed, "Two—four—six—eight. Who do we appreciate? Rowan. Rowan. Rowan!"

Rowan looked pleased but confused until I explained the "cheerleader with pom-poms" allusion.

For the next hour, he was a consummate host, unerringly finding something to appeal to each of his guests: explaining the origin of the battered trunk to Javier; lingering with Alex by the antique melodeon; showing Janet the silver-framed photograph of Jamie and his family.

When he saw Reinhard gazing raptly at one of the bookcases, he nudged me and whispered, "Library lust." As we wandered over, Reinhard carefully removed one volume and cradled it in his hands. "I still cannot believe you own a first edition of this."

I craned my neck, and he turned the book so I could read the faded lettering on the bright blue cloth cover: *Adventures of Huckleberry Finn, Tom Sawyer's Comrade.*

"Holy crap," I whispered.

Rowan smiled. "The first book I ever owned—and the first novel I ever read. I preferred travelogues and newspapers that offered me glimpses of the world. But I enjoyed *Roughing It* so much that Jamie's son Andrew bought me that."

"Do you know how much this is worth?" Reinhard asked.

Rowan shook his head.

"At a guess . . . twenty to thirty thousand dollars."

"Holy crap," I whispered again.

Even Rowan looked shocked. "Well, at least now I know I can support myself."

"You're not selling it," I told him flatly.

"No. It has too much personal history. But most of the other first editions are just . . . old books."

"You should have them appraised," Reinhard said. "I am no expert, but I have a friend who is an antiquarian bookseller. She will give you an honest estimate."

"Thank you, Reinhard." Rowan cocked his head. "I believe the other guests are arriving."

A few moments later, he ushered Lou, Bobbie, and Nancy into the living area. After the hugs, kisses, and backslapping concluded, I steered them over to Daddy. Nancy eyed him intently as she shook his hand.

"It's nice to meet you, Jack. Maggie's told me so much about you."

Lou settled for a more casual "Howya doin'?"

"Better," Daddy replied, drawing uncertain glances from Lou and Bobbie.

I brandished the plate of cucumber cups. "Hors d'oeuvres, anyone?"

"I won't lie to you."

"Rowan made the salmon mousse himself."

"I went through some bad times."

I tramped on Daddy's foot. "But right now, he's enjoying the party."

"Oh, sure. But don't get your hopes up. There aren't any mini-hot dogs."

It was only a matter of time before someone asked Lou and Bobbie about their status. Naturally, that someone was Mei-Yin who demanded, "When are we gonna hear WED-DING bells?"

Bobbie blushed. "Well, now that you mention it . . . next spring."

Rowan's voice rose above our excited babble. "This calls for more champagne!"

As we raised our glasses, I wondered if our friends would ever toast our engagement or witness our wedding vows. Then I silently intoned my "one day at a time" mantra and reminded myself to enjoy this moment, this day, and the company of good friends.

Half an hour later, I shooed Nancy, Bobbie, and Lou out to the picnic area to grab some pizza with the rest of the audience. Rowan shooed the staff off to the Smokehouse to get into makeup and costumes.

Our first party. And everything about it—except the hors d'oeuvres—had been wonderfully ordinary.

"Post-party depression?" I teased as Rowan collapsed on the sofa.

"Post-party exhaustion. Do you think they enjoyed themselves?"

"They had a wonderful time. How about you?"

"It wasn't as bad as I thought it would be."

"Didn't you have any fun at all?"

"Yes," he replied, a faint note of surprise in his voice. "Once I stopped trying so hard and just let things . . . happen."

"There's hope for you yet, Mackenzie."

He heaved himself off the sofa. "Stop patting yourself on the back and get to work, Graham."

I banished my uncertainties about the future, content to revel in the wonderfully ordinary task of cleaning up after our guests.

CHAPTER 32

QUIET PLEASE, THERE'S A LADY ONSTAGE

IF THE STAFF WAS NERVOUS ABOUT DADDY'S debut they hid it well. As we changed into our costumes behind the screens Hal had set up, there was a lot of good-natured teasing about *my* debut. Last year, I'd been too overwhelmed to take a role in the Follies. This year, my stomach was aflutter with nerves and mushroom pomponnettes.

When I emerged in my costume, the staff applauded. I laughed when I beheld my adorable forest creatures.

Over their tights, the staff wore shapeless knee-length serapes in various shades of brown and gray. Mei-Yin—our resident squirrel—had a bushy gray tail attached to her serape. Catherine had a bunny's powder puff. Alex's head was crowned with a stag's antlers. In his black eye mask, Javier looked more like a dashing cat burglar than a raccoon. But a morose-looking Reinhard won top honors with his enormous moose antlers.

"The cast will lose all respect for me."

"They'll be too busy admiring your rack," Hal replied. "Honey, my drapes are stuck again."

As Lee fiddled with the draping that hung over Hal's full-length mirror frame, the door to the Smokehouse opened. We all froze, but it was only Bea.

"My God," she said when she saw Mei-Yin and Reinhard. "It's *The Adventures of Rocky and Bullwinkle*."

Reinhard scowled. "If you have come to call places, please do so."

"Places!" she sang out, still grinning. "Break a hoof, Dad."

I adjusted Daddy's floppy dwarf cap. "You'll be great."
Please, please, please let him be great.

Rowan kissed my cheek. "Just have fun. Both of you."

I slipped out the Smokehouse door and eased aside so that Janet and Hal could squeeze in behind the backdrop that hung from the branches of the maples. The recorded overture blared from the speakers, prompting cheers and whistles from the assembled actors. When the lights came up to reveal Janet in her evil queen glory, they responded with a low "Oooh." But Hal got the first laugh of the evening when he pulled open his draperies. He'd kept the weird mask from the Disney cartoon, but the rest of his costume was pure Carmen Miranda, complete with a towering head-piece of apples.

There were some giggles when I launched into "I'm Wishing." And even more at Catherine's echo, which veered between Minnie Mouse and Marlene Dietrich. Lee got some laughs with Prince Charming's constipated voice. But Bernie's Huntsman brought down the house as he gamely attempting to stab me while inching forward in his walker.

The friendly forest creatures were a hit. So was the entrance of the dwarfs, who marched over from the breezeway carrying lanterns. I watched Daddy anxiously, but he "heigh-hoed" as fervently as the rest and shamelessly hammed up his sneezes: stuttering, staggering, regaining control, only to lose it again; clinging to a very un-Happy Reinhard; goggling at a very Dopey Javier; and finally unleashing such a storm that the rest of us careened around the acting area.

"You're doing great," I whispered to him. And was rewarded with a smile and a snuffle.

I danced with the dwarfs, spinning from one pair of hands to the next. It was almost like my dream, but I was so much happier now. Daddy had joined our dance and although Rowan could only watch from the shadows, his pleasure bubbled through me like the champagne we had sipped at our cocktail party.

When it came time for the Queen's transformation, I was the one watching from the shadows. As Janet drank her magic potion, the strobe light kicked in, making her contortions positively eerie. Her gown billowed as she whirled in a circle. The flash pot went off, emitting a small cloud of sickly yellow smoke. It cleared to reveal a hook-nosed, hunchbacked Rowan shrouded in a long, black cape.

The collective gasp from the audience was followed by wild applause. Awe changed to laughter when Rowan dipped his apple into the cauldron and pulled up a succession of different objects: a softball, a cantaloupe, and a scarlet brassiere with cups large enough for watermelons. I didn't know whether he used faery glamour to pull off the trick or merely some ordinary sleight of hand, but I laughed as delightedly as the audience.

When he arrived at the dwarfs' cottage, it struck me that this was the first time we would play a scene together in front of an audience. The few words we'd exchanged in *Carousel* didn't really count. Another first—for both of us.

"Make a wish," he croaked, proffering the shiny red apple.

For a moment, I forgot where I was. I just saw those familiar green eyes looking out from that almost unrecognizable face.

I wish I could help you find your place in this world. I wish that you could direct again. I wish you could let the staff into your life and discover how those friendships can nurture and sustain you. I wish you could trust me to share your worries. I wish I could give you a child with my red hair and your green eyes. I wish I could always be with you. I wish I could spare you the pain of watching me grow old and die.

Rowan's eyes widened. Then he lifted my chin and whispered, "One wish."

I snapped out of my daze and dutifully wished for my prince to come and carry me away to his castle where we would live happily ever after.

He pressed the apple into my hands. I raised it to my mouth and bit into it.

Colors exploded before me—probably some weird lighting effect that made the sparks in Rowan's eyes flash gold and silver and apple red like the fireworks we had watched from his balcony. The apple slipped from my fingers. I seemed to float to the ground, but that must have been Rowan's magic easing me earthward.

In the blackout that followed, he pulled me to my feet a good deal more brusquely and quick-stepped me behind the backdrop.

"I'm fine," I whispered, although I was still a little dazed. "Go die spectacularly."

His kiss bruised my mouth and shocked me back to reality. His spectacular death scared the shit out of me.

One minute, he was racing through the audience, pursued by a horde of screaming dwarfs and the next, he was scrambling up one of the trees by the Smokehouse. He edged his way onto a branch and looked down where I was huddled in the shadows, gnawing on my fist.

"It'll be great!" he whispered. Then he leaped for the Smokehouse roof.

There were a few screams from the audience. I nearly bit off my index finger.

A spotlight picked him out as he clawed his way up the roof. Although I knew he was just making it look difficult, I gasped each time he slipped. He struggled to his feet, hampered by his long skirt, then tiptoed along the roofline like a tightrope walker.

He paused to shake a fist at the dwarfs and suddenly lurched sideways. His arms pinwheeled as he fought for balance. I told myself he was acting, that his magic would protect him if the four mattresses behind the Smokehouse didn't, that we would laugh about this later unless I murdered him first.

He flung out a hand in a final, desperate effort to save himself. With a despairing screech, he toppled backward off the roof.

More screams, including mine. Someone seized my arm, and I screamed again.

"Get on the table," Bea whispered.

"What?"

"Your bier."

"Shit."

I snagged my foot in the draping around the bottom of the table. Then I disentangled myself and crawled onto my makeshift bier. The hinges creaked as Bea lowered the plexiglass lid over me. I folded my hands across my heaving chest and tried to take shallow breaths.

To the accompaniment of the Prince's "One Song," the crew hauled up the backdrop. My faithful dwarfs rolled the table forward and—I prayed—locked the wheels. Hal marched on to narrate the tale of the Prince who had searched far and wide for his fair maiden. The lid creaked open and I suppressed a sigh of relief as cool air flooded in.

Lee's lips touched mine. Then touched them again. He lifted me up and plastered a big wet one on my mouth, but when I refused to awaken, he abruptly released me.

As I flopped back on my bier, he whined, "She's supposed to be revived by true love's first kiss."

"Maybe YOU'RE not her true love," Mei-Yin declared.

The dwarfs lined up for their try at reviving me. Javier slobbered all over me in an appropriately Dopey way, but the rest were very decorous. Then it was Grumpy's turn. Mei-Yin ground her mouth against mine for so long that I finally tapped her on the shoulder.

She grinned. I glared. Then I got back into character and exclaimed, "Oh, Grumpy! It was you all along."

After which I went home with my dwarfs, the Prince danced off with his Carmen Miranda Mirror, and we all lived happily ever after.

＜＝＞

"If you ever scare me like that again," I warned Rowan after I'd changed into my street clothes, "I will kill you!"

"But wasn't it spectacular?" he asked, eager as a child.

"Spectacularly scary." I smacked him, then rounded on Mei-Yin. "And what was with that kiss?"

"You LOVED it!"

Our high spirits evaporated when we discovered Long waiting outside the Smokehouse. Daddy shrank back against Rowan. The rest of the staff clustered around him; whatever reservations they had, he was part of the pack—and Long was not.

Judging from Long's frown, he caught the "us against him" vibe. But he just smiled and said, "Congratulations, everyone. I can't remember when I've had so much fun. Although I nearly had a heart attack when you fell off the roof, Rowan."

"All carefully choreographed, I assure you."

Long's gaze rested on Daddy. "I can understand why Maggie was so eager to have you in *Into the Woods*. I'm sure you'll be a wonderful addition to the cast." He waved away Daddy's stammered thanks and shot Janet a rueful smile. "I guess this means I can only claim dinner."

She chucked him under the chin. "A very nice dinner."

As the staff hurried toward the breezeway for the reception, I lingered to thank Long. With Nancy's admonitions fresh in my mind, I was more than usually gracious.

His smile vanished. "I'm not giving him a free ride, Maggie. Just a chance to prove himself. And only because he's your father. If there are any outbursts or disturbances, I'll pull him from the show."

My chin came up. "I'm the director, Long. If he can't handle the role or causes any problems, *I'll* pull him."

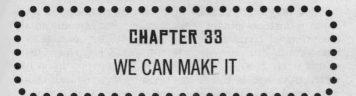

CHAPTER 33

WE CAN MAKE IT

THE NEXT MORNING, I SHARED A BRIEF farewell breakfast with Lou and Bobbie and Nancy, then plunged into rehearsals for *Into the Woods*. I'd always loved the show. Okay, maybe there was too much moralizing in Act Two and maybe the songs weren't as strong as those in Act One, but once I became executive director, I was determined to mount a production. It didn't matter that Rowan had done the show before. It captured the essence of the Crossroads: its history, its secrets, and its undercover mission of helping people find their paths through life.

Like all good fairy tales, it was about the wishes people make and the quests they take to fulfill them. A Baker and his Wife, cursed with childlessness by the vengeful witch from next door. A collection of fairy-tale characters— Cinderella, Little Red Ridinghood, Jack from "Jack and the Beanstalk"—that must break out of their predetermined stories and make difficult choices to survive. A lighthearted Act One that morphs into a dark and dangerous Act Two, in which consequences can be deadly and wishes can only come true through collective effort and sacrifice. And of course, the Mysterious Man, who abandons his wife and child, but returns to guide his son the Baker through the darkest hours of his life. Plus a great book by James Lapine and a Stephen Sondheim score that made you laugh one moment and cry the next.

What's not to like?

Alex suggested we start things off by running the prologue, a thirteen-minute musical scene that introduced all the principal characters. Since the prologue consisted of nine—count 'em, nine—interwoven scenes, I was more than a little nervous about the possibility of starting things off with a train wreck. But Alex's instincts were sound. There were stumbles, of course, but when they sang that final "and home before dark," there were cheers and whistles from the rest of the cast and high fives among the performers.

I watched my father whooping it up with the others and felt a wave of pride. Yes, Rowan and I had run his lines with him dozens of times. But Daddy had performed like the pro he once had been—and might become again.

We split up after that, Rowan and Alex working musical numbers in the Dungeon and Smokehouse, while I blocked onstage. By the end of the afternoon, I was so jazzed by our progress that I seized Rowan's hands and exclaimed, "Let's go out to dinner!"

"Out?"

"Alex and Mei-Yin are working 'Ever After' tonight. We've got the whole evening free. Let's celebrate!"

"Good idea," Alex agreed. "You've been chained to this place ever since you returned, Rowan. About time you got out and saw the town. What there is of it."

"But what about Jack?" Rowan asked.

"I'll take him along to dinner at Momma's."

"It's all settled," I declared. "I'll meet you in the lobby in half an hour."

I skipped up the hill and into the Bates mansion. Janet leaned over the upstairs railing and remarked, "Either you've decided to play Little Red Ridinghood or it was a good rehearsal."

"Into the town without delay to celebrate this perfect day . . ."

"A good rehearsal. I'm delighted. You can stop singing now."

"Into the Chatterbox, we may decide to share a milkshake."

"You and Rowan?"

I nodded and hurried up the stairs.

"He's actually leaving the grounds?"

I paused on the top step. "Sure. Why?"

"Nothing. Have a good time."

"You, too! Alex is bringing Daddy up to dinner."

"Oh, goodie."

"Stop. Daddy likes you."

"Yes. I know."

"What does that mean?"

"Nothing."

"You're full of meaningful 'nothings' this evening. Do you know something I don't know?"

"I know a great many things you don't know. I am—"

"Wise beyond your considerable years. Someday I hope to hear all about your date with Calvin Coolidge. But right now . . ."

"Go. Have fun. You can tell me all about it when you come back."

I laughed. "I only tell you about my awful dates."

But she'd already walked into her bedroom and closed the door.

By the time I selected a flowered skirt and scoop-necked blouse, my bedroom looked like a tornado had blown through. I left my cast-off clothes where they'd fallen, pulled on my sneakers, and threw a pair of sandals into my tote bag; no way was I ruining another outing by turning my ankle. I flew through the house, packing up additional supplies, and hurried back down the hill.

Rowan was waiting outside the barn.

"You look so pretty and summery."

I pivoted in a circle, my skirt swirling around my thighs. "And I feel as corny as Kansas in August."

His smile was oddly wistful. "Still in love with a wonderful guy?"

"Yeah. But you're nice, too." I grinned and pointed toward the road. "And . . . they're off!"

Like the nineteenth-century gentleman he was, he took my tote bag, but frowned as he inspected its contents. "Do you really think we need bottled water?"

"In case you get warm."

"Couldn't you just spray us with this thing?" he asked, pulling out the plant spritzer.

"Sure. But that's mostly to scare off the dogs."

Thunder rumbled faintly in the distance.

"Looks like it might rain," Rowan noted.

"I put umbrellas in the bag."

"Ah."

"We could take the car if you—"

"No."

As we walked up the lane, I yapped about our dinner options. With both the Bough and the Chalet closed on Monday nights, it came down to the Chatterbox or Duck Inn.

"Duck Inn is basically pub grub. But they have a liquor license."

"Ah."

"If you want a strawberry milkshake, though, we should go the Chatterbox."

"Yes."

"What are you in the mood for?"

His anxiety prickled through me.

"No biggie," I assured him. "Decide when we get to town. I'll eat anywhere. I'm just happy to be going out to dinner with you."

His power surged, laden with such apprehension that I drew up short.

"What is it? What's wrong?"

Sweat popped out on his forehead, as if conjured by my words.

"Rowan? Talk to me."

Instead, he sank onto the low stone wall.

"This isn't going to work."

"What isn't going to work?"

"I've tried, Maggie! You have no idea how hard I've tried. But I can't do this."

He's leaving me.

He swore he wouldn't.

Mom was right.

You misunderstood. He wouldn't walk out of your life again.

Oh, no? Watch him!
You know this man.
He's not a man. He's a faery.
He loves you.
Not enough.
Stop. Think. Don't blurt out something you'll regret.

I raised my eyes to heaven, hoping for some celestial guidance. All I found were thunderclouds piling up like dirty cotton balls.

I took a deep breath and asked, "What are you talking about?"

"This! Dinner!"

My breath leaked out in a shaky sigh. I sat beside him, mostly to keep my knees from buckling.

"If you didn't want to go out . . ."

"I *can't* go out!"

I shook my head, completely baffled.

"I can't go out to dinner. I can't even step into the road!"

"If you're talking about the curse . . ."

"The curse was lifted. But I am still bound."

Finally, I understood what must have happened on our abortive Fourth of July outing, why he was always inventing excuses to avoid going to town, why he was drenched with sweat.

I laid my hand over his clenched fist. "You know what this is, right? A classic panic attack. You were a prisoner so long that your body is going nuts at the prospect of leaving the property."

He jerked his hand free and stalked away. "I am well aware of the nature of my . . . dysfunction. That has not helped to effect a cure."

"Don't be so hard on yourself. This is only the second time—"

"No, Maggie. It's not the second time or even the twenty-second time. I tried to step into the road the first week I returned. Every night after Jack fell asleep, I walked up this lane. And every morning before dawn, I tried again—and failed again."

That long, lonely walk, shrouded in darkness but buoyed with the determination that this time, he would break free. And then the longer, lonelier walk back to his apartment, bowed down by yet another failure. Repeating that ritual night after night. Locking away his fear and humiliation in the daytime to present a confident facade to the world.

"He's actually leaving the grounds?"

Clearly, Janet had suspected the truth—just as Alex had picked up on Rowan's sexual frustration. They had their Fae power to guide them. I had only my human senses. And they had failed me. Why hadn't I looked deeper?

"Why didn't you tell me?"

He whirled around. "Because I was ashamed!"

The hot flush of his humiliation roiled through me. His angry eyes met mine. Then his gaze slid away and he slumped atop the wall.

Okay, Graham. You're the helping professional. Start helping.

He'd spent several lifetimes learning to lock away his emotions, consigning his fears and hopes and doubts to the unresponsive pages of his many journals. I had read some of those journals. Shared his bed. Heard his bitter confessions about the willful misuse of his power. I had felt his grief and anger, longing and despair resonating inside of me. I had even experienced the agony of being bound by iron. And still, I felt pitifully unprepared for this moment and all too aware that the words I chose—or failed to choose—might change our relationship forever.

Touch had always unlocked his emotions. And humor. This sure as hell didn't feel like a situation that humor could remedy, so I'd have to rely on touch.

I wriggled between his knees and rested my hands on his shoulders. A shudder rippled through his body, but his emotions remained carefully shielded.

"First off, I love you. And these panic attacks don't make me love you or respect you less. We'll deal with them. Together. But I can't help if I don't know what's troubling you."

"I didn't want to worry you," he mumbled.

"Worry me. Please. I don't have your power. I don't know what's going on inside your head. I either miss the clues or feel like I'm putting together a puzzle with half the pieces missing. We have to be able to talk. To be honest. And to trust each other."

His gaze finally rose to meet mine. "You thought I was leaving you."

Fucking faery powers.

"Yes. And then I stepped back and decided—"

"Not to kill me?"

His small smile left me wobbly with relief. But I knew my lack of trust had wounded him, even if he was carefully shielding me from his pain.

"I'm sorry I doubted you. I wish I could say it'll never happen again. But . . ."

"It will. Whenever we're put to the test."

"We're going to face a lot of tests, Rowan. And if you always know what I'm feeling and I'm always in the dark, it'll only make them harder. Just let me in. Tell me what you're thinking. If you blame me for doubting you—"

"No. I've had doubts, too. When I'm with you—or when I'm working—I forget about the obstacles. But at night . . . the Fae only require a few hours of sleep. That leaves a lot of time to think. And the night breeds . . . dark thoughts."

"But the sun is shining now." I scowled at the lowering sky and added, "Well, it's shining behind the clouds. And we have the whole evening ahead of us. We'll make dinner. We'll make love. We'll chase away the darkness."

His arms went around me. I cradled his head against my breast.

"Let's go home," I whispered.

"No."

Gently, he freed himself from my embrace. Then he rose and turned toward the road.

"You don't have to prove anything to me."

"I know. I have to prove it to myself."

He took a single step forward and stopped, the toes of his boots a mere inch from the black macadam—like the night of the *Brigadoon* cast party, when he had hovered just beyond the patio of the house he had vowed never to enter.

But he had reconsidered that vow, made in the first flush of anger and hatred for the Mackenzies who had imprisoned him. If he could enter Janet's house to comfort Helen after her heart attack, then surely, he could conquer his fear now.

He took a deep breath. Then another. A drop of sweat oozed over his eyebrow. He blinked it away.

A muscle jumped in his cheek as he gritted his teeth. A shudder racked his body. He wiped his palms on his jeans. Clenched and unclenched his hands.

And then his head drooped.

I stepped into the road and thrust out my hands.

"You can do this."

Rowan backed away.

"Take my hands. We can do this."

He shook his head and continued retreating.

"Rowan! Please!"

He bared his teeth. Then he threw back his head and bellowed his anger and frustration and defiance to the sky.

His unleashed power blasted through me. I staggered backward, gasping. Saliva filled my mouth, as hot and delicious as the rage scalding my body.

Like a berserker out of some ancient tale, he charged, hair streaming behind him, eyes wild and unseeing, mouth open in a roar of fury that tore an answering scream from my throat. The thunder of his footsteps shuddered through the earth, shuddered through my body.

And suddenly, I was laughing, fury banished by exultation, blood-pounding rage transformed into a light-headed giddiness that made me reel.

Hands grasped my arms, steadying me. Green eyes—still a little wild, still flashing with the echoes of his power—stared into mine.

The soft huff of his breath against my face.

The nasal blast of a horn.

We clutched each other and stared at the vehicle bearing down on us. Then Rowan whisked me into his arms and out of the road and we fell back against the stone wall, laughing and breathless.

The pickup truck eased onto the grassy berm. The driver leaned over to peer out the passenger window. I spied a familiar John Deere cap and beneath it, the frowning face of my board treasurer.

"Hi, Mr. Hamilton!"

"What the hell are you two doing? Playing chicken?"

"Something like that."

"Well, cut it out. You're too old for such foolishness."

Rowan whooped. I seized his shirtfront before he toppled backward off the wall.

"He been drinking?"

"No. We're just . . . we had a really good day."

Mr. Hamilton shook his head at the unfathomable
weirdness of theatre people. "Next time you have a really
good day, stay out of the road."

"Yes, sir."

His head withdrew into the truck, an anxious tortoise
retreating into its shell. I stifled a giggle with one hand and
waved good-bye with the other. Then Rowan and I exchanged grins.

"I couldn't walk into town now to save my life," I admitted.

"I'm not even sure I can make it to the barn."

I shoved a hank of wet hair off his forehead. "You did it."

"*We* did it. I'm sorry I lost control like that."

"It worked. That's what matters."

He raised my hand and pressed his lips to my palm.
"Have I mentioned that I love you?"

"Not for ages. An hour, at least."

"I love you, Maggie Graham."

"I love you, Rowan Mackenzie."

❧❧

We took a cool shower and made love. Fixed dinner and
made love again. I knew I should dress and go back to the
house before Daddy returned from rehearsal. Instead, I fell
asleep in Rowan's arms—and awoke in them the next
morning.

It was the first time that had ever happened. Every other
time I had slept in his bed, he woke long before me and only
returned to the bedroom when he sensed I was waking.
Maybe he had stayed with me to avoid disturbing Daddy.

Before I could ask, there was a soft knock.

So much for a clean getaway.

Rowan slipped out of bed and padded to the door.

"What is it, Jack?"

"Janet left something for Maggie."

"Leave it outside the door, will you?"

"Okay."

"Was there anything else?"

"I made coffee. And put out some crumb cake."

"Thank you."

"Rehearsal starts in an hour."

"We'll be there."

"I thought . . . until then . . . maybe I'd take a walk around the pond."

"Thank you, Jack. That's very thoughtful."

"See you at rehearsal. You, too, Maggie!"

"Okay!" I sang out.

Janet's mysterious offering turned out to be a shopping bag filled with a change of clothes, my makeup bag, a toothbrush, and a note that read, "Dear Heloise. Congratulations on breaking out of the cloister. Try not to appear too saddle sore at today's rehearsal. Janet. P.S.—please extend my congratulations to Abelard on *his* escape. It's about time."

I merely folded the note without reading it aloud. But Rowan said, "She sensed what I was going through, didn't she?"

"I think so." I gently traced the centuries-old scar at his wrist where once he had tried to kill himself to escape the degradation and agony of the iron.

"It doesn't matter. It's over now."

He stretched out beside me and I let my fingers drift across his chest, marveling yet again at its smoothness.

"Did you stay with me all night?"

"Yes."

"Just lying here? Awake?"

"I slept for a few hours. The rest of the time, I just listened to you."

It was impossibly sweet: Rowan holding me in his arms, listening to the soft sound of my breathing.

"You snore."

I bolted upright. "I do not!"

"You snore and snuffle and mutter and thrash. You're a very lively sleeper."

"I'm surprised you didn't sell tickets."

"It was endearing!"

"Snoring. Endearing."

"Yes. It was so . . . unexpected. Like you."

He pressed me back onto the mattress and kissed me. Expecting the usual developments, I was surprised when he rolled over onto his back.

"I've never fallen asleep with anyone. The Fae always sleep alone. Each in his own secret place. That way no one can find you when you're vulnerable."

"Well, it's always hard sharing a bed when you're used to—"

"It's more than that. I can't shield myself when I'm asleep. I've always worried that I might sense my partner's dreams. Or that hers could bleed into mine. I think that might have happened last night."

I fought down my panic. Although I knew Rowan would never deliberately invade my dreams, it still felt like my last bastion of privacy had tumbled.

"Say something. Please."

The upwelling of love caught me off guard. He could have used his power to sense what I was feeling. But he was deliberately shielding himself to restore the privacy I might have lost during the night.

"Well, I'll tell you one thing: we're not sleeping in separate beds."

His embrace was bruising, but his lips were very gentle as they roamed over my face. "Tell me what you dreamed."

"The same dream I've been having for months. I was alone in a forest glade . . ."

"Dancing with fireflies."

Another shiver of panic, but smaller this time and easier to subdue.

"I've had the same dream," he whispered. "All summer."

"All . . . ? But how is that possible?"

"I don't know."

"Did you see the staff? Were they there?"

"No. You were alone."

So it was not my dream, but his—or some strange blending of the two.

"You sensed my presence. I thought at first you would run away, but you waved your hand, beckoning me. And when I hung back, you ran across the glade and pulled me out of the shadows and ordered me to dance."

"God. Even in dreams, I'm a bossy cow."

"You started twirling around and told me to twirl, too. I was oddly . . . clumsy. But you took my hands and spun around and around with me. And the fireflies surrounded us in light—beautiful golden light. And we were laughing and happy. And then . . ."

"And then?"

"The fireflies vanished. And so did you. And I was alone in the dark."

The desolation in his voice shocked me. I rested my left palm against his chest and raised my right to cup his cheek.

"You're not alone. I'm right here. And I'm not going anywhere."

Neither of us wanted to state the obvious: that one day, death would take me away from him. Maybe that's why I kissed him so fiercely—to drive away that specter.

When he didn't respond, I kissed him again, more gently. I let my hands and my mouth offer the reassurance we both needed: that we would have thousands of nights together, thousands of days to work and play. We would celebrate the end of summer by walking in our woods. We would lie together, warm beneath our blankets, while snow silently drifted onto the skylights. We would see the first crocuses bravely pushing through the snow in the spring and stand on our plateau, admiring the fiery glory of autumn.

Trust me, my hands whispered as they skimmed over his back. Cherish what we have, my body urged as I guided him inside of me. Give me your doubts and your fears; I am strong enough to bear them. Fill me with your magic; I am brave enough to accept it.

His heart pounded against mine. His power ebbed and flowed, eternal as the tide. Golden sunlight poured through the skylights, caressing our bodies, seeping through flesh and bone and blood to dance inside us like a cloud of fireflies, the light pulsing to the rhythm of his power, the rhythm of our bodies.

A single note, bittersweet and beautiful, vibrating with possibility, blossoming into fullness. An answering chord, resonating with my love, my longing, my hope. Melody and harmony, faery and human. Bodies and hearts and spirits entwined in a single song that swept us over the edge of the precipice and carried us safely back to earth again.

Share my dreams and I will share yours. Offer me your heart and I will give you mine. Trust me, my love. And, together, we will defy all the powers of this world and Faerie to come between us.

ENTR'ACTE
THE JOURNAL OF ROWAN MACKENZIE

She astounds me. Her strength, her determination, her bull-headed stubbornness that sees every impossible obstacle as an annoying hurdle.

And her love. Not fascination, which I have encountered from many humans. Or awe, which the elders assured us was our due from such an inferior race.

Love.

As a child, I sniggered at the stories about humans who stumbled upon our kind and wandered mazed through the world for the rest of their days. I smiled indulgently at their depictions of our realm and dismissed as sheer invention those stories in which a human outwitted the Fae.

We knew all their tales. Throughout the ages, the Fae have slipped through the veil to lurk outside their homes or stand just beyond the light of their fires, watching and listening.

Only when I returned to Faerie and was inundated by the questions of my clan did I appreciate the symbiotic relationship that has evolved between human and Fae. If they are fascinated with us, we are just as intrigued by them: their minds, so easily controlled; their senses, so easily beguiled; the gamy smell of their flesh; the hairiness of their bodies. Try as we might to hide our wonder behind a facade of disparagement and detachment, we have always marveled at the fire they carry inside, the passion with which they devour life, the fierce emotions that roil through them: fury and joy; grief and longing; hatred and love.

Even after living among humans for centuries, I could not ad-

694

equately describe those emotions to my clan. When I tried, they regarded me with confusion and thinly veiled contempt.

What is more pathetic than a Fae in thrall to a human?

Yet Maggie has never made me feel pathetic. Furious, incredulous, uncertain, joyful, but never pathetic. Even when I revealed the shameful truth about my panic attacks and the recurring dream in which she always, always leaves me.

How can she love my weaknesses? Do they make me seem more human?

I must never suggest that; Maggie would fly into a temper if I equated weakness with humanity. Besides, so many of the human qualities the Fae ridicule as weaknesses are—paradoxically—their strengths: their blind loyalty to those they love; their willingness to accept the flaws of others; their ability to forgive.

I maintained a distant professionalism with Reinhard, yet he stores my belongings without ever knowing if I would return for them. I brushed off Alex's overtures of friendship for decades, yet he risks the possibility of being hurt again to try and forge a genuine relationship with me. Janet can put aside a lifetime of resentment to invite me into her home. And Maggie can forgive me for leaving and open her heart and her life to me again.

Will I ever understand them? Will I ever understand her?

Yet I trust her with my heart and my life. I have shared my secret name. I will even risk sharing my dreams. But how can I share the truth of what really happened on opening night of *The Secret Garden*?

It might be kinder if I did. It would help her understand Jack's determination to go on seeking the elusive portal to Faerie. And prepare her for the inevitable moment when he tells her he is leaving—again.

But she is so confident that this show will change him. And perhaps she is right. I have to give her—and him—the chance to find out.

So I will lock away the truth. I will let Maggie believe that Jack saw his daughter on the stage, that he rushed to aid his child in her moment of peril. I will let her overlook the obvious: that the peril had already passed when Jack leaped up, that child and father had already found each other, that it was only when the Dreamers drifted away that Jack cried out in despair.

Just as he cried out when my clan slipped into the forest on that long ago Midsummer.

Nearly thirty years since that night. And Jack is still running after the faeries who beguiled and abandoned him, his longing only whetted by the passage of years.

Oh, Maggie, your love is your greatest strength and your greatest weakness. It blinds you to the truth about your father—and the truth about me.

No matter how many times you pull me into the light, I will always have to retreat into the shadows. One day, you will grow tired of coaxing me out.

And when that day comes, I will lose you.

ACT THREE

EVER AFTER

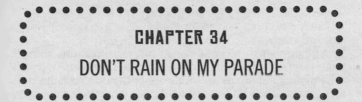

CHAPTER 34

DON'T RAIN ON MY PARADE

I FLOATED THROUGH THE NEXT WEEK on Cloud Nine. Performances for *The Secret Garden* were great. Rehearsals for *Into the Woods* were great. Life was great.

So what if Jessica was struggling with the role of the Baker's Wife? She'd get it eventually. So what if Kanesha was tentative? So was Cinderella in Act One. I'd make it work. I could make anything work.

The students playing Little Red Ridinghood and Jack blended smoothly with the adults. Our Baker was rock solid. Our Rapunzel was a terrific singer. Our two princes—one a Mackenzie, the other a professional—got along so well you would have thought they'd been friends for years. And they looked so much alike—tall, dark, and handsome—that Mei-Yin dubbed them TweedleTim and TweedleTom.

Directing Rowan was a breeze. He brought a hint of danger to the mysterious man that nicely offset the comic moments.

Best of all, Daddy was happy and confident. The reservations of his cast mates faded when there were no further outbursts or bragging about his past performances. As the week progressed, he even began joining them for meals.

I was thrilled that he was making friends, delighted that he was getting out into the world—and a little hurt that he could dump me so easily. I knew it was stupid. I was the one who had pushed him to mingle. Now, I was acting like an abandoned child.

699

Been there, done that, not doing it again.

I made up my mind to let Daddy fend for himself and enjoy my time alone with Rowan.

After which I promptly began lurking: inventing some vital item I needed at the grocery store so I could drive past the Ptomaine Stand at lunchtime, popping into restaurants for takeout while he was eating dinner. Hal chided me for reverting to Maggie Graham, Stalker. Janet advised me never to consider a career as a private investigator.

Rowan just said, "Let him go, Maggie."

"I am letting him go. I'm just following at a discreet distance."

"If you're so discreet, then why did Jack ask me if you were checking up on him?"

"Oh, God. What did you say?"

"I lied and said you were running errands."

"Did he believe you?"

Rowan gave me his "What do you think? I'm a faery!" look.

Debra's rendition of "Stay with Me" inadvertently put an end to my lurking. She captured the Witch's fury at discovering Rapunzel has admitted the prince to her tower, her bitterness at learning she is not "company enough," her fear about the dangers lurking in the world, and her tender plea for Rapunzel to remain a child, safe with the mother who loves her. As I watched that rehearsal, I realized I'd run through all those emotions in my relationship with Daddy. If I hadn't begged him to remain a child, I'd certainly shadowed him like an overprotective mother.

Been there, done that part deux.

I backed off and prayed that the greatest danger he would encounter in the world was the fat content of the Ptomaine Stand's burgers.

Our first run-through went so smoothly that I was shocked when the staff began speculating about when the other shoe would drop.

"We've got a terrific show," I protested.

"A terrific Act One," Alex corrected.

"So let's enjoy the moment."

"You know who you sound like?" Mei-Yin asked. "The BAKER'S Wife. Right before the giant SQUASHES her."

"A tree squashes her."

"The point is she gets SQUASHED."

I waved away Mei-Yin's observation. Of course, Act Two would be more demanding; the show got a lot darker, characters died left and right, and those that remained faced difficult choices. But the cast was strong and united, and I was confident we could pull it off.

Some of the credit went to Otis and Debra. With only the tiny part of Cinderella's father to master, Otis spent most of his time calming nervous Mackenzies and running lines with Daddy and the kids. Even the professionals seemed to rely on his easy laugh and quiet strength to ease them through the occasional rough patch. If Otis was the cast's unofficial den mother, Debra had become its head cheerleader, her acid humor balancing his warmth, her "let's get this done" practicality offsetting his easygoing attitude.

"She reminds me of you," Rowan commented as we shared a hurried dinner.

"Funny, talented, helpful . . ."

"Skeptical, bossy, opinionated . . ."

I tossed my half-eaten breadstick at him and exclaimed, "Finally!"

"Finally?" he repeated, neatly snagging the breadstick in mid-flight.

"A joke. You've seemed so . . . preoccupied this week."

I waited for an explanation, but he merely returned the breadstick to my plate.

"Look, if you're uncomfortable being directed by me —"

"No." He poked an asparagus spear and said, "Your mother's coming up next weekend to see *The Secret Garden*."

"I'll tell her to leave the spoon at home."

"I'm more concerned about her meeting Jack."

I sighed. "She can't. Not then, anyway. The last thing Daddy needs before Hell Week is that kind of drama. She's coming up the next weekend for *Into the Woods*. Maybe by then . . ."

"Why not wait, Maggie? Until the season's over. You have enough to deal with without telling Jack you're his daughter and engineering this meeting."

"But—"

"All we have to do is keep him out of her way for two weekends. Have Bernie go on as the Narrator the night she's here. Print up programs that list his name instead of Jack's. Let's save the drama for the stage."

While I hated the continued subterfuge, I knew it would save Daddy a lot of stress during *Into the Woods*. And it would give us more time to get to know each other, which would make the revelation that I was his daughter easier for both of us. Maybe by the time *Into the Woods* closed, he'd have worked out what he wanted to do next. Knowing he had his life in order would impress Mom far more than seeing him in yet another musical.

"It's a deal."

Rowan's relief surprised me; obviously, he'd been a lot more worried than he'd let on.

"So she's arriving Friday?"

"Saturday. There's some retirement party at Chris' law firm Friday evening."

"Then Jack and I will go to the cottage before the matinee—"

"We'll have to ask Janet to keep him under wraps. Chris wants the four of us to have dinner Saturday. Don't worry, I told Mom you'd make dinner here because we wouldn't have enough time to go out between shows. And don't yell at me for not telling you sooner. I didn't want you to start obsessing."

"I do not yell," Rowan replied. "Or obsess."

He spent the next fifteen minutes interrogating me about my mother's favorite foods. When I pointed out that this qualified as obsessing, he flashed a rueful smile. "It's just . . . it's our first meal together. I want everything to be perfect."

"All you have to do is wave your magic wand and we'd eat sawdust and think it was great."

"That would be cheating. I want her to see me, not my magic."

"Beguile her with mushroom pomponnettes instead of faery glamour?"

"I want her to accept me as a man. As a human."

Touched by his serious expression, I reached across the table and squeezed his hand.

"She will."

On Sunday, the other shoe dropped with God-like vengeance.

A storm knocked out the power around lunchtime. Bernie dealt with the hassle of canceling the matinee. Alex soldiered on with music rehearsals in Janet's candlelit parlor. Lee hooked up the generator to light the Smokehouse. After turning my script with staging notes over to Reinhard, I raced to the hotel.

Fortunately, most of our paying guests had checked out that morning. Frannie handed out flashlights to those who remained. Our backup generator churned out enough juice to power the emergency lights in the common areas and the coolers in the kitchen. We served up sandwiches and beer that evening, and cast members and tourists alike joked about our adventure.

After two days of staging scenes in the soggy meadow, the adventure had palled and the cast had begun sniping at each other. I soothed and cajoled. The staff churned out Fae power to ease the tension, focus tired minds, and boost confidence.

Much to my surprise, my father used his charm for the same purpose. He flashed that gap-toothed grin. He made silly jokes. He complimented cast members on their comic timing, their singing, their death scenes. And he seemed utterly sincere. Even when he shifted the charm to someone new, the person he'd just abandoned regarded him with an affectionate smile.

For the first time I understood why he had been so successful onstage and off. He made each person feel like the center of his world. He'd done it to me after the Ms. Pac-Man debacle just by asking me about my day and encouraging me to talk about rehearsals. I wondered if his behavior stemmed from genuine concern or a need for approval or simply a desire to avoid unpleasantness.

Frankly, I was too grateful about the results to care.

Cloud Nine might be a little gray, but at least it was no longer scudding over the horizon.

⋙⋘

The power came back on Wednesday morning. With that hurdle behind us, I set my sights on the next one: helping Jess find the strength and humor in the Baker's Wife.

"If she's so strong, why does she sleep with the Prince? Just because she quarreled with the Baker . . ."

"Her defenses are down. She lets herself be swept off her feet. She realizes it's a mistake, but it helps her understand who she is and what she wants—and to appreciate the life she has."

"And then she gets crushed by a tree."

"Well . . . yes."

"Is that supposed to be God's punishment?"

"I prefer to think of it as dramatic irony, but if God's punishment works for you . . ."

"No. It just seems so unfair. She makes one mistake . . ."

"'People make mistakes,'" I quoted from "No One is Alone." "Because she lingers with the Prince, she's under that tree when it falls. Because the Baker's father steals the magic beans, the Witch is cursed by her mother. And in revenge, the Witch lays a curse on the Baker's family. Act One is all about spells and magic and making choices. Act Two is about the consequences of those choices. Untangling the spells. Relying on ourselves instead of magic."

I might have been describing the history of the Crossroads Theatre—and my family. Rowan's fascination with humans led him to break his clan's rules about approaching them. Because he seduced an innocent Mackenzie girl, he was cursed by her mother and abandoned by his clan. In a vain effort to lift that spell, he worked another to call the Mackenzie descendants to the Crossroads. My father answered that call. And one fateful night, he stumbled on Rowan's clan and fell under the spell of their glamour.

Maybe this was the summer we untangled the spells and our lives.

Observing Jess' frown, I tried to get back on track.

"Her mistake makes her human—and vulnerable. And her loss forces the Baker to step up to the plate. Same thing happens with Jack and Little Red and Cinderella. They lose their lodestones and have to grow up. Like we all do. We learn to make our own choices, find our own paths. And if we're lucky, we find people along the way who can help us."

Mom. Rowan. Nancy. Helen. Everybody on the staff. They all guided me, no matter how many twists and turns the path took.

"The stronger you are, the harder your loss will hit the Baker—and the audience."

"I don't feel very strong. Especially around Brian."

"He's overcompensating."

"Because he doesn't trust me."

I hesitated. "Because he's scared. So he's trying to control the situation."

"Like the Baker."

Like me that first season.

Jess studied her script. She was one of those people whose appearance suggested that her primary goal was to slip through life unnoticed. Medium height, average weight, ordinary features, indefinite age somewhere between twenty-five and thirty-five.

And then she raised her head and I was struck anew by her thoughtful expression and the intelligence of those brown eyes. She was a quiet pool that seems unremarkable at first glance, but whose depths you discover on closer inspection.

Like Nancy.

"I know someone like Brian," Jess said. "Scared underneath and trying really hard to hide it."

Hard to say whether that "someone" was a parent or a lover or a friend—or what effect this summer would have on their relationship. But I finally understood why Jess had come here. And even if the choices that lay ahead were tough, I knew she had the strength to make them.

"Brian's a good guy," I finally said. "And a good actor. Talk to him. Work your scenes. If you need me to step in, I will. But I think you can handle this without me."

❦

Our Act Two run-through got off to a rocky start, but the solid performances of Debra and Rowan helped steady the others. The cast was close to mastering the rapid-fire lyrics of "Your Fault" and the intricate dance steps in the finale. And both Jess and Kanesha were beginning to bring out their characters' inner strengths.

I skipped Friday's performance of *The Secret Garden* to spend the evening with Rowan. He had to scurry down the back stairs from the kitchen now and then to smooth over the usual rough spots with his magic, but it was still nice to have some quiet time together.

When he returned from ensuring that Act Two was off to a good start, he refilled our wineglasses, lifted my feet off the sofa, and settled them across his lap. By the time he finished the foot massage, I had devolved into a state of boneless bliss.

But I couldn't help asking, "The show will be okay, right?"

"The show will be fine."

"Debra's great. Much better than I was when I played the role at Southford. I was good at the big moments, but I went for the cheap laughs."

"Well, that was before you came to the Crossroads."

"And you took me under your beneficent wing?" I raised my hands and salaamed as best I could from my reclining position. "I am not worthy, O great one."

"I'm not great," he assured me solemnly. "Just very, very good."

I stuck out my tongue. "Do you suppose she's a Mackenzie? Debra, I mean."

"I don't know."

"You don't?"

"It's not like they have a particular scent, Maggie. Or a plaid aura."

"I thought you always knew."

"Of course I knew. They were the only ones who came here. But I don't have a blood tie to the Mackenzies. Except to the staff, of course. If you're really curious about Debra . . ."

"The important thing is that she found something here she needed."

"Yes. A job."

"More than a job. She's mellowed since the beginning of the season."

"Maybe."

I pushed myself into a sitting position. "Are the Mackenzies supposed to have a monopoly on the Crossroads? Professionals and community theatre actors might need help, too, you know."

"The Mackenzies don't want a career in theatre."

"Neither do most of the others. Debra's the only one who's actually making a living at acting. The other 'professionals' are doing what I did: bouncing from one non-Equity job to the next and holding down a crappy job between gigs to pay the bills. Sure, some are hoping for their big break. But most just love the theatre too much to give it up."

"If they can't make a living at it, aren't we doing them a disservice by encouraging them to believe that they can?"

"I don't think we're doing that. I think—I hope—we're giving them skills that will help them succeed on and off the stage. Same as the Mackenzies. There must be thousands of people who need this place, who could learn something about themselves by working here. I want to give them that chance. It's not a betrayal of what you set out to do. It's just . . . expanding the mission."

Rowan frowned. "And magic? Where does that fit in?"

"The same way it always has. When you left, we all thought we had to become a normal theatre in order to survive. But it's the magic that makes this place special. I want that. I want this to be a place that changes lives, just like it changed mine. And I know that sounds like Maggie Graham, Helping Professional, but—"

"That's who you are."

"Are you so different?"

"I don't have your illusions about people. And I don't want you to be . . . disappointed."

"Are we talking about the theatre? Or Daddy?"

"Both."

CHAPTER 35
ONE NORMAL NIGHT

BY THE TIME THE MATINEE LET OUT Saturday, Daddy was in lockdown at the Bates mansion, dinner preparations were complete, and the air in Rowan's apartment was redolent with the earthy aroma of mushroom pomponnettes.

"You look beautiful," I told Rowan, who had donned his green silk shirt and black leather pants for the occasion.

"So do you," he replied, surveying my kicky sundress.

"Are you as calm as you look?"

"Absolutely. When Alison walks in, I'm going to call her Mom and give her a big kiss."

"You better be wearing a brass jock strap."

He laughed and shooed me downstairs to keep watch.

When Chris' Accord eased down the lane, I hurried out of the lobby and ran after it like an excited puppy. Mom crawled out of the car, submitted to a brief hug, and noted, "You look appallingly blissful."

"I am. How are *you*?"

"Tired."

She made a brief detour to greet some of the cast members who were enjoying the usual post-matinee supper in the picnic area. As soon as she turned toward the barn, her pleasant smile vanished. She marched toward the stage door like a prisoner about to enter Stalag 17.

"This is going to be a disaster."

"No, it won't," Chris assured me. But his expression was almost as grim as my mother's.

"Is it dinner with Rowan? Or something else?"

"It was just a really long drive."

We followed Mom up the stairs to the apartment. Rowan took one look at them and said, "You both look like you could use a drink."

As he ushered them into the living area, Chris gave a low whistle. Mom, of course, had seen it during her less-than-cordial meeting with Rowan two summers ago. Praying our dinner would go better, I darted around like a hummingbird on crack as I set out the hors d'oeuvres.

I heard another whistle and turned to find Chris examining the bottle of wine on the sideboard.

"You really pulled out all the stops, Rowan."

"Wait'll you taste the mushroom pomponnettes," I promised.

My mother's lips pursed; clearly, she thought Rowan was trying too hard. She thawed a little after her first glass of wine, but her chilly politeness was almost worse than outright rudeness. Rowan pretended not to notice, but when he went into the kitchen to put the lamb chops on the grill, I plunked myself on the sofa next to her.

"He's worked really hard on this dinner," I said in a furious whisper. "Could you at least try to meet him halfway?"

Mom had the grace to look abashed. She took a deep breath, put on a happy face, and said, "I thought Maggie was exaggerating when she praised your cooking. Now I know better. If you get tired of the theatre, you can open a restaurant in town."

Rowan glanced at me, then shook his head. "I'm already keeping a wary eye out for your spoon. I don't want to be looking over my shoulder for Mei-Yin's cleaver."

"Look on the bright side," my mother said. "A cleaver would be quick."

"Thank you, Alison. That *is* a comfort."

I began humming "Always Look on the Bright Side of Life." Chris obligingly chimed in with the whistles. Rowan laughed. Even Mom smiled.

Apart from her brief interrogation about how Rowan had spent his time away—and whether he had reconciled with his mythical father—dinner went more smoothly. But both Mom and Chris seemed . . . off. Maybe it *was* just the long drive. I hated to think of them enduring the return trip tomorrow.

When I mentioned that, Chris said, "We're not. We're going to stick around and play tourist next week."

I managed to avoid shrieking, but my face must have conveyed my panic because Mom said, "Don't worry. We won't be underfoot. We'll do some sightseeing and come back Thursday after *Into the Woods* opens."

"And since you'll be done with rehearsals," Chris added, "we'll have all day Friday to visit. Maybe go on a day trip, the four of us."

I banished the mental picture of Rowan vomiting out the back window of Chris' car and plastered a smile on my face. "That's great! I'm not sure if the Rose Garden Room's available next Thursday, but — "

"It's all taken care of," Chris said. "Frannie booked us into a room down the hall for Thursday night."

"Wonderful," Rowan said. "You'll have much more fun playing tourist than driving back and forth two weekends in a row. Where are you going? Or are you just going to wander?"

I gave a derisive snort; Mom was as likely to wander through Vermont as she was to hitchhike.

After favoring me with a quelling glance, she began describing their itinerary. Rowan astonished me by commenting on all the sites she mentioned and offering suggestions for others to consider. If I didn't know better, I'd have believed he had actually visited them.

"It's worth a side trip to see the Quechee Gorge," he urged. "The Grand Canyon of Vermont, they call it. If you don't want to walk to the bottom, you can still get a marvelous view from the bridge. Better still, take a hot air balloon ride. I've always wanted to do that." His expression grew dreamy. "Imagine floating through the sunset with the world drifting by beneath you. Like Phileas Fogg in *Around the World in Eighty Days*."

"It probably costs an arm and a leg," my practical mother noted.

"But for the experience of a lifetime . . ." Rowan sighed. Then he brightened. "You should come up for fall foliage season. The town will be crawling with leaf peepers, but there's a place nearby with incredible views. I took Maggie there for a picnic."

"It was our first date. Rowan packed up his entire kitchen—silver, crystal, bone china. And the food . . . poached salmon, grilled quail . . ."

"That's some first date," Chris said.

"It wasn't as romantic as it sounds. More like the opening round of a boxing match. Both of us probing, trying to find out what made the other one tick."

"But it was a beginning," Rowan said. "The first time we really opened up to each other."

As we shared a smile, an enormous sense of peace filled me. We'd come a long way since that afternoon.

My smile faded when I caught Mom studying me. Chris was studying Mom, his expression grave.

Was that why they seemed off? Were they having problems?

Stop borrowing trouble. The evening's finally going okay. Slice up the blueberry pie, dish out the ice cream, and thank God for small favors.

To my relief, they seemed to enjoy *The Secret Garden*. We waited in the green room to greet the cast and Mom found a special moment in each of the principal actors' performances to praise. But as Rowan and I walked them through the lobby, she said, "It's not an easy show, is it? The story, I mean. There's so much bitterness and anger and lost dreams."

"But there's a happy ending."

"Musicals are nice that way. Life is rarely so accommodating."

I shot a glance at Rowan, who obligingly dragged Chris over to examine a poster. I led Mom toward the parking lot and asked, "Is everything okay?"

"Yes. No. Sue's mother died."

Without thinking, I blurted out, "It took long enough." Then clapped my hands over my mouth, aghast at my insensitivity.

After staring at me in shocked disbelief, Mom threw back her head and gave a great bellow of laughter. Then she pressed her fingertips to her lips. We stood there like two "Speak No Evil" monkeys until she lowered her hand and whispered, "I said the very same thing."

"We're going straight to hell," I whispered back.

"Nonsense. She was a dreadful old harridan. And she made Sue's life a misery."

"How is Sue?"

The last traces of amusement fled. "Sad. Angry. Bitter. Guilty. The whole experience made me feel . . . old."

"You're not old!" Unwillingly, I noticed that the unforgiving fluorescent lights in the parking lot cast shadows under her eyes and deepened the faint grooves around her mouth. "Sixty-two is practically middle-aged these days."

"Only if you live to be a hundred and twenty," she remarked dryly. "When the morning paper comes, you know the first section I read? The obituaries. A sure sign I'm getting old."

"Or that you're ghoulish."

"Well, there *is* that."

"I wish you'd told me all this when we talked on Sunday."

"You sounded so happy. I didn't want to spoil that." She grimaced. "Instead, I spoiled dinner."

"No, you didn't."

"Promise you won't say awful things about me when I'm dead."

"I don't say awful things about you now! I don't think you're a harridan."

"And . . . ?" she prompted.

"And you very rarely make my life a misery."

To my relief, that wrested a smile from her.

"Hey!" Chris called. "Are you two finished whispering?"

Mom motioned the guys over and said, "I was being maudlin. Another sign of impending decrepitude."

"You're the least decrepit woman I know," Rowan said.

"Your opinion doesn't count. You're just trying to win me over."

"Am I succeeding?"

"I'm still deciding."

"Told you she was tough," Chris said. "You had *me* at the mushroom pomponnettes."

Mom hugged me. "It was a wonderful show, Maggie. And a wonderful dinner, Rowan."

The first time she'd ever called him that. Hard to tell

whether he felt the earth teetering on its axis, too. He merely shook her hand and thanked her.

"Breakfast at the Chatterbox?" I asked.

"No. Sleep in and get some rest. You have a busy week ahead. I'll call you Thursday when we get into town."

"Call me sooner if you want. To talk about the trip. Or . . . whatever."

"I'll call you Thursday," she said firmly.

As the car eased up the lane, Rowan said, "All in all, I thought it went pretty well." When I merely nodded, he asked, "Didn't *you* think so?"

"Yes," I assured him.

"She called me Rowan. That was a big step."

I hugged his arm. "Yes. It was."

"But . . . ?"

I told him about my conversation with Mom, adding, "I was afraid she and Chris were having problems." When Rowan remained silent, I asked, "They're not, are they?"

"I don't know," he replied. "I sensed something during dinner. A certain . . . sadness. Maybe it was the specter of mortality."

"But you don't think so."

"I don't know," he repeated. "But I'm glad they'll be able to spend some time together. They deserve a chance to relax and enjoy each other. And so do we. So let's have fun tonight and celebrate another successful show."

I nodded. But I wished I could skip the cast party. All I really wanted to do was hurry after my mother and find some way to dispel the sadness that shadowed her.

CHAPTER 36
SEE WHAT IT GETS YOU

■WAS RELIEVED TO DISCOVER THAT DADDY'S
■EVENING had been less stressful than Mom's. He had
grilled burgers with Bernie and Mei-Yin, helped Hal string
paper lanterns around the patio, and beaten everyone at
Monopoly. Apart from asking why we hadn't brought our
guests to the cast party, he seemed disinterested in our "out
of town friends." I provided a hushed summary of my evening to the staff while we were setting out beer and wine
and platters of food.

A rousing chorus of "The House Upon the Hill" her-
alded the arrival of the cast. Those who were making their
first pilgrimage to the Bates mansion surveyed their sur-
roundings with awe. The veterans made a beeline to the
dining room.

The partying began in earnest after the kids departed
with their parents. Most of the staff and crew left shortly
afterward; they had to be back at the theatre at nine o'clock
to begin loading in the set of *Into the Woods* and knew better than to incur the wrath of Reinhard and Lee by showing
up late.

I wandered through the house, laughing at some of the
war stories of our rehearsals and making a special effort to
spend time with the cast members who would be leaving
tomorrow. But the strain of dinner was telling on me and by
one o'clock, I was yawning.

"Time for bed, Cinderella?" Rowan asked.

"Past it. Mind if I bunk with you tonight? The party will go on for at least another hour."

He offered a convincing imitation of Long's leer. "I was hoping you'd suggest that."

"Just to sleep."

"No hanky-panky?"

"No."

"No makin' whoopee?"

"Uh-uh."

"Not even a little Graham on the half shell?" he whispered. And laughed as I frantically shushed him.

"Have you seen Daddy?"

"Not lately. Why?"

"I don't want him up to all hours drinking."

Rowan cocked his head and gazed thoughtfully at the chandelier in Janet's foyer. After about ten seconds, I said, "Hello? Earth to Rowan?"

"He's out back," he announced with a smug smile.

"If only you were that good with lost keys. I'll grab my stuff and roust him out."

"Meet you on the front porch."

I threw a change of clothes and some cosmetics into my carryall, snatched up my purse, and headed back downstairs. I breathed a sigh of relief when I stepped outside. After the stuffiness of the house, the cool air felt delicious.

Cigarette smoke drifted skyward, shrouding the patio in a haze. Cast members chatted together, some faces illuminated by the lamplight shining through the windows, others dyed pink and gold and bilious green by the paper lanterns hanging from the branches of the maple tree. Spying no sign of Daddy's signature white hair, I slowly descended the steps, guided by the soft glow of the luminarias in their paper bags.

A couple was strolling in the garden, their shadowy figures barely visible as they moved in and out of the small pools of light shed by the solar lanterns. I felt a pang of regret that Rowan and I had never wandered through the moonlit garden. But there would be many nights for that after the season ended.

The couple turned to each other. I expected them to kiss, but after a moment, they moved apart and started toward the house. At which point I mentally scolded myself for spying and directed my gaze to the lower patio.

The guttering flames of the tiki torches revealed Daddy sitting atop a picnic table, feet planted on the bench, elbows resting on his knees. As I drew nearer, his head turned and he lifted his paper cup in salute. That's when I noticed the champagne bottle lying on its side next to his thigh.

"How come you're sitting out here all alone?"

"Got too noisy for me."

His words were clear; maybe he hadn't had as much to drink as I'd feared.

"Plus, I was enjoying the view." He gestured toward the garden with his cup. "Did you see them?"

"It's bad manners to spy," I said primly.

"But you see some pretty interesting things. Want to know who it is?"

"I do not. They deserve their privacy."

"Then how come you're peering at them, trying to make out their faces?"

"I am not peering. I'm just . . . enjoying the view."

As the couple passed one of the post lanterns on the drive, I caught my breath. There was no mistaking the coppery gleam of the man's hair or the identity of the woman whose face was turned toward him.

Alex and Debra?

I froze as they mounted the steps to the patio, but they were too intent on each other to notice Daddy or me. When they were safely out of earshot, I whispered, "Oh. My. God."

Daddy giggled like a naughty boy. "Who'da thunk it, huh?"

"Rowan must have. I'm going to kill him for not telling me."

Was that why Debra needed to come to the Crossroads? To find Alex?

I reviewed every interaction I'd witnessed. They clearly liked each other and enjoyed working together. Debra joked with him. Alex teased her. But they did the same with me.

"Maybe they just wanted to take a walk," I said.

Daddy snorted in disbelief.

"Let's go back to the apartment. We'll pump Rowan for info."

"Sure you two wouldn't rather be alone?"

"I'm too tired to do anything but sleep. And I won't get much around here."

As if to prove my point, a dreadful rap version of "Come to My Garden" floated down from the house.

Daddy sighed. "Time was I could perform in the evening, party till dawn, and rehearse all day. Not anymore. Must be getting old."

It was a painful echo of my mother's words, but Daddy seemed rueful rather than sad.

"One for the road?" he asked, reaching for the champagne bottle.

I tossed my carryall onto the table. "Okay."

He righted the champagne bottle, poured a slug into his cup and handed it to me. Then he raised the bottle and said, "Here's to my first Hell Week in a couple of decades."

"The first of many."

I tapped my cup against the bottle and took a small sip. Daddy lowered the bottle without drinking.

"What? No toast?"

"Can't very well drink to that one."

"Why not?"

"I think we both know my acting days are numbered."

"We haven't even opened yet and you're throwing in the towel?"

"Oh, it's been fun. And I appreciate you taking a chance on me."

"There will be other shows, Jack. And better roles."

"It's not that."

"You want to get back into teaching?"

"Teaching? Hell, no. I got bigger plans." He glanced around the patio, then whispered, "Come on. You know."

I shook my head.

"I'm going to Faerie, of course."

The world became utterly silent, as if his words had swallowed the muted buzz of conversation from the upper patio and the ratchety chorus of night insects. From a great distance, I heard my croak of laughter. The hoarse caw of the crow in the maple tree. The jeers of the shapeshifters in the Borderlands, mocking me for imagining I could hold him here.

Daddy mistook my reaction for delight and laughed with me. If he had looked at my face, he would have realized his mistake, but his rapt gaze was fixed on the forest, a dark, formless mass barely visible in the light of the waning moon.

"Rowan said I shouldn't tell anybody, but I knew you'd understand."

Something wet on my hand. Champagne from the paper cup crushed between my fingers.

"Everybody thought I was crazy. My wife. The doctors. But I found a way in. Took me years, but I found it."

He rocked back and forth, hands gripping his knees, as if to restrain himself from racing into the forest.

"If only I'd come to Rowan in the beginning. It kills me to think of the time I wasted. Not that I regret reaching the Borderlands. I saw things you can only imagine. But I knew I'd only touched the tip of Faerie. Sometimes, I glimpsed it through the mist. And heard that music."

High-pitched and silvery, like the rippling glissando of a harp.

I must have made some sound because my father peered at me. "Don't worry. Rowan already told me he wouldn't leave. But he doesn't have to, see? That's the beauty part. He just has to open a portal and bam! I march out of this world and into the other one. Piece of cake. In a way, I owe it all to you."

All I could do was stare at him.

"Well, Lee helped. His lighting, anyway."

When I just continued staring, Daddy exclaimed, "*The Secret Garden*! The storm at the end of Act One. It was like Lee had been there that night."

His gaze returned to the forest. "For years, it was just bits and pieces. Like a dream you half recall the next morning. The leaves rustling in the breeze. The thunder rumbling off in the distance like timpani. The sky shuddering with heat lightning. The whole forest seemed to shimmer. But that wasn't the lightning."

He drew in a deep, trembling breath and let it out on a sigh.

"Oh, Maggie, if you could have seen them. You can't judge by Rowan. He's trying to pass as human. It was like they carried the light of the sun and the moon and the stars inside. And when they came gliding through the trees—like a cloud of fireflies ..."

Just like that other Midsummer. The fireflies dancing in the meadow. The glowing ball of light vanishing into the woods. The night Caren and I had come so close to discovering the secret of the Crossroads and glimpsing what my father had seen decades earlier.

"I'd forgotten most of it until opening night. But with the lights and the music and the Dreamers drifting onstage, circling around that little girl ... that's when all the bits and pieces finally fit together. And when the Dreamers left ..." His voice caught. "It was like I was losing *them* all over again."

My father leaping out of his seat. His desperate shout. That frail figure tottering down the aisle, arms outstretched.

It was not me he'd seen on that stage. It was not me he wanted.

He was reaching for them.

He had spent half his life pursuing them. Why had I been stupid enough to imagine he would stop?

"I begged Rowan to open a portal that night. But he wouldn't. He said I'd promised to do the Follies and *Into the Woods* and told me I had to honor my commitments. And he was right. It would have been wrong to walk out. But after the season's over ..."

I sank onto the bench. Daddy slid down beside me.

"He'll open a portal if *you* ask him. I know he will."

I forced myself to look into his eager face. "So you're just going to turn your back on this world?"

The steadiness of my voice astonished me. Even more astonishing was my calm—as if I'd always known I would face this moment and had been preparing for it since the night he had crept out of the theatre.

Daddy drew back, frowning. "Look, I'm grateful for everything you and Rowan have done. But there's nothing for me here."

"There's your wife."

"My ex-wife."

"And your daughter."

He shifted uncomfortably on the bench and stared off into the darkness. "She's better off without me."

"How do you know?"

"Because I know Allie. My ex."

My calm shattered. He was only one who had ever called her by that nickname. Mom had always hated it.

"She'd have taken good care of her. Brought her up right."

"You don't even want to see her? To find out?"

"I'd just screw her up. Again. Besides, she's a grown woman now."

"Thirty-four."

"Something like that."

"Not 'something like that.' Exactly that."

"So she's thirty-four. And I'm a crappy father for not remembering, okay?"

"No, Jack, it's not okay."

I slowly rose and stared down at him. I was shaking with anger and had to take a moment to regain control of my voice.

"Maybe your life got turned upside down because of what happened here. Maybe any man would have fallen apart. And maybe your wife had no choice but to divorce you. But you had a child. And you abandoned her."

"I did what I thought was best," my father mumbled.

"For you! You always did what was best for Jack Sinclair. A couple of visits after your wife kicked you out. A couple of postcards saying 'Daddy will always love you.' How many birthdays passed before she stopped hoping for a card? How many times did she cry herself to sleep, wondering why you had forgotten her?"

My father leaped to his feet. "I didn't forget! I never forgot!"

His breath was coming as hard and fast as mine, his eyes glaring with the same anger, his chin stuck out with the same belligerence. And he was blind to the resemblance.

"Even now, you can't see it, can you?"

His anger shifted into something else—wariness, perhaps. Or fear.

"What the hell are you talking about?"

From the direction of the house, I heard someone shout my name. Dully, I realized it was Rowan. Well, he'd started this tangled chain of events by calling my father to the

Crossroads. It seemed only fitting for him to be here for the big climax.

"Let me help you put the bits and pieces together, Jack. Just like opening night of *The Secret Garden*. Alison reverted to her maiden name after the divorce. And she changed little Maggie's name, too."

His eyes flew wide. He shook his head and stepped back, only to bump into the picnic bench and collapse gracelessly onto it. And all the while, his eyes remained fixed on my face, scanning my features the way I had catalogued his that first night.

"Oh, Christ . . ." he whispered.

The footsteps pounding toward us abruptly halted. Then they resumed, much more slowly. They stopped again, so close behind me that I could feel the heat of Rowan's body.

I wasn't aware of edging away until I discovered that I was standing much farther from the picnic table. Nor was I sure if I had unconsciously tried to distance myself from them or if I was trying to preserve the strange bubble of calm that surrounded me again.

Not calm, really. Emptiness.

"Why didn't you tell me? Why didn't either of you tell me the truth?"

He seemed strangely insubstantial—as if part of him had already left this world.

Rowan's gaze remained fixed on me as he quietly explained: Jack's fragile mental state, the shock, waiting for the right time. The same words he had offered when Jack discovered how much time had passed. Always, it seemed, we kept circling back, revisiting the links in the endless chain of spells and curses, explanations and excuses. Yet nothing ever really changed.

"I should have realized. There were so many clues."

I had been just as blind. Longing for the transformational ending of *The Secret Garden*, I had created the same kind of fantasy that Mary imagines in "The Girl I Mean to Be": the characters in a picture-perfect setting, all wounds healed, all wrongs forgiven.

If I had been less caught up in that fantasy, I might have recognized the clues Rowan had given me: his fear that I would be disillusioned, his plea to postpone Mom's meeting with Jack, his quiet warning that I needed to let him go.

So many clues—and I had ignored them all.

Like father, like daughter.

"I'm sorry, Maggie. If I had known . . ."

"Would it really have made a difference?"

Although I'd spoken gently, he winced.

"Would you honestly give up Faerie for me? For any-one?"

His hesitation answered me more clearly than any words.

I nodded and began walking toward the steps.

"Magpie . . ."

My breath whooshed out like I'd been punched in the stomach. Rowan's anxiety stabbed me. I flung up my hands, warding off Jack's words and Rowan's power. Then I slowly turned.

"I will always be your daughter, Jack. But I am not your Magpie. I'm Maggie Graham. The executive director of the Crossroads Theatre. Call tomorrow is at one o'clock."

I started up the steps, only to discover Alex hurrying down them and Janet watching from the upper patio. As Rowan started toward me, I shook my head.

"No."

Although my voice was little more than a whisper, both men stopped short.

Such a tiny word to hold such power.

Rowan spoke my name, his voice low and urgent, his power pleading with me to stay.

"No," I repeated.

I took the only escape route available and hurried down the steps to the drive.

CHAPTER 37

LEAVIN'S NOT THE ONLY WAY TO GO

TOO LATE, I REMEMBERED THAT I HAD PARKED MY CAR at the theatre after my morning trip to the grocery store. Not that I could have reached the garage anyway. I barely made it to the drive before I heard Rowan's footsteps behind me.

I veered up the hill toward the side of the house.

"Maggie!"

The ground was terraced, each level connected by a short series of steps. But it was a steep climb and I was panting before I reached the halfway point.

"Wait!"

The light streaming from the windows flung bands of illumination across the level ground at the top, but here, I had only my memory and the unpredictable moonlight to guide me. Twice, I stumbled, but managed to regain my balance and keep moving.

"Talk to me, damn it!"

I had no breath to talk and no desire to stop, although my body was drenched with sweat and my legs had begun to ache. As I mounted the final set of steps, a blur of movement to my right startled me. The next thing I knew Rowan was blocking my path.

It seemed childish to dodge around him. Worse, it was useless. He'd just pull his "faster than a speeding bullet" act to thwart me again.

He had the good sense not to touch me with either his

hands or his power. I didn't want to be touched by anything Fae at that moment. Janet, Alex, Rowan . . . all of them sensing every emotion, battering at my defenses. That was why I had left. With all their fucking magical power, you'd think they would understand that and leave me alone.

"Talk to me. Please."

"I can't do this, Rowan. Not right now."

I started walking. Rowan kept pace beside me.

"The evening of my panic attack. You said we had to be able to talk. To deal with things together."

"I also said we had to be honest."

He checked suddenly, but caught up with me a few paces later.

"I wanted to tell you the truth. But you were so happy during rehearsals for *Into the Woods*. I just couldn't bring myself to hurt you."

"I know."

Again he checked and hurried to catch up with me.

"But . . . I don't understand . . ."

"Glass houses, Rowan."

"What?"

"I've been lying to my mother all summer. Trying to protect her. Why should I be angry at you for doing the same thing?"

"But—"

"I'm angry at myself. For being stupid enough to believe he could change."

"Now that he knows you're his daughter—"

"He might stay out of some sense of obligation, but he'll always want Faerie more than me."

My voice cracked and I pressed my lips together. I felt more than saw Rowan's hand come up, but I just quickened my pace.

The parking lot was an oasis of fluorescent light. Rowan must have thought I was going to the apartment because he had to veer sharply to follow me to the car. As I fumbled for my keys, he slapped his palm against the window.

"Where are you going?"

"I don't know."

The hotel was booked. I didn't want to wake Hal. Besides, then I'd have to contend with Lee's Faedar.

"You shouldn't be driving when you're upset."

"I'm fine."

"Please. Let's go up to the apartment and—"

"I don't want to go to the apartment!"

"You can't just drive around all night."

"Maybe I'll crash in the lobby of the Bough. It doesn't matter! I just need to be alone."

"I'll take Jack to the cottage. You'll have the apartment to yourself."

"I need to get away, Rowan. From everything and everyone that reminds me of Faerie."

His hand slipped from the glass. His shocked expression shattered what was left of my self-control.

I blurted out an apology, flung open the car door, and slid inside.

"Are you coming back?"

His voice sounded hollow, as if every emotion had been drained.

"I'll be here for load-in."

It took three tries before I managed to shove the key into the ignition. I slammed the door and backed out so quickly that the car skidded on the gravel.

As I neared the top of the lane, I glanced into the rearview mirror. Rowan was still standing in the parking lot.

His small, lonely figure blurred. I gripped the steering wheel hard and hit the accelerator.

❦❦

I made it about half a mile before I pulled over and indulged in the release of tears. Then I blew my nose and kept going.

I drove aimlessly, grateful for the dark, winding roads that forced me to concentrate on my driving. But I kept seeing Rowan's forlorn figure. I was angry with myself for hurting him, angrier still that his persistence had driven me to it—and terrified to realize that I couldn't bear to be near him.

Had Mom felt like that when she kicked Jack out? Or had love leached away long before that?

Thank God, I had never told her that Jack had returned. Just imagining what I might have put her through brought on another fit of the shakes. Better to envision her sleeping peacefully beside Chris, untroubled by the ghosts of our past. Ghosts had no place in this world. And Jack Sinclair had no place in our lives.

The lyrics of "No More" kept running through my head, an ironic counterpoint to my turbulent thoughts. No more giants, the Baker pleaded. No more witches or curses or lies. But even he realized that he couldn't ignore them, any more than he could forget the false hopes, the reverses, the good-byes . . .

Damn Stephen Sondheim. Why did he have to write my fucking life into a musical?

I turned on the radio, hoping to drown out the lyrics, but the brief bursts of music vanished as soon as the car descended a hill.

At some point, I realized I was hopelessly lost. If my car had a GPS, I might have been able to punch in the name of one of the rare streets I passed. Lacking that, I just kept driving until I stumbled onto Route 9. Unsure of my bearings, I turned west. Within a few miles, I realized I was heading toward Bennington rather than Dale.

I wished I could keep driving. I wished I could crawl back into my protective bubble.

No more feelings. No more questions. Just running away. Escaping the ties that bind.

That was the Mysterious Man's solution. And Jack's.

Like father, like daughter.

But the Mysterious Man warned the Baker about the dangers of wandering blind. Which was exactly what I'd been doing for the last hour.

I could never outdistance my thoughts or escape the ties that bound me to the Crossroads. With every mile that separated me from the theatre, I became more conscious of them: the concern of my staff, the bewilderment of my father, and most of all, the anguish of the man who loved me.

The man I still loved. But my blithe confidence that we could surmount every obstacle had been shaken.

No matter how human he acted, Rowan was innately different. He had powers I would never understand, weaknesses he could never conquer. If I couldn't accept that, I should break it off now.

But would I be able to do that? Even if I wanted to? Maybe I was ensnared by Fae glamour as surely as my father. Or maybe that was simply the nature of love. Another sort of trap—and just as dangerous.

"Give him a chance, Mom."

"To do what? Break your heart a second time?"

"That won't happen."

"You know who you sound like? Me. Thirty years ago."

Was I repeating her mistake—trying to make Rowan over into something he wasn't, something he could never be?

Always more questions. Just different kinds.

But one thing I did know. Like it or not, I *was* Magpie, the child pounding her fists on the window as her father walked out of her life. And Maggie Sinclair, the girl who watched her identity disappear just as her father had. Without those girls, Maggie Graham would never have made that fateful journey to the Crossroads.

So many spells. So many ties. Blood and friendship. Duty and obligation. Commitment and love. How do you break free without dooming yourself to loneliness? Even then, the ghosts are always there, lurking in the shadows of memory. Sooner or later, you have to face them.

Rowan had taught me that.

I waited for a truck to roar past, then made a quick U-turn. Running again, but this time, back to the family I had been given and the family I had chosen.

Although I was driving faster, the odometer seemed to spin more slowly. By the time I coasted into Dale, my eyes felt like they were lubricated with sand. Main Street was deserted at this hour, but the streetlamps were so bright after the dark road that they made me squint.

I slowed as I approached the Golden Bough. It was tempting to hide out there, to snatch a few hours of sleep on one of the sofas in the lobby. But there were too many people back at the theatre who were waiting and worrying about me.

I was already gliding past the hotel when I saw the figure sitting on the porch steps. I tramped on the brake, and the Civic shuddered to a halt.

It seemed to take an hour to cross the street, yet my breath came so fast, I felt like I was running. All the while, Rowan sat there like a statue. Only when I reached the porch did I notice the unceasing tremor rippling through his shirt.

I imagined him hesitating in the parking lot. Running up the lane. Hesitating again as he reached the road before racing through the darkness to town—the town he only knew secondhand from the stories of others. Had he paused for a moment to take in his first view of Dale? Or simply hurried down Main Street, searching for the Golden Bough?

And then the long, lonely vigil, watching and waiting and hoping.

His breath caught as I raised my hand, then leaked out in a strangled sigh when my fingertips touched his cheek.

I drew his head to my breast. As he flung his arms around my waist, his power burst free, flooding my senses with tremulous relief, the ache of sorrow, and a stab of fear so sharp that I winced.

We had embraced like this the evening I had confronted him at the theatre, daring him to love me. Now, we clung to each other like survivors of a shipwreck, both aware of how close we had come to foundering.

I pressed my lips to his hair and breathed in his scent. Not the musky-sweet aroma of desire, but the bitter tang of fear and despair.

"Are you coming back?" he had asked. Stupidly, I had told him I would return for load-in. But he had known I would never walk out on the show. He had been asking if I was walking out on him.

Maybe it would always be like this for us—this pulling away and coming together. Maybe that was inevitable between human and faery. But I had to believe that we could bridge our differences, that love and trust and time would bind us together more strongly.

His silk shirt was damp with perspiration. I stroked his back, his shoulders, the knotted muscles in his neck, my hands silently assuring him of my love, my commitment. But silence had proven to be our enemy and caused too many misunderstandings. I needed to speak the words—as much for me as for him.

"I'm here, Rowan. I can't promise I'll never bolt again, but I will always come back."

The fear receded, but his sorrow whispered through me. And something else that made no sense to me.

Wonder.

When he raised his head, I saw only his eyes. So impossibly green. So clearly Fae. Only when his fingertips touched his cheek did I notice the damp track running down it, glistening in the light of the porch lantern.

"You made me weep," he whispered.

"Oh, Rowan. I'm so sorry."

"No. You don't understand. The Fae can't weep."

His gaze searched my face as if I were a stranger.

I brushed my fingertips against his cheek and drew back, startled. His tears felt . . . thick. Like the glycerin used in films to simulate real tears.

He seized my hand and brought it to his mouth. His lips closed around my middle finger, and he sucked it gently. Then he raised his index finger to my mouth.

Salty, yes. But also something sweet. Like honey.

"Am I becoming . . . human?"

I shook my head helplessly. "Maybe the Fae don't weep because nothing ever touches them deeply enough. But now that you've learned to love . . ."

"I've learned the fear of losing it."

The fear that had haunted his dreams this summer. And made him weep tonight.

"I just wish I hadn't been the one to teach you that."

"Who else could?"

I nodded, shouldering the burden of my guilt and the risks of loving him. Never again would I believe we could sail over every hurdle as easily as we'd conquered his panic attacks. The knowledge left me forlorn, as if we had lost something nearly as precious as what we had found tonight.

I took his hand and led him to the car, only to draw up short when I realized he couldn't possibly ride in it.

"I'll park behind the hotel. And we'll walk home."

His fingers tightened on mine. "We'll drive."

Tears rose in my eyes. I blinked them away and shook my head.

"We'll drive," he repeated.

I rolled down all the windows and turned the vents on high. Then I leaned over and opened his door. As soon as he slid inside and closed the door, I tramped on the accelerator and sped back to the theatre.

When I reached the lane, I slowed just enough to avoid ripping out the undercarriage of the Civic. Even before I stopped the car, he flung open the door and stumbled outside. I hurried around the car to find him gulping great lungfuls of air. But he didn't get sick. He just nodded gravely, as if he'd proved something to himself—and to me.

As I glanced up at the apartment, he said, "Jack's at the house. We didn't think he should be alone."

I thought longingly of Rowan's bed, then resolutely turned toward the house.

"You don't have to see him tonight."

"I'm not going there to see him. Janet will be waiting up. And Alex."

"How did you know Alex was—?"

"His car's still in the lot."

We walked up the hill hand in hand. The lights were still on in the house, but it was quiet now. As we neared the porch, the screen door swung open, and Janet and Alex walked outside. He was still in his tuxedo, although he'd removed his tie and jacket. Janet had donned her old terry cloth robe and she held my carryall in her hand.

"I'm sorry I worried you."

They nodded, their eyes on Rowan, their faces betraying the same wonder I had seen on his when he had wept. Although the traces of his tears were gone, Janet's power was strong enough to have sensed what had happened at the Bough.

If Rowan felt that his privacy had been invaded, I saw no sign of it. He even managed a weary smile when Alex gripped his shoulder.

"The important thing is that you're home," Janet said.

She nodded to Rowan and returned my hug with surprising fierceness. Then she thrust out my carryall and declared, "If you pull a stunt like that again, I'll evict you."

Rowan and I walked to the apartment in silence and undressed by moonlight. We were too exhausted to make love. It was enough to hold each other.

The last thing I remembered was the steady throb of his heartbeat under my hand.

CHAPTER 38
PROMISES, PROMISES

I HAD THREE JOBS DURING LOAD-IN: to set out the coffee urn and the Chatterbox pastries in the lobby; to clean up after the feeding frenzy; and to stay out of everyone's way in between. Usually, I enjoyed the camaraderie with the crew, but the events of the previous night weighed on me.

I had dreamed again of that glade in the forest. But instead of dancing with the fireflies, I chased after them, while Rowan chased after me, both of us helpless to capture what we sought. And when the fireflies abandoned the glade, we were left to stumble through the darkness, each blind to the other.

My dream or Rowan's or some tangled mix? I only knew that I awoke to that same forlorn feeling I had experienced on the steps of the Bough—and the fear that neither Rowan nor I was strong enough to follow the path we had chosen.

As the early birds on the crew swarmed the lobby, I saw Lee eyeing me with concern. I beat a hasty retreat into the house. The back doors of the barn were open. It reminded me of the ending of *White Christmas*, only instead of a Currier and Ives snow scene I saw Catherine and Javier wheeling a giant storybook through the breezeway—and Rowan walking out of the stage right wings as if he carried the weight of the world on his shoulders.

"Jack's upstairs. He was hoping to speak with you."

The other burden we both had to carry. This one, I would

have gladly thrust aside. But I had to face him sometime.
Better to clear the air now than have all those feelings sim-
mering during Hell Week.

"Would you rather talk to him alone?" Rowan asked as
I mounted the steps to the stage.

"You're as much a part of what happens to him as I am.
Just . . ."

"Keep out of it?"

"Keep your magic out of it. Unless he goes off the deep
end. Let us feel what we feel without smoothing out the
rough edges." As we walked through the wings, I asked, "Do
you think he *might* go off the deep end?"

"He's nervous about seeing you, but all in all, he's surprisingly calm."

Maybe subconsciously, he had suspected the truth and
been bracing for it, just as I had been braced for his revelation about going to Faerie.

Jack was hovering in the middle of the living area.
Against my will, I was touched that he had dressed with
such care, choosing khaki slacks and a short-sleeved shirt
instead of his usual shorts and T-shirt.

His smile was hesitant, like a kid who wasn't sure if he
was going to be scolded or praised. Maybe that was the real
Jack Sinclair. The boy who never grew up. My personal Peter Pan.

He waited for me to sit on the sofa, then glanced at Rowan
for direction. Rowan merely sat in one of the easy chairs and
after a moment, Jack perched on the other one.

He studied me uncertainly, the actor awaiting his cue. I
refused to give him one. If I was kind, he'd respond with
warmth and charm. If I seemed angry, he would try remorse.
This time, he would have to improvise. I just hoped that
whatever he said was genuine, not playacting.

He glanced around as if seeking inspiration, then blurted
out, "Do you hate me?"

Startled, I replied, "No, I don't hate you."

"That's what I kept worrying about. The only child I'll
ever have. What if she hates me?"

I found myself recalling the words in Rowan's journal:
*"His insecurity throbs like a heartbeat. He is so eager for me
to like and respect him."*

"I didn't want to leave. Or drop out of your life. But it was hard. Thinking about you. The longer I stayed focused on finding a portal, the easier it was to let everything—everyone—go. And I know that makes me a shitty father and a shitty husband, but . . ."

He paused, waiting for me to speak—probably hoping that I would deny it. When I remained silent, he added, "It was only after I got to the Borderlands that I could really let myself think about you."

Again, that hesitant smile.

"It's so hard to believe that you're all grown up. My Maggie—the one in my head—she's still a little girl, even though I knew that she—that *you* had gone to college, gotten a job. The Borderlands, it was always changing. But you stayed just the same."

It had been like that for me, too. Both of us frozen in time for the other.

"I just wanted to say . . . I'm sorry. I know that doesn't make up for anything, but . . ." He took a deep breath and slowly let it out. "If you want me to stay, I will."

I was surprised to feel my throat tightening. Last night, I had written him off, convinced that he had no place in my life. Now, my heart thudded against my breastbone.

"Why don't we just focus on the show for now? And on getting to know each other. If you still feel that way after *Into the Woods* closes, we'll talk about it then."

His relief was so obvious that it hurt.

You can't do this again. The endless cycle of hope and disillusionment.

"There *is* something we should talk about, though. Mom's coming into town Thursday. I haven't told her about you. And for now, I don't think we should."

"You want me to stay out of the way while she's here? Sure. Why upset her?"

I suspected he was more eager to avoid any potential unpleasantness than spare Mom's feelings, but I just said, "That means no going out with the cast. And Bernie plays all the performances while they're here."

"They?"

"Mom and Chris—the man she's been seeing for the last couple of years."

"She never remarried?"

I shook my head.

"Huh. I figured she'd settle down with some nice, steady corporate type."

His clear disdain for the nice, steady corporate type — like Chris — made me snap off a curt, "No."

"What? You blame me for that, too? I can't help it if she never got over me."

The man has ballocks the size of basketballs and an ego to match.

"Sorry to burst your bubble. She got over you a long time ago. But you'd hurt her so badly that it took years before she could trust a man again."

"It wasn't like everything that happened was my fault! She wasn't the easiest person to live with, either. Everything in its place. Everything just so. I can count on one hand the number of times she did anything spontaneous."

If anyone else had said that, I would have admitted the assessment was pretty accurate, but I was damned if I'd let him belittle her.

"Can you blame her? Living with you? Always running off. Gone for weeks at a time. If she wanted everything just so, it was to bring a little stability into her life. And mine!"

"She's been like that as long as I've known her. Always scared of life. Of taking a chance."

"She took a chance on you. Look where that got her."

"It was different in the beginning. I was the bad boy who jolted her out of her groove. And she loved it! But she couldn't just enjoy the ride. She had to start in on me to quit acting. Settle for a boring job like the one she had at the bank. Well, I wanted more!"

"And it was always about what *you* wanted, wasn't it?"

"I tried! I gave up theatre for teaching. And I stuck it out, even though there were days I wanted to put a bullet in my head. You know how mind-numbing the nine-to-five grind is. You tried it yourself before chucking it for the theatre."

"Then I chucked theatre for the nine-to-five grind again. I might still be doing it if I hadn't come here."

He stared at me in bewilderment. "I thought you were like me, but you're not, are you? You're like Allie." He jerked his thumb at Rowan. "And there's *your* bad boy."

"No."

"Right now, it's all romance and magic and hot monkey love. But a couple of years down the road, you'll be after him to change. To be ordinary."

"No."

"Or you'll start wishing you'd settled for a banker or a lawyer or a dentist. And then Rowan'll be out in the cold. Just like I was!"

"No!"

It was too close to the bone, too close to the fears that Rowan and I had shared in the night.

"You don't know anything about me. Or Rowan. I can't predict what the future holds for us, but we're going in with our eyes open. I don't know what the future holds for you and me, either. We've got a month to find out. Just don't sign on to become part of my life if you're going to bolt at the first sign of trouble."

"Maggie . . ."

"I'll see you at the run-through."

I stalked out of the living area and flung open the front door. The hammering onstage only added to the painful throb of my headache. I walked outside and sought the relative privacy of the Smokehouse.

As I sank onto a chair, the door opened again. Rowan circled behind me and rested his hands on my shoulders, but he used only the gentle pressure of his fingers to knead away the tension. Maybe he was still obeying my request to keep his magic out of this.

"What do you want from him, Maggie?" As I tensed, he added, "I'm not suggesting that you should excuse anything he's done in the past. I'm asking what you want from him *now*."

"I want him to be honest."

"But he was honest. Yes, he was trying to justify his behavior. But he was also very perceptive. About Alison. And us."

Which was why I'd gotten so angry.

"Was he right?" Rowan asked in that same quiet voice. "Do you want a nice, normal, ordinary life?"

I jumped up from the chair and shoved it out of the way. "Who doesn't? But I gave that up when I signed on to be executive director of this place. And I gave up looking for a nice, normal, ordinary guy when I fell in love with you. I don't want a banker or a lawyer. And unless Bernie will marry me, I don't want a dentist, either."

It killed me that his smile was so sad. The same smile I had seen at the end of our last summer when we knew we were going to lose each other.

I punched him on the chest with both fists and kept raining blows on him, driving him back against the wall.

"Goddamn it, Rowan. Don't you give up on us!"

I never saw his hands move. I just discovered my upraised fists trapped by his imprisoning fingers.

"Then don't you give up on us, either!"

His mouth claimed mine, bruising my lips. Then it softened, anger shifting into hunger, into the same desperate need I felt.

And then I heard Hal calling my name.

Rowan's hands fell. I stepped back.

"You should go see what he wants."

"Yes."

But we just stood there, staring at each other.

"I'm not giving up," Rowan said.

"Neither am I."

We sealed the pact with our usual handshake. Instead of releasing my hand, Rowan gripped it harder.

"Remember all those things I said about how the journey's never over and learning valuable lessons along the way?"

I nodded.

"I like your way better. Let's cut right to the happy ever after."

His smile was confident. But he was skilled at disguising his fears.

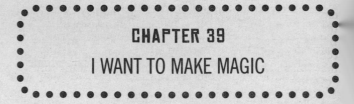

CHAPTER 39
I WANT TO MAKE MAGIC

JACK TIPTOED AROUND ME FOR THE REST OF THE DAY. Finally, I took him aside and assured him I wasn't angry. He assured me that he just wanted Rowan and me to avoid the mistakes he and Mom had made. I assured him that I understood. We assured each other to death and although it really didn't change anything, it did cut some of the tension.

The staff went into "circle the wagons" mode just like the night Rowan returned. Only this time the interloper was my father. I had to plead with Lee to refrain from ripping Jack's head off and beg Alex to stop looking at me with sad, puppy dog eyes. Hal bit his lip every time he saw me, Catherine patted me every time she passed, and Mei-Yin spoke in such dulcet tones that I wanted to scream, "I'm okay! Really!"

I knew they all meant well, that they loved me and were trying to help me deal with this situation. But I didn't know how to deal with it, either. What I wanted most was to thrust aside my personal problems and focus on the show.

As usual, Reinhard—ever stalwart, ever silent— understood that. He must have spoken to others because the hovering abruptly ceased and we all got back into show mode.

Everyone got a much-needed lift when we saw the set for *Into the Woods*. The cast actually applauded.

Like the characters in Act One, it was mostly two-

dimensional. Painted cutouts of two enormous trees framed
the stage, their branches curving over the proscenium arch.
Banks of twisted trees flanked a tiered rock formation at
center. Our local Cub Scout troop had collected the leaves
that Hal had laboriously added to the netting of the forest's
"canopy."

Rapunzel's tower and the tree that hosted the spirit of
Cinderella's mother were also trompe l'oeil miracles. Like
the three giant storybooks in place at the start of the show,
these were hinged and could be opened and closed by the
actors or crew.

I let the cast explore a bit, then sent them off to change
for the costume parade. It was the first time they'd seen
each other in fairy-tale drag and there was a lot of "oohing"
and "aahing" over the transformations. Jack's gray suit
looked natty if bizarrely out of place among the peasant
garb, uniforms, and ball gowns. Rowan looked more like an
adorable ragamuffin than a Mysterious Man; I'd have to
wait until he donned his gray wig and beard at dress rehearsal to get the full effect.

Not so TweedleTom. Even without the hair pieces and
ears, he looked wonderfully wolfish in his furry leggings and
tail, clawed gloves, and black sequined jacket. His bare chest
came in for almost as much comment as his costume, especially after his cast mates realized that the "fur" was all Tom.

"Watch out," Debra warned. "One of the locals might
skin you and set you out before a fireplace."

Everyone was on such a high afterward that I wished we
could plunge right into the run-through, but I knew we
needed to work the stickier bits of business first. So we spent
the next hour opening and closing the storybooks, the tower
and the tree; practicing the Wife's "fall" from the rock formation; and raising and lowering the "tree limb" on which the
Baker and Jack kept watch for the giant.

We'd flown in set pieces plenty of times, but never a
pair of actors. Lee had tested it for half an hour before
the costume parade, and although he assured Brian and
Connor that it was safe, they looked petrified the first
time they descended from the flies. By the fourth time,
though, Connor was having so much fun that he began
rocking their narrow platform like a Ferris wheel seat.

Brian shrieked. So did I. Lee shouted, "Quit messing around! Or I'll cut the bit and you'll do the scene on top of two stepladders."

We actually needed rolling stepladders so the actresses playing Rapunzel and Cinderella's dead mother could ascend to their bowers. Mira—the aforesaid dead mother—chose that moment to announce that she was afraid of heights.

"Did she even look at my sketches?" Hal demanded in a furious whisper. "Am I supposed to put the ghost of Cinderella's mother in a stump?"

"Let's just deal with it."

Even with two stagehands helping her on and off the ladder, she was still a wreck. In the end, Javier had to mount the ladder behind her and put his arms around her waist while Mira clutched the ladder's railing in a death grip and shakily sang her solo.

Through it all, Rowan sat in the front row, silently gauging how much magical help cast and crew might need on opening night.

We held the run-through after our dinner break. There was so little seat squeaking from Long that I actually swiveled around to make sure he was still there. He gasped so loudly at the Witch's transformation that I was glad Hal had permitted Debra to do the scene in costume.

When the run-through concluded, he shouted, "Bravo!" And as soon as I finished giving notes, he hurried onstage to praise the actors.

"The transformation worked beautifully," he told Debra as the rest of the cast trooped down to the dressing rooms. "I don't know how you managed it. No, don't tell me. You'll spoil the magic."

The transformation was anything but magical. Shrouded in a voluminous hooded cloak, no one could tell that Debra was already wearing her younger self's white satin gown and sequined slippers. After she drank the magic potion, she reeled upstage. While the audience was agog at the Mysterious Man's dying revelations, Debra was ripping off her flesh-colored clawed gloves, prosthetic nose, and bushy eyebrows. She stuffed those into a hidden pocket in her cloak, slid off her gray wig, and even had time to apply the red lipstick that had been secreted in the goblet.

A flare from the flash pot. A puff of smoke. Debra dropped her cloak and voila! The crone had transformed into a glamour puss. In the few seconds before the blackout, everyone was too busy gawking at the gown and the blonde wig to notice that the glamour puss still had age lines on her face.

The most magical moment in the show and we accomplished it without any faery magic at all.

It would have been cool if Rowan could have cast a glamour across Debra's features to make her look youthful, but it was simply too risky. Even when he had directed the production, he'd done it the old-fashioned way, unwilling to arouse suspicion.

After Long left, Debra asked, "Is that how you worked it when you played the Witch?"

"Hey! I never told you I played the role. Who spilled the beans?"

She glanced at the pit, and Alex sheepishly raised his hand.

"Sorry," Debra said. "Didn't mean to out you."

"It's okay," I said. "And no. We used a double at Southford. I ducked offstage; she staggered on in an identical cloak. Poof. Reveal. Blackout. Applause."

"That would be easier, you know."

"Yes, but it was so damn obvious. At least, the audience knows you're working hard."

"Especially with my hooked nose hanging off my face."

"That was only the first time. It looked great tonight."

And would look even better during the show. If Rowan refrained from using his magic to effect the transformation, he would certainly jump in to help Debra do so.

"Did the makeup read okay?" Debra asked.

"You looked beautiful," Alex replied.

He smiled up at her. She smiled down at him. Then Alex made a big deal about collecting his score and Debra hurried off to change.

As soon as was humanly possible, I dragged Rowan up to the apartment and demanded, "Is something going on between Debra and Alex?"

"They certainly light up around each other."

"They do?"

"Well, you wouldn't notice."

"No. Of course not. I'm a mere human."

"I only meant that there's nothing about their behavior to give them away."

When I filled him in on their moonlit stroll in the garden, his eyebrows rose.

"I thought you'd be happy."

"I've always hoped Alex would find someone to share his life. I just never imagined it would be someone like Debra." His expression grew thoughtful. "Then again, Annie was pretty domineering."

"You're kidding. I always pictured her as . . . well . . . like Helen. Sweet. Kind. Loving."

"She was. But she was also strong-minded. A match for Janet any day. Which was probably a good thing for Alex. Sometimes, he needs a push."

"Maybe we should—"

"No."

"You don't even know what I was going to say."

"You were going to suggest we give Alex a push."

"Damn faery . . ."

"Let them be, Maggie."

"You cast Lou and Bobbie opposite each other."

"And after that, I let them be."

"Sometimes people need a little push."

"And sometimes they need to figure things out for themselves. As you have reminded me on more than one occasion."

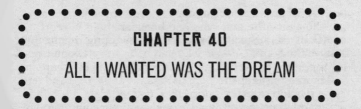

CHAPTER 40
ALL I WANTED WAS THE DREAM

THE EXTRA TIME WE SPENT WORKING THE
PROBLEM AREAS paid off. We were out of tech in
three hours instead of our usual five; even Reinhard was in
danger of ascending to Cloud Nine. When I settled into my
seat for dress rehearsal, I was filled with confidence.

The stage lights came up to reveal the open storybooks
with their fairy-tale characters in a frozen tableau: Cinder
ella by the hearth with her broom; the Baker and his Wife
preparing bread; and Jack and his Mother flanking Milky-
White, the wooden cow that resembled a giant pull toy on
casters. The right page of each book showed the interiors of
the three cottages. On the left, Hal had painted the opening
lines of the story in elegant calligraphy, each beginning with
the traditional "Once upon a time."

All that remained was for Jack to enter and utter those
same words to open the show.

Although I had seen him make that entrance a dozen
times, my heart still sped up when he strode out of the
wings. He nodded approvingly at the tableau and crossed to
his position by the stage right proscenium arch.

The spot came on.

He turned toward the darkened house.

And stood there.

For about two seconds, I thought he was milking the moment. Then I noticed his glazed expression.

He'd had his lines down the first week of rehearsal. Had

performed perfectly during the final run-through. But now Jack Sinclair—the man who had boasted about his performance as Billy Bigelow, who had given acting tips to the cast of *The Secret Garden*, who had been a professional actor for more than ten years—Jack Sinclair had dried up.

His mouth snapped shut. His Adam's apple rose and fell as he swallowed. Alex's head jerked stage right, his hands upraised to cue the pit band. Long's seat gave an ominous squeak. And still Jack remained frozen, blinking like the proverbial deer in the headlights.

Rowan would never leave him hanging out to dry. Maybe Jack was simply too terrified to respond to the gentle nudge of Rowan's power.

Seconds after the thought crossed my mind, Jack started visibly at what had to be a much stronger jolt of Fae power. He swallowed again. Opened his mouth.

"Once upon a time . . ."

The words came out in a strangled whisper. My heart went "da-DUM" along with the opening chords from the pit band. Instead of continuing the narration, Jack lapsed into silence. The actors forged ahead. I gripped the seat in front of me and prayed he would recover.

He did. But instead of introducing Cinderella's Stepmother and Stepsisters, he muttered the lines he had just missed.

The number went downhill from there. At some point, he simply stopped talking and stood there with his head bowed. Although critical information was lost—like the fact that Rapunzel was the Baker's sister—Sondheim's lyrics held the story together.

The director in me noted that with dispassionate interest. The daughter wanted to rush onstage and lead that dejected figure out of the spotlight's glare.

I was halfway out of my seat when he slunk offstage. As I sank down again, two hands patted my shoulders: Bernie and Catherine, silently lending their support.

The curtains parted to reveal the forest. I tried to concentrate on the wonderful maze of light streaming through the trees and the characters' journey into the woods, but I was too conscious of the minutes ticking away until the Narrator's return at the top of Scene 2.

I swiveled around and whispered to Bernie, "If he doesn't come back, I'll need you to go on."

Bernie nodded toward the stage. I whipped around and found Jack in place. He spoke his line clearly enough, but he seemed to be in a trance. I wasn't sure if he was grasping for words or if he was merely repeating the ones that Rowan was magically feeding him.

Three musical numbers passed before he returned to introduce Rapunzel. The glazed look had left his eyes, but only in the final moments of Act One did he seem to be in character.

I stayed away from the Dungeon at intermission, fearful that my presence would only distract him further. Instead, I hurried up the stairs to Rowan's apartment.

Although I had just seen him in full costume and makeup, it was still bizarre to be greeted by a Mysterious Man in long gray wig, false beard, and rag picker's motley.

When he asked, "How bad did it look?" I knew he was referring to Jack's performance rather than his appearance.

"After the meltdown? A little . . . robotic. But okay at the end. How much of it was you?"

"Most of it."

It was hard to tell if he was tired with all the age makeup. The weariness in his voice might only have been the same disillusionment I felt.

I followed him through the living area. His dining table now held an eight-bulb makeup mirror, a wig stand, and a partitioned makeup case filled with brushes and pencils, foundation and sponges, powder and rouge, vials of spirit gum and remover.

As he resumed his seat before the mirror, I asked, "Are you okay?"

"The top of Scene 2 was the worst. I had to calm Mira and feed Jack his lines. Very . . . schizophrenic." He plucked a makeup pencil from his case and began retouching the age lines on his forehead. "In the past, I've always directed my power at a group or an individual. Same power. One focus. This is the first time I've had to help two people with two distinct problems at the same time." In the mirror, his gaze met mine. "So I guess that's what I've learned from doing the show."

"And we haven't even opened yet." I rested my cheek lightly against his, careful to avoid smudging his makeup.

"Sorry I didn't have any power to spare for you."

"I'm fine. I just hope Jack makes it through Act Two."

"The Narrator's death occurs well before my resurrection. So I should be able to concentrate on him. If he needs me."

I straightened with a sigh. "Of all the problems I knew I'd face with him, I never expected this one."

"Neither did I. He seemed fine during warm-ups. No more excited or nervous than any of the others. It was only after he walked onstage that I felt his panic."

"Will he be able to perform tomorrow?"

Again, his gaze met mine in the mirror. "I don't know, Maggie. Maybe he'll work out his jitters tonight."

Jack seemed more confident in Act Two, but that might have been the effect of Rowan's power. Much as I wanted him to have the opportunity to perform, Rowan had others in the cast who might need him. I couldn't allow him to become Jack's personal Energizer Bunny. If Jack needed that level of support, I would have to pull him.

As soon as Lee brought up the house lights, Long hurried down the aisle toward me. Before he could speak, I said, "I don't know what happened with Jack." I kept my voice low, conscious of the cast waiting onstage for notes. "But I'll deal with it, okay?"

"I know you will. And I know you'll do whatever's best for the show. I just wanted to tell you I was sorry. For your sake and his. I know how much it meant to you to have him in the show. And I think it meant just as much to him."

His response was almost as unexpected as my father's meltdown. Funny thing was, I'd dealt with that calmly. Long's support brought me to the verge of tears.

He sighed. "I really should know better by now. When things go wrong, a lecture stiffens your resolve and kindness upsets you. Maybe one day, I'll figure out the rules."

"Maybe one day, I'll be able to take either the lecture or the kindness without losing it."

Long cleared his throat. "Yes. Well. The cast is waiting. I'll say something brief and inspirational and get out of your way."

All summer, I had dreamed of a new relationship with my father. Instead, I seemed to have stumbled into one with my board president. As we walked toward the stage, I recalled Long's habit of popping in at unexpected moments, of attending run-throughs and dress rehearsals as well as most of the performances. I'd always suspected he was checking up on me. Maybe he was simply lonely.

Long uttered his few inspirational words. My speech was equally brief and consisted mainly of telling the cast how proud I was—and that I wanted to run the Act One opening early tomorrow afternoon. After I staged the curtain calls, I let Jack leave with the rest of the cast, unwilling to ask him to stay behind and shame him in front of everyone. He hurried off to the Dungeon, visibly relieved at his easy getaway. It was Otis who lingered.

"He'll settle down," he assured me.

"I hope so."

He regarded me silently, then said, "It's tougher when it's family."

Without thinking, I replied, "Tell me about it." Then I stared up at him in shock. I hadn't told the cast that Jack was my father. And I knew none of the staff would reveal that, either.

"How did you know?"

"Didn't at first. Then I started noticing little things. Like the way you both stick your chin out when you're angry. And how you took such care with him. You're good to all of us, but it was different with Jack."

I nodded, still a little stunned.

"He hasn't figured it out yet, has he? That you're his daughter."

"He didn't know in the beginning, but he does now."

But only because I had told him. It revealed so much about both men that Otis—a relative stranger—had seen what my father had missed.

"Families can be one tangled up mess sometimes," Otis said. "Or the greatest blessing in the world. Usually both."

"At the same time."

"If there's one thing I've learned this summer it's to keep trying to untangle that mess. You taught me that, Maggie. Don't you go forgetting it."

The staff gathered in the green room and waited for the cast to leave before we began the debriefing. Jack was the last to emerge from the Dungeon. He flashed a nervous smile when he saw us and started when I took his arm and led him down the hall toward the production office.

"Can you believe I went up on my lines? I've never done that in my life. But I'll be fine for the opening."

"Why don't you sleep on it? You can let me know tomorrow if—"

"I don't need to sleep on it. I'm ready!"

I noted the truculent thrust of his chin with brittle amusement.

"Okay. I'll see you at one o'clock to run the opening. If that goes well, great. But if I think your nerves are getting the better of you, Bernie goes on."

Without a word, he stalked down the hallway and disappeared around the corner. I slowly walked back to the green room. I knew the staff would support whatever decision I made. I just hoped it was the right one.

"He says he can go on. I'm not so sure. I'll decide after tomorrow's rehearsal. Either way, Bernie, I need you to be ready. I can't risk a meltdown like we had tonight. If Jack's out, you can dress with the rest of the cast. Otherwise . . ." I glanced at Rowan, who nodded. "Use Rowan's apartment. It'll only undermine Jack's confidence if he sees you in the dressing room."

"Whatever you say."

"Javier, please make sure Bernie's armchair is stage right so we can move it out in a hurry if Jack folds."

"Do we really need the chair?" Bernie asked. "I feel like such an old fart sitting there."

"But you look like the guy who used to introduce *Masterpiece Theatre*."

"Only small, balding, and Jewish."

"It works, Bernie. Yes, it saves you from all those entrances and exits. But it's like you're actually telling the story to the audience."

"Maybe we should try that with Jack," Hal ventured. "I

could put together a storybook. A smaller version of the ones onstage. And paste his scenes into it."

Once again, I found myself torn between my roles as daughter and director. This time, the director won.

"We've all bent over backward to help Jack. Either he performs the part as rehearsed or he doesn't perform at all."

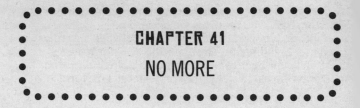

CHAPTER 41
NO MORE

JANET AND I WERE YAWNING OVER OUR COF-
FEE the next morning when she suddenly shoved back
her chair and jumped to her feet.

"What's wrong?"

"Rowan. Something's upset him."

"What?"

But she had already run out of the kitchen. By the time
I recovered from my shock and stumbled to the front door,
she was racing down the hill, bathrobe billowing behind her
like giant blue wings.

I tore after her, terrified that Rowan had been hurt. She
must have sensed my fear because she stopped at the bottom of the hill and waited for me to catch up with her.

"He's fine."

"Then . . ."

"I don't know, Maggie!"

As we approached the theatre, I noticed the stage door
hanging open. Then I saw Rowan standing in the picnic
area.

His wet hair hung in unruly tangles over his bare shoulders. Tiny rivulets of water oozed down his back. As we hurried toward him, his shoulders rose and fell. Then he turned.

"What is it? What happened?"

"It's Jack. He bolted."

"Bolted?"

"He said he wanted to take a walk. I could feel his rest-

750

lessness, so I agreed. I'd just gotten in the shower when I felt this stab of panic . . ."

I searched the treetops for the crow that must have frightened him. Only when I registered the sympathy—the pity—on Rowan's face did I finally understand.

Last night's bravado had crumbled. And instead of talking to me or asking Rowan for help, Jack had run off.

Why was I surprised? It was what he did best.

Rowan was still talking, but his voice failed to penetrate the roaring in my ears and the pounding of my blood and the pressure inside my head.

"Son of a bitch!"

I slammed my fist into the trunk of a tree.

The pain felt good, a refreshing shock to my system. Then, of course, my hand just hurt like hell.

Rowan's fingertips glided over the abrasions, trailing cool relief, just as they had that afternoon two years ago when I'd fallen in the woods. Circling back to the past yet again. This whole summer seemed like one endless circle with stumbles in all the same places.

"I'm sorry, Maggie."

"You're not his keeper."

"He's probably gone to the cottage. I saw him running . . ."

"Into the woods?" I gave a short, bitter laugh. "I thought he might bolt when he found out I was his daughter. Or when he learned Mom would be here."

But naturally, he was more concerned about his performance.

"I think he was too embarrassed to face you. To admit that he couldn't do it."

"And he thinks it'll be easier to face me after this?"

"He doesn't think, Maggie. He just reacts in the moment."

Which works great onstage. In real life, not so much.

"I'll get dressed and go after him."

"No."

No more stumbling around the circle.

No more chasing the false hopes and impossible dreams.

Just . . . no more.

The show was a huge hit. I was happy for the cast—
especially Bernie. The audience warmed to him the moment he walked onstage. He unhurriedly made his way to
the armchair, hung his cane over one of its wings, unbuttoned his suit coat, and eased himself onto the leather seat
with a little grunt. Then he surveyed the darkened house
with a smile that said, "Okay, folks. I'm settled in. You do
the same."

That was the only moment I felt really connected to the
show. The rest of the time I was far away, noting the laughter and the applause and—near the end—the occasional
sniffle. It was the same at the reception afterward: I heard
myself saying all the right things to the cast and the audience and the press, but it was like I was playing a role without fully inhabiting the character.

When Jack was still AWOL the following morning,
Rowan again volunteered to go to the cottage. I told him to
suit himself; I had no intention of accompanying him.

He was gone most of the afternoon and arrived at the
house alone. By then, I was dressed to meet Mom and Chris
for dinner.

"Was he at the cottage?" Janet asked.

Rowan nodded.

Stupid to feel relieved. As stupid as spending the day
worrying that he was lying in the woods with a broken leg
or a broken neck. Especially since I would have cheerfully
broken his legs *and* his neck after what he'd done.

"He's sorry he ran out," Rowan said.

"He's always sorry when he runs out."

"I took him some food. And clothes."

"You're kidding."

"I didn't think you'd want him to go hungry."

"I don't care if he starves!"

"You don't mean that."

"Don't tell me what I mean."

"You're just angry."

"And don't tell me what I feel! I'm just glad he's out of
our hair while Mom's here."

"And after that?" Janet asked.

"He'll get hungry."

"So it's back to the 'starve him into submission' plan?"

"I'm not ... look, he chose to run off. Why should we reward that behavior by ferrying food to him?"

"All right," Rowan said. "If that's what you want."

"Am I supposed to feel sorry for him? To plead with him to come back? I've spent too much of my summer—and my life—doing that. If you want to play Meals-on-Wheels, knock yourself out. Just don't expect me to play helping professional. Not this time. Jack can spend the rest of the goddamn summer at the cottage for all I care. The only way I'm talking to him again is if *he* comes to *me*."

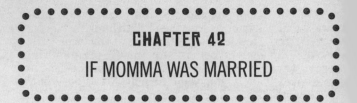

CHAPTER 42
IF MOMMA WAS MARRIED

TOOK A LOT OF DEEP BREATHS ON THE DRIVE to the Bough, knowing Mom would pick up on my emotions in a heartbeat. I just hoped I could put her off the scent by telling her it had been particularly hellish Hell Week. At least that wouldn't be a lie.

Although I was only a few minutes late, I found Chris pacing the lobby.

"Sorry. Last minute hair crisis."

"Not a problem," he replied, treating me to his usual affectionate hug. "Your mom's still getting dressed. Want to grab a drink in the lounge?"

"God, yes!" When my reply drew a startled look, I said, "Sorry. Aftereffects of Hell Week."

Might as well start planting the seeds now.

The lounge was only half-full, mostly locals enjoying a quick brew before heading home. We snagged two pints and hunkered down at a table near the back of the room. We both took fortifying swigs of ale. Then Chris thumped his glass on the table and said, "I wanted to talk with you. Alone."

For half a second, I thought he was going to tell me that Mom had finally accepted his proposal. But his gloomy expression hardly suggested a prospective bridegroom bubbling over with excitement.

"I asked your mother to marry me—again. And she turned me down again."

"But . . . why?"

"She says she's happy with the way things are."

"But you're not."

"I'm sixty-four, Maggie. I want more than sleepovers on the weekend and dinner on Wednesday. I want to go to sleep with her at night and wake up beside her in the morning. I want to vow before God and my family and friends to spend the rest of my life with her. Maybe that's hopelessly old-fashioned, but—"

"No. It's lovely."

I wanted the same thing.

Groping for something to reassure him, I said, "People stay in committed relationships for years without getting married. Look at Lee and Hal."

"At least they live together. She won't even consider that. Look, I know her marriage to your father was a disaster. And that it's taken her a long time to get over it. Hell, it took six months before she'd even go out with me. But she's been divorced for more than twenty years and we've been together for two. If she thinks I'll run out on her the way he did—if she doesn't know me any better than that by now . . ."

"You're nothing like my father. And she knows that."

Chris stared into his ale. "I'm sorry to unload on you like this. I just . . . I don't know what to do."

"We'll think of something," I promised.

◄═ ═►

Chris picked at his food, while Mom nattered on about the glories of Vermont. When our coffees arrived, he pushed back his chair and announced that he needed to take a walk.

Mom waited until the sound of his footsteps faded, then said, "He's even more transparent than you are. Obviously, he's told you everything."

I nodded.

"I don't know why he felt compelled to involve you."

"Because he didn't know where else to turn."

"Maggie, Chris and I have been over and over this. He wants to get married. I don't."

"Do you love him?"

"Don't be silly."

"Yes or no."

"Of course I love him," she snapped. "But I like my independence, too."

"Being married doesn't necessarily mean you lose your independence. Reinhard and Mei-Yin are hardly joined at the hip."

"That's different."

"How?"

"Because it is! Now let's drop this."

"Are you willing to risk losing him?"

"It won't come to that." Her fingernail tapped a nervous tattoo against her coffee cup. Then she must have realized what she was doing, because she folded her hands in her lap and asked, "Shouldn't you be getting to the theatre?"

"No."

We glared at each other and retreated to our coffees.

Another frontal assault would be ineffective; when Mom was upset, she tended to fight rather than withdraw or admit her feelings.

Gee, who does that sound like?

I attempted a conciliatory smile. "You could move in together. If you didn't want to take the plunge. That would—"

"Only encourage him to believe that, sooner or later, I'll agree to marry him."

I gave up on conciliatory and went for the bombshell.

"Is this about Daddy?"

Her coffee cup rattled violently against the saucer. "If you think I'm still carrying a torch for Jack Sinclair—"

"No. I think he hurt you so badly that you're afraid to take a chance with Chris. You're scared he'll leave you like Daddy did. So you're pushing him away before he can."

"Thank you, Dr. Phil." She flung her napkin on the table and signaled the waitress. "But I'm afraid our time is up."

I spent most of the show going over those conversations. I could understand if Mom didn't want to discuss her personal life with me—or take advice from her daughter. But if she refused to open up to the man she loved, the relationship seemed doomed. Her chance for lasting happiness was slipping through her fingers, and Chris and I seemed powerless to prevent it.

I could think of only one person who might.

I followed Rowan to his apartment after curtain calls. Without bothering to remove his makeup or costume, he poured us each a healthy slug of whisky, waited for me to take a sip, then sat beside me on the sofa. He nodded sympathetically as I described the problems Mom and Chris were facing, but when I broached my plan to deal with them, he drew back, frowning.

"You want your mother to talk with Jack?"

"I don't *want* them to talk. But I can't think of anything else that might jolt her out of the past and save her relationship with Chris."

"It's their relationship, Maggie. It's up to them to save it or not. I don't think we should be interfering in their lives."

"This from the faery who's been calling Mackenzies here for more than a hundred years."

"I called them, yes. But I never forced them to confront their problems."

"You pushed me hard enough."

"But I never said, 'It's all about your father.' I let you discover that for yourself. Over the course of three months. Do you really think your mother will take one look at Jack and decide she wants to marry Chris?"

"Maybe not, but—"

"And what if it makes matters worse? This isn't like giving Alex a little push toward Debra."

"Don't you think I know that? But I can't just stand aside and watch things fall apart. She's stuck, Rowan. And unless something happens to . . . unstick her . . . she's not only going to lose Chris, she'll never be able to move on with her life."

"Then let me use my power to—"

"No."

"I'm not talking about brainwashing her. Just reminding her that she loves Chris and doesn't want to lose him."

"She already *knows* she loves Chris and doesn't want to lose him. And when your power wears off, she'll be right back where she is now."

"At least, talk to Chris first. See if this is what *he* wants."

"I can't. If he's part of this, it will only convince her that he can't be trusted."

Rowan shook his head. "She'll be furious, Maggie."

"I know."

"She might never forgive you."

"I know!"

"Do you really want to risk everything? Not just Chris' relationship with your mother, but yours, too?"

"No! But I don't think I have a choice."

The next morning, though, I called Nancy before she left for work. I'd brought her up to date on The Life and Times of Maggie Graham when she made her opening night "break a leg" call. It took less than a minute to fill her in on the latest installment.

She was silent for so long that I expected her to offer the same objections as Rowan. Instead, she said, "I think they *should* meet. Not because it will save her relationship with Chris; that's something they have to work out for themselves. But she has a right to know about Jack."

"Even if he's . . . moving on at the end of the season?"

"I think so. But you know how I've hated this cat-and-mouse game you've been playing. Think how relieved you'll be to get everything out in the open."

Except the fact that my father was "moving on" to Faerie. And my lover was opening a portal so he could get there.

That afternoon, Rowan accompanied me to the cottage. I spent most of the walk steeling myself to face Jack again — and mentally vowing to keep our conversation short, sweet, and drama-free. This was a straightforward business proposition, after all, not a reconciliation.

Jack answered Rowan's knock. His smile faded when he saw me.

As he began stammering an apology, I said, "I need you to do something for me, Jack. And if you're willing, I promise that after the season is over, Rowan will open the portal to Faerie for you."

I watched the shifting play of emotions across his features: confusion, wariness, disbelief, shock — and finally, a joy so profound that tears filled his eyes.

Once, perhaps, he had regarded me with such joy. Now, only the Fae could evoke it.

After all that had happened, the upwelling of grief surprised me. Resolutely, I swallowed it down. I was accustomed to losing my father. The important thing now was to keep my mother from losing Chris.

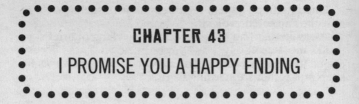

CHAPTER 43
I PROMISE YOU A HAPPY ENDING

OVER THE NEXT TWENTY-FOUR HOURS, my confidence eroded. After watching me pace the living area, waiting for Mom and Chris to arrive, Rowan said, "We can still call this off. Just leave Jack in the Smokehouse and send Alison and Chris off to do some sightseeing after lunch."

"Let's play it by ear. Maybe they've patched things up and we won't have to do anything."

One look at their faces convinced me that the "patching up" scenario was wishful thinking. When lunch concluded, I offered a silent prayer that I was not about to make the biggest mistake in my life and sat Mom and Chris down on the sofa. I sank into an easy chair. Rowan perched on the arm and took my hand between his.

"Mom. There's something I have to tell you."

"Oh, my God, you're pregnant."

"No! No. I am definitely *not* pregnant."

Mom heaved a sigh of relief. Then she frowned. "Well, you're not getting any younger," she noted in one of her maddening about-faces. "And if you two intend to stay together, I hope you've at least discussed—"

"Let's save kids for another day, okay?"

She studied me suspiciously, then leaned back on the sofa with a groan. "Oh, Lord. This is like those TV shows where the family stages an intervention to save their drug-addicted loved one. Only you're intervening in our relationship. Thank you, no."

"Mom . . ."

"Chris and I are grown-ups, Maggie, and we'd appreciate it if you would—"

"Daddy's here."

As Mom went rigid, I hurriedly launched into the same story I had fed Nancy weeks ago, a truer depiction of Jack's life than the version he and Rowan had concocted for public consumption: the letter that was eventually forwarded to Rowan; his cross-country trek; the chance meeting with a group of hikers that led him to a dilapidated cabin in the mountains; and his eventual return to the Crossroads with Jack in tow.

"I wanted to tell you all of this when you came up for *Annie*, but Daddy was . . . well, he was a mess, and I decided to wait until he was more like his old self, and I'm sorry to spring it on you like this, but I thought . . . I thought . . ."

My voice ran down. Mom stared at her clasped hands, her lips compressed into a tight pink line. Then her head came up and she fixed Rowan with a cold stare.

"Why did you have to interfere?"

"He's Maggie's father. And I knew she loved him. Should I have left him there? Living like an animal? Knowing he'd never survive another winter?"

"No. You should have taken him to a hospital."

"I tried. He ran away."

My mother's laugh was bitter. "That's his answer to everything. You could have notified the authorities. They would have removed him forcibly and seen to it that he got the care he needed."

"We were miles from anywhere, Alison. No cell phone reception. No roads."

"Then you should have lied! Taken him to town and turned him over to people who could help him."

"I couldn't do that. He'd put his trust in me."

"So you brought him here."

"Yes."

"Knowing it would only turn Maggie's life upside down."

"Yes."

"Knowing she was probably better off without him."

"Yes."

"And now what?" She turned that burning gaze on me.

"You're going to become his caretaker? Waste years of your life like I did?"

"It won't come to that."

"My God, Maggie! Don't you think I said that? I spent most of my marriage trying to change Jack Sinclair. And when I couldn't, I spent the rest of it trying to keep him from going off the deep end."

"He's better now."

"Running a telephone hotline doesn't qualify you to diagnose or treat mental illness. And unless he's given up this ridiculous search for ... other worlds ... then he *is* mentally ill and he needs professional treatment, whether or not he wants it."

"When you see him—"

"I have no intention of seeing him."

"What?"

"I've gone through hell for Jack Sinclair. I am not starting down that path again. And I pray to God you'll abandon it. Because there is no happy ending here. If he's sick, he'll have another breakdown—and another and another until you have no choice but to commit him. And if he *is* better, he'll leech off of you just long enough to get his life together and then walk out—again. Either way, he'll ruin your life and break your heart in the process."

"He can't break my heart. He doesn't have that power over me any longer."

Maybe the weariness in my voice convinced her that I was stating a fact rather than protesting.

"As for ruining my life, he won't be around long enough to do that. He's moving on after the season ends."

"Moving on? Where? To do what?"

"I don't know. Neither does he."

"Typical. And what happens a month from now—a year from now—when you get another desperate cry for help?"

I shrugged. "I'll help him."

"Then he'll hold you hostage for the rest of your life."

"He's my father. I can't just turn my back on him. But I won't allow him to hold me hostage. And you shouldn't either."

Her puzzled frown cleared. "Now I get it. Honestly, Maggie, did you really think I'd take one look at Jack and change my mind about marrying Chris?"

I avoided looking at Rowan, who had said exactly the same thing.

"Okay, it was a stupid idea!"

"No, it wasn't," Chris said quietly.

Mom's head snapped toward him. "Were you in on this?"

"No. But if Maggie had come to me with the idea, I would have said, 'Let's try it.' At this point, I'm willing to try anything."

"Then try accepting how I feel! All of you."

She grabbed her purse and started for the door.

"There's one more thing you should know."

With obvious reluctance, she turned to face me.

"Whether or not you want to see Jack now, you might see him tomorrow night. He's playing the Narrator in *Into the Woods*."

"I thought Bernie—"

"Bernie's his understudy. And he's playing the matinees. If Jack can't go on—"

"Don't pull him for my sake."

"It's not that. He froze during dress rehearsal. And ... couldn't go on opening night."

"Froze? Jack?" Mom shook her head in disbelief. "Of all the things you've told me today, that's the most unbelievable. Was it because of me? Did he know I would be here?"

"He learned that days ago. Just after I told him I was his daughter."

"He didn't figure that out himself? All he had to do was look at you. But that's Jack. Too wrapped up in himself to notice anyone else." Mom studied me for a moment, then nodded. "That's what you meant when you said he didn't have the power to hurt you any longer."

"Partly. But I've had a chance to get to know him this summer. And he's everything you always claimed. Charming. Clever. Childish. Self-absorbed. You warned me. So did Rowan. But I thought I could ... fix him. Talk about 'The Impossible Dream.' If something's really impossible, why waste time trying?"

"If you believed that," Rowan said, "you would never have risked loving me." He took my chin between his thumb and forefinger and tilted it up. "People do change, Maggie."

"You *wanted* to change."

"I wanted *you*. As far as changing . . ." His thumb caressed my chin. "As I recall, you pretty much had to drag me kicking and screaming the whole way."

"As I recall, I did a whole lot of kicking and screaming myself."

We stared into each other's eyes. Then we both became aware of the silence in the room. I ducked my head. Rowan cleared his throat and rose.

"Yes. Well. As Alison said, enough dissection for one day."

"Where is he?" my mother asked.

"Jack?"

"No, the Easter Bunny. Of course, Jack!"

"In the Smokehouse. Look, you don't have to—"

"I know I don't have to. Let's just get this over with."

"I'll bring him up here," Rowan said.

But Mom was already marching to the front door, leaving the three of us to scamper after her like schoolchildren following an impatient teacher.

Short of knocking her down, there was no way to reach the Smokehouse first to warn Jack. As it was, when she flung open the door and stopped dead, we barely managed to avoid piling up behind her like The Three Stooges. I edged past and found her staring at Jack in shock.

He acknowledged her reaction with a hesitant smile. "You should have seen me when I first got here. I looked like something the cat dragged in."

Maybe it was the use of one of her favorite phrases that made her shudder. Her hands tightened on the handle of her purse. Did she realize she was holding it in front of her like a shield?

The same way Daddy held his guitar when he met me.

"You look great," Jack said. "Pretty as ever."

My mother gave a disparaging snort. "Your eyesight is failing."

"Same old Allie."

"Not quite. Time changes everyone." She glanced at me. "Isn't that a song from some musical?"

"Maybe you're thinking of 'Time Heals Everything.' "

"The lyricist was clearly an optimist."

"The title is ironic," Rowan said quietly.

"In that case, I'll have to listen to it sometime."

A long silence ensued as they continued to study each other. Finally, Jack said, "Maybe we should walk down to the pond." He shot a pointed look at Chris. "So we can talk in private."

"Talk about what? Where you've been? What I've been doing for the last two decades?" Mom shook her head.

"Well, Maggie thought we should talk."

"Maggie thought the mere sight of you would send me running to the altar. This is Chris Thompson, by the way. The man I've been seeing for the last two years."

Jack and Chris exchanged stiff nods. Neither extended his hand.

"Maggie ought to know better," Jack said. "Once you make your mind up, there's no budging you."

"How do you know?"

"I just meant—"

"I know what you meant. You always thought I was hopelessly stuck in my ways."

"And you always thought I was a screwup."

"You *are* a screwup, Jack." Her voice was surprisingly gentle. "But our marriage was probably doomed from the beginning. The only good thing to come out of it was Maggie. She's the reason I'm here. Not to demand apologies or point fingers or stumble down memory lane. Now what is this nonsense about you freezing onstage?"

The abrupt shift in conversation left us all adrift. Jack shot me a reproachful glance and muttered, "It's been a long time since I performed."

"Are you saying you can't act any longer?"

"Of course I can act!"

"Then stop making excuses and do it! Rowan put his life on hold to find you. Maggie's turned this theatre upside down to make a place for you. It's time to step up to the plate, Jack. I'll expect to see you onstage tomorrow night. And by God, you better give the performance of a lifetime."

"It's only a small role."

"What's that old theatre proverb? 'There are no small roles, only small actors'?"

"I hate that saying!" Jack and I exclaimed in unison.

Our reaction drew a reluctant chuckle from Mom. "God, Jack. I can't believe you didn't realize she was your daughter."

"She's your daughter, too. First time she yelled at me, she said, 'An apology goes a lot farther than a shrug and a smile.' How many times did you remind me of that?"

"About a million."

I recalled the strange look he'd given me when I said that. But he still hadn't put the pieces together. Maybe he'd been afraid to try.

"So," Mom said, "if we're done here, I'll see you after the show, Jack."

"Allie? You don't . . . hate me, do you?"

"No. I don't hate you."

She sounded infinitely weary. How many times had he asked that over the course of their marriage? And how many times had she given him the same tired reassurance?

"All the hurt and pain and mistakes we made . . . it was a long time ago. I can even forgive you for vanishing from your daughter's life, because I think that was the best thing you could have done for her."

Jack nodded eagerly, but I was stunned that she could wave aside his abandonment.

"But while I might be willing to forgive the past, I am holding you accountable for the present. And the future. If you hurt Maggie again, I *will* hate you. You've been given a second chance to play a part in your daughter's life, Jack. Don't screw it up this time."

She strode out of the Smokehouse. Chris and Jack seemed shell-shocked by her vehemence. On Rowan's face, there was open admiration.

I ran after her. When she heard me calling, her steps slowed, then stopped.

"I'm sorry. I shouldn't have put you through that."

"No. You were right. I did need to see him."

"Are you okay?"

"Just . . . tired."

I hooked my arm through hers, and we walked toward the parking lot. Mom finally broke the silence to ask, "When you told him you were his daughter, did he ask if you hated him?"

I nodded.

"Still so desperate to be loved."

Rowan had written something similar in his journal. I wondered if Jack hungered for love or merely for expiation.

"Maybe that's why he became an actor," Mom mused. "All that love pouring over the footlights."

"That's not love. It's applause. Adulation."

"It's the only kind of love Jack could handle. The love of strangers. Real love requires that you give something in return."

"And that doesn't make you bitter?"

"I'm bitter about the wasted years. But I meant it when I said I don't hate him. Frankly, I don't feel much of anything. I never expected that. You love someone. You live together. You bring a child into the world. And in the end, there's nothing left. I find that very sad."

"It is."

"Maybe Rowan was right to bring him back, but I wish for your sake that you could have held on to your happy memories of him." She sighed. "How awful has it been for you?"

I watched Chris and Rowan walking toward us. Then I turned back to Mom and asked, "Do you want to go somewhere? Just the two of us?"

"Yes," Mom said. "I'd like that."

❧

We ended up at Woodford State Park. Although there were a couple of cars parked by the trail entrance, the lakeshore was deserted. It was an unprepossessing spot for a chat, the overcast sky as gray as the waters of the lake. The rack of canoes provided the only cheery note, the bright colors — yellow, red, orange — a startling contrast to the pine trees lining the shore like grim, green soldiers.

"It's not exactly Rehoboth," I said.

"More like the lake in that Montgomery Clift-Elizabeth Taylor movie. The one where he takes Shelley Winters out canoeing so he can kill her."

"That's a real pick-me-up."

"This from the woman who refers to Janet's lovely home as the Bates mansion."

We sat on a weathered wooden bench near the strip of sand that constituted the beach and I told her as much about my summer as I could. She punctuated my monologue with the occasional sigh, but her head jerked toward me when I described the night I ran away.

"I know. Another like father, like daughter moment."

"Maybe. But you came back. And the two of you seem okay now."

"I think so."

I could hear the uncertainty in my voice and feel my mother's intent gaze.

"The honeymoon isn't exactly over, but we've had our share of ups and downs."

"Good. That means you're going into this with your eyes open."

I'd told Jack we were. But were anyone's eyes really open when they were in love?

"When I met Rowan, I thought you were falling for a man just like your father. The boyish charm. The eagerness to please. And that strange watchfulness. Like he was gauging my reactions and choosing the most appropriate response."

That description of their first encounter was so accurate it was scary. And it was a scary-accurate description of my father, too.

"But I'll grant a lot of leeway to a man who'd spend months searching for his girlfriend's father. And who looks at you the way he does . . . like you were the only person in the room."

"The same way Chris looks at you."

Her cheeks grew faintly pink.

"Did Daddy ever look at you that way?"

"In the beginning. When he was trying to win me. But after he had . . ." She shrugged.

"So you're okay with Rowan?"

Mom sighed. "Yes. But he still scares me, Maggie. There are scars on that man's soul."

"Everybody has scars."

"But some can't be healed."

I wondered if she was talking about herself as well as Rowan, but I just said, "He's helped heal some of mine. I'm trying to do the same for him."

"That won't be easy. Rowan's a bit . . . murky at times, isn't he?"

"Yeah." It was my turn to sigh. "Is Chris ever like that?"

She stared out at the lake. "Chris is like the water in the Caribbean. So beautifully clear you can see right down to the bottom."

We returned to the theatre to find Chris and Rowan sitting on a bench by the pond.

"Seems everyone is gazing at water this afternoon," Mom noted.

"Actually, we just got back from a hike," Chris said. "Rowan showed me the plateau where you two had your first picnic. Talk about a romantic spot. Well. Not so much for Rowan and me. But if you two had been with us . . ."

I saw exactly what Mom meant about clear waters. His love for her shone through his eyes, his smile, the very way his body leaned toward her.

For a moment, she allowed her love to shine just as clearly. Then she frowned and said, "We should let Maggie and Rowan get ready for the show."

As their car pulled out of the parking lot, Rowan said, "I'm beginning to understand why you wanted to intervene. He's a good man. And they're good for each other."

"But I'm not sure they're going to make it. Or if I helped them."

"You opened the door, Maggie. Like I do when I call the Mackenzies. You can't push them through it, any more than you can push your father."

"That's not what you wrote in your journal the summer

he was here: 'If anyone can save Jack Sinclair from himself, his daughter can.' "

"You can't save someone who doesn't want to be saved."

"I suppose that's the lesson I had to learn this summer."

Rowan put his arm around my waist. "The summer's not over yet."

CHAPTER 44

YOU'LL NEVER BE ALONE

JACK APPARENTLY WANDERED UP TO THE HOUSE after the rest of us left the theatre. He was gone by the time I returned, but Janet said that they had spent the afternoon sitting in the sunroom.

"Just ... sitting?"

"He talked about the early days of his marriage. And when you were a little girl."

"Did it ever occur to him to share those memories with me?"

"Maybe he needed a dress rehearsal."

"Don't remind me of dress rehearsals."

"One thing I do know: he didn't want to be alone. Every time I got up to do something, he trailed after me like a lost puppy."

"You must have loved that."

"Actually, it was rather sweet." At my disbelieving look, she added, "Don't worry. I'm immune to Jack Sinclair's charm. But he's adrift right now. And a little lonely."

If so, he was back on track by the Saturday matinee when he swore up and down he was ready to go on that night. I just nodded and made sure Bernie was on standby. As soon as Jack headed down to the dressing room, I slipped upstairs to Rowan's apartment.

"How is he?" I asked.

"He seems fine."

"He seemed fine before he bolted."

"He won't bolt this time. He has something to prove —to himself, to Alison, and to you."

"That's what it took? Mom daring him to screw up?"

Rowan shrugged. "Stranger things have happened. Especially in this theatre."

When Jack reported to the green room for warm-ups, he seemed as calm as Rowan had claimed. And when Reinhard called places, he gave me a brisk nod.

I did the same as I slid into my seat next to Mom. She shrugged, but her hands relaxed their death grip on her purse.

The house lights began to dim. The murmur of conversation hushed. A program rustled. A seat squeaked. Someone coughed. I took a deep breath.

The lights came up on the stage, and there was a smattering of applause at the storybook tableau. Then Jack walked onstage.

I heard Mom catch her breath. Maybe it was the gray suit. Or the haircut he'd gotten in town that morning. He looked exactly like the nice, steady corporate type he had disdained — or the well-dressed English teacher he might have remained if luck or fate or faeries hadn't changed his life.

He strolled to his position. His gaze swept the darkened house. Then it returned to the center section where we were sitting. Maybe I only imagined that it lingered on Mom, but his smile was strangely wistful.

"Once upon a time . . ."

The orchestra launched into the opening number, the jaunty staccato beat of strings and piano driving the vocals of the cast and Jack's narration. As the characters made their wishes, two of mine came true: my father was performing again and my mother was witnessing it.

She chuckled at Cinderella's diffident description of the ball, laughed at the self-centered "agony" of the princes, but when the Witch implored Rapunzel to give up her wish to see the world, she became very still.

I knew "Stay with Me" would remind her of the years we had been estranged from each other, the eagerness with which I abandoned my childhood home for college. Each new job, each new role had been an adventure. I never thought about my mother returning to that empty house at the end of the day. When I thought of her at all, it was with a mingled sense of guilt and duty. She'd kept her fears and her doubts to herself and let me go my own way. I wasn't sure I could be as strong if I ever had a child.

Jack's performance surprised me. He brought a sly humor to the role I had never seen in rehearsal, as if he and the audience were sharing an inside joke. It was utterly different from Bernie's folksiness and made the Narrator's death even scarier.

When Bernie played the role, I always felt disbelief when that moment arrived. How could anyone throw this nice old man to the giant? It was like murdering Mister Rogers. Or Santa Claus.

This time, I shared all the Narrator's emotions: nervousness escalating to desperation; the momentary relief when his tormentors backed off; and then the terror of being dragged across the stage and shoved into the wings where the giant awaited her sacrifice. I felt oddly betrayed because Jack had promised the happy ending we got in Act One. If the joke could turn so viciously on him, no one was safe.

I shifted uneasily in my seat and heard others doing the same. It was as if the entire audience feared that something might emerge from the darkness to snatch us from our uncomfortable seats and our comfortable lives and drag us into the unknown.

Was that Rowan's magic or Jack's performance or some strange amalgam of the two?

The few light moments in Act Two shone brighter for that, but there was a nervous undercurrent to the laughter, as if the audience was still searching the shadows for danger. I floated in and out of the show, adrift in the shadows of memory:

My mother's pain throbbing through me as the Witch lamented Rapunzel's death, the muted sadness of watching me drift away all those years ago made sharper by the fear that she might lose me again to the siren call of my father's charm.

The sour taste of bile filling my mouth as the characters hurled accusations at each other, their bitter voices replaced by Rowan's and mine the night he revealed the truth about himself and about my father.

Shock turning my body rigid when the Mysterious Man appeared, no longer Rowan in his tattered costume but that terrified Rip Van Winkle who had tottered out of the theatre and back into my life.

No more visions.

Rowan's face, the unfeeling mask of Faerie. His voice, filled with familiar gentleness. As if the Mysterious Man's resurrection had rendered him both more otherworldly and more human.

Faery-green eyes weeping honey-sweet tears.

Rowan's face becoming my father's, filled with the excitement of exchanging the ties that bind for the thrill of the unknown. Brian's filled with my mother's weariness as she confessed that all the pain and anger and love had been reduced to ashes.

Once upon a time . . .

My father spinning tales about fantastic worlds. My mother cautiously explaining why Daddy had to leave. While I listened and watched, looking to them to learn what to be, what to feel, where to turn.

Careful what you say.

My eight-year-old self, staring at the newspaper clippings of Daddy's shows, wishing he would come back. My thirty-four-year-old self, staring at Jack's name in the program, wishing he would stay.

Careful what you wish for.

And hidden in the shadowy wings, the one who had cast the spell that brought father and daughter to the Crossroads; cast another to erase a man's memories of the magic that had touched him one Midsummer night; watched the unexpected consequences wrought by time and fate and human nature; and returned to restore order, only to discover that some spells are beyond Fae magic to repair.

Oh, careful what spells you cast, my love. For even you with all your power cannot always tell where they will lead. And then it is left to us to untangle them. Stumbling along the path, guided only by the magic we humans possess: determination, instinct, love.

Into the woods and out of the woods. And maybe—if we're very lucky—we earn our happy ever after.

The finale brought me back to the show. The audience clapped along with the music, as relieved and happy as if they had survived a dangerous journey. But after the red velvet curtains closed, my mother remained in her seat, staring at the stage.

I touched her arm lightly, and she started as if awakening from a dream.

"It was like the night I saw *Carousel*. When it seemed like you were singing to me. Only this time, I saw my whole life flash before me. The handsome prince who is charming, but insincere. The witch whose daughter keeps pulling away. The crazy man darting in and out, in and out . . ."

Clearly, whatever magic Rowan had worked had affected her, too.

Impulsively, I blurted out, "You know you won't lose me. No matter what happens with Jack."

Her eyes widened. "How did you . . . ? All right, now you're scaring me."

"I'm sorry. I just . . . that's what came to me. When I was watching tonight."

"Yes. Well. Let's just say I was grateful when Cinderella began singing 'No One is Alone.' "

"You're not alone," Chris said.

"I know," she replied, her voice as quiet as his. "And I know I'll never lose you, Maggie. I'm far too adept at hunting you down wherever you might go." Her nod was as brisk as Jack's before the show. "We'd better move along. Jack will expect to see us at the stage door."

Chris frowned, but followed us into the lobby. It took awhile to make our way through the crowd; people kept stopping to congratulate me. Their faces held a mixture of pleasure and uncertainty, as if they, too, were still feeling the effects of the show.

Friends and family members of the actors gathered in small clusters near the stage door. Jack hovered in the doorway, scanning their faces. Then he spied us and began edging forward, his head turning this way and that to acknowledge the congratulations.

His steps faltered as he approached us, his smile a little nervous.

"So. What did you think?"

"It's funny," Mom said. "I thought it would be a straightforward role. But you really held the whole show together, didn't you? And the moment they threw you to the giant . . . that was terrifying."

Jack's expression clouded. "Yeah. It was."

I wondered again how much Rowan had done to create the power of that moment. But Jack was watching me, clearly awaiting my reaction.

"It was a great performance. You took the role—and the show—to a whole new level."

"Thank you. That really . . . it means a lot." He shot a quick glance at Mom. "I guess you'll be leaving in the morning."

"Yes. So I'll say good-bye now."

She thrust out her hand. He clasped it gingerly. It was the first time they had touched and it lasted only a few seconds before both backed away. But they continued staring at each other, as if they recognized that this would be the last time they would ever meet.

"Maggie says you plan to leave after the season's over."

"Well . . . probably."

Mom blew out her breath impatiently. "What are you going to do with yourself, Jack? You're not a kid anymore. You can't just wander."

"I know, Allie. Maybe this time, I'll figure out where I belong."

"Still searching for enlightenment?" Her voice held resignation rather than the bitterness I remembered from my youth.

"Still searching, anyway."

"Well, someday I hope you find what you're looking for."

"You, too." He stepped closer. "Is he good to you?" he asked, ignoring the fact that Chris was standing a few feet away, glowering at him.

"He's very good to me. And very good *for* me."

Resentment tightened my father's features. Then it was gone, replaced by that same wistful half-smile I'd seen at the top of the show.

"I'm glad," he said, almost to himself. "You did a good job with our girl. I knew you would. But . . . well . . ."

"She's temperamental," my mother noted. "Like you."

"But she's got her feet on the ground. That she gets from you."

Did they see only the strangers they had become as they gazed at each other? Or the parade of their younger selves? The college students caught up in the first throes of romance. The young couple trying to keep that romance alive as he flitted from gig to gig. The happy parents, united in the love of their child. The older ones, torn apart by bitter quarreling and an obsession neither could understand.

For a moment, I thought they might embrace. Then Mom nodded and turned away. Chris tucked her hand into the crook of his elbow. My father watched them until they were lost in the crowd. Then he gave me a shaky smile and walked slowly back to the theatre.

People ebbed and flowed around me, their noisy chatter punctuated by occasional bursts of laughter. I felt removed from all the excitement and suddenly, very alone.

And then I felt them all around me. Reinhard's power, as steady as the throb of a heartbeat. Janet's as bracing as cold water on a hot day. Alex's warmth. Lee's protectiveness. Mei-Yin's determination. The quiet strength that was Catherine. The brighter flash of concern that was Javier. And for the first time—very faint—a bubbly upwelling of sympathy and love that could only be Hal.

And the center of all those separate powers and the source of most of them—Rowan.

I felt him slipping past the clusters of people behind me, making his slow, steady way toward me. His hands came down on my shoulders. His love rippled through me.

I leaned against him and closed my eyes.

No one is alone.

CHAPTER 45
TIME HEALS EVERYTHING

MOM'S DEPARTURE WITH CHRIS seemed to cue a mass exodus from Dale. The professionals bolted after the matinee to audition for their next gigs. The Bough emptied as the Mackenzies embarked on day trips. The local actors and staff resumed their everyday lives.

It was the natural order of a summer stock season, but my sense of loss was greater this year, knowing that my father would soon leave my life—and my world—forever. I'd hoped we could spend some of that time getting to know each other, but he left the apartment early every morning to walk in the woods and only returned as the light was waning.

"He'll come around," Rowan assured me. "In his own time."

But there was little time left.

Instead of using mine to research grants, I moped around the theatre. Alex, too, was moping, and I was certain it was because Debra had left for New York. When I found him drifting aimlessly around the garden Tuesday morning, I dragged him to the apartment for lunch.

"Look at us," I said. "We spend half the summer complaining about how overworked we are and we can't even enjoy our freedom."

"You need to start thinking ahead," Rowan said.

"We are," Alex replied gloomily.

"Thinking about the theatre, I mean."

778

I inscribed another figure eight in my gazpacho. "Debra had this idea for a murder mystery series at the Bates mansion."

Alex poked at his salad. "She mentioned that to me, too."

"It's not exactly part of our mission, but it might be fun. And it would bring in money. Do you think Janet would go for it?"

Alex shrugged. "She's always complaining that she's bored during the off-season."

He sighed. I sighed.

Rowan said, "What about that reading series you were telling me about? The one to showcase new works by Vermont playwrights."

"That's not until the spring. The scripts have just started coming in. But there's always the Christmas show."

"You're doing a Christmas show?"

"Do you even look at the program?" I complained. "There's been a notice in every one! We're doing *A Christmas Carol*. Long loves the story. Ghosts. Redemption. New beginnings."

The perfect summation of this season at the Crossroads.

"He loves all the children's roles even more: Cratchits and carolers and street urchins. He's sure we'll make a fortune. But so far, Alex and I haven't found a version we like."

Alex's fork clattered onto his plate. "My God. I'm so stupid. There's our version!"

"You guys wrote a musical adaptation of *A Christmas Carol*?"

Rowan nodded. "The first show we ever wrote together."

"Mostly as a lark," Alex said, "We started talking and the next thing you know, Rowan presented me with a draft."

"Why didn't you suggest it from the start?" I demanded.

"It felt wrong to do it without Rowan," Alex replied. "And once the season got underway, I was too busy to even think about Christmas."

"We'd probably want to make some changes," Rowan said. "We've both learned a lot about putting a musical together since then."

"The plot's not going to change," Alex replied. "And most of the songs are done. The orchestrations will take a couple of weeks, but—"

"Whoa, whoa, whoa!" I exclaimed. "You're starting school soon. When will you have time to—?"

"I'll make time! Besides, Rowan and I work fast."

"We wrote *The Sea-Wife* in six months," Rowan added, catching Alex's enthusiasm. "This is just polishing."

"If we put our minds to it, we could have the whole thing ready by mid-October."

"And begin rehearsals in early November," Rowan said.

They turned to me, a freckled face and a pale one, both alight with excitement.

"I'll need the completed script before the September board meeting," I warned them.

"But we're a known commodity!" Alex protested.

"A winning commodity," Rowan added.

"I still need to let them read it. If they want to."

Rowan shoved back his chair. "I must have a copy somewhere."

"I still have mine," Alex said, following Rowan into the office. "If you can't find yours, I'll dig it out this afternoon and—"

"Here it is!" Rowan crowed. "On the shelf with our other shows."

I found them sitting thigh-to-thigh on the floor, their heads bent over a green binder. I considered volunteering to make another copy, but they had already begun dissecting the opening number, exclaiming over some bits and groaning over others.

Reluctant to become an unnecessary third wheel, I wandered down to the production office and pulled out my lesson plans for the new after-school program for elementary school kids. I jotted some notes, went through my inbox, then slumped back in my chair.

Alex had something to look forward to when Debra left. Rowan had a project to fill the next two months. But the project I wanted to focus on—getting to know my father—was going nowhere.

So focus on something else, Graham.

I picked up the phone and called Long.

When I told him about the Mackenzie-Ross adaptation of *A Christmas Carol*, he exclaimed, "That's wonderful! I'll call the board today and let them know."

"Umm . . . shouldn't they vote on this?"

"A new musical by Rowan Mackenzie and Alex Ross? What's to approve?" Then he added, "They're not doing some radical reinterpretation, are they? The Ghost of Christmas Past wandering around in the nude."

"I sincerely doubt it. Apart from the sensation it would cause, it would be way too chilly for the poor actor."

"I suppose we do need an official vote. Boards can be so tiresome sometimes."

"Tell me about it," I replied without—as usual—thinking.

Long just chuckled. "I'll e-mail everybody today and ask them to weigh in. I'm sure they'll be thrilled. And once it's approved, I'll announce it before the remaining performances of *Into the Woods*. If you think that would be appropriate."

"It would be perfect."

There was a brief silence on the other end. Then Long said, "I didn't get a chance to speak with your mother after the show, but I saw her talking with Jack."

"It went okay. Better than I thought it would. But it was . . . stressful. For both of them."

"And for you. A lot to deal with in one week. And that show Saturday night! It was excellent," he hastily added. "But . . . strange. Harder to watch somehow."

When I told him my theory about Jack's performance and the joke that unexpectedly turned around to bite him—and the audience—in the ass, he said, "Yes, you might be right. But everyone I talked with afterward seemed delighted. Maybe it was just us. Because we were expecting one thing and got something different."

Much like Long himself. From the moment I'd met him, I had pegged him as one sort of man, but this season, he had turned out to be something else.

"Well, you must have a million things to do," he said. "And I need to get out those e-mails. I'll let you know as soon as I've heard back from the board."

I resisted the urge to keep him on the line, to soak up some of his excitement. Everyone seemed to be caught up in the Christmas spirit except me.

Rowan must have sensed that. He appeared in the doorway a few minutes later and said, "Alex has gone home to search for the music. We're going to meet tomorrow afternoon to play through the score. Want to join us?"

"Love to. When do I get to read the script?"

"How about tomorrow morning?"

"What's wrong with right now?"

"I thought we might walk into town. See the sights. Have dinner at the Golden Bough."

I jumped up and hurried around the desk. Then I hesitated. "Are you sure you're ready for this?"

"Absolutely."

I flung my arms around his neck and buried my face against his shoulder.

"He'll come around," Rowan whispered.

CHAPTER 46
LET'S TAKE AN OLD-FASHIONED WALK

OUR WALK TO TOWN WAS UNIMPEDED BY SLA-VERING DOGS. It was the cats that slowed us down.

A succession of furry wraiths darted through the grass and twined around Rowan's ankles, purring in adoration. When he attempted to remove the first one, it went limp, as if his touch had induced a fainting spell. The next treated his fingers to a lascivious tongue bath. When I tried to extricate the third, it shot me a disdainful glance, dug its claws into Rowan's pants, and hung on with grim determination.

We shambled and stumbled and shooed our way past the large houses outside of town, only to glance back and discover a line of cats trailing after us. Rowan broke into helpless laughter, then a tremulous rendition of "There's a Parade in Town," made even more discordant by the yowls of his admirers. When I pointed out that his Pied Piper act might blow his cover, he called on his magic to gently discourage his feline courtiers.

The human inhabitants of Dale were as curious as their cats. If they didn't exactly faint, they popped out of shops and restaurants to greet me and exclaim over Rowan.

"Do you know everyone in town?" he asked after our shouted conversation with Mrs. Grainger, who was a dear, but deaf as a post.

"It's a really small town."

But there was no denying that Rowan was a bigger draw than the Fourth of July parade.

As yet another wave of admirers approached, he seized my hand and pulled me into the General Store.

"Well, if it isn't Rowan Mackenzie," Mr. Hamilton exclaimed.

Every head swiveled in our direction. Fortunately, most were tourists, who went back to their browsing.

Rowan greeted Mr. Hamilton pleasantly, but his wide-eyed gaze swept the scuffed floorboards, the exposed wooden beams, the woven rugs that hung over the railing on the second floor, and the moth-eaten heads of various dead animals that eyed us glassily from the shadows near the rafters.

"This is what a General Store *should* look like," he declared. Then he spied the widowed Kent sisters making a beeline toward him and darted off.

Mr. Hamilton watched Rowan prowl through the narrow aisles filled with Vermont-made products plus a hodge-podge of stuff ranging from dishware to clothing to camping equipment.

"Doesn't get out much, does he? First time I remember him coming to town in all the years he's lived here."

"He was claustrophobic. Or agoraphobic. Something phobic."

"That's what I heard, too. Doesn't seem to bother him now, though."

"I think he got treatment. While he was away."

As Rowan clambered up the steps to the second floor— pursued by the indomitable widows—Mr. Hamilton frowned. "Not afraid of heights, is he?"

"Heights he's okay with."

For half an hour, Mr. Hamilton and I discussed the weather, the Blueberry Festival, and *A Christmas Carol*. Then Rowan zoomed up to the counter and paused to study the rack of postcards.

"That's what we need. A postcard of the theatre."

As he took off again, I exchanged a long look with Mr. Hamilton. "Why didn't we think of that?"

"Beats me. Every shop in town would carry them. Out-of-town ones, too, I bet."

"If we get them printed up soon, we could have them in stores by fall foliage season."

Mr. Hamilton tugged his right earlobe, a sure sign that he was calculating expenses.

"Why don't I work up some figures?" I suggested. "We can go over them before the September board meeting."

As he beamed approvingly, Rowan strode toward us again and laid two beeswax candles and a wallet on the counter.

"Who's the wallet for?"

"Me."

I refrained from pointing out that he had nothing to put in it. He hadn't made a dime all summer and had repeatedly refused to accept any of the money he had given to me.

After studying the glass jars of penny candy for five minutes, he selected a striped stick of sarsaparilla.

"Would you like one?"

"No, thanks. But let's get a licorice one for Jack."

I unzipped my purse and froze when Rowan pulled a wad of bills out of his pocket. With a proud smile, he paid for his purchases and carefully slid the remaining money into his new wallet.

As soon as I dragged him outside, I demanded, "Where did you get all that money?"

"Never mind."

"Did you sell one of your books?"

"Not an old one."

"*Which* one?" I persisted.

"*To Kill a Mockingbird.*"

"You own a first edition of *To Kill a Mockingbird*!"

"Not anymore."

"But how could you let it go? It's such a wonderful story."

"And I can still enjoy it whenever I like. Reinhard bought me a paperback copy after he arranged the sale."

"I should have known Reinhard was in on this." I lowered my voice to ask, "How much did you get for it?"

"Guess."

"Five thousand dollars?"

He glanced around before whispering, "Fifteen thousand."

"Holy crap!" I exclaimed, drawing giggles from two passing kids.

"Reinhard's holding most of it. I just have what's in my lovely new wallet." He glanced up and down Main Street. "Now where?"

"Hallee's. But we have to hurry if we want to get there before it closes."

Although Hallee's was just across the street, it took us fifteen minutes to escape the new tide of well-wishers that surrounded us. I groaned in disappointment when I discovered the door was locked. Rowan stared at the window display, transfixed.

"It's Hal's annual tribute to blueberries," I explained.

The display featured the usual assortment of scantily clad mannequins, all sporting blue lingerie: blue panties and bras, blue teddies and negligees. A mannequin in a blue corset cradled white bowls of blueberries beneath her breasts. Two male mannequins in tight blue briefs posed with pies like discus throwers. Off to one side, a mannequin in a blue negligee leaned languidly against a white picket fence. Her left hand toyed with her sparkly "sapphire" necklace. Her right proffered a single blueberry to the male mannequin— in obligatory blue thong—that reclined at her feet amid a veritable ocean of berries. High above, a blue moon smiled benignly.

"Merciful gods," Rowan breathed.

"Wait until apple season. He's planning a Garden of Eden theme."

Rowan was still mesmerized by the display when the door to the shop banged open and Hal flew out.

"Oh, my God! I can't believe it. You're here. In Dale!"

As he burst into "Miracles of Miracles," the door opened again and Lee walked out, grinning. "When Hal and I saw you through the window, we just about—"

"Do you like it?" Hal interrupted. "The display?"

"I love it. It's sexy and funny and inventive. Just like the man who created it."

Tears welled up in Hal's eyes. With a tremulous cry, he ran back into the shop.

Lee caught the door before it swung shut. "He's just verklempt," he told Rowan.

"Ver—?"

"Ask Bernie," Lee and I chorused.

As we entered the shop, the pink velveteen curtains at the back parted and Hal emerged, dabbing his eyes with a tissue.

"I'm fine," he insisted. "Lee, Maggie — talk among yourselves. I have to give Rowan the tour. Oh, where to begin? Accessories? Gowns? Nightwear!"

While Hal played tour guide, I idly sifted through a rack of camisoles and corsets.

"Who buys something like this?" I asked Lee, holding up a plaid prep school uniform with cutouts around the breasts.

"You'd be surprised. I just wish his high-end stuff sold as well as the kitsch. He makes out pretty well on the costumes he designs for the drag queens, but when he opened the shop, he planned to sell all custom-made clothing. People just aren't willing to shell out the bucks for it."

I glanced at Rowan and Hal, who were in hushed consultation in nightwear. "Mr. Hamilton and I were talking about making up a series of postcards of the barn. What if we expanded the idea to include note cards featuring Hal's artwork?"

Lee's face lit up. He seized my arm and dragged me over to Rowan and Hal. "I'm taking over the tour, Hal. Maggie needs to talk with you."

Hal was even more excited than Lee. "We could do different versions. Reproductions of the pen-and-ink sketch on the program. Original watercolor renditions of the barn. I could do a whole Dale Collection! The barn. The General Store. The town hall."

"Hallee's."

Hal shook his head. "The tourists will want Ye Olde New England Towne." He gasped and clutched my arm. "A gift shop. We need a gift shop with theatre tchotchkes. T-shirts, hats, note cards, books, posters. My posters!"

For a moment, we were both transported into the wonderful world of merchandising. Then I descended to earth.

"One step at a time. First, work me up some prices I can show the board. Then we'll tackle the gift shop."

We hurried over to share our latest brainstorm and found Rowan and Lee examining a pair of black leather boots with stiletto heels.

"Just what I need. I fall over my feet when I'm wearing sneakers."

"But think how well they would go with this leather bustier," Rowan said.

"I'd sweat like a horse. Come on, I'm hungry."

We made it about fifty feet down Main Street when a barrel-like figure stormed out of the Mandarin Chalet.

"So you FINALLY made it into town!" Mei-Yin exclaimed. "This calls for a CELEBRATION. A special DINNER!"

"That's what we were planning," I said.

Her eyes narrowed to slits. "Where?"

"Why, the Chalet, of course," Rowan lied smoothly.

"GOOD answer!" She flung out her arms. "WELCOME to the Mandarin Chalet. Where EAST meets WEST. And the ELITE meet to EAT!"

When dragons flank the doorway of a giant gingerbread house, you expect the interior to be a hellish amalgam of *Flower Drum Song* and *The Sound of Music*. I'd been shocked the first time I walked into the Chalet and found nary a dragon or cuckoo clock in sight.

The snow-covered mountains in the mural would have felt equally at home in Sichuan Province or Switzerland, as would the intricately carved wooden screen that separated the restaurant from the bar. Soft pools of light illuminated the tables, while the rose and gold accents conjured a glorious sunrise. Throw in the faint music that combined sounds from the natural world with harp and flute, and the Chalet felt like a mountaintop retreat or a relaxing day spa.

"So what do you THINK?"

Although Mei-Yin was beaming, a discordant twang of anxiety shivered through me.

"It's so restful," Rowan said. "Exactly what I need after all the excitement today."

Her relief surprised me; clearly, Rowan's approval meant as much to her as it had to Hal. But she just whispered, "Makes people STAY longer. And SPEND more."

She snatched up a sheaf of menus and marched off. Although it was only 6:30, the restaurant was already half full, mostly with the AARP crowd, all of whom regarded us avidly, all of whom expected us to stop and chat. When we finally reached the corner table where Mei-Yin waited impatiently, we both sank gratefully onto our chairs.

"Order whatever you want," Mei-Yin said. "Chinese, Swiss, Mexican . . ." She punctuated each cuisine by slapping a different menu on the table. "I'll have Max cook you up something SPECIAL." She slapped the wine list down, too, then snapped her fingers at a hovering busboy. "YOU! Clear off these utensils and bring out the REAL silverware."

"You keep the family silver here?" I asked.

"Just a couple of place settings. When Reinhard and I try out one of Max's new recipes, we like to do it up in STYLE."

More likely, she had brought the silverware in after Rowan's return in anticipation of the day he would dine at her establishment.

Rowan just thanked her quietly and watched her march back to the kitchen.

The restful atmosphere was somewhat undermined by the staff's obvious terror of offending their boss' special guests. Ice rattled like chattering teeth as the busboy tiptoed over with the water pitcher. Our server's voice shook as he announced the specials. Both relaxed so quickly that I knew Rowan must have called on his power to calm them.

Mei-Yin emerged from the kitchen with her stepson in tow. Max was a younger version of Reinhard from the premature gray of his brush cut to his stocky build. He even gave a little bow when Rowan rose to shake his hand.

"It's an honor to have you here."

"And a long overdue pleasure for me. But with all these choices . . ." Rowan waved his hand at the pile of menus. ". . . Maggie and I are at a loss. What would you recommend?"

As the two men launched into a protracted discussion of menu options, I brought Mei-Yin up to speed on recent developments. She demanded good dance music for Fezziwig's party and the opportunity to play the killer in our yet-to-be-approved Halloween murder mystery. But she also suggested that until we scraped together funds for a gift shop, we set up tables on the breezeway at intermission to hawk merchandise. And volunteered to teach some movement classes for the after-school programs if I got swamped. Which seemed likely given all the new initiatives.

Max announced our dinner selections. Rowan's main

course sounded like a phlegmy sneeze, mine like the worst salad ever imagined. They turned out to be veal strips in a cream sauce and a cold sausage salad that was unexpectedly delicious. Mei-Yin and Max lingered long enough to share a toast, then left us to savor our meal.

Dinner in town—another first. And Rowan's sweet smile made it even more perfect.

When we passed on dessert, our server brought us coffee and a small bowl filled with chocolate-dipped strawberries. What he didn't bring was the check.

"It's on the HOUSE!" Mei-Yin declared when Rowan called her over.

"I can't let you do that."

Once more, her eyes narrowed into dark, dangerous slits. "You gonna tell me what you'll 'LET' me do? In MY restaurant?"

"No, of course not. I just—"

"GOOD! It's SETTLED."

We thanked Max and Mei-Yin profusely. And after she had escorted us to the door, Rowan pressed a kiss to her cheek.

"You are a very gracious lady. And you made this an evening I will never forget."

Her happiness zinged through me, but all she said was, "Don't get run OVER walking home."

Rowan caught my arm as I turned toward the theatre. "What about the Bough? Don't I get to see all the changes you've made?"

"We could do that another time."

"Nonsense," he said, steering me down the sidewalk. "Besides, Frannie's feelings will be hurt if I don't stop in."

From the rapidity with which Frannie descended, I suspected she'd been watching our progress from the front windows. But Iolanthe still reached us first. I caught a blur of movement near the front desk. A moment later, she was draped over Rowan's boot.

"Cats like Rowan," I told Frannie.

"My goodness. I can't remember the last time I saw her move that fast."

"I can't remember the last time I saw her move."

Naturally, Frannie insisted on showing him around. And

naturally, Iolanthe insisted on accompanying us. But her burst of energy had faded and she yowled so plaintively that Rowan finally picked her up. She spent the rest of the tour cradled against his chest. Now and then, her paw came up to touch his cheek, as if she—like Frannie—had difficulty believing that Rowan Mackenzie was actually here. The cast members in the lounge took his presence in stride, but of course, they had no way of knowing they were witnessing a minor miracle.

Rowan declined a drink, but when we returned to the lobby, he said, "The hotel looks beautiful. It reminds me of Helen's sunroom."

Frannie and I exchanged startled glances.

"You're right," Frannie said. "Maybe it was Helen's spirit guiding us all along."

Rowan smiled. "Maybe so. She'd be so happy to know that you're watching over the cast."

"And even happier to see you two together again." As the grandfather clock struck ten, Frannie added, "It's late. You better run along. I'll give you the rest of the tour next time you're in town, Rowan. I'll even show you the room Maggie stayed in during her season. Where she laid awake nights dreaming of you."

"Frannie!" I protested.

"Well, you did, didn't you?"

"Yes! But you're not supposed to tell him that. It'll give him a big head."

"Rowan's head's just fine. Now scoot, you two."

Rowan carefully deposited Iolanthe in the inbox and we started for home. The streets were already deserted, everyone in Dale tucked in for the night. We said little, content to mosey along in silence. My heart was filled with happiness at sharing Rowan's adventure in town and my mind was buzzing with ideas for the theatre. Astonishing that Rowan's casual mention of a postcard could lead to so many new possibilities.

As we walked up the hill to the house, I said, "This has been a perfect day."

"Has it? I'm glad."

I stopped, struck by the eagerness in his voice.

"What?"

I was so stupid. I knew he'd suggested this outing because he'd seen how depressed I was. But even if he'd enjoyed seeing Hal and Frannie and Mei-Yin, he'd also had to
rub shoulders with strangers, endure an endless succession
of little chats, an endless exchange of stupid pleasantries. If
the cocktail party with the staff had been a challenge, this
afternoon must have been agony.

"What?" he repeated.

Before I could reply, the screen door creaked open and
Janet walked onto the porch with Jack trailing behind her.

Hands on hips, she surveyed us with a frown. "Well, I
hope *you've* had fun. *I've* been on the phone all goddamn
evening. Half the population of Dale has called to inform
me of Rowan Mackenzie's historic visit. There will probably
be an article in the next edition of *The Bee*: 'Local Recluse
Tours Town. Citizens Agog.'"

Rowan proffered the two beeswax candles. "By way of
apology." Then he produced the penny candy for Jack.
"Maggie thought you might like this."

Jack held the stick up to the porch lantern, then slowly
lowered it and stared at me. "Licorice. My favorite."

"I know."

An awkward silence descended. Janet poked her elbow
into Jack's ribs. He cleared his throat and said, "I was thinking. Maybe tomorrow, we could all go on a picnic. If you'd
like."

I stared at Janet, who enjoyed picnics about as much as
Rowan liked long car rides, and promptly burst into tears.

Jack looked horrified. Rowan put his arm around me.
Janet said, "Oh, for God's sake, stop bawling like a constipated calf."

I snuffled like a congested calf and said, "That would be
lovely." Then I remembered. "But Alex—"

"Alex called," Janet said. "He forgot he had a dentist appointment tomorrow. So he'd like to postpone playing
through the score until Thursday."

I knew damn well there was no dentist appointment. I
fought the return of the constipated calf and whispered,
"Okay."

"Good," Janet said. "I am now going to reheat my dinner
for the third time."

As the screen door slammed behind her, Jack said, "I guess I'll head down to the apartment. Unless you want me to take a walk around the pond."

"I think we're both a little worn out," Rowan said. "I'll see you down there."

"And I'll see you tomorrow," I said.

Rowan led me over to the old wooden porch swing. I listened to the mournful creak as we rocked gently back and forth, then asked, "Was it awful for you today?"

"No. Well. A little daunting. All those people . . ."

"I'm so sorry. I should have realized—"

"No," he repeated. "I loved seeing Hal's shop and Mei-Yin's restaurant and your hotel. All the places I've been hearing about for so many years. I just never expected such a welcome. Such . . . kindness. Humans really are quite magical, aren't they?"

"Kindness isn't magical."

"It is to me. Kindness, compassion, love. Those qualities are alien to the Fae. And innate to humans."

"But they're not magical."

"Yes, Maggie. They are. *You* are. Look at what you've accomplished this season. You helped your mother come to terms with her past. You forged a disparate group of actors into a company. You made the staff partners in this theatre in a way they never were when I was director. You laid the groundwork to make the Crossroads financially viable. You pushed and pulled and dragged me into this world that I had only glimpsed secondhand. You've done far more with your magic than I ever did with mine."

"How can you say that? I know what your power can do."

"But don't you see? No matter how beautiful or terrifying or extraordinary the magic of Faerie is, its ultimate purpose is to disguise. Human magic . . . reveals. I never understood that until this summer. It's like when I call the Mackenzies. My magic sets the stage, but human magic— your capacity to love, to change—that's what makes the drama unfold."

His smile was a little sad, as if the revelation had diminished him somehow.

I squeezed his hand. "I loved the nice, normal, ordinary

day you gave me. But I love your magic, too. You can calm me with a touch or carry me to the brink of ecstasy. You can make paper flowers bloom and help an actress overcome her fear of heights—and help heal a lost soul like my father. Your magic is the most wondrous thing I've ever known in my life. Never forget that. Or think that I want you to be like other men."

His love flowed into me and through me, as strong as the earth, as boundless as the sky.

My father had said that the Fae carry the light of the sun and the moon and the stars. And maybe they did. But Rowan's love shone with the soft glow of the fireflies that danced in our dreams.

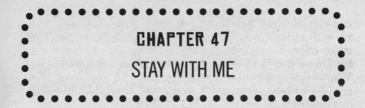

CHAPTER 47

STAY WITH ME

WE WERE BLESSED WITH A BEAUTIFUL DAY for our picnic, but the cool breeze reminded me that autumn was quickly approaching. The four of us tramped along the trail, content to savor the peacefulness. Occasionally, our pace slowed as we skirted a boggy area. In springtime, those places had been a riot of wildflowers: carpets of white-petaled bloodroots giving way to shy violets, yellow trout lilies, red trillium, and the green sprawl of jack-in-the-pulpit. Only after I'd walked the woods in spring did I fully understand what Alex had wanted us to capture during "June is Bustin' Out All Over": that giddy relief at feeling the world awaken.

When I mentioned that, Janet snorted. "And to think, she once thought spring peepers were birds."

"Well, who knew frogs could sing?"

"When she came back to the house one fine spring day and told me about the beautiful buttercups she had found, I decided to take her in hand."

"Marsh marigolds?" Rowan guessed.

"Yellow violets," Janet replied.

"Yellow violets?" Jack echoed. "Well, no wonder you got it wrong. Talk about your oxymoron."

"Thank you," I said. "And as for you two, cut me a break. I lived in cities all my life."

"You had Prospect Park," Rowan said.

"Which I hardly ever got a chance to visit."

"And the one in Wilmington. What was it called?"

Jack inscribed a slow crescent through the leaves with his boot.

"Brandywine Park," I finally said. "And it was hardly the hundred acre wood."

"Just some open space along the river," Jack added. "With picnic tables and barbecue grills."

A tiny step for mankind, but a giant leap for father and daughter.

The conversation drifted to other topics, but when we stopped at the ancient beech, I told my father, "The first time I saw it, I thought of that tree on the Brandywine. The one with the roots that could hide pirate gold or a family of gnomes."

Jack stared at me in astonishment. "I can't believe you remember that."

Rowan seized Janet's hand to help her ascend the hill to the plateau. After a moment's hesitation, Jack took mine. When we reached the top, we exchanged shy smiles like kids on their first date.

But that's what this was. And Janet and Rowan were the chaperones easing us through it with food and conversation and sensitivity.

We talked mostly about the theatre, but somehow our discussion of *A Christmas Carol* led to a comparison of Christmas celebrations in Dale and Wilmington, just as Rowan's story of building his first snowman with Jamie's children encouraged Jack to talk about the first time he went sledding and broke his nose.

During those two hours, I learned more about my father than I had ever known, including the shocking discovery that he'd had an older brother who had died when Jack was thirteen. Less shocking was the revelation that Jack had been considered "the bad Sinclair boy" who had grown even wilder after Jimmy's death.

Although he quickly changed the subject, it was obvious that acting had saved him from getting into serious trouble, that the theatre was more of a home than his parents' house. What better place to forget his troubles—as a teenager and as an adult? And what better way to do it than by becoming—for a few hours, at least—someone else?

I'd done it myself.

The stage was playground and therapist's couch. The one place we could safely explore our fears, our hopes, our deepest selves. A place where the laughter was approving, where we could bask in the applause and the admiration — and yes, the love — of our audience.

Little wonder he was drawn to Faerie. It was another sort of playground — more fantastical, more dangerous, and infinitely more alluring. And unlike a theatre where the magic vanished as soon as the curtain came down, its glamour never faded.

That was the first of many conversations with my father — and many walks in the woods. Somehow, it was easier to talk under the open sky, maybe because it allowed us to walk the trails in silence if we preferred.

Cautious at first, we skirted the difficult parts of our shared past to concentrate on the happy memories. But as the season neared its conclusion, we began sharing stories from the years after he had left. His were often confused and disjointed, the description of a glorious sunset over the red rocks of Sedona suddenly shifting into a vision of Stonehenge at sunrise — as if his memories were as mutable as the landscape of the Borderlands. At such moments, I glimpsed the fragile, confused old man I had met in June. It saddened me to realize how much of his life was lost — and frightened me to think that the glamour of Faerie would blot out his remaining memories.

Including his memories of me.

By piecing together his stray comments I managed to fill in some of the blanks of his final years in this world. Dark years, mostly, when his money was gone and he lived hand-to-mouth, picking up work where he could find it, staying in one place only long enough to make enough cash for the next leg of his journey. The homeless shelters he resorted to when there was no work and no money. The struggle to find the clarity of mind to continue his quest.

He was far more at ease listening to me talk about my life, offering only an occasional quiet comment. I had rarely seen his introspective side. And while I was grateful to discover this other Jack Sinclair, it made the prospect of losing him more painful.

Perhaps he felt the same for during the final week of *Into
the Woods*, his silences grew longer, his expression more
troubled. When we returned to the theatre Thursday afternoon, he suddenly blurted out, "I can stay. If you want me
to."

Once before, he had made that offer and been relieved
when I didn't accept it.

I nodded to one of the picnic tables and sat down op-
posite him. Choosing my words carefully, I said, "Of course,
I want you to stay. But most of all, I want you to be happy.
Do you really want to give up Faerie for this world?"

"I wouldn't have to give it up. Just . . . postpone going for
awhile."

"And what would you do here?"

"I suppose I could teach."

"Do you *want* to teach?"

His shoulders sagged. "Not really."

"It's okay to want Faerie. You've been looking for it
most of your life."

"It was all I had. But now . . . I just keep thinking about
what Allie said. About getting a second chance and not
screwing it up."

"We're bound to have regrets. No matter what you choose.
If you go, I'll miss you and you'll feel guilty. If you stay, *I'll*
feel guilty for keeping you from Faerie. And you might be
bored out of your skull."

My weak attempt at humor failed to evoke a smile.

"It's not like the clock runs out when the curtain comes
down Saturday night. Let's both think about what we want.
And talk about it again on Sunday."

His performance that night was more solemn, as if the
decision he had to make weighed on him. I listened to "Stay
with Me" and longed to speak those same words to him. I
wanted to protect him from the unknown dangers of Faerie,
to assure him that the theatre was his home, that I was his
home.

Rowan had told me that the night he returned. But
Rowan loved me more than my father ever could.

When Kanesha hobbled onstage, wearing her one golden
slipper, and began to sing "On the Steps of the Palace," the
song seemed an ironic commentary on my situation. Cin-

derella was trying to make a decision, too. And like me, she was stalling. Should she allow the Prince to find her or just keep running? Was she better off at home where she was safe but unhappy? Or with her prince in a palace where she would always be out of place?

It was a jolt to realize that her words reflected Jack's dilemma far more than mine. To stay or to run. To remain in the safety of this world or exchange it for the dangers of one where he would always remain an outsider.

Cinderella's decision was not to decide, but to leave a clue—a shoe—and let the Prince make the next move. A clever choice that neatly absolved her of responsibility.

Like Cinderella, my father was afraid of making a choice for fear it might be the wrong one. And like her, he had left his own clues: his assertion that he would stay—if I wanted him to; his fear of screwing up; his compromise of postponing his departure—and his decision—a little longer.

He had always allowed Mom to make the tough choices. He was waiting for me to do the same.

If I forced him to choose, he would stay. For a few weeks, a few months. That was easier than hurting me.

And if, like Cinderella, I chose not to decide?

We would drift along. I would offer him a role in the Halloween murder mystery. The role of Scrooge in *A Christmas Carol*. I would use the glamour of theatre to combat the glamour of Faerie. And for a few weeks, a few months, it might work.

But then the show would close and the New Year's celebrations would end. The long, dark days of winter would creep by. And faced with the piercing cold and the gray-white silence of this world, his eyes would turn to Faerie, the longing greater, the need to see it more urgent.

I would watch him grow increasingly restive and resent him. He would sense my reaction and feel guilty. The tentative relationship we had built this summer would slowly erode and we would end up angry and alienated.

Cinderella's song ended in a dizzying confection of clever rhymes and clever compromise. But although we had both learned something new, our choices were very different.

After the show, I found Rowan waiting for me at the top of the stairs. Whether he knew my decision, he certainly sensed my turbulent emotions. He poured two glasses of whisky and together, we waited.

Jack's steps slowed when he saw us sitting on the sofa. At Rowan's gesture, he sat beside me. Knowing a long preamble would only make him more anxious, I said, "I've been thinking about our conversation this afternoon. It means the world to me that you offered to stay. But you lost your heart to Faerie years ago. And that's why I think you should go there."

His head drooped, and he began to tremble. For a moment, I thought I'd made a terrible mistake. When he looked up, there were tears in his eyes.

"You're so much like your mother. So strong."

I took his hand between mine, feeling the rough calluses on his fingertips, the loose, dry skin on the back of his hand. He had been in the prime of his life when he found the portal to the Borderlands, but he was older now. Was desire enough to sustain him in that other world?

"It's okay, Daddy. Everything'll be okay."

A single tear oozed down his cheek. "It's the first time you've called me that."

"I lost you for awhile. And Magpie, too. But we found them again during these last few weeks. And they'll always be with us. No matter where we go."

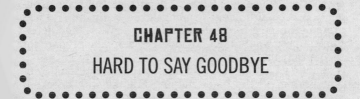

CHAPTER 48

HARD TO SAY GOODBYE

WHEN DADDY WALKED ONSTAGE FOR THAT FI-
NAL PERFORMANCE, his gaze fastened on me as it
had on Mom. His face held the same wistfulness. And his
voice was hushed as he spoke the magical words he had so
often used to begin one of his tales: "Once upon a time . . ."

That night, he offered me the tale of our lives: the charming, weak-willed prince; the marriage that began with passion and ended in separation; the baby who represented the
hope for the future; the young girl eager to see the world;
the stranger who emerged from the past to weave his way
into his child's life once again. The choices made. The lessons learned. The regrets. The losses.

Nancy sat beside me, her hand clasped in mine. She had
arrived without Ed, claiming he had a dreadful summer
cold. For once, her instincts were wrong. It would have
cheered me to share their joy, to see the blossoming of their
relationship, to know that on this night of endings, something wonderful was beginning.

But as the cast took their final curtain call, I decided
she'd been right, after all. It would be better to meet Ed in
September when he was more than an antidote for grief,
when the four of us could simply enjoy spending time together and share the happiness of being in love.

I moved through the cast party with Nancy and Rowan
beside me and the staff hovering nearby, their faces radiating
concern and love. It was eerily reminiscent of the *Carousel*

cast party on the eve of Rowan's departure. But I was stronger now. And although I would grieve for my father, I was grateful for the gift of time we had been given—and determined to use what time we had left to help him prepare for the journey that lay ahead.

But first, I had to deal with other departures. I spent Sunday morning at the hotel, helping Frannie with checkout and bidding a final farewell to my Mackenzies.

"Don't fret about your daddy," Otis said. "He's a tough old bird for all he looks like a good wind'll knock him over. And just 'cause he's leaving doesn't mean he'll never be back."

I managed a smile. My father had returned to me once, his resurrection as miraculous as the Mysterious Man's. But there would be no miracle this time. The choice I had made brought with it the knowledge that I would never see him again, never know if he was safe or happy—or even if he was alive.

"Well, *you* better come back," I said. "Bring Viola up for a vacation."

"You can count on it."

Debra was one of the last to leave. As she looked around the lobby, she said, "I'm actually going to miss this old place."

"Then you should consider a return engagement. I'm preparing the budget for a Halloween murder mystery night. If the board goes for it, I'll need someone to help run it. And then there's *A Christmas Carol*. You'd bring a new level of feistiness to Mrs. Cratchit."

"Great. Another mother with a dead child. Can't I just be a ghost and scare the crap out of kids?"

"The Ghosts of Christmas Past and Present are up for grabs. Rowan's got his eye on the Ghost of Christmas Yet To Come."

"Well, he's appropriately wraithlike."

"Name the role and you've got it. I can offer you the same fabulous salary you got this summer. And a room at your favorite Vermont hotel."

"At least, I won't roast like I did this summer."

"You won't sleep much, either. Every time the heat comes on it sounds like 'The Anvil Chorus.'"

"You really have to work on your sales pitch."

"Think about it," I urged her.

Caught by my serious tone, she nodded. "Okay. I will." She turned to go, then hesitated. "You survived without him most of your life. You can do it again."

Before I could reply, she strode out of the hotel, leaving me to wonder if she and I had traveled parallel paths through life.

I hoped I would find out, but only time would tell if I could lure her back to the Crossroads. No matter what Rowan said, people sometimes needed a little push. And my sales pitch wasn't really pushing. It was just my version of calling the Mackenzies. If Debra answered the call, I would sit back and let the drama unfold. And maybe tweak it a bit like any good director.

I was heading back to the front desk when the bell over the front door jangled again. I turned to discover Bernie and Reinhard walking into the lobby.

The last bird was flying home.

"You know, Reinhard doesn't have to drive me back today," Bernie said.

Much as I would have liked him to remain, I shook my head. How could I explain all the gear we were purchasing—or why Rowan and I were escorting my father into the woods instead of driving him to an airport or train station?

"You're the best," I whispered as I hugged him.

"I'll be back for the September board meeting. You need me before, you call."

Gregarious Bernie and gruff Reinhard. One had been my first friend in the cast. The other had begun as hectoring stage manager and become my rock. Always in the background unless a crisis arose. Always lending me his quiet strength. Advising me, scolding me, but never saying, "You must do this." He allowed me to take risks and hovered nearby in case I crashed and burned, hiding his worries lest they add to mine.

He was more of a father to me than my own.

Impulsively, I threw my arms around him. When I finally released him, his smile was strangely tender and I knew he had sensed what I'd felt. Then his frown returned and he said, "So. The hugging is finished. Now, we go."

I called Mom that afternoon. When I told her that Daddy was moving on, there was a long silence. Then she asked, "Are you okay?"

"I told him he should go."

"I figured that. Are you okay?"

"Yes. Mostly. It's the right decision."

"That doesn't make it easier."

"No. But it's not like when Rowan left. I have a life now. Things to look forward to."

"Do you want me to come up?"

"Not for my sake. But if you want to see him again . . ."

"No." Her voice was as firm as mine. "Good-byes aren't your father's strong suit. And we already said ours."

"How are things with you and Chris?"

Another silence, even longer than the first. "Things are . . . okay."

"Meaning . . . ?"

"Meaning we're working on it and stop prying."

"You pry into my life all the time."

"I'm your mother. That's my job."

"You sound like the Witch in *Into the Woods*."

"I didn't lock you in a tower for fourteen years. Or blind your Prince Charming."

"No, you just threatened to castrate him."

"Not lately. How is Rowan?"

"He's good. *We're* good."

I wished I could tell her that he had ventured into town three times since that first dinner. That he had endured the short car ride to Hill with just a trace of queasiness. That he had made similar trips to have dinner with Hal and Lee, to visit Reinhard's office and Javier's antique store. Instead, I talked about the final performances of *Into the Woods* and my mixed feelings at facing the end of another season.

As we were about to hang up, I asked, "Is there any message you want me to give Daddy?"

"No." Then she added, "Tell him to take care of himself. And try not to go nuts again."

Daddy and I both went a little nuts during the days that followed. We had agreed to give ourselves a week after the show closed to gather the supplies he needed. I sat him down Monday morning to create a list. We rush-ordered some things via the Internet and scoured the shops of Dale and Bennington for everything else. Between the freeze-dried foods and the all-weather gear, I felt like a mother preparing her little boy for his first camping trip—on Mount Everest. But at least, the frenzy of preparations distracted us from his imminent departure.

By Saturday, all that remained was the farewell barbecue at the Bates mansion. Neither Daddy nor I ate very much; the "Last Supper" overtones were all too obvious. But we did our best to keep up a good front until Rowan's blue-berry cobbler had been demolished and Reinhard rose from his place at the picnic table.

"So. Tomorrow Jack will leave us. And like all farewells, this one brings a mix of emotions. We are sad to see him go. Even I, who was not so sure that he should stay in the first place. But. He is about to embark on a great adventure. One he has longed to take for many years. And for that, we should be happy."

His gaze lingered on me for a moment before drifting around the table.

"Those of us who remain are very lucky. We know the joy of finding our heart's desire."

He smiled at Mei-Yin. Lee pressed a quick kiss to Hal's cheek. Javier rested his palm on Catherine's stomach. Alex stared at his plate, thinking of the wife he had lost and per-haps, the woman who might fill that void in his heart. Janet watched him. Then her gaze rose to my bedroom window. To Helen's bedroom window.

I twined my fingers through Rowan's. I'd always hated that line near the end of *The Wizard of Oz* when Dorothy announces that if she ever goes looking for her heart's de-sire, she will search no farther than her own backyard. If it isn't there, she tells Glinda, she never really lost it to begin with.

But sometimes, you don't know what you've lost. And even when you do, you might have to go farther afield to find it. It had taken me years to reach the Crossroads. My father had traveled much farther and spent far longer on his quest. And although he had yet to find his heart's desire, we *had* found each other.

"As Jack resumes his journey, I offer this blessing. One that my mother taught me a very long time ago."

Reinhard raised his mug of beer. Benches scraped against brick as we rose, bottles and glasses uplifted.

"May the road rise up to meet you. May the wind be always at your back."

Around the table, voices softly chanted the words of the traditional Gaelic blessing.

"May the sun shine warm upon your face, the rains fall soft upon your fields."

Rowan's arm around my waist. Daddy's eyes shining with unshed tears.

"And until we meet again, may God hold you in the palm of His hand."

It was the perfect ending to our dinner and to my father's season at the Crossroads. But when we returned to the apartment, we discovered the farewells were not quite finished.

"Christmas came early this year," Rowan said.

A giant wicker basket sat on the sofa, filled with assorted boxes wrapped in Christmas paper and bedecked with ribbons and bows. I understood now why Rowan had sent us ahead to the barbecue. He had been setting the scene — again.

"A few things from the staff," he said. "They thought it might embarrass you to open them at the barbecue."

"It's too much," Daddy whispered. "How will I ever thank them?"

I exchanged a glance with Rowan and said, "Write each of them a note."

"But what will I say?"

"I'll help you."

There was a Swiss army knife from Javier and Catherine, antibiotics and detailed instructions on their use from Reinhard. Mei-Yin had contributed a wicked looking cleaver, Bernie a dozen toothbrushes and enough dental floss to strangle the entire population of Faerie. Hal's small watercolor painting of the barn made my throat tighten. Lee's gift of aftershave and condoms made us laugh.

Alex's gift touched me the most. The tiny digital recorder came with a plastic baggie filled with batteries and a note that explained that he had programmed a selection of show tunes as well as two Crossroads musicals: *Into the Woods* and *Carousel*. If my father never saw my face again, my voice would be with him, singing, "You'll Never Walk Alone."

Daddy abruptly excused himself and hurried to the bathroom. By the time he returned, we both had our emotions under control.

There was only one gift left, a small envelope that bore Janet's handwriting. Daddy pulled out a rectangular piece of paper and gave a soft cry.

It was a photograph of me. Janet must have used an industrial strength telephoto lens to get the close-up of my profile. The sunlight streaming over my left shoulder turned my hair to fire. The right side of my face lay in shadow, but you could still see my pensive expression as I stared off into the distance, lost in thought.

"When was this taken?" Rowan asked.

"I don't . . ."

And then I remembered. It was the afternoon of Arthur's funeral. I'd gone out to the garden to seek a little peace before our final dress rehearsal.

"Midsummer's Eve," I whispered.

"You look so faraway," Daddy said.

I had seen that same look on his face, always at odd moments when he thought no one was watching. A little dreamy, a little sad. My father yearning for Faerie and I, for the lover I had lost to it.

"There's one more thing," Rowan said.

He held out a small manila envelope addressed to Janet. Daddy and I exchanged startled glances when we saw my mother's return address label.

"What would she be sending to Janet?" I asked.

"I think she wanted someone else to see it first. And decide whether to pass it along. There was no note. So we're not sure if she intended it for Jack or for you."

"You open it," Daddy said.

The top of the envelope had already been slit. Inside was a smaller envelope. From its size and shape, it might have held a greeting card. But it was another photo, its colors faded with age.

The bottom of the Christmas tree filled the background. Discarded wrapping paper and open boxes were scattered around it. I was probably four or five years old, dressed in my red-and-white candy cane pajamas with the feet. Crushed to my chest was Moondancer, the unicorn My Little Pony I had wanted so desperately. And sitting opposite me, his mouth open in the same round "O" of delight, was my father in his Rudolph the Red-Nosed Reindeer pajamas and goofy antlers.

Both of us so impossibly young, so impossibly happy.

"This is for you," I said as I passed the photograph to him.

My voice was as steady as my hand. But of course, I had seen that picture countless times. Its twin was in one of my old scrapbooks—pasted there by my mother.

Daddy's breath caught. He studied the photograph for a long moment. Then he walked over to his battered old backpack, unzipped a compartment, and withdrew something from it.

It was another photograph, the colors even more faded, the corners ragged. But it was the same Christmas. I was asleep under the tree, clearly worn out by the festivities. Moondancer was still clutched to my chest, but my head rested in my mother's lap. Her hand was frozen in the act of brushing my hair off my face. Hers was almost masked by the dark waterfall of her hair, but you could just make out the tender curve of her mouth as she gazed at me.

I wept then, as silently as my father. For the happiness we had known and lost. For the man who had safeguarded this photograph for decades. And for the woman who could forgo blame and resentment and anger to offer him another keepsake of that time—once upon a time—when we had been a family.

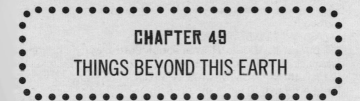

CHAPTER 49
THINGS BEYOND THIS EARTH

I SPENT A CHEERLESS MORNING HELPING DADDY write his farewell notes and listening to the incessant pounding of rain on the roof. I was on the verge of demanding that we postpone his departure when the rain abruptly ceased. Like a scene from a Biblical movie epic, the dark clouds parted and sunlight streamed into the apartment.

Daddy's mood brightened just as quickly. "Good-byes aren't your father's strong suit," Mom had told me. But his relief still hurt and as usual, I did a poor job of hiding my feelings.

"It's not that I want to leave," he explained. "I just hate dragging it out."

"Maybe it would be best to say your good-byes here," Rowan said. As I started to protest, he added, "I don't want you there when I open the portal. You know what happened to Jack after his encounter with my clan. It's even more dangerous for a human to look upon Faerie. All the legends tell us that."

"You told me most of the legends were crap."

"Most of them are. But the allure of Faerie is very real. Do you want to spend the rest of your life always seeking it, always wanting it? Will you risk everything we have here, just for a few more moments with Jack?"

I gnawed my lip, bitterly acknowledging the truth of his words. But I wasn't ready to say good-bye. Not yet.

Rowan sighed. "All right. Come with us as far as the cottage. You can wait there while Jack and I go on alone. Agreed?"

"Agreed," I whispered.

I put on my boots. Rowan shouldered Daddy's bulging backpack. Daddy grabbed his guitar and Rowan's knapsack and left the apartment without a backward glance. I wondered if he would leave me the same way.

The birds mocked me with their cheerful warbling, as did the chinks of brilliant blue sky that peeked through the forest canopy. The earth had a better handle on my mood, releasing my foot with reluctance each time I sank into a soggy mass of leaves and pine needles and mud.

The rain had transformed the low-lying places into swampland. We picked our way around the worst spots and tottered across others on fallen logs. The rain-slick leaves made climbing the smallest rise a monumental effort, even with Rowan steadying us as we clambered up one side and skidded down the other.

It was almost a relief to see the stone walls of the cottage through the trees. The glade lay deep in shadow, although sunlight still gilded the treetops.

Rowan gazed skyward. "We have a little time left. Let's rest here for a few minutes."

We scraped our boots against a rock by the doorway before traipsing inside. The first time I'd entered the cottage, I'd shuddered to imagine Rowan living in this gloomy little room. After slogging through the woods, I was just grateful to slump onto one of the benches flanking the wooden table.

Rowan unearthed supplies from his knapsack: a plastic bottle of lemonade, a crusty loaf of bread, a bunch of grapes, a hunk of cheese. He retrieved crockery plates and cups from the hutch near the open fireplace and laid them on the table as well. Then he took a bone-handled knife from a drawer and sliced off cheese and bread for us.

Daddy stoically shoveled food into his mouth. I picked at the grapes. Rowan studied me. Desperate to break the silence, I asked, "Is the portal nearby?"

"Not far," Rowan said evasively.

"Has it always been here? In these woods?"

"It's not a physical place, Maggie. The Fae can open a portal anywhere."

"Then why did we come all the way out here?"

"Opening a portal leaves traces of energy behind, no matter how carefully I seal it. Although they fade quickly, it would be unwise to draw attention to the theatre or Janet's house. And since my power is weaker than most of my kind, I have to choose a place where all four elements are present—earth, air, fire, and water."

We lapsed into silence again. When Daddy finished eating, Rowan carefully wrapped the remaining food in linen napkins. As he reached for the backpack, Daddy said, "I'll do that."

"All right. And then we'd better be going."

Rowan slung Daddy's guitar across his back and walked outside. Panic quickened my pulse as I hurried after him.

"Can't I go just a little farther with you?"

"No. And I want you to promise not to follow us." When I hesitated, he added, "I don't want to use my power to keep you here. I'll need all of it to open the portal. But if you won't give me your word—"

"I'll stay."

His arms came around me. "I know you want to be with him. But it's safer this way."

I swallowed hard and nodded. Daddy emerged from the cottage with his pack on his shoulders, and I swallowed again.

As many times as I had imagined this moment, I'd never come up with the right words of farewell. How do you say good-bye to a father you barely know but whose presence has been with you every day of your life?

As I groped for something to say, Rowan reached into the pocket of his jeans.

"I meant to give this to Maggie one day. But I think you need it more."

He thrust his fist toward Daddy and opened his fingers. I gasped when I saw the gold ring in his palm. Daddy backed away, shaking his head.

"Take it," Rowan said brusquely. "There are markings on it my clan will recognize. It might ensure your welcome."

"Or they might think I stole it."

"My chief warded it against theft. They'll know it came to you as a gift."

I gazed at the ring of faery gold—the ring Rowan had surely meant to give me on our wedding day. With shaking fingers, I plucked it from his palm. The ring was warm from his body and seemed oddly heavy for such a small circlet of gold, but if there were markings on it, they were too small— or too magical—for me to see.

Rowan's sweet smile brought on a fresh upwelling of tears. I blinked them back and held the ring out to my father. He slid it onto his pinkie, grunting a bit as he wiggled it over the swollen knuckle. Then we just stared at each other.

"I'm lousy at good-byes," he said. "But you know that."

"I wanted to buy you a gift. Like the staff did. Something to remember me by."

"Do you think I could ever forget you?"

They might make him forget. They might banish every memory he had of this world, including our years in Wilmington and these last two months.

"I just wish I had something to give you."

"Oh, Maggie. You've already given me so much."

Our embrace was clumsy, the stupid backpack making it hard for me to hold him. Finally, I wriggled my hands beneath it so I could hug him. Even after two months, he was still so thin I could feel every rib.

"Be happy, Magpie."

He wrenched free, staggering a little from the weight of the backpack. Rowan took his arm to steady him. Then he led my father away.

The leaves squelched obscenely as they walked across the glade. I swiped my fists across my eyes and followed the bobbing red backpack as it moved deeper into the woods.

I should have told him to be happy. I should have begged him to be safe.

I should have assured him that these last two months have been a gift. I should have promised him that he would always have a home at the Crossroads.

I should have asked if he had a message for Mom. I should have asked him to stay.

The backpack was just a red spot among the trees, as small as Rudolph's nose on those silly pajamas.

I should have told him that I loved him.

The red spot grew brighter as Daddy walked into a patch of sunlight. As I opened my mouth to call to him, it vanished.

Oh, God...

Something gleamed in the sunlight. A tiny spark no bigger than a firefly.

The ring. He must have turned back to look at me one last time. He must be waving good-bye.

I ran to the edge of the glade, waving frantically as I shouted, "I love you, Daddy!"

The spark disappeared. For just an instant, I glimpsed that spot of red. Then it, too, was gone.

Had he heard me? If not, Rowan would tell him what I had said. I tried to take comfort in that as I trudged back to the cottage.

I wiped off the cups and the plates and returned them to the hutch. Screwed the cap back on the bottle of lemonade and returned it to Rowan's knapsack. Found a broom in one corner and tried to sweep the drying mud from the floor. I looked around for another task—anything to keep busy— and spied something on the bed that interrupted the patchwork pattern of the quilt.

Even in the gloom, I made out the moose-headed cows. The T-shirt had been carefully folded and obviously left for Rowan. Daddy must have placed it there while we were outside.

I frowned when I saw a dark smudge on one corner of the shirt. As I attempted to brush it away, I touched something hard. Wood, I realized, as my fingers curled around it. I carried it to the doorway, seeking more light, but the glade was as shadowy as the cottage.

I fumbled around the hutch, feeling along shelves and opening drawers until I found a box of matches. I lit two candles and carried them over to the table. Then I sat down to examine the mysterious object.

It was a model of a bird a crow judging by the black substance that covered most of its body. Too dull and rough to be paint. Charcoal, perhaps. Was it some sort of protective talisman he had carved in the Borderlands to ward off the Crow-Men?

The body had been worn smooth. Only the grooves of

the tail feathers were faintly discernible under my finger-tips. The charcoal had chipped away on the wings and belly, leaving patches of bare wood. I stroked the belly gently, then frowned at the smudges I left behind and the white residue on my fingertips. Chalk?

Even then, it took another moment for me to grasp the truth.

Not a crow. A black-and-white bird, carefully carved, carefully painted with whatever materials he could find, and carefully preserved for decades to remind him of the child he had left behind.

His Magpie.

🐦

I don't know how long I sat there, sobbing. Minutes, prob-ably, although it seemed like hours. Finally, I rose and wiped my face with the same towel I had used to clean the dishes. Then I carried the magpie back to the bed and set it atop the T-shirt.

As I turned away, I noticed something pale peeking out from under the bed. I crouched down and picked it up.

The photograph must have slipped out of his backpack when he set out his gifts. I had to hold it close to the candles to determine that it was the faded picture of Mom and me, the photo he had carried for more than twenty years, pre-served just as carefully as the magpie.

I ran out of the cottage and plunged into the woods, shouting Rowan's name. He would open the portal at sun-set. There was still time to reach them. There had to be.

I skidded into a tree trunk and clung to it for a moment, gasping. The shadows under the trees were too thick to risk running. One misstep might bring the disaster of a twisted ankle, a wrenched knee. But my mind screamed at me to hurry.

I shoved the photo in the back pocket of my shorts. If I dropped it, if I lost it . . .

Don't think about that. Just keep moving.

I clawed my way up a slope, slipping and sliding on wet pine needles. At the top, I paused, trying to get my bearings. The sky was a deeper blue now, but up ahead, the trees thinned, and the light was brighter. All I could do was fol-low the dying sun.

I sidestepped down the slope, reeling from one tree trunk to another to keep from falling. When the ground leveled out, I quickened my pace. I forced myself to ignore the sharp stitch in my side, to concentrate on the next step and the next and the next after that. If I thought about my father vanishing from this world before I could reach him, the panic would rise like bile.

I searched the shadows for tree roots that might trap a foot, vines that could ensnare an ankle. But still, I tripped over something hidden under the leaves.

Pain lanced through my wrists as I tried to break my fall. My cry was cut off as I bellyflopped onto the ground. Precious seconds ticked away while I lay there, panting. Only when the cold dampness penetrated my T-shirt did I drag my forearms through the muck and use them to leverage myself onto my knees.

The light through the trees was now a rich orange-gold. The twittering of the birds grew louder as they saluted the sunset. But even their chorus failed to drown out the sound of splashing water.

I gave a hoarse croak of laughter when I realized how close I had come to sliding headfirst into the stream. I'd made so much noise crashing through the woods that I had failed to hear it. For once, my clumsiness had served me. Rowan needed water to open his portal and this stream meandered through the thin screen of saplings. Between them, I could make out the undulating line of the distant hills, dark against the bright stripes of the rose-colored clouds.

I staggered to my feet and clambered along the muddy bank, ignoring my sodden clothes and the cold that made my teeth chatter and the sharp throb of pain in my left wrist. As I neared the saplings, I opened my mouth to shout Rowan's name.

A hill blurred, and I blinked to clear my vision. But it wasn't the hill or my vision. It was the air just beyond the trees, roiling and churning as if caught in a whirlpool.

The whirlpool shuddered. A sliver of light cracked open the sky like a lightning bolt. But the lightning was golden. As golden as a cloud of fireflies.

The rough bark of a tree beneath my fingers. The golden

light blessing my eyes. The stream laughing as it tumbled over the hillside, past a small outcropping of rock below me, past a man with his arms upraised and another with a red pack and a guitar.

A rainbow shimmered in the air where the dying rays of the sun sliced across the thin cascade of water. A warm breeze caressed my face, carrying with it the dizzying aromas of roses and honeysuckle, ripe berries and sweet grass. And glorious birdsong that shamed the pitiful chirps from the treetops.

And music . . .

High-pitched and silvery, like the rippling glissando of a harp.

And singing . . .

The sweetest of harmonies, augmented by a deep vibration that pulsed through me like a second heartbeat. So might crystals sound if they could sing. So might the heart of the world sound if it could beat. Add one voice, change one thread of the song, and it would be diminished.

Then the chorus swelled, and as beautiful as it had seemed before, this was the sound of perfection. I yearned to be part of it, to blend forever in the pure, glorious, aching joy of that song.

Another rainbow, more beautiful than the first, growing out of the shelf of rock, arcing toward the portal of golden light where stars now danced like fireflies. A rainbow bridge, shimmering with otherworldly brilliance, pulsating with the steady tattoo of that heartbeat.

The man with the red pack places his foot on the bridge. His giddy laughter shivers through me and I laugh with him.

And suddenly, I am scrambling down the rocky hillside, slipping through the waterfall's spray, leaping onto the shelf of rock, running past the man with the upraised arms, running after the lucky one on the rainbow bridge.

"Maggie!"

My steps falter. I know that voice. It comes from behind me, so it must belong to the man with the upraised arms.

The man on the bridge hesitates and looks back. I know that face. But it is so much older than I remember.

The music urges me onward. The golden light fills my eyes. But another power rips through my chest, cleaving heart and spirit alike.

"Maggie! Please!"

The man and the bridge blur just as the hill did.

"Run, Jack!"

Something is wrong. Even the golden light seems to sense it for the stars are winking out one by one.

The man on the bridge starts running toward the light. I have to stop him. There is something I have to do, something I have to give him.

"Maggie!"

Three times, he has called my name. Three times for a charm. Where did I learn that?

Warmth enfolds me. A breeze kisses my cheeks. The scent of lavender fills my nostrils.

"Rowan will always carry you in his heart. We all will. Remember that, my dear. And know that you will always have a home at the Crossroads."

The breeze whips my hair across my eyes, obscuring the rainbow bridge and the flickering portal and the golden light of Faerie.

"Goddamn it, Maggie! Don't you give up on us!" that broken voice shouts.

The siren call of the music beckons me. The sweetest music I will ever hear in my life.

I cover my ears to block it out. And then I turn my back on Faerie and stumble into Rowan's arms.

FINALE AND CURTAIN CALLS

WAKE TO THE BLARE OF A CAR HORN. I cannot understand why the skylights have disappeared. Then I remember: I am in the guest room of Alison's home in Delaware.

I relax when I sense Maggie's presence somewhere in the house. I barely remember stumbling inside yesterday evening, nor when I have ever slept through an entire night. Hardly surprising after that hellish car ride.

Pale slivers of sunlight leak between the panels of fabric at the far end of the room. I realize now that they cover a sliding glass door. How strange that my bedroom in this house has one, too.

I slip on my dressing gown, pad over to the doors, and fumble in the gloom for a cord. The blinds ratchet open, treating me to a depressing vista: a grid of asphalt; a collection of narrow townhouses, and a fortresslike structure that must be the hospital. I spy a patch of green that might be grass, but no trees anywhere. Still, sunlight slants through the warren of buildings; we will have a nice day for the wedding.

I pull open the door and am greeted by the reek of car exhaust and gasoline and garbage. A blessing for humans that their senses are so muffled; how else could they stand to live here?

I shove the door closed and sink onto the bed. My muscles ache from vomiting, my stomach—my whole body—a

821

hollowed-out shell. That I survived at all is due largely to Maggie's new convertible.

When she suggested buying one, I pictured a long, sleek automobile with fins or one of those sporty little roadsters driven by international playboys and middle-aged men seeking to reclaim their youth. Our car is rather stumpy. But Maggie quoted a lot of initials that apparently proved it was a sound purchase in spite of its horrifying price.

I made it through Vermont, Massachusetts, Connecticut, and New York with only mild queasiness and windburn. Then we reached New Jersey.

The rain forced us to put up the roof. After that, we had to pull over every fifteen or twenty miles. I now have the dubious distinction of vomiting at every rest stop and exit on the southbound side of the New Jersey Turnpike. Doubtless, on our return trip, I will become acquainted with those on the northbound side, although Maggie has suggested another route that will allow me to see the "scenic" parts of the state.

I will have to take her word that they exist. After marveling at the incredible sprawl of New York City, I recall little of New Jersey other than that endless highway studded by giant signs advertising dating services, insurance companies, and an adult club. And an airport where the giant planes soared so low that I feared they would land atop us. The roar of their engines made me shudder as much as the car.

I force myself to my feet. After mistakenly stumbling into a closet, I discover the bathroom next door. I have to use a washcloth to turn on the nozzles in the shower, but the hot water revives me. As I reach for the shower curtain, I feel her entering the bathroom.

She perches on the toilet seat, still dressed in her long flannel nightgown and slippers. A steaming cup rests on the sink's faux marble countertop. I breathe in the scent of ginger that rises from the cup and from Maggie's body.

Her gaze sweeps over me, and a quiet smile blossoms on her face—the same smile with which she greeted me when she awoke in my bed. A night and a day after that mad dash through the woods with Maggie's body cradled in my arms and her blood bathing my hand. A night and a day after she looked onto Faerie and I thought I had lost her.

"How are you feeling?" she asks.

Like the discarded carapace of a cicada.

"Hungry."

"I'll make you some scrambled eggs and toast after you get dressed."

As she turns to leave, I climb out of the tub, carry her hand to my lips, and press a kiss to her palm.

"I love you," I tell her, as I have every morning since she returned to me.

"I love you, too," she replies as she always does. But this time, she frowns. "I'm okay, Rowan. Really."

But I can't help recalling that wild creature who laughed as she raced for the portal, heedless of the blood running down her leg where she cut herself on the rocks, heedless of the pain of her sprained wrist. Heedless of me.

She will always bear the scar on her knee. It is the other scars I fear more: the ones on her soul and her mind and her heart.

Her hands come up to caress my face. "I'm here, Rowan."

She said that the night we found each other at the Golden Bough. And promised then that she would always come back to me.

And she did. It still amazes me that she possessed the willpower to turn away from the portal. As often as I have claimed that human love is greater than the power of Faerie, it was only at that moment that I saw the proof of it.

I want to pull her into my arms. I want to bury myself in her softness and use my body to drive away the memories. But I cannot risk losing control of my power with Alison in the house.

Maggie flings a bath towel at me. "Get dressed. The wedding's in two hours."

"How's Alison?"

Her laughter refreshes me far more than the shower. "Solid as a rock. I'm more nervous than she is. Ever since she decided to take the plunge, it's been full speed ahead." Her kiss is brisk and businesslike. "Don't dawdle, Amaryllis."

I laugh at *The Music Man* reference and obey. But as I dress, my mind returns to that evening in the woods. Someday, perhaps, I will stop blaming myself for allowing her to come with us to the cottage. As for failing to sense her presence, I was almost as helpless as Maggie, all my power bent on opening the portal and holding it open until Jack made the crossing.

I almost lost him when I saw her. That outpouring of love, that desperate plea for her to stay . . . and the terrible knowledge that if I continued to use my power to try and stop her, the portal would collapse and Jack would be trapped between the worlds. Not in the Borderlands, but in that other land where legends claim lost spirits dwell.

Maybe Helen *was* there, just as Maggie insists. If I could not sense Maggie's presence, I could have overlooked hers as well. It comforts me to believe that her spirit was watching over us. Might still be watching over us.

But I am baffled by some of Maggie's other claims. The light and the music, yes. But I saw no stars inside the portal—just the green hills of Faerie barely visible through the misty sunlight. Did she imagine the stars and the rainbow bridge and that chorus of voices? Or does every human experience Faerie differently?

Reinhard and Janet were there to hear her halting recollections. When we exchanged glances, she asked, "Doesn't anybody believe me?"

"Of course, we believe you," I assured her.

She laughed a little when she realized we were parroting lines from *The Wizard of Oz*. Then she looked up at me and said, "But anyway, Toto, I'm home. Home."

That's when I knew she had truly returned, touched by Faerie but not lost to its power.

Janet urged me to banish her memories of the portal. But I recalled Maggie's insistence that humans sometimes needed to work things out for themselves. Her promise that, together, we could deal with my panic attacks. And most of all, that she had chosen me over Faerie. If she had the strength to do that, I must let her deal with the memories. And stay close so that I may help her.

But for now, I must push them aside. I will not allow them to spoil this day for Alison and Chris—or for Maggie and me.

I imagined that this wedding would be like those I had seen in the movies of *The Sound of Music* and *Camelot*. A glorious affair with hundreds of people in attendance, music swelling, and the bride and groom garbed in their finest clothes.

But there are only twenty of us gathered on Alison's tiny patio, mostly Chris' family and friends: his sons and daughter, their spouses, a small tribe of children, and a man named Frank whom everyone calls Biff and his wife Barbara whom everyone calls Babs. Instead of a white gown, Alison wears a simple dress the same pale blue as the October sky. Maggie's is the deep russet of an oak leaf.

A high wooden fence shields us from the street, but not from the second-story windows of the neighboring houses or the occasional blare of a car radio. At least, we are gathered under the open sky instead of inside a clerk's office.

The minister stands before the sundial. The white stole atop her robe is embroidered with a motley assortment of religious symbols. Apparently, this means that she is qualified to unite people of many faiths. Her welcome is pleasant but brief. Then Alison and Chris step forward. Maggie and Biff take their appointed places as maid of honor and best man.

It seems so . . . unceremonious, so lacking in the ritual that should mark this occasion. But I forget about that as Alison and Chris speak their vows. Her expression is as soft as it was in the photograph that Jack preserved. His is earnest, and he recites his words breathlessly, as if he cannot believe this is really happening.

Their love fills my spirit with joy, as does Maggie's tearful smile. I wonder if she imagines the two of us standing before our friends, speaking the words that will bind us together in the eyes of the world.

Janet assures me it will happen. She has even offered to arrange everything with the "acquaintance" she retained the last time she changed her identity. I would merely have to sell one of my first editions to pay for the false papers this person would procure. I had hoped to avoid that, to pretend I was an illegal immigrant and eventually earn a green card and then full citizenship. But even illegal immigrants have birth certificates and driver's licenses and credit cards. Don't they?

I wish I could seek Chris' advice, but that would mean more lies. And how can I put him in the position of honoring such confidences as my lawyer and withholding damaging information from Alison?

My concern for Maggie has absorbed me for the last six weeks, but soon, I must take steps. The board is preparing next year's budget. Even if I wait until May to sign a contract and receive my first paycheck . . .

A burst of applause interrupts my daydreaming. The ceremony is already over and Maggie is hugging her mother. I wait with Alison's friend Sue at the fringes of the small crowd to allow family members to greet the new couple first. As I step forward, Chris pulls me into a hard embrace. Alison shocks me by doing the same.

We troop into the living room where the caterers have set out hors d'oeuvres. I am—as Maggie would say—underwhelmed. But the others are too happy to notice what they are eating. And after several glasses of champagne, even I can look charitably upon limp asparagus spears wrapped in prosciutto.

I gravitate helplessly toward the children. A feast for the eye and the spirit. I approach them with caution, but their parents seem delighted by my interest, so I calm fretful babies and play horsey with the toddlers and try to nod intelligently as the older ones demonstrate the wonders of their handheld computer games. I am more comfortable when a little girl shoves a crayon into my hand and demands that I help her color two gremlins with the improbable names of Bert and Ernie.

I look up to discover Maggie watching me with that same quiet smile. I wish again that I might give her a child, but it is too soon to discuss that. For now, I will anticipate the birth of the newest member of the Crossroads family. According to Catherine and Javier, he—or she—will arrive shortly before the equinox. What more perfect symbol of spring could there be?

As Alison and Chris go upstairs to change, I abandon my selfish indulgence of playing with children to guide Sue onto the patio. We chat about Alison and Chris, but her mother's death shadows her happiness. I use my power to drive some of the shadows away. Perhaps before Maggie and I return to Dale, I will be able to do more.

Maggie runs out of the house and exclaims, "Hurry! They'll be leaving any moment."

As we rush toward the front porch, she orders me to grab a fistful of rose petals from the dish by the door. Rice, apparently, is no longer de rigueur.

The vista from the front porch is far more pleasing than the one from my bedroom. Although the houses are still lined up like soldiers, the tree-lined street soothes my senses. There are only a few golden leaves among the green. Autumn has just begun to touch Wilmington, while back in Dale, the fall foliage is nearing its peak.

A shout goes up behind us. Alison and Chris scamper through the crowd. We throw our rose petals and shout good wishes and wave as the car pulls away. It seems impossible that they will share dinner tonight in the Bahamas.

I doubt I will ever see the beautiful blue Caribbean. I would have to be carried off the plane on a stretcher. But I never thought I'd survive this trip, so perhaps there is hope for me yet.

In the meantime, there is still the beautiful gray Atlantic. Maggie has hinted that we might leave early and stay for a night at the Jersey Shore. I pray it is nicer than the Turnpike.

The guests disperse. The caterers pack away the leftovers. Maggie kicks off her shoes and collapses onto Alison's rock-hard settee with a grunt.

"Never wear new shoes to a wedding," she says, crossing her ankle over her knee to massage her foot.

"Let me do that."

She takes the precaution of stacking pillows at the end of the sofa; the carved wooden arm of the settee looks as comfortable as a shillelagh. Then she leans back and swings her feet into my lap. The slippery feel of her stockings sends a shiver of desire through me. As I dig my thumbs into the ball of her foot, she purrs like Iolanthe.

"I'm a foot rub whore."

"That's all right. I'm a grocery store whore."

She laughs. "At least foot rubs are sensual. You're the only man in the world who finds grocery shopping an erotic experience."

I close my eyes, happy to surrender to these memories, to exchange the light and music of Faerie for the glare of fluorescent bulbs and the soft drone of pop songs. Perhaps grocery stores are as alluring to the Fae as Faerie is to humans.

Shelf upon shelf of brightly colored boxes and cans. Fancifully named breakfast cereals like Count Chocula and Lucky Charms, which Maggie refused to purchase. Towering cumulous clouds of paper towels and napkins and toilet paper. Slabs of meat glistening beneath plastic wrap. Mounds of shrimp peeping out of the ice like buried treasure. Geometric stacks of apples—green and red and gold. Leafy vegetables reclining under a misty spray. The mingled aromas of fresh-baked bread and ripe bananas, coffee and cocoa, floor wax and fish.

And that deli department . . .

Earthy cheeses and salt-cured meats. Briny olives and phallic pepperoni. The lascivious pink of the hams. The plump curves of the roast beef. Whole chickens weeping thick tears of barbecue sauce as they revolve in basted bliss upon a spit.

It was all so beautiful, so bountiful, so . . . arousing.

We barely survived the short car ride home. I was too excited to be queasy—or to control my power. We dropped the groceries by the doorway, wrestled off the necessary clothing, and went at it on the office floor. Maggie was still laughing when she climaxed.

She laughs again as her toes investigate the bulge in my pants. "Someone's thinking of naughty things," she chants in a singsong voice.

"Someone wants to do naughty things," I chant back.

"Later. I'm too contented right now." She sighs. "They looked happy, didn't they?"

"Yes, they did."

"I can't remember the last time she seemed so happy."

"Did she ever tell you why she changed her mind?"

"Nope. She just announced that they were getting married and told me if I acted smug and self-satisfied, I wasn't invited." Maggie's smile is entirely smug and self-satisfied. "Sometimes, a little push is exactly what people need. Look at Alex and Debra."

"They're not at the altar yet. Debra's not even in Dale."

"She'll be there next week to prep for *Murder at the*

Mackenzie Mansion. A little murder. A little mystery. A little Cratchity Christmas cheer. Who knows where it might lead?"

I serenade her with a brief rendition of "Matchmaker." Her hand flails briefly, but I am safely out of range of her intended smack.

"Know what I think?" she asks.

"That Debra came to the Crossroads to find Alex."

"No, Mr. Smarty Pants Faery Man. I think Debra came to the Crossroads because she needed all of us. What we have there. Our family. Alex was just the cherry on the sundae."

Her expression softens. Is she recalling the morning she awoke to find Janet and Reinhard and I at her bedside? And the others crowding in behind us, their faces filled with such love, such relief?

This after the long vigil in the apartment. Lee prowling around like a caged animal. Mei-Yin snapping at everyone. Hal alternately weeping and declaring that it would be all right, that it had to be all right. Catherine and Javier making food that no one ate because they had to do something other than sit there and wait.

Janet's energy resonating with the same fear that had screamed through her the night of Helen's heart attack. Alex so bowed down with grief that he suddenly seemed an old man. And Reinhard who silently stitched her wound and bandaged her hands and wrapped her wrist. Only when he was certain that she was safe in mind as well as body did he leave the apartment—and return a few minutes later, his eyes reddened from weeping.

I shared their love, their anguish, their fear, their relief—and they shared mine. And in that night and that day, I became part of their family, as blood alone had never made me. The unexpected gift that came from that ordeal.

"Penny for your thoughts?" Maggie asks.

"Just thinking about family."

Maggie yawns hugely. "Better stop with the foot massage before I start snoring."

"We could always take a nap," I suggest casually.

"Yeah, yeah. I know exactly what kind of a 'nap' you have in mind."

"Well, you'd nap afterward."

"Mmm . . . let's wait until later. We can snarf down left-overs, watch a cheesy movie in the rec room, and make out."

My spirits brighten. We have often made love, but never made out. I understand it involves extensive foreplay.

"So what *would* you like to do?" I ask.

A look of determination crosses her face. "Let's go for a walk."

"On your sore feet?"

"Sucker. I just wanted a foot rub."

❧❦

We change into comfortable clothes and walk toward the towering buildings of downtown Wilmington. Then Maggie turns back. I wonder if she has forgotten something at the house, but we continue past it.

I let my hand brush against the trunks of the trees we pass. Their roots wreak havoc with the sidewalk, but their energy feeds me more than any of the food I consumed.

The houses on our right give way to an open tract of land. A pretty little brick church with a gambrel roof sits upon it. According to the sign, it is older than I am. I find it oddly comforting to find another relic of the past here, thriving in the shadow of the skyscrapers.

Beyond it, I glimpse a hillside of trees. I am so engrossed in them that I fail to notice the sound of rushing water until we reach the end of the street. I knew the Brandywine was close to Maggie's childhood home, but I never imagined it was only two blocks away.

Her good spirits have evaporated, and I realize that this is a test for her.

We take our lives in our hands as we dart across the roadway, dodging cars that are traveling far too fast. We follow a narrow canal that parallels the river — the millrace, Maggie informs me. The path is crowded with pedestrians, eager to enjoy the crisp afternoon. Dogs strain at their leashes as I pass, but a flick of my power deters them from further investigation.

Maggie has lapsed into an ominous silence, but when I take her hand, I receive a quick smile.

Although her mood worries me, my power swells in relief as we walk among the trees. Opening the portal drained me and my concerns about Maggie's recovery prevented me from spending September at the cottage as I usually do. Perhaps when we return home, I will go there. Maggie will be working. I can use the time to finalize the script for *A Christmas Carol* and still return to her every night.

We cross a small footbridge. I smile as my boots sink into the soft grass. So good to feel the earth beneath my feet again. Beyond the river, I spy a parking lot, some sort of statue, and an allée of cherry trees that must be glorious in the spring. When I notice the picnic tables, I realize this must be Brandywine Park.

"That's the zoo," Maggie says, pointing to some stone structures half-hidden among the trees. Her finger moves left. "You can't really see the monkey house from here. Not until the leaves fall."

But I *can* see a steep expanse of grass, which must be Monkey Hill, where she and Jack chased fireflies.

We have spoken of him only once. The morning she awoke, I reassured her that he was safe. She wept because he had left without the photograph; even the reminder that he still had the other two failed to console her.

I expect her to talk about him now, but we merely re-trace our route. Instead of turning up the street to her mother's house, she leads me toward a terrace of white stone overlooking the river. I lean against the railing, my senses cheered by the water eddying around the rocks in the shallows.

Maggie's anguish rips through me.

My hand automatically reaches for her. She is standing as still as a statue, gazing across the river. I cannot imagine what has upset her. Then I notice a partially uprooted stump clinging precariously to the bank.

"Is that . . . ?"

She nods, and the tears in her eyes overflow.

I put my arm around her and gaze at the remains of the tree that sheltered pirate treasure and a family of gnomes and a little girl's dreams.

Maggie dashes away the tears with the back of her hand. "Talk about symbolism."

Her chin trembles, but she thrusts it out defiantly. She

refused to succumb to Faerie. She will not collapse under the weight of this sight. She is as strong as the roots of the gnome tree that stubbornly resist the efforts of nature and man to dislodge them.

Her defiant expression fades and she takes a shaky breath. "I just wish I knew if he was safe. If he was happy."

I don't care if he's safe or happy. Twice, Jack Sinclair has nearly cost me the woman I love. Had he been anyone else, I would never have spent all those months searching for him.

But he is Maggie's father. And for her sake I say, "The ring will ensure at least one night of hospitality. And with his talent for song and storytelling, I believe my clan will let him stay. Happy? I think so. As much as he might regret leaving you, he's better off in that world than drifting aimlessly through this one."

"And what if they tire of him like they did before?"

Doubtless they will. Jack can be fitfully entertaining, but I cannot believe he will hold their interest forever. But again, I search for words that will reassure her.

"It's just as likely he'll tire of them. With so many clans to visit, so much else in Faerie to see, I can't imagine Jack staying in one place very long."

"A wandering minstrel."

"Aye."

She smiles, and I silently bless Gilbert and Sullivan.

"Let's go back to the house," she says, "and open a bottle of wine."

When I hesitate, her brows come together in a puzzled frown.

I had always intended for this moment to take place on the plateau with the glorious autumn foliage for a backdrop. But even a faery director must occasionally improvise. And this place, this moment when past, present, and future converge feels right.

I take her hands and stare into the face I love more than any in this world or the other—and all the beautiful words I have memorized evaporate. Instead, I blurt out, "Marry me."

Brilliant, Rowan. Just brilliant. What woman could resist such a poetic outpouring?

Yet Maggie's eyes are shining and her face glows with an inner radiance more glorious than the afternoon sunlight.

"Yes," she whispers. "Oh, yes."

Her mouth is soft against mine, but her arms are strong and sure as they pull me closer.

I grope for the ring in the pocket of my jeans, then hesitate. She notices the gesture and the hesitation, and a small tremor ripples through her.

"I'm sorry. I should have given you the ring later instead of reminding you—"

Her fingertips press gently against my mouth. "Reinhard was right. Every parting holds joy and sadness. Maybe it's fitting that every new beginning does, too. I'll look at this ring and remember the other one. But I'll also remember that it might keep him safe. That you brought him back to me and gave us this summer and helped him find his heart's desire." Her thumb traces the outline of my lips. "I've already found mine."

My hand trembles shamefully as I slip the ring onto her finger. As she stares down at it, I resist the urge to probe her emotions. I chose the ring within moments of walking into the jewelry store in Dale. The bands of gold and silver to represent the intertwining of our lives. Emeralds for her birthstone and mine—at least according to the false birth certificate Jamie procured for me long ago. And the diamond because . . . well . . . an engagement ring is supposed to have a diamond.

Now, I only notice that the diamond is small, the emerald chips flanking it even smaller. I should have bought a more expensive ring. I should have let her choose one herself.

She holds her hand before her face. Then her eyes meet mine.

"It's perfect."

She flings her arms around my neck and I hold her tightly. A horn blares. We look up, startled, as a car whizzes past. Two young men stick their heads out of the windows, grinning and pumping their fists. I don't know whether they're cheering or jeering. And I don't care. Maggie's softness fills my arms, her scent fills my nostrils, and her happiness fills my spirit.

Abruptly, she pulls away. "I have to call Mom. And Nancy.

And Janet and Hal and Reinhard and . . . no. Tomorrow. I'll call them all tomorrow, Scarlett. Tonight is just for us."

For the first time since Jack's departure and her brush with Faerie, the shadows are gone. They will return, of course. You cannot have sunlight without shadow.

But the past cannot hold us hostage. And to my dazzled eyes, the future shines more brightly than the golden light of Faerie.

Laura Resnick

The Esther Diamond Novels

"Esther Diamond is the Stephanie Plum of urban fantasy! Unplug the phone and settle down for a fast and funny read!"   —Mary Jo Putney

DISAPPEARING NIGHTLY
978-0-7564-0766-7

DOPPELGANGSTER
978-0-7564-0595-3

UNSYMPATHETIC MAGIC
978-0-7564-0635-6

VAMPARAZZI
978-0-7564-0687-5

POLTERHEIST
978-0-7564-0733-9

THE MISFORTUNE COOKIE
978-0-7564-0847-3

To Order Call: 1-800-788-6262
www.dawbooks.com

Kari Sperring

Living with Ghosts

978-0-7564-0675-2

Finalist for the Crawford Award for First Novel

A Tiptree Award Honor Book

Locus Recommended First Novel"

"This is an enthralling fantasy that contains horror elements interwoven into the story line. This reviewer predicts Kari Sperring will have quite a future as a renowned fantasist."
— *Midwest Book Review*

"A satisfying blend of well-developed characters and intriguing worldbuilding. The richly realized Renaissance style city is a perfect backdrop for the blend of ghostly magic and intrigue. The characters are wonderfully flawed, complex and multi-dimensional. Highly recommended!"
— *Patricia Bray, author of The Sword of Change Trilogy*

And now available:

The Grass King's Concubine

978-0-7564-0755-1

To Order Call: 1-800-788-6262
www.dawbooks.com

DAW 206

Once upon a time...

Cinderella, whose real name is Danielle
Whiteshore, did marry Prince Armand.
And their wedding was a dream come true.

But not long after the "happily ever after,"
Danielle is attacked by her stepsister Charlotte,
who suddenly has all sorts of magic to call upon.
And though Talia the martial arts master—
otherwise known as Sleeping Beauty—
comes to the rescue, Charlotte gets away.

That's when Danielle discovers a number of disturbing facts: Armand has been kidnapped; Danielle is
pregnant; and the Queen has her own Secret Service
that consists of Talia and Snow (White, of course).
Snow is an expert at mirror magic and heavy-duty
flirting. Can the princesses track down Armand and
rescue him from the clutches of some of
Fantasyland's most nefarious villains?

The Stepsister Scheme
by Jim C. Hines
978-0-7564-0532-8

"Do we look like we need to be rescued?"